Lapland Underground

THE COMPLETE SERIES

BY HOLLY BLOOM

DIGITALLY SIGNED BY AUTHOR

Holly Bloom x

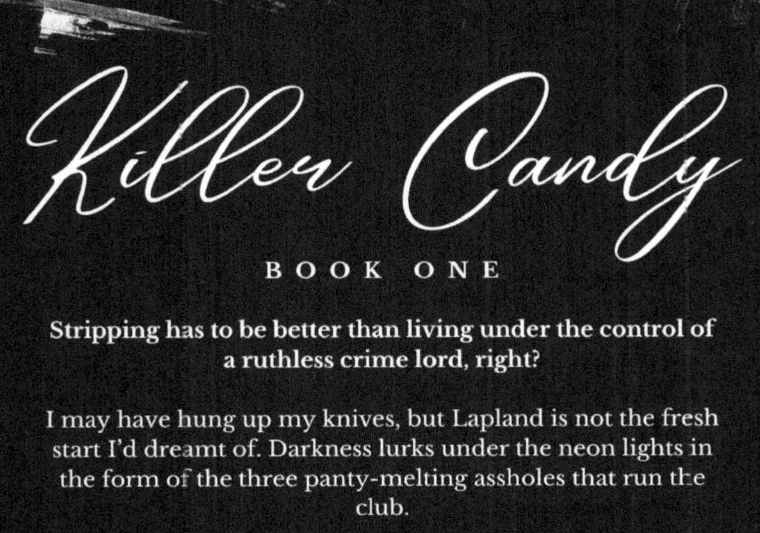

Stripping has to be better than living under the control of a ruthless crime lord, right?

I may have hung up my knives, but Lapland is not the fresh start I'd dreamt of. Darkness lurks under the neon lights in the form of the three panty-melting assholes that run the club.

Zander, West and Rocky are exactly the types of dangerous men I'd sworn to avoid.

They want me to play by their rules, but I'm nobody's puppet. Sexy smirks and inked muscles won't stop me from getting what I really want. Revenge.

Everyone better watch out because my name is the only sweet thing about me...

Prologue

KITTEN

"You like this?" Raphael grunted. His hand pumped up and down his dry shaft like he was trying to yank his damn cock off. He took the phrase choking the chicken to a whole new level. "You want a piece of this, huh?"

Once upon a time, he may have been considered attractive. Now, he was old enough to be my father. His belly hung over the dirty waistband of his jeans, trying to escape. That, and the Jacobson signet ring on his finger, made me want to vomit.

Instead of throwing up, I ran my tongue over my red lips and stared at him in wide-eyed wonderment. The type of smoldering look to con him into believing a drop of his cum would be the best present he could give me. I had the whole 'innocent but a freak in the sheets' look nailed to perfection.

"I love it!" I moaned, kneeling before him to give an eyeful of my cleavage. It was no accident I'd chosen to wear a killer black dress to show off my best assets. "You are *so* big!"

Well, as big as my pinkie finger chopped in two.

Men gobbled up compliments over the size of their dicks every single time. Why did they all think their spunk was spun from fucking gold? Give me a chocolate milkshake any day of the week.

"You're a bad girl, aren't you?"

A high-pitched, sickly sweet giggle erupted from the back of my throat. Eurgh, it made me cringe to think about what the job had reduced me to. In another life, I'd have made a damn good actress.

Well done, Kitty. I could almost hear Hiram purring in my ear. *You've got him right where you want him.*

Sweat dripped down Raphael's forehead from the exertion. Getting hard at his age must take some effort. The poor chump looked like he'd run ten marathons. If he wasn't about to die, I'd have warned him about friction burn and given a lecture on the benefits of lube.

"Suck it," Raphael ordered. He pointed his man meat in my face like a small angry marshmallow. Hell, I'm sure he'd whip it out for anyone who looked in his direction because he was so fucking proud of it.

I tried not to gag as I took the disgusting slug into my mouth. I'd need to get a tetanus shot and gargle disinfectant for weeks to feel clean again afterward. Raphael didn't notice. Men like him were used to getting anything they wanted. A blow job was just another transaction. I'd bet he went through more whores than underwear judging from the look of the stains.

Raphael groaned and pushed my head down deeper. His sticky pubes smelt like fried chicken left in the sun for weeks during the height of summer. His eyes rolled back in his head. "I'm close."

Fuck, no!

Enough was enough.

I may be a professional, but I still had limits.

I bit down as hard as I could. Sinking teeth into flesh is more difficult than it sounds. A penis isn't quite as easy to chew as your standard hotdog. The situation played out the same every time. First, a brief pause when the guy doesn't know what's happening. After that, the pain and panic set in like someone lit their balls on fire.

"Fuuuuuuuuuuuuuuuuuuuuck!"

Raphael screamed like a wounded animal. He grabbed a fistful of my hair. His shit wouldn't fly with me. He may be bigger, but I had all the power. I once watched a documentary about how crocodiles kill their prey. That's exactly what I liked to do.

I locked my jaw down in a motherfucking death grip and ripped straight through. Thrashing around didn't do him any favors. The more he struggled, the more he tore.

Oomph. A kick to my stomach loosened my hold enough for the bastard to pull away.

"You crazy bitch!" he yowled, clutching onto his split dicklet. *How disappointing.* I'd been hoping for a clean break. He staggered to his feet to make a desperate hobble for the door. "Somebody help!"

In his eagerness, he tripped over the corner of the rug and landed with a thud. What better way to be found? His pants around his ankles and spouting blood from his dick like a fountain. It had a poetic ring to it. After building his wealth on the exploitation of others, this was exactly what he deserved.

"No one is coming," I said, wiping his blood from my chin with the back of my hand. I'd been waiting to do this for a long time. I wanted to savor every second. He'd spent the last thirty years trafficking and selling underage girls. The fucker was gonna pay for what he did. "It's just the two of us."

"Why are you doing this?" He trembled. Seeing him like this made me realize how weak and pathetic he really was. How could I have ever been afraid of him? There was nothing impressive about picking on those who couldn't defend themselves. "What do you want?"

He reached for my ankle, but my reactions were quicker. Didn't he know stilettos could be as sharp as knives?

"This isn't my first rodeo," I hissed, driving my heel straight through the palm of his hand and pinning him to the floor.

He didn't bother calling out this time. Raphael may be a monster, but he wasn't stupid. There was no point in pleading when we both knew he wouldn't be leaving the room alive. His body would soon be decomposing in an acid-filled oil drum or chopped up and forced through a meat mincer… I hadn't decided yet.

"W-w-who are you?" he stammered.

I seductively ran a hand up my thigh, pulling the fabric away to reveal a blade tucked into my stocking. His gaze traveled to the distinct red scar. The letter R. A letter he had burned into my skin with a hot poker years before.

"What's the matter, honey?" I cocked my head to the side. "Do you remember me now?"

His eyes blackened with fury. The twisted sicko had never expected this day to come. I wanted him to die knowing exactly who had brought him down. Before he could say another word, I took my knife to his throat and slit it wide open.

I grinned down at my work. "Karma's a bitch, right?"

CHAPTER

One

THREE YEARS LATER...

I pulled up outside the strip club. Unlike every other building on the block, the pink neon sign hadn't succumbed to graffiti. That could be for two reasons, either: the owners took care of the joint, or the vandals were scared to get close. If it was the latter, the people inside were bad fucking news, which was the last thing I needed. But what other choice did I have? Taking off my clothes would beat living on a dumpster-diving diet, or worse…

Selling my jewelry had gotten me this far but, now, I was on my own and out of diamonds. I needed to make rent on my new place. It was a total dive and the cheapest apartment in town, but it was *mine*. If I could keep up with the payments. Apart from that, the only thing I owned was a beat-up old car stolen from a gas station a few months back. It'd been a miracle the cops didn't pick me up before I switched the plates.

It's not like I hadn't *tried* to look for an ordinary job. I'd wasted weeks canvassing neighborhoods for work in rundown diners and stores. Snotty hiring managers took one look down their noses at me and said they had no positions available, despite the clear-as-fuck vacancy sign still hanging in the window. People tend to make certain assumptions when you have tattoos, pink hair, and fake tits. *Judgmental jerks.*

Let's be real though, I'm hardly an employer's wet dream. A twenty-one-year-old with no qualifications or experience — well, none that'd be traditionally accepted anyway. Unlucky for me, being 'trained to kill assholes who deserved it' was not a pre-requisite on a barista job application. That's why I decided to move to Port Valentine. There were other ways to make money in a town like this… if I wanted to.

Over the decades, its rundown streets have been an epicenter for illicit activities. But, before resorting to my unconventional ways, I wanted to try something that didn't involve slashing throats.

Lapland was my best bet.

It wasn't exactly what I had in mind when I left Hiram to live a normal life. Then again, what did someone as damaged and broken as me know about normal? The only thing I knew for sure was that I needed cash. Fast. Stripping was a realistic option and playing a role would be nothing new. Besides, I'd done a hell of a lot worse than batting my eyelashes, shaking my ass, and twirling around a pole for money before.

I'd parked far enough away from the door to be concealed from view. As I turned the handle to get out, a crashing noise stopped me. Had I imagined it? Old habits were hard to shake when you'd spent years watching your back. I took a deep breath to pull myself together — hell, I'd been less jittery when I'd seduced a congressman!

Moments later, the side entrance to Lapland burst open. Three shaven-headed beefcakes dragged a sniveling man into the alley. From a glance, I could tell his nose was broken, and, judging from his whimpering, he'd probably bust a few ribs too. The gang of baldies threw the guy to the floor and gave a signal to someone inside.

This is where the fun would begin.

A giant mountain of a man filled the entire door frame; almost as broad as he was tall. Imagine a literal embodiment of The Hulk, but not green and covered in tats. A distinct diagonal scar ran from his cheek to the corner of his mouth, which curled into a snarl. His biceps were so big he'd be able to fold the guy on the floor up into a suitcase as easily as making an origami bird.

I knew a killer when I saw one.

The Hulk didn't make his move straight away. He was biding his time and making it clear who was in control. I couldn't risk lowering the squeaky window to hear what they were saying, but I'd be damned if I could look away.

I'd bet the guy on the ground had shat himself and offered up his only child on a plate by now. You'd be shocked to find out how low people sunk once they realized their life was balancing on a knife edge. None of them seemed to understand bribery, almost always, made things worse. When someone decides you're going to die, there's nothing you can do about it.

The Hulk pulled out a gun. He could rip someone's head straight off their shoulders with his bare hands in his sleep. Wasn't using a weapon a bit of a cop-out? A little too easy? Or, perhaps he did it so often that he didn't feel in the mood to pound bones to a pulp tonight? The thought sent a shiver up my thighs.

I liked how he had no idea that I was hiding in the shadows, watching him. It's rare to get the chance to see another artist at work and, there I was, getting my own private show. A unique insight into the mind of a beast. I should want to get away. After all, it'd been me who had wanted to leave my old life behind and start afresh. Maybe I'd been naïve in thinking I could ever get on the straight and narrow.

The muscled monster squeezed his finger on the trigger. I didn't even blink as the gun fired and splattered chunks of brain all over the bricks.

The Hulk looked down at the remains with a grim smile of satisfaction, making the hairs on the back of my neck stand on end. It was an expression I knew all too well. He'd done what he had to do. I'd found someone like me. Someone who had danger running through their veins. If you cut him open, he'd bleed havoc and destruction. He was the last person you'd want to run into in the dark and every father's worst nightmare rolled into one.

The beast kicked the corpse for good measure and disappeared inside. I slunk back in my seat, as his merry band of security appeared to tidy the mess he left behind. It'd be a nasty clean-up job, but nothing a jet wash couldn't fix.

What did it say about the club if people weren't afraid to shoot someone in a spot where anyone could walk on by? Shady underground shit had to be going on within those walls.

The best thing to do would be to drive away and pretend I'd not seen anything, but I wasn't about to do that. Danger had a strange way of drawing me in and, perhaps, it was time I accepted an ordinary life wasn't for everyone...

———

Inside, Lapland was definitely not an icy kingdom home to Santa's workshop. Picture crushed red velvet, black leather, low lights, and drapes hiding one too many dark corners. It was seedy enough to attract the drunks and give the appearance of being *just* another strip club, but something more sinister lurked in the shadows. This was a place where dirty deals were struck; where players exchanged cash under poker tables and lives were traded like gambling chips.

The air had a distinctive smell too: whiskey, cigars, cheap perfume, and a whiff of desperation... or that could have been the group of suburban dads hoping to get their dicks wet when their wives were away for the weekend. *Fucking idiots.* They didn't know how lucky they had it.

Hawk-eyed girls clad with sequined pasties worked the crowd, looking out for the guys with the biggest wallet and lowest self-esteem. You could spot the more experienced hosts a mile away, already grinding on laps in high-backed booths. Under UV light, those seats would glow like they were freaking radioactive.

Across the floor, dancers writhed on poles and in cages on several podiums, but it was easy to see where the main action happened. Spotlights pointed at the stage right in the heart of the club. It was higher than the other platforms, like a prized spot in a trophy cabinet. In the middle of it, a ten-foot pole painted with red and white stripes resembled a giant candy cane. Whoever danced there would be the star of the show for the evening. That's where the big money was and where I needed to be.

The barmaid glared at me from underneath blunt bangs that looked like they'd give you a paper cut if you accidentally brushed by. Her black bob streaked with fiery red made her porcelain skin look almost iridescent, and an inverse labret stud drew my attention to a cupid's bow so sharp it looked like she'd penciled it on with a fucking ruler. Aside from that, the main thing I noticed? Her fake as fuck expression told me she thought her shit didn't stink.

"What do you want?" she eventually snapped, after serving everyone else in sight.

"Vodka," I said, unperturbed by her complete lack of customer service. "Double."

"Ice?" She looked like she'd rather be glassing me with a bottle instead of pouring a drink out of one.

I smiled, which only seemed to piss her off more. "Of course."

The bitch slammed my drink down on the counter and shoved it toward me. One sip was enough for me to realize she'd cut it with water. I downed it one.

"Another," I demanded.

She narrowed her eyes. Clearly, she wasn't used to being challenged.

"Have it your way," she said, as I handed over my last five-dollar bill for an even more diluted excuse of a vodka. I wasn't dumb enough to give her a reaction — not yet, anyway. There would be plenty of time for games later but, right now, I'd come on a mission.

"Who do I speak to about getting a job around here?" I asked.

"You want to work here?" She raised one perfectly plucked eyebrow and crossed her arms over her chest. "Not going to fucking happen."

I was seconds away from tearing her septum piercing straight out of her face and attaching it to the back of my car when a voice behind me froze my feet to the spot.

"Oh really, Vixen?" A voice so fucking cold it'd make the flames of hell turn to ice. "Since when do you have that authority?"

"We don't need someone like her, Zander," Vixen spat, looking at me in disgust. "Just *look* at her."

"As one of the Sevens, you should remember I'm the boss and this is my club," Zander said, holding up a hand to silence her. I hadn't heard of the Sevens before, but I assumed it was the name of the gang in charge. A gang he was the leader of. A gang I should avoid if I knew what was good for me. "And I choose my girls."

My girls.

His words should make me want to run, but I didn't. Instead, I turned to find myself staring into the stormy gray eyes of a devil in a perfectly fitted black suit. A chokehold of tattoos enveloped his throat and crept over the top of his crisp white collar. An inked silhouette of a single rose adorned the side of his face; the thorns cut across the razor edge of his cheekbones like a warning to stay away. If we were in a fairytale, he would be the type of prince who'd fuck the princess senseless, destroy her happily ever after, and... she'd still be begging for more.

"You." His dead stare locked on me with such an intensity it made the rest of the room fall away. "What's your name?"

"Candy."

"Candy, what?"

"Uh..." I stalled, looking around for inspiration and landing on the first thing in sight. "Cane."

Okay, it sounded a *little* ridiculous. But I'd have to own it. It shouldn't be hard, considering I'd already spent most of my life explaining to people that Candy was my actual name and not something I'd made up to sound cute. Cute is the last word I'd use to describe myself.

My full name is Candy Green, but it'd been years since I'd gone by that identity. The story behind my name is a funny one. When my two-week-old baby self got dumped on the doorstep of Evergreen kid's home, my fate had been sealed. Every abandoned baby was automatically given the last name 'Green' and whoever discovered them was given the honor of choosing the first name. Unfortunately, the brat who found me was a toddler with a sweet tooth.

"Candy Cane?" Zander repeated. The corner of his mouth twitched up in what could be the beginning of a smile or a snarl, but it was too hard to tell.

"Yep," I said, popping the p. "That's me."

He paused, as his eyes trailed up and down my body with the precision of an X-ray machine. They lingered a little too long on the stretch of skin where my crop top ended and shorts began. That one look told me all I needed to know. He had the power to tear people down, rip them apart, and shatter their souls into little pieces. Lucky for me, I wasn't made of glass.

Finally, a twisted panty-dropping grin spread over his face. "You have one dance."

"You've got to be kidding, Zander," Vixen objected. I got the feeling she would give anything to claw my eyeballs with her pointed talons. "You're out of your fucking mind!"

"Show Candy backstage," Zander ordered. His decision was final. "What difference will one more slut make?"

———

Vixen stayed silent as I followed her into the dressing room, where twenty other girls were practically pulling at each other's extensions to get closer to the mirrors. You'd think they were preparing to go on a catwalk, not the stage of a seedy titty bar.

"Who is *she*?" a girl hissed.

"The boss picked her out," Vixen declared.

Everyone spun around to stare me down. What a great start. I'd only just walked in, but they had already made me public enemy number one. There was nothing like slicing someone open before throwing them into a shark tank.

"Her?!"

"Have fun competing for the top spot." Vixen blew me a sarcastic kiss, making me hope she'd get a yeast infection in her skin-tight leather pants. "You're up last if you're still here by the end of the night."

"Lapland is only for the best." A leggy brunette cornered me. I resisted the urge to roll my eyes. Since when did strippers have a fucking A-Lister status? I must have missed the memo. "We don't have room here for trash."

"You're right, Bella," a blonde with a dodgy nose job agreed. "Cupid's always has openings, though."

"Even they are not *that* desperate," Bella added, looking pleased with herself as the rest of the group snickered in response. "They want high-class escorts."

I stood my ground. This wasn't a fucking playground, and her attempts to intimidate me wouldn't work. Bella may be the Queen Bee around here, but I didn't have a problem getting stung.

"Why don't you take it up with Zander if you have a problem?" I asked, cocking my hip and planting my hand there.

Bella flinched at the mention of his name, then regained her resting bitch face.

"You're only in the trials for the freak factor," Bella said. "You didn't think he was serious about you dancing here, did you?"

"What's wrong?" I questioned. "Are you feeling threatened, Bells?"

Everyone drew a sharp intake of breath. Bella may rule over her minions, but someone would have to put bullets through my kneecaps to get me to bow down to her throne.

"Listen up, you little whore!" Bella loomed over me. Puh-lease. Did she really think the sight of her underboob would make me beg for mercy? I'd survived being tortured and locked in a prison basement for months. After that ordeal, it'd take more than unnaturally perky breasts for me to break out in a sweat. "Lapland has a certain reputation. They're not going to let in trailer trash. Everyone knows the top spot is mine."

Bella didn't *want* the top spot, she needed it. She'd be lucky to get another three years out of dancing before the partying and botched plastic surgery forced her off the main stage. Youth didn't last forever, and she fucking knew it. It would make taking her crown even sweeter.

"We'll see," I said, with a shrug.

"You'll regret—"

A megaphone requesting Annabella's presence on stage stopped her from finishing whatever threat she was about to throw my way.

I yawned. "And here I thought this would be a slumber party."

"This isn't over," she hissed in my ear, before flouncing away in a fog of cheap perfume.

Yep, I guess that meant we wouldn't be having a pillow fight and sipping hot cocoa arm-in-arm any time soon. Whoever said girls should stick together talked utter bullshit. We lived in a dog-eat-dog world and these girls were thirsty bitches.

My cell phone vibrating in my pocket jolted me back to reality like a taser shot in the ass. Stripper wars were the least of my problems. This could only be one person.

Missing me yet, Kitten? The message read.

Yeah, like a hole in the fucking head.

The mouthy brown-nosing blonde felt like now would be a great time to face off against me. "Where are you going?"

"I'm getting a drink." I clenched my fists, readying for a fight. "Do you have a fucking problem?"

"I don't know who you think you are; swanning in and—"

I was on top of her before she even saw me coming. I grabbed her pony-tail and twisted it around my knuckles like I was preparing to go into a boxing ring.

"Unless you want to have your nose rearranged again," I said, yanking her head back with full force. "I'd shut the fuck up and tell me you don't have a problem."

The rest of the sheep shifted nervously in their seats, but none of them made an effort to move. Since when did applying bronzer to your cleavage become more important than helping a friend? Spineless assholes. If they had each other's backs, they'd be all over me and I wouldn't stand a chance.

"N-n-no problem," Blondie yelped. "I don't have a problem!"

"That's what I thought," I sneered, releasing her and hoping none of them noticed the slight tremor in my voice.

———

Way to fucking go, Candy!

I'd lived in a world of violence for so long that it came as naturally to me as breathing. It'd been six months since I'd left Hiram, and he knew exactly how to get under my skin.

Missing me yet, Kitten?

I'd been a fool to think he'd let me go so easily. I may have worked hard to win my freedom, but it didn't change how Hiram saw me. He'd always believe I belonged to him. That I was his. I'd thought our contract would be enough to hold him at bay. Hiram might be the most twisted motherfucker around, but he was a man of his word. Even if he didn't plan to break our agreement, it didn't guarantee he wouldn't try to find a way around it and destroy me... again.

If he came for me, I'd have to be ready this time.

Over the last five years, Hiram had molded me into an unstoppable killing force. He'd made sure the sweet and innocent girl I used to be was gone. She'd been replaced by a fucking lion who could play him at his own game. I knew all his old tricks. Hiram was a dirty player, but he'd trained me to be a worthy opponent. The text was his way of toying with me. It'd only be a matter of time before he played his next move. All I could do was wait until he showed his hand.

Right now, I had to address more immediate concerns. I needed to get my head together before I attacked another stripper and blew any chance I had at getting a job. Up on the main stage, Bella humped the pole to the beat of the music. One look at her smug, money-grabbing face made me want to punch something. I needed to...

"Hey, watch where you're going!"

I wiped my watery eyes from the force of the blow. Goddammit, I'd been too busy fantasizing about breaking Bella's legs I'd walked face-first into a human built like a literal fucking house. What the hell were his pecks made from? Bricks?

Oh, shit.

One glance confirmed my suspicions.

It was him.

The killer in the alleyway.

"Why aren't you backstage?" Vixen appeared out of nowhere. "This isn't a whorehouse. You need to do more than just spread your legs to get paid here."

For once, being called a whore was a welcome distraction. I could deal with a snarky bitch like Vixen any day of the week, but the hulk-like man? I didn't trust what I'd say if I opened my mouth around him.

"I'm getting a drink," I replied, not daring to look up at the beast at her side.

"No alcohol on the job." Vixen scowled, then addressed the man. "West, our guest has arrived."

I followed their gaze to a booth where Zander was clinking glasses with a man with cropped dark hair and a sharp nose. He was traditionally handsome but made me uneasy. I'd been in enough tricky situations to trust my gut feeling and something about him made my skin crawl. When his guest looked the other way, Zander expertly emptied his glass into the ice bucket with one seamless motion. Judging from Vixen's eyes darting back and forth, a deal was going down and it was important nothing fucked it up.

Vixen zeroed in on me again like a hungry Rottweiler. "What are you still doing here?"

"Struggling to control your girls, Vix?" West mocked. The deep husky growl of his tone simultaneously made my blood run cold and ignited a fire between my legs. "We don't need airheads running around here. Girls like her are only good for one thing."

"Here I was thinking you were enjoying my company," I quipped back, then instantly regretted it.

God help me. Why couldn't my damn smart mouth control itself? I knew exactly how trigger-happy this man could be.

"I wouldn't even pay for your company," West said, causing Vixen to cackle.

"You said you wanted a job," she snarled. "So fucking prove it."

———

The other dancers mustn't have been as stupid as I first thought. On my return to the dressing room, none of them were brave enough to look in my direction without their Queen Bee around. My little performance with Blondie had sent them all a clear message. Play with gasoline and you're gonna get burned.

As a late addition to this evening's line-up, there were no spare costumes for me to wear. Whilst the rest of the girls strutted around in tiny scraps of fabric, I had to get creative. Bella may think this was a classy club, but I knew from experience how powerful men had an appetite for things that were a little less refined.

I took scissors to my crop top to shorten it even further and leave it sitting just under my boobs. My denim shorts were basically hot pants anyway — thankfully, they were so well-worn I could move in them fine. I hit the jackpot by finding black tape at the back of the lipstick drawer and used it to cover my nipples. It'd sting like a bitch to pull off, but I needed to rock the 'down and dirty' look. If it meant having X's over my tits then that's what I had to do.

"Now, for the final dance of the evening!" The host's introduction rang through the club. Did they *have* to make my entrance sound so dramatic? "I present to you, Candy Cane!"

I piled my pink waist-length hair into a high ponytail and slipped off my boots. They were great for kicking men in the balls but not so good for hanging upside down on a pole. The audience would have to deal with the fact I wasn't eight feet tall, in skyscraper heels, like everyone else.

The beat from Marilyn Manson's 'Tainted Love' cover played as I stepped into the spotlight to take the stage like it was my fucking territory. I may not have a diamond G-string up my ass, but that didn't mean I couldn't work my way around a pole. Lapland may only be reserved for the best, but I would show them what it meant to be real.

As I climbed the striped pole, I tried not to think about how Zander and West were sitting somewhere in the audience. I hadn't always been a natural performer, but Hiram's training forced me to shred every one of my inhibitions. Now, stripping for a crowd came as easily to me as brushing my teeth in the morning. At the top of the pole, I locked my ankle in place and dropped into a perfect leg hang which made the clapping go wild.

The chanting started getting louder.

I whipped back upright, straddling the metal between my legs, and gave the audience a cheeky wink before corkscrewing down into an angel pose. You didn't honeytrap as many men as I had without having a few moves in your repertoire. I needed to hold on long enough to get them panting.

I shook my hair out of the ponytail and dropped to the floor, giving the crowd a good eyeful of my booty. Five crisp fifty-dollar bills fluttered down at my feet, which felt like a middle finger to the more distinguished dancers who were hellbent on throwing me onto the sidewalk.

I looked up to catch the eye of my admirer who I recognized as the guest Zander had been entertaining. Behind him, Zander whispered furiously in West's ear.

"I have more where that came from," their guest bragged, pulling a thick roll of cash from his pocket and confirming my earlier instincts.

The only people brave enough to carry around that much dirty money knew no one would be stupid enough to try to steal it. I dubbed them the 'Untouchables'. They could be gang leaders, drug lords, corrupt politicians, or media moguls who had so much filth on corporations they could bring them down with a single click. It didn't matter which category he fell into. Money was power, and he had a shit tonne of it.

I bit my lip and leaned forward to tease him with a glimpse of my cleavage. He tossed another bill my way. This was too easy.

Bella better be watching from the wings and taking notes because I wasn't going to make it rain... I'd make it fucking pour.

CHAPTER
Two

"You've got to be fucking joking!" As usual, my zero-filtered mouth acted before my brain had time to catch up. "Did you even see me dance?"

No one could question whether I'd outperformed the other dancers during the trials. The crowd got so crazy there were calls for an encore at the end of my routine. I'd made five hundred dollars from Zander's creepy guest too — shouldn't she be showing me a little gratitude? My motorboating skills would have helped to sweeten whatever deal they were making.

"Bella has the top spot," Vixen repeated to the group, then turned to me. "The sooner you learn your place here, the better. If you want to stay, you're starting right at the fucking bottom. If you don't like it, I'd suggest you walk out the door and never come back."

"You'd be doing us all a favor to crawl back to the gutter you came from," Bella chimed in.

Oh, I'm sure she'd love that. The bitch may wear my crown, but we both knew she didn't deserve the top title. The fact I'd earned it didn't matter. In Lapland, it would never be a fair fight when nobody played by the rules. Bella had another thing coming if she thought I'd roll over and give up so easily. Her days were fucking numbered.

"If I'm not dancing," I said, "then, why did you even call me back here?"

Vixen smirked as the evil cogs turned in her mind, reminding me of a nutty professor planning the apocalypse. She must have had serious shit happen in her own life to be this determined to make mine miserable.

"You're going to be our new cleaner."

I flashed her my most dazzling smile which I usually reserved for right before I rip off somebody's toenails. "When do I start?"

She'd underestimated me if she thought scrubbing spunk off seats would scare me away. Unlike the other bimbos, I was no stranger to getting my hands dirty. Breaking a few nails had to be better than breaking bones for a living, right?

"Tomorrow." Vixen eyed me with suspicion. "You'll be first here and last out at night, is that clear?"

"Crystal," I said. "Whatever you say, *boss.*"

I may start by mopping the floor, but I had no intention of staying at the bottom for long. The only way to bring down a hierarchy was from the inside, and there was serious money to be made here. If I couldn't dance for tips, I'd have to figure out what operation Zander was running… and how I could use it to my advantage.

———

Zander may be the boss of Lapland's underground business and the elusive gang known as the Sevens, but Vixen ruled over the daily running of the club. Her Majesty ruled with an iron fist and nothing was good enough for her exacting standards. She'd screamed for twenty minutes at the delivery guy because a bottle had accidentally smashed in transit; I counted myself lucky she'd only asked me to clean the urinals three times over.

"Well?" Vixen appeared in the dressing room, where I was busy buffing the mirrors. She had a nasty habit of materializing like the Grim Reaper when you least expected it. "When're you going to change? We're opening soon."

"Nobody mentioned a uniform."

Since when did you have to dress up to clean toilets? My comfy as fuck jeans and baggy T-shirt were all I needed.

"We're a strip club, if you haven't noticed," Vixen spoke in a slow, patronizing drawl. "You'll be clearing empty glasses on the floor. You can't wear *that.*"

"Fine." I crossed my arms to stop myself from shoving the cloth down her throat. "Where's my uniform?"

"Here," she said, placing a bag down and leaning back against the wall to watch my reaction. "It'll be perfect for you."

"Wow." I glowered at the contents. A French maid outfit complete with matching stockings. Couldn't she have tried to be more original? "I can see you put a lot of thought into it."

The costume had been bought from a budget fancy dress store meaning

I'd look even less like the other dancers in their boutique lingerie. It could have a silver lining, though. Rich men had a thing for maids, so maybe I could find a way to work it for extra tips.

"Don't even think about speaking to customers," Vixen snapped as if she'd read my mind. "We have hosts for that. All you need to do is collect empty glasses and clean up the mess. Think you can handle it?"

"Just about," I muttered.

Oh, honey... you have no idea what I can handle.

"My cousin may have picked you out, but that doesn't mean you're fucking special." Her eyes flashed in warning, showing a whole new level of crazy lurking under the surface. Vixen and Zander being related explained why he hadn't fired the charmless psychopath yet. "You don't want to make an enemy of me, Candy."

"I'm the one you should be worried about," I murmured under my breath, as the bitch stomped away in her New Rock boots.

Vixen may think she's an ice queen, but it wouldn't be enough to extinguish the inferno that burned inside me. Being around Zander made her untouchable at work, but it didn't make her invincible. She wouldn't know what hit her if I went Guy Fawkes on her ass. If I didn't need the money, her house would already be burnt to the fucking ground and I'd be dancing in the ashes.

My first shift didn't improve after changing into my compulsory uniform. I flashed my panties every time I bent over in my short dress. Sleaze balls took it as an invitation to pat — yes, fucking PAT — my ass. The slimy bastards didn't even leave a tip because they thought it was the correct way to show their gratitude for collecting empties. With their manners, it's no fucking surprise they had to pay women for company.

The club was quieter on a Sunday night, as no big performances were scheduled. Bella and her followers had descended upon the floor to reel in horny desperados for private dances. Judging from her overzealous hair swishing, Bella would give the old guy with false teeth a lot more than a lap dance by the end of the night. He'd already ordered the best champagne and Bella hung on his every word, lighting up every time he swiped his platinum card.

Out of the corner of my eye, I clocked Vixen slipping out from behind the bar to the side entrance. Shortly after, she resurfaced with two men by her side, donning a rare smile. Only one thing would make her grin like that: cold, hard cash. I pressed myself against the wall and edged my way around a group of drunken revelers to get a closer look.

Vixen showed the guests into a private booth and, a few seconds later, she emerged alone. The dancers were too busy grinding on stranger's boners and the customers were too distracted by trying not to cum in their pants, to even notice people slipping in undetected under their noses. Nothing got past me, though. I'd lived in a world where survival depended on noticing what other people missed. Everyone knows if you're oblivious, you're as good as dead.

Over the next hour, more men arrived. The same thing happened each time. Vixen had the whole slick routine nailed. You didn't have to be a rocket scientist to work out there must be a hidden door somewhere. There was barely enough room to house two people in the space — let alone seven!

Whatever was happening, I wanted in.

———

I planned my move carefully. As soon as Vixen went to greet the next arrival, I positioned myself close to the booth and waited for the perfect moment. Then, like clockwork...

"Oopsie!" I stumbled from the shadows and, miraculously, found myself in the arms of a stranger. I mean, what had Vixen expected from a ditzy, clumsy maid who lacked the coordination to be a dancer?

The man looked down at me. "Well, aren't you a sight for sore eyes?"

"You're my hero!" I beamed at my savior as he helped me to my feet. The fabric of his suit was expensive to the touch, and the thick gold chain around his neck almost blinded me. "Thank you."

It was a cliché move, but it's a classic for a reason. What man doesn't want to save a poor damsel in distress? The helpless princess always lands the handsome prince or, in this case, a ticket to a private gathering taking place in a strip club.

He spoke in a strong New Jersey accent, "You need to be careful where you're stepping in those heels."

"I'm so clumsy." I shook my head and squeezed his arm in thanks. "If you hadn't been there to catch me, then I don't know what I'd have done..."

Vixen bared her teeth in a lackluster attempt at a smile. "Don't you have work to be getting on with, Candy?"

If looks could kill, the daggers she was shooting would have impaled me. Luckily, even she wasn't stupid enough to make a scene in front of a client. Who knew she had it in her to be so professional?

"You can't be all work and no play, Vix." The man playfully nudged her in the ribs — a move that would have had many others castrated. "Why don't you give the girl a break?"

"Vixen's right." I bit my lip and pulled down the hem of my dress to flash an extra pop of cleavage his way. Yet another classic maneuver that never failed. "I should get back to work. I'm sorry again for being such a klutz."

It would only take... 3... 2...

"Candy, is it?" The man held out an outstretched hand. "I'm Vinny."

"It's so rare to meet a proper gentleman."

Vinny was in his fifties and, from his puffed chest, I could tell I'd hit his sweet spot. Underneath the tough guy act and firm grip, he was still a stickler for old-fashioned values. No one got to the top of their game without doing some damage, but he'd be the type who'd feel bad after killing a man who had a wife and kids at home.

"I've had an idea!" Vinny's eyes lit up in excitement, still completely oblivious to the subconscious mind games I'd been playing. "I think this little minx may just be the good luck charm I need tonight."

"Me?" I gasped and put my hand to my mouth in mock surprise. "A good luck charm?"

"You know the Sevens' rules, Vinny," Vixen warned. "No girls."

"I'll tell you what, how does an extra ten G's to seal the deal sound? I'll also forget about the little favor Zander owes me?" he suggested. "Tonight is a game amongst friends after all."

Vixen paused to consider his proposal, then nodded sharply in agreement. "Done."

"Now, tell me..." Vinny pulled open the curtain and led me into the booth. "Are you as sweet as your name suggests?"

"Oh, Vinny." I giggled. "You have no idea..."

What can I say? The fairytale formula gets proven results. No one expects Sleeping Beauty to have a knife under her pillow.

Vinny loved the sound of his own voice. From the moment we passed through the not-so-secret door and down the hidden staircase; all I had to do was laugh whenever he took a break for air. Whilst he was blathering, I made a mental note of the door's keypad combination when he typed it in. 6-9-6-9. Real fucking mature, but remembering it could come in handy someday.

"I'm feeling really lucky tonight, Candy," Vinny exclaimed, rubbing his hands together. "What d'you think? Am I gonna win big?"

Once upon a time, Vinny may have been a big shot. Now, he had more money than sense and only enjoyed having a pretty young piece on his arm to stroke his ego. The most pathetic part of all? He didn't realize it only made him look more desperate and irrelevant. It wouldn't be long until he faded into insignificance entirely and the wolves closed in to take his place.

"Definitely," I chirped, playing the part of the personal cheerleader he wanted me to be. All I needed was pompoms to shake along. "I'm your good luck charm, remember?"

We made our way through the underground corridor, where closed doors beckoned me like shiny invitations. Most women fantasized about their dream weddings, but me? I got my kicks from unearthing secrets people wanted to stay buried. I was damn good at it, too. One of the first lessons Hiram taught me was how money could buy you anything, but knowledge had the power to rip it all away. Empires, careers, and lives can be destroyed in an instant when information gets into the wrong hands.

"This is our stop." Vinny opened a door for me to pass. "Ladies first."

Black leather chairs surrounded a poker table. The smell of cigars, whiskey, and testosterone hit me like a cum shot to the face. I'd been in rooms like this many times before. A scent combination like that meant the big boys were here to play. I was about to discover who sat on these thrones and ruled the kingdom.

As soon as my heel hit the tiles, heads snapped around to gawp in my direction. I bit my tongue to stop myself from making a joke about whiplash. You'd think this was the first time they'd ever seen a woman.

"No girls allowed." A gigantic figure rose from his seat. Trust the fucking Hulk to have a problem. He was on a constant man period. "Rules are rules."

Vinny waved his hand nonchalantly. "Vixen agreed Candy will accompany me."

"She didn't run it past me," West hissed. "Or the rest of the Sevens."

How many people made up the Sevens? So far, I knew West, Vixen, and Zander… was that all of them? Or were more monsters skulking around in the shadows who I hadn't met yet? I made a mental note to find out.

"Come on, West!" another player, the same bag of shit who'd made my stomach turn and tipped me generously last night, said. "I've always had a soft spot for maids."

"Candy is with me this evening," Vinny said stiffly. From the change in Vinny's tone, he wasn't a fan of the guy. Either that, or he didn't want to have wasted ten grand for someone else to pull me from under his feet. Men acted like dogs; they loved to piss on women to claim their territory. "She is *my* guest."

West shot a venomous glare in my direction. Being in the company of others gave me immunity, and we both knew it. I didn't allow myself to think about what would happen when he next got me alone.

"You sit next to him and don't say a word," West ordered.

I nodded dutifully, enjoying the way a vein protruded from his forehead in anger. He seriously needed to work on keeping his emotions in check. If he kept going like this, his blood pressure would put him in an early grave before someone from a rival gang did.

"She won't be any trouble," Vinny promised, pulling out a chair for me to sit down. That was easy for him to say when he had no idea who he'd really invited along. "Will you, Candy?"

"No, sir." Well, not tonight anyway. "You won't even know I'm here."

"Atta girl!" Vinny patted my thigh. "See, West? Everyone's happy!"

Well, almost everyone. I wasn't exactly overjoyed at the prospect of having to act like Vinny's fucking golden retriever for the evening.

"Let's fucking play," West growled. He returned to his chair, which was larger than the others to accommodate his muscular frame, and nodded for the dealer to shuffle. I'm surprised he hadn't ground his teeth to the bone with how hard his jaw was clenched. Someone needed to teach him how to cut loose.

The dealer started to lay down the cards. It was time for the real games to begin. I may have entered the lion's den, but none of them suspected a new predator was now in their midst.

———

As the night wore on, it became obvious Vinny didn't know a rat's ass about poker. Being clueless didn't stop him from laying down twenty big ones on a shit hand. It was easy to see why everyone treated him like royalty here. He burned through cash and expensive liquor faster than a car lit up by a petrol bomb.

"What do you say, Candy?" Vinny asked, already pulling out a fat roll of cash. He had more money on him than Mr. fucking Monopoly. "Winner takes all in the last game?"

Between fluttering my eyelashes and flicking hair over my shoulder, I'd been watching the players closely. Three of them, including Vinny, knew fuck all about playing the game. They'd only been invited to make up the numbers and crank up the pot. The remaining four all had some skill, but West was the one I had my eye on. He knew his way around the deck but the big guy wasn't playing to win. No, he'd carefully orchestrated the game like a conductor by pre-empting every move to strike up a perfect balance of wins and losses. Just enough to give the players a flavor of victory to keep them reaching into their pockets and coming back for more.

"Why don't we make things a little more interesting?" The suggestion came from the heavy tipper perve who had spent most of the evening ogling my tits from across the table. "Candy should play."

The muscles in West's neck tensed. "You know the rules, Cheeks."

From listening to their conversations, I learned Cheeks was a bent cop drunk on power. He seemed to know everything that was going on in Port Valentine, or at least that's what he wanted everyone to think. If something dirty was going down, you'd bet he'd be around to smooth things over and collect a cheque for his troubles. Cheeks could be schmoozing the Mayor one evening and making sure an arms delivery arrives without a hitch the next. He had to be a twisted bastard to make an oath to protect people, then help murderers and rapists stay on the streets.

"I'll buy her in." Vinny counted out a stack of crisp hundred-dollar bills. "What do you say?"

"Be a sport!" One of the older gents clapped West on the back in encouragement. "What harm could it do?"

West could treat me like the devil incarnate all he liked, but hello? It's not like I'd asked to play. Letting me join a game was a small commiseration for having to sit around listening to this group of animals measuring the size of their dicks for hours.

"I'll let her play, but it's your money you're wasting." West shrugged. "You don't pay a girl like *that* to use her head."

As if I hadn't heard the same line before. A good ole misogynistic spreading the legs quip grew old fast. For someone smart enough to mastermind an illegal casino, West was surprisingly unobservant.

"Tell you what." Vinny refilled his scotch. "We'll go 50/50 if you win."

"But I've only played a few times before..."

It pained me to act all dumb and innocent, but it got the response I wanted.

"Don't they play poker at the trailer park?" West rebutted, taking my bait.

The prick. Didn't anyone ever teach him never to underestimate an opponent? I'd been planning to go easy on him, but it was about time someone taught him a lesson. By the time I'd wiped the floor with him, he'd be slurping his words through a straw.

"You ignore them, darlin'," Vinny said. "You're my good luck charm tonight, remember?"

Vinny may be a schmuck, but he'd lost thousands tonight. The least I could do was get him back the money he'd paid for my invitation. Besides, the winning pot now stood at fifty grand and the extra money would come in handy. Rent was due in a few days, and I craved food with more nutritional value than a packet of mac and cheese.

———

"What did I tell you, Candy?" Vinny grabbed my face and kissed me on both cheeks. "You're my lucky charm."

"Oh my gosh, I can't believe it," I said, dragging out my words to do my best bimbo impersonation. "I guess it must be beginner's luck."

West's stare cut through my core like molten lava as his eyes flicked from me to the straight flush laid on the table. He knew this had nothing to do with luck. If only he'd seen through my bluff sooner. Who would have suspected the pink-haired stripper was a poker pro?

West threw down strong moves throughout the game, but he had diverted his attention to the other players long enough to give me the upper hand. It wasn't until the river he noticed something was wrong. By then, it was too late... he was already drowning.

Over the years, I'd accompanied Hiram to casinos and watched from the shadows. Learning the rules of poker was one thing, but it wasn't enough to make you a winner. The game is as much about analyzing the other players as the cards. It's a good thing people are easier to read than books because I've cataloged the full fucking library. I'd never lost a game.

"It's the first time I've won in ten years," Vinny said. He scooped up the prize pot with all the glee of an addict getting their next shot of snow. Technically, I'd won... but I wouldn't ruin this moment for him. Logically, he'd have to 'win' at some point, right? "I had a good feeling about you, Candy."

"I just can't believeeee it!" I crooned.

"I'm a man of my word," Vinny said, slipping me my cut of the cash. *Thank you very much.* It'd sort my bills for the next year. "You buy yourself something nice, won't you?"

"Oh, I will."

I stashed it inside my bra and flashed West a sparkling smile, which he met with a scowl. The puppet master wasn't happy to learn he hadn't been the only one pulling the strings.

"You're a lot more than a pretty face, Miss Cane," Cheeks leered. Yep, this 'pretty face' actually had a brain and the ability to ram a corkscrew down his urethra without hesitation. "Why don't I take you up to the bar and buy you a drink, huh?"

Before I could respond, West cut in.

"She has work to do," West said, saving me the effort of coming up with an excuse. Although, I had a funny feeling he wasn't trying to do me a favor. "If she still wants to keep her job."

"He's right." I threw my hands up in the air to signal it was a completely hopeless case. "I need to clean up in here."

Thankfully, Vinny was too caught up in his winning high and the potential of making a dent in the bar's liquor stash to object. Thank fuck. My sweet and stupid act was souring fast. How did people smile all day without their face aching like they'd sucked a dragon chode? It was a full-on workout routine.

Cheeks winked at me over his shoulder as the party filed out. "I'll be seeing you soon, Candy."

The only place I'll be seeing you is in hell, motherfucker!

The man tipped well, but my intuition didn't lie. Learning he was a bent cop only proved it. I'd need to give Cheeks a wide birth, even if it meant having to face the wrath of West with no crowd immunity.

———

West slammed the door shut behind the last player. Hopefully, the building had firm foundations because the floor shook from the force. I braced myself for the worst, but West didn't say a word and whipped out his phone. On the screen, he pulled the club's CCTV footage and watched them move along the basement corridor. He waited until the final figure slipped back into the club, then turned to face me.

It was just the two of us.

Alone.

Just breathe, Candy. It's not fucking hard. You do it all the time.

"Where did you learn to play like that?"

West took a step closer and backed me into a corner. The walls suddenly felt like they were closing in. If it wasn't for his delicious smell — a mixture of rum, sandalwood, and a fancy cologne I couldn't remember the name of — I'd have thought he'd put a bag over my head and this was an astral experience.

"What's wrong?" My voice came out breathier than usual. "Upset about being beaten by a girl?"

"Don't fucking push me."

He punched the wall to the right of my head. The plasterboard breaking snapped me back into the moment, but I didn't flinch.

"Is that supposed to scare me?" I asked.

He could do better than that…

"It should do."

One wrong move would be like waving a red flag under the nose of a raging bull, but I never ran from confrontation.

"What're you going to do?" I cocked my head to the side and arched an eyebrow in mild bemusement. "Take me to the parking lot and shoot me, too?"

He spluttered. "How did you—"

"Chill out, okay?" As much as I enjoyed making him squirm, I didn't want to have to answer Zander's questions if West ended up tearing apart the entire room. "Your secret is safe with me. But, a little tip for next time, maybe you should be more careful next time you take out your garbage?"

West looked at me. Like, *really* looked at me. As if he was only seeing me for the first time. "Who the fuck are you?"

"I'm just another airhead," I said. "Remember?"

Why did it feel so fucking good to be noticed by him? I'd been the one who'd insisted I wanted to skip into the sunset to live a normal life and look at me now! I stood face-to-face with a cold-blooded killer who had the tattooed muscles of an alternative Greek god. The worst thing of all? I didn't even care. Hiram may have been right all along when he said some people were destined to become monsters.

"We split the money down the middle," West growled, returning to his usual grisly self. "It's club policy."

"Club policy, or Seven policy?"

He narrowed his eyes. "Both."

"How about we make a deal?" I suggested, twirling a strand of hair around my finger. "I'll split the cash *if* I'm promoted to dancer and you give me permission to burn this outfit as soon as I take it off."

"Done." His mouth quirked upwards at the corners. Then, just as quickly, the ghost of a smile vanished. "What the fuck did you say your name was again?"

"Candy," I said. Remember that. I may sound sweet, but I'm the type of girl who'd break your teeth if you cross me. "Candy Cane."

West averted his eyes as I pulled the cash from the front of my dress. Well, who knew he could be such a gentleman? It pained me to part with the money, but I needed to play the long game. If I could make this amount in one night, think how much more I could earn over a few months… if Zander and his gang trusted me enough.

"Be careful, Candy." His stare scorched me with a soulless intensity only serial killers possessed. "You don't want to make an enemy of me."

"Don't worry," I said, sashaying out of the room on my heels. "I'll go easy on you next time."

My face broke out into a grin at the crash of a table being upturned behind me. I guess that's one way to deal with your masculinity being threatened by a stripper dressed as a maid. He didn't scare me. Not when I'd already been to hell and back.

I didn't run from the darkness… I fucking welcomed it.

CHAPTER
Three

I strutted into the dressing room like I owned it. "Did you miss me?"

If only I had a camera to film their reactions. Jaws hit the floor quicker than Bella dropped her panties for a wrinkly millionaire with saggy balls. From my observations, that was almost faster than the speed of light.

"What is *she* doing here?" Bella turned to Vixen in accusation. "I thought *she* was the help, not a dancer."

"*She* has a name," I reminded her.

"We've had a staff restructure," Vixen explained, refusing to admit her authority had been overruled. "It seems some of our clientele have lower standards and Candy will be filling the gap."

The bitch never failed to miss an opportunity to twist the knife in, but it didn't matter. We both knew the real reason why I was still around. All West had to do was click his fingers to get what he wanted. She wasn't as all-powerful as she thought. That would be killing the control freak inside her.

"None of our clients are that desperate." Bella tried to wrinkle her nose but the botox made her look constipated instead. "She was more suited to cleaning the bathroom."

"If you want me to be Cinderella, what does that make you?" I asked. "One of the ugly sisters?"

"You think you're so clever, don't you?" Bella snarled. "You won't last here. You're not the right fit."

"That's what everyone said to Cinders before she tried on the slipper. Haven't you read until the end of the story?" I asked. "The future doesn't look good for you"

She'd die old, ugly, and alone with only her bitter heart and poisonous tongue for company. Not that I believed in happily ever afters for people like me. They didn't exist. Life was no fucking fairy tale. Love was an excuse adults used to justify sleeping next to the same fat snoring bastard for fifty years.

"You bring any more trouble here and you're out, Candy." Vixen pointed one of her black-painted claws my way. "And I don't give a shit what West says."

Boss from hell, much? I resisted the urge to give her a one-finger salute as she stomped out of the room, cursing under her breath.

"West?" Blondie wailed, almost falling off her chair. I'd heard rumors she and West were seeing each other. Her reaction only confirmed it. I didn't understand how West could be interested in someone with zero backbone... or why the thought of him fucking a Barbie-wannabe made me want to rearrange her face.

"He wants to see me dance." I shrugged like it was nothing and made myself comfy at a vacant dressing table. "That's not a problem, is it?"

Blondie kept her mouth clamped shut. Almost scalping her must have made a lasting impact.

"She's lying, Scarlett," Bella said, patting her arm. "Ignore her. West is interested in you."

"What do you think? Will West like it?" I held up a lipstick. If winding them up was a sport, I was going for a gold medal. "Mm, it tastes like sour cherries."

"West wouldn't be interested in a slut like you." Bella looked down at her nose like I was a piece of shit caught in her stiletto and smiled knowingly to herself. "West likes classy women, just like Zander."

I snorted. Surely they weren't naïve enough to think they were living in a stripper version of the Stepford Wives? These men were using them like taps to get their dicks wet on demand. If Bella wasn't such a bitch, I'd feel bad her only source of genuine pride was wearing the fact the boss boned her like a badge of honor.

"At least I don't need to bang the boss to hold down a job," I pointed out.

I may have been an expert seductress in the past, but I'd never had full-on sex with any of my marks. It was another one of Hiram's rules. Not that I'd have wanted to. My vagina was a complete no-peen zone. The closest I'd got to sex was biting cocks off, although I wouldn't really count it. There's a blurred line between pleasure and pain but severed penises cross the line.

"They wouldn't want you, anyway. Who knows what diseases you have?" Bella scoffed. "I bet you don't even know how many men you've slept with."

She couldn't be any further from the truth. It wasn't hard to keep count when only one guy had ever been inside me...

One guy who I'd never been able to forget.

One guy who had single-handedly been the catalyst for ripping my entire life apart.

Falling for him was the biggest mistake I'd ever made, and the most soul-shattering part of the whole thing? I'd been stupid enough to believe he loved me when the only real desire he had was to screw me, then screw me over. The bastard handed me over to Hiram like a gift-wrapped present. If our paths ever crossed again, I'd make sure he lost more than his cock for what he did.

"At least every one I've fucked still had their own teeth," I said, dabbing the corner of my mouth to perfect my lipstick. It was exactly the same shade as a two-day-old bloodstain. "Can you say the same, Bells?"

"You're going to wish you never said that." Bella's cheeks flushed red in anger. She had no reason to be annoyed when I was only telling the truth. If she was happy to trade gummy kisses for cash, then she should fucking own it. "There is a hierarchy here, and you? You're right at the bottom. No one crosses me and gets away with it."

She threw her long dark hair over her shoulder and flounced away with Scarlett. *Good fucking riddance.* I needed to concentrate on my winged eyeliner without worrying someone would stab me in the back with a curling iron.

"You don't want to get on the wrong side of her," someone whispered in my ear.

I turned to face a petite beauty. She wore her glossy purple hair in two cute buns on the top of her head and looked like a legit anime character from outer space. I'd seen her around a few times. She kept quiet and tried to blend into the background. Apart from the quirky hair color, she was essentially my total opposite.

"Bella will make your life hell." She spoke so softly that I struggled to hear, but something about her vibe made me warm to her instantly. She didn't have an ego like the others. "Bad things happen when she targets you."

"Thanks for the warning, but I don't need it," I replied. "She doesn't scare me."

"She should," she whispered, glancing around to make sure none of the minions were listening. They were all too absorbed in their reflections to pay us any attention. "I don't agree with what she does, okay? It's just easier this way."

Something being easy didn't make it right. Everyone else may be okay with getting squashed under the Queen Bee's massive fucking superiority complex, but I wouldn't stand for her bullshit. If she wanted a war, I was going to put on my big girl pasties and bring it.

"What's your name?" I asked.

Her eyes widened in shock. I may as well have asked whether she liked to take it up the ass. In Lapland, bitches were hiding around every drape waiting to tear you down. A simple question, with no ulterior motive, came around as often as a customer wanting you to put more clothes on. *Fucking never.*

"It's Mieko."

"Well, Mieko," I said, "I think it's about time someone taught those bullies a lesson, don't you?"

Mieko didn't answer, but a tiny smile flickered over her lips as she turned away to fix her false eyelashes.

It looked like I'd found an ally in the hive.

———

West may have gotten me promoted, but Vixen wanted to make damn sure I started at the bottom. I'd spend the evening trying to flog diluted shots and avoid being molested by the creeps who had crawled in from the gutter.

"Come and sit with me," a chubby man leered, beckoning me over with a fat finger. I'd rather lie under a bus and ask the driver to run me over, but I smiled politely on the off-chance it'd earn me a few dollars.

The man had a round pink face that looked like sliced ham. Immediately, my thoughts moved to how easy it would be to strip his layers of fat away with a blade. As I approached, the clammy sweat of his paws seeping through my shorts made me want to throw up in my mouth. He gave my cheek an extra greedy squeeze like he was trying to force the last of the ketchup out of the bottle.

Hell fucking no, did he just do that!

I placed the tray down on the table carefully. Spilling the merchandise would only give Vixen another excuse to get rid of me.

"If you touch me again," I bent down to whisper in his ear and sunk my nails into his arm, "I'll fucking break you."

"But I thought you were selling," he whimpered. "One of the girls told me you were."

I tightened my grip. "Selling, what?"

He squealed like a piglet. If I didn't need this job, I'd take great pleasure in roasting him over an open fire. Bella waved over at us from the other side of the club. If rumors were being spread about me, it was no fucking mystery where they were coming from. A big bullseye had been planted on my booty from the moment I'd stepped through the sparkly silver doors.

"Bargain blowjohhh—Yowchh!"

His wrist would snap with another swish of my hand. From his quivering bottom lip, he fucking knew it too. For him, losing the ability to move his right hand would be worse than losing a best friend. How else would he fill his time?

"Candy." Vixen's glacial tone made me drop his trotter. Goddammit, he'd live to jerk another day. "You're up in the cage."

"I'll see you soon, handsome," I said, flashing the lump of lard my pearly whites. He didn't know how lucky he really was. No one ever laid a finger on me without paying for it. Not anymore.

I followed Vixen to one of the three cages and spotted Mieko kicking ass in another. Holy shit, the girl was flexible. She flew around like a crazy trapeze artist. I couldn't help wondering what had led her to this place. She could do better than this seedy joint with such raw talent.

"At least your hands won't be able to stray behind bars," Vixen hissed.

"Maybe they wouldn't need to if people kept theirs to themselves."

"What's wrong? Did he undercut your little operation?" She locked the cage behind me. It's a good thing we had a barrier between us because I'd have loved nothing more than to wipe the smirk off her smug face. "I heard you were offering ten dollars to swallow."

I may be under Vixen's lock and key for now, but she had to remember wild animals could do damage when they were unleashed.

———

I knew now why Mieko wound herself around the cage like a circus performer. The less time you spent on the ground, the less opportunity the foot fetish guys had to stroke your toes. I'm all for people having their kinks, but I was not in the mood for anyone to play a game of little piggies on me.

A sticky-fingered bastard yowled as my heel trapped his forefinger underfoot. "Ouch!"

Oops. A girl can't help it if she's ticklish, right?

Thankfully, a toe-ring wearing dancer distracted the group of footsies away from my podium. The cheap piece of sterling trash was a twenty-carat diamond in their eyes. With them gone, the minutes passed quickly. It was easy to forget the club was filled with people. When I went into my own world, everything else became background noise.

My teachers used to call me a daydreamer for staring into space. It didn't win me any popularity contests in class. The other kids called me a freak — not that they dared say it to my face. *Spineless assholes.* There was an unspoken rule at school not to mess with the Evergreen group home kids. If you did, there was always the risk of your daddy's BMW being burnt to a metal crisp or your garage turning into a meth lab when you were on vacation. The Evergreen kids were trouble, and I was guilty by association.

"Oh, look!" The distinct whine of Bella cut above the bass like the scraping of frost in a freezer. "Vixen said she wanted to keep the chlamydia outbreak under control. Up there, she can't infect anyone."

Sticks and fucking stones. I'd been up against bullies like her my entire life. To survive growing up in Evergreen, you didn't just need thick skin... you needed a bulletproof vest. If Bella thought she could break me by spreading a few rumors, she was even stupider than she looked.

Whoever said drama got left behind when you graduated was a liar. The truth is, high school never ends. If you don't believe me, look at any politician. Corruption goes all the way to the top. There's nothing you can do. When I was younger, being invisible was my way of coping. Now, I'd take down the system with a sledgehammer if I had to.

"Are you even listening, Candy? Hey!" Vixen rattled the bars to get my attention. "I said, Zander wants to see you. Now."

What had I done wrong?

Vixen escorted me through the building. Correctional officers had more trust in convicts than she had in me. What did she think I was going to do? Make a bomb out of lube in the ladies? Raid the clubs' lifetime supply of tissues and rubbers? Pfft, they had nothing worth stealing — at least on the upper levels, anyway.

A bronze plaque reading 'The Boss' emblazoned on Zander's office door could either be a stroke of irony or a hint at his inflated ego. I'd put money on the latter.

I scowled as Vixen raised her hand. "I am capable of knocking myself."

"Have it your way." She grinned, pushing it open and shoving me inside. Who doesn't want to make an entrance with the grace of Bambi on roller skates after a nasty LSD trip?

"You should have knocked." Zander's chair faced away, but I detected the underlying contempt in his tone. "Did no one ever teach you manners?"

"I must have missed that lesson."

The rest of the dancers seemed happy to throw each other under a moving train, but I was no snitch.

Zander slowly turned and gestured towards a chair that looked as comfortable as a medieval torture device. "Sit."

"If you're going to fire me, just get it over with." I put my hands on my hips and didn't move an inch. "I didn't even hurt the bastard's wrist. It's not my fault he was a fucking crybaby—"

"What are you talking about?"

Way to go, Candy. I may as well have put an apple in my mouth and hogtied myself. *Just don't say anything else.*

"I'll only ask one more time." Zander drummed his fingers on the desk impatiently. My heart jolted at the sight of the 'no mercy' tattoo over his knuckles. For most people, they'd see that as a bad omen. But I had to drag my mind out of the gutter to stop thinking about what other ink might be hiding underneath his flashy suit. What the fuck was wrong with me? "Sit."

I plonked my ass down. At this point, did I really have anything to lose?

"What do you want?" I asked.

"Are you always this direct?"

"It depends." I lifted my chin to meet his unblinking stare. "Are you always this mysterious?"

"Tell me about the poker game." He reclined and propped his feet on the desk. "Where did you learn to play poker?"

I shrugged.

He raised one eyebrow, making his rose tat dance. "Now, who is being mysterious?"

"I got lucky one time," I said. I wasn't about to spill my life story to a stranger because West was a sour loser over being beaten by someone with tits. "So what?"

"Your act may have fooled Vinny, but this isn't a game." Zander's face turned to stone, giving me a glimpse of the predator prowling under the surface. "When I ask you a question, I expect you to fucking answer it."

He looked at me like I was a freshly baked cookie he wanted to sink his teeth into. Zander was no amateur. If he took a bite, he'd leave no crumbs behind. He'd devour you whole and wipe any trace of you from existence.

"You got your cut," I replied. "What more do you want?"

"Your cooperation."

Unfortunately for him, cooperation wasn't usually one of my strong points.

"West is taking you on a date next Friday," Zander continued. "There's a high-stakes poker game at Briarly Manor I'd like you to attend."

I'd heard enough whispered conversations in the dressing room to know Briarly Manor was the multimillion-dollar estate of a family, who'd made their fortunes through generations of drug smuggling. Nobody stayed at the top for that long unless there was something to fear. And the Briarly's? They were a fucking institution in Port Valentine. But it wasn't playing poker or visiting the manor that bothered me about Zander's proposal…

"You want me to help you win," I said, reading between the lines and putting aside my reservations. What's the worst that could happen if I went on a fake date with a man who hated my guts? "What do I get out of it?"

"Keeping your job and a new dress." My skin prickled as he looked me up and down with distaste. "West can't be seen with someone who looks like *that*."

"The arrangement doesn't work for me." The last time I checked a pretty dress didn't pay the bills and, given the Briarly's reputation, there would be a lot more at risk than losing money. "I want twenty percent *and* a pair of Louboutins."

If Zander wanted to dress me up like a doll, then he'd need to give me the full fucking package. When I left Hiram, I had the clothes on my back and as much jewelry as I could wear without arising suspicion. Beautiful shoes had always been a guilty pleasure of mine... or maybe I just really enjoyed how they could do serious damage? Either way, watching Bella choking on her veneers when she found out about my new gift would be priceless.

Zander threw back his head and laughed; a sound that would give Lucifer himself the chills.

"Brains and a pretty face." He let out a low whistle. "You'll get five percent *if* you win."

Before I could argue, Vixen charged into the office unannounced. She had the crazed manner of a meth addict hunting down their next fix. The chick's default mode was angry, but this was on a whole new level.

"You sent Red after the Razors?" she blazed. "Are you insane? There will only be three of the Sevens left by dawn. If he fucks this up, they'll kill him!"

Red, whoever he was, must have got himself wrapped up in seriously messed up shit to have whipped the ice queen into this much of a frenzy. She had also inadvertently answered another one of my questions. I now knew who the members of the Sevens were: *West, Zander, Vixen, and... Red.* Despite the name, there were only four of them. Although, they may be down to three if Vixen was right. If the elusive fourth member was anything like the others, maybe his imminent death wouldn't be a bad thing.

"Red knows what he's doing," Zander replied coolly. "Ask him yourself tomorrow."

Vixen's nostrils flared like a bull preparing to charge. It was not the answer she'd wanted.

"What the fuck are you still doing here?" She turned on me, the nearest thing to a punching bag in sight. "Get back to work!"

As much as a Vixen-Zander showdown would have been entertaining to watch, you'd have to be missing brain cells to risk being sucked into the middle of that hurricane. When I reached the doorway, Zander called after me.

"Oh, and Candy?" As if he'd let me walk away so easily. "Don't ever think about lying to me again. It could be the last thing you ever do."

How could someone have the bone structure of an angel, but be a fucking demon on the inside?

———

"Where have you been?" Bella descended upon me like a vulture as soon as I stepped back onto the club floor. "You're late."

"Late for what?" I rolled my eyes. "Don't tell me you've been missing me already?"

She pointed up at the empty stage. The club lights were dimmed, and the spotlight pointed at a big fat nothing. *Fuck.* After my whirlwind conversation with Zander, it completely slipped my mind I was part of the line-up.

"How much longer?" An impatient drunk threw a beer can. "We want boobs! We want boobs!"

The crowd grew more restless with every passing second like a bunch of sugar-starved toddlers at a birthday party. If they were gagging to see a half-naked woman, they'd be better off going home to their long-suffering girl-friends or watching porn. Hadn't they heard of the internet?

"Get up there," Bella ordered. "Now!"

I bit my tongue to stop myself from telling her to go fuck herself and that I'd perform in my own sweet time. However, it wouldn't be long before Vixen returned. She was already on the warpath tonight, and I'd be damned if I was gonna be a casualty of her bad mood.

"Better late than never!" The announcer introduced me as I strutted onto the stage. "But will she be worth your wait? Candy Cane, everybody!"

The song 'Wicked Ones' by Dorothy blasted from the speakers. All I had to do was throw down a few simple moves to keep the pond scum happy. I let the rhythm wash over me and allowed my body to respond to the music. I gyrated my hips, moving slowly, trying to hypnotize them with my sway-ing. The leeches couldn't get enough of it. Dollar bills were already being tossed my way.

It wasn't until I began to climb the pole that an uneasy feeling swept over me. Bella and her army of tramps were standing shoulder-to-shoulder at the bar with shit-eating smirks on their faces. If those bitches were happy, some-thing was wrong.

By then, it was already too late...

The moment I dropped into a rainbow pose, I saw the large bucket precariously balanced on the drapes above my head. All it took was the quick tug of a rope for it to overturn completely, showering me in a red and sticky substance.

"What the hell is this?" a customer gasped, wiping his spattered glasses. The liquid had sprayed every man in the front row. It'd be interesting to hear how they'd describe away the stains to their dry cleaners. Now, that would be a story worth writing about.

Mieko was easy to spot in the crowd. Her eyes were like saucers and a shaking hand covered her mouth. Hey, at least I had something to be thankful for. No one could fake a reaction like that, so she mustn't have known about Bella's plans to go Carrie on me.

Now, it made sense why Bella was so eager to get me on stage. It would have been difficult to source this much pig's blood at short notice — maybe she'd sampled the butcher's special sausage? In any case, it was hard not to be impressed by how little time it had taken for her to orchestrate this master humiliation plan.

It was a shame her efforts would be wasted, though. Hadn't anyone ever told her the show must go on? I flipped upright to let the metallic-tasting liquid run down my face and twirled down the pole to end in the splits.

Choke on a big fat pig's dick, Bella.

The audience went wild as I shook my hair and flipped onto my front to crawl through the puddle. It soaked my white clothes through as I writhed around and caressed my curves. It wasn't every day you went to see a strip show that ended like a scene from a slasher movie.

Lucky for me, I was no stranger to bathing in blood.

Thunderous applause filled the club as the song ended. Against all odds, Bella's plans to sabotage me had spectacularly backfired and I'd pulled it off. She'd not considered how good I looked in a wet T-shirt. This may have been my baptism of fire, but she was the one who'd got burned like a rasher of crispy bacon.

At the back of the crowd, Zander watched on with a stare as dark as the secrets he kept. A wicked grin crept over his lips as I caught his eye. He raised a glass. A part of me felt a twisted satisfaction at drawing his attention, whilst my instinct sensed it was anything but good fucking news.

I ran my tongue over my lips and savored the metallic taste on my tongue. Zander may be the big bad wolf around here, but Little Red wasn't a helpless young girl anymore. She'd got lost in the woods and turned into a woman with a hunger for blood... and an appetite for monsters with face tattoos.

"Can you smell something rotten?"

As usual, Bella's nasal voice grated on my soul like freshly mani-cured nails down a chalkboard.

Scarlett sniffed the air. "I can't smell anything."

"Look!" Bella elbowed her in the ribs and nudged her head pointedly in my direction. "Over there."

As much as I was over the drama in the club, I'd actually been looking forward to my shift. Anything was better than spending another hour in my mold-ridden apartment. My teeth had only just stopped chattering from the three hours I'd spent scrubbing blood off my scalp with cold water.

"How funny, the only thing I can smell is a dried-up old cum rag. Oh, wait…" I said, smiling sweetly as my eyes landed on her. "That must be you."

Bella pursed her lips. It was rare for her to be in this position. No one else had dared to stand up to her and keep coming back for more. She'd better get used to it because I always came back swinging.

"I really should thank you for last night, Bells," I continued. "I made a sweet stack of Franklin's."

I planned to save every dime. Unlike Bella, who spent her earnings on coke and designer clothes, I needed a fallback plan. You didn't get as high as I did in Hiram's ranks by making friendship bracelets and singing Kumbay-fucking-ah. Bad people wanted me dead and, if any of them came sniffing around, I needed to get the hell outta town in a flash.

"Make the most of it while it lasts," Bella said. "Because I'm only getting started."

Bella may have been smart enough to not pull the rope herself at yesterday's show, but she was unknowingly wrapping another tighter around her neck. Getting into a war with me was not one she would win.

————

The club felt emptier than usual. Zander and West sat in their usual booth, where Bella and Scarlett hung off their arms like flies buzzing around shit. Their simpering giggles made me want to slice out their voice boxes and rip off my ears. Bella had clambered onto Zander's knee, and Scarlett looked like she was trying to light a fire in West's lap. I was busy wishing their cocks would shrivel up when a voice crept up behind me.

"Hello there, beautiful," it said. I painted on my fake-ass smile and turned to face Cheeks. His gaze was automatically drawn to my chest. The guy was incapable of looking any girl in the eye for longer than two seconds. "I've been looking for you everywhere."

"Well, you've found me…"

I'd already started weighing up the best escape options in my head. The last time I'd seen the bent cop was at the poker game when I'd hoped it would be the last.

"I'm going to a Maven party tomorrow night. It's an exclusive crowd, if you know what I mean?" Well, duh. You'd need to have lived under a rock for years to have not heard about the insanity that goes down at the Maven. "It's going to be a crazy night."

"Mhmm." I did my best to feign interest as Cheeks bragged about his connections. The guy spouted more shit than an explosive bout of diarrhea after popping a pack of laxatives. "Yeah, it sounds crazy…"

"Vixen told me it was your night off." Oh, I bet she had. I'd been trying to forget about it. Working kept my mind busy, and having an entire day with no plans was not something I was used to. "So, how do you fancy being my plus one?"

My mouth hung open.

No.

Fucking.

Way.

An invitation to a Maven night was one of the rarest tickets in town. Scratch that, it was like finding a fucking red diamond in the dirt. People traveled from all over the country to visit the underground club. It only opened a handful of times a year. Hiram's cronies, who'd done business in this area, had told me about it before. Sometimes, Hiram even went himself.

Rumor had it they completely redecorated after each party because things got... messy.

As much as I didn't want to breathe the same air as Cheeks for any longer than necessary, it was hard to deny the prospect of going to the Maven had piqued my curiosity. Before I had time to reply, Zander appeared out of nowhere like a black cloud of doom ready to rain down hell.

"She's not going," Zander said flatly.

"This is a Maven party we're talking about," Cheeks insisted. "Why don't you let the girl speak for herself, Zander? Candy would like to go, wouldn't you?"

It was probably the first time in his life that Cheeks had requested a woman speak up for herself.

"My decision is final," Zander said. I opened my mouth to speak, but Zander shot me a look in warning. "You're not going."

Who was he to tell me what to do? He'd spent the evening wrapped around his in-house floozy. He was my boss — not my fucking keeper.

"It's my night off." I crossed my arms. "I don't see a collar around *my* neck."

As if to illustrate my point perfectly, Bella sidled up to Zander like a mangy cat. Her inflated lips were pouting so hard they resembled a severe case of hemorrhoids.

"Babe," she whined, pawing at Zander's arm. Her tone was ten times past desperate. If you dipped your dick into that level of crazy, you deserved to have it cut off. "You said we'd have some special time tonight."

"What good is a loose pussy to me?" Zander growled. She dropped her hand and yelped as if he'd slapped her. "You'd have to pay me to fuck you."

If Bella wasn't such an egotistical psycho hellbent on screwing me over, I *might* have felt sorry for her. But I didn't.

"You can't keep all your girls on a leash," Cheeks said, ruining his moment of redemption by slapping Bella's ass as she slunk away. "Why don't we let Candy decide?"

"I'll think about it," I replied.

Zander's stare scorched into my skin like he was trying to brand me as his own. He needed to get it through his skull that I wasn't his property, especially if he wanted me to be a part of screwing over the Briarly's on their home turf next week. Not every girl in Lapland would do what he wanted on command.

"I'll pick you up here at ten." Cheeks took anything other than a straight 'no' to be a yes. Then he winked at Zander, adding, "She won't regret it."

Zander's eyes were dead inside as he watched Cheeks leave the club and disappear into the night. This spelled out a disaster waiting to happen.

"You won't go to the party if you know what's good for you," Zander warned. His breath sent goosebumps racing down my spine as he leaned in closer. "Every action has consequences."

A sane person would see his words as a threat, but I never ran away from a challenge. Zander thought he could break me, but I'd put myself back together more times than I could count, and maybe... *just maybe*... a small part of me wanted to see exactly what consequences Zander had in mind.

————

"He's really into me," Bella told Scarlett as they reapplied their lip gloss for the millionth time. How many layers of gloss would it take for them not to be able to speak again? "Have you noticed? He can't keep his hands off me tonight."

I disguised my snort of laughter as a bad fart from within the bathroom stall. I couldn't believe what I was hearing. What part of him saying 'you'd have to pay me to fuck you' didn't she understand? You had to admire her ability to bounce back.

"Can we double-date?" Scarlett asked. "West is, like, so... tall."

West was a lot of things, but *tall* wasn't the first thing that sprang to my mind when I thought of him.

"Zander just wants us to be alone, sweetie," Bella replied. "He's been begging to take me to a new French restaurant opening. Can you believe it?"

Puh-lease. The only place Zander would take her for dinner was the fucking kennels where the specials were a bowl of dog food and a side serving of cold shoulder.

Scarlett sighed. "You are *so* lucky."

"I am," she agreed. "Just think how much a man like him is worth. I can't wait for him to take me shopping."

Zander blowing her off like a used sex doll wasn't a deterrent when she was only interested in his bank balance. How was it possible for your vision to be so clouded by dollar signs that you'd throw yourself at someone who treated you like a hole in the wall? Maybe I was old-fashioned, but I believed sex should mean something and be with someone you cared about.

After they left, I gave it a few minutes to make sure the Queen had returned to her throne. Bella may be happy to pretend things were fantastic, but Zander's dismissal will have made her more resolved to mark her territory. It wouldn't be long before the hive was abuzz with the news of my Maven request which would only give them more reason to make my life unbearable.

As I made my way back to the bar, a clumsy idiot stepped right into my path. The drink in his hand went flying over the pair of us and...

Fuck.

This couldn't be real.

"Candy?" The glass slipped through his fingers, shattering with a smash. "Is that you?"

It couldn't be, could it?

"What are you doing here?" I demanded, praying he didn't notice how much my hands were shaking. I'd been dreaming about this moment for years, but being caught off guard and drenched in tequila was never part of the plan.

"I could ask you the same question," he said, taking in my hot pants and crop top. His deep brown eyes looked troubled, and his caramel skin bore more scars than before. Good, I looked at them with satisfaction; I hoped they'd fucking hurt. "Last time I heard you were working with—"

"Why pretend you give a shit, Rocky?" My adrenaline kicked into overdrive, and I pulled my pocket knife out of my bra. I went nowhere without it. "I could gut you right here if I wanted."

I wasn't the same helpless girl he'd left behind five years ago. Back then, we were teenagers from the wrong side of the tracks who dreamed of getting out of a shitty situation. I'd been too young to see him for what he really was. Now, I knew the truth.

Rocky Marshall had no heart.

He was pure, unadulterated evil.

"If you touch me," Rocky said, "you'll have Zander to answer to."

His voice was just as I remembered, but malice had replaced any hint of playfulness. Did he seriously think him knowing Zander would stop me? I held the blade to his stomach. It would take seconds to make an incision and run with his entrails down the corridor like a party streamer.

"Let him come," I spat through gritted teeth. I pushed the knife in deeper, enough for a round pool of red to seep through the white fabric of his shirt. "Maybe he'll even finish the job if he finds out what you did to me?"

His rough hands closed around my throat in a flash.

"You don't know what you're talking about," Rocky hissed, using his full body weight to slam me backward into the wall and fingers to crush my windpipe. "I saved you."

"Saved me?" My mouth twisted into a snarl. He may think he has the upper hand, but I gripped the handle tighter. "You *sold* me!"

Rocky faltered, loosening his hold. "You think you know the full story, but you know nothing."

"I know everything I need to." None of his bullshit would change what happened. A few hours after I'd lost my virginity to him, Rocky delivered me to Hiram like I was nothing more than a pepperoni pizza. He knew the life he was signing me up for when he'd handed me over. The bastard doused me in gasoline, struck the match, and left me to burn. I walked through fire and came back stronger every time. Now, I'd become an inferno that'd tear down his entire world. "I'm going to hurt you just like you hurt me."

"Go on. Do it." He pressed his muscled frame closer toward me, forcing the blade in further. "I dare you."

I hated Rocky with every fiber of my being for what he'd done, but the heat of his body against mine stirred something else inside me... which made me detest him even more than I thought possible.

"Everything has always been a game to you, hasn't it?" I said. He'd played with my life. Trusting him had been the biggest mistake I'd ever made. "You won't get away with it."

"I know you don't want to hurt me, C," Rocky murmured.

He was right about one thing. I didn't *just* want to hurt him. I wanted to make him suffer. He needed to feel the pain of having his heart cut out and ripped to pieces as he'd done with mine.

Vixen's sharp voice hit me like another drink in the face. "What the hell is going on here?"

Neither of us spoke. Rocky's hands wrapped around my neck and me holding a knife to his crotch must have been an interesting sight to stumble upon.

"Do I have to make a new rule about no S&M in public places?" she sneered. "It didn't take you long to meet the new resident whore, Red."

Red?

No...

Rocky couldn't be...

"What can I say, Vix?" Rocky took advantage of my surprise by swiping the knife from my hand in a slick motion. "I've always had a sweet tooth."

"Don't let Zander catch you with a blade," she scowled.

Rocky winked and pocketed my weapon. "What he doesn't know won't hurt him."

Vixen shook her head in mock disapproval, but her shield had significantly thawed. I'd never seen her attitude rise above freezing before. The boy I'd grown up with would never have been friends with a slave driver like Vixen. It was only more proof he'd never been who said he was. That person had never really existed. All the time we'd spent together was built on lies.

How had the boy who broke my heart transitioned into the man now known as 'Red'?

"And, Candy?" Vixen's frosty glare returned with vengeance. "Don't think screwing one of your new bosses will change your place here. Go and sort the costume closet, before I change my mind about firing your ass."

I caught Rocky's eye. "I'll watch out for the skeletons hiding in there."

He may be one of the Sevens, but I would never follow his orders. His quick thinking and smooth move may have saved his balls this time, but the clock was already ticking down. History had a way of coming back to life and biting you in the fucking ass.

———

"Are you okay?" Mieko ambushed me amidst the growing piles of funky-smelling latex littering the floor. "I swear I didn't know what they were planning yesterday."

"I'm just peachy," I said. Well, if you didn't count learning one of my new bosses was responsible for destroying my entire future.

"I never thought she would do something like that." Mieko grimaced. "All the blood everywhere…"

"Are *you* okay?" I pressed gently.

"Fine," she replied, a little too fast.

Unsaid words hung in the air. We didn't know each other well, but I recognized a haunted look when I saw it. She shot me a small smile that said *thank you, but I'm not ready to talk*. Hell, I understood better than anyone how some wounds could take a lifetime to heal.

"I wanted to talk to you about something else." Mieko chewed her bottom lip. "I overheard the girls talking tonight. Apparently, they found a video of you."

"A video?"

"A…" she said, then mimed, "sex tape."

Laughter bubbled out of me like a popped cork. I mean, come on, have you ever known a stripper who was too afraid to say the word 'sex' aloud?

"What's so funny?" She frowned in confusion, which only made her even more endearing. "Aren't you worried?"

Mieko's concern was sweet, but Bella's childish pranks were the least of my problems. The bitch would get what she deserved eventually but, right now, the only revenge I could think about involved spilling the blood of a man who I'd fantasized about killing for years.

I shrugged. "It'll be a fake."

Anyone could trawl through the internet to find someone with a similar body type or pay a shady hacker to do a deepfake job. The only semi-compromising footage of me ever taken had been used for blackmail. It didn't look great when married politicians were filmed in a hotel room with a hooker, did it? Hiram would never have allowed it to leak into the public domain. Covering your tracks was one of his rules. He was too thorough to let anything lead back to him… or me.

"How many hours do you think it took her to find my porn star doppel-gänger?" I asked. With any luck, the actress would have a killer bod and I'd be able to use it to my advantage. "No wonder she was begging Zander for the D tonight."

A giggle escaped Mieko's lips and, within seconds, the pair of us were wiping rolling tears from our cheeks. I'd lived in the darkness for so long I'd forgotten how freeing it was to laugh again. When I lived in Blackthorne Towers with Hiram, my only real happiness came from my friendship with Crystal… but it was too painful to remember.

"I'm so glad you're here, Candy," Mieko said, blotting her mascara. "I'd never be brave enough to stand up to her like you do."

Not yet, anyway. Mieko may not realize it, but I sensed she was stronger than she gave herself credit for. All she needed was more confidence and belief in herself. If she hung out with me for long enough, she'd be kicking ass in no time.

"There's nothing wrong with lying low," I pointed out. "Sometimes it's the only thing you can do."

In this cut-throat world, we all did what we had to do to survive. Everyone had their own pasts and demons to battle. It just so happened mine sat in the next room with my knife in his pocket.

Mieko glanced up at the clock. "Vixen will be wondering where I am."

"Go," I said, throwing a pair of cum-stained stockings at her face. She shrieked in horror. "I'll see you in there."

A lone soldier couldn't do the same damage as an army when it came to taking down a hive, but having Mieko on my side would help to take the bitches in Lapland down.

If I found one more pair of unwashed crotchless panties, I'd…

Shit.

Bile rose in my throat at the buzz of my cell phone. Only one person could make this evening any worse. I looked down at his latest text.

Want to come home yet, Kitty? Just say the word.

This was the bastard's way of testing me.

I knew exactly how Hiram's mind games worked. He wanted to assert his dominance and remind me of where he felt I belonged. He didn't under-stand that Blackthorne Towers had never felt like a proper home. Ever. I may have had my own room, but it changed nothing. Deep down, I'd always known what the place was. A five-star fucking prison. If he wanted me back, he'd have to drag me across the country in a body bag.

"What are you doing on your phone?" Vixen roared, blowing up like a volcano and almost shattering my eardrums. She didn't even look at the rows of outfits that I'd spent the last hour organizing by color. Freaking color! I'd be lucky not to have caught a sexually transmitted disease from the pieces needing dry-cleaning. "You're supposed to be working."

"Why don't you buy a whip and be done with it?" I muttered under my breath, pressing delete and stashing my cell away. If only erasing Hiram from my life would be as easy.

"Scarlett's disappeared, and it's her shift at the bar," Vixen continued. No doubt she'd disappeared down a backstreet to give someone a cheeky hand job. "I need you to cover her. You have worked behind a bar before, haven't you?"

"Sure have," I lied. I mean, how hard could it be?

———

Everyone had gathered around the main stage to watch Mieko dance, leaving very few customers waiting to be served, which suited me just fine. We were in the hazy stage of the evening, where people were already too wasted to care what they were drinking anyway.

A storm rolled in over the bar as I ducked underneath to collect a clean stack of glasses.

"I told you." I recognized Rocky's voice instantly. My body tensed, knowing he was only inches away. "It's all good, man. It's under control."

"That's what you said last time," West replied in a low rumble. "Remember what happened then?"

"Enough." Zander silenced them both. "We can't afford any more mistakes."

"There won't be any," Vixen hissed. Whatever they were up to left no room for error. That meant one thing. Danger. "We'll talk later."

I rose to my feet slowly, hoping to draw as little attention to myself as possible. It failed. Zander detected the smallest sign of movement like a bloodhound.

He clicked his fingers. "Bourbon."

At least it was something I knew how to pour.

I decanted a shot and slammed it down with a bang. He may look like a gentleman in his suit, but wearing a fancy tie didn't excuse having no fucking manners. Then again, who needed to say 'please' when girls dropped their panties for you at a single glance?

"When he says bourbon," Vixen snarled. "He means Old Rip Van Winkle that we store *under* the bar. Not the cheap gasoline we serve to customers."

"Here's an idea," I said, unable to stop the words from firing off my tongue. "Maybe you should treat your colleagues with a little respect?"

"Don't even pretend we're on the same level." Vixen's jaw clenched. "I'm nothing like you."

"Oh, honey. I think we're a lot more alike than you think." I met her seething stare. "I know a cold, hard bitch when I see one."

Vixen looked like she'd fallen straight on her ass, as West threw his head back and laughed. I'd pay for that another time but not being thrown out on the street instantly felt like a win.

"She has you there, Vix," Rocky agreed, looking at me with a mixture of shock and admiration. The teenage girl he used to know wouldn't have dared to call someone out. She would have preferred to blend into the background and pray no one noticed her. Because of him, that girl no longer existed. "Maybe you should take her advice?"

"Of course, you'd say that," Vixen said. "You've only been home five minutes and already—"

Zander twisted his head sharply. "Already, what?"

I used to be able to tell what Rocky was thinking. Under Zander's scrutiny, I could have sworn a flicker of fear crossed over his moody features. Then, just as fast, it vanished.

"Is it a crime to check out a new piece of ass?" Rocky shrugged, returning to his zero-shits-given attitude and lightening the weird tension between them.

Rocky wanting to keep our history a secret from his fellow Sevens didn't surprise me. Whatever motivations he had for keeping quiet suited my agenda. If no one knew about us, there would be no reason for anyone to suspect me when he ended up dead.

"That piece of ass is going to the next Briarly game," Zander said.

"If the shoes fit," I added.

"I can handle it on my own," West grumbled, crossing his arms. The giant killing machine was pouting and it was freaking adorable. Did he even realize he was doing it? Making him sulk might become one of my new favorite hobbies. "I don't need any help."

"We'll see," I said, making him pout harder.

"In that case," Rocky raised his glass, "let the games begin."

Bring it on, motherfucker.

He had beaten me once but, now? I played to win.

Five

I teased my pink hair into loose waves. To play it safe, I'd opted for a slick of red lipstick and a smoky eye. You couldn't go wrong with a classic combo, right? Besides, a Maven night was no high-society event. It was a place where shit went down and things got dirty.

Every action has consequences.

Zander's words sprung into my mind as I pulled on ripped black high-waisted shorts over fishnet tights. It paired well with my loose white crop top, which was thin enough to show off my leopard print bra and the snake tattoo which coiled from my hip to rib. I didn't know what the dress code was, but this should fit the bill.

Against the paleness of my skin, my beautiful pair of traditional inked roses stood out on my collarbones. Permanently altering your body wasn't for everyone, but it had offered me a lifeline. I traced a finger over the dagger tattoo on my thigh to feel the scar hidden underneath. The dagger plunging into a colorful heart had been my second big 'fuck you' tattoo.

Getting inked had been a healing process, allowing me to take control and reclaim my skin as my own. Who gave a shit about what other people thought? My opinion was the only one that mattered. Decorating my skin with stunning artwork reminded me of who I wanted to become every day: a bad-ass bitch who didn't answer to anyone. Including Zander.

I didn't care about defying his orders. A Maven invitation was just that. *A Maven fucking invitation.* This was a once in a lifetime chance to go to one of the most exclusive clubs in the country. I wasn't about to throw it away because my boss demanded all his girls lick his shoes clean.

———

From the cab driver's reaction, my whole look must have worked together because the perve nearly crashed the car checking me out in the rear-view mirror.

"Pull up here," I demanded. I'd rather walk two blocks to Lapland than have him know where I worked. Having one creep like Cheeks hanging around was bad enough. I didn't need a fan club. "Anywhere's fine."

"The pleasure is all mine," he said, attempting to rub my hand as I handed him the bills. The creeper wouldn't be washing his palm for a week.

I waited until his headlights disappeared before walking in the right direction. Thankfully, I'd chosen not to wear heels and it wasn't far away. My trusty pair of black knee-high boots were perfect for dancing and their steel toe caps doubled as a great ball cruncher. As I turned down the next street, an uneasy feeling came over me.

Someone was watching.

I was not alone.

In my pocket, I closed my fingers around my pepper spray cleverly disguised as a lipstick case. Sure, I could go straight for the throat, but that wasn't what normal girls would do. Killing someone would draw too much unwanted attention.

Footsteps grew closer behind me. I reacted fast. I spun around, wielding my lipstick and ready to blast the fucker.

"Woah!" Rocky jumped back. He stood six feet away with his hands up. "Can we talk?"

I turned and kept walking in the opposite direction. He wasn't worth wasting my spray on. That'd be too kind. When I made my move, I'd make it count. Rocky sped up in pursuit. The bastard used to be on the football team, so I stood no chance of out-running him.

"Hey!" He caught my wrist and pulled me into an alleyway. "All I want to do is talk."

"Most people would take the fucking hint," I hissed, yanking myself out of his reach like his fingers were on fucking fire. "What do you want?"

"Zander told me about Cheeks." He put his hands against the bricks on either side of my head to box me in. "You're going, aren't you?"

I jerked my chin upward to meet his furious glare. "What I do is none of your business."

"Cheeks is a bad guy." Rocky was the last person in the world who had any right to lecture me. "You should stay outta his way."

"Don't tell me you're concerned about me now," I mocked. "It's not like you cared when you handed me over to the fucking devil."

Compared to Hiram, Cheeks was as threatening as the tooth fairy.

"What happened to you..." Rocky sighed, chewing his lip to think of the right words. It didn't matter what he said. Nothing would be good enough. "I had no choice."

"No choice?" I laughed bitterly. "Of course, you had a fucking choice."

His shoulders slumped like his entire body had caved in, then stood to run a hand through his dark floppy hair.

"I never wanted to hurt you," he whispered.

"Too fucking bad," I snapped. "What did you think would happen to me? I'd skip off into the sunset at Blackthorne Towers?"

Growing up in Evergreen wasn't easy for anyone. We first met when I was fourteen and Rocky was two years older. The other kids never tried to talk to me, but he hadn't been like the rest of them... or so I'd thought. The two of us used to hang out, share a joint, and talk about how we wanted a better life. Over time, we grew closer and our friendship turned into something more. Something I thought was special. We had a dream of starting afresh together, somewhere new, away from all the bullshit. Then it all fell apart...

"I did what I had to." Rocky looked down at his sneakers. I noticed the outline of something in his pocket. Something that belonged to me. "There was no other way, C..."

Rocky had been so much more than someone I used to date. He'd been my best friend. My rock. The person I trusted more than anyone else in this screwed up world. If something got stolen from my room in Evergreen, he made sure I got it back. Whenever I felt upset, he brought me candy to cheer me up. We didn't have much between us: no family, no money, no home, but we had each other... and hope.

"There's always another way," I snarled. "You didn't even fucking try."

When Rocky kissed me for the first time, it shocked me. I didn't understand how he could have been interested in someone like me. Back then, I was the weird freak who everyone avoided. Rocky was the opposite. He'd been popular. The cool, funny guy everyone picked first in gym. Even though we were different, I still believed him when he said he loved me... and was stupid enough to have loved him back.

"I get that you don't trust me. I don't blame you," he said, shuffling from one foot to another, then meeting my gaze with a newfound determination. "But I'm trying to look out for you. Fucked up shit happens at the Maven. It's not safe."

"I'm not the same girl you used to know." I narrowed my eyes. "I don't need anyone to look out for me. I can handle myself."

Betrayal and pain had twisted my soul in ways that made it impossible to put back together. I could kill a man in less than thirty seconds and castrate him in less than ten.

Rocky sighed. "Zander won't be happy when he finds out."

"Zander isn't my fucking keeper."

"You don't want to get on the wrong side of him, C. Zander and West are like my fucking brothers, but that doesn't make them good people," Rocky warned, stepping forwards to close the gap between us. "Disobeying an order will have consequences. You know that, right?"

"I'm not afraid of consequences," I said. "Not anymore."

He gently stroked one finger down my cheek, leaving a burning trail behind. "Maybe you should be," he whispered.

Wham! I slammed my knee into his groin like I was doing a kick-up with a soccer ball. He groaned, steadying himself against the wall to stop himself from falling. It'd be a while before he'd be able to move again.

"Don't ever touch me again," I hissed, pushing aside the tingling left behind by his touch and reaching into his pocket to retrieve the knife he'd stolen. "I'm taking back what's mine."

I stormed towards the neon lights. My skin may scream out for more, but my heart would never forget the feeling of being ripped out and blasted to smithereens.

———

After ensuring Rocky would piss red for days, I needed a drink. Fast.

"Double vodka," I barked at Scarlett, who, for a change, had shown up to her shift on time. It was most likely a rare stroke of luck over her ability to read the time, as there was nothing but air in her blonde weave. "Don't even think about watering it the fuck down either."

It was still early, and Cheeks hadn't arrived to pick me up yet. Typical. Where was the louse when you needed him?

Bella surrounded my barstool and formed a circle around me with her cronies. "Look who it is."

"It's always a pleasure, Bells." I downed my drink in one. It hadn't even touched the sides. I could drink men twice my size under the table. "Another."

"You know," Bella smirked, pulling out her phone and dramatically scrolling over the screen. "A certain video is going around."

"Really?" I played dumb. "What video?"

"You never mentioned you'd been in porn before," Bella drawled. "I'm not surprised. Everyone knows you love the attention, but who would want to watch that?"

The others giggled behind her like a pack of hyenas staring down at a dead carcass. I'd already lost my shit with Rocky once tonight, and Bella was treading a very thin fucking line.

"Your technique isn't even that great..." she continued.

As she was about to spin the screen around, a quiet voice piped up behind her.

"Zander is looking for you," Mieko squeaked.

Bella turned like a starving shark, and her nostrils flared like she'd got a whiff of a fresh kill. "Where?"

"In the back," Mieko said.

"Get out of my way!" Bella shoved her followers to the side. If she was driving, she'd have mown down every person who stood between her and Zander without batting an eyelash. Had no one ever told her desperation was unattractive? Zander wanting his cock sucked was not a life and death situation. "Move!"

Mieko caught my eye and nudged her head to the left, gesturing for me to follow.

"Is everything okay?" I asked.

"We don't have long before Bella finds out I lied..."

Mieko's voice trailed off as I followed her into one of the private booths. Something had to be seriously wrong for her to risk bringing down the full wrath of the Lapland monarchy on her head. Bella would not be happy when she realized the boss's boner wasn't waiting for her.

I pulled the drape closed behind us. "What is it?"

"I know you weren't worried." Mieko wrung her hands. "But you need to see this."

She passed me her phone, which displayed the still-image of a hotel room. Room 29. Adrenaline sent my heart racing like I'd robbed a fucking bank.

Fuck.

It can't be... but, it is... fuckety-fuck-fuck-FUCK!

I hit play.

"I'm so sorry, Candy," she whispered, having the decency to avert her eyes as the scene played.

In the video, a man with hairy legs and a fat belly perched on the edge of a bed. Only the lower half of his body was visible, but I could almost smell his reeking body odor through the screen. A few seconds later, a blonde-haired woman stepped out of the bathroom wearing a silky black robe. It was like watching a stick of dynamite explode in slow motion and knowing exactly what would happen next.

I clenched my teeth to stop myself from retching. "How long does it go on for?"

"I didn't watch it," Mieko said. "As soon as I realized what it was."

My retinas were burning, but I couldn't bring myself to look away. The woman peeled off her robe and stroked her curves over expensive lingerie. Her hair color may be different, but there was no mistaking it was me.

I fast-forwarded, being assaulted by a frame of Raphael Jacobson's dirty hands holding my head down. The slimy feeling of his *thing* in my mouth was hard to forget. Worse, if anyone found out his identity and what happened to him… I was dead.

I skipped to the end of the clip, where it abruptly cut off. If it continued for a second more, Raphael's dick would be flapping around his thighs and he'd be bleeding out on the floor.

My mouth was dry and words came out in hoarse breathy rasps. "Did Bella say where she got her claws on this?"

"She said someone sent it to her," Mieko said. "Who would do something like that?"

I knew someone who would.

There was a bitter irony in the fact I used to make videos to blackmail others. Now, the roles had been reversed. I'd offended Hiram by ignoring his attempts to contact me. This was my punishment. He wanted to show he had the power to destroy me. Raphael may have been an evil son of a bitch, but there were still people interested in finding out why he'd disappeared. And who was responsible.

If Hiram had held onto this, what other evidence did he have?

During the years I'd spent with him, he must have been storing incriminating evidence in case I ever dared to leave. He may have agreed to my release, but he never promised to stop following me or leave the past behind. Hiram must have sent Bella the video because he knew I'd see it. He knew exactly where I was.

"Who else has seen it?" I pressed, even though I already knew the answer.

Mieko gulped. "Everyone."

My tongue turned to sandpaper. I didn't care that the stripper bitches had seen it. Hell, I knew most of them had featured in a porno at some point. No, what bothered me was how nothing happened in this club without the Sevens knowing. If Zander and West didn't make enough jokes about me being a whore already, they sure would now.

"Candy," Mieko called after me, but my feet were already moving. "Wait!"

I didn't know where the fuck I was going, but all I knew was I needed to get out.

Far away from here.

———

I raced through the back of the bar towards an exit. As I threw the door to the kitchen open, I stopped dead in my tracks. Ahead, a girl sat astride the counter with her legs spread as someone chowed down on her pussy like an all-you-can-eat buffet.

The life-size barbie threw her head back. "Ohhhhhhh, Vixen."

Her moans were overly theatrical, which meant that Vixen didn't give good head or the girl had an even better reason for faking it. It also explained the mystery of how Vixen hung out with hot guys all day and didn't break out in a fucking sweat.

"What the fuck!" Barbie's thighs slapped together around Vixen's head so tightly that it's a wonder her brains didn't leak out her ears. A part of me hoped it would. Anything would help distract me from the memories of my time with Raphael flooding my senses.

"What're you looking at, huh?" Vixen snarled, standing and wiping her mouth as if she'd been snacking on a bag of chips.

"Isn't she the whore from the sex tape?" the girl asked. The longer I looked at her, the more she resembled a plastic toy that had been left in the sun for too long. "Babe, she was filming us."

I hadn't even realized Mieko's phone was still in my shaking hands.

"You may want other people to watch you fuck," Vixen's girl sneered, "but not everyone's into that."

"I wouldn't—"

Before I could finish telling her how no one would be interested in watching her groan like a dying horse, she ripped the cell straight out of my clutches. My reactions were too slow. I had to use all of my self-control to squeeze my eyes shut and block the images trying to take over my mind.

She pressed play, and the sound of Raphael's voice filled the room.

"You like this, huh?"

It felt like a weight had been strapped to my chest.

I was sinking.

Every breath more shallow than the last.

I needed air.

I may have made sure Raphael would never hurt anyone again, but his voice still haunted my nightmares. Often, it was the last thing I heard before waking up screaming in clammy sheets. Hearing it again transported me straight back.

When I'd first moved to Blackthorn Towers, Hiram believed every girl should go through, what he liked to call, a 'breaking in' period. Raphael took his job as 'the breaker' seriously. He was a sick bastard who got his kicks from causing inexplicable pain. He got hard off your tears and laughed through every bloodcurdling scream. Three days in a dungeon with Raphael would be enough to make the strongest person beg for death — let alone a sixteen-year-old girl. That's what Hiram wanted; he needed you to be willing to do anything to stop the pain. After Raphael broke your bones, Hiram stepped in to break your fucking spirit.

"What's wrong with her?" Vixen's girl giggled. "What a fucking freak."

They were still talking, but I couldn't hear a word. My vision blurred like a television set losing signal. I vaguely made out Mieko's phone, bouncing off the wall and hitting the floor with a smash, but it seemed so far away. I gripped the counter to stop myself from falling. The only thing worse than having a breakdown was having one in front of people who were already waiting for any excuse to tear you apart.

"Just leave her," Vixen said. She sounded like she was underwater. "Let's go, Charlene."

The two of them linked their sticky fingers together and pushed past me like I was invisible. With them gone, I slumped down the wall and started to count back from five hundred in intervals of seven.

500…

493…

It was the only thing that worked.

486…

I'd do it for however long it took to force the memories back into their coffin.

63…

Footsteps hitting the tiled floor made my head snap up. Fresh bleeding moons cut into my palms and stung from my clenched fists, but the discomfort grounded me enough to get my shit together. *Raphael can't hurt you anymore,* I reminded myself, *he's dead.*

"Cheeks is looking for you." West scowled down at me with his arms crossed over his muscled chest. "He doesn't like being kept waiting."

"Fuck you." I sniffed, wiping my eyes with the back of my hand and standing before he could see. "Go to fucking hell."

"Calm down, Pinkie." West's silver-plated canine winked at me under the fluorescent light. He didn't smile often, and it made the hairs on the back of my neck stand on end. "I don't bite."

"But I do."

My teeth had torn straight through Raphael's flesh like razor blades. I'd slain a monster that night, and I'd fucking enjoyed every minute of it. Killing him had been the best birthday present Hiram had given me, and I didn't regret it. Just like I didn't regret leaving behind my life under his rule.

The video may only be the start of his plans to get me back, but I couldn't let him win. I'd weighed up my options. I could pack a bag and flee, but what good would it do? He'd hunt me wherever I went. No, the best thing I could do was wait for him to come to me. I stood a better chance of survival if I knew the area. Besides, I had other reasons to stick around…

Stripping in Lapland may not be the future I dreamed about, but I was only beginning to scratch the surface of the Seven's operations. Powerful people were close by and there were opportunities to make money. The Briarly Manor poker game would help. Port Valentine also offered me something I couldn't get anywhere else. Revenge on the one person to blame for the fucked up mess my life had become. I wasn't going anywhere until I'd mounted Rocky Marshall's bleeding heart on the candy pole.

West paused. "Maybe you will survive a night at the Maven after all."

"Aren't you going to tell me not to go?" I asked, cocking my head to the side. Rocky and Zander had already made their opinions pretty clear. "Everyone else around here seems to enjoy telling me what to do."

"It's your funeral." West shrugged. "But I do have one piece of advice."

I snorted. "And what's that?"

A wicked grin spread over his face as his electric blue eyes met mine. "Don't do anything you wouldn't want to be caught on film."

"I'll try to remember." I'd rather scrape my skin off with a cheese grater than let West get under it. "Do you get off on watching trailer trash now?"

"If I want to see someone suck cock." West's voice became a dangerously low growl. It had an animalistic quality that made my legs feel shaky again. "They'd be choking on mine."

"Get outta my way." I shoved him and bruised my shoulder in the process. I really needed to remember his muscles were hard enough to cause serious damage.

West's laughter followed me. If the sword in his pants was as big as his head, I'd bet he'd break my jaw. Getting down on my knees for West would be like bowing down at the devil's altar, and… a twisted part of me couldn't help but like the thought.

———

The sight of Cheeks was enough to extinguish any faint flutters West had ignited in my core. I wrote it off as being down to the shock. Adrenaline could do weird shit to our brains.

"Hi, gorgeous." Cheeks dropped a wet kiss on my cheek, which made me cough because of the strength of his cologne. He needed to come with a hazard warning label. "I've been looking for you everywhere. Not having second thoughts, are we?"

Tonight had seriously messed with my head. I didn't want Zander to think I was following his orders, but partying was the last thing on my mind. Plus, I didn't have a gas mask. A few more minutes around Cheeks would bring on a fucking migraine.

"Actually, about that—"

"Before you say anything else," Cheeks interrupted. His shoulders tensed like I'd poked him with a cattle prod. He pulled a USB stick from his pocket. "There is something on here that I'm sure you don't want anyone to see. One of your dancer friends sent me a video she thought I'd be interested in."

"You're too late," I said. Being a cop and having a badge didn't give him the authority to blackmail me. The Maven may be a once in a lifetime opportunity, but it wasn't worth throwing my principles out the window for. Rule number one: don't take shit from a dirty slime-ball who thinks he has the upper hand. "Everyone's already seen it."

"As much as I loved watching you, that's not what I'm talking about." Cheeks ran his tongue over his lips. Eurgh, he made my skin crawl. Those pixels would be the closest the fucker ever got to touching me. "There was something else in the video that interested me more. Did you know that only one family wears that particular ring?"

An icy shiver trailed down my spine.

How the hell hadn't I noticed the ring before?

As much as I hated to admit it, Cheeks was onto something. With the right technology, someone could easily sharpen the video enough to see the crest on Raphael's golden ring.

Raphael Jacobson hadn't only worked for Hiram. Sure, he regularly worked in Blackthorne Towers to break in the new girls, but he was part of a family whose fortune was built on sex trafficking. Raphael had been the youngest of six brothers and the black sheep of the family. He'd been too disorganized to get involved with the operational side and too unpredictable to procure girls, so he did his own thing. When he went missing, his family thought he'd crossed the wrong people and got himself killed. He was too much of a liability to be missed, and they were grateful his disappearance didn't bite them in the ass. Still, the other Jacobsons wouldn't be happy if they found out what happened to their baby brother. It didn't matter how much of a pain in the nuts he was; they were still blood.

I needed to tread carefully. Leaving Hiram's rule and starting over hadn't erased my past. All the big underground criminal organizations and networks were interconnected. Cheeks might have even heard rumors about the Kitten, Hiram's mysterious female protégé. If he had, or if he shared the video with any of his associates, Hiram coming after me wasn't the only danger I faced. The list of people who held grudges against me filled a motherfucking bible.

"I think the Jacobson family would be interested to know who their brother was screwing," Cheeks continued. He may know who the guy in the video was, but he didn't seem to suspect my involvement in Raphael's death. "Don't you?"

"He paid for sex all the time," I said, playing along with his assumption. If Cheeks believed I worked as a prostitute, then I wouldn't need to kill him... yet. "What's the big deal?"

"I'll bet a piece of ass like you doesn't even know what happened," Cheeks gloated. He didn't know he was talking to Raphael's murderer. "Didn't you hear?"

"Hear about what?"

"Your client disappeared around the same time the video was filmed." If Cheeks spent the same amount of time doing his actual job as he did jerking off to a grainy porno, then the town's crime rates wouldn't be so damn high. "I checked the time stamp."

"Really?" I gasped. "No way."

"I'm sure his buddies would like to have a chat with one of the last whores to fuck him." Cheeks leaned in closer, almost knocking me out with his toxic smell, to whisper in my ear, "I know you're nothing but a sweet ripe pussy, but they may not see it that way. Not all men are as gentle as me."

I had to grind my teeth together to stop myself from snapping his fingers. "I don't do that anymore."

"Sure you don't." Cheeks tucked one of my loose tendrils behind my ear, but the underlying threat lingered. He wanted me to go to the Maven and would not take no for an answer. "I've already ordered a cab."

I fluttered my eyelashes. "Sounds perfect."

Well, as perfect as using pliers to peel my toenails off one by one in a vat of battery acid...

"I thought that's what you'd say." Cheeks smirked, stashing the USB safely into his pocket and pulling out a jewelry box. "I almost forgot, I got you something special to wear."

He opened the lid to reveal a diamond choker. It looked like a tacky, sparkly dog collar. Not the type of accessory anyone would choose to wear to a rave known for its brawls. Diamond knuckle dusters would have been more appropriate.

"It's beautiful," I lied. "Can you fasten it for me?"

From across the bar, Rocky's eyes burned into us. He watched our every move like a lion prowling in the undergrowth, ready to pounce on his prey at any second. I turned around and held my hair up. Rocky jumped to his feet, causing his stool to screech across the floor. It looked like I'd touched a nerve. He needed to get it through his skull that my life, and the decisions I made, were none of his fucking business.

"Everyone will know you're mine tonight," Cheek said. His slippery hands snapped the clasp in place. "See? All mine."

The cool stones felt heavy around my throat. I tipped my chin upwards to meet Rocky's thunderous glare in defiance. His fists were balled at his sides. His usually brown eyes turned black, penetrating me with a venomous fury that wanted to poison the deepest depths of my soul. He'd never been an angry person before but, now, I saw a whole new side to him. A monster lurked under his clenched jaw, begging for release.

"Let's go." I shot Cheeks my best attempt at a charming smile, but it turned into more of a grimace. Luckily, he was too busy staring down my shirt to notice. "I think I heard a car outside."

As much as I relished the chance to make Rocky suffer, I couldn't afford for him to compromise my plans. I needed to lull Cheeks into a false sense of security, so I could wipe evidence off his devices. It'd be easier to kill him, but murdering a cop was never a good idea, even one as icky as Cheeks.

Keep your friends close and your enemies closer, right?

CHAPTER
Six

The cab ground to a halt at the rusty gates of an old shipping yard. Some girls got taken to fancy restaurants, but girls like me? We were taken on dates to places that looked like fucking crime scenes. Metal containers in varying shades of rust loomed above us like skyscrapers, surrounded by a graveyard of broken machinery. I hadn't expected a red carpet, but this? It wasn't exactly impressive for somewhere so infamous.

"We're here." Cheeks declared proudly like we'd pulled up at the Four Seasons.

We waited until the cab disappeared before heading towards a hole in the barbed wire fence underneath a danger of electrocution sign. As if that would keep the type of people on the guestlist out.

"Ladies first." Cheeks eyed the warning warily and proved me wrong. It turned out even the Maven had a handful of cowards attending. "After you."

I rolled my eyes and ducked under. It was an eerily still evening, like the opening scene in a horror movie. When evil acts take place, they leave behind a residual energy you can feel in your bones. My intuition told me this yard had more ghosts than a fucking cemetery. This was where many people had drawn their last breaths. Half the containers were probably stuffed with rotting corpses who held grudges.

Cheeks led us deeper into the metal jungle.

"How much further?" I asked.

Where was everyone? I'd expected axe-wielding murderers to be jumping out from every unlit corner. This was supposed to be a wild, hedonist's wet dream.

"Not far," he said. "We're nearly there."

We turned a corner and approached the filthiest container of them all. From its appearance, it looked like it had been at the center of an atomic bomb drop with large dents on the top and sides.

"This is the VIP entrance," Cheeks bragged.

"No champagne?" I muttered sarcastically. It wasn't exactly a luxury retreat.

Cheeks pounded on the door, then jumped a few steps back like he was playing a game of ding-dong ditch. Suddenly, the metal groaned to life to reveal a small gap. Out of it, an arm shot out and pressed the barrel of a gun into my forehead.

I didn't flinch.

Please. If they were going to pull the trigger, I would be dead already. It wasn't the first time someone had pointed a weapon in my face; although I'd be mighty annoyed if the ring of gunpowder ruined my make-up.

"Don't worry, princess. Let me handle this," Cheeks said. He stepped in to play the role of savior and mumbled a few hushed code words to grant us access. Had he forgotten he'd been the one quivering behind me a few seconds ago? It's not like he was saving me from imminent death.

The gun lowered, and the hinges swung open to let us inside. If this was the VIP entrance, I didn't even want to think about what other shit you had to do if you came in the other way.

"In," the doorman grunted. It was hard to make out his features from the number of piercings on his face. How the hell did he towel dry without catching one of those things? I only had my belly button pierced, and it hurt like a bitch whenever it got caught. The pierced troll stepped off a steel trapdoor and nudged Cheeks with the gun to pass. "Go through."

"Ladies first," Cheeks insisted.

Chivalry had nothing to do with it. The guy was a fucking limp dick. The feel of his sweaty hand on the small of my back made me want to scrub my skin clean with a scouring pad.

The killer bass hit me as soon as the trapdoor opened. It revealed a rickety metal staircase that vibrated with the volume of the music and looked close to collapsing. The stairway to hell led down into an underground cave where a swarm of people was crammed inside. Strobe lights mounted in the rock face bounded off every uneven surface.

Now, this was the Maven.

The dance floor was a fast blur of tits, leather, and tattoos. Chains hung from the walls like a medieval torture chamber, and bloodstains smeared the stone like cave paintings. This is what happened when you stuck all the worst people in the same place. A total cesspool of fuckery.

Cheeks pulled a vial out of his pocket and sprinkled white powder on the back of his hand.

"Want some?" he offered, snorting a line. "It's the best in town."

"Maybe later."

The night was young, but a bubbling tension already lurked under the surface. I needed to stay alert. It would only take the smallest thing for the whole situation to explode. Although, helping Cheeks get off his face wouldn't hurt.

We edged through the writhing bodies to the bar.

"Absinthe," Cheeks barked. He pointed at the dusty green bottle with wide, dilated eyes.

Cheeks chugged his down in one. Thankfully, they'd mixed it with water for me. No one but Cheeks wanted to drink that shit straight. Every mouthful burnt the back of my throat, but the minty flavor was good. It's what you'd get if you mixed petrol and mouthwash.

Cheeks slapped his empty glass down. "Another!"

"I'm gonna go to the bathroom," I said.

His high had kicked in, which made it the perfect time for me to slip away. With any luck, he'd have passed out by the time I returned. All I'd need to do was grab his cell, the USB, and his house keys to destroy any copies of the video. Then, somehow, figure out a way to take it down for good.

"Hurry back," he slurred.

I wouldn't be seeing any green fairies in the underground lair tonight; the only creatures around were horned fucking demons.

———

I scanned the packed crowd, trying to discern whether I recognized any faces. Hiram and his cronies only traveled to Port Valentine occasionally, but it didn't hurt to be too careful. So far, no one looked familiar, meaning there was no reason to make a hasty escape... yet.

I passed a group of brawling men who were a storm of fists and metal. Judging by the tattoos on their necks, they were from rival gangs. Behind them, a harem of young half-naked women surrounded an old guy, and a dominatrix led three barking men around on collars. Rules were non-existent.

"Want some company?" A straggly-haired man wiggled his tongue through the gap where his two front teeth should be. "I promise I won't bite."

Well, duh. He probably had to blend all his meals and suck them through a straw.

"If you want to keep the teeth you have left," I said, grabbing him by the scruff of his neck. "I'd think carefully about what you say next."

"Frigid bitch," he grumbled. He couldn't grasp how looking like he'd crawled out of the sewer may explain why someone wouldn't want to screw him. It was easy to understand why men subjugated women when rejection shattered their fragile masculinity.

I stopped myself from following him as he scurried off to try his luck on the next nearest vagina in sight. Forcing the Teenage Mutant Ninja Turtle's wrinkled grandad to kiss the ground may help release my pent-up anger from Cheeks's blackmail attempt and Rocky wanting to control me, but it was too much of a risk. I couldn't justify the attention it'd draw with Hiram breathing down my neck.

"Hey, watch where you're going!" A man called after me as I barged into him.

Wait… his voice sounded familiar.

I spun around to look up at the face hidden underneath the baseball cap. The surprise in his eyes mirrored my own.

"Q?!" I gasped, blinking hard to make sure I wasn't hallucinating. Surely, no amount of absinthe could resurrect the dead? Hell, I was sure Q's bones were dust by now! I'd always known Q was a stealthy lone wolf, but it was almost impossible to believe that someone could stay under Hiram's radar for so long. He had vanished without a trace after... what happened. "Is that really you?"

We first met in my early months of living in Blackthorne Towers. During my breaking-in period, Q had been kinder to me than the others. He'd tried to look out for me as much as he could. With the way things turned out, he must regret it now.

Whilst Q had never been one of Hiram's crew officially, he had been one of his most trusted allies until he disappeared. It had taken Hiram months to find a replacement. No one else could clean money quite like Q. What he could do with the filthiest dollars overnight was nothing short of magic.

"You shouldn't be here." Q grabbed me by the arm and dragged me to the side of the pit. All the while, his eyes darted around the crowd like he was expecting gunmen to descend upon us any second. "It's dangerous."

"What are you doing here?" I stammered. "I thought you were dead. Everyone did."

The last time we saw each other was forever scorched into my memory; Q was covered in blood, jumping into the back of an ambulance. The look of horror on his face was something I'd never be able to forget. Even though it'd only been a year ago, it could have been a decade. Time hadn't been kind to him. Q was in his late thirties but looked older. His shoulder-length sandy hair was flecked with gray, and deep lines were carved into his skin. That's what happened when you went on the run and hid from Hiram.

Q put a hand to his lips. "Are you here alone?"

"I don't work with *him* anymore." The last thing I wanted was for him to think this was a trap. "I got out."

"He let you go?" Q frowned.

"Well, not exactly…" I paused. "It's a long story, but we made a deal."

"She always knew you'd find a way." Q shot me a tight-lipped smile, but pain hid behind it. The pain left behind by the absence of someone he loved. Who *we* both had loved. He ruffled my hair, like he used to do, then added, "Look after yourself, kid."

He turned his back on me and melted into the crowd like the invisible man, leaving so many questions unanswered. *Where had he been all this time? How had he evaded Hiram? And would he ever forgive me?* Instead of running after him, I stayed rooted to the spot. Q was entitled to his privacy. I owed him that much, at least. Maybe our paths would cross again one day, and we could finally talk about what happened… until then, knowing he was still breathing would have to be enough.

A girl shoved past, jolting me back to the chaos. "Move, bitch!"

For once, I couldn't find it in me to snap back a snarky response. Seeing Q had felt like a dream. It'd made defying Zander and Rocky's recommendations worth it. Even my worries about the video leak faded in the glow of knowing Q was alive. If he had started over, then maybe there was still hope for me. With the buzz of alcohol and newfound optimism, I set out into a tunnel that led further underground to find out what other secrets the Maven may be holding.

On my way, I passed ten couples either fucking or in different stages of undress. Seemingly, you had to battle past several orgies to go for a pee. I turned a corner to find myself face-to-face with a man lounging against the wall with his hands behind his head. I recognized the rose face tattoo and the smug smirk in an instant.

What the fuck was he doing here?

It took me a few seconds to register the two girls down on their knees, taking it in turns to pleasure him. Neither one was Bella. Zander averted his gaze from one of the dick suckers to catch my eye, then winked. Yes, he fucking winked.

"Enjoying the show?" Zander asked.

What kind of psycho stops to have a conversation when someone is giving them head? If he was trying to make me uncomfortable, it wouldn't work.

My cheeks heated in fury. "You didn't say you were coming tonight."

He wouldn't allow me to go to the Maven, but it was fine for him to do whatever the hell he liked. How was that fair? One girl pulled away and mumbled a few words in a language I didn't understand. To my surprise, Zander responded fluently. Whatever he said gave them added encouragement as their heads returned to bobbing around like they were raving to a song only they could hear. All the while, his eyes didn't leave mine.

"I'm not," he said, then grinned wickedly, "yet."

"You're a fucking hypocrite," I spat, turning on my heel.

I'd rather see Cheeks again than stand around watching Zander drop his load.

———

The atmosphere in the club had taken a dangerous turn. The rising testosterone levels in the air could have impregnated a virgin, and a few more drops of spilled blood threatened to start a full-on cage brawl. Pieces of rock falling from above covered the crowd in a cloud of fine dust, as it crumbled under the thumping beat. If people didn't end up killing each other soon, everyone might get buried alive by the end of the night.

Cheeks staggered towards me. "Where've you been?"

It was impressive he was still standing with the amount of absinthe and coke in his system.

"I couldn't find you."

At that moment, the action in the middle of the dance floor erupted. A man pinned another to the ground and started pounding into his face like he was trying to shape it into a burger patty. This was what everyone had been waiting for. Seconds later, bodies flooded into the pit and turned on each other with swinging fists. Sweat, fury, and pure blood lust turned everyone into animals. The darkness had been unleashed, and there was no going back.

"Le'sssss go." Cheeks grabbed my wrist in a vice-like grip and pulled me to the exit, as his instincts kicked in.

The man was a coward right down to the bone. Cheeks may be a police officer by vocation, but he let others do his dirty work. We both knew he stood no chance if anyone threw a punch his way. They'd roast him over a barbecue and eat him alive.

"Leaving so soon?" The dungeon troll guarding the VIP staircase scowled, looking down at the crowbar in his hand like he was considering smashing it over Cheeks's head. I wished he would. Seeing Q had made this evening extra special, but being splattered in the asshole's brains would be the perfect cherry on top.

The crack of a gunshot and a bullet ricocheting off a nearby wall sent Cheeks flying forwards.

"Move!" he yelled, barging past.

The guard spat at his feet. Too fucking right. The Maven was not a place where you came to run from a fight. It seemed a shame to leave when it was just getting exciting, but I couldn't paint the town red every time I went out — especially when my sexy, insane boss was jizzing somewhere in the shadows.

Cheeks half-ran up the steps, nearly yanking my arm out of its socket. "Hurry up!"

The extra height gave us a bird's-eye view of the riot breaking out below. I glimpsed Zander's thorny face diving into the middle of the pit. His energy hadn't been drained along with his balls. I hoped the fight had ruined his happy ending. With any luck, someone would give him a black eye or break his perfectly defined cheekbones. Although any injury would only make him look more rugged and… *don't even fucking go there,* I willed myself. Those types of thoughts would send me over the edge of a dangerous cliff I wouldn't be able to come back from.

"I'ss nice we're alone," Cheeks said, releasing his hold on me as we exited the container.

Spotlights flickered overhead and cast shadows through the drizzling rain. There was nothing to suggest that complete carnage was unraveling beneath our feet.

"I'll call a cab," I said, heading towards the sound of the highway.

"Why so quick?" Cheeks's hand closed around my cell, leaving grubby fingerprints on the screen. "What's the hurry?"

I quickened my pace. "It's been a long night."

"But I think we should get to know each other," he said, then paused for a few seconds to remember the right word, "better."

"You're wasted."

"And you're *mine* for the night." His expression turned quickly to rage as his temper boiled over. It's funny how he was too scared to face off against the big boys underground but had no problem trying to intimidate a woman who only tipped over five-feet tall. "You're not going anywhere."

"I'm going home," I said firmly. "Alone."

"No, you're not." He snatched my phone from my hands and threw it against the metal side of a container, like a child unwilling to share his favorite toy. There goes the second one that had been destroyed in my possession. Clearly, I was cursed. "Not until you give me what I'm owed."

I glared up at him through my thick lashes. "I owe you nothing."

"You knew what you were agreeing to." He pointed at my neck. "Remember?"

"Not anymore." I ripped the choker from my throat, sending stones bouncing and rolling into the darkness. Diamonds were overrated, anyway.

"You ungrateful whore!" Cheeks lurched forward and struck me hard across the face. The metallic taste of my blood was bitter on my tongue, but it made me feel more alive than I had in weeks. "No one disrespects me!"

"Just fucking watch me," I said, spitting the blood from my mouth on his shiny shoes.

He had messed with the wrong girl.

The stumbling bastard lunged again, but I was ready. My fist smashed into the center of his face. The satisfying crack of his bone felt wonderful beneath my knuckles. It had been too long since I'd heard that sweet sound. There was nothing I hated more than a person who picked on someone who was half their size, who they believed would be an easy target. Cheeks was a sniveling piece of vermin who hid behind his badge and had only gotten to where he was by brown-nosing the most powerful.

"Fucking bitch," Cheeks gasped, falling to his knees and holding his gushing nose like it was a fatal wound. "Call an ambulance."

"What's wrong?" I asked. "Is your mommy not here to kiss it better?"

"Call an ambulance," he begged.

"On what cell?"

"Come on," he pleaded. "This is all just a m-m-misunderstanding."

The only misunderstanding was him thinking I'd do whatever he wanted. I may have done a lot of things in my life that I wasn't proud of, but I still had my own rules. One of them was to only kill people who deserved it. Rapists, murderers, and traffickers were my favorite men to hunt, and Cheeks? Well, he fucking deserved it.

"You have something that belongs to me," I snarled. I knelt by his side and frisked his pockets. The closest to any action he'd be getting. He was too weak to resist, as I pocketed his phone and swiped the USB stick. He didn't have any keys, so I'd have to think of another way to get any additional copies. "Enjoy the rest of your night, Cheeks."

His eyes widened in panic as the realization of sleeping rough in a shipping yard festering with criminals set in. This wasn't how he'd expected the evening to end. "You c-c-can't leave me here!"

"Yes, I fucking can," I said. A part of me wanted to finish him off. Instead, I compromised by kicking his left side hard enough to break a rib. "And don't ever lay a finger on a woman again, got that? Consider this a warning."

———

Cheeks's yowls faded into the distance as I reached the edge of the perimeter and slipped back through the hole in the fence. I'd already deleted the video from his phone and the cloud. Now, all I had to do was destroy it. On the other side, a car screeched to a halt and its headlights almost blinded me. The window lowered.

"Get in," West growled from the driver's seat. "Buckle up."

I didn't have any better offers. It was either: accepting a ride, or having to hitch back looking like a hooker from a zombie apocalypse. As soon as I slipped in next to him, we sped off into the night.

"This makes us even," he snarled.

"Giving someone a lift doesn't equate to covering up a fucking murder," I snapped. "But it's a start."

West scowled. "What happened to your face?"

"Nothing I couldn't handle," I said, wiping my bloody knuckles on the expensive leather seats. I didn't know a lot about cars but, if he could afford this set of wheels, he could pay to get the stains out.

His biceps tensed under the thin fabric of his T-shirt. The roar of the engine was deafening as we raced down the empty highway. Maybe getting into a car at night in the middle of nowhere with a killer hadn't been a great idea after all.

Suddenly, and without warning, West slammed his foot down on the brake. Hard.

The tires squealed in objection.

We lurched forwards so fast that my insides felt like they were about to burst out of my skull. If we weren't wearing seatbelts, we'd have flown straight through the windshield like rag dolls.

"What the fuck are you doing?" I shrieked as we came to a halt.

A cocky smile spread over his face. "Just seeing what you can handle."

West usually came across as the sullen and moody type. Go figure it took almost giving me a heart attack to make him grin.

"So, you're trying to test that theory by killing us?"

"You seem to be doing a pretty good job of trying to get yourself killed on your own," he said. "Tell me what happened tonight."

"It's none of your fucking business." I tried the door. Walking home in the cold would beat riding alongside a crazy man who thought he was Mad Max. "Let me out!"

"I want you to tell me what happened," he pressed. "As long as you work in the club, you're my business. If someone hurt you, I'll deal with them."

A laugh escaped my lips.

West's brows furrowed. "What's so funny?"

"You pretending to give a shit," I said. West had taken every opportunity to rip me to shreds since the poker game, so seeing this new protective side of him had caught me off guard. "I'm not a damsel in distress, and I don't need you to fight my battles. I do just fine on my own."

"Cheeks hit you, didn't he?" West's expression was blank and unreadable, which made it even more worrying. I couldn't tell what was going on behind the muscles in his twisted mind. "Leave his cell with me."

"How did you—"

"It doesn't matter." West shut me down instantly. "You're not the only person who has a grudge against Cheeks."

I waited for him to elaborate, but he stayed silent. That was all the asshole was willing to share.

"Fine." I shoved the phone into the cupholder. I was only giving it to him because I'd already cleared what I needed to. He'd be doing me a favor in getting rid of the damn thing. "Are you going to tell me what you'll do with it?"

"No," he said. Of course, he wouldn't trust someone like me with such information. Whatever he had planned, it better be good. "Now, are you going to let me drive you home or what?"

"Only if you promise not to drive like a maniac." My heart rate still hadn't returned to normal after our emergency stop. "And only because I don't have a better offer."

He turned the key in the ignition and didn't say another word until the car pulled up right outside my apartment block. Lapland wasn't the kind of place that kept the personal details of its employees on file.

I raised an eyebrow. "Are you stalking me now?"

"I think what you're trying to say," he said, "is 'thank you'."

"You lost my gratitude when you almost killed me."

I jumped out and slammed the door shut with a bang.

"Oh, and Pinkie?" West called. I didn't give him the satisfaction of turning around. "No one else needs to know about this."

Another secret I'd have to add to our growing list.

After doubling up on aspirin and gorging on junk food, I sauntered into Lapland with all the self-confidence I could muster. The dull ache in my head from last night hadn't fully lifted, but physical pain was the least of my problems. Zander knew I'd defied his orders by going to the Maven, and there would be consequences to pay. As if a hangover and slight concussion weren't bad enough…

I'd barely cleared the entrance when Rocky descended on me like a vulture. I wasn't the only one who'd had a rough night. He wore a loose hoodie over a pair of ripped jeans, and his crazed eyes were bloodshot.

"What happened? Who did that to you?" Rocky grabbed my arm, his fingers digging into my skin like he was holding on for dear life. "I told you not to go. I tried to warn you."

I may have respected his opinion once, but he'd lost the privilege long ago. His interference in my life had destroyed it. He was fucking delusional if he thought pretending to look out for me now would make up for the ultimate betrayal he committed.

"And I told you I don't do as you fucking say, remember?" I looked down at his groin in warning. "Move out of my way before I do some more serious damage."

He sighed and raised his hands in surrender. A wise move. A knee in the gonads had taught him to know better than to argue with me.

I headed straight for the dressing room, ignoring the other dancers' curious stares. There used to be a time when I was too shy to look anyone in the eye. Now, I walked into any place like I was fucking royalty. Confidence was easy to fake and no one could tell the difference.

"Oh my gosh!" Mieko dropped her comb and rushed to my side. "What happened to you?"

"I'm fine." I waved away her concern with a sweep of my hand, then winked. "You should see the other guy."

She dropped her voice to a whisper. "Are you sure you should be working?"

Bella's bat-like ability to detect vulnerability must have gone into overdrive because her chair spun around so quickly that the motion was a blur.

"Look who it is, everyone," Bella declared. "Frankenstein has arrived. Doesn't she look like a monster?"

"Frankenstein was the creator," I pointed out. Back in High School, gothic horror had been one of my favorite genres to read. "If you're going to insult me, at least get your fucking facts straight."

"No one wants to see someone with a face like yours dance," she sneered.

"Do you want me to level out the playing field?" I cracked my knuckles. "Let's see who does better."

Her smile froze momentarily as she weighed up whether I was bullshitting. Was saving face worth more than getting her own smashed up? She better think carefully, because I wasn't in the mood to be tested.

"What's going on here?" Vixen stormed in, then did a double-take in my direction. "You're not performing looking like that."

I played dumb. "Like what?"

"Like you've just walked out of a fucking ring."

The bruises on my face had matured like a fine wine; no amount of concealer could hide the bluish hue underneath. Not to mention my puffy bottom lip, which looked like someone had slipped when injecting filler.

"Maybe she's right, Candy," Mieko agreed. "You should rest."

"I'm fine," I insisted. Laying on the sofa planning Rocky's demise and binging trash TV wouldn't pay me. "I'm here to work."

"Not here," Vixen said. "Come back in a week. We'll see if your job is still around then."

"A week?" I spluttered, following her out and ignoring the snickers from the hive. "Can't I wear a mask?"

After dancing in a shower of blood, getting down in a balaclava didn't seem too outrageous.

"I'm done with your avant-fucking-garde performances," Vixen hissed. "You may have been able to charm Zander, but it's not going to work on me. My word is final. Lapland has standards."

"Fine, I won't dance." Now didn't seem the right moment to comment on how low her standards were if she let Bella front the show. Instead, I tried to level with her to strike up some kind of compromise. "But there must be something else I can do?"

"I thought you were too good for cleaning," she said. It'd only been a matter of time before she threw that back in my face. Bargaining with her was harder than taking blood from a heroin addict. "Remember?"

"C'mon, Vix." Rocky came over to intervene. "Cut her some slack, huh?"

He could shove his 'help' right up his ass. His trying to help only made me more infuriated. I wasn't the defenseless kid he used to look out for. The only thing he needed to be watching was his own back because I was coming for him.

"What the fuck is wrong with you, Red?" Vixen turned on him like a hungry Rottweiler and jabbed a finger into his chest. "You've been acting weird since you got back. The girls are my fucking business, not yours. You need to get your shit together. You're a mess!"

Rocky scratched his left ear like he always used to when he was trying to hide something. Would Vixen still think so highly of her precious Red, if she knew what he'd done to me? Hell, who was I kidding? The bitch would give him a medal.

Before Rocky could reply, Zander and West joined us. Zander wore his usual perfectly pressed black suit. He must have held his own in the Maven pit because all he had to show for it were minor cuts over his knuckles. It only made me hate Cheeks even more. I'd missed out on seeing Zander in action because of his spinelessness.

"What're you two arguing about now?" West asked.

"Red thinks I should cut her a little slack," Vixen explained. "We run a strip club, not a fucking freak show!"

"Speaking of shows," Zander said, turning his attention to me, "did you enjoy yours last night, Candy?"

Rocky's eyes flitted between the pair of us in confusion. The truth was, I'd been trying not to think about what I saw in the tunnel. Everyone knew Zander used women like tissues, and they were happy to be disposable for him.

"I've seen better," I answered with a casual shrug. "It didn't last long."

"You defied a direct order," Zander said. His gray eyes burned into mine like we were the only two people in the room. "I told you there would be consequences if you went to the Maven."

Was that a threat, or a promise? A shiver ran down my spine. Apparently, my beat-up face wasn't enough to serve whatever punishment he had in mind.

"What consequences?" I challenged, squaring my shoulders.

"You'll see."

"You can't let her go to the Briarly game now," Vixen huffed. "Not unless West doesn't mind looking like a wife-beater."

"Hey!" West slammed his glass down hard enough for it to crack. "She's not fucking going if—"

"Enough." Zander's steely tone signaled the conversation was over. "No more business talk here."

Vixen whirled around to face me. "Why are you still standing here? I told you to come back in a week."

"You heard her," Zander said. "Go."

"What about—"

"We'll be in touch," Zander interrupted. "But remember what I said, Candy."

The club fell into a hushed silence. In a seedy place, that only meant one thing. Serious trouble had strolled in off the sidewalk.

"He said he had to come in." One of the bald security guards hurried over to report to West and jerked his head toward a swaying figure. "I didn't know what—"

West raised his hand to silence him. "We'll take it from here."

Holy shit.

"You!" Cheeks's shrill voice echoed through the building as he pointed a shaky finger at me in accusation. "You sneaky fucking whore! What did you do with them? What did you do?"

He stumbled down the steps, and the floor cleared to make a path for him to pass. He looked almost unrecognizable. He was filthy, still in last night's blood-soaked clothes, and covered in bruises from head to toe. Both of his eyes were so swollen he couldn't see where he was going and kept tripping over his own feet. Sure, I'd given him a good beating, but he'd still been coherent when I'd left — well, coherent enough to have tried to attack me. After I'd gone, someone else must have got to him... but who?

"How did you do it?" Cheeks slurred, then mumbled a series of nonsensical sentences no one could understand. "All the copies... the... gone."

"I don't know what you're talking about," I said.

I may not be performing tonight, but we were certainly giving everyone a show.

"You heard her," West growled. He planted a firm hand on Cheeks's shoulder, making him cry out in pain. "It's time to go."

"Not until she gives me them back. They're mine. Mine!" Cheeks shouted, wrestling to free himself. With his free hand, Cheeks grabbed my shirt and yanked me closer. The smell of vomit and liquor on his breath made my stomach heave. "I'll hand you over... I'll tell... I swear..."

"Get your hands off her," Zander warned. He unbuttoned his shirt cuffs and rolled up his sleeves to reveal more beautiful ink. "I won't ask you again."

"But, she—"

Zander threw a right hook that sent Cheeks toppling backward like a stack of Jenga blocks.

"You don't know who... you don't know..." Cheeks wailed as West yanked him to his feet. "You... mistake... she... you don't know who..."

Rocky moved to create a human wall between me and Cheeks. Seeing him stand next to West made me realize just how much he had filled out over the years. Rocky had always been tall and toned, but his shoulders were now broader and his muscles more defined.

"What the fuck is he talking about, Candy?" Vixen asked.

"How am I meant to know?" I rebutted. "Just look at him. He's on something!"

Roaring sirens outside grew closer.

"If you've brought trouble to our door, I swear I'll—"

Ten armed officers charged through the doors and flooded inside, drowning out the rest of Vixen's threat. Complete mayhem broke out. A stampede of clicking heels and high-pitched squeals echoed around the club as dancers fled into the backroom. Several customers ducked under tables to hide or scampered to the nearest bathroom in a desperate plight to flush whatever substances they had.

My heart hammered in my chest.

Why were they here?

Had someone tipped them off?

Did Cheeks tell them about my links to Raphael?

"Over here," one cop roared, beckoning the others to follow and heading in our direction.

Running would only make me look more guilty. This was it. The moment I got locked away forever.

"Get him," another said, as Cheeks tried to make a run for it.

They swarmed down on him in a flash. He stood no chance against them all.

"No!" Cheeks screamed in objection. They forced his struggling body to the floor and pinned his limbs in place. "This is a mistake!"

"Look what we have here." An officer pulled a bag of white powder from his back pocket. "Roy Checkersford, you are under arrest. You have the right to remain silent."

Last night Cheeks had carried a small vial of coke, but this would have been enough to tranquilize the entire dance floor. Even Cheeks wouldn't be stupid enough to carry around so much gear. West's words came flooding back: 'I'll deal with him.'

"No!" Cheeks thrashed around like a fish out of water. "Please, Billy! No! That's not mine! It's a setup... I can ex-explain!"

West watched the scene unfold with little interest. *Was it possible he'd orchestrated the whole thing?* His expression was as blank and unreadable as ever. Goddammit, it was easy to see why the guy was good at poker.

"Save it, Cheeks." The officer took great pleasure in forcing his colleague roughly into cuffs. Cheeks may have powerful connections outside of work, but it didn't look like they had made him a popular guy on the force. It was nice to know there were still cops who took their oath seriously. "You'll be going away for a long time."

"But it wa-wasn't me," Cheeks wept.

Watching him cry like a baby almost made my decision not to kill him worthwhile... *almost.*

———

The club buzzed with speculation as soon as the cops cleared out. Watching a powerful figure, like Cheeks, being escorted in a police van sent a massive statement. A big fuck you to the status quo and to those who pulled the strings in Port Valentine. The fallout from his arrest would be worse than the Chernobyl exclusion zone.

"Get everything under control, Vixen," Zander ordered.

She nodded curtly. A police raid was akin to throwing a grenade at Lapland's reputation for discretion. No doubt she'd have an empty bar by the time she'd finished smoothing over this mess.

"All of you." Zander signaled to the rest of us. "My office. Now."

From his rigid posture, he was using every ounce of his self-control not to explode. This was not a situation I wanted to get caught up in.

"If I'm not allowed to work—"

"Don't fucking test me, Candy," he said through gritted teeth. "Fall in fucking line."

This wasn't a battle worth fighting. Tension rose with every step. I felt like a naughty child being called to the principal's office; although Zander's punishments would be worse than writing an apology letter or a page of lines.

"Do you know what this means?" Zander reeled as soon as the door closed behind us. "The Briarlys are going to be furious. You know who they'll blame."

It didn't surprise me to find out the Briarlys had Cheeks on their payroll. Dirty cops helped crime families from the inside all the time; whether that was by feeding them information, helping them cover their tracks, or smoothing over any misdemeanors. It also explained why Cheeks carried a lot of cash. A family as prolific and wealthy as the Briarlys would have to pay damn well to ensure law enforcement looked the other way.

"But we didn't do anything," Rocky said. "Cheeks has fucked a lot of people over. It's not our fault he got sloppy and got caught with coke."

"Sloppy doesn't exist in our world." Zander paced back and forth. "I'm only going to ask this once. What do you know?"

Zander studied each of us. West didn't flinch under his scrutiny. He stared back at Zander with bored indifference. If West had gone against his fellow Sevens to handle Cheeks in his own way, then that was his prerogative. It was not my story to tell.

"What was he talking about, Candy?" Zander pressed. His piercing eyes searched my face for any hint of hesitation. "Copies? What did he mean?"

"He was talking shit like a crazy person," I dismissed. West wasn't the only person in the room who had a good poker face. "Nothing he said made any sense."

"You shouldn't hide anything from me, Candy."

"Come on, Zander." I rolled my eyes. "Anyone with a brain cell could see he'd lost his mind. The guy was too jacked up to function."

Zander pulled a gun out of his suit jacket and placed it on the desk. He turned to West and Rocky. "Why don't you two leave us alone?"

Rocky tensed at my side but inclined his head. Both of them obeyed and filed out. No one would dare question Zander's authority. Being stuck in a soundproof room with a gun and my boss was not an ideal situation.

I jutted my hip. "Well?"

Zander didn't reply. He let the silence stretch out to try to make me squirm. His tactic wouldn't work. If he gave me a recliner and a margarita, then I could chill here all night without saying a word if I had to. I'd spent a lot of time in solitary confinement in Blackthorne Towers, and my company was often better than the alternative.

"You've defied me once before," Zander said eventually. He cocked his head to the side, trying to figure me out. "Why should I trust you?"

"I could ask you the same question."

Trust was something to be earned. Zander knew better than anyone. Above all, I had to look out for myself. No one else was going to. I'd come into this world having to fend for myself, and that's the only way I'd get through it.

Zander picked up the gun and took a step forward.

I didn't move, but my heart rate started to rise. It wasn't the gun that made me nervous, but the thought of being so close to someone who wanted to ruin me. My vision wavered as his smoky bergamot aftershave enveloped me. He smelled nearly as delicious and dangerous as he looked.

"Do you always have an answer for everything?" Zander leaned in closer, the heat of his breath tickling my neck. "Anyone would think you had a death wish."

The feel of the cold metal running up my bare leg made me shiver.

"Maybe I do," I said.

Zander's knuckles gently grazed my skin as the gun slipped in between my thighs.

"I don't know what you're hiding." His stare scorched into mine as the gun slid further underneath my tiny skirt. "But I'll find out."

I tried to ignore how Zander's inked fingers brushing against me were setting every nerve ending in my body on fire. *How could something so bad feel so fucking good?* I didn't fear him shooting, but I'd rather die than give Zander the satisfaction of knowing the effect he had on me if he were to slip a few inches higher.

"I had nothing to do with his arrest," I said. "That's all you need to know."

Zander studied my face, then pulled the gun away and tucked it back into his waistband. Whatever he saw in my expression must have satisfied him. I smoothed down my skirt and flicked my hair over my shoulder, like having the barrel of a gun pointed at my pussy was a normal occurrence. He'd get pleasure from knowing he'd rattled me, and I refused to give him it.

"Do you like playing games, Candy?"

I arched an eyebrow. "Games?"

"No one takes me for a fool," Zander said. "When I play, I win. Every time. Whatever you're hiding, make no mistake, I will find out. And if you cross me, there—"

"There will be consequences," I finished the end of his sentence for him. "I know."

"You have no fucking idea," he spat. As much as Zander tried to portray the image of someone with full self-control, an unpredictable demon lived inside him that liked to rear its head when people least expected it. "Listen carefully to what I'm about to say. On Saturday, you're going to help us win the poker game at Briarly Manor. You will not see a cent because of the trouble you brought in tonight."

"But we had a deal."

"A deal you broke the moment you stepped into the Maven," he snarled. "You should be fucking grateful for the opportunity."

"What's stopping me from walking out of here and not helping you at all?"

"Nothing," Zander said, then paused to give the illusion he was deep in thought. "Unless you want the police to find out your new little friend's secret. What's her name? Mieko? Don't you think they'd be interested to know how she killed her own father?"

"You're talking bullshit," I said. A Care Bear seemed more likely to be an axe-wielding psychopath than the sweet girl who was too embarrassed to say the word 'sex' aloud. Sure, she'd seen some messed up shit, but killing her dad? She didn't seem capable of squashing a fly, let alone another person.

"Am I?" He stroked his chin, drawing attention to his perfect jawline. "Why don't you ask her yourself?"

The real question wasn't whether Zander was telling the truth about Mieko. It was what he was capable of and the depth he'd be willing to sink to.

"You're not a snitch."

Not snitching was the only rule all criminals held as fucking gospel. Snitches get stitches didn't become a truth universally acknowledged for no reason.

"Maybe not, but how sure are you?" He wouldn't mind screwing decent people over if it meant getting what he wanted. "Is it a risk you're willing to take?"

He was a master manipulator who could burrow under your skin and dig up vulnerabilities. It didn't matter whether he was lying. Seeing Q yesterday had brought back memories, and I'd already vowed I'd never let another innocent life be ruined because of my choices.

"Okay, I'll go to your fucking game." I scowled. "But I have one condition."

"This wasn't up for negotiation."

"Neither is this," I said. "If I do this, I want Mieko's history to stay buried. Forever."

"That depends."

"On what?"

Zander grinned wickedly. "On whether you can play by my rules."

Every fiber of my being screamed in objection. After leaving Hiram, I'd sworn never to follow someone else's orders again. Especially when those orders came from a gang leader who had serious control issues.

"Fine." I pursed my lips. Backing down wasn't usually in my nature, but this was an exceptional circumstance. Letting Zander believe he had the upper hand was the lesser of two evils. Allowing him to think he'd won would get him off my back long enough for me to pursue my personal agenda. "I'll try."

"Good," he said. "Just don't forget what happens if you break them."

There would be consequences.

Eight

A loud banging on my apartment door rudely interrupted my dairy coma. If my nosey neighbor had come to tell me to turn the TV down again, I'd blast metal at full volume for the rest of the day. Since when was the sound of Queer Eye so offensive? I didn't thump on her door every time she argued with one of her boyfriends.

"I'm coming," I shouted.

Since the Sevens had banned me from working in Lapland until my face healed, I'd spent the week involuntarily getting to know a little too much about the people who lived around me. In fact, the most productive task I'd done was turning my sofa into a blanket cocoon and devouring two tubs of ice cream in sixty minutes flat.

The knocking persisted.

If the TV was loud enough for her to walk across the landing, then she should have damn well heard me.

I swung the door open. "I already told you—"

"Before you slam the door in my face." Rocky stepped forward to wedge his foot in the gap. "I have something for you."

He held a large shiny shopping bag that looked like it was from a fancy boutique I'd never be able to afford.

"Leave it there," I directed, nodding at the ground like it was a suspicious package and I was part of the bomb disposal unit. "Then back away."

"Aren't you going to invite me in?" he pressed.

"What's going on? What's that racket?" My neighbor's shrill voice floated over from across the hall. She shuffled out of her apartment with her hair still in rollers. She wore a leopard print silky robe and balanced a cigarette precariously in her hand. She looked Rocky up and down with distaste, then tutted. "Isn't it a bit early for gentleman callers? It's a scandal!"

"Can it, lady," I snapped back. Hello, we weren't in the 1920s anymore. Besides, she was hardly one to talk. I knew all about what *she* got up to. Wasn't it pathetic that even my sixty-year-old neighbor had a more active sex life than me? "If you don't want your husband to know what you get up to during the day, then you'll keep your mouth shut."

Rocky snorted in laughter.

From the look of shock on her leathery face, I may as well have flashed her my boobs. She cursed under her breath about the youth of today and left a trail of ash behind her as she stomped back inside. Hopefully, she'd think twice before bothering me the next time I binged a box set.

"Can I come in?" Rocky asked again.

He was the last person I wanted to invade my space, but I knew Mrs. Leopard-Print-Robe would already have a glass pressed against the wall. Reluctantly, I stepped aside to let him pass. "You have two minutes."

"Looks like you've been having fun," he said, taking in the half-empty ice cream tub and spoon balanced on the coffee table.

"What do you want, *Red*?"

He smirked down at my pink fluffy feet. "I like your slippers."

Goddammit, those soft cushioned clouds really brought down my badass vibes. I'd been rocking the no make-up and messy bun look all week. Why get ready when the only plans I had involved pressing a button and eating my body weight in sugary goodness?

"My face is up here." I snapped, noticing his gaze lingering on my chest. I'm pretty sure my white vest was see-through. "Give me the fucking bag."

He cleared his throat.

"This is for you to wear at the game tomorrow." Yep, he could 100% see my nipples through this thing. "A car will pick you up at eight."

I ripped open the bag and shredded the pink rose-smelling tissue paper. Inside, a beautiful white dress had been neatly folded on top of a shoebox. It was one of the most stunning dresses I'd ever seen. Not that I'd let him know that.

I held it up and half-shrugged. "It'll do."

"Zander wants to know if it fits." Rocky planted his ass in the center of my blanket cocoon and draped his arms over the sides of the sofa like he owned the fricking place. "If it doesn't, I'll exchange it."

I checked the label. "It'll fit."

"Aren't you going to try it on?"

"And give you a private show?" I scoffed. "I don't think so."

"What about the shoes?"

I opened the lid to reveal a brand-new pair of Louboutins. *No fucking way.* I'd never been a materialistic person, but those beauties were a piece of wearable art. They were also worth more than everything I owned put together.

"They're the right size." I took great care in relaxing my facial muscles. My happy dance would have to wait until after Rocky left. "I guess they'll do too."

"Good," he said flippantly, completely oblivious to the value of the heels. Either that or becoming a Seven had completely changed his perception of money. When you'd come from a place of poverty, it was hard to leave that mindset behind.

"You've made your delivery," I said. "You don't have to stick around."

Rocky didn't move. He looked up, trying hard to keep his gaze fixed above my shoulders. "Your face looks better."

"I'm a quick healer."

The bruises had faded enough to make them easy to cover, but the cut on my lip would be harder to hide. A faux lip ring should do the job nicely. It's good I knew how to rock a disguise better than anyone.

"I see you still have a sweet tooth." Rocky picked up my spoon and took a whopping mouthful of my ice cream. If I didn't already want him dead, I would now.

I snatched the tub from his evil clutches. "Don't you know eating a girl's cookie dough without permission is the douchiest move on earth?"

"Mmm." He licked his lips to taunt me further. "My favorite!"

I threw him a filthy look. "You can go now."

"While I'm here," he went on, ignoring me, "I wanted to talk to you about something else."

"And I don't want to listen to anything you have to say."

How many times did I have to shut him down before he got the message?

"Zander has eyes in jail." He knew that would get my full attention. "Cheeks has started talking. We heard from the doc that he was drugged and beaten. The fucker wouldn't be breathing if I'd gotten my hands on him."

Well, that was one thing we agreed on.

"What else have you heard?" I probed. It wouldn't be practical to kill Rocky here but, if the cops were closing in, this could be the last chance I'd get.

"He's squealing to anyone who'll listen that it was a setup." Rocky watched me closely for a reaction. "But he's not given any names."

Cheeks cared about maintaining the image he'd created over the years. He'd never want to admit how he'd got his ass beat by a stripper, who he'd tried to assault at an underground rave. It'd be too damaging to his macho persona.

"What do the cops think?" I asked, savoring the creamy goodness on my tongue. It tasted all the sweeter to know it was Rocky's favorite and he wouldn't be getting another bite.

"It's not the cops we're worried about. They've always known Cheeks was dirty, but the bastard has always had someone else to cover his ass." Rocky's brows furrowed in concern. "I've been thinking about something Cheeks said when he was last in the club. He mentioned a video, and if he was talking about—"

"The one of me?" I cut in. "You've seen it then? Old habits die hard."

He winced, but let my comment wash over him. "Where did it come from?"

"Why does it matter?" I slammed my spoon down. If things got ugly, I needed both hands ready. "You've already added it to your wank bank, what more do you need to know? It's not like you see women as any more than objects."

"Did Hiram have anything to do with it?" he asked. "I just thought if he leaked the video, then he might have had something to do with what happened to Cheeks."

"How the hell should I know what *he* is doing?" I snapped. The mention of his name in my apartment was akin to talking about anal sex to a nun. Hiram may have leaked the footage, but messing around with law enforcement wasn't usually his style. When he wanted revenge, he'd slam a person into the trunk of a car and make sure they never saw the light of day again. "If I were you, I'd be looking closer to home."

"Forget I said anything," he said, shaking his head. "I wanted you to know the video is gone, too. I made everyone turn over their cells after Cheeks's arrest. They made no other copies. Outside of Lapland, Cheeks was the only person Bella sent it to. You don't need to worry about anyone else seeing it, okay? I didn't mention to Zander where I thought it came from..."

"Doing one good thing doesn't make up for what you've done." I narrowed my eyes. "Do you expect me to be grateful?"

"Look, Candy." Rocky sighed. "I know you're angry with me but—"

"But, what?" I placed the Louboutins carefully back in their box. If blood was going to get spilled, the only true crime would be wrecking those babies. "I think I'm entitled to be angry."

"I know you'll never forgive me for what I did." He rose from the sofa, making the room shrink around us. "And I don't fucking deserve your forgiveness, so I'm not gonna ask for it or make any excuses. But I do want us to try to get on or... be civil, at least."

The old me would have crumbled into his arms. It was the one place where I'd felt safest. Now they spelled out danger. I didn't know whether the person I used to love had ever existed, but I *knew* I couldn't trust the man he'd turned into. Rocky had always been handsome, but he'd grown a hardened edge over the years. His eyes held the secrets of a person who had seen too much darkness, and the new scars on his body showed he hadn't gotten away unscathed.

"Be civil?" I laughed in his face. Rocky was no longer my harbor. He was the fucking storm who had sent me crashing into the rocks and taught me that no one could be trusted. "We will never get on. Ever."

"What happened to you, C?" Rocky asked. "I don't even recognize you anymore."

"You happened to me," I spat. "Now, get the fuck out of here."

He sighed. "Be ready at eight tomorrow, yeah?"

He paused on his way out and looked like he wanted to say more, but shook his head and decided against it. All I had left for company was the melted cookie dough, which served as a reminder that all good things came to an end.

———

Getting ready for the poker game at Briarly Manor had been a marathon activity. After a day of taming my body fuzz and blow-drying my hair to perfection, all I had to do was the final touches. Nothing could go wrong tonight if I wanted to be in with a chance of helping the Sevens in the future.

"Come on, get in!" With one last tug and a huge inhale, I pulled it up past my ass. "Finally!"

Despite having to be a contortionist to squeeze into it, my new dress was comfortable to wear. It was long-sleeved and sat mid-thigh, but the plunging V-shaped neckline more than made up for the lack of skin coverage.

I spun around to admire my reflection. "Perfect."

I'd gone for a smoky eye and red lip to match the white dress. My tattooed skin against the white fabric combo made me look like an angel who'd got turned away at heaven's gate. Living in sin was always more fun anyway, right?

I did a few bunny hops to make sure my boobs stayed in place. I didn't need to add a nip-slip to the list of things I needed to worry about. Thankfully, the tape kept them strapped down.

Whilst my cleavage looked epic, it still surprised me whenever I looked in the mirror and saw my new breasts. Honestly, I hadn't even wanted the procedure done. A few years ago, I'd been whisked away in the middle of the night and woke up as a D-cup. I hadn't been completely flat-chested before, but going under the scalpel molded my body to meet the bullshit ideals of the men I needed to seduce. All of my experiences since had reaffirmed how men who judged girls on their bra size were grade-A assholes.

Over time, I'd grown to embrace and accept my new look. My shape may have been altered to meet other peoples' ideals, but I'd never fully be free if I allowed that to become my story. Getting ink, dying my hair, and reclaiming my body had unlocked me from an internal prison where I'd remained trapped for too long.

"Shit," I cursed, glancing at the time and grabbing my purse.

I needed to follow the instructions exactly.

Albeit breathless, I made it outside my apartment block at eight o'clock exactly. Right on cue, a black Range Rover pulled up with West glowering behind the wheel. I couldn't help feeling a little disappointed. I'd been expecting a yellow Ferrari, or something more flashy. These poker games were the perfect opportunity for the richest to show off their wealth. Why waste such a chance?

"Aren't you a little under-dressed?" I asked, slipping into the passenger seat. If it wasn't for the blood spatters up his arms, he could have come straight from the gym. Holy shit. My eyes were drawn to West's lap like a fucking magnet. Whoever designed gray sweats had to like dick because why else did they show off an asset like a fucking frame? I forced myself to look away from the obvious bulge visible in his pants.

"I had some business to attend to." He scowled. After our spin the other night, I should have known better than to wind him up. The tape wouldn't survive the whiplash. "We're swinging by the club first, so I can change."

"You've been very busy with *business* recently," I said, keeping my gaze fixed firmly ahead and clenching my thighs. I needed to distract my mind with the least sexy thing I could think of. "How is Cheeks?"

"I should be asking you the same question."

"I only broke his nose and ribs." I shrugged. "What I want to know is how you pulled it off."

"Me?" The car ground to a halt at a red light. "Getting him busted on a drug charge isn't my style, Pinkie."

"But you said you'd deal with him."

"If I had," West said, his eyes were soulless, like the very first time I saw him in the parking lot, "there would be no mess left behind.'

"If you didn't do it, then who did?"

A horrible sinking feeling in my gut told me Rocky's suspicions about Hiram's involvement may have been right. It was too much of a coincidence for his arrest to happen right after being seen at the Maven with me.

"If I did know anything, which I don't, do you really think I'd tell one of our strippers?" West asked. From his snide tone, the answer was pretty fucking clear. He saw the dancers as lower-class citizens. Lucky for me, I knew my real value and didn't rely on an arrogant prick to dictate my status. "Being able to play poker and catching Zander's attention doesn't make you any better than the rest."

"Are you always this charming when you take a girl out on a proper date?" I questioned. "Because you seriously need to work on your game, if you want our act to be convincing."

"This is a one-off," he hissed. "Don't get used to it."

"Are you that delusional to think I'd actually want to get used to hanging out with someone who acts like a fucking asshole? Don't flatter yourself," I snapped. Contrary to his belief, looking hot didn't compensate for acting like a total jerk — even if it made him a whole lot easier to look at. "We've got a job to do. That's all."

West gripped the wheel hard like he wanted to tear it off, as we pulled up at the club.

"Zander is waiting."

"Well, what are *you* waiting for?" I demanded. "Are you going to open my door, or not?"

Tonight was all about business, and I was going to make sure West put in the work.

Going to Lapland in this outfit would be like lighting a stick of dynamite, but entering with West on my arm? Well, that'd be enough to blow the entire place up. Bella had already drawn up her battle lines. It was time for me to ignite the war.

Eyes raked over us from the moment we stepped inside. Shitting in a cup would have drawn less attention than this. At the other end of the bar, Scarlett burst into tears. Strike one.

"I'll be back soon," West muttered. "Try not to cause any trouble while I'm gone."

"I'll try," I replied, then added under my breath, "but I can't make any promises."

As soon as West left, Mieko bounded over like an excitable puppy and launched into my arms. I wasn't used to physical affection, but it was sweet to see how much she cared and confirmed I'd made the right decision. After striking a bargain with Zander, I'd made up my mind not to tell Mieko what I'd found out. We all had secrets we wanted to keep buried. If Zander's information was correct and Mieko had killed her father, then he must have been a monster to push her to do it. Besides, who was I to judge? I'd lost count of the number of lives I'd taken.

"Hey, go easy!" I laughed. My make-up had taken time, and I didn't want to leave here looking like I'd stepped straight outta the circus. "You know I didn't die, right?"

"I've been worried about you." She pulled away. "I would have called, but—"

"Shit, your phone..."

With everything else going on, I'd completely forgotten that Vixen's plastic girlfriend had smashed Mieko's cell into smithereens.

"Don't worry, I have a spare." She pulled another out of her bra like a magician would yank a rabbit out of a hat. "I lost all my numbers though."

"What have I missed here?" I noticed a commotion at the bar as Bella fussed around Scarlett like a mother hen. They kept glaring in my direction like I was the spawn of Satan. "Well, apart from the usual."

"Bella's been even more unbearable," Mieko groaned. "I heard Zander broke it off with her."

After seeing him in action at the Maven, she had a lucky escape — not that she'd view it that way. All Bella cared about was her crown. Zander ending their arrangement threatened her position.

"Everyone's been talking about what happened to Cheeks. Rumors have been going around that you went to the Maven with him because you were going to buy drugs," Mieko said. Being heartbroken must have really affected Bella's imagination if it was the best she could come up with. "Vixen has even banned everyone from talking about him. If she hears anyone say his name, she'll fire them on the spot."

I glanced over at Bella and crossed my fingers. "Here's hoping."

Damage control was one of Vixen's areas of expertise, and it was more important than ever. Lapland didn't need any extra attention when it was the Sevens' base for an underground illegal poker ring... and whatever other shady operations were happening.

"Enough about what's been going on here," Mieko said, then lowered her voice. "How are you feeling about tonight? Is it true you're actually going to Briarly Manor?"

"Does everyone else know about it?"

"I don't think so." She blushed. "I *may* have overheard the Sevens talking earlier."

"Even better," I said. The best way to bring down a clique started by breeding insecurity. "Have you been to the manor before?"

"Only once," she admitted, wrinkling her nose. "I didn't like it. It's one of the oldest buildings in Port V, and it has a creepy vibe. I swear it's haunted."

I winked. "Don't worry, I'll keep an eye out for the ghosts."

"It's not the ghosts you need to look out for," she warned. "The Briarly family founded this town. Bryce Briarly practically owns it, and he makes all the rules. Tonight is a chance for anyone who is anyone to meet, throw away money that normal people could only dream about, and decide how the rest of us mere mortals should live."

"So, as fucking usual, it's a boy club," I summarized. Luckily for me, people who thought they ruled the world rarely saw what was right in front of them. Just like the players in Lapland's underground game, they would never see me coming.

"I don't know what you're planning, and I don't want to know. But just be careful, okay?" Mieko said. "Bryce is not someone you want to mess with."

Before I got the chance to delve deeper, Bella stomped over with a sniveling Scarlett in tow. Their expressions were murderous.

"What were you doing with West?" Bella demanded.

"What I do in my spare time is none of your business," I said.

"Wait!" Scarlett's mouth hung open. "Are those Louboutins?"

For someone with cotton candy for a brain, she could sniff out a pair of designer shoes quicker than a piranha detecting a drop of blood.

"Do you like them?" I twisted my ankle to give her a better look. If I wasn't the one wearing them, I'd have been drooling with jealousy too. Zander may not be paying me a cut for my help tonight, but these shoes cushioned the deal and came with the bonus of infuriating Bella. "They were a gift from Zander."

"Zander?" Bella put her hand to her chest like I'd shot her. "You're lying. Why would he give anything to you?"

The guys chose the perfect moment to make an appearance.

"Why don't you ask him yourself?" I suggested as they neared.

Holy shit balls. Zander looked fucking insane in a pinstripe black tux, and his sharply trimmed beard signaled he meant business. It was the first time I'd seen West dressed smartly, and he scrubbed up well. Too damn well. The buttons on his shirt strained under his massive pecks, which made me realize why some women had a thing for men in his suits.

"We're leaving," Zander said to me, nudging his head at the exit.

"Before we go," I said, knowing we had an audience, "I never got the chance to thank you for the shoes."

"I'm glad they fit." His words caused Bella's face to crumple like a wet paper bag. "The car is waiting."

"But... she..." Bella stammered, losing her ability to speak.

It wouldn't last for long, but I shot her a smug smile for good measure. "I'll see you tomorrow, Bells."

Tonight, I dropped the bomb. I would have to deal with the fallout later.

CHAPTER
Nine

A black stretch limousine lay in wait for us, taking up most of the narrow dingy street.

Zander held the door open. "Ladies first."

His gentlemanly act didn't fool me. The last time we saw each other, he'd almost stroked my vagina with a gun. Zander kept a lot of things hidden under his mysterious inked exterior, but manners were not one of them.

"Sweet ride." I exhaled, leaning back into the sleek leather seats.

Plush velvet lined the walls, and it boasted a host of flashy features: a large fold-down plasma TV, sound system, mini-fridge, a disco ball, and a giant number seven spread over its ceiling. It was more like a vacation destination than a car. The lavish sheepskin rug was the only thing I didn't like... fuck knows who had rolled around on it before.

Zander grabbed an expensive champagne bottle from the icebox and poured himself a generous glass. I coughed pointedly. Like, hello? If he hadn't noticed, three of us were here.

"You two need to stay clear-headed." Zander put his feet up, almost reclining entirely. All he needed was someone feeding him grapes to complete the overall picture. "I have other matters to deal with tonight."

"I didn't know you were coming along," I said, watching with envy as he refilled and downed it like water.

"And miss a chance to go to Briarly Manor?" Zander gave a hollow laugh. "I don't think so."

West grimaced, his arms pressed to his sides. Why did I feel like I was missing part of the story?

"Are you ready for tonight, Candy?" Zander asked. "Can you handle it?"

"Handle it? Please!" I scoffed. "I'm not an amateur."

West coughed. "Bullshit."

"Listen up, asshole. Let me tell you how it's going to go down." I swung around to face him and flipped my hair over my shoulder. I meant fucking business, and I wouldn't let him ruin our chances of winning tonight because of his oversized ego. "I can read a room better than anyone. If I scratch my ear, it means fold. If I run my hands through my hair, it means to lay down more chips. If I spill my drink, it means we get the fuck outta there."

"She has you there, West." Zander let out a low whistle and tipped his glass in my direction. "I'm impressed. You've thought this through."

"As I said, I'm no fucking amateur." I shot daggers at West. "Were you taking notes, West? Or, do you need me to repeat myself?"

"How can you still think having her around is a good idea, Zander?" West's face reddened. Healthy competition was new to him. "I told you, she's fucking reckless."

"What's wrong, West?" I fluttered my eyelashes. "Feeling threatened?"

"I don't need help from you." West pouted, balling his fists in his lap. "I can win on my own."

"Only if you don't underestimate other players again," I reminded him. I would never let him live that down. "I can help you, and you know it."

"If we're going to pull this off and walk away with fifty thousand dollars," Zander said, pausing to look between us, "then everyone needs to believe you're a real couple. Can you both do that?"

I lifted my shoulder in a half-shrug. "Depends."

"On what?" West growled.

"Whether you can behave yourself."

"You little—"

"See?" I said. Teasing him was easy, and I couldn't help myself. His moody pout was just too fucking irresistible. "We're even arguing like we're married already."

Married couples bickered, right? They did in movies, anyway. In reality, I'd known no one who had a successful marriage. Growing up, the only people I saw getting hitched were those who had knocked up a townie and super religious parents orchestrated the whole thing. Under Hiram's wing, I'd been to a few weddings, but most of those had underlying motives too. Marriages of convenience, pairing off people to call a truce between rival families, or gold-diggers seeking to land a fortune from killing their spouses. Marrying for love only existed in chick flicks.

"Enough," Zander snapped. "This isn't child's play. You need to make it convincing, or we'll all have to face the consequences."

I peered out the window. "Holy crap."

The car climbed a steep hill to a gothic mansion looming ahead. I hadn't taken Mieko's warning about ghosts seriously enough. The place looked haunted as fuck. If the walls could speak, they would have stories to tell. When one family had sustained their grip on a town for generations, the manor had to have a bloody history. How else would the Briarlys have ruled over Port Valentine for so long? No one stayed in control by being nice.

"Welcome to Briarly Manor." Zander rubbed his hands together. "Let the games begin."

———

"Ready?" West laced his gigantic fingers through mine as Zander held the door open for us to follow. His huge hand completely entombed my own.

"Let's do this." I nodded. "It's showtime."

My dress was too tight to wear panties, so getting out of the limo had to be a slick maneuver. Thankfully, I avoided pulling a Britney to the gaggle of men smoking cigars. An onlooker held up eight fingers followed by nods of agreement from the others. I didn't even want to know whether he was rating me or the car, but that set the tone for what I should expect.

Rich entitled pricks. They would get what they deserved when we cleaned out their wallets by the end of the evening.

"This is how the other half live, huh?" I murmured.

I'd never seen so many expensive cars in one place: Maserati, Ferraris, Lamborghinis, and even a gold-plated Bentley. A red carpet led up a stone staircase to the entrance where butlers, who looked like they'd come straight from an English period drama, handed out flutes and canapés.

"Make the most of it," West said, guiding me towards the house. "It's the only time you'll ever come here."

"We'll see about that." If tonight went well, he may have a partner, whether he liked it or not.

Inside, a gigantic staircase split into two in the center of a hall, which was five times the size of my entire apartment. Marble floors, oak-paneled walls, oil paintings, and a chandelier made a grand statement. Whoever designed the room had spared no expense to show off how much money they had.

"Would you care for a drink?" a server offered.

"Why, thank you." I ignored West's disapproving glare. We were there to win, but that didn't mean I couldn't enjoy myself along the way. "Would you like one too, honey?"

West grunted in response. He wouldn't dare say anything to risk shattering our happy couple illusion so soon.

With my pink hair and their tattoos, the three of us stood out amongst the crowd like clowns at a funeral. Most of the guest list consisted of middle-aged and graying men, accompanied by much younger female companions who were being paid to be there. Everyone in this room had something to prove. Everything was a competition from who had the best car to who had the hottest piece on their arm.

How had we secured an invitation? This wasn't somewhere the guys would usually be seen dead at.

"Zander!" A smug young man with a British accent swanned over to greet us. He was handsome in a red-faced, boyish way and looked like he'd go for tea and scones with members of the royal family. "Good to see you. I'd almost thought you'd been avoiding me."

"I've been busy," Zander replied coolly.

"I'm surprised your little club is still open," the man said, overlooking our frosty reception. "West, it's always a pleasure. Are you ready to give the game your best shot?"

"I'll try," West snarled, although I'm pretty sure the only shot he wanted to take was a bullet straight through the obnoxious fucker's forehead.

"You do that." He clapped West on the shoulder, then turned his attention to me. "Who is this pretty thing?"

"This is Candy," West said. "She's mine."

"Giles," he said, holding out his hand for me to shake. I hated him already. "Giles Briarly."

"Sorry," I said in a sassy tone that implied the opposite. I held up my glass and my other hand interlinked with West's. "My hands are full."

"Aren't you a feisty one?" Giles wiggled his eyebrows suggestively and nudged West in the ribs. "I've always liked my girls a little less refined."

He had the Briarly name, but that didn't stop him from being one of the world's biggest douchebags. I'd met men like Giles before. Men who had come from a long line of generational wealth. They'd been born with a silver polished butt plug up their ass and expected life to be laid out on a platter. The worst thing is, it normally was…

"I told you," West growled. He tightened his grip on me. I couldn't tell whether it was because he wanted to hold me or himself back. Either way, I'd have broken bones if Giles kept this act up. "She's all fucking mine."

Giles smirked, causing West to crush my knuckles further. "If you say so."

If we'd been anywhere else, West would have knocked him out by now. But things didn't work like that in high society. People still hated each other, but scores got settled differently. They replaced fists with cunning plans and scandals to cause financial or political ruin.

"Let's talk business, Giles," Zander said, gesturing to an adjoining room. Smart move. He needed to get him out of West's range fast. If Giles opened his mouth one more time, I'd never be able to tie my shoes again. "Somewhere more private."

Giles winked. "Don't miss me too much, Candace."

"It's Candy." I glowered as Zander steered him away.

Good fucking riddance.

West waved a server over. A few moments later, they returned with a whiskey on the rocks. He knocked it back and ordered another.

I raised an eyebrow. "I thought you wanted to have a clear head."

"That was before we ran into Giles Briarly."

"Would you mind not taking your anger out on my hand next time?" I suggested. "I can't feel my fingers."

"Shit." He loosened his grip instantly. "Giles knows how to get under my skin."

"I have a feeling he knows how to get under everyone's skin," I said. "Let's keep moving."

We followed the flow of people into a library-turned-bar. Bookshelves covered every wall from ceiling to floor. I doubted the Briarlys had even read any of the books in their vast collection. They probably used first editions to wipe their asses.

A small group gathered to admire one painting on the wall.

"Look at the technique," someone drawled.

Another nodded. "One of his finest pieces."

"You can really feel the emotion behind it," I mimicked sarcastically. Whoever painted it must be prestigious, but it looked to me like someone had vomited over the canvas after a messy night out. "When does the game start?"

"After the torture ends," West muttered, leading me away from the art snobs. "They love to stretch it out."

"You were pretty convincing back there with Giles," I said. He'd owned the whole protective boyfriend routine. "Maybe you're not such a terrible actor after all."

"I'm full of surprises." He picked up a canapé and swallowed it whole. "What's the point of these tiny things?"

"More money than sense," I answered, popping one in my mouth. The whole thing was as disappointing as premature ejaculation. It was over before I'd even had a chance to appreciate any of the flavors. "Give me a burger and fries any fucking day."

I spotted Giles and Zander re-entering with two gorgeous brunettes. It looked like they'd sorted whatever important 'business' they had to discuss.

West leaned against one of the old bookcases and gave me his undivided attention. "You look nice tonight."

"You don't have to pretend," I said. "They can't hear us from over there."

"Who says I'm pretending?" West put his hands around my waist. The heat from his fingertips radiated through the fabric and sent my heart racing. With palms the size of baseball gloves, they could almost wrap right around me. "Are you always bad at taking compliments?"

"Only fake ones."

He pulled me closer. "How do you know they're fake?"

I couldn't think straight, knowing the arms holding me had smashed skulls into dust.

"I know men like you." I ran one of my red nails down his chest. "You'll say anything to get what you want."

"What do I want, Candy?" West brushed a loose strand of hair out of my face, and I had to stop myself from dislocating his wrist. Our every move was being watched and monitored. I couldn't fuck this up. As well as blowing our cover, it'd ruin any chance I had of being part of any future schemes. "Tell me."

"You want money," I said. "And you want to win."

"I don't *want* to win," West said. His hands slid down to rest on the small arch of my back above my ass. "Winning is inevitable."

"Are you always so fucking full of yourself?" I narrowed the space between our bodies until I almost pressed my tits against him. Two could play at that game. If West wanted to give Zander a show, then who was I to let him down? "Or, are you trying to impress me?"

"Has anyone ever told you that you'd be a lot hotter if you kept your mouth shut?"

I leaned in closer, so close our lips were almost touching. "So I've been told."

"Maybe you should take the hint," he murmured, allowing his lips to gently brush against mine.

It was too bad he'd missed the memo saying I didn't give a shit what other people thought. No man would ever put me in a muzzle. And this bitch? She wasn't afraid to bite. West would learn that the hard way.

"Ouch!" West pulled away to check his lip for blood and his eyes darted around the room. I wasn't stupid enough to do it when people were watching. "You're fucking unbelievable."

"I don't kiss on the first date." I smirked, running my tongue over my sharp canines. "Now, if you'll excuse me, I'm going to reapply my lipstick."

———

I needed to give West time to lick his wounds. He was so used to having free rein in the candy store that he didn't like being told he couldn't have every treat on the shelf.

Three men were talking in hushed tones by the staircase, which piqued my attention.

"But they arrested him." One of them raised their voice in frustration, "Isn't there anything we can do?"

"What if someone gets to him?" another questioned. "What does that mean for us?"

"Cheeks was our man," the third cut above the rest, silencing the others the moment he opened his mouth. He was the ringleader. His tone was sharp, flippant, and oozing with the arrogance that came with a life filled with everything money can buy. Something was vaguely familiar about him, but I couldn't place it. "A move against him is a strike against us. Someone will pay for this. I will make sure of it."

It was no surprise Cheeks made his bucks sidling up to a bunch of men who thought they were Port Valentine's answer to the Illuminati. His getting locked up threatened their dominance, and they'd make sure the responsible party would suffer.

"How can we find out who did it?" one asked.

"Secrets never stay hidden for long." Their leader made a steeple with his fingers. "All we have to do is wait until the time is right."

"Are you lost?" Zander's chilling whisper in my ear sent a shiver down my spine.

I whirled around. "You shouldn't sneak up on people."

"Why aren't you with West?" he hissed. "He's looking for you."

"Relax, it's not a crime to pee." I rolled my eyes sarcastically. "Besides, I was doing some… research."

The more I learned about these people before the game, the easier it would be to squeeze cash out of their stuffed pockets later. Staying glued to West's side wouldn't help us get the right information. I needed to find their weaknesses to exploit their vulnerabilities.

"I asked you to win the game." Zander's voice was a dangerous low whisper. "Not poke around in Briarly business."

"I didn't—"

Suddenly, the leader of the group I'd overheard was headed in our direction. He was probably in his seventies but looked younger. He dressed in a smart silk suit, and his silver hair was immaculately groomed.

"Zander." The older man approached us with open arms. Instead of looking tired with age, his extra years had only made him more shrewd. "Someone told me you'd decided to show your face around here."

"What can I say?" Zander shrugged, burying his hands in his pockets. "I had nothing better to do."

"Who is this with you?" The man scanned me up and down like a fucking barcode. Every movement and look felt calculated like he was already ten steps ahead. "A girlfriend, perhaps?"

"She's with West," Zander said.

"Pity." He sniffed. "Then again, you were always a disappointment. Aren't you going to introduce us?"

"Candy, this is Bryce Briarly." Zander looked at him with utter hatred. "My father."

Wait, hold up! Zander was a motherfucking Briarly?

"It's nice to meet you, Bryce." I molded my face into an unreadable mask to hide my shock. "You have a beautiful home."

Zander being a Briarly explained our invitation to the poker night and his general my-shit-doesn't-stink attitude, but it didn't answer the other million questions rattling around my mind. Why was a Briarly running a strip joint in the worst part of town when he grew up in a fucking manor?

"I always like it when my son brings his friends home." Bryce's thin smile didn't meet his unfeeling eyes. Now, I saw the family resemblance. "Enjoy your evening, Candy."

He glided past to greet late arriving guests, stopping only briefly to whisper in Zander's ear. From Zander's stormy expression, it didn't look like a friendly father-son conversation about their next fishing trip.

"Keep fucking walking," Zander hissed, taking my arm. "You have a job to do."

"When were you going to tell me?"

"It's not relevant," Zander dismissed. His fingers cutting off my circulation told me we wouldn't be discussing his lineage any further. "You're here for one reason only."

Back in the library, our chances of winning the poker game were dropping fast. The scene unfolding was a catastrophe waiting to happen. West was still standing where I'd left him, but he wasn't alone. He and Giles were in a heated conversation, which threatened to spill into a full-on brawl. At this rate, we wouldn't even make it to the table.

"This is what happens when you can't follow instructions," Zander said.

"It's not down to me to keep West under control," I snapped. I'd not seen West this rattled since I'd beat his ass at poker. Whatever Giles had said to provoke him was making its way through his veins like poison. "Do I look like a babysitter?"

"You said you wanted this job." Zander pushed me forwards. "Fucking prove it."

I didn't need to be a mind reader to know who would be held responsible if West unleashed The Hulk. There wouldn't only be consequences for me, but for Mieko too. I had to make sure that West didn't lose control. Not until we'd rinsed the bastards dry, anyway. Hitting them in their wallets was how we would make them pay.

"Babe, I've been looking for you." I re-joined West and put myself in between them. "I've missed you."

West had once told me he'd never hurt a woman, but now I wasn't so sure. I'd played enough computer games to know Bowser was never afraid of mowing down Princess Peach if it meant winning a race.

"Why you'd miss that gorilla is beyond me," Giles scoffed.

He knew exactly what he was doing, and how to press West's buttons. If it wasn't in my best interests to diffuse the situation, I'd be first in line to cut out his tongue with a scalpel.

"Let's go for a walk," I whispered in West's ear. His entire body shook with the power that threatened to burst free. The muscled hurricane had the potential to tear through the library and leave thousands of dollars of damage in his wake in seconds. "We can go outside?"

The dead lock behind West's stare told me all I needed to know. He had already passed the point of no return. Unless I acted fast, Giles's head would be the next stuffed animal mounted above the fireplace.

"I'll kill him," West roared. "I'll—"

Before he could finish talking, I did the only thing I could to distract him... I threw my arms around his neck and brought his mouth crashing down against my own.

He responded like lightning. His arms squeezed around me like a fucking python, devouring me in his darkly delicious smell. I had instigated the kiss, but West was now in charge. His lips consumed me in a hot, explosive frenzy. His tongue slipped into my mouth, and the sweet taste of his fury engulfed all of my senses. All I could do was hold on tightly as the hurricane swept me away.

One of his hands slipped through my curls, whilst the other snaked around my waist and pulled me deeper into the storm. He kissed me like I was the very air he needed to breathe. Like I was the only way to satiate a ravenous hunger and... I fucking hated myself for loving every second of it.

The shrill sound of a ringing bell brought us both to reality with a thwack. We sprung apart. Giles had disappeared, and Zander was smirking up at us from a red high-backed chair which gave him a front-seat row to our show. Next time, I'd remember to charge him.

West whipped his head around to look at the crowd filing through large wooden doors. "It's starting."

"Can you get your shit together?" I murmured into his shirt, leaving a red lipstick mark on the edge of his collar. Nobody would question who West belonged to. "We've got a job to do."

"Let's fucking do this." West nodded. His anger still lurked underneath the surface, but the murderous rage within him had been caged... for now. "Oh, and Pinkie?"

I kept my stare firmly fixed on the poker room. "What?"

"So much for not kissing on the first date."

"Screw you." I cracked a small smile, daring a glimpse up at his swollen lips. Well, shit. I was now the one who needed to pull myself together. This was just business, okay? I only did what I had to do. "Let's bleed them dry."

Ten

West draped his arm around my shoulders and strode forward with purpose. We were like two soldiers heading into battle. Our tattoos were our armor, our fists were our swords, and our minds? Well, I needed to get mine out of the gutter after the kiss we'd shared.

"Remember what I said," I reminded West as we headed towards the poker room. I played the role of nagging girlfriend so perfectly that no one would guess I'd never had an actual relationship before. "Don't do anything stupid."

West scowled. "I'm not on your fucking leash."

"You are tonight," I said. "I'll even put a collar around your neck if it'll help."

After his earlier outburst, what the hell had he expected? I'd brought him back from the brink of eruption. I hadn't thrown myself into the fire for him to ruin things. I'd do whatever needed to be done to stop the night from turning into a bloodbath.

"Be careful, Pinkie." West shot me a warning glare, making me tingle in parts that should be unacceptable in a public place. "You wouldn't want to make me angry again."

We passed through the gigantic wooden doors. A full forest would have had to be cut down to construct them. Somehow, I doubted sustainability was high on Bryce Briarly's agenda. Beyond them, an impressive room with a domed ceiling had a poker table positioned in its center.

The crowd parted for us to make our way past. West's little performance in the library hadn't gone unnoticed, and no one wanted to get on the wrong side of the scary tattooed beast. Hell, I didn't blame them. Those people may have seven zeroes after their bank balance, but they couldn't buy a backbone.

At the table, players had already taken their seats. A black rope barrier around its edges separated them from the swarm of onlookers.

"Right this way, Mr. Parker." A guard manning the border opened the gap for West to pass.

Before he went up and over the front, I caught West's arm.

"Don't do anything I wouldn't do, honey," I simpered for the benefit of the guard, but my stare was laser-focused. Hopefully, West could read me well enough to understand the underlying threat behind my words. "Good luck."

"Don't miss me too much." West bent down to kiss me roughly on the cheek. He almost had me convinced until he added menacingly under his breath, "I don't need your fucking luck."

West spoke too soon. As soon as he took his designated seat at the table, Giles pulled up a chair opposite. The two of them sat eye to fucking eye with locked jaws. All I could do was hope for the best because we were past the point of a make-out session saving the day. From here on, I needed to trust West to keep his cool. We had a plan, and we needed to stick to it.

As we'd agreed, I circled the table to get a read on the nine other players like a shark planning a strike. The men came from all walks of life, from stuffy politicians to obnoxious business executives. They were all powerful people Bryce had collected over the years, who influenced the town in some capacity. None of them would be seen dead in a place like Lapland. If they wanted to see a girl undress, they had enough money stored in offshore accounts to hire an entire penthouse to rival the Playboy mansion.

Whilst West battled to keep his anger in check, I had a more pressing challenge ahead. I needed to look like I was trying to blend in and socialize. The thought of mixing with these assholes was even more torturous than staring at Giles's smug grin. Even though I could talk the talk, I'd never felt comfortable rubbing shoulders with people who'd never done a day of washing up in their lives. How can you trust someone who had never scraped grease from a pan? They lived in their ivory towers with no clue about what went on in the real world.

The game was just another evening of light entertainment for them. Sure, they wanted to see who'd win, but the outcome didn't matter when they were all loaded and could afford to throw dollars to the wind. None of them understood how this amount of money had the power to transform lives.

Bryce Briarly rose from the poker table and chimed on a glass to get everyone's attention. A hush swept over the room like he'd cast a fucking spell.

"Welcome, ladies and gentlemen!" Bryce extended his arms in the air like he was some kind of prophet. From the round of applause that followed, he may as well have turned water into whiskey. "This is our biggest prize yet."

West caught my eye, and we exchanged a look of mutual understanding. A quarter of a million dollars was on the line. We were not leaving empty-handed.

As the clapping died down, Bryce's chest had visibly inflated like he'd fed off their admiration.

"Let the game begin," Bryce declared.

Daddy Briarly would not miss the opportunity to crush his minions in a game. Losing was not in his nature. He was used to other people rolling over to give him what he wanted, which would make navigating a win even more difficult. It was one thing coming here to screw over rich strangers, but it was another to know that we were trying to dupe Zander's fucking family. When we got through it, Zander had some serious explaining to do.

As the dealer shuffled, a voice with a familiar New Jersey accent crept up behind me. "You and West are together, huh?"

I spun around to face Vinny. The last time I'd seen him, he'd been pass-out drunk from celebrating his big win... after he'd given me half his winnings for being his lucky charm.

"It's so nice to see you again." I adjusted my pitch to the same high-pitched whine I'd used at the Lapland underground game. "It's been too long."

His previously friendly demeanor had crumbled, and the cogs in his brain were turning. Shit. We hadn't planned for this. With all the drama this evening, we'd fucked up by allowing him to slip underneath our radar. While I was trying to stop West from murdering Giles, Vinny had been watching from the shadows all along and jumping to the wrong conclusions.

"So, it was all a fix?" he demanded.

Come on, Candy. Channel your inner ditzy gold-digger!

"You've got it all wrong, Vinny." I swatted his arm playfully, hoping charm alone would be enough to diffuse the situation. "We didn't start dating until after the game."

"You owe me money." Vinny put his hands on his hips in a power stance. Now, I was getting a glimpse of his mob boss alter ego. "I want it back."

On the plus side, his assertion that we were a proper couple meant we'd put on an Oscar-winning performance. It's a shame that it also threatened to tear down the house before the dealer laid a card. All it would take is for Vinny to sound the alarm for others to suspect there was more to West and I's 'relationship' than staged sexual chemistry.

"You heard me." Vinny advanced forwards. "I want it back, or I'll tell everyone how the Sevens run a rigged ring."

Before I could reply, two suited men swooped down on Vinny like vultures. Each of them grabbed one of his arms.

"Hey!" Vinny tried to shake them off, but they held on fast. "What do you think you're doing? You know who I am!"

"You're not on the guest list," one sneered.

"There's been a mistake. I was invited!" Vinny's raised voice drew the room's attention. From the poker table, Bryce watched the unfolding scene in bemusement. "Ask Bryce. He'll tell you."

Bryce raised his watch to his mouth to communicate with his men through their earpieces. It's a damn good thing that I could lip-read. "Take him outside," he ordered.

Vinny looked between the men and Bryce in confusion, then realization set in as Bryce's lips curled into a cruel snarl. All the color drained from Vinny's face as their grips tightened. He may have been invited to the game, but that didn't mean the host intended on him staying until the end.

"No!" Vinny shook his head wildly. "You can't do this!"

Vinny tried to thrash around, but it was hopeless. He wasn't as young as he used to be. His resistance was futile against the strength of the two trolls. It had only been a matter of time before someone took him out. He may have been important once upon a time, but it was inevitable someone would make a move to replace him eventually. The screech of his shoes against the newly polished floor made me cringe. If Vinny hadn't threatened to blow the lid on the Seven's illicit operations, then maybe I'd have intervened. Instead, I stood by and watched as they dragged him out of the room like a bag of garbage.

His cries of objection slowly faded. A few moments later, the sound of a muffled gunshot rang through the building.

"Someone needs to get their car to the shop," an idiot guffawed over his caviar, mistaking the noise for an exhaust backfiring. It was easier to dismiss anything that threatened his perfect rose-tinted view of the world than face the brutal reality of Bryce Briarly being a cold-blooded murderer.

He may have been able to fool some people in the room, but I noticed who stood a little straighter. Those were the ones who knew exactly why Bryce had lured Vinny to the game. Those were the people we had to watch out for.

"Don't even think about causing a scene," Zander hissed in my ear.

"It's nice of you to finally show up." Where had he been all this time, anyway? With West and I busy doing his dirty work, he'd probably been busy hooking up with a leggy brunette on a four-poster bed. "Vinny almost blew our cover. Your father has done us a favor."

We both watched as another player slid a thick envelope across the table to Bryce. The content of the envelope was the price of Vinny's life.

"My father's favors usually come at a high price," Zander said drily. If Bryce could orchestrate a brazen murder in the middle of a party, what else was he capable of?

"Now that outstanding business has been taken care of," Bryce said, clapping his hands together. I could see where Zander had inherited his ruthlessness from. Growing up in this house of horrors with a beast of a father would be enough to screw up any child. "It's time to play."

Zander whispered, "You know what you have to do, Candy..."

"I do," I snapped, "and I don't need you fucking reminding me."

Zander chuckled to himself as I stomped away. If he thought Vinny's death would distract me from our mission, then he was wrong. I knew exactly what I had to do. The game was on, and there was only one thing on my mind. Winning.

I started by doing a few laps of the room and engaging in mindless small talk to blend in. All the while, I gave West the right signals and watched from the corners. My initial assessment confirmed most players were mediocre. Only three of them posed actual competition, including Giles and Bryce. Although, the cards were the least of my worries. I couldn't hear what was being said from behind the barrier, but West's shaking arms were enough of an indicator that trouble was brewing. We couldn't afford any more fuck-ups.

"It's almost time for the interval," Zander said, re-joining me.

"An interval?" My mouth fell open. What happened to playing a simple game of poker without the bullshit theatrics? "This is poker, not fucking Broadway."

"My father enjoys putting on a show." Zander downed another shot. In the past hour, I'd lost track of how many he'd ordered. It was impressive how little of an impact hard liquor had on him. "It's what he does best."

"Clearly." I pressed my lips together to stop myself from saying something I'd regret. "Giles looks like he's enjoying himself."

"My cousin has always enjoyed causing trouble..."

"It must run in the family." I narrowed my eyes. "Didn't Vixen want to come along to the family reunion?"

"Don't mention her name here." He grabbed my wrist, and his cool gray eyes turned into burning hot coals. The monotonous drone of a pianist playing didn't even break Zander's furious stare. His fingers pressed hard into my wrists as a warning. "Not now. Not ever."

"What's going on?" West's question broke up the moment.

"Nothing." I ignored West's frown and yanked my wrist from Zander's grasp. If Zander wanted to censor what came out of my mouth, he should have given me the full story before throwing me into a snake pit. "I'm going to the bathroom."

"I'll come with—"

"I don't need a fucking bodyguard to pee, okay?" I jabbed a finger into West's chest to silence him. "Try not to kill anyone when I'm gone."

"Don't wander too far," Zander called after me. "If you get lost, you might not be able to find your way back."

There may be ghosts haunting these corridors, but none of them could scare me. When you've already looked death straight in the face and laughed, you had nothing left to lose.

———

A helpful server pointed me toward the nearest 'powder room'. I wove through the manor's corridors, passing several locked doors. Behind one of them, Bryce's men would be busy zipping Vinny's corpse into a body bag. They extinguished everything Vinny had built over the years the moment they pulled the trigger. In his final moments, would Vinny have thought it had all been worth it? It's a question I asked myself.

The grand sweeping staircases of Briarly Manor reminded me of a place I'd been to six months before. A place where I had slashed Giovanni Romano's throat for my freedom.

I was never naïve enough to think Hiram would let me go willingly, but I knew he'd strike a deal if he thought it'd be impossible for me to win. Our terms were simple: I kill Romano, and he permits me to leave his service, or I stay his Kitten forever. Giovanni was the oldest brother in a family who had controlled the drug scene of half the country for years. He had recently taken over as the kingpin; his house was a fucking fortress, and his entourage made him virtually untouchable. Hiram knew killing him was basically a suicide mission, but he'd underestimated how much I'd wanted to get away… and it'd cost him.

Getting into the Romano house was easy, seducing him was a breeze, and killing him was even quicker. Getting out undetected posed more of a challenge, but Hiram had trained me well. He'd created the perfect weapon in me. It kept me up at night wondering whether my freedom had been worth the final cost. Romano may be dead and not able to hurt anyone else, but Hiram had taken over part of their business. I may have gotten away, but it'd come at the expense of expanding Hiram's empire.

Pull yourself together. I reminded myself, pushing thoughts of Giovanni Romano's dead body from my mind. *You have a fucking job to do.*

As I turned a corner, an open door caught my attention. I pressed myself against the wall and shimmied to get a closer look. My first reaction was to vomit in my mouth and get the fuck away. The sight of Giles Briarly plowing a blonde over a marble sink was enough to put me off eating any more canapés. Her high-pitched, grating moans made me want to rip my ears off… well, shit. It looked like the Briarlys had the same taste in women.

"Have you missed me?" Giles panted between thrusts.

Vixen wouldn't be too pleased to find out what her girl was doing at a gathering they'd banned her from attending. Being cheated on was bad enough, but finding out it was with a member of your fucking family? Not even she deserved that, especially if your cousin was a bastard like Giles balls-deep Briarly.

"Yes," Charlene squealed. "So much!"

Despite the urge to rinse my eyes with rubbing alcohol, I forced myself to stay rooted to the spot. The pair knew each other, and the fact I hadn't seen her downstairs amongst the rest of the party seemed even more suspicious.

I pulled out my phone and hit record. Karma was about to come around and bite her on the fucking ass. Seeing them fuck for thirty seconds would be enough evidence, right? Vixen didn't need to watch him finish too.

"When I win tonight, we'll fuck on a bed of money." Giles took a break to check out his reflection in the mirror. "They won't even see it coming."

"But you can't know you'll win, right?"

"Oh, but I do. Let's just say I've called in a favor," Giles said, then winked. "I'm unbeatable."

Of course, the bastard had resorted to fixing the whole fucking game! Giles knew West would thrash him with his eyes closed if they were playing based on skill. I needed to get to West and Zander before the game started. We needed to get the hell outta Briarly Manor before Giles cleaned us out… unless, I came up with a better idea.

———

Out of the corner of my eye, I spotted the dealer loitering in the hall. If Giles wanted to play dirty, then I could play him at his own fucking game. With each step, I swayed my hips to draw attention to my curves and painted a sultry pout over my lips.

"Do you have a minute?" I put a gentle hand on the dealer's arm and stroked it gently. He gulped as I bit my lip and looked up at him through my lashes. "There's something I want to show you. Giles sent me."

"Sure!" The idiot grinned like he'd won the jackpot. He'd been too busy working out how to bend to Giles's demands to notice that I'd arrived on West's arm. "But I have to get back to the game in a few—"

"It won't take long," I insisted, taking his arm to lead him in the opposite direction from the party. I had to act fast before Giles returned downstairs. "You don't want to upset Giles, do you? It's something he thinks you'll really like."

The first door I tried was unlocked, and we stepped into a study. I clicked the door shut behind us and twisted the lock. We couldn't be disturbed.

"What do you want to show me?" The dealer loosened his tie. "Giles said nothing about—"

His voice trailed off as I stepped forward to run my hands up this thigh. His erection caused a tiny tent in his pants. Unfortunately, I was no fucking gift from Giles.

I leaned forwards to whisper in his ear, "How much is Giles paying you to cut him the winning cards?"

"I don't know w-w-what you're talking about," he stammered. "Is this some kind of weird foreplay?"

"Oh, I think you know exactly what I'm talking about." I grabbed his balls. "How much is he giving you?"

"YOWCH!"

"If you want to have children, I'd suggest you answer the question." I tightened my hold and dug my nails into his scrotum. "Tell me what I want to know."

"Three," he gasped as tears ran down his face. "Three percent, okay?"

"I'll tell you what…" I relaxed my grip a little. "You can walk away from this room on two legs if you play it straight for the next half."

Giles may be a fucking cheat, but that didn't mean we had to lower ourselves to his level. If we won fairly, there was no way anyone could question the integrity of the win.

"What about the money?"

"Would you rather have a little more cash in the bank or be able to walk?" I asked. "Or, would you rather I tell Bryce Briarly how you were trying to con his son's business partner out of money? I think he'd do a lot worse than break your legs if he found out."

All the color drained from his face. Thankfully, he seemed to know even less about the Briarly family than I did, as the mention of Bryce's name alone was enough to spook him.

"Okay, I get it," he whimpered. "Fine, I'll do it! Just let go, please!"

"Good." I released my hold, and he fell to the floor. "You can tell Giles you made a mistake when dealing the cards. Understood?"

He nodded meekly, rolling around and cradling his balls like they were wounded animals. Hopefully, he'd be able to get up and handle the rest of the game.

"And don't even think about crossing us," I warned. "Or, you'll face the consequences."

———

Zander and West immediately stopped talking the moment I returned.

"Don't let me interrupt," I muttered sarcastically.

"We'll talk later," Zander said to West before marching in the direction of the bar. The longer we stayed here, the worse his mood seemed to get.

We were supposed to be a team, but these guys didn't seem to know the definition of the word. Rule number one of working together was not to leave a person in the dark. If they wouldn't let me in on their plans, then I was going to keep my little conversation with the dealer quiet... for now.

"You took your time," West grumbled.

"What's wrong?" I asked. West had made it perfectly clear he didn't want my help, so I'd have thought he'd have been happy if I didn't return. "Were you scared they dragged me off to shoot me like they did to Vinny?"

"That's not funny."

"Are these nights always so eventful?" I snagged a miniature cheesecake from a server's tray. Holy shit, vanilla and blueberry goodness exploded over my tongue. One bite wouldn't cut it. "You can leave them with me."

The server frowned. "The whole tray?"

"You heard the lady." West took it from their shaking hands. It was easy to forget how intimidating he must be to strangers. "If my girl wants the tray, she's getting the whole fucking tray."

I crammed two more in, and a moan escaped my lips. What more could a girl want? A muscled man holding twenty mini cheesecakes? This was as close to heaven as you could get.

West grinned down at me wickedly. "How much more can you fit in?"

"Fuck you," I retorted, sending cream dripping down my chin. West wiped it off with a swipe of one finger, then popped it into his mouth to lick it clean.

"You're right." He nodded in approval. "These do taste good."

"Hey," I objected as he grabbed the last one. The entire lot had only lasted a few minutes between us. God damn him for making me share. "No fair."

He demolished the bite-size dessert in seconds. "I'm the one playing, remember?"

"You don't need the extra energy." I scowled. "If you're sitting across the table from Giles, we don't want you tearing his head off."

"Speaking of the bastard, where is he?" West looked around the sea of jerks. "It's not like him to miss an opportunity to work the room."

I snorted. "He's busy working on other things..."

West eyed me with suspicion, but I didn't elaborate. It wasn't fair to tell him about catching Giles with his pants around his ankles before I told Vixen. She may be a bitch but, if it was the other way around, I wouldn't want to be the last person to find out that my cousin had been fucking my girlfriend.

"Incoming," West muttered, right in time for me to put on my fake smile.

"West, Candy, how nice to see you together," Bryce acknowledged us with a smooth demeanor. He'd spent years putting on a polished front to hide who he really was. He reminded me of a politician who shook hands with the poor, only to make their lives even more unbearable. "Are you enjoying your evening?"

"Very much," I lied. Spending time with a load of rich assholes and listening to someone get shot was hardly my idea of a fun night out, but I'd never let it show. "They were some great, um…. canapés."

"My son's friends are always welcome here," Bryce said. From his tone, it sounded like Zander's friends were about as welcome as a pack of rabid dogs. "Where is Zander? I was hoping to catch up with him this evening."

"He had to take a call," West replied smoothly.

"Always business before pleasure. Later then." Bryce motioned for someone to join us. "Have you met my nephew, Candy?"

Giles swanned over, still busy fastening his shirt buttons. Charlene, Vixen's girlfriend, was nowhere in sight. After watching one too many movies set in England, I'd thought British men were sweet and charming. Giles had completely shattered that illusion and dashed any hopes I had of finding my Mr. Darcy across the sea.

"We've already met," I sniffed.

"He studied economics at Oxford before moving to the States," Bryce bragged.

Formal education didn't impress me. Books can teach you a lot of things, but they don't tell you what you need to know to survive. How does understanding the theory of relativity help when four men corner you on your walk home? How does memorizing the periodic table assist if you have to create a new identity and start over? The knowledge I needed to stay alive couldn't be found in the lecture theatre of a fancy college. I learned all I needed to know from the streets.

"I'm sure Candy doesn't want to hear about my history, Uncle." Giles tutted. What I wanted to know was why he'd moved over here and how he'd got his feet firmly under the Briarly table. "She's not used to being around such civilized company."

"I think we have very different definitions of civilized," I replied. I put my hand on West's arm to steady him, hoping the sugary cheesecake bites of dreams weren't like spinach to Popeye. "I know exactly what kind of company I like to keep."

"I like this one." Giles laughed. "She must be a tough one to handle, isn't that right, West?"

Every word coming out of his mouth only made me hate him more. Nothing was more terrifying to a man than a woman who knew her power and wasn't afraid to use it. Giles was about to find that out in the next half of the game.

"I like a woman who knows what she wants," West said through gritted teeth.

"If this is the type of woman you're offering, maybe I should pay your little club a visit?" Giles winked. He saw strip joints like shopping malls, where he could take his pick and buy whatever he wanted. No matter what the media says, society still isn't an equal place for women. In elite circles and old institutions, gender differences are even more pronounced. Wrinkly men still sat around tables making the big decisions, which made it easier for pond scum like Giles to bring women down. "I'm sure you have quite the selection."

I bit my tongue so hard that the taste of blood filled my mouth. Some feminists argued stripping helped to support the patriarchy, but screw that. Dancers worked damn hard pulling tricks to make their money. Customers didn't exploit us. If anything, it was the other way around. We'd bat our eyelashes to get what we wanted, which gave us a power that men like Giles could only dream about.

"Our girls dance," West growled. "They're not for fucking sale."

Bryce glanced down at the gold Rolex on his wrist. "Let's take our seats, gentleman."

I caught West's eye. "Have fun."

If this conversation was a prelude to the type of shit Giles was going to spout over the next half of the game, West had deserved the last cheesecake.

"I don't know much about poker." I giggled along with a boring aristocrat, watching the game unfolding over his shoulder. "What can you tell me about it?"

We were almost on the last hand.

"It's all very exciting," the man replied, then launched into a lengthy explanation about the rules. I nodded along animatedly as he talked. It turned out he knew fuck all about poker but loved chatting with anyone who made the mistake of listening to him.

I had hoped Zander may have been able to save me from the company of the rich and entitled, but he'd disappeared. From the amount he'd been drinking, he'd probably passed out in a shadowy corner somewhere. I didn't blame him. As a child, having a family seemed like the best thing in the world. After meeting the Briarlys, I wasn't so sure. What was worse: having no family at all, or one filled with fucking monsters?

I'd been on my own from the start. Abandoned on the steps of Evergreen in the depths of winter, wrapped in a blanket at only a few weeks old. If I hadn't been screaming at the top of my lungs to draw attention to myself, I wouldn't have lived until morning. That night set the precedent for the rest of my life.

Fighting to survive was all I'd ever known. The only two people who had promised to protect me had let me down. First, Rocky had shattered my hopes for a future by handing me over to a vicious crime lord. Next, Hiram had sworn to take care of me. It'd been his way of manipulating me into staying under his control forever. Before Blackthorne Towers, I'd thought I might have had a chance of an ordinary life: college, marriage, kids... but I'd been stupid to think that would even be possible for someone like me. Whatever the future had in store, I'd come to expect nothing.

The aristocrat broke me out of my reverie. "This is the last turn."

A hushed silence swept over the room as the tension mounted — even the gossiping crowds broke up their conversations to watch. The winner was going to take all.

"I'm going all in," West said, sliding his entire mountain of chips into the center of the table.

His hand was mediocre, but he was doing all he could. The only chance he had was by trying to bluff his way through. I raked my hands through my hair and shook out my curls. He needed to pile on the pressure to shake the others.

West's confidence caused three of the remaining players to fold and cash in what they had left. They were all financiers who spent their days calculating risk. West's smug smirk had them all fooled. Their small-minded analytical brains wouldn't expect to be outsmarted by a tattooed thug. Quitting whilst they were ahead would save face and a lecture from their wives later.

Bryce was up next.

"And we're down to the last two," he declared, folding in a surprise twist.

I'd already calculated Bryce had the best hand on the table. The fucker wasn't quitting because he was afraid to lose. Bryce got his kicks from pushing two opponents together and sitting back to watch them fight to the death — or, in this case, to win a quarter of a million dollars. That was where the real entertainment was for him.

It was now between West and Giles. I caught the dealer's eye, and he winced. The poor guy still wasn't able to stand upright.

"I'll match you." Giles pushed his pile into the middle and unclipped his diamond-studded watch. "I'll even throw this in."

"Giles loves his watch." Zander suddenly materialized by my side, watching and calculating every move. "He wouldn't risk it, unless—"

I raised one eyebrow. "Unless, what?"

It wouldn't be long until the house of cards shattered Giles's gigantic ego. He'd be coming into paper tissues instead of fucking cash at the end of the night.

Everything came down to this moment.

This was it.

Giles and West laid their cards in front of them.

The smug smile on Giles's face turned to fury as his eyes flitted from the dealer to the table.

"We won?" I covered my hand over my mouth in mock disbelief. And the best part? We hadn't had to cheat our way to the top either. "I can't believe it."

I followed Zander to join West at the barrier.

"How the fuck did you do that?" Zander murmured. If I didn't know better, I'd say he sounded impressed.

"I don't know what you mean," I replied coyly. Giles was used to getting what he wanted, but this victory was something he would never have won. "It was a *fair* game."

The dealer busied himself counting the chips and lining a black leather briefcase with stacks of cash. Charlene would be disappointed about not getting the happy ending she was waiting for.

"Now I can treat you to the vacation I promised, Candy," West said, wrapping his arm around my waist. He was going the extra mile to make our act convincing. "Just point at the map and tell me where you want to go."

Giles's cheeks turned a deeper shade of red with every passing second like he was about to throw a tantrum. *Boo-fucking-hoo.* Was diddums unhappy because he didn't get his way?

"Good game, Giles," Zander addressed his cousin. "But not good enough."

"Why don't you try the watch on, West?" I suggested. It was worth almost as much as the winnings. "It'll make you look so much more civilized."

"Nothing can make an animal seem civilized," Giles hissed. He looked like he wanted to rip the watch straight out of my hands. "You should use the money towards that business of yours. Charities are always looking for donations."

"We're leaving." Zander's vicious tone could have cut through steel bars. "Now."

"Going so soon, son?" Bryce asked.

Zander drew himself up to full height. "We have other business to attend to."

Bryce's lips pressed into a firm, disapproving line, but he didn't argue.

If we were in a movie, this would be the moment when the credits rolled. The camera would follow the three of us walking side-by-side down the manor steps in slow motion. Then it would zoom into the case, swinging in West's hand.

———

As soon as we got into the back of the limo, Zander popped another champagne cork. He didn't care that the foam sprayed all over his suit; in fact, it was the happiest I'd seen him all evening.

"Our win calls for a celebration."

"So, we're allowed to drink now?" I grinned and watched Briarly Manor fade into the horizon. I was in no rush to return.

"Tell me," Zander said, "how did you know Giles was cheating?"

"Does it really matter?" I raised my glass in a toast. I hadn't forgotten what Zander said to me in his office. He may be trying to figure me out, but he was still no closer to discovering my secrets. If I had anything to do with it, they would stay hidden. "I handled it."

West clinked his glass against mine. "Cheers to that."

My rumbling stomach caused the two of them to stare at me like I'd dropped a massive fart.

"Hello? What are you both staring at?" I demanded. "All we had to eat were those tiny canapés."

Zander pressed the button to lower the screen through to the driver and gave him hushed instructions. Within no time, we'd pulled up outside a fast-food joint where Zander ordered three of everything on the menu. When we pulled up outside my apartment, I'd eaten a lifetime's worth of mozzarella dippers and the guys looked at me like a monster who'd devoured an entire village. It's like they'd never seen a girl eat before.

West cleared his throat. "We'll see you tomorrow."

"Yeah." I wiped my mouth on the back of my hand. "I guess you will."

The night may have ended on a high, but real life was no movie. This wouldn't be the end. In fact, this might only be the beginning…

CHAPTER
Eleven

After the hive watched me leave with West and Zander, my next shift at Lapland would be as pleasant as walking naked into a wasp's nest. Girls like Bella did anything to protect what they had. They stung when they felt threatened. But I wasn't going to wear a fucking beekeeper suit; instead, I wore my gorgeous pair of new shoes. Confrontation didn't scare me and, if I had to face the swarm, I wanted to look damn good doing it.

As soon as I stepped into the club, the sight of Vixen gnawing on the face of her melted Barbie girlfriend welcomed me.

"Oh, it's you." Charlene tore her face away from Vixen's long enough to look me up and down like a piece of roadkill she'd scraped off the sidewalk. It's a wonder she could even sit down after seeing how hard Giles pounded into her last night. "Have you come over to add to your porn collection?"

The only collection she was getting added to was the list of people who'd crossed me and got what was coming to them. I'd been deliberating over whether it was worth telling Vixen what I'd seen last night, but now? There was no doubt in my mind. Hopefully, she'd learn to lock the door before banging in a bathroom next time.

"I need to speak to you, Vixen," I said. "Alone."

"This better be fucking good," she snarled, giving Charlene a parting kiss, which I'm sure would be their last. "I'll be right back."

"Don't get too close to her, babe." Charlene smiled smugly. "You don't know what you'll catch."

The tunnel between Charlene's legs was the only thing around here that Vixen would catch something from, but I held my tongue. I already had the ammunition to wipe the smirk off her rubbery face without getting my hands dirty.

I led us away from any prying ears. "I don't think you'll want this to be overheard…"

"You can't tell me anything that I don't already know," Vixen said. "Zander and West told me what happened last night."

"Not everything." I held out my cell and pressed play. Vixen's eyes widened momentarily, as she realized who was on the screen. There were no mistaking Charlene's wails and Giles slapping against her like a wet fish. Sure, I could have used this information to blackmail Charlene, but… exposing her as a cheat was the right thing to do. Plus, I'd be pleased to never have to hear her fake orgasm again. "I thought you should see it."

Vixen snatched it from me and watched it again. Then again.

"Why show me this?" she asked. Like me, Vixen had trained herself to keep her emotions under control. Hiding your feelings was a way of protecting yourself. It stopped other people from seeing your weaknesses. The only problem was when you kept them buried for years, you started to question whether you had any feelings left at all. "You didn't have to."

"No one deserves to be cheated on," I said. "Not like that."

"Who else knows? West? Zander?"

"Nobody," I confirmed. "I came to you first. I thought you'd want to handle it personally."

For the first time, a look of understanding passed between us. Maybe we weren't so different after all.

"Get back to work, Candy." Okay, I was wrong… that bitch and I were nothing alike. I guess expecting a thank you was a little too much to ask. "You were ten minutes late today, so you can make up the time by cleaning the stage at the end of the night."

I headed to the dressing room to leave Vixen to ponder her next move when Rocky called me over. He sat slumped over a table by the bar with an array of empty glasses around him. He looked like he'd fall straight off the stool if someone poked him with a straw.

"Did you enjoy yourself last night?" he asked.

As soon as I was within a six-foot radius of him, the lingering smell of pot hit me. "It looks like you're starting early."

"Congratulations," he slurred. His bloodshot eyes confirmed he was high… and drunk. "You won the game."

"You're a mess." I sniffed the air. "Have you even showered today?"

"Who needs to shower?" He took a swig straight from the bottle. "You didn't listen. I told you to get outta here when you had the chance."

When we were teenagers, Rocky had been the life and soul of any party. He was the funny joker who could make anyone laugh, but he'd never gotten out of control. The person in front of me was nothing more than a shell of a human. What had happened to him over the last five years to be in this fucking mess?

"It looks like you've had enough," I said. "Maybe you should sleep it off?"

"No!" He slammed the bottle down on the table and poured another glass. The liquid sloshed over the sides, but he didn't notice. "It's only enough when I say it's enough."

I went to take his drink away, then stopped myself. Why was I allowing myself to feel sorry for him? What Rocky had done to me was unforgivable. The only thing I should be thinking about was how I was going to kill him.

"Fine," I hissed. "See if I give a shit if you drink yourself into oblivion."

The truth was, I did care. But only because it would be too fucking easy for him to die from alcohol poisoning. He needed to suffer. Just like he'd made me suffer.

"You should have listened to me." He shook his head. "You don't... you don't know what it's like here."

West slapped him on the back. "Hitting the hard stuff already, Red?"

"Join me, bro," Rocky said. "Le'ss party..."

West sat down without looking in my direction. A small part of me was disappointed, but I had no reason to expect any more. The poker game was purely transactional. Everything had been an act, including the kiss we'd shared. Now, it was back to business as usual and treating me like a piece of furniture.

"Enjoy your night," I snapped. "Some of us actually have work to—"

Over on the dance floor, a woman's cry drowned out the deep bass and the rest of my sentence. It sounded like a demented chicken trapped in a metal box.

"No, babe," Charlene wailed. Her anguish almost sounded believable. If it wasn't for the hard evidence I'd shown Vixen, Charlene's blubbering may have resembled heartbreak convincingly enough. Instead, she was digging her own grave with every shoulder-wracking sob. "You've got it wrong!"

Mieko emerged from the dressing room in a sexy black latex dress to see what all the fuss was about. She must have used an unthinkable amount of baby powder to slip into it.

"What's going on?" Mieko joined me and followed my gaze. "Oh, shit."

"It looks like Charlene isn't going to win the most faithful girlfriend of the year award."

"But I love you!" Charlene desperately tried to cling to Vixen. "You can't leave me! You love me!"

"Get the fuck outta here," Vixen spat. The fake tears and performance had no effect on her. "And tell my cousin I said hello."

"How did you…" Charlene's mouth opened and closed like a drowning roach gasping for air. I may be a little late to start my shift, but having a front-row seat to this was something I had to see.

"I have eyes and ears everywhere." Vixen shot her a filthy glare. "Don't even think about stepping foot in here again. Or else."

Charlene grabbed her purse and nearly tripped over her feet to get to the door. What was the sense in hanging around now her cover was blown?

"Oh, and Charlene?" Vixen called after her. "Lock the fucking door next time."

"Good fucking riddance," I mumbled under my breath.

Mieko's jaw dropped. "Did she mean Zander?"

"Her *other* cousin," I said. "Trust me, the less you know about him the better."

In the last twenty-four hours, Giles had lost his undercover mole and his prized Rolex. It wouldn't take him long to work out who might be responsible and, when he did, he wouldn't take losing lightly. Briarly blood ran through his veins and the desire to win was engrained in his DNA… no matter the cost.

"Poor Vixen." Mieko fiddled with her earring. "Do you think she'll be okay?"

I didn't like cheaters as much as the next person, but this was Vixen we were talking about. While I wasn't going to stick on a party hat and do the conga, I wouldn't lose any sleep over someone who'd spent the past month trying to make my life hell.

"She seems fine to me," I said. We watched on as Vixen barked an order at a security guard. Some girls got knocked down and cried into their pillows after a breakup, but Vixen? She was the type who came back swinging. "See? She's just peachy."

"Don't you feel sorry for her?"

"Has anyone ever told you that you're too fucking nice for your own good?" It was easier to feel sympathy for a dog gnawing on a corpse than it was to pity Vixen, who tore down everyone to make herself feel better. "Vixen's a big girl. She can take care of herself."

Mieko sighed. "She deserves better."

I shook my head in disbelief. "Whoever ends up with her will deserve a fucking medal."

"She's not *that* bad…"

"Are you sure?" I asked. At that moment, Vixen spun around in our direction. The look of pure anger could have turned us into stone. "Now, seems like the perfect time for me to change."

There was no way I was risking getting my ankles snapped under her massive New Rock boots. If Mieko thought something was redeeming about her, that was her prerogative.

"Don't leave me alone with her," Mieko squeaked as Vixen charged forward.

"I thought you said she's not that bad." I laughed and slipped away. "Good luck."

———

Bella lay in wait. She'd been building up for this moment all night. I could practically smell her frothing at the mouth and ready to attack.

"Why did Zander give you those shoes?" Bella demanded.

"These old things?" I flaunted the heels from every angle. "I guess he thinks I'm a really hard worker."

"You've been fucking him, haven't you?" She rose from her seat. Up close, her make-up wasn't as flawless as usual. Her foundation was cakey and sat in her skin's creases, which drew extra attention to all her fine lines and blemishes. "Tell me!"

I inspected my nails. "Not all of us have to fuck the boss to get what we want."

"You think you're better than the rest of us, don't you?" Bella edged closer. "Because you're not. You're not special."

"You have a little something under your nose." I pointed at the hint of lingering white powder. After a week off, I had better things to do than waste time arguing with a paranoid cokehead. "You might want to look in the mirror."

She scowled and wiped it away, but she wouldn't let it hold her back. "Zander was going to take me on a date."

As if on cue, Scarlett stepped inside, flanked by two more of Bella's closest minions. An ambush? How interesting. It was like being back in high school around the popular girls who thought they were God's gift because they had the bounciest hair. No one ever taught them beauty was only skin-deep.

"West was going to take me out too," Scarlett chipped in.

"If I wanted to hear both of your dating histories," I said, "then I'd have booked the night off."

Bella's nostrils flared. "You're a fucking slut."

"If you want to hurt me." I looked her up and down. "Then I'd think again."

These girls fought with their words, but they'd be no match for my fists. I didn't want to resort to violence, but if I had to yank out a few hair extensions to make a point, then I'd do what I had to do.

"Oh, we're not here to hurt you." Bella threw back her head and cackled like a possessed banshee. She looked to the girls with trained precision and nodded. "Take them."

A second later, two of the bitches dived to the floor to knock me off balance like human fucking bowling balls. I fell on my ass like a stack of skittles, whilst Scarlett was perfectly positioned to wrench the shoes straight off my feet. It felt like we were in a Cinderella retelling gone wrong.

Bella clapped her hands. "Bring them here!"

Scarlett held the shoes as if they were a crown ahead of a coronation. Meanwhile, another accomplice disappeared and returned with a trash can. The smell of gasoline filled the room.

"Put them in," Bella ordered.

A flash of pain crossed over Scarlett's features, but she bowed her head and dropped my Louboutins in with a tinny crash. All I could do was watch on in horror as Bella gleefully lit a match and threw it in. The flames engulfed my only prized possession. They may as well have destroyed the fucking Mona Lisa. As much as I wanted to, I didn't retaliate. One wrong move and the entire club could go up in smoke.

Suddenly, someone charged the door open.

"What the hell is going on in here?" Vixen barged in and sent Scarlett tumbling to the floor. Bella should have known better than to leave the weakest link guarding the door. "Is that a fire?"

Vixen stared into the smoldering pile of leather, and then at my toes. She took a sharp intake of breath. "Are those fucking Louboutins?"

Vixen seemed more horrified at the charred remains of my shoes than when I showed her the video of Charlene fucking Giles — perhaps she was human, after all.

Bella threw her hands in the air and dropped the matches from her shaking claws. "I c-c-can explain."

"You don't have to." Vixen took one look at them and back at Bella. "You're fired."

"Wait, what?" Bella spluttered. "It was only a joke!"

"Well, I'm not joking." Vixen advanced towards her. "Find a new fucking job."

"Vixen, please!" Bella's eyes filled with tears. No amount of begging would save her now. She'd got caught red-handed with a smoking bin. Her fate was already sealed. "I need this. You know I'm the best dancer here. It won't happen again."

"It won't, because if you don't get the fuck outta here in the next thirty seconds, then those shoes won't be the only thing on fire," Vixen threatened. If she didn't already have a job, she'd make a shit tonne of cash as a dominatrix. She'd have grown men crying like babies in minutes. "Don't fucking push me."

Mascara ran down Bella's cheeks as she grabbed her coat. She took one last pleading glance at Vixen and opened her mouth to grovel more, but hastily shut it again. Who knew she could make smart decisions? With that, she rushed out sobbing with snot dripping down her face. My shoes may be a pile of burnt ash, but it had been worth it to bring Bella's reign to an end. Every war has casualties. She'd blown up her own fucking crown, and things were going to change.

"Going somewhere?" Vixen whirled around to face Bella's minions, who were slowly edging backward. After watching their monarch get dethroned, none of them wanted to be next on the guillotine. Vixen stared at them, one by one. "The rest of you should consider this a warning. Now, get the fuck out of my sight."

They all nodded furiously. I didn't know anything about Vixen's past, but her threat alone looked enough to make the girls shit their pants in fear. As they filed out, Vixen offered her hand to help me up.

I took it. "I was all down for burning her on the stake."

A trace of a smile fluttered over her lips. Then it vanished.

"This changes nothing," she spat. "We're even."

"Got it," I said, wiping myself down. Hell, I'd take what I could get at this stage. We may be a long way off from a truce, but I respected someone who paid back their favors.

———

Mieko rushed over to me. "I've been looking for you everywhere."

"I had to find a spare pair of shoes." I grimaced. The drab pair of stilettos on my feet were the only things that fit me, and a blister was already forming over my heel.

"I heard what happened." From the serious expression on her face, you'd have thought a family member had died. "I'm sorry about the shoes."

"They can be replaced," I said. Well, not on my wages… but I'd already allowed myself a two-minute silence to mourn for their loss and then strapped on my big girl panties. Like people, it was pointless getting attached to material possessions when everything could be taken away at a moment's notice. "Plus, Bella getting fired was a real consolation."

"Speaking of replacements…" Mieko shifted nervously from one foot to the other, as she tried her damnedest not to smile. "I've just spoken to Vixen, and she's offered me Bella's spot."

"No way, congratulations!" Mieko was the most flexible of all the dancers and deserved recognition. If she wanted to, she could join the circus or be part of a theatre show but, if she had to stick it out here, I wanted her to be the rightful star of the show. "You've earned it."

"I feel like I should thank you."

"You don't need to." I held up a hand to silence her, then winked. "Thank Bella. She's the one who dug her own grave."

"Not because of that," Mieko said. "Things have been different around here since you started. You don't take any shit. You've made me see that I don't have to be a doormat."

Compliments weren't something I was used to, especially from other women. Girls were always so quick to bring each other down but, with Mieko, she wore her heart on her sleeve. We couldn't be more opposite. Whilst I'd mow down anyone who stood in my way, she preferred to be invisible.

"You've never been a doormat," I said. "You're a survivor."

"You think so?" She looked up at me through watery eyes. Goddammit, I'd purposefully not wanted to make any real friendships, but I couldn't help feeling protective over her. "If you knew some of the things I'd done..."

"I know you've always done what you had to do," I interrupted, noticing her retreating into the safety of her head. We didn't need to talk about her past. Not if she didn't want to. "Why don't we focus on celebrating tonight, huh? You've gotta kick ass on stage."

Mieko beamed. "You got it."

"Do you think it's too soon to sing Ding Dong the Wicked Witch is Dead?"

Mieko collapsed in laughter, then groaned and clutched her sides. "This dress is too tight to laugh this hard."

"How the hell do you pee in that thing, anyway?"

She shook her head. "You don't want to know."

Making enemies came naturally, but making friends? It was still an unfamiliar territory, but it felt fucking good to have fun and act like a normal twenty-one-year-old for a change.

———

My voice was hoarse from cheering so loud. Mieko's performance was an incredible success — even Vixen didn't offer any criticism. Bella's prior minions had scurried around like headless chickens trying to stay out of my way, which suited me just fine. Now the monster's head had been cut off, they didn't know which way to turn.

"Are you sure you don't want me to wait?" Mieko paused at the entrance. "I can help?"

"It's fine," I insisted. Vixen needed to find a way to way to punish me for my late arrival, which had landed me extra cleaning duties. It made no sense for both of us to suffer through it. "I'll see you tomorrow night, okay?"

"If you're sure?"

"You're running up the cab fare." I pointed the brush toward the noisy engine running outside. She couldn't argue with my logic. "Go!"

I swept up the explosion of gold confetti over the stage; it looked like a fairy had jizzed all over the place. Luckily, I was no stranger to cleaning up messy scenes. I'd take cleaning up the glitter to entrails any day. The club felt strangely empty. Vixen was somewhere in the back, working on the books, and the guys had left earlier. Rocky picking fights with the customers hadn't gone down too well, so Zander and West had taken him elsewhere to cool off.

The sound system was still on, and I hit play. The song 'Gasoline' by Halsey whirred into life.

How could I resist such a tune?

Whenever I danced in front of a crowd, I was hyperaware of needing to put on a show. Everything was an act to make the audience happy; a combination of conscious movements and flattering angles to make guys reach into their wallets. When I danced for myself, it became something else entirely.

As a teenager, I'd used my beloved CD Walkman to drown out the arguments from the surrounding corridors in Evergreen. It had been a hot summer evening when I'd first discovered the power of dance. The police had raided the room directly below mine. I'd locked my door and drew the curtains to seal out the chaos. All I wanted to do was take out my frustration, and dance gave me a way to do it.

Dancing could make even prisoners feel free. During the months trapped in my apartment in Blackthorne Towers, music became my lifeline again. It helped time pass quicker and made it easier to forget where I was, and the person I'd become.

In Lapland, the bright lines shone down over me. Performing on an empty stage had an unsettling, almost ironic, beauty. Dancing for no other reason than pure pleasure. I embraced the cool metal of the pole and pirouetted around it. Instead of grinding, I climbed up, then slowly twirled back down. As a treat, Hiram had once taken me to see an Italian ballet. I didn't understand what was happening, but it was still the most beautiful thing I'd ever seen. Sure, dancing on a pole could be sexy… but it could be a graceful art form too.

The song faded to a close, and slow applause broke out from the back of the room. I snapped my head up into the shadows to see Zander step forwards and approach the stage.

"You gave quite a performance."

In seconds, I'd gone from feeling like I was flying to being stuck in a police interrogation room with nowhere to hide. I couldn't bring myself to meet his gaze and quickly returned to sweeping up the remaining pieces of confetti. "I'll be done in a sec."

"You don't have to stop on my account."

"I need to get home."

Zander had watched me strip back my layers of armor and let myself go. Knowing he had watched the video of me giving head was one thing, but seeing me in my most raw, vulnerable state was an even deeper violation. No one got to see that. Ever. Letting my guard down around him, or anyone, was something that couldn't happen. I wouldn't allow it.

"Why don't you join me for a drink?" He inclined his head towards the bar. "We could call it a tip for an exclusive show."

"I wasn't giving *you* a show."

"Have a drink with me, Candy."

"Is that one of your rules?" I challenged. "If I say no, will there be consequences?"

He paused, and my heart thundered at the sight of the sly smile spreading over his lips. Whatever made Zander grin meant trouble. "Would you like there to be consequences?"

"Fine," I snapped. Giving in would be less hassle all around, and it's not like I had any other plans. "Just one."

He pulled out a chair for me to sit down. "Espresso martini?"

"Sure." I shrugged. "Why not?"

Zander moved with purpose behind the counter. Watching him work was mesmerizing. Every flourish and pour was deliberate and calculated. He spun the shaker around in his hands better than any bartender. As he shook it, the sleeves of his shirt rode up to expose more inked skin. I forced myself to look away. Unfortunately, that didn't stop my mind from straying to what was lingering underneath.

"Why didn't you tell me you were a Briarly?" I asked.

He raised one eyebrow as he expertly poured the cocktails. "Would it have changed anything?"

"It'd have been nice to know what I was walking into," I quipped.

"Think of it as a test." He pushed the glass towards me. Holy hell, one sip was enough to tempt any angel down to the gates of hell. It tasted of fucking creamy coffee perfection. "When people hear the Briarly name, there are certain expectations."

"Do I strike you as someone who gives a shit about expectations?" I questioned. "I told you I'd help you win, and I did. Even if it meant fucking over your own family."

"I may have been born into the Briarly bloodline, but that doesn't make them my family." Zander tensed. I'd hit a nerve. "A name is nothing. It's just empty letters. The Sevens are my real family. I got to choose them myself."

"So, you wanted to start over?" I probed. He had gotten the chance to see me open up on stage. Now it was his turn to answer some of my questions. There was more to him than the face-tattooed womanizer who acted like he had everything figured out, even if he didn't like to show it. "Why here? Why Lapland?"

"You mean, why did Bryce Briarly's son choose to open a strip club and not join the family business?" Zander laughed coldly. "You've met my father. What do you think?"

"Fair point," I murmured, recalling Vinny being dragged into the hidden depths of the manor. "Has he always been like that?"

"We've talked enough about the Briarlys." Zander circled the bar and pulled up a chair next to me. "Why don't you tell me how you learned to dance?"

"I'm self-taught."

"That's not what I asked." Zander brushed a loose hair off my collarbone. The feel of his skin on mine sent a shot of adrenaline racing through me. Either that or the caffeine was kicking in. "You can't hide from me, Candy."

"You have your secrets." I drained my glass. "And I have mine."

"For now." He leaned back, resting his arms behind his head. Confidence oozed from every pore of his body. He'd be able to convince someone that signing over all their worldly possessions to him would be a good idea. "I was wrong to pair you with West last night."

"Wait, what?" I crossed my arms. Without my input, West would have never made it onto the fucking table, and Briarly Manor's library would resemble a bomb site. They needed me. "We won the game."

"You did." Zander looked at me like I was lying naked on a plate, ready for him to devour. "But I didn't like sharing you."

"I'm not a piece of fucking property you can put your claim on."

"You agreed to play by my rules," he said. "That makes you all mine, Candy. No other man can touch you without my permission."

"That was never the deal." My body shook with anger. "No man tells me what to do."

"You've never met a man like me before," Zander said. "Besides, I think you like it."

He reached out to stroke my cheek, but I grabbed his wrist before he got too close.

"I've finished my drink," I snapped. "You can clean the rest of the fucking mess up yourself."

I didn't know what scared me more: Zander thinking I was his, or how he was right... a small part of me liked it.

CHAPTER

Twelve

Zander got under my skin. Just as he had wanted to. He'd caught a glimpse of a part of me that I kept hidden from the world, and I fucking hated it. Every time I thought about him watching me dance, my collar bone seared like a fresh scar where his finger brushed against me. It could have been worse, though…

I stroked the hidden scar on my thigh, a memento from the darkest period of my life. It was shaped like the letter 'R'. When I arrived in Blackthorne Towers, Raphael tortured me to make me more pliable to Hiram's future demands. As his final sadistic act, Raphael tied me down and took great pleasure in branding me with his initial. It was his signature mark. The sick bastard.

When I killed him, he'd known exactly what was coming when I lowered my stockings. I'd never forget the look of pure disbelief in his eyes. Raphael couldn't understand how someone so broken could put themselves back together enough to bury his twisted ass. His initial was no longer the mark of a victim; it was the sign of a warrior. I'd covered it with a beautiful piece of ink, but the raised skin underneath still provided a daily reminder of what could happen if you found yourself out of control. Something I wouldn't allow to happen in Lapland.

'That makes you all mine.' Zander's words floated back to me. Even remembering them sent a shiver down my spine. 'No other man can touch you without my permission.'

Zander was a control freak who liked to have everything his way, so I needed to be careful. I had to play by his rules to stay in Lapland until I dealt with Rocky, but there was another problem. Zander's touch may have seared my skin, but it had left me wanting more, which made me even angrier. How was it fair he looked like a fucking angel? Every fiber of my being knew he was a monster, exactly the type I'd sworn to avoid. Yet, my body betrayed me whenever he was around. Why couldn't I be attracted to stable men who held down boring office jobs? Seemingly, even my hormones were programmed to self-destruct mode.

The doorman nodded at me as I stepped into the neon lights with my head held high. "Evening."

Being attracted to someone was different from acting on it, I reminded myself. Rocky was smoking hot, but it didn't stop me from wanting to kill him. West had the body of a God, but an ego bigger than his fucking biceps. Attraction meant nothing. Besides, Zander already had enough women throwing themselves at his feet. I wouldn't fall for his high cheekbones and smoldering smile. He needed to get it through his head that I'd never become one of his fucking groupies. Instead, I wanted to know more about the man behind the rose tattoo and his family of the Sevens.

Mieko hurried over to greet me. "You don't want to go into the back."

I raised my eyebrows. "Oh, really?"

Mieko should know telling me not to do something would have the opposite effect. The raised voices of Lapland's management team in a stand-off were coming from behind the door leading to the back corridor. I positioned myself at an angle to listen in and get a sense of what was going on through the frosted pane.

"What do you mean they're working together, Red?" Zander spat out each word like an angry bullet. "It was your job to make sure this didn't happen."

"Calm down!" Vixen positioned herself in the middle of the two men. Everyone knew telling someone to calm down was the equivalent of splashing accelerant on a fucking fire. If Vixen had any sense, she'd back out of the way before Zander took her down as collateral. "Look, it's not his fault."

"You know as well as I do what this means. Now, we've got to fix this fucking mess," Zander snarled. "Don't defend him."

Vixen sighed and reluctantly stepped aside. Water was already up to her knees, and the Sevens were sinking faster than the Titanic. Like Rose, she knew this was a losing battle. She had to cut Rocky loose and leave him for the sharks.

"They were taking time to think about it. I thought we had them," Rocky explained. "How was I supposed to know they'd get a better offer?"

West shook his head. "This is all because of the fucking watch, isn't it?"

"It's more than that," Vixen said. "We all know that it was only a matter of time before they reached out to one of the local gangs, after what happened with Cheeks."

"I'll try to talk to the Razors again?" Rocky offered. "See what they—"

"The deal's already done," West dismissed. "It's too late for negotiations."

"This is on you, Red," Zander growled, giving a glimpse of the devil lurking underneath the perfectly pressed suit. "The Razors were ours, and you lost them. Now, the Briarlys have control over the whole fucking town."

Zander stormed past the others. He marched into his office and slammed the door behind him, making the frame rattle. Maybe it's not a bad thing that the room was sound-proofed after all.

Mieko tapped my shoulder, making me jump out of my skin.

"Told you so." She smirked, then her expression turned to worry as she grabbed my arm and pulled me away in time for the Sevens to storm back into the club. "That was close."

"Care to fill me in on who the Razors are?" I asked.

I'd heard their gang name thrown around casually, but didn't know where they fit into Port Valentine's criminal eco-system. Wherever you went, there was a hierarchy in the streets. It started at the bottom with petty thugs and runners, then went all the way up to the whales at the top of the food chain who could swallow everyone else whole. Whoever the Razors were, they were now at the center of the latest shit storm.

"They think the name makes them sound tough, but they're only kids," Mieko said. "Most of them skip school or have already dropped out. They hang out on the project on the edge of town in Bayside Heights thinking they're gangsters. They steal cars, set fires, the usual stuff, you know?"

When people had nothing to live for, they did stupid shit. It wasn't hard to risk everything if you had nothing to lose and, sometimes, crime was the only way for kids like them to make a living. Most of the people Rocky and I had grown up with were now behind bars for making those same decisions. It had started when they were young and now; they bounced in and out of facilities like human pinball machines.

"I've heard things." Mieko looked over her shoulder to check the coast was clear. "Apparently, Zander wanted to bring the Razors in on some of his operations to help them get up on their feet."

"Zander doesn't exactly strike me as the charitable type." If Zander wanted the Razors to work for him, then he must have had a hidden agenda. As someone who had grown up with everything, he had no reason to care about what happened to a group of down-and-outs from the wrong side of the tracks. "What would happen if, say, the Briarlys had the Razors in their pocket?"

"The Razors may be kids, but there are a lot of them." Mieko's eyes widened. "They have the numbers and manpower to do serious damage. If the Briarlys have control of them, then they'll be wanting to prove themselves and there will be no going back. They'll be running heavy drugs in no time."

"The Briarlys are big in the drugs scene, huh?"

If the Razors were young and impressionable, they'd be easy to manipulate by a puppet master, especially one as experienced as Bryce Briarly. What's another wayward kid getting wrapped in drugs to him? With control of the Razors, Bryce would have an army of young men at his disposal who were eager to prove themselves and stupid enough to die trying.

"The Briarlys are big in a lot of scenes." She played with her skirt hem, then nudged her head toward Vixen approaching. "We shouldn't talk about this here."

I nodded and grabbed my tray of shots. If Bryce was drawing up battle lines against his son, then any customer could be one of his spies.

———

Filling in as a shot girl officially sucked. No one was interested in buying anything from me, without expecting something in return, and my cheeks ached from smiling. To make matters worse, a group of businessmen had come to town for a conference, so the club was even busier than normal. Thankfully, most of the suited newcomers were being entertained by a group of blonde dancers. They seemed to favor the ex-cheerleader type, which I certainly was not. Thank fuck, even listening to snatches of their conversations about stock options made me want to tear out their tongues.

As I patrolled the dance floor, doing my best to dodge any wandering hands, I recognized a face in the crowds. Sandy hair, flannel shirt, ripped jeans, baseball cap. I blinked to make sure I wasn't seeing things. Yep, it was definitely him. *Q.*

I'd thought seeing me again at the Maven would have chased him away, and it would be the last time we'd ever see each other. Relief washed over me. The fact he didn't run had to count for something, right? It showed he trusted what I'd said. If he believed I was still working with Hiram, he'd already be on the other side of the country by now.

As I pushed my way through the crowds to get to him, someone else blocked my path. West strolled over to Q and shook his hand. What the fuck? There was an easiness to their body language that came from familiarity. How did they know each other?

I wasn't the only one who looked shocked. Q's eyes landed on me. He froze on the spot. Shit, I needed to speak to him. To explain. Before he got the chance to ruin everything I'd been building by telling West what he knew.

I charged forwards, almost sloshing the entire tray over them both. "Drink?"

"Not now." West scowled down at me like an annoying fly he wanted to swat and made a shooing motion. "Go."

"Maybe I could interest your guest in a private dance?" I wasn't about to give up. West's flexing muscles didn't intimidate me. Too much was at stake. My eyes burned into Q's, hoping he'd take my bait. "What do you say?"

"A dance sounds great," Q said. His stare didn't leave mine. This was not a conversation we could have in the middle of the dance floor. "I'll catch you later, West."

"Fine." West gritted his teeth as if it was anything but fine. My interruption may have annoyed him, but I was in full-on damage control mode.

"Why don't you follow me?" I tried to keep my tone light, but my smile faltered. Hopefully, West wouldn't be able to tell anything was amiss. I needed to keep calm, at least on the outside, anyway. "This way."

I led Q into a booth and drew the curtain behind us.

"Why are you still here?" Q asked. He remained standing. I didn't blame him — just being in here made me feel like I needed to get checked out at a sex clinic. "I thought you were passing through on business?"

"I could ask you the same question," I said. "If you hadn't noticed from the tray of shots, I work here."

"I thought you were at the Maven for…" He paused. "Other business. I know you said you left Hiram, but—"

"Don't talk about him here," I snapped. Now it was his turn to look on edge. Q had never been someone who engaged in physical combat, and he knew exactly what I was capable of. I softened my voice to put him at ease. "I meant it when I said I was trying to start over, okay? I'm not working for him anymore. I've cut ties."

"How do I know you're not lying?"

"You don't," I replied. I didn't blame him for being suspicious. Hell, he'd be stupid not to be. Knowing what he knew about my time at Blackthorne Towers, it's a miracle he even agreed to come into a booth alone with me at all. "But do you really think Hiram would have let me work here?"

He mulled things over in a long silence.

"I never thought he'd set you free, Kitty." Q shook his head eventually. "How did you do it?"

"That's a story for another time." One no one else could find out about. Knowing I was the one who killed Giovanni Romano wouldn't just be a death sentence for me, but for them, too. "And I go by Candy now. My real name, remember?"

I always hated it when Hiram called me Kitty, but I wasn't the only one with a nickname. Everyone in Hiram's circle went by a code name. Including Q. In fact, I didn't even know what his real name was.

"What are the chances we both end up in the same town?" Q asked. He was a maths genius. It came with the territory of money laundering. He would already be running through the stats in his head and calculating the low probability. "Two people on the run from the same person."

"Coincidence? Fate? The pull of Port Valentine on people like us? Whatever it was, we're here now." I exhaled. I couldn't do anything to prove to him I wasn't lying, even if I wanted to. "And I'm not leaving. Not yet."

"I wonder why," he muttered sarcastically. The way he looked at me made my skin squirm like he could see right into the inner workings of my mind where revenge plans were forming. Was I being paranoid? Q had no way of knowing Rocky and I used to know each other, did he? It was hard to hide from someone who knew the darkness I was capable of. "I thought you'd left that life behind."

"I have," I insisted. Well, I'd left behind the part about following other people's orders at least. "That's why I want to talk to you about what happened the last time we met."

When I was younger, I believed everyone made their own luck. Life had proved me wrong. No one who grew up in Evergreen got out unscathed, and I'd been no exception. My upbringing set me up for failure. It didn't matter how hard I'd tried, or the dreams I used to have, I couldn't escape it. It's rare to get the chance in life for a second chance. This town offered me the chance to right Rocky's wrongs, but maybe it also offered something else… the chance to make amends with Q.

"We don't have to talk about it." He stood up straighter and cleared his throat. "Crystal knew the risks."

Crystal was my confidant during my year in captivity under Hiram's control. She did other jobs for him, mainly involving entertaining his guests on their visits. As I started doing more work of my own, Crystal helped me master my disguises. All she needed was a make-up bag and a wig to turn you into a different person. Over time, we slowly became friends. Unluckily for her, Crystal didn't know it would be the biggest mistake she'd ever make.

"It didn't have to happen," I murmured. Crystal knew what Hiram was capable of, but she also showed me that there was more to life than killing on command. "It's my fault. I want you to know that if I could go back and switch places with her, then I would."

As I'd spent more time with Crystal, Hiram felt threatened by another influence in my life. His hunger to control me overshadowed everything, and everyone, else. There was no level he wasn't afraid to sink to, and the worst thing of all? I didn't even see it coming…

"You didn't kill her, Candy." Q placed a gentle hand on my arm. "It wasn't on you."

Crystal was a one-off. She was my sunshine in a place filled with darkness. She taught me to laugh again and reminded me of a world outside of my prison… and she was the love of Q's life.

"How can you say that?" My voice trembled. I took a deep breath to regain control of my emotions. If I let them out, they'd hurtle from me like a train. "He killed her because of me."

The night she'd died, we'd been working in a casino seeking intelligence on one of Hiram's competitors. It'd become a regular fixture in my calendar after Hiram trusted me enough to leave the tower. Crystal and Q had planned to make their escape that evening. I'd never forgotten how happy she was, talking about how they were going to start a new life together. Hiram had other ideas.

"You don't know that," Q said.

"If it wasn't for the stupid tattoo, it'd never have happened."

Not long before it happened, Crystal had snuck me into a tattoo studio with Q's help. I got a tiny inked diamond on my ribs, and she got a tiny candy cane on her hip. It was our way of signifying our friendship forever. Wherever we were in the world, we would have always had each other. Somehow Hiram found out about it. Permanently changing my body without his permission was a punishable offense. Crystal paid the ultimate price for my wanting to do something for myself…

"Who helped get you into the studio?" His face contorted in pain as if he'd ripped off a bandaid. A year may have passed, but the pain was still raw. "You're not the only one who Hiram wanted to punish. What if Hiram found out that I was going to skip town?"

"He had no way of knowing," I said. Neither of them had shared their plans with anyone but me. The only thing worse than Crystal's death was believing Q had blamed me for it. "I swear I never said anything. I'd never have done that to you, either of you. It's what she wanted. I wanted you both to get away and be happy."

"We both know Hiram has other ways of finding information," Q said. "Maybe I got sloppy? He could have caught a trail of what I was planning."

"This wasn't your fault, Q," I whispered. "You didn't pull the… you didn't kill her."

We both stood in silence, remembering those last moments. Crystal and I had been walking to meet Q, where we were going to say our last goodbye. Before we reached him, an unmarked car pulled up alongside us. One minute, we were talking about her future. The next, she was lying lifeless in a pool of blood. Losing Crystal shattered us both and changed our lives in so many ways.

Q refusing to let go of her body, as the ambulance arrived, was the moment I decided I was going to leave Hiram. In the past, I'd believed he was tough on me because he cared. Killing Crystal finally broke his spell.

"Maybe not." He avoided my gaze. "But that doesn't make it any easier. I still think about what I could have done. If I got there earlier, would things have been different?"

"You can't think like that," I said. "She wouldn't have wanted you to. She'd have tried to kick your ass if she heard you talking now."

"You're right." Q laughed and wiped his eyes. "She'd have been proud of you, you know. For what you're doing."

"She's the one who made me believe it was possible, even when I didn't." I managed a half-smile. "I only wish she was around to see it."

"Me too." We shared a watery look of understanding. We may not be working for Hiram anymore, but we shared a bond. We both missed Crystal and, even though it was bittersweet, it felt good to talk about her again. "I think she'd have liked this place."

"She'd have loved the costumes…"

"I better be getting back." Q nudged his head. "West isn't someone who likes to be kept waiting."

"Wait!" I stopped him. After our conversation, I'd almost forgotten why I'd dragged him into this disease-ridden booth. "How do you know him?"

"Around here," he said, "I'm known as Cupid."

Cupid? Hang on a fucking minute! I'd heard that name before. Then it hit me.

"You run the escort agency?"

"That's where my nickname came from. It kinda goes with the whole town's vibe, doesn't it? People have expectations when they come to a place like Port Valentine." He shrugged. "Girls have always worked these streets, but I give them a safe place to come to. If I can get them out, I try. It's what she would have wanted."

Crystal was a sex worker when they first met. Running Cupid's was his way of trying to make sure no one else would end up in the place she did. Finding herself as part of Hiram's entourage.

"So, why do you need to speak to West?"

"We have a mutual agreement," he explained. "The Sevens help me with security. I help them with… other matters. Running a business has its uses."

It made sense. Q needed some kind of business for the money to run through. The Sevens had struck lucky in finding him. They wouldn't get a better launderer anywhere.

"Does that mean I'll be seeing you around more?" I asked.

"I swing by from time to time, but I keep my distance," he said. "Don't worry, kid. You have your past, and I have mine. Let's keep it that way, huh?"

"Deal."

As soon as we left the booth, West was lying in wait, prowling around like an animal in heat.

"Well..." Q shot a nervous look at West, then fished out two fifty-dollar bills and handed them over. "Thanks for the dance."

"I'm here anytime," I said. "You know where to find me."

West glared at me in fury. What the hell had got his balls caught in knots? He wasn't to know I hadn't given Q a dance. Shouldn't he be happy that I delivered fantastic customer service? Lapland was supposed to make them money after all.

Q nodded his cap. "I'll see you around, *Candy*."

"We're one dancer down because of you." West scowled. I resisted the temptation to remind him that it was Vixen who had fired Bella. I should be flattered he thought a lowly dancer like me would have such responsibilities. "You're on the late-night cleaning shift again tonight, got it?"

"Got it," I chirped back. "No problem."

West's eyes widened in surprise. Let's face it, obedience wasn't exactly one of my biggest strengths. Usually, I wasn't one to disappoint, but working an extra hour wouldn't bring my mood down.

"Good," West growled, turning on his heel with Q in tow.

Nothing would bring Crystal back. But, wherever she was looking down on us, she'd be happy that Q and I had found each other again. For the first time in a long time, I felt a little lighter. There was only one other thing I had to do to make this happy feeling complete. It'd only be a matter of time before I got my chance.

Apart from scrubbing the urinals, the biggest downside to working the late shift was trying to catch a cab home. I'd already been standing outside for twenty minutes. Where was my ride? What was the point in ordering something for a specific time when it didn't show? I began walking to see whether the car was at the end of the road. If not, I'd already resigned myself to having to walk the hour across town in heels. Blisters beat shivering out in the cold, right?

Suddenly, the sound of crunching metal and muffled shouts drew my attention. Usually, this wasn't the type of street where people stopped to see what was happening. Everyone knew keeping your head down and minding your own business were the unspoken rules of the street.

However, something compelled me to investigate. Trouble drew me in, like a vampire compelled to drink from an open wound. I knew I shouldn't, but I couldn't help myself. More than likely, it'd only be a few drunken guys in a brawl who I'd be able to take out with my eyes closed.

I peered around the side of an abandoned building into the alley. It was a thin street, narrow enough for only one car to fit through. Halfway down, a group of five men in balaclavas loomed over a groaning body. They drove their feet into the curled up figure like they were playing a game of soccer.

"Hey, assholes," I called out. "It doesn't exactly look like a fair fight."

I slipped my fingers underneath my waistband to feel the reassuring coolness of my trusty knife as I made my way toward them. I didn't need a blade to win a fight, but when it was five against one? It wouldn't hurt to have it ready to grab at a moment's notice.

"Turn around and go the other way, princess." One of the masked attackers, who was twice my size, looked me over. He seemed to be the leader of the group. "We're not playing games."

"I can see that," I said, continuing my advance. "But isn't it a bit of a coward's move to jump someone who can't defend themselves?"

They had bound their victims' hands behind his back, making it almost impossible to escape. It didn't look like kicking was the only damage they'd inflicted from the pool of blood. As I got closer, the man lying on the concrete twisted around to look up. It was hard to make out his features because his face was so swollen, but I'd recognize those dark brown eyes anywhere.

"Get out of here, C." Rocky rasped, trying to heave himself up but failing miserably. "Go!"

It'd be easy to turn away and leave them to beat him to a pulp, but... this wasn't how I wanted Rocky to go.

"Is this your girlfriend, Red?" another taunted, kicking him again. "How do you think she'll enjoy seeing your brains spill outta your head? Will she like that?"

I was close enough for my nostrils to be assaulted by the smell of overpowering body odor. Had these oafs not heard of deodorant? It was worse than standing in a guy's locker room.

"Maybe we'll play with her before finishing you off?" another leered. "How would you like to see me fuck her before you die, Red? We'll show her how cowards can fuck."

"Don't fucking touch her," Rocky threatened. He gritted his teeth to fight against the pain as he maneuvered himself to his knees. As soon as he was up, one of his attackers delivered a sharp blow to his jaw, which sent him slamming backward.

"What're you gonna do, Red?" they mocked. "Let's see how brave you are now."

Rocky wrestled to get up again. The bindings and his injuries made it too difficult. At the rate the blood was coming out of his wounds, it was surprising that he hadn't already lost consciousness.

"Kill me." Rocky spat blood at their feet. "But leave her out of this."

I crossed my arms. He couldn't be serious. Even after being beaten to a pulp, he still thought I was a damsel in distress. From where I stood, he was the only one who needed saving. His begging was about as useful as waving a burger in front of someone who hadn't eaten in days and expecting them not to eat it. Showing weakness would only encourage them more.

"Do you want to have fun with us, princess? You should have listened to your boyfriend when you had the chance." The leader talked down to me like I was a child, then nodded at one of his henchmen. "Take her while we finish him."

"I wouldn't do that if I were you," I warned as a thug stepped forward.

"What're you gonna do?" He lunged, but his reactions were slow. I easily stepped out of his reach. He may be a wall of fat and brute strength, but he wasn't quick on his feet. "You little—"

The ogre charged again, but I dodged him and stuck out my foot. The lump of lard fell face-first into the wall. *Eat a fucking brick.* Before he had the chance to retaliate, I grabbed the metal lid of a trash can and sent it crashing into the side of his head.

"What the—" The sound of his skull shattering drew the attention of one of his cronies. "You bitch."

"Bring it on," I mumbled under my breath, as he abandoned his attack on Rocky. It's a good thing I'd tied my hair up tonight. Things were about to get messy, and it was a pain to wash blood out my lengths.

"We're going to have some fun with you," he sneered. "Then, we'll cut your throat and let your boyfriend watch."

"Is that supposed to scare me?" I narrowed my eyes, channeling my inner animal and bringing her to the surface. "If you want me, you'll have to catch me."

He dove and pinned me to the wall. His sweaty hand closed around my throat.

"You weren't that hard to catch." He smirked. That's right. I'd give him a moment to enjoy his perceived victory before I snatched it out from under him. I had always enjoyed that part. The part where they thought they had the upper hand. His breath reeked of cheap beer, which made me want to heave as he pawed at my shirt. "How about we see what's under these clothes?"

Perfect. He was right where I wanted him. The man was of a short and stocky build. His height gave me the right angle to lean in, and... I went straight for his ear, tearing it off the side of his head with my teeth. His skin ripping sounded as satisfying as whipping off a wax strip after a few months of regrowth.

"Fuck," he wailed, letting me go and dropping to roll around in pain like a kid who'd been told they had to leave a playdate. "Help! Someone help!"

Looking to his leader for assistance was his second mistake. Didn't anyone ever tell him it's a rookie error to lose sight of an opponent? I spat his ear into his lap and plunged my knife into his neck. The fountain of blood spraying up my arm let me know I'd hit the major artery. Bullseye! The sound of him choking would make a sweet lullaby.

"Holy shit!" Another turned their attention to me. "What did you do?"

Becoming a killer didn't happen overnight. It was something you built up an appetite for. The first time I'd killed a man, I'd expected to feel something. Remorse, guilt, and sadness, but... those feelings never came. It was easier to live with the thought of taking someone evil out of the world than letting them live. There was no reason to fear evil when I'd become someone who could destroy it.

"What's the matter?" I wiped the blood dripping down my chin with the back of my hand. "Don't you want to play anymore?"

The leader laughed. "Do you really think we're scared of you?"

"You should be," I said. The bodies of their two friends lay motionless in my wake, like tombstones displaying the magnitude of my destruction. They were going to be next to meet the monster who lived inside me. "This is your last chance to run."

"You're a crazy bitch!" The taller of the three cast a telling glance at their getaway car. I had to take him out first because he was the only one smart enough to start to plan their escape route.

"So I've been told." I grinned, flashing them my canines. "But I'm the last crazy bitch you'll ever meet. Say hello to the creature from your fucking nightmares, boys."

The next five minutes passed in a blur. My body went into autopilot as I worked like an artist, focused on creating a masterpiece. Their lives were my canvasses to toy with. Every slash, stab, punch and kick added an extra stroke to the perfect picture. By the time I'd finished, it looked like a pack of starving lions had gone wild. Someone needed to award me a public service medal for taking those assholes off the streets. Now, I had only one thing left to do.

I kicked a body out of the way to get to Rocky, who was curled up in the fetal position. He was still alive... just.

"I've been waiting years for this." I knelt at his side and listened to his shallow breathing. My shaking hand held the bloody knife to his throat. It'd only take a few seconds to slit it open and watch the life drain from him. "You betrayed me and now you're going to pay."

"Do it then." he gasped. His voice was rough with pain, but he didn't move or resist as the blade dug into his skin. "Kill me."

This wasn't how I'd imagined it going down. I'd played the scenario through in my head so many times that it felt like a movie I'd watched on repeat. I had wanted to make him understand how much he'd hurt me and let him plead for mercy — not beg to fucking die!

"Before I do, there's just one thing I want to know," I hissed. After all these years of wondering, it was time to get the answers he owed me. "I want to know why you did it."

Rocky's gaze found mine in the dark. He was now a stranger, but he still had those same brown eyes. The eyes of the boy who'd smuggled me candy, who'd taught me how to blow smoke rings, who'd watched the stars at my side, and who'd convinced me I had a chance of a normal life… only to burn those hopes to the ground.

"If I didn't do it, they'd have killed you," he said. His body went rigid from the agony, but he didn't look away. "I knew what Hiram was, but I couldn't… couldn't… lose you."

"You're lying." My hand gripped the hilt tighter, hovering before making the last cut. He would say anything to save his skin, but I wouldn't fall for his lies again. "Tell me the truth."

"I did what I did because I loved you, C," he murmured. "I still do. I've… always loved you. It's only ever been you."

His eyes flickered shut as his voice trailed off.

"Rocky?" I shook him, but his limbs slackened under my grasp. His body didn't want to fight anymore. "Rocky!"

This wasn't how it was supposed to happen. I'd been looking forward to my moment of redemption for years, but why did it suddenly feel so wrong? If he died, I'd never know if there was any truth in what he was saying. Did he really have no choice at all?

"What the fuck happened here?" Zander's voice behind me sent the knife slipping through my fingers. "Is he alive?"

I fumbled around, trying to find Rocky's pulse. "It's slowing."

"Go back to the club." Zander threw me a set of keys. What would the scene have looked like through his eyes? "Get Vixen and go to the bunker. Now."

"Don't you want to know what—"

"There's no time. Get out of here," Zander ordered. Five dead guys surrounded me, but Zander didn't even blink as he took in every detail. He may as well have just walked into a kid's birthday party. "I'll fix this."

My head nodded along, but it didn't feel like it was attached to my body. The only thing I could focus on was Rocky's last words.

'It's only ever been you.'

Fourteen

I tore off my shoes and raced to the club. A rogue glass shard dug into my foot, but pure adrenaline stopped me from registering the pain.

"Fuck," I swore as I grappled with Zander's keys. Why the hell were there so many? How did he even fit them all in a pocket? "Stupid fucking-fuckety-fuck keys!"

I struck lucky. It only took the third try for it to click open. A light whirred on like I'd breached a prison alarm, and Vixen's shrill cry echoed through the building. "Who the fuck gave you a key?"

"I don't have time to explain." I dragged a table behind the door. The barrier wouldn't be enough to stop someone if they wanted to come in, but it'd slow them down and the noise would give us enough of a warning to act. "We need to hide now."

It might only be a matter of minutes before someone came looking for the five masked men. This would be the first place they'd check. Hopefully, Zander could clean up against the clock, because whoever they were taking orders from would not be happy when they discovered they were missing… or what I'd done to them.

"Hang on—" Vixen began. As soon as I spun to face her, she looked like she was staring into the face of a resurrected corpse. "Holy fucking shit."

If she couldn't force out a bitchy remark, then I must look like hell.

"Where's the bunker?"

Her eyebrows raised in surprise. "How do you know about that?"

"We don't have time for one of your fucking interrogations." I waved the keys under her nose. We both need to get to a place of safety. "It's Zander's orders, okay?"

Vixen eyed me suspiciously but nodded. "Follow me."

We cut through the private booth and headed down the secret staircase into Lapland's underbelly, where the Seven's secrets lurked. I recognized the room where we played poker games, but we pushed on. Vixen stormed ahead. I had to half-run to keep up with her pace. Eventually, we came to a stop outside a door that looked like a janitor's closet.

"This is it," she said, holding out her hand for the keys. She didn't even flinch at the sight of my bloody arms and the slick metal. "Let me."

Once inside, there was hardly enough space for the two of us to stand next to each other. The only other thing in the room was a shit tonne of spiders and an ancient-looking filing cabinet, which had been pushed against the wall.

"Are you sure this is the right place?" I asked, swatting a cobweb.

She scowled and pushed me out of the way. "Move."

Vixen pulled open the third drawer and ruffled around amongst a ream of paperwork. A few seconds later, a mechanical clicking noise caused the entire cabinet to slide to the right to reveal a hidden passage.

"That's some serious Batman shit," I murmured, following her through the concealed entrance.

Vixen sealed the opening behind us by pressing a button on a control panel. The Sevens seriously valued their security to put those measures in place. We then went down a further set of narrow stairs to join an underground tunnel. Emergency lighting buzzed into life overhead to illuminate the way. Like the Maven, Lapland's hidden depths went even further beneath the surface than I'd first thought. What was it with this town and underground bunkers?

"Here we are," Vixen said, as we came to another sealed door that required a code to open. Vixen punched it in too quickly for me to make it out, but it beeped in agreement and swung open. "Welcome to the bunker."

It wasn't a large room, but thought had been put into its design to make the most of the space. There were two comfy-looking sofas, an armchair, a television, a dartboard, and a well-stocked drinks fridge. Imagine a doomsday bunker for bachelors, and you'd hit the jackpot. It'd be a great place to kick back and unwind away from the chaos of the strip club above.

I sunk into a chair. Who cares about blood stains, when the Sevens had won a quarter of a million at the poker game? They could afford to get it reupholstered. Vixen sat down opposite. She stared at me with an intensity that made me squirm; I couldn't tell whether it signaled concern or the fact she didn't trust me.

"So, are you going to tell me what the fuck is going on?" she asked.

"Roc-Red got jumped."

"How bad was it?" Vixen's guarded expression didn't change, but the slight edge to her tone told me what she really wanted to know.

"He was still breathing when I left… just." I looked away. "It didn't look good. It was one against five."

She stood up and kicked the vending machine hard enough to rattle its contents. "What happened to you? Why're you covered in blood?"

"I'm not one to run away from a fight," I said. Vixen didn't need to know the full story, but Zander? He'd want to know how those five men ended up dead, and I needed to get my story straight. "Let's just say, they got what was coming to them."

"You're a psycho, you know that?" From Vixen, I'd take that as a compliment. "Who even are you?"

"Do you have any pain relief?" I needed to change the subject before we got into dangerous territory. Plus, the initial adrenaline was wearing off. A dull pain shot down my shoulder, from where a fucker had got a nasty right hook in before I buried a blade in his gut.

"Here." She passed me a pack of pills and a cold can of beer to wash them down. "Your feet are cut."

I shrugged. "It looks worse than it is."

She frowned, rummaging around in the cupboard and retrieving a first aid kit. "I'll clean them."

"Now, there's a sight I never thought I'd see."

"I'm not doing it for you. I'm doing this for Red," she snarled. "The Sevens don't owe anyone anything. They don't need your help."

I snorted. Vixen had no idea. Helping dab my wounds didn't come close to making up for the massive five-year hole in my life that Rocky owed me. How would she go about repaying that favor? Feed me fucking grapes whilst wearing a toga?

"Maybe I should have left him to die then?" I snapped. "He wasn't doing a good job of fighting his battles when his hands were tied behind his back."

"Hold still," she ordered, then yanked the shard of glass out of my heel with a pair of tweezers. "Done."

"Motherfucker!"

Vixen smirked as she rubbed the wound roughly with disinfectant. She was about as gentle as fucking Godzilla. The bitch was taking way too much pleasure in my suffering.

"I saw you two together, remember?" Vixen continued. "Don't get your hopes up. Red doesn't do girlfriends. Never has. Never will."

I took another swig of beer to drown out the stinging pain and winced. "Should I be touched you care about my feelings?"

"I don't," she retorted. "I'm telling you how it is. In the four years I've known him, girls have tried and failed. He's not interested. Red won't tie himself down."

I did the math in my head. For so long, I'd believed Rocky's and I's connection had been built on a lie. But if he hadn't had a girlfriend during our time apart, could there have been an ounce of truth in what he'd said? Part of me wanted to believe I'd been wrong, but that was a fool's way of thinking. It didn't matter whether our feelings were real. It changed nothing.

If Rocky had thought he was saving my life by handing me over to Hiram, he'd have been better off killing me himself. Hell, at the bare minimum, he could have given me some warning to help me understand, instead of luring me to my fate. How he treated me is not how you treated someone you loved.

"Don't worry, I have zero interest in being a Seven groupie."

"That makes you one of the only ones." Vixen rolled her eyes, then wrapped my foot. "All done."

"Thanks," I muttered. To her credit, she'd done a good job. It clearly wasn't her first rodeo. "So, what do we do now?"

"We wait." She pulled out a metal tin from under the sofa and opened the lid to reveal sweet green buds which filled the room with a distinct earthy smell. "Do you smoke?"

"Sometimes."

Well, not since the days I'd spent with Rocky back in Evergreen. Our favorite spot to hang out used to be on the roof of an abandoned warehouse. I pushed the memories of our time together away and coughed to clear the lump forming in my throat. Rocky's life hanging in the balance should be a celebration. Why did it feel like the opposite?

"Red always keeps an emergency stash." Vixen ground the buds into a powder and carefully rolled out a perfect joint. "Smoking it will teach him a lesson. Stupid fucker is always getting into shit."

She lit up and inhaled deeply, then passed it over. Why the fuck not? Getting stoned may not be the answer to my problems, but it'd help me relax long enough to answer any questions Zander threw my way upon his return.

I let the smoke fill my lungs and embraced the heady feeling. Neither of us said another word as we passed the joint between us. Smoke hung above our heads with the questions we didn't know the answers to. The swirling mist morphed into shapes and faces, but there was no more we could do. It was a waiting game.

———

The weed, or pure exhaustion, must have taken over because loud thumping interrupted my dozy haze. I shot bolt upright like someone had given me an electric shock. Vixen was even quicker. She was already up on her feet and swinging the vending machine away from the wall. If I hadn't pulled my legs back fast enough, she'd have decapitated my ankles.

"Another one?" My mouth fell open. "This place has more secrets than a fucking carnival house."

The new passageway led away from the club, which meant it must connect to a wider network of tunnels that sprawled underneath the town. It was a smugglers' dream.

"How is he?" Vixen asked.

Zander and West stepped into the bunker from the outside. Considering they'd spent their evening disposing of five bodies, the pair looked unscathed. If it wasn't for the flecks of blood over West's brow and the scuffs on Zander's shoes, the pair wouldn't have looked out of place at Briarly Manor.

"Alive," West said. His eyebrows raised as he looked me over. I'd almost forgotten I looked like a fucking butcher. Blood had congealed and dried hard on my clothes. "He's stable."

"Thank fuck!" Vixen's shoulders slackened. She may be frosty on the surface, but she couldn't hide how much she cared about the guys. "Who's with him now?"

"Our best men are on it," West replied. "No one will get close to him."

I'm not sure how I'd expected to feel at hearing the news. One of the main reasons I wanted to stay in town was to kill Rocky. Despite that, I let out a breath I didn't realize I'd been holding onto.

Zander sniffed the air, and his expression turned to fury. "Are you both fucking stoned?"

I suppressed the urge to collapse in a fit of giggles. The two of them had cleaned up five dead bodies for me tonight. The least I could do was try to show some courtesy.

"How else could we entertain ourselves down here?" Vixen asked. "You were the one who wanted to fucking seal us away."

"For your own protection," Zander snapped, starting to pace the room. "And for good reason. We found out who was behind the hit."

"Who?" she asked.

"The Briarly heavies came for Red." West winced. The Briarlys were even more fucked up than I'd first thought. What kind of father orders a hit on one of his son's friends? "They were some of Bryce's best."

"Red went against my orders and approached the Razors again to make them change their mind. The hit on him was my father's way of sending a message to stay out of Briarly business. They were only meant to scare him,"

Zander explained. His unfaltering stare lingered on my bloody clothes, making me shift uncomfortably in my chair. How was I to know they didn't intend on killing him? They sure sounded set on the idea. "Now, they're dead. All five of them."

"Jesus…" Vixen dropped to the sofa and ran a hand through her short hair. "When this gets back to Bryce, he won't let this go. How?"

"We've dealt with it. There's no proof," Zander said. "But secrets in this town never stay buried for long."

"This is the start of a fucking war." West pressed his lips together in a determined line and cracked his knuckles. "We have to be ready."

"And we will be," Zander said. "But, for now, West is going to take you back to the hotel."

"This is our home," she objected. "Why should we run away scared? We don't want to show weakness."

"This isn't open for discussion, Vixen," Zander shut her down.

"Zander is right, Vix," West said. She opened her mouth to argue but stopped herself. They already had enough enemies without turning on each other, too. "It's better we don't stay here for a while."

"Fine." She bowed her head, and the two of them made to leave.

I stood to follow them out. What I needed more than anything was a shower. There'd be no hot water left, but it'd beat having a heart-to-heart with Briarly Junior, who looked like he wanted to burn a hole through my head with his glare.

"Where are you going?" Zander blocked my path. Well, it'd been worth a try. "You're not going anywhere."

"I can give Candy a ride to her apartment?" West suggested. He looked even more uneasy about leaving me alone with Zander than I felt. If Zander killed me down here, no one would ever find my remains. "It's on the way."

"I said, she's not going anywhere," Zander snarled. "Candy and I need to talk. I'll see she gets home."

"Whatever you say, boss."

Their footsteps faded down the tunnel, and Zander sealed the tunnel behind them, leaving us alone.

———

Zander studied me from across the bunker.

"Will this take long?" I crossed my arms. "In case you haven't noticed, I need to wash, and I'm not in the mood for an inquisition."

"I don't care what you're in the mood for." He took a step closer. "Care to explain why I had to dump five bodies in the lake tonight?"

"The lake? Really?" I sighed in an exaggerated way. "Is that the best you could do?"

My head still felt weird, like it was floating in the clouds. If it wasn't for that, maybe I'd have held back my bitchy remarks. As much as it pained me to admit it, Zander had saved my ass. I didn't have the resources to make one person disappear with a click of my fingers — let alone five. Still, it was disappointing he couldn't have been more imaginative. It wouldn't be long before the bloated blobs floated to the surface or washed ashore.

"I improvised." Zander's nostrils flared in a don't-fucking-push-me way. "What would you have suggested?"

"Burning them? Dissolving them in acid?" I started counting them on my fingers. "Digging a mass grave in the middle of nowhere? Pigs? Take your pick."

"How did a girl like you learn how to do such terrible things?"

I gulped. "There's a lot you don't know about me."

"I'll find out, eventually." His lips curled into a smile as he took a strand of my hair and twisted it around his finger. The way he looked at me sent a lightning bolt shooting down between my legs. Even though I looked like I'd stepped out of a slasher movie, he made me feel like a piece of meat he wanted to sink his teeth into. Now, I needed a cold shower for other reasons. "But, for now, why don't we make a deal?"

"I'm listening."

"You can tell me exactly what happened tonight. Divulge every gruesome dirty detail, or..." He leaned in closer to whisper in my ear, making me shiver as if someone had twerked all over my grave. "You can do a job for me."

"Let me guess. I'll get no payment for that too?"

"What price would you put on keeping your secrets a little longer?" Damn, he could see right through me like my skin was fucking glass. He had me by the nipples, and he fucking knew it. "I've done you a favor tonight. Now it's your turn to do one for me. You want us to be friends, don't you?"

Friends? *Fucking please.* There was nothing friendly about the way he looked like he wanted to crawl under my skin and eat his way out.

"What's the job?"

"West is going on a debt collection trip tomorrow," he said. "With Red in the hospital, you can accompany him. We'll call it a trial."

"A trial, for what?"

"You'll see." A smug smirk spread over his face. "What do you say?"

"I'll do it," I agreed. If I had to go on an excursion with the big man to get Zander off my back, it'd be better than the alternative. How hard could it be? Besides, it'd been too long since I'd seen West's sulky pout. "But I don't think your golden boy is going to be happy with me tagging along."

"You seemed to enjoy yourself last time," he said. "You know how to put on a good show, remember?"

"I-I-I don't know what you mean," I stammered. "It was just business."

Thankfully, the blood spatters covered the blush spreading over my cheeks at the memory of kissing West. How could I still be lusting after a kiss from someone who regarded me as highly as a cigarette butt in the gutter? I'd never smoke a joint again if it turned me into a pathetic mess.

"Tomorrow will be strictly business, too," Zander said. "You're all mine, remember?"

"You've seen what I can do." I stared him down. "Don't you realize that no man can own me now? I don't need someone else's protection."

Zander's chilling laugh echoed around the empty room, drawing attention to the fact we were the only two people in a room under layers of dirt.

"What's so funny?"

"Oh, I know you don't need my protection, little one." He put his hand under my chin and forced me to look at him. "But I think you know as well as I do, I get what I want. When I say you're mine, that means I own you."

"Well, you can't fucking have me."

I wouldn't be afraid to take him out if I had to, but Zander was a worthier opponent than the apes outside. He had already employed his most dangerous weapon against me. His brain. I wouldn't make the mistake of underestimating him.

"Can't I?" Zander grabbed my waist and pulled me closer. How was it possible for someone to smell so good after dumping five bodies? The heat from his palms made my sides tingle. "What's stopping me from having you right now?"

"You mean, apart from me ripping your balls off?" I pushed him away, ignoring every primal urge in my body begging for inked hands to explore me. "You're an arrogant bastard. I'm not your plaything, Zander."

"No, you're not like the others," Zander said. "But I will find out what you're hiding sooner or later."

"I need to go home. Now."

Zander opened the vending machine passageway and stepped aside. "A car is waiting at the end of the tunnel."

"Aren't you a gentleman?" I murmured sarcastically under my breath.

"Don't play games you can't win, Candy." He held out a flashlight. As I went to snatch it, he caught my wrist. "You don't want to see me when I'm angry."

"Likewise," I hissed. "Or, didn't five dead guys already prove that?"

When we were together, the two of us drew darkness out of each other. Breathing in the same air was fucking intoxicating like an outside force pulling us into a black hole. The harder I fought against it, the more it felt like I was drowning, but letting go? That was even more terrifying. I marched straight into the blackness and didn't look back. I wouldn't let him win. Ever.

"Remember what I said, Candy," Zander's voice echoed after me. "I always get what I want."

The darkness may be my fucking home, but I wasn't the only one used to living in the shadows. Being alone was one thing, but it was another to know Zander was right by my side. Ready to consume me.

CHAPTER

Fifteen

For a change, the sunlight slipping through the threadbare curtains didn't wake me. Instead, the sound of someone hammering on my front door like they were trying to knock it off the hinges did.

"What the fuck?" I murmured, rolling over to check the time and see it was only eleven am.

Whoever was ruining my sleep was going to get a piece of my fucking mind. I'd only had three hours of sleep after my return from the bunker. It'd taken an hour to scrub off the blood, and my skin resembled hamburger meat after the ordeal.

The pounding on the door continued. If they knocked any harder, their entire fist would burst straight through the wood. I slipped out of bed and winced from the sharp pain in my heel. I'd have to walk on my tip-toes to avoid the worst of it. I peered through the keyhole to see West huffing like a dragon trying to breathe fire from his nose. He needed training.

I yanked it open as he rose his hand once more. "Are you trying to break down the fucking door?"

"I thought you were expecting me," West said. "When you didn't answer, I thought—"

"I overslept, okay?" I noticed my nosey neighbor's door squeak open and ushered him in before she made any rude remarks. "You can wait inside."

West's eyes strayed downwards. In my groggy state, I hadn't realized my oversized T-shirt flashed the bottom of my ass. Before my overtired brain could bark out a comment about clawing his eyeballs, a flicker of concern passed over his strong features. For someone with a poker face, I'd already worked out one of West's tells. His brows scrunched up slightly when something worried him. I recognized the minute movement from the time he'd left me alone in Zander's office after Cheeks's arrest and, again, last night.

"Are you sure you're okay, Pinkie?"

He frowned at my cut knees and the gnarly bruises decorating my thighs. You'd think I'd have learned that hot pants weren't the best thing to wear when fighting in the streets. Apart from the pain in my foot, I didn't register any other discomfort. I remember a time when my entire body had been a tapestry of different colored bruises in various stages of healing. It was something you got used to.

I wasn't ashamed of my battle scars, but West's pitying looks would drive me insane. The sooner he realized I wasn't a pretty princess who feared breaking a nail, the better. I'm the type of girl who ripped fingernails clean off to get what I wanted.

"I'm fine," I snapped, turning on my heel and not caring whether he saw my ass cheeks. "I'll be five minutes."

I got dressed quicker than the Flash; throwing on a pair of leggings and a comfy hoodie. As I returned, West jumped. I'd caught the fucker red-handed rooting around the papers on my table. Did he honestly think I'd be stupid enough to leave anything compromising lying around for anyone to find?

I cleared my throat. "Looking for something?"

"What really happened last night?"

I raised one eyebrow. "D'you think you're going to find the answer on my table?"

If he wanted to find out more about me, he'd have to dig a little deeper. The only thing he'd find in my apartment were local takeout menus, too many empty ice cream cartons, and overdue bills.

"You could have got seriously fucking hurt," he said. "Zander said he stepped in—"

"Oh, yeah." I laughed. It was typical of Zander to take all the credit and play the fucking hero. "I don't know what I'd have done without Zander to save me..."

"Why did you get involved?"

"Why do you care?" I countered, pocketing my trusty chapstick. You couldn't kick ass when your lips felt like a two-hundred-year-old women's shriveled labia after soaking in a five-hour bath. "Don't we have a job to do? You seemed pretty eager to get going when you woke up the undead with your banging."

"You're only coming along for the ride." West may have dropped it for now, but our conversation was far from over. "Leave me to handle it."

"Have it your way," I said. "I'll be around to supervise."

He shot me his famous pout and stomped off. What a diva. As we left, my neighbor's scathing remarks stalked us down the stairwell. "That's her second gentleman caller, you know. Waking up the entire block!"

"Do you cause trouble everywhere you go?" West asked.

"I don't cause it," I replied. "Trouble finds me."

We were traveling in a slick black Mercedes. How many vehicles did West own? I didn't think I'd ever seen him in the same set of wheels.

"What do you think?" West admired it like he was reviewing his mail-order bride. Men's relationships with cars would always be a mystery. "She's a beauty, huh?"

"When you're done jerking off over the paint job, let's get this over with." I slammed the door shut and killed a little piece of West's soul. It served him right for my rude awakening.

As I slid inside, the smell of fresh coffee and hot cinnamon sugary goodness hit me instantly. It reminded me of a fairground that used to come to town every year when I was a kid, not that I ever went on the rides or bought any food. Evergreen kids didn't get those kinds of privileges. But I'd never forgotten lusting after the cotton candy, popcorn, and corn dogs.

"I didn't have you down as a morning person." West shoved a paper bag of mother-freaking goodness into my hands. Now, I felt a little bad about shutting his baby's door so hard. "I thought you might be hungry."

"You got me donuts?"

"Hey, I can always take them back," he grumbled. "If you don't want them."

"I didn't say that," I said, clutching onto the devil's food. No one would take them from me if they wanted to keep their hands.

West grinned and turned on the ignition. "That's what I thought."

Goddammit, he'd found my kryptonite.

On the outside, West came across as a tough as nails brick wall of muscle who could crush you harder than a plastic bottle underneath a bus. But maybe he had a softer side. Any guy who greeted me with coffee and donuts couldn't be a total monster, right?

"Where are we heading?" I took a bite and let out a small moan. Who cares where we were going? The only thing I needed to know was where the hell he had bought these from. Every bite felt like an orgasm exploding on my tongue. "These are so freaking good."

Back in Blackthorne Towers, Hiram put great emphasis on the importance of maintaining my figure. I followed a strict diet of shakes, salads, and other boring-as-shit foods that made wood shavings look appetizing. Keeping chocolate away from me had been a big mistake. My first rebellious act, in opposing Hiram's regime, was eating a bar Q smuggled in. I hid it under my duvet and savored every mouthful. It felt like someone had given me the key to Willy Wonka's factory.

"They're the best in town," he said, swinging a right onto the highway. "We're heading out to Shade Vale."

I groaned. "I didn't realize this was going to be a road trip."

It'd be a five-hour round-trip easy. After my actions the night before, this had to be another way for Zander to punish me. He may have put me on a 'trial', but the only thing he was trialing was my fucking patience, which was diminishing the closer I got to finishing the donuts.

The stark ringing of a phone bursting through the speakers almost made me spill coffee over myself. The in-built fancy display showed who was ringing. It was no surprise who was on the other end of the line.

Zander's voice filled the car. "How is Sleeping Beauty this morning?"

The bastard knew how to wind me up.

"Screw you," I mumbled.

Zander laughed. "As charming as ever, I see."

"How's Red?" West asked. "Any news?"

"He's still out cold," Zander said. "Vix's staying at the hospital today..."

The rest of his words washed over me. Rocky had been my metaphorical voodoo doll for the past five years. Him lying comatose in a hospital bed was something I'd dreamed about when my mind escaped to the darkest places. Why did it no longer feel like a victory?

After a few minutes, the line went dead.

"Buckle up, Pinkie," West said. "You're in for a bumpy ride."

"Tell me something I don't already know."

I'd moved to Port Valentine to start over, but old faces lurked around every corner. First, there was Rocky, then Q... it wouldn't be long until my past caught up with me, but for the time being? All that spanned ahead of us was the open road and the likelihood of having to watch West beat the shit out of someone at the end. I couldn't allow myself to think about anything else.

———

"Why buy me a coffee if you didn't want to stop to pee?" I returned to the car after he'd finally agreed to pull over at a rest stop. "You're the one who loves your leather seats so much."

Our honeymoon donut period had officially ended. We'd been bickering for the past hour. It started with who should pick the radio station. I wanted to listen to rock, whilst he wanted to listen to jazz. Next, we argued over his need to hit the gas like we were in a formula one race when there was no fucking need for it. My bladder, almost bursting, was the final straw. If I got a UTI after this trip, then he'd be paying the fucking bill.

"You could have gone behind a tree…"

"I'm not an animal like you." I glowered at him. "That wasn't a fucking compliment, either. How much further is this place?"

"Not far," he said, checking his beloved sat nav. He was especially fond of the machine's smooth accent, which made me want to throw it out the window. I wouldn't be surprised if he got off to her purring dulcet tones: continue on, take a sharp right, and you'll cum in your fucking pants.

"Are you even going to tell me about what we're here to do?" I asked for what felt like the millionth time.

"I already told you," he said. "You won't be doing anything."

"You're fucking impossible," I said, cranking up the music which he'd switched back to his station in my absence.

After a long frosty silence, the car approached an old junkyard and ground to a halt outside the rusty gates.

"Is this the place?" I asked.

"Yes, but—"

I'd already unbuckled my seat belt and jumped out before West could lock me inside. He may want me to stay behind, but Zander had given both of us this job. We were in it together, whether or not his pouty ass liked it.

"I thought I told you to stay in the car," West growled, driving along slowly at my side. "I made myself clear."

"I was feeling travel sick," I replied. He'd be the first to complain if I vomited over his pristine dashboard. "You really need to get the suspension sorted."

West's fists clenched on the wheel. Any word said against his car was akin to preaching about satanism to a priest.

"If you're coming in," he hissed, pulling to a stop, "keep your mouth shut and let me do the talking."

"Me? Talk out of turn?" I held my hand to my chest. "I wouldn't dream of it."

We made our way through the yard. It was the kind of place where you walked in constant fear of getting your skull crushed by an ancient television falling from a precariously piled stack. What kind of business could the guys have here? Comparing this place to Briarly Manor was like comparing a juicy rare steak to a burger that had been half-eaten by a rabid dog.

"Don't touch anything," West warned.

"No shit." I rolled my eyes. "I'm not a total idiot, and being squashed by an eighties sofa isn't exactly the way I want to die."

He snorted and strode forwards with purpose. His tight black T-shirt left little to the imagination, and I noticed a bulge tucked into his waistband. I had to do a double-take before realizing it was a gun. Out of the piles of scrap, a grimy trailer came into view.

"This is it," West said, rapping on the tin door. I squinted through the dirty window, but a build-up of grease, dead flies, and yellowing blinds made me give up any hope of seeing anything useful. Although, the radio playing suggested someone was inside. West knocked even harder. "I know you're in there, Eddie."

A moment later, the door creaked open to reveal a sniveling man. He wore a gray oil-smeared vest, which may have been white once upon a time. He looked to be in his forties, with a bulging beer belly, bloodshot eyes, and an unshaven face. Before he even had the chance to speak, I immediately disliked him.

After working with Hiram and mixing with his associates, I'd honed my instincts. My bad vibe detector could pick creeps out of a crowd easier than a metal detector could find a can. It didn't matter what walk of life they came from; they all had one thing in common. A distinct aura that made my skin crawl.

"Long time no see." The man wiped his nose with his hand, then held it out. When he realized West had no intention of shaking it, he awkwardly shoved it back into his pocket. "What kind of business can I do you for today, West? I've got some things you might be interested in."

"I'm not here for business today." West put a foot in the doorway. "I'm here to collect."

The little color in Eddie's cheeks drained away in a blind panic. The spineless rat attempted to grab the handle, but his body couldn't move quick enough and West's leg was one mighty doorstop.

"I didn't do it," Eddie wailed. One of the first signs someone was lying was how quick they were to beg. "Come on, West. We're friends, aren't we? How long have we known each other?"

West barged inside and pressed his gun into the middle of Eddie's chest. We had no time to listen to his bullshit.

"Please!" Eddie raised his hands. "It wasn't me, I swear!"

This was a textbook case. Now he was trying to shift the blame to someone else. Yet another pointless attempt to avoid a beating. Not taking accountability usually only ensured you got hit five times harder.

"We can do this the easy way or the hard way." West pressed the barrel of the gun harder into him. "It's your choice."

"What about your girl? She doesn't want you to hurt me." Eddie looked at me through his piggy eyes for support. Unfortunately, he was looking in the wrong fucking place. He wouldn't find any sympathy there. "A nice girl like you doesn't want to see him hurt me, do you?"

"Actually," I said, "I don't mind at all."

"You fucking whore!" Eddie screeched. Well, he turned quicker than I thought.

West struck him across the face with the gun with a smack. "Don't fucking call her that."

"Sorry, I'm sorry," Eddie whimpered, clutching his cheek, which was puffing up like he was sucking a gobstopper. "I don't know what you want, okay? I'd help you if I could, you know I would."

"You know why I'm here," West said slowly. "Give me what I want."

"I don't know. Please, I swear!"

West ignored his begging and delivered another blow. One after the other. Two of Eddie's last remaining teeth flew out of his mouth and landed at my feet, but I didn't make a move. I stood back in the shadows and watched West's beast erupt. Unlike most fighters, West didn't tire. The relentless beating only seemed to amplify his energy.

"Stop, please! You win!" Eddie wheezed. He'd curled into a shaking mess, lying in his feces and smearing the brown stain over the floor as he rolled around in pain. "Fine, I'll give it back. I'll give you what you want."

I expected West to stop, but he didn't. Pounding the guy with his fists had silenced his rational brain into submission. He'd entered the zone. The zone in which the power of another life lay at your mercy.

"Enough, West." I stepped in against my better judgment. "He'll give us what we want."

As much as this creep deserved to die, it wasn't the job we'd been given. We were there to collect. After having to clean up my mess yesterday, Zander would lose his shit over another bloodbath. Eddie spluttered blood over the floor — at least he wasn't dead, yet.

"West!" I shouted as he delivered another bone-shattering punch. "You're going to kill him!"

West's eyes were devoid of all emotion. He looked at me like he'd never seen me before. The supposed gentle giant who'd bought me donuts had vanished. In his place, the monster staring right through me wasn't even a human being anymore. The only thing it craved was blood.

For fuck's sake! West had been the one who insisted he didn't want me to be involved, but what other choice did I have? I launched forward to catch West's wrist. His whole body resisted and shuddered. The sheer force of his rejection sent me crashing into a pile of junk stacked in the trailer's corner. The bang must have stirred something in the depths of West's subconscious as he froze and turned to face me.

I staggered to my feet and brushed myself off. "Get out of here, West."

West looked from me to Eddie like he'd woken from a sleep and didn't know how he'd got there.

"Go," I repeated.

He turned and stormed out, pulling the door clean off its hinges.

"Listen here, you useless sack of shit." I ducked down next to Eddie and yanked his head upright by his thinning hair. "Tell me where it is, or I'll call West back in here to end your miserable existence."

"Under the chair," he rasped. "Tube..."

"A tube?" I pressed. "Eddie?"

Damn it, the bastard had lost consciousness. I dropped my hold and stepped aside as the growing puddle seeping through his pants got dangerously close to my sneakers.

Fantastic. A tube? What the hell did that even mean? The chances of finding anything in this hoarder's paradise were slim, and it didn't help that West hadn't told me what we were looking for. My nose wrinkled at the smell coming from the empty food cartons surrounding the mangy armchair. As I knelt to peer underneath it, I expected a demon to pull me under and drag me into the depths of hell. Thankfully, a half-eaten rotten sandwich was the worst I had to deal with.

You can do it. I took a deep breath and shoved my arm underneath to disturb the piles of wrappers. West owed me a manicure after this. Amongst the trash, a small cardboard tube around six inches in size nestled between empty chip bags. This had to be it, right? After all, it'd taken Eddie a few snapped fingers and broken ribs to reveal its location.

"It's been a pleasure doing business with you, Eddie," I said, stepping over his unmoving body and out into the fresh air with the package safely in my pocket.

All I had to do was tame the beast long enough for us to get the fuck outta there. Finding West wasn't difficult when I could follow the sound of smashing metal.

"Feeling better?" I called. He kicked a massive dent in a refrigerator with the force of a steamroller in response. "I'll take that as a no?"

Sweat dripped down his face from exertion. "Don't come near me," he panted.

When I first saw West outside Lapland, I wondered why he'd chosen to shoot the guy. Now I understood. When West loses control, he can't stop himself. He would keep going until he tore everything in sight to shreds... or until someone was dead.

"West?" I ignored him and picked my way through the rubble. "Look at me."

"I can't," he grunted through gritted teeth.

He pummeled the fridge so hard that the skin over his knuckles split open — even the blood trickling down his arm didn't stop him. He kept going and going, delivering blow after blow, like a car hurtling full speed towards a cliff's edge.

"I said, look at me," I repeated.

"You shouldn't see me like this." He didn't look angry anymore; instead, his face contorted in excruciating agony. "Stay back."

"I'm right here." I took a step forward with my hands raised in the air. "Come back to me, West."

He gulped. "Don't come any closer."

"It's okay," I soothed, reaching out to him slowly. His eyes followed my every move, but his body stayed frozen in place as if he feared what he might do. "I'm not going anywhere."

The seconds stretched into eternity as I took his gigantic hands in mine. His blood slipped between my fingers like we were entering a binding pact. I knew how it felt to lose control when your body spiraled into a place of no return. You needed something to ground you and bring you back to reality to stop you from drowning in a sea of your own making.

His hand eclipsed mine and held on tightly. "Aren't you scared I'll hurt you?"

I shook my head. Him asking the question told me all I needed to know.

"You shouldn't have seen me like this," he murmured. "I'm a monster."

"I think everyone can be a monster sometimes," I said, squeezing his hand. "Let's get back to Port Valentine, okay? I can drive."

West looked at me like I'd just stepped out of an alien spaceship. From his horrified expression, you'd think I'd decapitated Eddie and offered him his head mounted on a stick. He may lose control of his temper, but he'd rather die than give someone else control of his car.

"I'm driving," he said, grabbing his keys and marching to the car. "That's final."

"Do you have to walk so fast?" I had to run to keep up. "I'm not going to hot-wire it."

"I wouldn't put it past you," he said, pausing and peeling off his T-shirt.

Fuck, how was it even possible for someone to be so defined? His body was a freaking work of art. From his sharply defined pecks to the tattoos which spread from his neck onto his torso like a delicious trail. His ink was an intricate mix of black and gray images telling a story, which I could stare at all day… but shouldn't.

Get a grip on yourself, Candy!

West tore the fabric apart with his bare hands, then used the strips to wrap his knuckles and clean up some of the blood with the rest. Nothing suppressed a murderous rage more than the threat of wrecking your car's interior. If he was back to worrying about his precious seats, the beast inside him must have slinked back into its cave to hibernate once more.

What the fuck is wrong with you, brain? Under the sun, sweat glistened in every crease of his muscles — those big, bulging muscles. *I'm telling you to look away, can't you read my signals?*

I tried the car door.

"You're not getting in like that," West growled, throwing me the bloody tatters to wipe my own hands.

It would never be perfect, but it'd do.

Back in the car, a half-naked West seemed to take up twice the amount of space. Had it really been so cramped on the drive over? Hopefully, the rolling scenery would be a distraction from the literal Adonis sitting a few inches away.

"Fuck!" West slammed his hands against the wheel. His fury still lurked in the danger zone like a town sat on the edge of a forest fire. All it would take is for the wind to change direction, for the blaze to spread and burn your house down. "The package…"

"You mean this?" I pulled out the tube quickly, extinguishing any further risk. "I mean, you didn't exactly let me in on what we were here to collect."

West's eyes widened. "How did you—"

"It doesn't matter." I handed it over. "Now, are you going to tell me what's inside it?"

"You're telling me you didn't look?"

"I didn't exactly have the time," I reminded him. Funnily enough, making sure he didn't kill anyone or hurt himself was higher on my list of priorities.

West flicked the lid open and slipped out a rolled-up painting of a woman. From the discolored edges, it looked old. The subject was strangely familiar, but I couldn't place her. She looked to be in her late twenties or early thirties, and she could have easily been a model. Pretty blonde curled hair, red lipstick, a pearl necklace, and a beaming smile… whoever had painted her had captured her spirit.

"Who is she?" I craned my neck to get a closer look. "She's beautiful."

"You've already seen enough." West rolled it up carefully and sealed it back inside, then slammed it into the glove box. "Let's get outta here."

Minutes passed by, and my unanswered question still hung in the air. Whoever the woman was, she must have meant something to someone for us to come out to the sticks to pick it up. What was so special about it to make it worth beating the shit out of someone for?

West was the first one to break the silence. "Zander can't know you've seen the painting."

"Then why did you show me?" I challenged. "I thought the Sevens weren't supposed to keep things from each other?"

West wrenched the wheel to the right, causing the car to swerve off-road.

"What the fuck is wrong with you?" I screeched as he slammed on the brake. My heart skipped a beat like someone had thrown me off the edge of a building. "Why do you always have to do that? You—"

Before I could say anything else, West's mouth was on top of mine. The warmth of his lips was both intoxicating and suffocating at the same time. We'd already kissed before at the manor. But this? This set my entire freaking body on fire.

Candy! A distant voice in the back of my head tried to jolt me to see reason. *You shouldn't be doing this! You should know better!* I mean, I should… but why couldn't I stop?

Knowing what West was capable of didn't frighten me. It only strengthened the irresistible draw I felt toward a man who could rip me apart. I knew exactly what kind of demon lurked beneath West's muscled surface, but I couldn't think straight as his tongue explored my mouth and penetrated my fucking soul.

The heat radiating off his skin ensnared all my senses, rendering me powerless under his touch. I didn't resist when his blood-smeared hands cupped my face and pulled me closer. I kissed him back hungrily like he was my favorite snack that I hadn't eaten for weeks. I slid my hand over his tatted chest and caught his lip between my teeth, then…

BEEEEEEEEEEEEEEEEEEEEEEEEEEEEP!

The sound of a passing car brought us both thudding back to reality.

"Fuck," West pulled away, breathless. "This shouldn't—"

"—have happened." I finished his sentence and adjusted my top, trying to muster what I hoped to be a business-like tone. Instead, I sounded like a sultry porno actress.

"Zander can't know about this," West said. For someone under Zander's thumb, he did a pretty good job of breaking his orders. "Not ever."

"Agreed. It was a mistake." A big stupid head-fuckingly wonderful mistake that would bring down the wrath of Zander's consequences, if he ever found out about it. "It can't happen again."

In my defense, it wasn't like I'd been the one to instigate it. How else was any sane person supposed to react in that situation? Demons attracted demons, and a girl's willpower could only stretch so far. What I didn't understand is why West kissed me. The two of us were alone, and he had nothing to prove. Or did he?

"I'll take you home." West's gaze lingered on my swollen lips and swallowed hard. "Then I need to take over at the hospital."

The sound of the engine drowned out my racing pulse. We'd completed the job and picked up the painting, but I didn't feel victorious. The men in Lapland had infiltrated my life in more ways than one. Rocky had broken me, Zander wanted to own me, and West? Well, who knew what game he was playing…

CHAPTER
Sixteen

"Have you heard about what happened to Red?" Mieko asked. "Apparently, it happened right outside the club. It makes me not want to stand outside at the end of the night. It gives me the creeps."

I hadn't seen her since the night the Briarlys put a hit on Rocky, which seemed like a lifetime ago. After my collection job with West, Zander permitted me the rest of the day off before returning for my next shift. Pfft, I deserved a vacation after saving Rocky's ass and stopping West from killing Eddie at the junkyard. Although West must have relayed a censored account of our collection trip, otherwise Zander's reaction wouldn't have been so friendly.

"Maybe he had it coming?" I pointed out. "Good people don't get jumped for no reason."

She didn't know how close Rocky had come to dying, and I wasn't about to fill her in. I had Vixen to thank for the fact my involvement in the event had been erased.

"You have a strange sense of humor." Mieko shook her head. "Talk of the devil, I heard he only got out today."

Rocky strode over to the bar with a slight limp. If he noticed everyone staring, he didn't let on. His facial swelling had gone down, but he sported an assortment of bruises and cuts. I didn't miss the micro-flinches he made with each breath. Bruised ribs and a stab wound hurt like a bitch. It was the least he deserved. The fucker should feel lucky he could breathe at all.

"Good for him," I muttered, looking away. The other dancers may want to treat him like an injured soldier, but I wasn't about to pander to him.

"Look!" Mieko nudged me. "He's coming this way."

The theme tune to the movie Jaws played in my head as Rocky headed in our direction. Flouncing off was an option, but what would it achieve? It'd only postpone the inevitable. We'd have to face each other at some point.

"Can I steal Candy from you, Mieko?" Rocky asked. "We need to talk."

"Sure thing," she squeaked and hurried away.

"What is it?" I demanded, planting my hands on my hips. If he expected me to ask how he was healing, then he'd be waiting for an eternity. "I'm busy."

People watching our every move made my skin prickle. Being the center of another Lapland scandal wouldn't do my popularity any favors. All of Bella's ex-minions may have learned it wasn't worth getting on the wrong side of me, but it didn't stop bitchy rumors following me around like toxic gas. I didn't need to invite any more bad karma into my life.

"Let's talk somewhere private," Rocky suggested, nudging his head away from the prying eyes. "Zander's office is free. Meet me in there?"

"Okay," I agreed reluctantly. "But you only have five minutes."

"That's all I need."

———

I slipped into Zander's office, where Rocky was already waiting. When I looked at him, it was like staring into the face of a ghost.

"Well?" I tapped my heel against the floor. The awkward silence stretching out made me regret not killing him when I had the chance. "You dragged me in here to talk, so talk."

"Where do I start?" He sighed. "Life didn't turn out how we expected, did it? I never thought we'd be standing here like this."

"You shouldn't even be standing here at all."

When someone defied death, they joined an elusive club of the walking dead. Rocky owed his membership to my weakness. A weakness I should never have shown.

"I've got you to thank for that," he said. "Zander told me the fake bullshit story, but I know you were there. I know what really happened."

"You had a nasty fall." I flicked my hair over my shoulder. "Your mind is playing tricks on you."

"I remember you coming into the alleyway, and then..." Rocky's voice drifted away, then returned stronger. "You killed them. All of them."

"Do you realize how crazy you sound?"

"You should have killed me, C," Rocky said. "After everything I've done to you. I'd have killed me too."

"If you're trying to say thank you," I spat. "Save your breath."

"You don't get it. I wanted you to do it. It's what I deserved!" He kicked Zander's desk with a bang, forgetting about his injuries, then stumbled towards me. He grabbed my shoulders with both of his hands and stared into my eyes with a wild intensity. "How do you think it feels to know I'm only alive because you fucking spared me?"

"The only reason I spared you was because you caught me off guard," I sneered, meeting his gaze with fury and trying to ignore how his hard grip burned through my shirt. "Even on your deathbed, you were lying."

He dropped his arms to his sides. "It wasn't a lie."

"You expect me to believe you had no choice?" I laughed coldly. "That there was nothing you could have done?"

"I was a selfish fucking kid, okay?" he said. "I know it's my fault. All of it. Don't you think I've hated myself for it every fucking day? If I hadn't got wrapped up in that gang, then taken you to the fucking clubhouse, none of this would have happened..."

Sometimes people can pinpoint a time in their life when everything changed. They don't realize it at the time but, after that moment, nothing would ever be the same again. That night was mine, and I remembered it well.

It'd been a hot summer evening. Rocky was close to graduating. We'd spent most of the night sitting at our spot on the warehouse roof, sharing a spliff and talking about how we couldn't wait to get away from this dump. On our way back to Evergreen, Rocky got a text to swing by a place they called 'the clubhouse' to pick up drugs. He'd been working for a local gang and dealing to save money for college. I didn't like it, but it was the only way for him to make enough money to get away... which is what we both wanted more than anything.

When we arrived at the clubhouse, there was a party going on. Everyone was wasted, so Rocky made me wait for him across the street whilst he picked up the goods. The first flutter of the butterfly's wings altered everything. If I had stuck with him, maybe things would have been different. He'd been trying to protect me from the assholes inside, but neither of us knew who else was prowling the streets. That's when I met Hiram for the first time.

Back in the present, Rocky paced the room.

"If I could go back and change it, I would," he continued. "I'd have stopped us from going. He'd never have seen you. He'd never have taken you away!"

"When Hiram wants something, he'll do anything to get it."

"He said he'd kill you, C." Tears pooled in Rocky's eyes as he choked out his words. "If I didn't hand you over, he said he'd slit your throat. I was a selfish fucking kid stuck in a messed-up world, and I didn't know what to do. I couldn't think of another way."

"You could have fought for me!" I shouted. "You didn't have to hand me over!"

"What would have happened if I said no?" Rocky pressed. He would have known a man like Hiram didn't make empty threats. Hiram would do whatever it took and, if someone didn't give in, he'd have no problem taking them out of the equation. "Come on, C. What chance did a seventeen-year-old dealer, like me, stand against the state's biggest crime lord?"

A bitter twang of pain twisted my gut. Deep down, I knew he was right. Rocky's resistance would have been futile, but it still didn't make it hurt any less.

"You could have warned me," I whispered; my voice cracked. "You could have explained what was going on."

"I didn't want you to know what I'd done. I couldn't face it until it was too late…" He sniffed and wiped his eyes. "After he took you, I didn't give up. I tried to find you, I—"

"Wait," I interrupted him. "You tried to find me?"

"A few weeks after they took you, I went to Blackthorne Towers and saw the prison they were keeping you in," Rocky said. Then his expression darkened. "Hiram made sure I wouldn't come sniffing around again. The bastard set me up."

I racked my brain to think of anything that happened in my early days of captivity that could have hinted at Rocky trying to find me, but nothing jumped out. Back then, I'd been kept in the dungeons without sunlight. The days passed in a blur when you were in a living nightmare you couldn't wake up from.

"When I tried to break into one of the back entrances, the guards warned me away," Rocky explained. "A few days later, the cops picked me up. I got two years in juvie on drug charges. That's where I met Vixen."

For Hiram, getting sent to prison was a relatively light punishment. Rocky's earlier compliance in handing me over must be the only reason Hiram didn't plant a bullet between his eyes.

"So, you joined the Sevens after you got out?"

Slowly, I started to piece together the timeline of what had happened since we last saw each other.

"Vix told me her cousin could give me a job, so we both came here," he said. It made sense now why the two of them were so close. "But I didn't give up on finding you. I'd go away for weekends to trail around the city, following whispers about what Hiram was up to. I heard nothing about you. I had to be careful. I knew if he caught me next time, then I wouldn't so lucky. Then Cupid showed up in town…"

I exhaled deeply. "Shit."

"I recognized him as soon as I saw him," Rocky continued. "He was there the day I went to Blackthorne Towers. I made a deal with him. He'd tell me everything he knew about you, and I wouldn't share his past with anyone else."

"Then you gave up on me again, right?"

"What would you have done, C?" he asked. "I didn't know if you'd even remember me after all of Hiram's brainwashing. Q told me how Hiram would kill anyone who got close to you, and how you followed his orders. I thought you were under his spell. If I'd found you, how would you have reacted?"

I ignored his question. Both of us already knew the answer. If Rocky had tracked me down, I wouldn't have needed to get Hiram involved. I'd have killed himself.

I changed the subject. "Why didn't you tell the Sevens about me?"

"I was fucking ashamed, okay?" Rocky hung his head. "Telling them wouldn't change anything. None of them could hate me more than I hated myself."

Seeing him like this should make me want to rub my hands in glee like a supervillain, but all I felt was emptiness. Both of us had spent time behind bars over the years. The only difference between us was that I'd been freed from my shackles. Rocky's guilt kept him locked up in his mind. No amount of bodily pain I could inflict would ever come close to the mental torture he'd put himself through. My time with Hiram had made me stronger, but Rocky? It had shattered his soul into a thousand pieces.

"I wanted things to be different in Lapland," Rocky went on. "Zander values loyalty more than anything. I vowed to never make the same mistake again. And I won't. Ever."

I shrugged. "Talk is cheap."

Rocky's explanation made his actions easier to understand, but it didn't change what had happened. Turning off the contempt in my brain wasn't as simple as flipping a switch. How could I ever trust a word that came out of his mouth? He'd deceived me once before; he could do it again.

"I know words mean shit, but I'll prove it to you," Rocky vowed. He held my gaze, reminding me of the fierce protector I thought he used to be. "I don't expect you to forgive me, but I'll spend my life trying to make it up to you. If you'll let me."

My snarky ass mouth found itself speechless. An apology couldn't erase the past. It didn't magically take away the scars or memories. It didn't scrub out the terrible things I'd done or change the person I'd become. But if nothing had changed, then why did everything suddenly feel so different?

"I need to get back to work," I mumbled, feeling around for the door handle. Hell, I needed to get as far away from him as possible. "Your five minutes are up."

———

Back on the dance floor, my head reeled from Rocky's revelation. What was I supposed to do with the information? It'd always been easy to blame him for putting me in a terrible situation. I hated Hiram for who he was, but I hated Rocky even more for who he had pretended to be. His betrayal had hurt more than anything Hiram had done.

If Rocky was telling the truth, then he was also a victim. His name could be added to the growing list of people whose lives Hiram had destroyed. But could I forgive him for the part he had to play in how my life turned into a fucking horror movie overnight? The old me believed in second chances, but was that something I was still capable of? Becoming the Kitten had changed me beyond recognition. Protecting myself had to be my number one priority.

"What did Red want to talk to you about?" Mieko asked. "I just watched him leave."

"Nothing," I lied. She didn't need to know about the tangled web of trouble I was caught up in. "Damn, is that the time? I'm up next."

I performed my pole routine with the same level of enthusiasm as a professional chef tasked with boiling an egg. No one seemed to notice. Everyone was too busy drooling over my tits to care if I was smiling — well, apart from West, who didn't even glance in my direction at all. He and Zander sat in their usual booth donning grave expressions; whatever plan they were concocting hinted another storm was rolling in.

It wasn't a shock that West couldn't bear to look at me. Why would he want to be reminded of his dirty little slip-up? I'd already rationalized what had happened on our way back from the junkyard and drawn the only viable conclusion. He'd kissed me because of the adrenaline rush that came from beating Eddie to a pulp. People did crazy shit when they were buzzed, right?

West didn't have to worry about me telling Zander, though. He wasn't the only one who was ashamed of their actions. I should have punched him in the mouth, regardless of whether an inked six-pack was on full display. With Rocky back on his feet, the last thing I needed was to create more drama with another member of the Sevens. Kissing West is a secret that needed to stay buried... alongside how fucking good it'd felt.

"Your performance looks like torture," Vixen barked, and broke my reverie. That made at least one person who hadn't been staring at my tits. "Would it fucking kill you to smile?"

"Maybe I don't want to fucking smile all the time."

"I thought I was the miserable bitch around here," she said. "You can help me clean up tonight. Someone's called in sick."

"Do I have a choice?" I asked, even though I already knew what her response would be. If an awful job needed doing, she'd put me at the top of the list without hesitation.

"Do you want to keep your job?"

"I'll help," Mieko piped up. She was so light on her feet that I hadn't even realized she'd been listening in. "I really don't mind."

"You don't have to—" Vixen began.

"It's okay, I want to," Mieko insisted.

Vixen and I looked at her like she'd declared she wanted to lick a homeless man's asshole. Who would volunteer to wipe down those disgusting urinals with a smile on their face?

"Suit yourself," Vixen said, scouting out the joint for any signs of trouble. *Bingo.* Her eyes locked on a customer who looked ready to vomit all over the expensive sound system, and she gritted her teeth. "I'll catch you both later."

She stomped away to crucify her next target. The poor guy didn't know what was coming…

"She's going to eat him alive."

"She was right about your performance, though," Mieko said. Fine, make that two people who looked above my cleavage. "Are you really sure everything is okay?"

My phone buzzed in my pocket, and I checked the screen. It was an unknown caller. Getting a new phone and number was never going to keep him away for long.

"It will be," I murmured grimly. "I'm gonna get some fresh air."

This wasn't a conversation that I wanted to be overheard.

———

I had three choices: hang up, leave town, or speak to a man who'd make Lucifer break out in a sweat. The choice was simple. I let it ring a few more times — just long enough to piss him off, then held the cell to my ear.

"Hello, Kitty."

"Hiram," I replied, keeping my tone even and level. "This is unexpected."

Texting me was one thing, but calling meant Hiram was advancing. His urge to infringe on my life and invade was an itch he needed to scratch.

"You haven't replied to my messages." Hearing the contempt in his voice put me on edge. Hiram hated being kept waiting. The old me would have never dared leave him in the lurch, but I didn't follow his orders anymore. I was in control of my own life, even if he hadn't accepted it yet. "I was beginning to think you were avoiding me."

"I've been busy."

"I know all about that." His bitter laugh made the hairs on the back of my neck stand on end. He wanted me to feel like he was watching me. Another of his classic manipulation techniques. "I hear you've made quite a statement in Port Valentine, Kitty."

"No thanks to you." Anger built inside me like hot molten lava. "Care to explain how a certain home movie got sent around my place of work?"

"Think of it as a reminder of the good times," Hiram said. "Besides, you should be thanking me."

"Thanking you?" I snorted. "For what?"

"You owe me a favor for taking care of your little police problem," he said. "You wouldn't want me to think you're ungrateful now, do you? You know I'd never let anyone hurt you, Kitty. I'm always watching."

Fuck… *Cheeks.*

Rocky's suspicions had been right. My fucking ego had come back to bite me. Going to the Maven with Cheeks may have annoyed my new bosses, but it'd come at an even bigger cost. Hiram's favors had a hefty price tag.

"I didn't need your help," I said. At the Maven, I'd kicked the hell outta Cheeks and taught him a lesson. The only thing locking him up achieved was starting a bigger war between the Sevens and the Briarlys. Knowing Hiram, that was no fucking accident. "I had it under control."

"I'd be careful what you say next," Hiram warned. "You know I don't like it when my work is unappreciated."

"What do you want, Hiram?" I demanded. "You didn't call me to gloat, did you?"

"How long are you going to carry on with this act, Kitten?" he asked. "You need me. We both know you're going to come back home where you belong."

"That's never going to happen. We had a deal, remember?" My entire body trembled with rage. "No matter how many fucking favors you do for me."

"Remember, Kitten," he hissed, slamming a fist down on a hard surface. "Favors can be undone."

The line went dead.

Cheeks getting out of prison didn't scare me. I could make a pathetic weasel like him cower by raising a pinkie finger. But it wouldn't be long until Hiram decided he was done with playing games at a distance. When he came for me, I needed to be ready. Death would be the only way to stop him and, even though I was one of the best, I didn't have the resources to match him.

I took a deep breath and headed back into the pink lights of Lapland. I'd spent years working solo, but I would have to form alliances to stand any chance at defeating Hiram. The problem was, being a bitch hadn't exactly won me a lot of friends. Right now, Rocky's promise to make amends and whatever weird connection I had with the Sevens may be my only hope. But first, I needed to find out whether they could be trusted…

"This is fucking gross." I grimaced at Mieko as I peeled a used rubber from the sticky booth floor. This was supposed to be a strip joint reserved for dancing, but some dancers didn't mind giving a little extra shimmy for cash. "Remind me why you volunteered for this again?"

"We can share a cab home this way. After what happened with Red, I don't think anyone should travel alone," Mieko said. If she knew the full story, then she'd have no qualms about leaving me to fend for myself. "Besides, I won't be able to sleep for ages. Not after the show."

"You were amazing." She truly was. The girl was crazy talented. If strip tease ever got recognized as a sport, Mieko would be a world champion. "I don't know why you're still working at this dive."

Her cheeks flushed. "I like it here."

"Where do you think you're going?" Vixen's shrill voice hit us from the other side of the building, like a foghorn.

"Out," Zander shot back. Mieko and I kept our heads down. We knew better than to stand between Vixen and the guys. "We have a job to do."

Zander, West, and Rocky were dressed head-to-toe in black. They looked like they were about to conduct a bank heist. A balaclava hung out of Rocky's back pocket, and my imagination ran wild about what West might be hiding inside his bulky backpack.

Vixen put her hands on her hips. "Why didn't you tell me about it?"

"I've been busy," Zander dismissed. "And I'm the boss around here, remember?"

"We'll be back by sunrise," West said, then winked. "Don't wait up."

"Hey, you two!" Rocky called over to us. "I'll leave money here for your cab."

"They're not charity cases," Vixen snapped. "This is their fucking job!"

"They're staying late, aren't they?" He placed down more cash than we needed. "It's the least we can do."

"Thanks, Red." Mieko smiled brightly and waved. "Have a good night."

"Anytime, Mieko." His gaze met mine. "Get home safe."

I scowled and turned my back on him to mop the floor furiously. It'd take a lot more than a few bucks to prove he truly wanted to make amends.

"Clean up when you get in." Vixen looked at all three of them. "And bring me breakfast from the place that does good pancakes."

Rocky bowed. "Will that be all, Your Highness?"

"For now," she said, cracking a rare small smile. As much as she tried to be a bitch, she thawed considerably when Rocky was around. After finding out they were in juvie together, it made me question what must have happened for them to have created such a close bond.

Zander checked his watch and nodded. "Let's move."

The men exchanged looks like were telepathically communicating in a secret language. It was strange seeing how they worked together as a unit. Whenever Hiram gave me a job, the success rested entirely on my shoulders. As did the risk. With the Sevens, they worked like a well-oiled machine. Each of them had their role and part to play.

A blustery gust of cold air ripped through the club as the trio departed. What were the Sevens planning this evening?

"Come on," Mieko whispered as soon as they'd left. "You can't lie to me and say nothing is going on between you two now."

"Who?" I played dumb. Now didn't seem the right time to bring up the secret kiss I'd shared with West or Zander's desire to lay claim on me.

"You and Red, obviously."

I sighed. "Look, it's complicated..."

"Most things are," she said.

"It's not what you think, okay?"

"Whatever you say!" She smirked, then wiggled her eyebrows. "But I can see the way he looks at you."

"We're in a strip club, not a rendition of The Notebook," I snapped. The only male attention I attracted fell into three distinct categories: those paying me to take off my clothes, those I lulled into a false sense of security before I killed them, or those with the power to destroy me. "Real life isn't like the movies."

"You can deny it all you want, but you can't fool me," she said. "I can see what's going on."

"Maybe you should focus a little more on sweeping and less on making up imaginary theories about my love life?" I grumbled. "Then we'd finish up faster."

Mieko stuck her tongue out. "Only because you know I'm right."

She couldn't be any more wrong, but it was easier to let her believe the only thing I had to worry about in my life was whether a guy liked me.

———

"What do you think?" Mieko held up a lipstick. We had almost done cleaning and working together had made the late shift bearable for a change. "Do you like this shade?"

I waited until the moment she was about to try the color on. "I wouldn't use it unless you want to catch herpes..."

She dropped it on the floor, and I snorted with laughter at the look of horror on her face. The cosmetics left in the dressing room by the bimbo army should come with a fricking warning label. I'd seen the state of the men they sucked face with.

Suddenly, a crash from the other room startled us.

Mieko looked around nervously. "Maybe the guys forgot something?"

They'd only left an hour ago. Zander would never leave for a job unprepared. Precision and organization weren't just skills to add to a resume, they helped you to survive in our world. The amateurs didn't last in this game. I may not have superhero senses, but my intuition told me when something didn't feel right.

A few seconds later, a glass smashed.

Something was wrong.

"Wait here," I instructed Mieko. "I'll go check it out."

"I'm coming with you!"

We had no time to argue about why that wasn't a good idea; instead, I shoved a bottle of hairspray into her hands and said, "Spray first, questions later, got it?"

"Got it." Mieko nodded, wielding it like a weapon. At least she could spray someone in the eyes and incapacitate them long enough to escape.

"You don't want to do this." Vixen's voice floated down the corridor as we edged closer. I put a finger to my lips and pushed the door to the club floor open gently, gesturing for Mieko to follow. "The Briarlys sent you, didn't they?"

"You took out five of their men," the squeaky-voiced intruder replied. He'd pulled his hoodie over his face and stood with his back to us. His clothes hung off him in an awkward teenage way. "Now, someone has to p-p-pay."

Mieko dropped the hairspray bottle with a bang. Well, there goes our cover...

He spun around to face us and confirmed my suspicions. He couldn't have been older than sixteen. I knew Bryce Briarly had recruited the Razors, but sending someone so inexperienced into a situation like this without supervision was a fucking disaster waiting to happen. You wouldn't let a toddler loose with a chainsaw for the same reason.

"Stand back." He pulled a gun out of his pocket with a shaking hand. "Stand back or I'll sh-sh-shoot her!"

"Get outta here," Vixen hissed at Mieko and me. The chick had more guts than most men I'd seen in the same position. "I'll handle this."

"We're not leaving," I said, standing firm. Zander would never forgive me for it. "We're staying with you."

"I'll d-do it," the boy stammered. "I'll bl-blow her brains out."

"If you were going to do it," I rebutted, taking a step forward, "you'd have done it already."

He pointed the gun at the bottles behind the bar and gently squeezed on the trigger. Then nothing.

"You've still got the safety on," I pointed out. Clearly, he'd never shot a gun in his life. "Why don't you put it down?"

"You don't want to kill anyone, do you? We can talk this through." Vixen tried to reason with him in an uncharacteristically soothing tone. "This isn't what you signed up for. We can help you and the rest of the Razors get out."

"I have n-n-no choice," he yelped. "If I do this, I'm in. If I don't, he'll k-k-kill me."

This only confirmed what we already knew: Bryce Briarly was a mother-fucking monster right down to the core. This boy soldier's life meant nothing to him.

"There's always another way." I took another step closer to him and Vixen. "You don't have to do this."

"Don't move!" He pointed the gun at my face. "I'll do it, I will! I'll shoot you all!"

"You don't even want to murder one person," I responded, not breaking a sweat. "Do you seriously think you could kill two? Or, three?"

"I have to!" His bottom lip quivered. "He said I had to do it..."

"Why do you think Bryce Briarly would send one of his newest recruits to do such an important job?" I probed. This guy was nothing more than walking target practice. "He knows you won't succeed. Even if you kill all three of us, do you think Zander Briarly would let that go?"

I watched my words sink in. If he didn't kill Vixen, Bryce would kill him. If he killed us, Zander would kill him. Either way, the poor kid was fucked. Bryce had already sealed his fate. One way or the other, Bryce planned for the boy to end up dead. His death would be nothing more than a statement to prove a point about who was really in charge in this town.

"We can help you get out of this," Vixen said. "It's the only way."

"No one can help me," he screamed. His eyes darted around the room in panic and he flapped his arms around wildly. "I have to do this!"

The situation was escalating. I caught Vixen's eye and gave her a micro-nod. People did stupid things when they panicked. We needed to shut this down. Right fucking now.

I grabbed a glass from a nearby table and threw it at the wall. His momentary surprise gave Vixen an opportunity. She shot forwards like a cannonball, rivaling a star football player, and knocked the gun from his hands. The weapon slid across the shiny floor. I dove to retrieve it… but the kid was closer.

He'd recovered from the shock of being tackled faster than expected and skidded toward the gun. Then he picked it up the wrong way and…

"No!" I didn't realize the scream was coming from the back of my throat until it was too late.

A single gunshot fired straight through his chin, ripping through his flesh like it was made of butter. He hadn't even noticed the safety switch got knocked off in the fall. Now, he lay dead in the middle of the floor with a bloody mess where his head had been a few seconds earlier.

Bullets are no joke. They don't discriminate. That's why children should never play with guns.

———

"Fuck!" Vixen clutched her stomach. She'd got caught in the spray zone and splatters of brain covered her clothes. It's a good thing she only wore black. "I think I'm going to be sick."

She turned her back on the body and retched.

Tonight should never have happened. His life had meant nothing to the powerful older man who'd played with it. What happened may have been an accident, but Bryce had sentenced him to death before he'd even had the chance to live. Hell, he could have been any of the Evergreen kids I'd grown up with. When you had no family, you became an easy target for exploitation. Isn't that where it all went wrong for me too?

I took a deep breath and thought back to my earlier conversation with Rocky. Would he have ended up lying dead in a pool of blood if he'd resisted luring me to my fate? Hiram had also put him in an impossible situation where he saw no way out.

"Mieko?" I turned back. Her thin frame shook madly like someone had doused her in ice water. "Mieko? Can you hear me?"

Silent tears fell from her eyes, leaving black mascara smudges streaming down her cheeks.

"Go sit in the back," I said. "We'll take care of it."

My automatic reflexes were kicking in. It wasn't the type of neighborhood where people called the cops whenever they heard a gunshot, but who knows what else Bryce could have in store? This could be a warm-up. There was no time to think about why the boy was sent to Lapland. Or whether I was to blame because I'd killed five of Bryce Briarly's men to save Rocky. We needed to focus on clearing up the mess left behind.

"No." Mieko sniffed, wiping her eyes and meeting my gaze with a newfound determination. "I'll help."

"Vixen, do you have any guys you can call?" I asked. "What about the club security?"

"We can't call them!" Rising panic grew in her voice. "Not with this. They can't be trusted when it comes to Briarly business."

"It looks like this we'll have to sort this ourselves then." I sighed. What was the point in having stooges if they couldn't do the jobs you needed them for? "Do you have any garbage bags? Duct tape?"

"I mean, yeah," she murmured, wiping the vomit from her mouth, "I think so... somewhere..."

"Get them," I ordered. "We need to move. Fast."

Vixen nodded and disappeared without saying a word. She needed to draw her attention away from the dead body before she went into shock.

"What are we going to do?" Mieko asked, avoiding looking anywhere above the boy's shoulders.

"Clean up," I said. "Are you sure you can do this?"

Mieko nodded grimly as Vixen returned with the materials. This wasn't the type of cleaning we'd expected to be doing, but I was no stranger to body disposal. I had Hiram's lessons to thank. Any idiot could kill another person, but not everyone could get away with it. Covering your tracks was the most important part.

I remembered the first time I'd watched someone die. It'd been a messy scene, not dissimilar to this one. Hiram wouldn't let me look away as he tortured and killed a so-called traitor. Listening to the man beg and watching his life explode before my eyes changed me as a person. The man lost his life, but I also lost a part of my soul that day. It blew apart my belief that everyone had something redeeming about them and let me see the truth. Some people were born evil, and nothing could change it.

"We need to move him before rigor mortis sets in," I said. "Vixen? Are you ready?"

"I... I..." Vixen shook her head. "I don't think I can do this."

Her chest heaved and her breathing came out in short bursts as she gasped for air.

Fuck.

I slapped her hard across the face before a full-blown panic attack took over. She'd thank me later.

"I need you to be in this," I said, placing my hands on her shoulders. "You can freak out later, okay? But, right now, we need you."

"Okay." Vixen gulped as my red handprint spread over her cheek and brought her back to her senses. Underneath the tough girl act, she had a sensitive stomach. I'd always assumed she'd played an active role in Zander's schemes, but her behavior proved me wrong. Was it possible Zander tried to protect her from the violent parts of his life? "Tell me what I need to do."

"Both of you start at the legs," I instructed, like a drill sergeant. "I'll take the head... or what's left of it."

Together, we wrapped and taped the body in black bags like an oversized present. Vixen kept gagging but, as soon as we covered his face, she regained some of her self-control. I made a mental reminder to never take her to see a gore movie.

"What now?" Mieko asked.

We were all sweating from the exertion but couldn't stop. We couldn't afford to take a break. We had to finish this. I surveyed the scene to see what we were working with. Usually, I preferred to be prepared, but we'd have to improvise...

"Get the curtain," I said. "We can roll the body onto it and slide it across the floor to the exit."

"But that's the stage curtain," Vixen objected. "It's velvet!"

"If you haven't noticed, we have a dead body in the middle of the fucking dance floor," I pointed out. "Is having to buy a new curtain really your biggest problem right now?"

"I guess it needed replacing anyway," she mumbled, as Mieko scampered away to unhook it.

Next, we needed to get the body off the premises. With the security staff unavailable and the other Sevens out on a mission of their own, we would have to do this ourselves.

"How many cars do you have?" I asked Vixen.

"I've got the keys to West's entire collection," Vixen said. Well, who'd have guessed West's love of cars would come in handy? "His garage is at the end of the block."

"We'll take two," I decided. "Pull them up at the side."

Meanwhile, I'd do a rough clean to remove the chunks of flesh and the huge blood splatters. We could do a deep clean after we'd disposed of the body, but getting rid of the most obvious signs that a crime had taken place would help if anyone came looking whilst we were gone.

The three of us were panting after we'd dragged the body over to the open door. Vixen had already opened the trunk of the car, which concealed us from view, so all we needed to do was get the wrapped package from the floor into the back. It was easier said than done. For a skinny guy, he weighed more than he looked. Talk about dead weight…

"Three, two, one," I counted down. After heaving and pulling, we managed to bundle him in. Our muscles would ache tomorrow. Who needs to lift at the gym when shifting a dead body gives you an intense workout?

Mieko wiped away the hair stuck to her head. "Why do we need two cars?"

"Because," I said, patting the hood, "we're going to light this baby on fire."

Vixen let out a low whistle. "West is not going to be happy."

"Shit happens." I'd originally planned on pushing the car into a ravine, but I changed my mind after seeing the spare can of gas in the trunk. It was West's fault for keeping his cars so well-maintained. "Now, all we need is a screwdriver and clean clothes."

"Already done." Vixen nodded at a bag thrown into the front seat.

I raised an eyebrow. "How did you pull that together?"

"Zander insists on keeping one in every car." Well, I had to give Zander credit when it was due. Damn, he really was a professional. I respected someone who planned for every eventuality. "Where are we heading?"

"We can drive around until we find somewhere?" I suggested. "Unless either of you—"

"I know a place," Mieko said quickly.

In an ideal world, I'd have preferred to scope out the location first, but we didn't have that luxury. We needed to get this done before the sun came up.

"Lead the way." I threw Mieko the keys to the escape car. Vixen couldn't be trusted behind a wheel, after her panic earlier. "We'll follow."

"Wow!" Mieko's eyes widened at the red Jaguar. "I've never driven one of these before."

"Go easy on the gas," I said. "The last thing we need is the cops pulling us over."

We didn't need to add any other bodies to our pile to burn…

"How did you learn all this?" Vixen asked, wincing as the car went over a bump in the road and the body lurched inside the trunk with a smack.

"Learn, what?"

"Strippers don't usually know how to clean up dead bodies."

"It doesn't matter." I kept my stare locked on Mieko's headlights ahead. We'd been driving for a while, and the neon lights were far behind us. "All that matters is we clean up this mess before one of us is framed for murder."

"Why didn't you leave when I told you to?" Vixen pressed. "He could have killed you both."

"We may not be best friends," I said, "but I wasn't about to stand by and let him shoot you."

If the situation was reversed, I doubt Vixen would have shown us the same level of courtesy.

"I thought I could deal with it," she murmured. "I thought he only wanted to scare me. I didn't think—"

"It was an accident," I interjected. No amount of over-analyzing the situation would bring him back. The only thing it would do was fuck with her head. "There's nothing you could have done. He was a dead man walking. It was better he choked on his own bullet than whatever Bryce would have put him through."

"But we could have pushed the Razors harder." Vixen wrung her hands over and over. Seeing a dead body was as normal to me as seeing a dog in the street. It was easy to forget not everyone was used to being surrounded by violence, and they'd need more than a quick breather to recover after a traumatic event. "They never should have made a deal with the fucking Briarlys. We were trying to help them."

"Why were you trying to help them, anyway?" I asked. "Don't take this the wrong way, but the Sevens don't exactly come across like a soup-kitchen type of gang."

"We're not complete assholes." She scowled. Well, they could have fooled me. "All of us know how easy it is to go down the wrong path."

"Too fucking easy," I agreed. I squinted down the open stretch ahead. I hadn't seen another car for the last twenty miles. Abandoned farms crumbling by the roadside were the only sign people had been here before. "Any idea where Mieko is taking us?"

"Beats me." Vixen shrugged, wrinkling her nose. "I'm not exactly a country girl."

Mieko's car suddenly made a sharp turn to the right, into a patch of overgrown woodland. Even in the daylight, the dirt road would have been impossible to spot if you didn't know it was there.

"Oh, fuck!" Vixen retched at the noise of the body thumping against the metal. Riding alongside a cadaver wasn't exactly first-class travel. "I'm going to—"

"If you're gonna hurl, do it in the footwell." What difference would it make if the car was about to turn into a burning wreck? She could vomit all she wanted over West's precious upholstery, but I didn't want to be picking it out of my hair for the rest of the night. The smell had a way of lingering even after you washed it. "Aim it away from me, okay?"

We continued until we were deep in a thicket of trees, which opened up to reveal a clearing. As we turned the next corner, Mieko pulled to a stop. Vixen managed to keep herself together long enough to stagger out of the car before I'd even pulled on the brakes.

I looked around. Up ahead, a ramshackle cabin stood nestled between the trees. It didn't look like a cute gingerbread house; instead, it resembled the scene of a horror movie. If anyone camped here, they were asking to be woken up by a crazy axe-wielding lunatic.

"What is this place?" Vixen asked.

"My dad used to bring me down here when I was a kid. No one else knows about it. He left it to me," Mieko said, her voice devoid of all emotion. This place didn't hold happy memories for her. "I've not been back for years."

"After tonight, you won't have a reason to come back again," I said gently, then returned to the task at hand. We could be sentimental later. "Now, let's get to fucking work."

I started by removing the registration plates to lessen the chances of the wreckage being linked back to us, then we worked together to splash petrol throughout the car's interior. The chemical fumes made my eyes water, but they beat the smell of decomposing flesh any day.

"We need to take our clothes off," I prompted.

We had spares to change into from Zander's bug-out bag. If there was ever a doomsday apocalypse, I knew who to come to.

"What?" Vixen stuttered. "Why?"

"Don't tell me you're shy. You've seen us half-naked a hundred times." I rolled my eyes and pulled down my shorts. "We need to get rid of the evidence. You're covered in brains."

"Fine," Vixen relinquished, adding her clothes to the pile to burn.

Mieko froze.

"Mieko?" I asked. Maybe this place was getting to her. I don't know how I'd cope if I had to return to my old cell in Blackthorne Towers. "You good?"

She flushed, pulling off her clothes and putting on the clean ones quickly. "Yep, all good."

"Great," I grumbled, looking down at myself. The shirt I'd pulled over my head hung down past my knees like a dress. I looked like a fucking house-elf. "Looks like I got West's."

A giggle escaped from Vixen's lips. I'd never heard her laugh before — not like a girlish schoolgirl, anyway. She slapped a hand over her mouth like she couldn't believe she made such a sound. We were basically holding a funeral, and she may as well have just burped the alphabet.

The guilty look on Vixen's face set Mieko off. Before we knew it, the three of us collapsed into hysterical laughter until we were cackling like witches. Emotions came out in unexpected ways. My stomach and face ached as Vixen handed me a lighter.

"Should we say a few words first?" Mieko paused. "It doesn't feel right to just... you know."

She was right. The least we could do was try to honor him in some way. The kid may have tried to kill Vixen, but he was desperate. If he'd been able to get the right help and support, none of this would have happened. Bryce was the real one to blame... and he wouldn't get away with it.

"I'll do it," Vixen volunteered.

She cleared her throat, then recited 'Eldorado' by Edgar Allan Poe perfectly. Mieko and I gawped at her like she'd been body-snatched by an alien before our eyes. Who knew there was more to her than enforcing the Seven's rules?

"What?" Vixen snapped after she'd finished. "I like poetry."

"That was beautiful." Mieko sniffed, dabbing her eyes.

Vixen hung her head. "Thanks."

"Now," I said, "let's burn it down."

The three of us stood side-by-side and watched as the flames whooshed along the trail we'd created. The fire swallowed the car in a ball of hungry flames. Even from a distance, the wall of heat made our eyes sting and throats scratch. None of us moved, though. The blaze was mesmerizing. We were all transfixed in equal awe and horror at what we were seeing. I couldn't be sure of what Vixen and Mieko were thinking, but I knew this moment would stay with us for the rest of our lives.

———

None of us spoke on the journey back, but I didn't allow my mind to wander. Our ordeal wasn't over yet. I went through a mental checklist of what we had to do to deep clean the scene, going over each step. Some people recited meditative mantras to keep calm, but not me. Who needs them when you're calculating how many gallons of bleach you'll need?

"Where do we start?" Vixen asked as we arrived back. She nervously inspected the spatters of blood over stools. Some things were beyond saving.

We'd have to burn the soft furnishings — no amount of cleaning would erase the DNA traces left behind.

We divided the work between us and worked in silence. When we'd finished, our hands were raw from scrubbing. It'd take weeks to get the smell of products out from under our nails, and we'd have to bathe in cocoa butter to make sure our fingers didn't look like they'd aged fifty years.

I surveyed the scene with satisfaction and wiped the sweat from my brow. "I think we're done for now."

You'd never guess someone had shot themselves dead in the club earlier. My body was exhausted, but my mind wouldn't be able to rest. Not yet.

"You can both crash here," Vixen said.

"I'd rather—" Before I finished speaking, a flicker of fear crossed Vixen's face. She hadn't offered out of the goodness of her heart; with the guys gone, she didn't want to be staying here alone. "I'll stay, but only if I get first dibs on the shower."

"We all have our own showers." Vixen led us up the stairs to the apartment above the club, which she and the guys shared. "Make yourself at home."

Mieko's eyeballs almost popped out of their sockets. "Woah…"

Their pad was more like a freaking penthouse. A huge flat screen, a pool table, and a gigantic corner sofa took up the full length of the room. The three of us could all lie together on it in a starfish pose and still not be touching. It was all open plan with an adjoining state-of-the-art kitchen, which looked like it'd never been used.

"We used to all have our own places, but we ended up staying here most nights." Vixen explained. "Zander figured we may as well renovate."

"No fucking kidding," I murmured under my breath.

"You guys can sleep here." Vixen gestured at the sofa. It looked more welcoming than the bed I had at home. "I'll get blankets. Follow me."

She led us through the living space to continue the tour like we were in an episode of MTV Cribs. Someone with great taste had carefully chosen everything from the carpets to the curtains. It was luxurious, but not in a way that you were too afraid to kick off your sneakers and relax.

"All of our bedrooms are en suite," Vixen continued. "There's a master bathroom at the end for guests."

"You could fit, like, four people in that shower." Mieko peeked around the door like a child eying up a pile of presents on Christmas morning. "I've never even seen one like it before."

"Go ahead, Mieko," I said. She deserved it after tonight. As for me, anything with hot water would be better than the torturous cold hose-down I'd become accustomed to. "Before I change my mind."

"You can use West's bathroom, Candy." Vixen pushed open his bedroom door. "He's a clean freak."

Holy shit. Vixen wasn't exaggerating. West's bedroom and bathroom were absolutely spotless. No photographs or any personal effects were lying around. It looked more like a hotel room than somewhere someone lived permanently. I mean, what kind of psychopath lined up their shampoo bottles in size order?

———

"What the hell?" I returned to the living area smelling of West's expensive sandalwood shampoo to find Vixen had transformed the room into a blanket fort. How had she put this together so fast? "Who even owns this many comforters?"

"It's like a proper slumber party," Mieko said gleefully, balanced on a mountain of pillows braiding her hair.

"What's next?" I raised an eyebrow. Seeing one of the Razors shoot themselves in the head was one thing, but this totally threw me off balance. "A pillow fight?"

That's what they did at slumber parties, right? When I was a kid, no one ever invited me to stay over at their house. The only invitations I got were from the older guys in Evergreen wanting me to give them blowjobs for a couple of dollars. *Fucking assholes.*

"Ignore her, Vixen," Mieko said. "I think it's great."

Vixen pulled out a bottle of vodka and took a swig. She must have one permanently shoved up her vagina because she seemed able to whip one out at a moment's notice. "Drink?"

"Why the fuck not?" I took it from her. It burned the back of my throat, but I liked the warmth spreading through my body afterward. "It's not like we'll be able to sleep."

Mieko cringed at the strength of the vodka but took a shot. "Doesn't this feel like a dream?"

Vixen collapsed on the sofa. "More like a nightmare…"

"Do you think he had any family?" Mieko asked. We all knew who she was talking about.

"Bryce chose him because no one would miss him." I shook my head and swallowed another mouthful. "The bastard."

"If his family is anything like mine, then he was probably better off not knowing them at all," Vixen pointed out. "Family causes nothing but trouble."

"Let's cheers to that." I held up the bottle. "To family! Who fucking needs them?"

Eighteen

"What's going on?"

The sound of men's voices brought me out of my alcohol-induced slumber. I looked up to find West peering down at me like a specimen in a science experiment. We may have overtaken their man cave for the night, but none of them were more surprised than me to be waking up in the Seven's apartment. It felt like we were in a fucked-up reality TV show — except we had more to worry about than which random guy we'd hooked up with the night before.

"Can you keep it down?" Vixen groaned from a pile of cushions. Beside her, an empty bottle of spirit confirmed my worst suspicions and explained the pounding in my head. "Some of us are trying to sleep here."

"Not anymore," Zander replied, snapping the overhead light on. "Does anyone care to explain to me why my club smells like a morgue?"

"Where's my fucking coffee?" Vixen croaked.

"How did you know we'd be here?" I asked, eyeing up the breakfast in Rocky's hands.

"Hey!" West objected as Rocky handed me a coffee, which had his name on it.

"Delicious." I took a sip. Perfect, that'd help shift the soul-destroying hangover. Things always seemed to taste better when they were someone else's. "Just how I like it."

"Would you like a coffee, Mieko?" Rocky offered.

She poked her head out of the blanket fortress. "Do you have any juice?"

Who could say no to someone as sweet as Mieko? For once, even Zander was too stunned to make a comeback.

"What would you prefer?" Rocky opened the fridge like a personal butler. "Orange, or mango?"

"Orange," she said, smiling shyly.

"How was your road trip?" I asked. They were all still wearing the same clothes. I did a quick assessment: no blood, no cuts, no bruises, no black eyes, and no missing teeth. It looked like they'd gone for a fucking stroll. When, in the meantime, we had to get rid of a dead body.

"It's none of your business." Zander crossed his arms. "I'm the one that should be asking the questions."

I rose from my mass of covers like a zombie rising from the dead.

"Hang on!" West's mouth fell open. First, I'd taken his coffee. Now, his shirt. The big guy was learning a valuable lesson in sharing today. "Is that my shirt?"

"A fucking shirt should be the least of your worries," I snapped. "What the Sevens do may be none of my business, but it became my business when one of the Razors broke into the club with a gun last night. Where were all of you then, huh?"

"Do you all have to be so loud?" Vixen brought down a pillow over her face. I'm pretty sure her alcohol level was still way over the legal driving limit judging by the slight slur to her words. "At least wait until I've had a fucking coffee..."

"They did, what?" Rocky gasped. He didn't register the juice he was pouring had spilled over the sides of the glass and onto the countertop. Poor Mieko may not get her juice after all. "You're kidding, right?"

"We'll tell you everything," I said, "after we've eaten breakfast."

No one should head into battle on an empty stomach. Besides, the pancakes smelled fucking divine...

———

"Tell me again." Zander leaned back in his chair and pinched the bridge of his nose after hearing Vixen's garbled version of events for the third time.

"What more do you need to know?" I asked. We didn't need to relive all the gory details over and over. "The boy showed up, held Vixen hostage, shot himself, and we cleaned up. End of story."

"Why didn't you call?" Zander turned to Vixen in accusation. "We could have dealt with it."

"Because you told me not to disturb you, remember?" she said. Well, that and the fact she was too busy freaking out to think straight. "It doesn't matter, anyway. We sorted it."

"Not all women need a man to come to their rescue, you know," I said. We were up against a ticking clock. Waiting for the Sevens to swoop in to save the day had been out of the equation. "We can't depend on a knight in shining armor to appear whenever a body needs disposing of."

"There's still one thing I don't understand." West paused. "How did you get out there? To this place in the woods?"

Goddammit. We'd almost gotten away with smoothing over the general details. Mieko looked down at her clasped hands, and I took a keen interest in the sofa stitching. We were keeping our mouths shut. Neither of us wanted to be caught in the middle of a family feud. Vixen would have to own up to it alone. He may forgive her... just.

"We may have borrowed your car," Vixen said. There was more tension in the room than when Vixen had a fucking gun pressed to her head.

West's jaw clenched. "Which one?"

"The Range Rover..." she said, her voice trailing off.

"Where is it now?"

Vixen didn't respond. Where was her usual no-bullshit attitude when you needed it? Someone needed to put him out of his misery.

"We burnt it," I said matter-of-factly, shoveling a large forkful of pancakes into my mouth before he could ask any more questions.

West's hands balled into fists. I recognized that look. The Hulk wanted to say hello. He jumped to his feet, flipping the table and sending our plates smashing to the floor. Wouldn't throwing a chair have been enough? Those heavenly chocolate chip pancakes didn't deserve to be wasted.

"Come on, West. It had the biggest trunk," Vixen called after him. Somehow, it didn't seem to help the situation. "Wait!"

West was already halfway across the room. He slammed the door behind him with so much force that the entire block will have heard it. Hopefully, he'd cool off before discovering I'd messed up the order of his shampoo collection...

"I suppose you were the mastermind behind all this?" Zander's icy glare landed on me. He could make a compliment sound like the biggest insult. "What about the car plates?"

"Do you think I'm a total moron?" I rolled my eyes. He wasn't the only one with experience in this area. "We removed them."

"I'll get a sanitation team over to clean the club and send someone to remove what's left of the car." Zander's fingers were already flying over the keys on his cell to make the request. "If Mieko has connections to the disposal site, we want nothing coming back to us."

"I haven't been there in years," Mieko mumbled. Her eyes glazed over. Whatever happened to her in the cabin had left lasting damage. The only regret I had about last night was Mieko having to visit that place again. I knew all too well the fear of returning to the places in my nightmares. "My dad used to take me hunting when I was a kid. No one knew we were out there."

"We can't be too careful," Zander said. For once, I agreed with him. We couldn't take any chances with Mieko, regardless of how loose she thought her associations with the location were.

"Were any of you hurt?" Rocky asked. "I can give you a ride to the emergency room?"

For three guys who spent twenty-four hours a day together, their reactions couldn't have been any more different. West couldn't control his anger long enough to stick around, Zander focused on damage control, and all Rocky cared about was whether we needed a bandaid.

"We're fine," Vixen said. "Quit fussing."

"Maybe you should go and check whether West is okay?" I suggested. "He's the one who needs his blood pressure checking."

Zander's brows lowered, letting me know I was treading a very thin line. So fucking what? When you'd spent your whole life walking across a tightrope, you had no fear of falling.

"A car is waiting outside for you both." Zander looked to me and Mieko. Fucking typical. We'd helped save his cousin's life, but were being thrown out without as much as a thank you. Would he have preferred to return to find Vixen's brains splattered all over the walls of his precious club? Gratitude didn't cost a cent. "We have family business to take care of."

"I'll see you out," Rocky said.

"No," Zander ordered, stopping him in his tracks. "They don't need a man to come to their rescue, remember?"

"Touché," I spat.

"We'll see you at work tonight." A snide smile spread over Zander's face. "I would hate for the other dancers to think you were getting special treatment."

I grabbed Mieko's arm and marched out before we had to clean up another crime scene.

"Thanks for breakfast," she called back.

"Don't thank them!" Mieko was too polite for her own good. "Zander Briarly can go fuck himself."

———

"You don't mind me being here, do you?" Mieko asked nervously. We'd both returned to my apartment after being ousted from the Lapland penthouse like unwanted cockroaches. "I just didn't want to be alone... not yet."

"It's fine." I handed her a spoon. Unsurprisingly, the only thing I had in my freezer was ice cream. There were very few things caramel creaminess didn't make a little more bearable. "Dairy and sugar make everything better, right?"

"We might need more ice cream." She sighed. "I don't know what would have happened if you weren't there. I froze. But you... you knew exactly what to do. If you didn't step in, Vixen could have died."

"But she didn't," I reminded her. When you faced a life or death situation, your natural human instincts came out. Every moment was a battle for survival, and only the fittest made it through. "If you hadn't been there, how would we have known where to take the body? We'd have ended up shoving it in the freezer for the cops to raid."

"That place we drove to—"

"You never have to go there again," I cut her off. "Zander is going to get rid of the car. There'll be no traces left behind."

"My dad was a wicked man." Mieko's eyes misted over. "He used to hurt me. He'd take me out there, and..."

"You don't have to talk about it if you don't want to." I reached out and took her hand. "You don't need to explain yourself to me."

"Last night wasn't the first time I saw a dead body." Her voice cracked. "My dad. It was an accident. I didn't mean to hurt him. I just wanted him to stop, but I... I... I..."

"You don't have to say it. I know," I said. Physical affection wasn't usually my thing, but I pulled Mieko into a hug. In my arms, she felt so small and fragile. I stroked her hair whilst she wept over my shoulder. "It's okay. It's all going to be okay. He can't hurt you anymore."

Mieko reminded me of how I used to be. When I first started killing, I felt a pang of sadness whenever I took a life. Not for my victims — those fuckers deserved it. But I felt like I'd lost a part of myself I'd never be able to get back. I grieved for a more innocent time, where I knew nothing about how to sever the jugular artery and hoped for a life away from the confines of Evergreen. Now, crying didn't help me release my emotions. I preferred to spill blood over tears. In my twisted way, killing had become a form of therapy.

"How did you know?" Mieko sniffed.

"Because we're the same," I said. "People like us do what we have to do to survive."

"You've done what you had to do to survive too, haven't you?"

"Sometimes there's no other way." After my fifth murder, the numbness set in. Society deems murder unlawful, but wouldn't it be an even bigger sin to allow monsters to walk the streets and ruin even more lives? Mieko did what she had to do to protect herself and, one day, I hoped she'd make peace with her choices. "After a while, you start to realize that bad people aren't worth your tears. You may not feel it right now, but you're stronger than you think."

"Thanks." Mieko shot me a watery half-smile, then grabbed the tub of dreams. "Do you have any more of this?"

"I'm sure I can find some," I said.

"How do you think Vixen's doing?" Mieko asked. Even after everything that had happened in the last twenty-four hours, she was still worrying about other people. "Zander seemed pretty mad at her, didn't he?"

"Vixen can fight her own battles," I said. It didn't matter what Vixen did, Zander's fierce protectiveness over her would forgive her for anything. "Why do you suddenly care about her so much?"

"I don't!"

"Hold on a second," I said, turning to face her. "Are you blushing?"

"N-n-no!" she lied.

"You can't be serious." I shook my head. "You have a fucking crush on the ice queen, don't you?"

"I don't!" She could deny it all she wanted, but the look on her face told me otherwise. Now, it made sense why she'd defended and felt sorry for Vixen in the past.

I winked. "Sure, you don't."

"Besides, she's not an ice queen." Mieko sulked. Damn, she liked Vixen even more than I'd first thought. "There's more to her than that."

"Just because she recited a verse of poetry doesn't make her any less of a bitch," I pointed out. "But if anyone can make her melt, it's you. Don't say I didn't warn you, though."

Freezer burn hurt like a bitch.

———

As per Zander's orders, Mieko and I arrived for our shift bang on time. There was no way I'd give him the satisfaction of complaining about my hangover, either. No matter how bad my head ached.

"Candy," Scarlett sauntered over on stilt-like heels to greet us. One wrong step and she'd break her legs. "I have a message for you from Zander."

Something felt off… and it wasn't just the lingering sensation from knowing a kid died where we were standing.

"I didn't realize you were his messenger now," I replied. Scarlett must be next in line to straddle the king of Lapland. It wouldn't be long until the crown fucking jewels crushed her like they had her predecessor. "Have you taken up Bella's position as lapdog?"

"He wants to see you in his office." She swished her blonde locks over her shoulder so dramatically that it almost slapped me in the face. "Like, right now."

"What do you think he wants?" Mieko whispered. "Do you think he's still mad?"

"It's Zander," I said as if that was explanation enough. "He's mad all the fucking time. Whatever he wants, it can't be good."

If Zander wanted to fire me, then I'd go out with a bang. Although, hopefully, not in the form of a gun aimed at my labia... again.

"Good luck." Scarlett shot me a fake smile. "You'll need it."

I stormed across the club; my rage growing with each step. I barged into Zander's office without knocking. Why should I play by his fucking rules after his complete lack of gratitude this morning? When he earned my respect, I'd repay it in kind. Until then, he could kiss my ass if he expected me to bow down to his orders.

Zander looked up in disapproval and frowned. "I told you to knock."

"What does it matter?" I challenged. "You were the one who summoned me."

"Take a seat, Candy."

I threw myself down with a huff. "Well?"

"Last night can't go without consequences. You know that, don't you?" Zander drummed his fingers on the desk. "I want you to do something for me."

"If you want me to run another errand, forget it," I snarled. "Why should I do another job to save the Seven's asses and not see a dime for it? If you want my help, you'll need to pay—"

"I want you to leave town," Zander interrupted. He pulled a black briefcase from under the desk and slid it toward me. "This is your cut from the Briarly poker game. You can use it to start over."

"Start over?" My mouth fell open. "You can't just order me to leave."

"I've already made my decision," Zander dismissed, checking his watch in boredom. "There's been a string of disasters since the moment you arrived. We are done cleaning up the mess you leave behind."

"My mess?" I grabbed the suitcase and hurled it against the wall in fury. If he wanted to see a fucking mess, then I'd make his office look like a department store after the Black Friday stampede. "Where were you when I saved Red's life? Where were you last night when a kid held up a gun to Vixen's head?"

"That's exactly my point," Zander said. "All of this started when you came to town."

"Things have been fucked up around here long before I arrived," I sneered. Zander rose to his feet, fists clenched, his stare searing with pure hatred. He didn't realize this was only me warming up. The truth fucking hurt and he'd been used to getting his way for too fucking long. "Don't pretend you're too blind to see it."

"I see everything."

"If you did, you'd be fucking thanking me!" Hell, he should be down on his knees licking my shoes. "If it wasn't for me, Red and Vixen would be dead."

"If it wasn't for you, we wouldn't be in a war with my father," Zander spat in accusation. "His men wouldn't be dead, and last night would never have happened."

"What happened last night was an accident," I said. "You were already in a war. You just didn't want to admit it. If I were you, I'd want me on your side."

"Take the money, Candy."

"I don't want your fucking money!" I kicked the briefcase. "Everyone else may be too afraid of you to say what they really think, but you don't scare me, Zander. You never have."

Suddenly, the office door flew open.

"You can't do this." Vixen fell inside, panting. "You can't fire her."

"This is my club," Zander growled. "I can do what I want."

"Correction!" She raised a finger. "It's *our* club. You told me I can decide which dancers we hire."

"Are you sure about that, Vixen?" Zander asked. "Do you really want Candy to stay?"

"Yes," she confirmed. Who knew burning a body together would win over Vixen's support? "I do."

"Have it your way, Vixen. I'll allow her to stay on one condition…" Zander paused for dramatic effect and his lips curled into a smile, "Candy won't be a dancer. She will become one of us. A Seven."

"What?" I spluttered. "Who says I even want to be a member of your twisted gang?"

"You said that we should want you on our side," Zander replied, using my own words against me. "This is your chance."

"You can't bring someone in without consulting everyone," Vixen intervened. Was she already regretting her choice to vouch for me? "That's not how we do things. It has to be a group decision."

"Let's put it to a vote then," Zander said. As if on cue, West and Rocky filed inside. Both of their expressions were blank. Had this been Zander's plan all along? Did he try offering me money as a final test to prove my loyalty, or was this another one of his mind games? "Are there any objections to Candy joining the Sevens?"

I expected West to speak up. After admitting to torching his car, there was no way he would want me to join his precious gang. If he didn't hate me, then Vixen had spent every waking minute trying to make my life hell. I couldn't imagine she wanted to keep me around. Even Rocky had tried to persuade me to keep my distance… but, a minute later, none of them had spoken.

"It's settled then. We're all in agreement," Zander said, turning to face me again. Had I entered an alternate universe or something? "Joining the Sevens is a lifetime deal. When you're in, there's no getting out."

"This must be your idea of a sick joke," I stammered. "How can you want me to join you? You don't even know me."

Rocky wrung his hands. Well, most of them didn't….

"But we will." Zander said. "Or, you can take the money and leave town. It's your choice."

Could I really trust the Sevens enough to put my life in their hands? I'd always been a lone wolf, but the threat of Hiram loomed over my head like a black cloud. I stood no chance of destroying him on my own, but maybe if I had these guys behind me…

"What's it going to be, Candy?" Zander's eyes burned into mine like hot coals. "Are you in, or are you out?"

I looked at the four people around the room. They were mouthy screwed up violent criminals, but they were also broken… like me. The Sevens had unparalleled loyalty to each other. Even though I would never get my happy ending, maybe it would be possible to find a place for myself somewhere amongst this gang of misfits.

They may have a battle with the Briarlys on their hands, but I was raging a war of my own. I had everything to gain and nothing to lose. What they didn't realize was adding me to their ranks wouldn't help them. It would only rain down a hell of a lot of complications and make them regret ever asking. My decision would change the rest of my life… and theirs.

"I'm in."

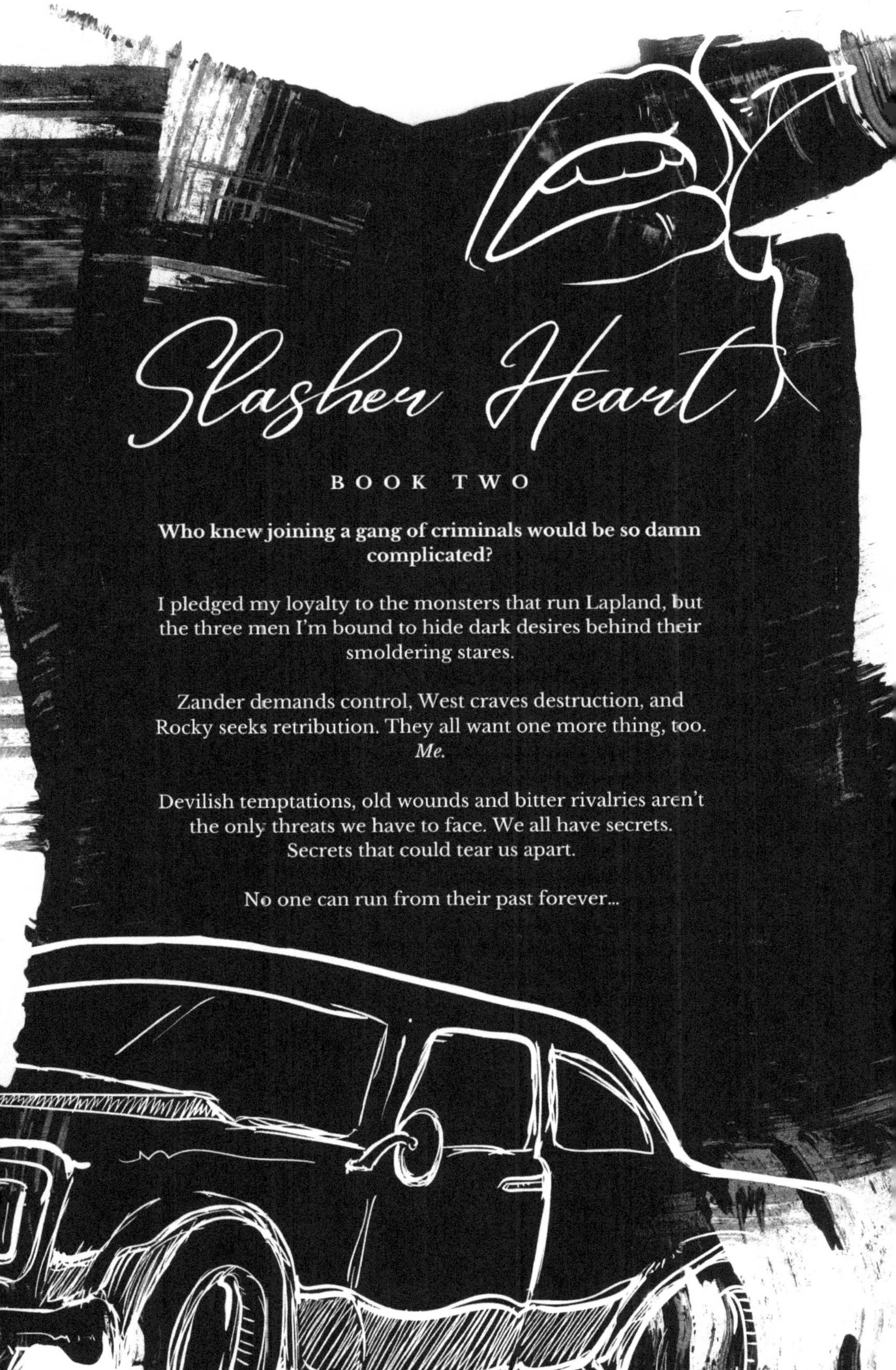

Slasher Heart

BOOK TWO

Who knew joining a gang of criminals would be so damn complicated?

I pledged my loyalty to the monsters that run Lapland, but the three men I'm bound to hide dark desires behind their smoldering stares.

Zander demands control, West craves destruction, and Rocky seeks retribution. They all want one more thing, too. *Me.*

Devilish temptations, old wounds and bitter rivalries aren't the only threats we have to face. We all have secrets. Secrets that could tear us apart.

No one can run from their past forever...

Prologue

ZANDER

"Why did you do that, Zander?"

How dare she question me?

I made the rules.

They all knew it.

"Zander? Are you fucking listening?" Vixen crossed her arms over her chest like a petulant child. "Have you lost your damn mind?"

"You were quick to defend her." I turned away to signal our conversation was over. "Aren't you pleased? This is what you wanted."

"I didn't want you to fire her ass," she hissed. "But I didn't mean for you to make her one of us, either. This is a big fucking deal."

"It's done," I replied dismissively with a wave of my hand. "I trust you'll make her feel welcome."

Vixen had always been fiercely protective of the Sevens. She found it hard to trust people after her upbringing. We all did. She saw a new member as a threat, but it gave her no authority to question my decisions. The Sevens answered to me. The last word was mine, and mine alone.

"You're fucking insane," she blasted, slamming my office door shut.

Good. Now, I could finally be alone with my thoughts at last. Vixen didn't know it yet, but her intervention saved me a job. Candy would have become a Seven eventually, but Vixen's agreement had never been guaranteed. I couldn't have planned it any better myself...

The pink-haired stripper, who knew her way around a knife better than a butcher, intrigued me like no other woman had. Women were there for me to fuck. There was no space in my life for emotional ties, but Candy? She was different. When I looked into her eyes, defiant darkness stared straight back. The same blackness that consumed me enveloped her perfect curves. She didn't run from the shadows. She lived and breathed them.

'Everyone else may be too afraid of you to say what they really think, but you don't scare me, Zander... you never have.'

No one had ever dared to speak to me like that. Ever.

Her blatant defiance made me want to wrap my hands around her neck and choke her as much as I wanted to throw her against the wall and take her from behind. Her tongue was vicious, her words poison, and her fuckable red lips enough to make me hard instantly.

At first, I'd thought she was just another girl who'd walked in off the streets of Port Valentine wanting to make a fast buck. But she wasn't like the others. She was so much more than that. After seeing the mincemeat she'd made of my father's finest men, I knew she was special.

Candy may not know everything about me or the Sevens, but she'd accepted my offer for a reason. When the briefcase of money didn't entice her, that's when I knew for sure. She was one of us. As expected, she passed my test and didn't run. Although, there was still time for her to wish she had...

Candy may be a Seven now, but I craved more than her loyalty. Under my rules, no one else would ever fucking touch her again.

Candy would be mine.

CHAPTER

One

CANDY

.

"**D**id you even read the dress code?" I arched an eyebrow at Vixen's skin-tight leather pants and the harness wrapped around her torso. How could her boobs even breathe in that thing? Taking it off and letting the twins hang loose at the end of the day would be the biggest relief. "You know you look like a dominatrix, right?"

"That's what I was going for," she replied smugly, applying her third coat of black lipstick. How were they not permanently stained? She hadn't worn another shade since I joined the Sevens. My presence put her in a constant state of mourning. "All I'm missing is chains and a whip."

"It wasn't supposed to be a compliment."

When I first started working at the club, I'd never have dared say something like that. Now, our relationship had changed. Sure, I still wanted to rip her piercings out of her face... but we could *almost* spend an entire evening together without wanting to kill each other. Who knew disposing of a body would be such a great bonding experience?

"I still don't see why I can't stay behind." As well as being the world's biggest perfectionist, Vixen complained like it was an Olympic fucking sport. "Do we really all have to go tonight?"

"It's my coming-out party, so yeah." I tied my hair into a high ponytail to ensure my new tattoo was visible. I'd opted to get the number seven inked behind my ear. "We all have to be there."

"No one gave me a coming-out party," Vixen muttered, adjusting her top so the matching tattoo on her collarbone peeked over the black lace. Every member of the Sevens had one. It was our mark and a way of showing we were in this for life. When I was younger, I'd grilled Rocky about joining a gang. Times had changed, and I'd done exactly what I'd sworn to never do. "For joining the Sevens, or when I came out as gay."

"Would you have wanted one?" I arched an eyebrow. "A coming-out party?"

"Maybe," Vixen said, then paused, "but I guess hooking up with my math teacher pretty much sealed the deal."

"No shit…"

"She was hot." Hot or not, she will have been the last woman Vixen slept with who had a brain. For someone who saw through people's bullshit, she was completely blind when it came to airheads with zero personality. "It sucked when we got caught by the principal."

"How did that go down in your fancy private school?" I asked. Picturing Vixen in a posh uniform was even more ridiculous than imagining the Queen of England twerking around a pole in tassels. "Did they kick you out?"

"I may be a Briarly by blood, but I didn't grow up with all the same luxuries as Zander." She laughed bitterly. Our conversations about the Briarlys never went too deep. Vixen and Zander were cousins, but they'd grown up differently. Every time I tried to probe them about their backgrounds, I got nowhere. "Where I went to school, no one gave a shit what went down… but I lost my extra credit."

Before I could press her, the devil himself walked in. How many suits did Zander own? He had one for every occasion. This sleek black number and bow tie had to be one of my favorites — not that I'd ever tell him that. If his ego could be turned into electricity, it would generate enough to power the entire Eastern Seaboard.

"The car's waiting," Zander declared. From his grim expression, you'd have thought we were about to embark on a funeral march. It wouldn't kill him to crack a fucking smile. After all, the outing had been his idea.

I clipped in large silver hoop earrings. "It can wait a little longer."

"You have two minutes, Candy," Zander ordered. "Or, you can make your own way there."

I held my hand to my mouth and gasped. "You mean West will actually let us borrow a car?"

Vixen snickered. We'd got to a point where it was *almost* acceptable to laugh about the Range Rover inferno — not to West's face, though. None of us had a death wish. One mention of the ruined car would send him into all out destruction mode. I'd lost count of how many bottles he'd smashed in an enraged frenzy. Fuck knows how the club pulled any profit when The Hulk loved playing whack-a-mole with the liquor.

"I mean it, Candy." Zander shot me a sharp warning glare, turning to stalk away then stopping abruptly to add, "Don't fucking push me tonight."

We were heading to an exclusive charity auction in town. The event was a bullshit charade, orchestrated by Bryce Briarly, to show the world he was a decent community-serving human. He wasn't fooling anyone. Zander's father was no better than the global oil companies that donated money to help with climate change. He was the problem. In fact, Bryce would prob-ably use the proceeds to enlist more impressionable kids to his ranks.

"Have you always been such a mouthy bitch?" Vixen asked.

I smirked. "Always."

"It wasn't supposed to be a compliment," she mimicked, lacing up her knee-high boots. They definitely wouldn't fit the black-tie dress code, but no one would dare criticize a Briarly. Not if they knew what was good for them. In Port Valentine, the Briarly family was royalty. They'd ruled the town for as long as it'd been on the map. Zander may have seemed to shun his father's fortune, but it didn't change his blood.

"Are you ready?" Rocky burst into Vixen's room. I'd been spending a lot of time in the Sevens penthouse above the club, but I still wasn't used to the guys barging in unannounced every two seconds. "If we don't leave, Zander is going to—"

Rocky stopped talking as soon as he saw me.

"What?" I looked down to see whether my period had come. Thankfully, Aunt Flo hadn't waved her magic wand yet. It wouldn't take a lot to ruin my skin-tight white bandage dress. I'd used almost an entire roll of tit tape to keep the twins in check because of the plunging neckline. "What're you staring at?"

He cleared his throat. "N-n-nothing."

It was weird to see Rocky all dressed up. Out of all the guys, he avoided attending formal functions. They weren't his scene. Unlike Zander, he hadn't opted for a bow tie. The top buttons of his shirt were open and his shirt untucked, giving the impression he'd already gone out and the night was over.

"Tell Zander to quit getting his panties in a twist," I said. "Or, are you afraid he'll shoot the messenger?"

"Knowing Zander," Rocky murmured, "it wouldn't surprise me."

Becoming a Seven hadn't automatically given me an all-access pass to the secrets in Zander's arsenal. He still didn't trust me enough to tell me every-thing about his underground empire. The only thing I'd been 'permitted' to take over was running Lapland's poker ring, whilst Zander tasked West with other covert operations. I understood trust had to be earned, but my patience would only last so long. I'd already spent too much of my life in a cell in Blackthorne Towers, and Zander couldn't keep me locked in the basement forever.

So far, we'd stayed quiet about me joining the Sevens. Now, our silence was about to break. After the auction, everyone would know I'd joined their twisted family. News travels fast in Port Valentine. Stepping out of the shadows as the newest member would paint a target on my back visible from outer space. Zander and the guys had enemies waiting to stab them in the throat around every corner. Bryce's army didn't frighten me, though. The only thing I worried about was Hiram's reaction. My evil ex-master wouldn't be happy to discover I'd publicly sworn allegiance to someone else.

So far, only Rocky and Q knew my history. A new tattoo didn't mean I was gonna spill my guts. If Zander wanted to keep me in the dark about everything going on, why couldn't I do the same? Everyone was entitled to secrets. The only problem was, Zander didn't know the dangerous game he'd become part of by letting me join them. When Hiram came for me, all of us would have to be fucking ready.

Vixen looked out the window and groaned. "Do we really have to go in the fucking limo?"

"Can you even hear yourself?" I rolled my eyes. "It's a fucking limo."

She wrinkled her nose. "Do you really want to sit down on a seat that would flash up like a crime scene under UV?"

"I guess you have a point." I pushed the image of the guys getting hot and heavy out of my mind. They may be juicy eye candy, but they were also assholes. Besides, I couldn't think of them like that. We were business associates. Everyone knows you don't shit where you eat. "Let's get this over with, okay?"

"I can't wait to see my uncle's face when we crash his motherfucking party." She spat out the word 'uncle' like it was a nasty STI — the type that'd make a dick sprout green blisters. Who could blame her? I'd be the same if Bryce Briarly was a relative of mine. Being a foundling had some advantages, at least.

The last time I saw Bryce was at the poker game in Briarly Manor, his millionaire gothic mansion, which held more secrets than Gretchen Weiners' hair. We attended the game for business, but the auction was going to be a social call. I didn't intend on being civil. Bryce lost that privilege when one of the Razors bled to death in the middle of Lapland's dance floor. It'd shown me the true monster he really was.

The crisp night breeze was a refreshing change to the sticky heat of the club. Under Lapland's neon sign, West rested his arms against the limo like a star in a cologne commercial. His sleeves were rolled to his elbows, and his suspenders hugged his pecks. He looked like he'd thrown off a jacket and was ready to launch into a fight. That, and the sight of his tattoos against the whiteness of his shirt, made my stomach flip. I'd only seen him a handful of times since joining the gang and never for more than a few minutes at a time. Whatever task Zander had given him meant he rarely visited the club. Seeing him again reminded me of how *big* he was. Did he have to get clothes custom-made to fit his biceps?

West held the door open. "Ladies first."

"Since when do you have fucking manners?" I grumbled as I got into the limo to join the others, thinking back to Vixen's comment and how the guys had dissolved women's panties in the backseat a thousand times before.

"I see you carefully considered your outfit, Vixen." Zander, already sprawled across the seats, sighed and shook his head. "My father will not be pleased."

"He can go fuck himself." She uncorked a bottle of champagne and managed to close her mouth over its end before the flow of bubbles erupted. After taking a swig, she wiped her mouth. "Besides, no one is going to be looking at me tonight. I'm not the main attraction, remember? No one is going to miss *those*."

"Hey," I snapped at her pointed look at my cleavage. Maybe it'd been a little too much of a risqué choice. "My face is up here."

She winked, passing me the bottle. "And so is your tattoo."

"Is everyone clear about what's happening tonight? We are going to the auction to show my father we are a force to be reckoned with." Zander's gaze lingered on me as he spoke. "I don't want any nasty surprises."

It's not like I purposefully went out of my way to cause trouble. I couldn't help it if I got caught in the middle of shit when it went down. Zander still hadn't gotten over how I'd saved Vixen and Rocky's life without his help. It was lucky for them I was around, otherwise, the two fuckers wouldn't have survived.

"It's a charity auction," I reminded him. "Not a shoot-out!"

"Oh, there's one more thing." Zander pulled a small velvet box out of his pocket and pushed it into my hands. "I got you a gift."

"A gift?" I frowned, half-expecting it to explode. "What is it?"

"Open it," he encouraged. "You'll see."

Inside the box, a large blood-red stone sat nestled on a silver band. The intricate design looked like two snakes coiling together to hold the ruby in place. I slid it onto my wedding finger and it fit perfectly. A ring like this would have cost more than feeding a family of four for a year.

"Well?" He studied my reaction. "What do you think?"

"It's okay." I shrugged and tried to keep my expression neutral. 'Okay' didn't cover it. It was the most beautiful damn ring I'd ever seen. "How did you know my size?"

"Lucky guess." Zander smirked, then turned to West. "How do you feel about your upcoming nuptials?"

West scowled. "I don't see why we have to do it this way."

I glared at him. Having a reputation as his soon-to-be gang wife wasn't exactly the statement I wanted to make, either. "Believe it or not, being your cock block is not my dream come true."

"We've been over this. It's part of the plan," Zander hissed. Of course, the elusive 'plan' he still hadn't divulged to anyone else yet. "Everyone already thinks you're a couple."

"How are you getting on with this plan of yours?" I pressed.

He'd better have a good reason for branding me as West's woman. The element of surprise could have its advantages later down the line. After all, no one expected a stick of dynamite to be planted inside a fleshlight. If anyone played with me, I'd blow their dick clean off.

"That's none of your business," Zander growled. "You'll know when you need to."

"Enough. No fighting on family night," Vixen said. Who knew she could be a decent mediator? "We're already facing enough people who want us dead. We don't need to turn on each other."

———

The auction was taking place in the town hall, an old building in the center of Port Valentine usually reserved for special occasions. As soon as our limo pulled in, the sight of Giles Briarly almost made me ask our driver to turn around. Giles, Zander and Vixen's English cousin, stood like he had something mounted up his ass. A reporter wearing a press badge from the local newspaper fussed around him with a camera while he lapped up the attention.

"Calm down, Vix." Rocky stepped into damage-control mode as Vixen ground her teeth like she was chewing on a mouthful of rocks. It was the first time Vixen had seen Giles since I showed her the video of him screwing her ex. "She wasn't even worth it."

"That's not the point," Vixen snarled. "It's the fucking principle."

"Let's wait until he's away from the camera, at least," Rocky reasoned. Vixen's verbal lashing would not be something worthy of a front-page news story. "You think you can do that?"

She nodded, but the look of determination glinting in her eyes meant we'd all have to watch her closely. If Giles wasn't careful, his philandering hands would be sold as one of the exhibits.

"Remember why we're here," Zander said. "We've come to make a statement. We're the Sevens, and this town? It's going to be ours."

"Let's fucking do this," Rocky agreed.

Zander got out first, followed by West. The big man paused, turning back and extending his open hand.

"Take it, there." Vixen shoved me forward. "He won't bite!"

Reluctantly, I took it. It was the first time we'd touched since West almost crashed his car on our way back from the junkyard. He'd pulled over to kiss me with a possessive hunger that I'd avoided thinking about since. It was a kiss that never should have happened. A kiss he wanted to erase from existence.

Even in five-inch strappy diamanté heels, West towered above me. As we stepped forward into the crowd waiting outside, widened eyes and frozen smiles gave us the reaction we'd hoped for. They hadn't been expecting us. Zander sauntered over to Giles, whose charm quickly turned bitter at being upstaged by our arrival.

"We were not expecting you tonight, cousin." Giles's lips curled into a snarl. "Or your posse of waifs and strays."

"I assume our invitation got lost," Zander replied coldly. "Nothing happens around here without us knowing about it."

"I almost forgot you were still around, Vixie." Giles turned to her with a sly grin. He knew how to push her buttons and enjoyed every second of it. "I'm sure we'll have the chance to catch up this evening."

"In your fucking dreams," Vixen hissed. Someone needed to get her to the bar before she scooped out his eyeballs and used them to garnish a Dirty Martini. "Stay the fuck away from me tonight, unless you want your balls to be auctioned off with the rest of the junk Bryce is selling."

"Let's go inside," Rocky said, tactfully steering her away. "Now."

West didn't utter a word as we climbed the stairs. I may as well have been holding hands with a walking robot. What the fuck was his problem? Inside the hall, several circular tables were set up in front of the stage where the auction would take place. Amongst the attendees, I recognized a few faces from the Maven and the poker game at Briarly Manor. No one spoke. Instead, hushed whispers followed us as we strode through the crowd. Nothing attracted attention more than uninvited guests.

Bryce Briarly caught sight of us from across the room and made a beeline like a vulture descending on a carcass. I smoothed down my hair to flash the newest addition to my tattoo collection and flaunt the massive rock weighing down my finger. Bryce didn't miss it.

"What a pleasant surprise," Bryce addressed Zander sarcastically, then his frosty glare rested on Vixen. Even a chainsaw couldn't carve the tension in the air. At Briarly Manor, Zander told me not to mention

Vixen's name around his father. If she got this kind of reception, it was easy to see why. Bryce looked at her with utter hatred. "And you brought *her*."

"Happy to see me?" Vixen countered. If Bryce's hit succeeded, she would be rotting in the ground. "It's always good to see you too, Uncle."

"Why don't we get a drink?" Rocky took her arm gently. His thoughtfulness continued to take me off guard. I still didn't know how he and Vixen met in juvie, but he took care of her like a younger sister. "It's a free bar."

I may never be able to forgive Rocky for what he'd done in the past, but I understood his motives after hearing the full story. Hiram left him with no choice. As a Seven, I had to abandon my plan to kill him. Besides, he owed me. What good would a corpse be when Hiram came to collect? Rocky's promise to do anything to make amends were only words, but a day would come when I'd need to cash in my favor.

"West, Candy." Bryce acknowledged our interlocked fingers with a curt nod. "I see congratulations are in order."

I held up my hand to show off the jewel, which glinted under the light. "They are."

"Have you set a date?" Bryce asked.

"Not yet, we have so much to plan," I said. Yeah, like how we could take down the entire Briarly fucking empire. "But we're working on it."

"I'm sure you are." A hint of a challenge lurked beneath Bryce's words. "We're glad to have you here this evening."

"Giving to charity isn't your usual type of endeavor, father," Zander said.

"What can I say? So many children in this town lack direction," Bryce said. To a bystander, it almost sounded like he gave a shit. "I'm in a fortunate position to give back to our special community."

"How generous of you," I hissed through gritted teeth. West squeezed my hand in warning. If more damaged kids fell into his clutches, the only thing Bryce would give back to the community were unmarked graves. He wanted to enlist every lost man in town into his criminal operations. "We all know how much you care about giving young people direction."

On Bryce's orders, his newest recruit accidentally blew his own brains out when he'd shown up at the club to kill Vixen. We'd gotten rid of the evidence, but Bryce was no fucking amateur. He knew we had something to do with the boy's sudden disappearance. Bryce's plan to avenge the loss of his men backfired, all too literally.

"I didn't plan the event alone," Bryce said, gesturing to his right. "In fact, I think you will all be pleased to see a friendly face back in town."

A man with his back turned and spun around to face us.

Motherfucker.

How hadn't we heard about this?

Zander's face turned to stone as he addressed the man. "Welcome back, Cheeks."

"Didn't you know he was released?" Bryce clapped Cheeks on the shoulder as he joined us. We hadn't been the only people keeping secrets over the last few months. "Cheeks is working for me full-time."

Even Bryce Briarly's influence couldn't get Cheeks out of jail. Only one person was powerful enough to overturn Cheeks's damning conviction. The same person who was responsible for putting him behind bars... *Hiram.*

"Missing evidence," Cheeks announced proudly. He grinned to reveal a newly gap-toothed smile. When we last spoke, Hiram threatened that favors could be undone. This was his doing. "They threw the case out at court."

Prison hadn't treated him kindly. Convicts were not likely to welcome a former cop with open arms — even someone as crooked as Cheeks, who was more of a criminal than most of them. He'd lost weight and a broken nose had ruined his facial symmetry. Being a shadow of his former self only made him more dangerous. Losing his career cost him everything. He was a man with nothing left to lose.

"I've been enjoying my freedom," Cheeks continued, nodding his head towards a trio of women who giggled like starving hyenas on command. They'd better be getting five times their usual rate to put up with his limp dick. "You'd know all about that, West."

"I'm taken," West said.

"For now." Cheeks smirked. "Didn't you hear that Penelope Cole is back in town? Does *she* know about your engagement?"

West didn't blink, but his jaw tensed. He wanted to keep his cool, but this came as a shock. Who the fuck was Penelope, and why did the mention of her name spook him?

"I told you," West growled, "I'm fucking taken."

"And we couldn't be happier," I added.

"We have some final preparations to take care of." Bryce shut the conversation down, as Cheeks cackled by his side. If they auctioned the opportunity to knock out his remaining teeth, I'd be the top bidder. "Enjoy your evening."

One glance at Zander's face signaled the night had gotten off to a rough start. We had aimed to surprise them, but Bryce was always one step ahead and ready to sucker punch at the final second.

Zander spun to face West in accusation. "Did you know she was back?"

West shook his head.

"Who is she?" I asked.

They both ignored me. As usual, my questions fell into the fucking abyss.

West clenched his fists. "I need a fucking drink."

He stormed over to the bar, where Vixen and Rocky already had a row of shots lined up, and downed them all in quick succession.

Zander grabbed my arm to stop me from following. "Keep an eye on West tonight."

"He's a big boy. I'm sure he can take care of himself," I said, pulling myself free and pretending to check a non-existent watch on my wrist. "Oh, look at that. It's time we hit the free bar before West empties it."

Zander scowled but trailed after me to join the others.

"I don't see why you wanted to come here, Zander," Vixen grumbled, sliding glasses to each of us like we were part of a production line. "Rubbing shoulders with your daddy's rich friends is not how we should be spending our Friday night."

"Oh, it gets better. Just wait until you see our favorite ex-convict." I pulled up a stool and took a drink. The gold flakes from Goldschläger cutting my insides were the least of my concerns. "Cheeks got out."

"When?" Rocky's expression darkened. "Where is he?"

"Don't even think about it," Zander warned. His calculating gray eyes scanned the crowd carefully. Did he have another reason for bringing us here, aside from presenting me as West's trophy wife? "We're not going anywhere. Not until after the auction."

"What're they going to be auctioning, anyway?" Vixen flicked through the catalog and yawned. The pages were filled with boring antiques you'd be able to pick up at a garage sale for fifty cents apiece. "These people have already got rooms filled with shit they don't use."

"I think they will appreciate the Sevens donation," Zander said.

"Our donation? Since when?" Vixen crossed her arms. "We're giving something away? You've got to be fucking kidding me."

"It'd be rude to show up empty-handed." Whatever Zander had planned suddenly made the evening a lot more interesting. "Wouldn't it?"

W est's brooding presence loomed over me like a dark cloud. He'd been a pain in the ass from the moment we arrived. We were meant to be working together but all he wanted to do was sit at the bar pouting while the other Sevens circled the room to gather intelligence. Everyone knew Bryce's guests would lower their guard and inhibitions after they'd downed enough champagne to sink the Titanic.

"We're supposed to be a happy couple, remember?" I reminded him. The last time I checked, I'd done nothing wrong — unless you count burning his beloved car, but that happened months ago. He couldn't hold it over me forever. Besides, the Sevens had enough money to buy ten more of them in an instant. "Are you planning to ignore me all night?"

"If you'll let me."

West took hot and cold to another level. With Zander and Rocky, I could at least try to guess what they were thinking. Zander cared about revenge and satisfying his desires. He made his demands clear, even if I ignored them. On the other hand, Rocky laid out his emotions for the world to see and used humor to conceal his pain. But West? He was fucking impossible to read. One minute, he almost crashed a car to kiss me. The next, he'd barely spoken for weeks on end.

"What the fuck is wrong with you?" I lowered my voice, thinking back to Cheeks's earlier revelation and being unable to stop the words that came next. "Are you too busy thinking about *Penelope*?"

It was no secret the Sevens had an appetite for women. I mean, they owned a strip club, which was akin to living in a fucking sweet shop for any straight guy with a penis. West's little black book was probably thicker than the entire Harry Potter series.

"Don't go there." West's furious stare burned into mine. "You have no fucking idea what you're talking about."

"Why don't you enlighten me?" I challenged. He didn't intimidate me, and I wasn't about to back down. "You know, open your mouth and verbalize something?"

"You think you have us all worked out," West hissed. "You may have joined the Sevens, but that doesn't make you one of us. You know nothing."

"And whose fault is that?" Being kept in the dark was getting boring. The whole point of joining a gang was to get a slice of whatever pie they were sharing. I didn't sign up to be left outside like a tethered dog and watch as they tucked into a sweet blueberry slice. I'd become a Seven because I wanted to be all in, not be a fucking extra. "If you talked to me, then maybe I'd be able to help?"

I may not have as much personally invested in bringing down the Briarly empire, but Bryce fit my 'type' perfectly. Whenever I killed, I assessed men based on my special criteria. He fit into the rich exploitative asshole category snugger than Cinderella's slipper. Murdering innocent people wasn't my jam, but when someone deserves it? Well, who was I to deprive them of a taste of their fucking poison?

"Help?" West snorted in disbelief. "I don't think so."

"If you didn't want me to stick around, then why didn't you say so?" All he had to do was say no, and then I'd have disappeared from their lives forever. Each of the Sevens had to agree unanimously for a person to join. "I'm only here because you didn't object."

His hands curled into fists the size of small soccer balls. "I should have."

We glared at each other. Neither of us wanted to be the first to break the silence. Vixen strode over to cut the tension, "Are you having your first fight?"

"West is getting cold feet," I said. "Isn't that right, *honey*?"

"I'm fucking done here." He jumped up, causing his stool to skid across the floor and tip over from the force. Onlookers cast a nervous look in his direction. "I'll see you at home."

"I don't know what's got into that asshole lately." Vixen let out a low whistle and shook her head, as we watched the crowd part for him to pass. No one wanted to stand in his way. "Believe it or not, he's normally the sweet one."

Yeah, as sweet as a Toxic Waste candy…

West's departure didn't go unnoticed. As if on cue, Giles sidled over to us like a piece of roadkill resurrected from the dead. Thankfully, Vixen had the sense to excuse herself before we made any more of a scene.

"How nice to see you again, Candy." Giles dropped a kiss on both my cheeks. On British TV, it seemed charming. In reality, having someone's germ-filled mouth on your skin made you want to head straight for a chemical peel. "I see your fiancé doesn't know how to behave in public. If I were you, I'd be reconsidering my nuptials. Don't tell me that big ogre really knows how to satisfy you?"

"You're the last person who should give advice about pleasuring a woman," I said, reapplying my lip gloss. The last time we were at Briarly Manor, I ruined his plan to sabotage the game and exposed his secret relationship with Vixen's ex-girlfriend. If I hadn't seen him and Charlene screwing, who knows how many diseases Vixen would have caught from sharing a girl with a piece of shit like Giles?

"I was impressed to find out you're an avid photographer," Giles said with a snide look on his face. Charlene must have squealed about the video. It wouldn't have taken long for him to put the pieces together. Judging from his new date this evening, their romance had been short-lived when her time as a Lapland spy ended. "And a talented blackmailer too."

"I'm sorry." My eyes widened innocently. "I don't know what you're talking about. But I do enjoy wildlife photography in my spare time."

"Can I give you some friendly advice?" Giles leaned in closer. Another inch and he'd be waddling around with gigantic balls for the next week. "If I were you, I'd watch your back."

What was a posh overgrown schoolboy going to do? I don't know what subjects they taught at private schools in England, but I'm sure the curriculum didn't cover the same material as my lessons with Hiram in Blackthorne Towers. While he'd been slaving away over textbooks learning Einstein's theory of relativity, I'd got an education on how to circumcise a cock with a vegetable peeler. Which was the more valuable life skill?

I looked over Giles's shoulder to see Rocky sneak up behind him. "What's going on?"

"Nothing." Giles attempted a smile. He looked like a starving alligator baring its teeth. "We're just having a friendly catch-up."

Rocky saw right through Giles's bullshit. "Nothing is ever friendly with you."

"We never see you anymore, Red," Giles said, changing the subject. "Do you have permission to be outside? I heard my cousin keeps you locked away. Then again, you're used to being in a cage."

"If you don't step away from Candy in the next ten seconds." Rocky lowered his voice to a threatening rumble and closed the gap between them. "You'll find out why I got locked up in the first place."

"Have it your way." Giles laughed coldly, then turned to face me. "Remember what I said, Candy."

I rolled my eyes. How could anyone take a threat seriously when it was aimed at your tits? If he got distracted by my cleavage, it wouldn't take much to throw him off during a fight.

"Are you okay?" Rocky asked as soon as Giles was out of earshot. "What did he want?"

"I didn't need your intervention," I snapped. "I had the situation under control."

"It's not you I was worried about," Rocky muttered. "West should never have left you alone here. Not with all these assholes around."

"Surely, you're not worried about Cheeks?" I raised my eyebrow. "I kicked the bastard's ass once before, and I'll do it—"

"Would you stop running your mouth for a second?" Rocky's fingers closed around my arm to silence me. If it wasn't for his serious expression, I'd have made my voice even louder. "Act natural and follow me."

"Hey," I objected as he yanked me violently to the edge of the room with a surprising amount of strength. "I thought you wanted to act natural."

Rocky ignored me as we came to a stop and nudged his head toward the entrance. "When you were busy talking to Giles, someone else walked in…"

I followed his gaze to a skinny, wiry man in glasses. He looked like a banker and was deep in conversation with Cheeks. With his flashy suit and spectacled face, the stranger fit right in with Bryce's guests. But he wasn't here for the auction.

Holy motherfucking shit.

My mouth went dry. "How did you know?"

"Remember when I said I tried to find you after Hiram took you? I went to Blackthorne Towers," Rocky explained. "I recognized him from one of my trips. Who is he?"

"They call him the Blackbird."

The Blackbird worked for Hiram.

As much as he had a God complex, Hiram couldn't be in a thousand places at once. He liked to have eyes everywhere and had an army of minions to do his bidding. The Blackbird was one of Hiram's surveillance experts. We'd worked together many times before, and now? I was his mark.

"Should we leave?" Rocky asked as his eyes flickered to the nearest exit. "We can go right now."

"No," I insisted. "He's not a threat."

The Blackbird was in town to gather intelligence and report back to his master. In the old days, he used to do the same for me. He'd compile a file on my target and hand it over for me to finish the job. He may have his nose in every dark corner of people's business, but he'd never want to get caught up in any real action.

The Blackbird's eyes met mine from across the room.

Rocky's body vibrated in anger. "I'll fucking kill him."

"I'm not scared of him." I grinned at the Blackbird and wiggled my fingers to invite him to approach. "Let him come to us."

The Blackbird took the bait and headed in our direction. It was the first time anyone from my old life had dared show their face in Port Valentine, which meant Hiram was progressing.

"Good evening." There was no ounce of friendliness in the Blackbird's tone. "Can I steal a moment with this lady?"

"I'm not going anywhere." Rocky drew himself up to full height at my side. "Whatever you've got to say to her, you can say in front of me."

"As you wish." The Blackbird raised his eyebrows in mild bemusement. "I haven't seen you in the longest time, Kitten."

"What brings you out this way?" I countered. "A little far from home, don't you think?"

"I'm here on business." His beady eyes analyzed my expression to search for a sign of weakness. Too bad I already knew his tricks. He'd get nothing out of me. "I hear you've been settling into Port Valentine, *Candy*. You've built quite a reputation in a short space of time. I've been told you have a new tattoo and are getting married."

No doubt Cheeks had been running his mouth. It'd only take one mention of my name for him to spill his guts. After our night at the Maven, I'd abandoned him in the shipping yard licking his wounds. The next time I saw him, he'd been beaten to a pulp and the cops slapped handcuffs on his wrists. If Cheeks still couldn't remember what happened in the missing time, it was natural he'd hold me responsible — even if he'd never admit it to anyone else. Why would he want to confess to being roughed up by a stripper?

"It's none of your fucking business," Rocky growled.

"Is this the lucky man?" The Blackbird looked him up and down then frowned. "You look familiar."

"Actually, my fiancé just left," I replied hastily. "He had urgent business to take care of."

"Shame." He sniffed. "I'd have liked to make his acquaintance."

"Don't hold your breath for a wedding invitation," I snarled.

"Why don't you come home to share your news?" the Blackbird asked. "You've been away for too long. We're basically family after all these years."

"The people in Blackthorne Towers were never my fucking family. This is my home now," I said, narrowing my eyes but keeping my voice quiet enough to avoid unwanted attention. "What's wrong? Are you too scared to tell him the news yourself?"

Hiram would not be able to ignore news like this. After years of having me as his prized possession, this would make him explode.

"He'll find out soon enough, Kitty," the Blackbird said. We both knew 'killing the messenger' took on a literal meaning when Hiram was involved. "He's planning a vacation."

"I hear Hawaii is nice this time of year," I snapped.

"Is that the time already?" The Blackbird checked his watch and tutted. "I have somewhere else to be this evening, but I'm sure we'll see each other again soon."

I didn't take my eyes off his cheap suit until I watched him leave the building. He'd got what he came here for. What would he do with the information? If Hiram found out I was engaged and a member of a gang, the Sevens would be in immediate danger. A revelation like this would force Hiram to act quicker.

"Do you want to get some air?" Rocky suggested. "We can have a look around the rest of the town hall."

"Sure, why the fuck not?" I sighed. "It's not like things can get any worse."

First, my new 'fiancé' had gone AWOL on the night we'd announced our engagement. Second, the Blackbird's appearance turned my new life into a ticking time bomb. I wasn't naïve enough to think I could run from my past forever, but I wasn't ready to share it with the Sevens yet. If West regretted his decision, how could I trust them with my darkest secrets?

We slipped out of the main function room and walked through the corridors steeped in local history. Rocky pulled a hip flask from his blazer pocket. "Drink?"

I took a large swig. The further we got from the auction, the colder it got. Thankfully, Rocky's whiskey provided a much-needed alcohol jacket. We opened a door to a long narrow room that looked to be a file storage area. Small windows along one side allowed slices of moonlight to creep in and highlight layers of undisturbed dust resting on the cabinets.

"Remember how we used to go exploring?" Rocky asked as he knocked cobwebs out of his face. His head almost skimmed the ceiling. "It's like old times."

"Hardly!" I snorted. As teenagers, we'd spent summers exploring abandoned buildings and warehouses around where we grew up. Part of the fun had been setting out on an expedition and not knowing what we were going to find. "We'd never have been able to get into a place like this without someone calling the cops."

"They'd have thought we'd clean the place out," Rocky said, then chuckled fondly at the memory. Evergreen kids had a bad reputation that followed us like a contagious disease. Whenever we entered a store, the cashier's eyes never left our hands until we were back outside. "Do you miss it? Evergreen?"

"I don't think about the past." Surviving meant looking forwards. You could learn from the past, but you couldn't live in it. Nothing could change it. "Not if I can help it."

Rocky changed the subject. "Why did West leave?"

"He's not used to someone asking him hard questions," I said. "Is he always used to getting his way?"

"West doesn't do emotions. He prefers to smash things." Rocky paused as his expression turned somber. "You and him... are you... you know?"

"Wait..." I stopped in my tracks. "What?"

"I don't know, I thought you might—"

"It's called acting," I hissed. The kiss we shared didn't count. It was a mistake. I flicked my hair over my shoulder to avoid meeting his probing gaze. "It's strictly business."

"I'm glad you're here." A small smile crept over Rocky's lips. "I wanted you to stay."

"Aren't you the one who told me not to?" I raised an eyebrow. "You said it's too dangerous for me to be here, remember?"

"That didn't mean I didn't want you around," he said. "Besides, you seem to be able to take care of yourself these days."

"Maybe you should leave me to fight my own battles then? I could have handled Giles and the Blackbird myself."

"You've fought battles alone for too long." Rocky turned solemn. "I meant it when I said I'd do anything to make things right with you."

I refused to have this conversation. What good would listening to his groveling do? I turned my back on him to avoid seeing his puppy dog eyes and continued on. "I don't need your fucking pity."

"There is something I still don't understand," he called. I'd reached the end of the corridor. *Fuck.* A brick wall blocked my path, forcing me to turn around and face him. "Why didn't you kill me when you had the chance?"

"Most people would say thank you and move on."

"I want to know why." Rocky stepped closer. "All I need to hear you say is that you didn't want me to die."

I could handle a confrontation with Rocky, but facing my feelings? That was terrifying, especially when I couldn't make sense of my actions. Killing him was something I'd desperately wanted to do, but something stopped me. Why couldn't I do it?

"Why can't you just let it go?"

"I can't." He reached out to stroke my cheek. A few months ago, I'd have broken his fingers. Hell, I once wouldn't have hesitated to disembowel him on sight. But his touch scrambled my thoughts and made me light-headed. "Because I can't let you go, C. I never have. I never will."

"Rocky…" My voice faded into the distance as I looked into his eyes.

"I need to hear you say it," he repeated. "You wanted me to live, didn't you?"

"What difference does it make?"

"I want you to admit it." The heat radiating from his body sent tingles racing over my skin. "You didn't want to let me go either."

"Rocky, I can't—"

Before I could finish my sentence, his lips silenced me.

The last kiss we shared had been years before, but so much had changed. We were no longer the two kids who dreamed of a better future. Rocky had grown into a man, and I'd become someone the old me wouldn't recognize in a mirror. Both of us bore fresh scars, held dark secrets, and had done unspeakable acts, but… if we'd both changed so much since our first kiss, then why did it suddenly feel like everything was the same?

I *should* want to push him away.

I *should* want to rip out his tongue and make him choke on it.

I *should* want to leave this town and never look back.

But, like the night I held my knife to his throat, I was rendered powerless.

My body responded to his kiss like a flower, turning to the sun, desperate to catch the last rays before darkness closed in. Rocky cupped my face like he held the entire universe in his hands. His mouth explored mine like it was the last thing he'd ever taste, and his body anchored me to the present like we were the last people left on Earth.

"I've missed you, C," he murmured, tracing the length of my collarbone gently with the tip of his finger. "So fucking much."

In the movies, this would be where I'd collapse into his arms and we'd swear our undying love to each other. Everyone knows real life doesn't work that way. True love doesn't exist. Our relationship was complicated, our history messy and our colliding again? Another fucking disaster waiting to happen.

How could he have gone from the top of my hit list to someone I made out with?

Reality burst the surrounding air with a bang, and realization rained down on me faster than a flash flood. It didn't matter that being in his arms felt like returning home. I needed to remember that 'home' didn't exist. It was nothing but a pile of ash because he'd set any chance we had of a future in flames. He'd ruined it. He'd ruined everything.

I pushed Rocky back, knocking him off balance.

"What's wrong?" His eyes widened. "I thought—"

"You thought wrong."

"I may not want you dead." I stripped all the emotion from my tone. "But it doesn't mean I want you."

"You're lying, C!" He grabbed my arm to stop me. "How can you say that after—"

"Don't." I shut him down. "We're only here because we have a job to do. The auction is about to start."

Rocky had broken my heart once before. He'd never get the chance to do it again. No one would. After what happened, a gaping hole was left in my chest from where he'd blown it to smithereens.

————

Zander's glare of disapproval burned into us as we walked back into the main hall. "You're late."

"It's not even started yet," I said, hoping he didn't notice my breathlessness from moving as quickly as my heels could carry me. Zander's stare had a disconcerting way of seeing past any bullshit. "We're here now, aren't we?"

"Where have you two been, anyway?" Vixen asked, as Rocky and I took our seats in stony silence. I'd vowed not to look at him again all night. What happened between us could never happen again. "You missed me almost knock out Giles."

"Quiet!" Zander silenced her as the auctioneer took to the stage.

I struggled to pay attention through the bidding war. The usual items you'd expect to see were sold for ridiculous prices: vases, jewelry, spa days, personalized photoshoots, and indulgent picnic baskets. Who even went for a picnic in winter? The prizes were meaningless, anyway. They were nothing but an elaborate ruse to keep wives or mistresses happy. While they appeared to be bidding on luxurious goods, it was a facade to hide the real trading happening under the tables. They were leveraging drugs or the services of the Briarly goons under the guise of charity. It made me sick.

"Finally, we have a last-minute addition from an anonymous donor," the auctioneer's voice boomed, causing Bryce to straighten in his seat as an item concealed by a red curtain was wheeled onstage. Zander leaned forward. This was the moment he'd been waiting for. The auctioneer pulled back the curtain to reveal a large framed painting. "And here we are!"

That was it? I'd wanted something a little more dramatic: an active bomb, or a severed head on a podium, perhaps? However, judging from Bryce's reddening cheeks, his perfectly controlled exterior was crumbling.

He hated surprises, and the last-minute auction prize had ruined his evening.

"No fucking way." Vixen's mouth fell open. "How? I thought he got rid of them all..."

"Not all of them," Zander replied smugly and raised a glass in his father's direction.

I looked at the portrait again. I'd seen it once before. It was the same picture West and I collected from the junkyard. The women's beauty was even more apparent blown up on a large canvas. Whoever she was, Bryce Briarly wanted her to be forgotten.

"Who is she?" I asked.

"My mother," Zander said. Most families had their fair share of problems, but the Briarlys took it to an extreme. No amount of therapy could heal the issues they had; analyzing their family dynamics would be enough to send a shrink crazy. "It's a story for another time."

The auctioneer signaled for bids to begin. Watching Zander and his father felt like being in the middle of a ping-pong game. The rest of the room observed with bated breath, both mesmerized and horrified.

"It's too much," Vixen hissed. The war between them reached a boiling point. The bidding had racked up to an eye-watering one hundred thousand dollars. It blew my mind how people could play with huge amounts of money like pocket change. "You need to stop."

"I will." Zander raised the paddle once more. "Soon."

"Do we have two hundred thousand dollars?" the auctioneer called.

Zander didn't move.

The slam of the hammer confirmed Bryce's win. "Sold!"

"You were bidding him up, right?" I whispered.

"Perhaps." Zander shrugged, then winked. "He doesn't need to know I made copies."

"Now, that's over with, can we finally get out of here and get home?" Vixen asked. "I'm done with these people."

Rocky slammed his glass down. "A-fucking-men."

"Change of plan," Zander cut in to dash their hopes, "we're staying in a hotel."

"A hotel?" Vixen groaned. "You've gotta be fucking kidding."

"Quit it!" I nudged her in the ribs. Wherever we stayed would beat returning to my dump of an apartment. "What the boss says goes."

"If I'd known it'd only take a hotel room to get you to comply," Zander murmured under his breath, so only I could hear, "then I'd have booked one sooner."

"Before you leave, cousin." Giles arrived at our table like a foul smell. "I want to thank you for your generous donation on behalf of the whole Briarly family."

"You may be the new Briarly heir, Giles." Zander rose from his seat, spitting out the words like bullets. "But it doesn't mean you'll ever be part of this family."

The landscape had been set for an upcoming battle.

CHAPTER

Three

Holy hell, the bedsheets were Egyptian cotton. They were even softer than the white, fluffy robe wrapped up around me like a fucking cloud. I fully intended to take it when we checked out.

"Do you want more ice cream brought up?" I asked, flicking through the television channels.

With Zander and Rocky staying on another floor, I wouldn't miss the opportunity to take advantage of room service when Zander's would cover the bill. Sharing a room with Vixen was bearable when you had an unlimited stream of desserts, complimentary slippers, and mini soap bars in cute shapes.

"I still don't get why we have to stay in a hotel." Vixen tucked into a piece of decadent chocolate cake, topped with a gold leaf. "We could have taken a car back. Fuck knows, we have enough of them."

"Come on, I bet this beats your cell in juvie…"

"Don't pretend like you know my history," she snapped. "You have no idea."

I rolled over to face her. "Why don't you enlighten me?"

"It was no fucking sleepover." Vixen's face darkened. "You had to stick together if you wanted to make it through your years at Redlake. Not everyone was so lucky."

"Redlake?" I nearly fell out of the bed. "You mean *the* Redlake?"

The place was infamous. A few years back, Redlake Juvenile Corrections Center made national headlines when an undercover operation revealed horrifying details of what prisoners endured under the wardens' care. The entire place got shut down. Ex-detainees were paid to cover up the worst of what happened and were forced to sign NDAs. Maybe that's why I'd never heard either of them mention their time there before. Paying for silence hadn't stopped the rumors from spreading, though…

"I told you, not every member of the Briarly family grew up in the fucking manor," she said bitterly, then changed the subject. "Now, it's your turn. Are you going to tell me why lover boy did a runner at the auction?"

I admired the ring on my hand, which still felt alien, and shrugged. "I guess we had our first lover's tiff."

"He's been acting so weird recently." Vixen shook her head. "He needs to snap out of it before he screws shit up."

"I mean, it didn't help that Cheeks told him Penelope was back in town…"

She stabbed her sponge violently. "I bet the bastard loved delivering that news."

"So?" I probed. "What's the deal? Who is she?"

"It's not my story to tell," Vixen said, then pursed her lips while wrestling with her urge to tell me more. She decided against it. "All you need to know is that she hurt him. She's no fucking good for him. If I get my hands on her again, I'll wring her scrawny neck."

"Are you always so protective?"

"Only when he could do better," she said pointedly. Although, I doubted anyone would match up to her high standards.

"How long have you known West?" I asked.

She and Zander were related, Rocky had joined the Sevens after their stint in juvie, but where did West fit into the picture?

"As long as I've known Zander," she replied. "He and Zander went to boarding school together. He used to stay in the manor during summer break."

"West?" I spluttered. "He went to boarding school?"

Unlike Zander, he didn't seem the type to have been born onto a golden throne. What else didn't I know about the gang I'd sworn my loyalty to forever? Each new scrap of information only raised a thousand more questions.

BAM!

Our hotel room door swung open. I jumped to my feet like an abominable snowman and flicked open my knife. It's a good thing I carried it at all times. I clasped its hilt and held it out, ready to slash whoever stepped inside.

Zander clicked the door shut behind him. "Easy, little one…"

"You could have fucking knocked." I reluctantly tucked the blade back into my pocket. "What do you want?"

Zander's lip curled in disapproval as he surveyed the empty plates and glasses. Liking to snack wasn't a fucking crime. Zander was a possessive asshole who thought him making the rules made me his property. If he knew everything that happened at the auction, our midnight sugar boost would be the least of his worries.

He looked at the two of us. "Did you really think tonight was just an excuse to have a sleepover?"

"How were we supposed to know you had other plans?" I challenged. "You don't exactly like sharing your plans with the rest of us, do you?"

"You knew I made the rules when you agreed to join us," Zander snarled. "Don't question me."

"The rules?" I laughed coldly. "What I *expected* is for you to tell us what's going on. From what I've seen so far, the only thing you want to do is taunt daddy dearest."

"If I wanted your opinion," he said, the darkness behind his eyes stirred, "I'd have asked for it."

"Can't you guys keep it down?" Vixen yawned, cranking up the volume on the cartoon she was watching. "This is my favorite."

Zander snatched the remote and cut short the episode.

"Killjoy," she muttered.

"When I agreed to join the Sevens, I didn't think I'd be playing the role of the trophy wife," I continued. "When I say I'm in, it means I'm all in. I expected *more*."

"You want to be all in?" Zander reached into his pocket. If he made a move to hurt me, I wouldn't hesitate to shred his expensive suit into ribbons. Instead of drawing a gun, he retrieved a key card and held it out. "Now is your chance to prove it."

I snatched it from him. "Go on."

Nothing intrigued me more than a challenge.

"We're not the only ones staying in this hotel tonight," he said. "This is the key to the penthouse suite where my father is paying for Cheeks to stay."

"You want me to kill him, right?"

Zander threw back his head and laughed in what looked to be genuine amusement. "Patience, little one."

"Is that a no?" I sighed. Killing Cheeks wouldn't be the worst way to end an evening. After my encounter with Rocky, I could do with expelling the extra energy.

"I appreciate your enthusiasm," Zander said. "But don't you think you've racked up enough bodies in your time here already?"

I bit my tongue. Based on my previous record, I'd basically lived as a nun since arriving in Port Valentine, but Zander didn't need to know that. Up until this point, both of us had honored our agreement. He wouldn't probe into my past, as long as I followed his rules.

"If you don't want me to kill him, what do you want me to do?"

"Cheeks had a little *too* much fun with some girls." Zander pulled a USB stick from another pocket like a magician would pull a rabbit out of a hat. What else was he hiding behind the pinstripes? "One of them ended up in the hospital with a broken jaw."

Vixen threw her fork, sending chocolate sauce flying over the room. "What a piece of shit."

I recalled how handsy Cheeks was when we went to the Maven. He'd messed with the wrong girl. If I hadn't known how to defend myself, the night could have had a different outcome. You'd think the bastard would have learned his lesson. I'd already given him a warning. It's time he got a little refresher he'd never forget.

"How did you get the footage?" I asked. As I said it, I already worked out the answer, "Cupid."

One of my old connections, Q — known to everyone else as Cupid — worked closely with the Sevens. As well as being the best money launderer in the biz, he ran a safe house for women trying to get out of prostitution and to make it safer for those who had no other choice. Q despised nothing more than a man who laid a finger on a woman. He'd be happy to bring a bastard like Cheeks down.

"I'm sure our old friend wouldn't want this video falling into the wrong hands," Zander said, dangling the stick in front of me like a carrot. "What do you think?"

"Fine." I took it. "What do you want from him in return?"

"I want eyes and ears on my father," Zander said. Anything less than killing him seemed like a waste of my fucking time, but I had to follow his orders. "I trust you can be very persuasive?"

Knowing Cheeks, it wouldn't take much persuasion to get him to do what I wanted. The gutless bastard would be scared of returning to jail and ruining what was left of his pretty face. Unlike cats, roaches don't have nine fucking lives.

I pouted. "Are you sure you don't want me to bring you his head?"

A small ghost of a smile haunted Zander's lips. He understood the darkness. Like me, he lived and breathed it.

"When we've got what we want from him, I'll let you do the honors," he promised. "But we're doing this my way first."

I wouldn't trust Cheeks to butter a slice of toast — let alone pass along sensitive information on Bryce. However, Zander must have logic behind his motives. If we wanted to take down the Briarly empire, we needed access to Bryce's inner circle. Cheeks had been at its center for years. He'd also made his dislike of the Sevens clear, so Bryce would never suspect him of working with us.

"Fine," I said. "We'll try it your way."

"You wanted to prove yourself," he said as he turned to leave, "so fucking prove it."

Challenge accepted.

"How do you do that?" Vixen stared at me open-mouthed as Zander slammed the door behind him. "He never compromises."

"I'd hardly call that a compromise," I said. "Maybe he likes the thought of Cheeks's head as a Christmas gift? It'd look good on top of the tree. "

She snorted. "You're seriously fucked up."

"So I've been told." My mind was already racing with the possibilities of how we were going to pull this off. "Now, go back to watching cartoons. I've got work to do."

"*We* have work to do," she corrected.

"I work better alone."

"You're part of the Sevens now. We're in this together, remember?" A slow smile spread over Vixen's face. "Besides, I wouldn't mind teaching the bastard a lesson."

"Have it your way," I said. "Just try not to throw up around blood this time."

———

"Finally!" Vixen sighed. For the past two hours, we'd questioned whether Cheeks would return to the hotel at all. "Where the fuck has he been?"

From our window, we watched Cheeks stagger drunkenly down the street with a woman on his arm. It's no coincidence Zander had chosen this room. It gave us the best vantage point of the entrance. Had the painting stunt been a warm-up to throw Bryce off the real reason we'd decided to gate crash?

"He's wasted," I said. He couldn't walk in a straight line. "He won't be getting it up tonight."

"Nothing kills a boner more than a gun pointed in your face."

"But we don't have a—"

"Actually," Vixen interrupted, pulling up her pant leg to reveal a Glock, "we do."

After being held at gunpoint, she'd spent a lot of hours at the shooting range over the last few months. Society teaches little girls to play with dolls and finger paint, whilst boys play with tanks and soldiers. In reality, every woman should know how to defend themselves. What's going to help save your life: learning how to get out of a chokehold or how to make a chicken pot pie?

"I've been practicing," she said proudly.

"I'm impressed." I grinned, then nodded twice. That was our signal. "Let's fucking do this."

We had a limited time frame to work with. It wouldn't be long before the maids started their morning rounds, so we had no margin for error. We had one chance and no room for mistakes. I also couldn't shake the feeling this was another of Zander's games. After cleaning up five bodies I'd left behind, he knew exactly what I was capable of. He wanted to test my self-control... and my loyalty.

After giving Cheeks enough time to stumble to the penthouse, we slipped out of our room and up the three flights of stairs to his floor. Thankfully, his taste for finer things had its advantages. We had no adjoining rooms to worry about.

"Shh." I pressed my finger to my lips, as Vixen didn't cushion the slamming of the stairwell door.

"Chill out." She rolled her eyes. "We've got this."

I pulled out the key card and held up three fingers to begin the countdown. We could use the element of surprise to our advantage.

3... Vixen raised her gun...

2... I swiped the card in the slot...

1... it flashed green.

Bingo. We were in.

I turned the handle.

"Who is it?" Cheeks slurred from the bed. "Another whore come to join us?"

We charged inside. The sight of Cheeks in his underpants groping a girl in skimpy underwear turned my stomach. Angry marks around her throat made me want to defy Zander's orders, but I took a deep breath. As much as it pained me to leave the fucker breathing, we had to stick to the plan.

"Get out of here," Vixen hissed at the girl, spotting Cheeks's wallet and throwing it at her. *Nice touch.* "Keep the change."

She ran without turning back, leaving the three of us alone. Hiram taught me a target's first move would always reveal their hiding place when taken by surprise. Cheeks lurched towards the bedside table. He knew better than to travel unarmed. Unlike him, I didn't need a weapon to feel comfortable. My most dangerous weapon was my bare fucking hands. As soon as his body twitched, I knew what he was gonna do and acted quicker than The Flash.

"Fuck!" Cheeks cried as I slammed the drawer shut on his fingers. As soon as his body twitched. *Nice fucking try.* Unfortunately for him, he couldn't move as quickly as a girl high on four bowls of ice cream. "What're you doing here?"

Vixen pointed her gun at him. "You're going to listen to what we have to say."

"C'mon, Vix. You're not going to shoot me." Cheeks laughed. "You're not like your cousin."

She cocked the weapon and aimed at his head. "Do you want to test your theory, Checkersford?"

"So you've not come here for a three-way?" he mocked.

Prison must have had an effect on him. Before, he'd never have dared speak out when staring down the barrel of a gun. Not killing him was really testing my self-restraint. *Do not kill him,* I repeated over and over like a mantra. *Do not kill him.* Instead, I slammed the wood shut on his fingers again to teach him a lesson. Would broken bones teach him to keep his grubby hands to himself, or would I have to cut them off next time?

"Do we have your attention now?" I asked. "There are worse things we could do to you, or don't you remember?"

"Okay, I'm listening," he yelped. "Let me go!"

I paused, looking at Vixen, who nodded. I released his hand and, while he massaged his broken joints like a whimpering baby, I retrieved his gun from the drawer and emptied it. What could he do with no bullets?

"Cover yourself up." I wrinkled my nose in disgust at his shrinking erection and threw him a robe. "We need to talk."

"Talk about what?" he sneered. "How you put me in jail? I'm under Bryce's protection now. He won't be happy when he finds out about this!"

"Bryce's protection only goes so far," I warned. Bryce may rule the town, but he was not invincible. "Will you do the honors, Vix?"

"Gladly," she replied, plugging the USB stick into the TV and pressing play.

The CCTV footage of Cheeks entering a bedroom with two girls flickered onto the screen.

"We'll leave it there, shall we?" I suggested, hitting pause at his first strike. None of us needed to watch the gory scene unfold. Everyone knew what happened next and, if he didn't agree to our proposal, the rest of the world would, too. Nothing would give me greater pleasure than exposing him as the monster he truly was. "Have you seen enough?"

Cheeks paled. Where was a camera when you needed one? It'd be good to capture the look of horror on his face. The threat of going back to jail was a surefire way to sober anyone up. "How did you get that?"

"Not so untouchable now, are you?" I grinned triumphantly. We had him by the fucking balls. "It doesn't matter where we got it. The only thing you need to worry about is what we're going to do with it now. You have a choice to make."

"What do you want?"

"Bryce Briarly trusts you, doesn't he?"

His face went as white as the crisp bed linen. "You want me to be a... spy?"

"You said yourself you're under his protection." I shrugged. "We need you to be the Sevens eyes and ears. That won't be too difficult, right? I mean, your head is already stuck so far up Bryce's ass."

"I can't be a mole. If he found out..." Cheeks's voice trailed away, thinking about what punishment Bryce might inflict. Forgiveness was not in his nature. "If I got caught, he would—"

"Well, you better not get caught then," I cut him off. He was out of his mind if he thought we'd pity him.

"How much do you want to get rid of the video?" Cheeks begged. "What's your price? Girls like you always have a price! Don't forget I know what you used to do and the circles you screwed around in."

"I don't want your money," I snarled, ignoring Vixen's curious stare watching me out of the corner of my eye. She didn't need to know Cheeks believed I'd fucked powerful men, like Raphael Jacobson, for money. The leaked video Hiram sent Bella when I first came to town had given me a reputation that was hard to shake. "I'm a fucking Seven now. And, if I were you, I'd start showing women a little respect."

"What if I won't do it?" His bottom lip trembled. "What happens then?"

"I'm sure your old friends will be happy to see you back in jail." I shot him a sparkling smile and ran my tongue over my canines. "I bet they've been missing you..."

"You w-w-wouldn't," he stuttered. "I know things about all of you. I can tell!"

"Who are you gonna tell? What evidence do you have?" I cocked my head to the side. He had nothing on us and he fucking knew it. "Who would believe a cokehead ex-cop? You've got nothing left."

"If I do this, what's in it for me?"

"You're only breathing because we still have a use for you," I snapped. "If you help us, the video disappears and you get to live. Think of your heart still beating blood to your cock as a gift."

"Fine," he relented. "I'll do it, okay?"

"Don't even think about crossing us." I threw him a look of pure menace. "We'll be in touch."

"Fucking bitches," he murmured under his breath.

Unlucky for him, I heard every fucking word.

"I've forgotten one thing..." I slowly spun around and punched him square in the nose. His bones cracked underneath my fist, and blood sprayed over the luxurious Texas king. The biggest tragedy was wrecking the Egyptian cotton.

"Fuck," he groaned into a pillow. "What was that for?"

"Never lay a hand on a fucking woman again," I said, grabbing a fistful of his hair and forcing him to look at my wild smile. "Next time I won't be so gentle. Understood?"

"Okay, okay," Cheeks wailed, shuddering at my murderous expression. "I understand."

"I think we're done here." I stood back to admire the blood running down his face and dusted my hands. "For now."

Vixen nodded in agreement, following me out. Punching him was a personal bonus. It's a shame we couldn't finish the job…

"You broke his nose again. Zander won't be happy," Vixen said as we headed back to the comfort of the lower floors. "What was *that*?"

"What was *what*?" I replied coyly. "Zander never specified the level of force we could use, did he? All he wanted was for Cheeks to be on our side."

She grinned. "My mistake."

It'd be our little secret. What Zander didn't know wouldn't hurt him. He may be the boss of the Sevens, but he would never be the boss of me.

———

We returned to our room to find Zander lounging over my bed like a Roman god and Rocky stuffing his face with the last of the cake we ordered.

"Well?" Zander demanded.

Before we had a chance to answer, Rocky jumped up from his chair with so much force one of its tiny legs cracked. Why did hotels insist on putting decorative chairs in every room? How many people broke them? Apart from throwing down your clothes, they served no fucking purpose at all.

"Are you hurt?" Rocky asked. He eyed the blood seeping between my fingers. "Your hand—"

"It's not mine," I snapped. At this point, I'd had more blood on my hands than lotion. It's a good thing red is my color. "We're fine."

Zander met my gaze. "I trust the job is done?"

"Do you really need to ask?" I narrowed my eyes. "I said I'd do it, didn't I? I keep my word."

"Good." He cracked his knuckles and made Vixen cringe. "That's step one."

"So?" I sat down opposite him on the bed. "What's step two?"

"Patience," he purred. "You'll see."

"Before we move onto whatever step two is," Vixen interjected, scouring the room service menu again, "can we order more food?"

"Gold leaf cake?" I suggested, making Zander's lip curl in annoyance. What was his fucking problem? It's not like he didn't have the money.

"Let's go for breakfast," Rocky said. "We'll go to the diner on the way home. The one that does the waffles you like."

Vixen threw down the menu. "Deal."

"Candy?" Rocky looked over hopefully. When he pulled that face, he reminded me of a wounded puppy. Goddammit. How could his eyes still have that effect on me? Sleep deprivation must be influencing my reasoning ability. "What do you say? Waffles?"

"I need to shower first." I may not have had a decent night's sleep in our beautiful room, but hell no would I be missing out on a hot shower. Washing in my apartment was akin to an icy hose-down. "You guys go without me."

"We'll wait," Rocky insisted.

"Okay, I'll come," I agreed grudgingly. I wasn't getting out of this one. "But they better be great waffles."

Rocky smiled, reminding me of the teenager I used to know. "You won't be disappointed."

Suddenly, I felt light-headed. Thoughts of our earlier kiss flooded my mind. A few months ago, I could have taken his life. Getting my revenge had been one of the main reasons I'd stayed in Port Valentine. How could a flash of a smile and the invitation to eat waffles send me spiraling to a place I'd sworn never to return? I needed to get my shit together. Joining the Sevens and sparing his life didn't mean falling back into his arms. I couldn't allow my guard to slip around him… not again.

CHAPTER
Four

I rolled my eyes at Zander's earlier text.

Car is waiting outside. Bring an overnight bag.

Did he get his kicks from being mysterious all the time? He only ever told us the bare minimum. After our night at the auction, I'd hoped he may become more forthcoming about his plans. His whole 'puppeteer' act was growing old real fast. One person couldn't run an entire fucking show. Wasn't the point of a gang to do things together?

"It's good of you to show up," I muttered, tapping my foot impatiently, as Zander stormed into his office with West in tow. They both had serious stony-faced expressions.

This was typical of Zander. After summoning me, he'd left me to twiddle my thumbs for half an hour. Didn't he know I had a bunch of Netflix shows waiting to be watched? If a series got spoiled, I'd hold him personally responsible. Likewise, if I got back pain after sitting in this uncomfortable as fuck chair, I'd sue.

Zander took a seat behind his desk opposite me. "I've got a job for both of you."

West stayed standing in the doorway like he couldn't wait to get away, and grunted like an overgrown gorilla. *How charming.* Couldn't he use words now? My PMS raged like a bitch, but West gave me a serious run for my money. The last time we saw each other, he bolted without explanation. Judging by the scowl on his face, his bad mood hadn't lifted. I didn't know who Penelope was, or what she meant to him, but West needed to get his head in the game if we were going to work together.

"Is this part of your big plan?" I asked, resting my elbows on the wood and leaning in closer. "What's our next move?"

"I told you to be patient, little one." Zander lounged back with an all-knowing smirk. "This job is related to something else. You and West are going to head to the Seven Sins casino in Hammerville."

Another road trip with West wasn't top of my list of things I wanted to do. At the junkyard, West almost killed a man. If I hadn't acted quickly, we would have had a dead body to deal with and no package. It was a dumb stroke of luck I found the painting amongst the trash in Eddie's trailer — not that Zander needed to know it'd been a disaster. If Zander found out about what really happened, he'd never send the two of us out again... especially if he learned about the kiss we shared on the ride home.

"What do you want us to do?" I questioned, keeping my back turned away from West. "Don't you have enough money?"

We'd won a quarter of a million dollars at the poker game in Briarly Manor. How fast did he burn through cash? Apart from the new club floor, the Sevens hadn't made any major investments. He had to have other motives, besides topping up his piggy bank, to warrant us traveling four hours to a casino in the middle of nowhere.

"This isn't about money. I want you to pay a visit to the manager," Zander said. "West will know what to do next."

Leaving the job in the hands of a man who could only speak one syllable didn't seem like a fantastic idea, but Zander said no more. If I wanted clear instructions, I should have referred to my daily fucking horoscope.

I jutted out my hip. "Why can't Vixen go instead of me?"

I used sass to cover my apprehension. My last trip to a casino ended in watching my best friend bleed to death on the sidewalk. Crystal wanted to skip town and start over with Q, but Hiram's men gunned her down before she got the chance. I couldn't do anything to stop it. Her death had been one of the worst moments of my life, and it showed me who Hiram really was. Pure fucking evil. Would visiting Seven Sins bring it all back?

"Because you're a couple now, remember?" Zander hissed viciously. How could I forget when I had to wear a ruby ring on my finger to declare my ownership like a fucking collar? I couldn't take it off in case it shattered our ruse. "And because I asked you."

"Lucky me!" I rolled my eyes sarcastically. Now, I knew how Harry felt when he got singled out by Voldie for being the chosen one. Why couldn't I be a fucking Neville?

"It's one night," Zander said. "I'm sure you can play nice for an evening."

"I'm not the one you should be worried about," I said, throwing West a filthy look that bounced off his muscles like they were made from iron. His jaw clenched, but he didn't break his sulky silence.

"Remember my rules, Candy," Zander warned, then began tapping away on his keyboard to show we'd been dismissed.

"I guess we'll see you tomorrow then," I muttered, then turned to glower at my new partner in crime. "I'll wait outside."

———

After spending two hours of the drive in frosty silence, West's snarky attitude was pushing me over the fucking line. Adjusting the AC had been our only form of interaction. We'd launched a passive-aggressive war over stable temperature. Whenever he turned it up, I'd flip it down. He had no appreciation for my freshly blow-dried hair, and I wouldn't let him ruin my hard work.

"Would you fucking stop it?" I yelled, slapping his hand away as he reached for the switch again. Usually, I wouldn't be the first to break a silence. But we were on a business trip. Someone had to back down for the greater good. I'd be the bigger person if he was gonna keep acting like a fucking child.

"Stop what?"

The bastard.

"You know what," I hissed, narrowing my eyes at him. "I don't know what shit you have going on, but could you at least try not to ruin my hair in the process?"

West didn't respond. He kept his gaze fixed on the stretch ahead and pretended he hadn't heard me.

"Are you going to keep trying to ignore me this whole trip?"

"If I can," he replied, "but something tells me I'm not going to have a choice."

"Why don't we have it out, huh?" We needed to sort out his issues before he derailed our plans. He couldn't lose control. Not again. Next time, I might not be able to bring him back from the brink. "I won't let you fuck this job up because you're distracted."

"I'm not distracted."

"Look," I said, trying to reason with him, "I know hearing your old piece of skirt is in town must be like a kick to the balls but—"

He slammed his foot on the gas, his voice rising above the roar of the engine. "Be careful what you say next, Pinkie."

"Point proven!" I gripped the edge of my seat as we flew down the highway like part of a high-speed chase. "Real fucking mature, West."

"You need to stay out of my fucking business," he growled. "You don't know what you're talking about."

"I know if you don't slow the fuck down, we'll be splattered over the highway for the next two miles. And another one of your cars will be a fiery wreck."

He relented slightly, slowing to a speed that wasn't in the triple digits.

"Sorry," he murmured. At least he had the decency to look remorseful. Every time I rode in a car with West, I put my life in his hands. "I used to race… and I forget sometimes."

"Clearly." Interrogating West about Penelope when he was behind the wheel was a massive no-no, so I focused my attention on our task ahead. "Are you going to tell me why we're going to see the casino manager?"

"Nico is an old friend," West said. "We have some business to take care of."

"So, we're going to have a reunion?"

"Something like that..."

"How enlightening." Hadn't he learned his lesson after keeping me in the dark last time?

I craned my neck to look out the window as we drove past the 'Welcome to Hammerville' sign. Someone had crossed out the town's name and scrawled 'hell' over it. What a great omen. We kept on going, passing buildings that had fallen to ruin, then pulled into the parking lot of an aged motel. If it wasn't for the lights inside, I'd have thought it was closed down.

"We're staying here?" I asked. The two-story building looked like it'd burnt to the ground and been rebuilt using mismatching materials. It wouldn't meet any building codes. "Really?"

"What's wrong? We need somewhere to stay after visiting the casino." West grinned, the first real smile that had crossed his lips in weeks. His silver-plated canine glinted maliciously in the sunlight. "Is it not up to your standards, princess?"

"You've been to my apartment, right? You're the one I'm worried about," I scoffed, wiping the smile straight off his smug face. "I bet this was nothing like your private school."

He looked at me in anger. "Who told you about that?"

"It's not a secret, is it?"

"Wait here," he spat. "Don't fucking go anywhere."

When he returned, I looked from him to the lone key chain swinging around his finger. "Just the one?"

He raised an eyebrow. "Don't you think it'd look suspicious for a newly engaged couple not to be sharing a room?"

"It doesn't look like the sort of place where people ask questions," I said, nudging my head toward someone scoring crystal meth at the opposite end of the lot. Couples staying in separate rooms was the least suspicious activity going on. "But, be warned, I may stab you in your sleep if you snore."

Our room was on the second floor. The place had a damp, stagnant odor of rat piss and cheap pine air freshener to mask it. It's the kind of motel you'd take someone to before driving out to the woods and shooting them in the head.

West scowled as he surveyed the set-up. "I asked for a twin room."

"We're a couple, remember?" I rolled my eyes. "Don't worry, I won't bite. Hey, we can make a pillow wall, if you like?"

He threw me a dirty look. Would we both fit in the bed? It looked like a double and, for West alone, it'd be a tight squeeze. My cheeks heated at the thought.

"I'm going to hit the shower," he said. "Then we'll head out."

"But it's not even six yet." I checked the grimy clock on the wall, which ticked at an annoyingly loud volume. "Aren't we going at night?"

"We're going to dinner first."

"Like a date?" I teased.

He slammed the bathroom door behind him. The sound of water hammering down drowned out my laughter. I guess a date with The Hulk may not be the worst thing in the world…

———

West took longer than any person I'd ever known to shower. What did he do in there? Knowing his obsessive cleanliness, he probably had to deep clean the entire bathroom before stripping down.

He returned in a cloud of heady cologne. He wore casual attire; his white T-shirt displayed his tattoo sleeves and accentuated his masterpiece of a body. How many hours did he spend working out to stay in shape? Even in a simple tee and jeans, he wouldn't look out of place in statue form at an art gallery.

I twirled around to show off my outfit. "What do you think?"

While he'd been using up all the motel's water, I'd salvaged my frizz with a blow dryer that almost electrocuted me. Thankfully, I'd packed the right clothes for the occasion. I'd stolen a tight leopard print dress from the costume closet at Lapland before any of the dancers had a chance to wear it. The stretchy fabric hugged my curves and the spaghetti straps showed off my rose tattoos.

West's voice came out in a low gravelly rumble, "It's okay."

After joining the Sevens, Zander gave explicit orders that he didn't want me to dance anymore. I may have followed his rules… so far. But it didn't mean I couldn't take advantage of the Seven perks, like raiding the closet whenever I liked. I pulled on my leather jacket to complete the look. "You sure know how to charm a girl, West."

West grunted. His opinion didn't matter, anyway. The dress made me feel like a wild cat who couldn't be tamed. No one would get past me. Whatever lay ahead, I was ready to kick fucking ass.

"Where are you taking me then, husband-to-be?"

"I know a place."

He always knew the best spots to go for food. I still hadn't gotten over the orgasmic donut breakfast he'd once brought me, so my expectations were high.

A man wolf-whistled in my direction as we headed to the car. I wiggled my fingers in greeting. Hey, at least someone noticed when I'd taken over an hour to get ready. Before the poor guy had time to speak, a single glare from West turned his face ashen. No one wanted to be mown down by a man who looked like a fucking Transformer. *What a cock block.*

I pouted as West held the door open. "Do you have to ruin all the fun?"

"Just get in the fucking car, Pinkie," West warned, slamming the door closed as soon as I swung my ankle inside. He got in after me, cursing under his breath.

"You seem to know where you're going," I commented as we drove through the back roads of Hammerville. Apart from motels, bars, fast food joints, and an array of strip bars, there were no other signs of life. It reminded me of downtown Port Valentine. Another perfect hedonist's escape.

"Of course, I do." West chuckled. "Don't tell me you haven't worked it out yet? You don't think it's an accident the casino is called *Seven* Sins, do you?"

"I..." I faltered. I'd dismissed the name as a coincidence, but I should have known better. "You mean, we fucking own it?"

"Yeah, but the place pretty much runs itself now. All we do is check in now and again," West explained with a shrug. "We only lived here for a few years, but it was where the Sevens were born. It's how we got our name."

"Why didn't you tell me before?"

I'd thought they'd always lived in Port Valentine, close to the confines of Briarly Manor. What made them leave and start over, then want to return later? It's not like Zander and Bryce had a strong father-son bond. They hated each other.

"Don't you like surprises, Pinkie?" West asked, taking a sharp turn.

"No." I scowled, annoyed with myself for not figuring it out sooner. "Are there any more hidden businesses you're not telling me about in godforsaken towns in the middle of bumfuck nowhere?"

"No, that's it." West laughed. "Despite how it looks, Hammerville isn't all bad. It has Big Al's. Trust me, it's the best steakhouse you'll ever visit. The place is hidden away. Only the locals know about it. Look, it's up ahead..."

I raised my eyebrows. It may have the best steak but, from the outside, the building looked close to falling apart. A gust of wind threatened to blow the windows from their frames and the restaurant's faded sign was unreadable. "Are you sure things haven't changed since you were last in town?"

"Trust me," West said. "It's the best."

Sure, biting cocks off had made me less picky about what I put in my mouth, but I was still choosy about what I'd swallow. West better be right.

The bell above the door alerted the server to our presence. A plump older woman hobbled over. It was hard to tell whether she was seventy or ninety. Either way, she looked too old to be working. Upon seeing West, her cheeks reddened in delight. She hurried over and threw her arms around him.

"It's been too long," she cried, squeezing him tightly. "Why'd you not come to visit me anymore, huh?"

"Easy, Pattie. I've been busy, but I'm here now." He laughed. Was that a blush on The Hulk's face? "Still looking as good as ever."

"You're not getting off that easy!" She swatted away his compliment with her notepad and turned her attention to me. "And who is this young lady? Is this your girlfriend, West? She must be pretty special for you to have brought her to Big Al's."

"This is Candy," he introduced grudgingly.

"It's good to meet you, hon," Pattie said, then turned her head to West. She had a warm aura that made you feel at home instantly. "You never bring girls in here, do you?"

He scowled to hide a smile. They were obviously fond of each other.

"I'll take ya'll to your favorite booth," she said, leading the way to a corner booth in the back. "You two lovebirds take your time with the menu."

"We don't need a menu." West shook his head as we sat down. "We'll both take my usual."

"Coming right up," she chirped. If Pattie's smile wasn't so damn contagious, I'd have snatched the menus straight out of her hands to decide for myself.

I folded my arms and pouted as she hurried away. "I don't like guys ordering for me."

West winked. "You'll enjoy *me* ordering for you."

With his track record of providing delicious food, I'd take the risk. Besides, seeing Pattie again had started to lift his energy-sucking mood. Maybe our trip wouldn't be unbearable after all...

"You used to come here a lot, huh?" I asked.

"All the time." He draped his hands over the side of the booth. "You'll see why."

I rolled my eyes. "Why did you and Zander pick here to open a casino? You could have gone anywhere."

"To get things up and running, then—" He cut himself off, realizing he'd revealed too much. "Let's just say, people don't ask many questions here."

"Now, I'm intrigued." I leaned forward and dropped my voice. They'd laid deep roots, which meant our visit was about more than reuniting with an old friend. "So, there's more to this place than the Seven Sins?"

"Forget it," he warned as his eyes darted around the restaurant. We'd have to have the conversation behind closed doors. Whatever business they'd started, West didn't want it to be broadcast around a small town where rumors spread like wildfire. Pattie returned to place two cool beers down and cut the lingering tension. "Thanks, Pattie."

She pinched his cheek like he was a child. "It is so good to see you again, Westie."

I raised an eyebrow. "Westie?"

"Don't," he growled.

"Okay, so you don't want to talk about your time here..." I took a long swig, leaving behind a perfect red lipstick smudge on my glass. "Why don't you tell me about how you and Zander met instead?"

"Why do you care?"

"I'm curious," I said. "You keep saying I don't know you. How can I if you don't let me?"

"We met when we were kids," he said after a long pause. "My ma died before I started school. My pa worked for Bryce. I used to spend summers at the manor with Zander. We were the only kids around."

I found it hard to imagine either of the two men as young boys. Between them, I'd bet they got into their fair share of trouble. With Port Valentine's overlord and a henchmen for a father, neither of them stood a chance.

"When my pa died on a job, Bryce took pity on me," he said bitterly. "Paid for me to go to school. He said it's what my dad would have wanted."

"And was it? You know, what he wanted?"

"I wouldn't know." West drained half of his glass. "The only thing my pa cared about was screwing whores and sorting his next fucking fix. He didn't give a rat's ass about what happened to me. If he didn't give a shit when he was alive, why'd he care if he was dead? The Sevens are my real family."

Family was about more than the blood running through your veins and the Sevens? They'd chosen and formed their kin.

"What was school like?"

"I knew what they thought of me." West shrugged like he didn't give a shit, but I could tell he was trying to cover up his true feelings. Being an outcast had affected him more than he wanted to admit. "Why did a hillbilly with a dead meth addict dad have to share their corridors?"

I related to West's feeling of not belonging more than he knew. As a kid from the Evergreen group home, I'd never felt a sense of being part of something. In grade school, I'd sat down in the canteen, and others at the table got up to move. It scared them that my misfortune might tarnish their own charming, perfect lives. We were the kids you didn't want to get paired with on a group project. We didn't get invited to slumber parties. We got picked last for sports. In High School, Rocky had been the only exception because he made the football team.

"But everyone knew who paid for me to go," West continued. "Even as kids, they knew better than to mess with a Briarly."

"I don't know whether you were lucky or unlucky."

"It's a question I've asked myself. The jury's still out," West said. "Enough about me. It's your turn."

Thankfully, Pattie spared me from answering. She arrived balancing two massive plates of steaks with fried mushrooms on her arms. It looked out of this freaking world.

"Cooked just how you like 'em." She slapped the gigantic mounds of food in front of us. "Medium rare."

Thank fuck he hadn't burned them to a crisp.

"You've always had a great memory, Pattie," West said.

"I never forget an order." She beamed and slapped him playfully with a towel. "I'll be back with the rest of it."

My mouth fell open. "The rest of it?"

Poor Pattie had to make multiple trips. West's 'usual' comprised pretty much everything on the menu. Enough to feed five people easily.

I lifted my fork to my mouth. "Well, here goes…"

My tastebuds launched into cartwheels. *Holy shit. What seasoning did they use?* I rarely ate mountain man-sized portions, but I refused to waste a mouthful of heaven. Thankfully, my dress was made from a stretchy fabric.

"I told you." West grinned from across the table. "Just wait until you try the mashed potatoes."

"Mmm!" They were whipped up, perfectly smooth, and deliciously buttery. A small moan escaped me, and West's eyes rested on my lips. "They're fucking good."

"Does that mean you'll let me order for you again?"

I licked my fork clean. "Maybe."

Who was I kidding? He could order for me anytime. Even if we didn't go anywhere else, our meal had made suffering through West's sulk worth it. If I was on death row ordering my final feast, this would be my go-to.

"Do you always scout out the best places to eat wherever you go?"

"It's a hobby," he said. "Not that I need to eat out since living with Zander. He makes a mean steak..."

"Zander is a good cook?"

The thought of our scary suited boss donning an apron made me almost choke as I fought back a giggle. There again, Zander's meticulous nature would be well-suited to following a complex recipe. He'd execute a meal with fine-tuned culinary precision.

"Don't tell him I told you," he said. "Can you cook?"

"You'll be lucky if I made you a slice of toast without burning it." I snorted. Give me a body to dissect over making a Thanksgiving meal any day. I'd never had access to a proper kitchen to hone my skills. In Blackthorne Towers, Hiram's chef cooked me a diet of rabbit food. Since then, packet mac and cheese has become my specialty.

"Maybe I can ask Zander to teach me?" I joked.

West gripped his fork tightly, making his knuckles go white and his eyes darken. "I'm sure Zander wants to teach you a lot of things."

His sudden change of mood cast a thunder cloud over our booth, and we ate in silence. After we finished, West left a stash of cash on the table and a generous tip for Pattie.

"Let's go," he ordered. "We've got business to do."

I t felt too soon after Crystal's death to step into a casino, but I did my damndest to make sure West didn't notice my shaking hands. I ran through my mental checklist: tits out, lip gloss on, head held high… *you've got this, Candy.*

"Mr. Parker." The security guard on the door bowed his head so low his beefy chin vanished into his neck. "Welcome back."

West took my arm. "Welcome to Seven Sins."

As soon as my heel hit the sticky carpet, a suited man in his forties strode over to greet us. His teeth almost glowed from too many whitening strips, and his slicked-back hair hinted he took longer than a Lapland dancer to get ready.

"West!" The stranger opened his arms wide. "I heard you were in town."

West grinned. "News travels fast, Nico."

"You brought company too?" Nico held out his hand. "Let me introduce myself. I'm Nico, the manager here. It's a pleasure."

"Candy," I said. Nico's handshake reminded me of a flaccid dick coated in lube. "It's always nice to meet one of West's old friends."

"Why don't we all go somewhere to talk over a drink?"

"We can't stay long," West warned.

Thankfully, the casino was smaller than those I was used to. It was a rundown joint, where people came to kill time on a stopover. We wove through the sea of whirring slot machines. Cameras followed our every move as if someone was watching behind the lens. If Nico worked for us, why were we being followed?

"West!" A high-pitched woman's voice screeched above the dinging sounds as we made our way across the floor. She swanned over with the air of someone who looked good and fucking knew it. I hated the bitch already. "Nico told me you were in town."

West froze momentarily. "I thought you were in Port Valentine."

"I fancied a change of scenery for the weekend." She shrugged and ran her tongue over her lips suggestively. "That's not a crime, is it?"

"I'm Candy." I stepped in to interrupt whatever moment they were sharing. We were away on business, not to get him laid. "We haven't met."

"It's Penelope," she said dismissively, keeping her gaze firmly set on The Hulk. "Have you missed me?"

Shit. This was his *Penny.* The girl who'd fucked him up. Her straight glossy hair sat around her waist, but it looked too thick and shiny to be real. She had perfectly tanned skin, a toned body, and legs that went on for days. Hell, she looked airbrushed. How was it ever possible for a human being to be so freaking perfect? She'd hit the lottery gene pool jackpot.

"What are you doing here, Penny?" West asked while his eyes searched for the nearest exit.

"Why don't we have a drink for old time's sake?" Penelope sucked in her cheeks to emphasize her lips as she trailed a manicured finger up West's inner arm, making me want to yank the skinny twig straight out of its socket. After that, I'd take great pleasure in displaying her doe-like eyes in a pickle jar. "I know you've missed me."

Why had my blood turned to lava? I needed to pull myself together before I exploded and turned the casino into a crime scene. We were in town to speak to Nico. I couldn't screw this up if I ever wanted Zander to trust me with more than the club's underground poker ring.

West's face remained an unreadable mask. "I'm here on business."

"Maybe later?" Penelope winked; her hungry eyes searing into West like she wanted to devour him whole. "I'll see you soon."

Not in my fucking motel room.

She walked away, swaying her hips like she was trying to hypnotize West into following her.

West shot Nico a filthy look in accusation. "You told her I was here?"

"I told you, news travels fast." Nico threw his arms in the air. I didn't trust him. The way his forehead was glistening with sweat told me he was lying. "We'll go into the private bar. We won't be disturbed."

In other words, we were running away from West's stunning ex, who they were too scared to say no to. If the overwhelming urge to break her limbs hadn't overtaken me, I'd have gladly told her to fuck off. Not that it was any of my business. It's not like I should even *care* what West does. But I couldn't have him screwing someone else and ruining our bullshit couple charade, right?

Nico led us into a separate room, clicking his fingers to order a round of cocktails I couldn't pronounce the names of. He looked at me nervously. "Can we talk freely?"

"I'm not another one of West's whores," I snapped, sweeping my hair from behind my ear to flash Nico my tattoo. "See?"

"She's one of us now," West confirmed, causing Nico's tense shoulders to relax. "Anything you have to say, you can say in front of Candy."

Nico eyed the ring on my engagement finger. Something Penelope had missed when she was busy groping West's muscles. The guy didn't miss a trick. "Do we have something to celebrate?"

"That's irrelevant." West shut him down, wanting to keep the meeting on track. "How's our operation going?"

"You know how it is, West." Nico sighed, waving for a server to bring another round. "With Red gone, the production quality is not the same. The guys miss him."

"He couldn't stay here forever," West said. "You know he had to come back to Port Valentine. He only came here to get you started. Show me the books."

"Certainly," Nico obliged, calling over one of his minions to bring out the papers. He may be working for the Sevens, but the growing sweat patches under his arms indicated our visit made him nervous. "I think you'll be pleased."

The pair of them then poured over the pages for the next hour talking figures, while I gritted my teeth, downed mojitos, and pretended it wasn't the first time I'd heard the Sevens ran a motherfucking drugs operation from Hammerville.

"I've seen enough," West said eventually. "Cupid will be in touch soon."

"Perfect." Nico bared his teeth in what he intended to be a smile as his shoulders sagged in relief. "We'll speak again soon, I'm sure."

"Why didn't you tell me?" I demanded as soon as Nico sidled away and we stepped outside. "You're fucking drug suppliers."

"We don't *deal* drugs," West corrected me. "We *grow* them. It's not illegal in this state. Not anymore, anyway. Why do you think Zander took Red on? The guy's a natural."

Somewhere along the way, Rocky must have graduated from smoking pot to growing it. He'd always liked to smoke a joint when we were in school, but I bit my tongue. West didn't know about the past we shared. No one did. It'd only bring more complications when our lives were already consumed by chaos... and we had a growing list of people who wanted to see us brought down.

Logistically, I understood how Lapland and the casino worked as a storefront. Q came in to clean up the cash from the drugs and poker games to make the figures look legit, but something didn't make sense. "Why do you need to use the casino to clean the money, if it's legal to grow?"

"Look, we don't sell our product to everyone the State would consider legitimate, okay?" West shifted on his feet. "Some of our stock goes elsewhere. That's where the casino comes in."

"So, you're not directly dealing drugs," I summarized, "but you're helping other people to do it."

"Look," West lowered his voice, "kids need to make an income, okay? People need medicine and can't get it. We help where we can."

"And profit off of it," I added.

"We're not complete fucking monsters," West said. "We let them keep some of the profits."

"So, you're running an illegal charity? It doesn't seem like a very *Seven* thing to do."

Since when did a gang care about giving back to society? I thought I'd joined a gang of hardened criminals, but there was more to the Sevens than what they showed on the surface. Could they really be up to the challenge of taking someone like Hiram down?

"You know nothing about what it means to be a Seven," West snarled as his cheeks flushed in anger. He turned to storm away at triple speed. "Keep up if you want a ride, Pinkie."

———

We'd only been back at the motel for five minutes when the aggressive knocking started. If the guy from the parking lot was too wasted to get into his room, I'd make sure he slept well by throwing him off the fucking balcony. Instead, I swung the door open to find myself staring at a beautiful brunette.

Penny.

"Can I help you?" I demanded. How the fuck had she found out we were here? Was the bitch stalking us? I'd check our car for trackers before leaving.

"You can't." She looked through me like my skin was made out of plastic wrap. "But he can."

Without waiting for an invitation, she barged inside.

West paled. "What are you doing here, Penny?"

"I knew you'd be pleased to see me." She unbuttoned her coat and let it fall away from her body to reveal a lacy red lingerie set like we were in a romantic movie. Who even did that in real life? I may as well have been a fly on the wall for all she cared. "Have you missed me, baby?"

"Cover yourself up," West said. He didn't look down. For a man who could lose control quickly, his ability to stand firm under the circumstances was an impressive feat. Most guys would have already dropped their pants and been balls-deep by now. "Tell me why you're really here."

"What's wrong?" Penelope pouted, trailing a finger over cleavage to draw him in. "You're not still mad at me, are you?"

"It's time for you to go," I intervened. If they wanted to have a raging domestic, they could have it elsewhere. "You can take your perky tits to someone who actually wants to see them."

"Sweetie, I don't know who you think you are." Penelope looked down her pointed nose with an air of smugness and entitlement that came from a lifetime of getting whatever she wanted because of her looks. I could see why Vixen wanted to wring her neck. "But I'm not going anywhere."

"I think you misunderstood me," I hissed back. "It wasn't a request; it was a motherfucking order."

Penelope was a beautiful woman, but more deadly than a siren. She could lure men from safety and send them crashing into the rocks with the snap of her bra strap.

"Who even are you?" she asked in irritation, finally starting to acknowledge I was a living human. "I'm sure he'll still pay you for the hour if you ask nicely."

"Don't speak to her like that." West stepped between us. "Don't even fucking look at her, Penny."

Penelope's jaw dropped. "You're defending her?"

Game on, bitch.

"I'll defend her every single time." West's voice came out in a low possessive rumble. "Because she's my fucking fiancée."

Well, shit... I couldn't help but like this protective streak. It may all be for a show, but I'd enjoy it while it lasted.

"You can't be serious!" Penelope gasped in horror. "This must be some kind of joke."

"Does this look like a joke to you?" I wiggled my finger at her in triumph. Even the International Space Station couldn't miss the massive red rock. "We're getting married. Get over it."

"This is your way of punishing me, isn't it baby? You don't really want to marry *that* trash." Penelope grabbed West's arm. The thought of him choosing to marry me for anything other than spite was too much for her small mind to comprehend. "I know you were angry with me, but I'm back now. We can start over, can't we? Isn't that what you want?"

Her whining voice and crumpled face made her look like she'd been sitting on the toilet for hours trying to take a shit and failing. She may be pretty on the outside, but she was rotten to the fucking core. Her short-lived relief at thinking she had figured everything out didn't last long.

"We're over, Penny," West said, his tone devoid of all emotion. "We've been over for years."

"But you love me." Her desperation filled the room like a gas chamber as her bottom lip quivered. "You've always loved me!"

"Not anymore," West said, looking at her with dead eyes. "I used to *think* I loved you, but I realized long ago you were nothing but an easy fuck and not even a good one."

"So, you're going to marry this whore?" she snarled, showing her underlying vicious streak. "When you could have me."

"I wouldn't want you if you were the last woman on earth," West spat, wrapping a strong arm around my waist. "Candy is everything you're not."

"You heard him, *sweetie*," I said, narrowing my eyes at her. "Get the fuck out of *our* room."

"You can't get rid of me that easily, West," Penelope threatened, grabbing her coat off the floor and pulling it tightly around herself. "I know everything, remember? *Everything*."

———

"Psycho bitch ex, much?" I checked the door was triple-locked behind her. It wouldn't surprise me if she tried to sneak in when we were sleeping to steal a strand of West's hair to clone him. "Are you going to tell me about her now? What happened with you two?"

West paced. I'd seen him lose his temper before, but this? It was different. Something was clawing at his insides and eating him up.

"We were on and off for years," West said, frowning like he couldn't believe it himself. "We met at boarding school. Her family had different ideas of who she should be dating. That's what happens with old money. They always want you to date their 'own kind', but we kept seeing each other in secret. Part of her liked the notoriety of screwing the guy from the other side of the tracks. After we graduated, she left for college. We'd planned to elope. One weekend I turned up at her dorm to surprise her and caught her fucking someone else. Someone from our fucking school..."

He trailed off, lost in his thoughts. Despite his tough facade, the anguish in his eyes gave me a glimpse of his vulnerable side. A side he didn't want anyone else to see. He'd opened up once and never wanted to feel the pain of betrayal again. A pain I knew all too well.

"It'd been going on for years. Her seeing him behind my back when they spent summers in the Hamptons," he continued, the words tumbling out before he could stop them. "Their families wanted them to get married. They had the whole thing set up. The next thing I knew, the pair were engaged. A few years after they got married, his family went broke, and Penny lost everything. Then she found me again. She told me she'd made a mistake and spun me a bullshit line about how she'd changed. I gave her a second chance. She needed cash, so I helped her, then she fucked up again. I caught her screwing a fucking ambassador. It was never about me at all. It was always about money."

"Couldn't her family have helped her out with cash?" I asked.

"Penny's family may come from old money, but they're going extinct," he explained. "Apart from a name and fancy house, they have nothing. All she cares about is staying at the top."

"Shit, West. I'm sorry." I meant it. He'd given her everything, and she'd fucking burned him. I knew the feeling. The feeling you'll never be able to trust anyone again. "What does she have on you? She said that she 'knows everything'?"

"She knew me and Zander in school." West looked away, avoiding my probing gaze. "Stuff happened."

I waited for him to elaborate, but he didn't. It wasn't a line he was willing to cross… yet.

"You may not be able to hit a girl," I said, breaking the silence. "But I have no objection the next time she comes around."

West laughed. "You're a crazy bitch, Pinkie."

"Sure am," I said, owning it proudly like a Girl Scout badge. They needed to add it to the handbook. They should teach little girls how to look after themselves. "I may be a crazy bitch, but you're a damn good actor. You didn't have to say all that stuff to Penny about us."

He ran his hands over his shaven head, drawing attention to the angel tattoo scene on his bicep. "You don't get it, do you?"

"Get, what?" I frowned, replaying back our conversation. Had I missed something? "Your ex is a gold-digger who cheated on you twice and appeared out of nowhere like a nasty bout of herpes. It's fucked up. I get why you left the auction after hearing about it. It's okay to admit that shit gets to you."

"You think she is the reason why I left the auction?" West's blue eyes pierced mine. "It's not about her. None of it is. I don't give a shit about Penny coming back to town."

"Then why your man period?"

"This is about you."

"Me? What have I done wrong?" I'd been doing a damn good job of pretending to be a dutiful wife-to-be. "I've done what Zander told me to. Just like you and the other Sevens. Does my presence upset you so much you can't bear to stick around the club for longer than one fucking drink?"

"You don't understand."

West punched the wall without warning, adding another dent to the many imparted by other angry men. Where had his Shakespearean dramatics come from? Whenever he didn't know how to express himself, he went straight to smashing shit up.

"Hey, stop!" I caught his bleeding fist to stop him from pummeling it again. I was more worried about him bringing the crumbling building down than him hurting himself. The motel's structural integrity violated a thousand building regulations. Another outburst from West could leave us buried under a pile of rubble. "Help me understand, okay?"

"You want to understand?" His eyes burned with passion. "I made a mistake."

I dropped his fist, my heart beating faster. "What did you do?"

"Do you really want to know?"

I nodded.

"You're going to regret this," he warned.

I put my hands on my hips and looked up at his imposing figure. If he wanted to intimidate me, it wouldn't work. "Try me."

My mouth went dry as he stepped closer. The pounding in my chest drowned out the sound of the highway and the rats scratching above.

West's body collided with mine at full force, as he brought his lips crashing against my own and stole my breath away. Like the first time we kissed in Briarly Manor, my body responded to his touch involuntarily.

"Do you understand now?" West pulled away gasping for breath. "You're the mistake I made. A mistake I can't stop thinking about making again."

"But you don't even want to be in the same room as me," I stammered, still reeling from our kiss. Ever since our junkyard trip, West had done everything in his power to stay out of my way. "I thought you didn't even want me here."

"Ever since our kiss, you're all I've thought about," West hissed. His words didn't come out as sweet or kind, they burst from his mouth in a bitter fury like something poisonous he wanted to expel. "Your snarky mouth, that sweet fucking ass of yours… it's like you enjoy taunting me. I can't get you outta my fucking head."

He kicked the bed frame causing the weakened wood to crack. How was I supposed to respond? West's kiss set my body alight… but it didn't mean it was the right thing to do. The Sevens were a gang. We couldn't mix business with pleasure, right?

"West!" I pulled him back before he snapped the damn thing in half. "Can you stop smashing shit for two seconds?"

"I want you, Candy." West stared at me with a burning intensity, like he wanted to burrow deep into my brain and discover my deepest secrets. "But I can't fucking have you. You know the rules."

"The rules?"

"No one can touch you," he said. "Zander's orders."

"Zander may be the boss of the Sevens, but he doesn't own me." A wave of hot prickling anger spread through my limbs. Fuck Zander. What right did he have to tell me, or anyone else, what to do with their bodies? If I wanted West, then I'd have him on my fucking terms. Nobody owned me. "I'm not a piece of fucking property."

"You're playing a dangerous game, Pinkie."

I stood on my tiptoes, slowly edging closer. My lips grazed against his teasingly. Had I decided to act to annoy Zander, or because I wanted West as much as he wanted me? I wasn't sure, but it was too late to back out now. "Fuck the rules."

West didn't need any further persuasion. When his lips responded to mine this time, we had no audience. No Zander watching in a chair, no room of ogling old men, no stream of oncoming cars or worries about prying eyes. It was just the two of us. Alone. That's why it was so dangerous. When no one else could intervene, how would I know when to stop when the urge to jump his bones consumed my entire body?

His hands slipped under my ass and hoisted me into the air like I was weightless. He pulled me closer, yanking my dress up to my hips. His giant monster hands gripped my cheeks so hard he'd leave marks, but I didn't mind. I wrapped my legs around his torso, my thighs gripping him tightly, to feel every hard muscle of his body pressed against mine.

"You have no fucking idea how much I've wanted you," he whispered into my mouth as if scared the world would collapse if he spoke too loudly. Maybe it would. Maybe this would destroy everything.

I sunk my teeth into his lip in reply. I couldn't have said anything even if I'd wanted to. West groaned, slamming my back into the wall and causing a part of the ceiling to fall at our sides. The whole fucking building could come crashing around us and it wouldn't stop me from wanting to be devoured by his passionate fury.

His tongue probed my mouth with an urgency. A thirst we couldn't quench. The heat of his body made my skin burn with longing, but it wasn't enough. No, we weren't close enough. Not yet. My nails clawed his back and drew blood. I didn't care. Hell, I wanted to. I wanted to claw every inch of him to mark what was mine. What Penelope couldn't have. The cool metal of West's belt rubbing against the heat of my lace panties left neither of us questioning whether we wanted this.

When was the last time I'd been this close to a man and wanted him to take me? I couldn't remember. But I needed to feel West more than I needed oxygen. Suspended in mid-air, there was nowhere for me to escape, and I didn't want to. I pushed my hips against the rock-hard bulge in his pants. West was a big guy and, unsurprisingly, his cock was a monster of its own. I reached down to undo his belt... then...

The cold ring of his cell pierced through our ragged breathing, causing West to break away.

"Leave it," I murmured in his ear.

West's lips trailed down my neck as we let it ring out, then...

It started again.

"I should get that," West murmured, his voice low and husky. "It might be Zander."

Well, shit... way to kill the fucking mood with a sledgehammer.

He placed me down gently like a rare fragile artifact he was scared to break. What happened to the raging beast who'd slammed me against the wall minutes before? After talking hurriedly in grave hushed tones, West hung up.

"Well?" I demanded. "What is it?"

"We need to go back." His words were heavy and loaded. He was talking about more than being summoned to Lapland. "Zander needs us."

"Fine." I smoothed down my dress and grabbed my packed bag. "I didn't want to stay in this dive, anyway."

What would happen when we returned? Would West go back to pretending I was a pain in his ass? Between Zander's rules, my history with Rocky and the fire I'd ignited with West, joining the Sevens had become even more complicated. Being bound to three dangerous men would open up a whole new world of unexpected threats.

CHAPTER
Six

By the time we arrived at Lapland, my head pounded from the heavy metal West blasted for the entire journey. It suited me. Better to pop a few aspirins, if it meant avoiding conversation and drowning out thoughts about my recklessness.

The gravity of my mistake started to sink in the closer we got to Port Valentine. What the fuck had I done? Seeing West and Penelope together touched a territorial nerve which made me forget everything I knew about men. The fucker turned me into melted putty in his massive hands. After our junkyard trip, I should have known better.

I knew men like West. They said anything to get a piece of the action. Hell, I'd bet he was sexually frustrated after seeing his stunning ex and settled for the backup option. The only person with a vagina in a block radius he didn't have to pay to screw. I should never have stopped him from smashing up the motel room. All the words he'd said? They were textbook lines. I needed to remember he was a player, like the rest of the Seven men.

As soon as we were back at the club, I flew from the car like a starving lion released from a cage before he'd put on the parking brake.

"Candy," West called, but I didn't look back.

We needed to put distance between us, and I needed to get my shit together to stop freaking out over what *almost* happened. My young naivety got me into this fucked up world in the first place. Why would West be any different?

Men were manipulators. They would say anything to get what they wanted – especially if 'anything' had a pair of tits and a hole between their legs. Criminals like the Sevens never had honorable intentions. They treated girls like toys. West used to hook up with Scarlett, another dancer, when I first came to town. If Zander hadn't called, I'd have become another name in his little black book, which I'm sure was already the length of Paradise fucking Lost.

"Candy!" Mieko greeted me as I rushed into Lapland with her usual sunny smile. "Vixen told me you were out of town for the night."

"Change of plan."

She nudged me gently. "It can't have been that bad, right?"

"What do you mean?" I snapped.

She raised her eyebrows. "You look like you want to rip someone's head off."

"Sorry, it's been a long day…" It wasn't Mieko's fault I'd offered myself to West on a plate. I only had my cock-starved vajayjay with questionable judgment to thank for that. "Is there space for me on tonight's schedule?"

"I think so," she said. "Vixen wouldn't mind, but didn't Zander say he didn't want you dancing now you're a Seven?"

"I couldn't give a flying fuck what Zander says." Thoughts rattled around my head like wrestlers in a mosh pit. Without a vibrator in hand, dancing was the only way I'd be able to find a release and empty my worries away. "I'm taking the stage."

"I'm not going to stand in your way!" She held up her hands, then surveyed my outfit. "You better change though."

Mieko made a good point. A wiggle dress wouldn't accommodate the splits. Besides, the delicious scent of West's cologne had absorbed into the fabric and I didn't need a reminder of how fucking good it felt to be pressed against his perfect abs.

I stormed into the dressing room like a tsunami. "Get out!"

The dancers obeyed, dispersing like a herd of sheep running from a wolf. None of them dared to argue. Since getting my initiation tattoo, they knew my upgraded status in Port Valentine. They feared me, but it didn't stop the bitches from complaining whenever they thought I wasn't listening. I could fire any of them with a flick of my wrist, but why waste my time with childish games? My real worries were far bigger… like how I'd kissed Rocky at the auction and fallen into West's arms a few days later.

I chose a neon pink dress that crisscrossed over my stomach and left little to the imagination.

It's showtime!

As I stepped onto the dance floor, a figure stepped out from the shadows. He'd been waiting. The furious look on Zander's face catapulted my heart to the back of my throat. He couldn't have rigged a camera in the motel, could he? I wouldn't put it past him. The guy's obsessive control issues were off the charts.

"Vixen told me you wanted to dance," he spat. "It's not what we agreed on."

If this was Zander's reaction to me grinding on a pole, I wouldn't want to see how he'd respond if he found out about the other agreement I broke… and who else I'd been getting close to.

"It's not a crime to let your hair down," I replied. "Why did you call us back, anyway? It doesn't seem like you need *me* to do anything else."

"West had other pressing business to attend to," he said, proving my point, but refusing to let me off so easily. "You're a Seven now. We have a reputation in this town."

"I may be part of the Sevens, but you can't control every part of my life. It's called having fun. Maybe you should try it?" I suggested. "Enjoy the fucking show, Zander."

I marched past, fully aware he'd get a glimpse of my ass due to the swishing fabric. What better way to make an exit?

The night was well underway, and a large bachelor party filled the dance floor. Dancers flitted around them like flies around shit, picking the group apart by beckoning individuals away for private dances. Everyone knew they had deep wallets when a last night of freedom was at stake.

"I see you've dressed up." Vixen looked me over with a smirk. "If you wanna dance, you better get your ass up on the stage before Zander pulls the whole fucking show."

"That bastard is not canceling me," I said. "Clear the fucking way."

"I thought you'd say that." Vixen winked. Having her as an ally came with advantages. She didn't care about calling out her cousin when he deserved it. "Mieko chose the song."

I took to the stage as 'Erbody But Me' by Tech N9ne blasted from the speakers. *Nice choice.* Everyone's eyes turned to look up and watch my every move. Most people hated performing for a crowd. I used to be one of them until I realized being seen came with power. Captivating an audience gave you the power to portray whatever you wanted. You could become an entirely different person. Performing rendered the real me, and the parts I didn't want others to see, invisible.

The rest of the song passed in a blur. I allowed my body to move to the rhythm, pushing aside the memory of West's eyes trying to pierce past my bullshit. Shimmying for strangers was easier. It was safe. Getting added to their wank bank wouldn't hurt me — not like The Hulk and his monster dick, who had the potential to penetrate more than my pussy...

"You were freaking hot," Mieko complimented as I stepped off the stage, and she readied to take my place. Her leather catsuit would not disappoint the hecklers.

"Says you." I blew her a kiss. "Now go break some balls."

Dancing had been the right decision. Zander may be in a sulky mood, but what was new? He'd need to get botox soon, because of the constant frown etched on his face. Performing had been exactly what I needed to blow off steam and think more clearly.

"Hey!" A stranger approached. He was standing in the front row during my performance and belonged to the bachelor party. "Can I buy you a drink?"

He was handsome in a clean-cut kinda way. Someone with a cheeky grin and enough confidence to sink the Titanic — the type who worked as a banker in the city and drove a fancy car to show off his status.

I shrugged. "Why not?"

It could be good for me. Maybe hanging out with a guy who wasn't a badass criminal would help cleanse my palette? The more I hung out with the Sevens, the less control I seemed to have over my desires.

"You're not the groom, are you?" I asked, eying him suspiciously as he ordered us tequila shots. Once poured, I took them straight from Scarlett's hands. You could never be too careful accepting drinks. I should know, as I used to slip drugs into my target's cocktails when working for Hiram.

"Hell no!" He laughed. "I'm the best man. I enjoyed your show. You're a good dancer. How long have you been doing this?"

I licked the salt from my hand, took the shot, and sucked the lime in record speed. "How about we dance?"

If I wanted to make conversation, I'd see a fucking therapist. I took his hand and led him to the center of the dance floor. Mieko was killing it on stage, but the man never took his eyes off me.

"You're stunning," he shouted in my ear.

As the beat dropped, he placed his hands on my hips. I turned to grind against him. His hands pulled me closer, allowing my ass to feel the half-tent pitching in his pants. At his touch, I felt nothing. No fireworks, no excitement, nada, zilch... zero. I may as well have been doing sudoku.

What the hell was my problem? There was nothing wrong with the dude. I spun around and put my arms around his neck. The thought of kissing him was about as appealing as drinking a cold cup of English tea. Even dancing with him bored the living shit outta me. Why did my body only respond to no good criminals? There were more guys in the world than Zander, West, and Rocky! I had to try, at least...

One minute, we swayed to the music. The next, the poor guy was hit with the force of a truck and lay sprawled on the floor clutching his face. The crowd stopped dancing to watch, backing away to create a circle around them.

Zander towered over him, fists clenched. "Nobody touches my girl."

"Hey, man," he stuttered, wincing as he rubbed the spot where Zander delivered his blow. He'd be sporting an attractive black eye tomorrow. "I didn't know she was yours. I was only messing around."

Zander grabbed his collar and hauled the banker to his feet. Two security guards were already waiting. Zander threw him into their arms, ignoring the objections from the rest of the party. "Escort him from the premises."

"What the fuck, Zander?" I demanded. As Lapland's owner, he seriously needed to re-read a customer service manual. "You didn't have to throw him out."

"My office, Candy." Zander rolled up his sleeves. He locked his eyes on me, seething in anger. "Now."

———

Being led into his office felt like doing the walk of shame after a regrettable one-night stand. As soon as we were inside, Zander turned the lock behind him.

"Are you going to explain yourself?"

"I've done nothing wrong," I said. "We were only *dancing*."

"Don't fucking lie to me, Candy." Zander stepped forward menacingly and loomed over me. He was so close that he had to incline his head for me to see his eyebrows lower in fury. The light cast shadows over his face, high-lighting his rose tattoo. The thorns inked into his cheeks looked sharp and ready to draw blood. "I'm not just talking about the man out there who placed his dirty hands on you. Do you think I'm too stupid to see how you've got West and Red wrapped around your little finger?"

"I don't know what you mean," I lied. I couldn't waver or show weakness. He'd see straight through it. When you said something with enough confidence, it almost became a reality – right?

"I told you, you're all fucking mine," he whispered; his breath sent chills racing down my spine. "You know my rules."

The hint of a threat should scare me, but it didn't. Why does being in the company of an ordinary man make me want to call it a night, but I get drawn in by a man who has the power to kill me? Zander's words didn't make me feel intimidated… they excited me.

"But I haven't broken them."

Well, I'd gotten close with West but what Zander didn't know wouldn't hurt him.

"Actions have consequences, Candy." Zander placed one finger to my mouth to silence any further objections. "You already know that, don't you?"

My breathing heightened. "What are you going to do?"

"Turn around," he ordered.

"Wait, what—"

"You agreed to follow my rules, remember?" He pressed his finger into my lips harder. "You're going to do as I say."

When Zander gave orders, he had a way of putting you under a spell. Instead of telling him to fuck off, I obeyed. I turned my back, feeling his presence looming behind me.

"Bend over," he instructed.

"Excuse me?" I tried to turn, but Zander caught my hips to stop me. "What the fuck, Zander?"

"You heard me," he purred, holding me firmly in place. "Bend over my fucking desk, Candy."

Resisting wouldn't end well for either of us.

"Fine," I agreed. If Zander thought he could humiliate me, I'd prove him wrong…

I made a show of stretching my arms out in front of me, slowly lowering myself forward. My tiny dress hitched up my thighs, riding up my ass to give him a good view.

His hands stroked the back of my thighs. "Very good."

Zander's fingers danced over my skin so gently that it made me question whether he was touching me at all. My encounter with West had been a primal fiery embrace, but with Zander? His moves were calculated. Deliberate. He enjoyed taking his time to plan every single stroke.

His fingers slipped into my inner thigh and caressed my delicate skin with unexpected tenderness. I should tell him to stop. I should want to put an end to it but, instead, I stayed silent. If this was his way of testing me, then I wouldn't back down.

While I was vulnerable, with my butt raised like a kitty wanting attention, this position meant I didn't have to think. Dancing helped to calm my thoughts, but Zander's touch? It calmed my body. My nerve endings were tingling, anticipating where his fingers would brush next. It's all I could focus on.

Zander's palms slid up the back of my thighs, applying a little more pressure, then… HOLY FUCK.

Thwack!

Zander spanked my ass so hard it made me yelp in surprise. If I looked in a mirror, his red handprint would be staring back.

"You have been a bad girl, little one…" Zander tutted. "Bad girls deserve to be punished."

He yanked up my dress to completely expose my sparkly G-string. The rattle of his belt buckle and leather sliding loose made my pussy clench. In Blackthorne Towers, I'd been inflicted with pain but never like this. I tried to stand, but Zander's grip held me down firmly.

"I won't hurt you," Zander promised, sensing my shift. "But I am going to teach you a lesson. A lesson I want you to remember."

"Zander, I…"

I let out a small moan as his hand softly caressed my cheeks, running his fingers over the burning mark he'd left behind. Taking a moment to appreciate his work.

"What a fucking ass," he admired, delivering another sharp blow with his hand in the crease where my ass met my thighs. The sting made me gasp aloud. "This is what happens when you break my rules. You like that, don't you, little one?"

I did. *Fuck.* I did.

Zander ran his leather belt over the backs of my thighs, warming me up for what was to follow. My shoulders tensed, anticipating the pain. When he swung and struck my whole body jolted. Hard enough to make a satisfying crack, but gentle enough that it wouldn't bruise. I sensed he was holding back. He didn't want to hurt me.

Then, he struck again, two quick blows in quick succession, perfectly delivered to give the same pain. The thudding feeling coursing through my body wasn't pain, but pleasure and excitement from not knowing what was coming next… a release I desperately needed.

He dropped the belt to the floor with a clang. "Now, everyone will be able to see that you're mine."

But Zander wasn't done yet. He stroked the raised marks, then trailed his fingers downwards. He used his hands to gently part my legs further, allowing enough space for him to dip between my legs and stroke my heat through the silky fabric.

"Fuck," I moaned.

He could feel my wetness. I couldn't hide the effect he had on me. His teasing was torturous. He expertly navigated his way to my clit and gently rubbed in slow circles to prolong my suffering.

Shit, I wanted more. If he felt this good through the fabric, I couldn't even imagine how amazing it'd feel to have his skin against mine. I bucked backward against his hand in encouragement.

Suddenly, he stopped. Zander withdrew his hand and stepped back. "I think you've learned your lesson now."

"You're a bastard." I stood up breathlessly and pulled down my dress, acutely aware my face was as red as my fucking ass. For punishment, I'd expected him to rip off a few toenails. What kind of twisted game was he playing? Getting a girl close to orgasm and then stopping took torture to a whole new level

"Actions have consequences, remember?" Zander grinned wickedly and popped one of his fingers into his mouth to taste me. "Delicious."

"Let me out," I hissed through gritted teeth.

He unlocked the door. "It was my pleasure."

———

Leaving Zander's office felt like leaving an alien spaceship after being probed. I had to splash my face with ice water and change my panties pronto.

"I've been looking for you everywhere!" Vixen burst into the bathroom and found where I'd been hiding. Thankfully, my heart rate had almost returned to normal. "What are you doing in here?"

"Nothing," I replied defensively. "What do you want?"

"We've got a gift from Cheeks." She waved a brown envelope in front of her face like a fan. "Our little chat in the hotel room worked."

"I still don't trust him."

Cheeks was a slimy handsy prick who accepted bribes for personal gain and slid through life with zero morals. The Sevens may have damning evidence that could put him behind bars, but it only scratched the surface of the crimes he'd committed over the years. Breaking a prostitute's jaw wouldn't be the worst thing he kept hidden.

"Neither do I," Vixen admitted. "But I trust Zander."

She may trust Zander's motivations, but I couldn't figure out what went through his head. Every time I thought I'd worked him out, he threw another curveball. If he was as calculating with business as he was with his hands, we should have nothing to worry about.

"Have you opened it?" I asked. Whatever information Cheeks passed over better be good. If we were going to work with the scum of society, I wanted it to be worth our while.

"Not yet, it's addressed to Zander." Of course, because it's out of the question that anyone other than Zander could pull the strings around here. "How was he?"

"How was..." My voice trailed off, thinking I'd misheard her. Why did my brain instantly go there? Of course, she wasn't asking about how skilled

Zander was at getting me to the brink of an orgasm. I recovered quickly. "Sorry, what?"

"How is Zander? He dragged you into the office like it was the fucking reckoning, remember?" She looked at me funny. "I've had to give out free drinks to the bachelor party to make up for him throwing out the best man. Is he still in a bad mood?"

"Yeah, well..." I mumbled. "I think he's over it now."

"Thank fuck Zander didn't break any bones. The groom threatened to press charges," Vixen went on. My ass hadn't been the only one to face punishment after I decided to dance with a stranger. "That is, until West made an appearance. The guy wanted to have all his teeth for the wedding photos."

"West is back?"

"He went straight upstairs," she said. "What happened in Hammerville? He looked like shit."

"Penny happened."

"What was she doing there?" Vixen's jaw dropped. "I thought she was in Port Valentine."

"She followed us," I replied. "You were right about her. The bitch has a neck I'd pay to strangle."

Vixen snorted. "You'll have to join the fucking queue."

Raised voices outside the club piqued our attention.

"Want help breaking it up?" I asked hopefully. Smashing a few heads together may release some of my frustration.

"Do I look in the mood to be mopping blood off the floor all night?" Damn, she knew me too well. "Call yourself a cab, and I'll see you tomorrow."

Heading home early wasn't a bad idea. I'd been on a complete head-fuck rollercoaster in the past twenty-four hours. From getting steamy in the motel room to being bent over a freaking desk. This was not what I'd signed up for when joining the Sevens.

The universe wasn't done kicking my ass yet, though. I checked my cell to see three unread messages flashing on the screen. All from the same person.

Having fun?

It's been too long, Kitten.

I'll be seeing you soon.

I couldn't afford any more distractions, especially not in the form of three perfectly sculpted Seven men. Hiram was coming, and I had to be ready... we all did.

CHAPTER
Seven

It'd been two days since Zander carried out his 'punishment', and I could finally sit down without feeling a sting, which made me more excited about the evening ahead. There's only so long I could put with Zander's smug sideways glances at knowing his prints were burned into my ass...

"Are you sure you don't mind me coming along?" Mieko sat cross-legged in front of my dirty mirror. A plethora of cosmetics surrounded her like a spell-casting circle. "Won't they mind?"

"I told you already," I said, running the straightener through my hair to iron out the final kinks. "I want you there, so you're coming. I'm a Seven too, remember? What I say goes."

We were heading to the Smoker for what Zander called a 'Sevens night'. Despite the pretense of going to have a good time, he would have an ulterior motive for our attendance. Zander always did. Why else go through the effort of getting us on the VIP list? The Smoker is an exclusive club in Port Valentine that opens every full moon in an abandoned warehouse. It's renowned as a cool hang-out, where they sell drinks so expensive you'd think they contained unicorn tears and centaur jizz.

Conveniently, Lapland had to close its doors for the evening because Vixen decided to get the dance floor re-done for the second time. After the urgent replacement job following the kid's death, Vixen hadn't stopped complaining. After hearing her bitching for weeks, Zander finally relented and agreed to get it done again. When Rocky called me earlier, he'd said she'd been whipping the workers to get it finished quicker.

Mieko fluttered her thick eyelashes. She'd drawn a perfect winged cat-eye, complete with shimmering purple shadow, which made her look like an otherworldly goddess. "Is this too much?"

"It's never too much," I said, then smiled coyly. Vixen will be blown away."

"I don't know what you mean," she replied with indignation. Although her sparkling eyes told another story.

I rolled my eyes. "Sure you don't…"

Mieko's secret crush on Vixen blew my mind. Even more baffling than Mieko liking her was Vixen's complete obliviousness. How hadn't she noticed Mieko hanging off her every word like a lovesick puppy? For someone quick to call out bullshit, Vixen couldn't see what was right under her septum piercing.

"Your hair looks great with that outfit," Mieko said. With her help, I'd freshly dyed my tresses to a vibrant shade of fiery pink, which complimented my red dress. It had a floaty layered skirt with a lace corseted bodice — the perfect balance of an angel on the bottom but a devil up top. "Is there anyone *you* are trying to impress tonight?"

"Nope," I said, popping the p. "Is there anything wrong with a woman looking good for herself?"

"Of course not, but I'm just saying." Mieko shrugged but wasn't about to let the topic go so easily. "One minute, I thought something was going on with you and Red. Next, you're in a fake engagement with West and Zander knocks out any guy who looks in your direction. All I'm saying is, you could have any of them if you wanted to. You'll have to pick eventually, right?"

"It's not like that," I insisted as my cheeks heated. Hopefully, my bronzer covered their rosy glow. "We *work* together."

Business first, I reminded myself, that's how it needed to stay. I never intended to get caught between three guys, especially when bound to stay in a freaking gang with them forever. Mieko was right. I couldn't have them all. I needed to think with my head and ignore whatever weird pull I felt towards them before it ended in fucking disaster.

"Whatever you say." Mieko applied deep plum lipstick with a smug smirk, seeing right through me. Goddammit, it was okay for me to wind her up about Vixen, but not the other way around. "When will they be picking us up?"

I checked my new phone. After Hiram's last messages, I changed my number. None of the Sevens had questioned my excuse of accidentally stepping on my last one in platform shoes. It wouldn't keep Hiram at bay for long, but it gave me a few days without worrying about his unexpected calls. He enjoyed playing games, so why make it easy for him?

"They're bringing the limo around in five."

Mieko's eyes lit up like a kid being told they could eat as much candy as they wanted before bed. "I've never been in a limo before."

"Don't get too excited. With all of us squeezed in, it won't be much better than a school bus…"

Well, one with fancy champagne and bulging male muscles instead of whining kids with runny noses and juice boxes.

Mieko peeked through the curtains and squealed in excitement. "They're here."

Incessant beeping from the street signaled Vixen's impatience. She had a habit of forcing the drivers to press the horn to hurry people along. They were too scared to question the crazy bitch who hated waiting.

"Let's do this." I linked Mieko's arm in mine and led her out of my apartment. "The Smoker, here we come!"

When I first arrived in town, I swore not to get close to people. With Mieko, it was different. After getting rid of a body together and learning about her troubled past, we'd grown closer over the past few months. I never thought I'd have another true friend after Crystal's death, but Mieko was slowly re-teaching me the value of female friendship. Sure, I also had the Sevens… but I wouldn't be making them friendship bracelets anytime soon.

———

"Are you okay, Mieko?" Vixen frowned as we slipped into the limo. "You look a little… off."

I held back a snicker. Mieko was completely unprepared to see Vixen's bustier, which hoisted her boobs up into two perfectly shaped mounds. The girl knew how to make an impact.

"Y-y-yes, I'm fine!" Mieko squeaked, averting her eyes to the first thing in sight. "Wow! This cupholder… it's amazing. It really can hold cups. It's the, um… perfect shape."

Vixen yawned. "Is it?"

"Where are the guys?" I raised an eyebrow at the empty seats. Hell, I'd canceled my boxset binging plans for this shit. "What's the point in calling a Sevens night if you're not even going to show up?"

"Something came up," Vixen replied, pouring three Russian vodka shots. "They'll join us there later."

I raised my drink in toast. "Who'd have thought we'd have another girl's night so soon?"

Vixen rolled her eyes and clinked her glass against mine. "Fuck the guys."

I almost choked. Of course, she didn't mean *literally* fuck them. Why was that the first conclusion I jumped to? Perhaps it'd be best if they didn't join us later. My vagina needed a break from their presence.

"I've never been able to get into the Smoker before," Mieko said. The guest list was exclusive and invitations were almost impossible to come by.

"The Briarly name has some perks." Vixen shrugged. The name also came with downsides, like having your relatives order a hit against you. "We know a guy. Let me know next time you want in. I'll sort it."

"Why don't we play a game?" I changed the subject. "Never have I ever."

"Why the hell not?" Vixen reclined, while Mieko looked like she wanted to shit herself. "We've still got a whole bottle left."

"I'll start," I said. "Never have I ever disposed of a body."

"Hey!" Mieko objected but took a sip anyway. "You're supposed to say things you haven't done."

"Fine…" I sighed. It'd be a short list. "You go next."

"Never have I ever been to jail."

"Is that the best you got?" Vixen laughed, taking a drink. "Okay, never have I ever killed someone."

Mieko and I both drank. What would happen if I made this a little more interesting?

"Never have I ever had a crush on someone I've worked with," I said.

Mieko narrowed her eyes and took a sip, but Vixen didn't notice. Was she incapable of seeing anything that might be good for her? She indulged in airheads, cigarettes, and spirits… but someone like Mieko didn't even come across her radar.

"Never have I ever kissed my boss," Mieko rebutted. "Candy, you need to drink. You kissed West!"

"He's not my boss," I replied, hoping the next question wouldn't ask whether a Seven had left bruises on my ass. "We're all equals."

"Look!" Vixen pointed outside as the limo started to reduce its speed. "We're here. Welcome to the Smoker."

The Smoker looked like any other abandoned warehouse. A gigantic building made from steel and grimy glass windows. You wouldn't look twice at it in the daytime, but, at night, it was lit up like a Christmas tree. Flashing lights bounced off the walls, music pulsed from every corner and mini fire pits burned to keep revelers warm.

"This way," Vixen instructed, leading us out of the car like soldiers heading to battle. She stormed straight to the front of the long queue, where we were let in straight away. No one would be brave enough to accuse a Seven of jumping a line.

"Isn't this place insane?" Mieko whispered in my ear as we stepped into the party. The building was broken up into multiple rooms with DJs playing different genres of music. There were small bars in each area, but the main space-age bar spanned the entrance lobby. Its sleek and sophisticated appearance contrasted the rundown warehouse which gave it an effortlessly cool vibe, and it was surrounded by tall tables for people to rest drinks and chat.

"I've got Zander's card," Vixen declared proudly, waving a platinum before our eyes. "Let's have a good fucking time, huh?"

———

After doing too many shots in weird and wonderful flavors, we descended on the dance floor. Considering Vixen spent most of her time in Lapland ordering dancers around, she had surprisingly great moves. Maybe she'd consider taking to the pole one day?

"Shit." Mieko gasped, pointing through the throng of moving limbs. "Look!"

The crowd parted for two men to pass. West's lip was split open, and his face twisted into his signature scowl. At West's side, Rocky didn't seem to be hurt, but his furious glare made him look ready to disembowel anyone who looked at him.

"What happened?" Vixen asked them as they joined us.

West grunted in response, and Rocky shoved her out of his way to head straight for a drink. What had gotten their panties in a twist?

I smirked up at West. "Nice lip."

"Don't fucking go there," he snarled.

Considering men didn't get periods, they experienced worse mood swings than any woman I'd ever known. How would they cope if they had to deal with cramps and bleed out their peens once a month?

"Is someone going to tell us what the fuck went down?" Vixen placed her hands on her hips, staring West down like they were in a quick draw contest. "Who did that to you?"

West nudged his head in Rocky's direction. "Ask *him*."

Vixen's jaw dropped, as Rocky returned. She spun around in accusation and jabbed a claw into his chest. "*You* did this to him?"

"We had a disagreement." Rocky shrugged like it was nothing, but his shoulders remained tense. Landing a punch on West was impressive. Had he taken The Hulk off guard? "So what?"

"It's no one else's fucking business," West spat.

"Where's Zander?" I asked, expecting they would have arrived together.

"He has somewhere else he needs to be," West replied flatly. Typical. Zander was holding onto more secrets the rest of us were not privy to. Why did he suggest coming to the Smoker in the first place, if he had other plans? "He's not coming."

"Let's go dance in the other room. I hear Ash and the Basilisks playing. They're my favorite band!" Vixen turned to me and Mieko without addressing the guys. There was no point when they were standing with their hands in their pockets like moody teenagers forced to attend a family function. "Are you both coming?"

"My feet hurt. I'm gonna find somewhere to sit down," I lied, then whispered in Mieko's ear, "you can thank me later."

I'd be her wing woman and stay with the guys if it gave her the chance to make her move. Alcohol had lowered Mieko's inhibitions, so who knows? She had to act on her crush soon or forget about it. She couldn't waste her life pining after Vixen.

"Suit yourself," Vixen called, grabbing Mieko's hand and pulling her away. Mieko looked back at me in wide-eyed surprise and beamed. Playing the role of Cupid was new to me, considering I usually acted as the Grim Reaper.

"Not in the mood to party?" Rocky cocked his head to the side. He only acted snarky when something was bothering him... or someone. "Are you too tired?"

I looked between the two of them. "Are you going to tell me what happened tonight or not?"

Neither of them said a word, letting the stony silence stretch out as they didn't look at me or each other. You'd need a sledgehammer to lighten their fucking moods.

"Fine!" I threw my hands in the air. I wouldn't be getting any answers until my pubes turned gray and my labia shriveled into prunes. "If we're not gonna talk, can we dance at least?"

"But you said your feet hurt," West said, looking down at my red open-toed heels with straps that tied around my ankles like they were the devil.

"Well, they're feeling better now. See?" I wriggled my toes. "Let's go into the other room."

Rocky frowned in confusion. "Since when do you like hip-hop?"

Like Vixen, I was also a huge fan of Ash and The Basilisks. Who didn't love heavy metal bands fronted by a kick-ass female singer? Ash was a freaking rockstar. But, if Mieko was going to pluck up the courage to make her move, we needed to give them space.

"Since when do you know what I like?" I snapped, marching onwards while the two of them trailed after me.

I pushed through until we were in the middle of the dance floor and let my body move to the music. I tried to ignore the simmering unrest growing between my companions as they stood still, shooting daggers at each other. Were they out of their minds?

"Come on," I encouraged them. We were not playing a game of musical statues, you had to move in the middle of a fucking rave. "Dance!"

West brushed my hair away from my face to lean in close and whisper in my ear, "Your ring looks good in this light."

I held it up in front of me and the ruby glittered under the strobes. I couldn't go anywhere in public without it if we wanted everyone to believe our act. My ring *was* pretty. Considering the unlikelihood of me marrying for real, I was pretty damn happy if this was the closest I'd ever get.

"It's too flashy," Rocky sniped.

I pouted. "Don't tell me you're jealous we're getting married?"

Rocky's expression turned thunderous. He moved behind me, placing his hand on my waist and forcing our bodies to move together to the beat. Had it suddenly got very hot? Or, was I slowly being suffocated in the middle of a man meat sandwich?

"Your ring means nothing," Rocky said, so only I could hear, "I know the real you, remember?"

"We're here to dance." I stepped out of his grasp. "Not talk."

West took advantage of the opportunity by grabbing my hand. He drew me closer to him like a fish on a line. His leg slipped between mine, coaxing mine apart and rocking our hips in time. Because of his size, I'd expected West to have zero rhythm but, from the way he moved, he knew exactly what he was doing. *I bet dancing isn't the only thing he's good at*, my vagina taunted like a bad yo' momma joke. What the hell had gotten into her? She was like a fucking rose in desperate need of watering.

I spun away from West, then raised my arms in the air and brought them back down over my sides, trailing down my curves. West closed the gap between us, cradling my swaying hips with his giant hands. While my ass circled West's crotch, Rocky stood in front of me and pulled my arms around his neck. If Zander was around, he'd knock both of them the hell out. He'd made it clear he wanted to be the only one to touch me.

Grinding in a club wasn't against the rules. We were supposed to do this, right? It was all innocent. If dancing would get the two of them to play along nicely, it was in everyone's best interest. Zander wouldn't want them to make a scene and attract unwanted attention. The Sevens had to present a united front. What other choice did I have?

We were so wrapped up in the moment we didn't notice a figure watching us from across the warehouse. A figure who crept up behind us to ruin our evening as soon as the song ended.

"Hello, Kitty." A chilling voice snapped the invisible thread tying me to West and Rocky. "Pleased to see me?"

Hiram.

———

The floor turned to water beneath my heels. I struggled to stand. Even the party seemed to go into slow motion as I turned around to face him. I knew he would come to find me. Hell, I'd been expecting it since I'd left Blackthorne Towers... but now it was finally here? It'd come too fucking soon.

Hiram flashed me his twisted smile, making me want to carve his eyeballs out with an ice cream scoop. He was in his forties but looked younger. Most women would find him attractive. You could mistake him for a handsome doctor if you didn't know any better. As he'd aged, Hiram had only grown a sharper and more menacing edge. He liked to take care of his appearance and wore an expensive navy suit, which he'd think nothing of ruining with the blood of his victims.

Rocky sprung into action, pushing me behind him to provide a blockade of muscle. He stared Hiram straight in the face and growled, "You need to leave."

West's hands held onto my waist to stop me from falling. In the ocean, fish could sense predators coming. West may not know who Hiram was but, judging from how hard his fingers dug into my sides, he knew a shark was in our midst.

"Where are your manners? You are forgetting who you're talking to." Hiram tutted at Rocky like a child who didn't know any better. "Don't you remember what happened last time we met?"

Rocky stepped forward, but I was quicker. I grabbed his arm to stop him before he did something stupid. "Don't!"

Hiram never traveled unprotected. If I hadn't been so fucking distracted, I'd have noticed eyes watching us from all angles. If Rocky made a move to kill Hiram, his men would be on top of us faster than a detonating bomb.

"I've missed your spirit." Hiram's bitter laugh made my stomach churn, as his evil glare didn't leave mine. "You look at home here, Kitty."

"Why are you in Port Valentine?" I spat through clenched teeth. Around us, partygoers danced to a new song, but we stayed rooted to the spot. "What do you want?"

"I wanted to see if it was true with my own eyes." His gaze strayed to my hand and locked on my ring. "The Blackbird was right. It looks like congratulations are in order."

"They are," West responded, placing his hands on my hips protectively. "Do you have a problem with that?"

"You can do better than a caveman, Kitten," Hiram said as his lips curled into a smile. He surveyed West with mild amusement, disregarding him like an annoying mosquito he could swat away. "He's not good enough for someone as special as you."

My stare burned into Hiram's unflinchingly. He had taken me by surprise, but I wouldn't give him any more satisfaction. He had ruined my fucking life. He was the monster who had allowed Raphael Jacobson to torture me mercilessly. He was the bastard who groomed me into submission. He'd transformed me from a shy kid to a woman who could slit throats on command.

During five years under his control, I went to hell and back. He showed me the darkest corners of the human psyche. He filled my head with images too graphic to be included in a horror movie. Hiram wanted me to be his protege. He gave me the skills to bring any man to their knees, but his training would be his undoing.

He believed he taught me everything I needed to know, but he was wrong. I learned the most valuable lesson on my own. Unlike him, I didn't *only* kill to further my agenda. Sure, it helped... but I killed because I wanted to take out fuckers who deserved to be wiped from existence. I killed people because it made the world a better place, and I did it with a fucking smile on my face. Hiram would never understand because he wasn't capable of feeling anything or caring about anyone other than himself. And, like the other beasts I'd put into the ground, I wanted my smile to be the last thing he ever saw.

"Quit the bullshit," I snapped. "Why are you here, Hiram?"

"You changed your number," Hiram replied with a shrug. "You know I don't like being ignored."

"Maybe you should take the fucking hint?" Rocky suggested, cracking his knuckles. "She doesn't want to speak to you. Not now. Not ever."

"You used to be so accommodating when you were younger." Hiram stifled a yawn, then narrowed his eyes. "Maybe I should have killed you when I had the chance? I still could. All it'd take is the click of my fingers, but I won't... not yet. Where's the fun in that?"

"I don't know who the fuck you are," West said, talking in a calm, arrogant drawl, "but Candy is ours."

"Did you hear him, Kitty?" Hiram threw back his head and cackled like a Disney villain. "*They* think you belong to them. We all know the truth though, don't we?"

"The only person I belong to is myself," I said, stepping out of West's grasp and standing on my own. "I'm a Seven now. But I'm assuming you already know that otherwise, you wouldn't be here. You're a long way from home."

"You never used to respect gangs," Hiram said, unperturbed by the two guys at my side, who looked like they were ready to beat his face to a pulp. He looked pointedly at Rocky. "No loyalty, remember?"

"You know nothing about loyalty," I said, hoping the music would drown the slight waver of my voice. Hiram had a doctorate in manipulation. He thrived in misery. Fucking with people's minds was his number one pastime. "I'm done with your fucking games."

"All I wanted to do was stop by to say hello," Hiram said, adjusting his tie. All the bravado was foreplay, leading up to the main climax. I wanted to give him blue fucking balls and cut straight to the point. "I thought you'd be pleased to see me."

"Do us all a fucking favor and say what's really on your mind."

"I'm not the only one who is playing games, Kitten." Hiram's expression turned frosty as he stepped forward and ran a finger down my cheek. He lowered his voice to make sure no one else could overhear. "I'm here to remind you of where you belong. I came to ask you to come home. It'd be easier for everyone if you agreed and came quietly."

"Over my dead fucking body," I snarled, jerking my face out of his noxious reach.

West and Rocky straightened up, gearing for a fight. If I ordered them to kill him, they may have a chance of snapping his neck before Hiram's men swooped in. But, if they did, none of us would get out of the Smoker alive.

"Pity. Everything could have been so much simpler." Hiram smiled wryly and checked his golden wristwatch. "I'm sure we'll see each other again soon. Remember, Kitty, I have eyes everywhere."

Hiram turned his back on us and melted into the crowd as if he'd never been there at all. *Was that it? He was giving up so easily?* My heart hammered in my chest, looking around to see whether snipers were ready to shower us with bullets. Instead, the party continued. Everyone was oblivious to the devil who lurked in the shadows.

"Is anyone going to tell me who the fuck he is?" West asked. "Why was he calling you Kitten?"

I had no time to give him answers.

Not now.

Not here.

My adrenaline kicked into overdrive, and I took off at speed. I raced through the mess of limbs, shoving people out of my way as I passed. Our Sevens night was officially over.

Hiram came to Port Valentine to spook me. He wanted me to know he was close. He wanted to reassert his dominance and make it clear he'd never let me go. When would it end?

I burst out of the warehouse, gulping the cool night air and letting it fill my lungs. My body shook — not from fear, but from being consumed by a wave of venomous anger. Hiram wanted to force me into a corner. His bitter poison sought to pollute my new life.

"Candy!" Rocky barreled out the exit after me. He hurried over to try to wrap his arm around my shoulders, but, instinctively, I shoved him back and winded him instantly. "I didn't see him. I swear—"

"Don't fucking touch me," I hissed. How could Rocky make me feel better after Hiram's reminder of his betrayal? Why did he think he could step into the same role he played in Evergreen as my protector? We were adults, everything had changed. "Leave me alone, Rocky."

"Candy, please!" He staggered forwards, clutching his chest like a wounded soldier. "This is what he wants. You know that, don't you? He wants to tear us apart again."

Rocky's betrayal had cut my soul so deeply that it'd become a permanent open wound. Whenever it scabbed over, a fresh reminder was enough to rip it open and make the blood pour all over again.

The Sevens limo sped around the corner and came to a stop at our feet. West swung the door open. "Get in."

"Don't!" I stopped Rocky from following. "Not now."

"You heard her," West spat as I slid into the backseat next to him. "Call a fucking cab."

Rocky's face fell as I slammed the door shut behind me. I may as well have stabbed him in the gut. If I didn't get away from him, maybe I would. When my anger boiled over, I didn't trust what I was capable of. Rocky had apologized and vowed to make up for his actions, but seeing Hiram brought it all back. Would I ever get past what he'd done?

The wheels screeched as we sped away, leaving Rocky alone in the dark… just as he had left me.

———

West's eyes watched me closely like he expected me to explode. "Do you want me to take you home?"

"Can we drive around for a bit?" I tipped my head back, finally breathing easier again, and stared up at the number seven on the roof. "I don't care where."

Driving around in the dark was better than being alone in my apartment and dwelling on what Hiram's next move may be. He didn't enjoy losing. It wouldn't be long before he returned to collect what he thought was rightfully his.

Neither of us spoke again for what seemed like an hour until West finally cleared his throat. He opened a secret compartment concealed in the back of a seat and pulled out an aged whiskey. He poured us both a generous serving. I'd bet Zander usually offered us the cheap shit, and this is where they kept their real supply.

He pressed the glass into my hand and asked surprisingly gently, "Are you going to tell me who he is?"

"No." I downed the amber smokey liquid and held it out for a refill. It was a drink to be savored, but I didn't give a shit. The fiery fuel burned my throat and distracted me from the thoughts rattling around in my mind. "I don't want to talk about it."

"Sharing goes two ways," West said, filling me up again. "You said yourself you're a Seven now."

I drained the glass and wiped my mouth with the back of my hand. "Not everything in my life is up for negotiation."

"I think you've had enough," West said. He pried the glass from my fingers. "If you won't tell me, how does Red know who he is?"

"Why don't you tell me why Red split your lip?" I asked, changing the subject. West kept his mouth sealed shut. "You're not so keen on sharing now, huh?"

Point fucking proven. I wouldn't be able to keep my secret from them forever. News of what happened would soon get back to Zander. When he heard, he wouldn't let it go until he discovered the truth. But it didn't stop me from wanting to hang onto my past a little longer.

West frowned, taking my hand in his and turning my palm up to face him. "You're bleeding."

I'd gouged small crescent moon indentations into my skin from balling my fingers into tight fists. Damn it, stiletto shaped acrylics had seemed like a good idea when Mieko persuaded me to let her fix my nails.

"I'm fine." I snatched my hand away and closed it. I didn't need his fucking concern.

"He didn't seem happy about your engagement..."

"Did you not hear me the first time, asshole?" I snapped, narrowing my eyes. "I said, I don't want to talk about it."

"He seemed possessive." Possessive wasn't strong enough of a word to cover Hiram's obsession. When he sunk his teeth into you, he'd never let you go. When you escaped his reach, he'd do anything to get you back. "I guess we both have crazy exes."

My eyes blazed in anger, digging my nails further into my skin and relishing the pain. "He's not a fucking ex."

Hiram manipulated me into doing his bidding. He enjoyed watching me kill other men, but he'd never touched me. Not like *that*. I wasn't an object of desire to him, but a pet. A loyal dog tethered to him by a fucking collar.

West reached out to take my hand again and uncurled my fingers.

"Want to know a secret?" he murmured under his breath, almost as if he was talking to himself. "I don't have self-control. I mean... when I start, I can't stop."

"What does it feel like?"

"I can't think. I can't feel. There's nothing stopping me. All I can think of is the next punch. The next strike." He traced over the backs of my fingers tenderly. His touch was so soft it almost tickled, like running a feather over your skin. "It started after my pa died. My anger. They put me on the school boxing team to help me channel it. During my first fight, this *thing* inside me... it took over."

A shadow dulled the twinkle in his eyes. I recognized the look. I saw it in the mirror whenever I remembered watching Crystal die.

"What happened during the fight?" I asked, not sure whether I wanted to hear the answer.

"The kid almost died." He dropped my hand and avoided my gaze. "He would have if Zander hadn't pulled me back. Bryce had to pull so many strings to stop the school from expelling me."

When you had a big enough cheque book, it was possible to brush anything under the plush carpet.

"He even paid some of the other kids to stay quiet, including Penny," West continued, hanging his head in shame. "That's what she was talking about in the motel room when we were in Hammerville. Bad things happen when I lose control."

Seeing West's guilt made me hate Penelope even more for her use of emotional manipulation, but I tried to keep my anger in check. I didn't want to spiral when he'd only just started to open up.

"But you stopped in the junkyard," I pointed out, remembering what happened when he released the beast inside of him. The man was a walking powerhouse. He'd be capable of tearing anyone apart limb by limb if he chose to. "You could have killed Eddie, but you didn't."

"Only because you stepped in." West took a swig of whiskey straight from the bottle. "Whoever the guy in the Smoker was, I know he's bad fucking news. Monsters recognize monsters."

"You didn't recognize me," I said, taking the bottle from him and slugging its contents. It has been barrel-aged in a Scottish cave for decades and cost hundreds of dollars, but it still tasted like engine coolant. "Remember?"

He smiled. "You're not a monster, Candy."

"Oops, my bad. What was it you called me the first time you saw me?" I muttered sarcastically, allowing words to spill from my mouth like vomit. "An airhead?"

"Are you always looking for a fight?" He scowled. "The universe isn't against you."

"Isn't it?" I don't know whether it was the alcohol or West's words causing tears to spring to my eyes. "You may have no self-control, but at least you have somewhere you belong. You're getting better. Hell, you could have killed Eddie in the junkyard, but you didn't. Look at me. I'm fucking broken, West. There's no fixing someone like me."

"You belong here." His index finger stopped a rogue tear from sliding down my cheek. I blinked the rest away, refusing to let myself break down in front of him. "I don't know what he did to you, but I won't let him near you again. I won't let him hurt you. Ever."

Words meant nothing. West didn't know what Hiram was capable of or the influence he had. His empire and reach spanned the entire country. After Hiram absorbed part of the Romano empire, he'd become one of the most feared and powerful men in the criminal sphere. From drugs to human trafficking, Hiram got involved in it all. He ended lives in the blink of an eye. He was an unstoppable force. Was there even any point in trying to fight him? What chance did I have?

"You don't know him like I do." I sniffed. "He won't stop, West. Not until he gets what he wants."

"What does he want?"

"Me."

West put his muscular arm around my shoulder and pulled my shivering body close. I hadn't even realized I was shaking but didn't have the energy to object. Being cocooned in his warm muscles and scent made me feel safe... for now, at least.

"You are a Seven, Pinkie," West murmured into my hair. "He can't have you. You belong to us now."

Maybe I did, I thought, as tiredness took over...

Where the hell was I?

I woke in a mild state of panic, grappling with the thick white freshly laundered sheets like a fish caught in a net. My eyes darted around the impeccably tidy room. It looked like the lair of a twisted OCD serial killer who covered his tracks.

"Morning." West emerged from the adjoining room in a cloud of steam, wearing nothing but a towel wrapped around his waist. I guess my prediction wasn't wrong…

If my heartbeat wasn't already erratic, it sure was now. Intricate grayscale tattoos adorned West's muscled torso. I could spend days looking at him and still find something new in his ink each time. "How did I—"

"You fell asleep on the drive," he explained, then raised his eyebrows as I peeked under the covers to find I was still wearing my dress from the night before. Across the room, my shoes and handbag were neatly stacked. "Don't worry, I slept on the sofa."

"Thanks for... you know," I mumbled.

"Sorry for waking you," he said, then wrinkled his nose. "I don't use other people's bathrooms."

Waking up to a half-naked man was not the worst sight to see in the morning, but I wouldn't tell him that. Instead, I rolled my eyes.

"Are you hungry?" he asked. "Zander's making food."

"I think I'll shower first," I replied cautiously, expecting him to kick up a fuss about me invading his sterile en suite.

"Be my guest," he said. "It's all yours."

I stumbled awkwardly out of his bed and onto my feet. I needed to get myself away from The Hulk when all that stood between me and his monster cock was a precariously tied towel.

I breathed a sigh of relief as soon as I slammed the bathroom door behind me. Inside, West had already laid out a folded fluffy towel and one of his clean shirts for me to wear, alongside two mini bottles of rose-smelling fancy shampoo. If he ever wanted to start over, maybe he could find success by opening a hotel? Although, he'd probably try to kill anyone who left a mess behind...

———

After showering, entering the Sevens penthouse kitchen felt like entering a parallel world. Had Hiram killed me last night, and the afterlife resembled a gang edition of the Real Housewives? Zander busied himself behind the counter, while Vixen, Rocky, and West sat waiting impatiently around the table.

"Take a seat," Zander ordered as he finished serving up pancakes and carried them over to the table where a selection of treats was already laid out. He handed me a plate with a serious expression on his face like I was a famous chef about to sample his food. "Enjoy."

"Finally!" Vixen threw me a look of disdain as I sat down next to her, and her stomach grumbled loudly. "Can we start now?"

"You didn't have to wait on my account," I said, diving straight in and stabbing the waffle on top of the enormous pile she had her eyes fixed upon.

Vixen stuck her tongue out. "Bitch."

It's funny how fast life could change. A few months ago, most of the people around the table couldn't bear to be around me. Now, our lives are intrinsically linked.

"Holy shit." I exhaled after taking my first bite. I'd loaded my waffle with maple syrup, bacon, and chocolate chips — was there really any other way? "These are so good."

West told me Zander was a good chef, but damn! His breakfast game was unreal. Why did we ever need to eat out when he knew his way around a waffle iron better than Bella, my old stripper nemesis, knew how to give a blow job?

"Did you sleep well, Candy?" Zander asked.

There was a sharp undertone to his voice, which put me on edge. I looked at West for help, but the giant was too busy filling his plate to notice. Opposite West, Rocky sipped a black coffee and didn't touch any of the food. The tension between the two of them hadn't lifted after last night.

Suddenly, the door to the living area creaked open and everyone spun around to watch Mieko sheepishly stumble in wearing last night's clothes.

"What are you doing here?" I asked.

Mieko's cheeks pinked. Judging by the rips in her tights and the lack of grazes on her knees, it looked like someone acted in a hurry.

Holy shit… finally!

My wing woman duties paid off. Hiram may have ruined my evening, but at least some of us had a good time. Although, if Vixen hurt her, I'd kick her ass… regardless of her Seven status.

A smug grin spread over my face and I turned to Vixen, "Is *your* guest joining us?"

"Of course she is." Vixen pulled out a chair for Mieko, like her sleeping with my best friend wasn't a big deal. "You need to try these pancakes, Mieko."

Mieko smiled shyly as she slipped into place at Vixen's side.

"We're expecting another visitor," Zander said.

The buzzer rang as if he'd planned it perfectly. Zander was either psychic or had cameras linked to his wristwatch. He disappeared to answer it and returned seconds later with Q.

The guys nodded at Q in greeting, Mieko squeaked a hello to introduce herself, and Vixen simply scowled. All the while, I kept my stare focused on Zander. What game was he playing?

"Take a seat, Cupid," Zander said. "Thanks for coming at short notice."

From the sheepish expression on Q's face, this wasn't one of his usual house calls. Zander had summoned him…

Shit. Zander wanted answers, and by inviting Q, it meant he'd already found them.

This wasn't *just a* nice breakfast.

It was a fucking ambush.

I threw Zander my filthiest look in accusation and dropped my fork. "How long have you known?"

He calmly met my gaze. "Long enough."

"Why didn't you say anything?" I demanded, crossing my arms. My life wasn't a fucking book anyone could read. I'm the only one who could tell my story. "We had a deal."

"Look," Q began, shuffling awkwardly in his seat, "after the night at the Maven—"

"I'm asking Zander," I snapped, shutting him down.

Q held his arms up to surrender, then slouched back to hide behind Mieko to avoid having to look at me. *Smart move.* He knew better than to get in my way. He'd never enjoyed confrontation and knew what happened when I lost my temper.

"I didn't break our deal," Zander said. "I didn't go looking for answers. Cupid came to me."

Finding out about Hiram coming to town must have been what it took for Zander to reveal his hand. If he hadn't, how much longer would he have kept the knowledge stored away?

"It wasn't your story to tell, *Cupid*," I snarled.

"I didn't want the same thing to happen to you as..." Q's voice trailed away as his thoughts strayed to Crystal. "I didn't tell Zander any details. All I told him was how we knew each other from... before."

Wanting to make sure Hiram didn't kill me may be an honorable reason for divulging my past, but it didn't make me any less furious. Why hadn't Zander said anything before?

"Is someone going to tell me what the fuck is going on?" West slammed his fists on the table, making it rattle, and looked at the three of us. "It's to do with him, isn't it? The guy who showed up last night."

"Mieko, you should leave," Zander said. "This is Seven business."

"No," I objected as Mieko rose to her feet. This was *my* business and Mieko was a friend amongst a table filled with assholes and hidden agendas. "She's not going anywhere."

Mieko shot a nervous glance at Zander and stammered, "I don't mind going..."

"I want you to stay," I insisted. "I don't wanna go over this story again, and I want you to hear it."

Mieko had already told me her biggest secret. It's only fair she heard mine. I may have to put my trust in the Sevens because of our business arrangement, but I didn't owe them the same level of loyalty I owed her. The night she helped Vixen and me dispose of a body showed me she was someone who I could trust.

"Fine." Zander relented with a sigh. "Mieko can stay."

She sat back down obediently, and Vixen squeezed her hand. She must be as skilled in the bedroom as she was on the pole to get the Ice Queen to show affection.

"Someone needs to talk," West growled. His cheeks reddened in anger and accentuated his scar. "Now."

I took a deep breath. Whether I liked it or not, my past was going to be laid bare for everyone to see.

"The guy who showed up at the Smoker is the biggest kingpin on the west coast," I began. "You name it, he's involved: drugs, women, weapons... the whole fucking deal. I used to work for him. For the last five years, I was his right hand."

"What kind of work did you do?" West pressed.

"Would you shut the fuck up and let her talk, West?" Vixen snapped, then turned back to watch me intently. "Go on, Candy…"

"I did bad things," I admitted. "Bad things to bad people. Extortion, arson, theft, murder… you name it, I've done it. Fuck, I don't even know how many people I've killed. I lost count at thirty. It wasn't just my job, it was my whole life. Whatever he said, I did without question. I was under his spell. Until—"

Q cleared his throat.

"Until I saw who he really was," I added hastily. He didn't need reminding of the day Crystal died. "All that matters is I got away. When I left, we made a deal. I did… something… in exchange for my freedom. We even had a contract written up. But a deal changes nothing in Hiram's mind."

"Hiram? You mean *the* Hiram?" Vixen gripped the table and looked at Q for confirmation. He nodded. She knew enough about Q's decision to forge a new life to connect the dots. "Fuck…"

"So, that's how you knew how to dispose of a body," Mieko murmured.

"Hiram trained me." I nodded. Something he would wish he hadn't one day. "He taught me everything he knew."

"Like, an assassin school?" she asked.

I couldn't help but laugh. Only Mieko could make my time with Hiram sound like a scene out of Harry Potter.

"Blackthorne Towers is more like a fucking prison," I explained. "Five years there is enough to send anyone insane. Hiram manipulates people. He has… his ways. Ways of breaking people down until they're nothing more than his puppet."

"And he wants you back to work for him," West hissed through clenched teeth. "I won't let it happen."

"You don't know what Hiram is capable of or the power he has," I said. "This is all a game to him now, but he's never going to stop. Not until he gets what he wants."

"How did you get into it?" Vixen questioned. "How does a guy like Hiram even go about recruiting a kid? You must have been young when he took you to Blackthorne Towers."

"Sixteen," I confirmed, catching Rocky's eye. He hadn't told the Sevens about our shared past, because he was ashamed. Knowing what he'd done would change their perception of who he was. He wanted to make amends and, just because I'd never get over his betrayal, it didn't mean everyone else had to make him suffer for his mistakes. "I guess I fell in with the wrong crowd."

Or fell in love with the wrong person…

Rocky took a deep breath and cleared his throat. "You don't need to cover for me, C. Not anymore."

Zander's head whipped around to stare at his friend in surprise. "What's going on, Red?"

Q must have told the truth when he said he hadn't told Zander everything. It wouldn't please a control freak like Zander to know he didn't know the full story.

"You don't have to do this, Rocky," I said. I respected how he wanted to take accountability for his actions, but he hadn't thought this through. Didn't he know his admission could get him kicked out of the Sevens? Or worse...

"Everyone needs to know what I've done, Candy." Rocky held his head high and met my gaze. "I've lied to you. All of you."

"Red?" Vixen's voice shook. "What're you talking about?"

"Candy and I knew each other when we were kids. We grew up together in Evergreen," he said. "When Candy says she fell in with the wrong crowd, she is talking about me. *I* was the wrong crowd. *I* made a deal with Hiram. *I* was the one who handed her over to that bastard. It's my fault she ended up in Blackthorne Towers and lived through those years of torture. It's all on me. All of it."

Rocky had apologized to me before, but talk is cheap. Actions spoke louder than words, and this? Him confessing his sins to the Sevens? It changed everything. Maybe... just maybe... this could help me on my journey to fully forgiving him.

A stunned silence descended over the table at Rocky's revelation. Vixen's mouth opened and closed like she couldn't decide what to say first. Zander looked between Rocky and me, trying to discern whether Rocky was telling the truth, then gritting his teeth when he realized he was. Mieko caught my eye; her only concern was checking whether I was okay, while Q continued to hide behind her to blend into the background. West was the first to act.

He jumped up like he'd taken an adrenaline shot straight to the heart. "You did, what?"

"Sit," Zander ordered.

West's nostrils flared as he considered charging at Rocky.

"Please, West," I pleaded. "Let him explain."

Reluctantly, West returned to his seat. Even though he was looking at Rocky like he wanted to tear his balls off.

"Let me get this straight," Vixen said, trying to wrap her head around his story, "you two *both* grew up in Evergreen?"

"Yep," I confirmed. They already knew Rocky's history. Them knowing we were forged in the same screwed up system is all they needed to know.

"Why didn't you say anything, Red?" Vixen addressed Rocky with the ferocity of a hungry hyena. After forming a close bond together in juvie, she'd take not knowing his secret the hardest. She put him on a fucking pedestal. "Why didn't you fucking tell us? Why didn't you tell *me*?"

"It was, and still is, the biggest mistake of my life." Rocky's eyes sought solace at the bottom of his cup. "I was ashamed, okay? I was a stupid kid and thought I was doing the right thing. But I was wrong... so fucking wrong."

"I knew there was something between you," Vixen declared, putting the pieces together. "When you came back from seeing the Razors months ago, Candy held a fucking knife to your balls. I brushed it off, but shit! Why didn't you say anything then? You had a chance."

"How do you think it feels to be constantly reminded of the worst thing you ever did?" Rocky asked, hanging his head in shame. "Whenever I look at her, it's all I see. I did something terrible to the one person I cared about more than anyone else."

"You cared about her?" West growled, wanting to get to the bottom of our relationship. "So, what were you? Friends? A couple?"

"It doesn't matter what we *were*," I stepped in to stop West's line of questioning. I'd already revealed enough. They didn't need to know every detail of my life, including how Rocky was the person I'd lost my virginity to. It was irrelevant, and nobody's fucking business. "It was a long time ago, okay? So much has happened since then. Now, we're just two members of the same gang. That's it."

"You should have told us, Rocky," Vixen snarled, turning on him without pity. "We're *supposed* to be a family."

"All families have secrets," I muttered.

The Sevens had more than most.

"Don't defend him." Zander's commanding voice made everyone sit up straighter. He sent Rocky a glare so chilling it could have stopped a volcano from erupting. He would not let this go lightly. I don't know what made him madder: how he didn't know about our connection or learning what Rocky did. "Get out of here, Red."

Rocky nodded solemnly, leaving without saying another word. Unanswered questions hung in the air.

"Pinkie, if I knew—"

"Don't." I held up my hand to interrupt West. "I don't want to talk about it again, okay? You all know now. There's no more fucking secrets, and I think it's time I go too."

After laying out my past like a road map, it zapped all of my energy. I may have just woken up, but all I wanted to do was crawl back under the covers and never come out.

"Wait up!" Vixen grabbed my arm as I stood to leave. "Do you even know what day it is?"

"Funnily enough, checking the calendar is not something I'd had time to do today," I snapped sarcastically.

"It's Christmas Eve." With everything going on, I'd completely spaced on the date, despite the dancers being dressed like elves in the club for weeks. Although, with a name like Lapland, it was like Santa's dirty grotto all year round. "You're staying with us for Christmas."

"I'd rather be on my own."

Vixen crossed her arms and put on her strongest boss bitch voice, "This is not up for negotiation."

"But I don't have my things."

"I'll get a driver to take you home and bring you back," Vixen said, then turned to Mieko."What are you doing for the holidays?"

"I mean, I didn't have any—"

"You're staying too," Vixen decided, with an air of finality. There was no point in arguing when she hadn't given either of us any choice in the matter. "You too, Cupid. We're a fucked up family, but we're all sticking together. No arguments."

"I'll sleep on the sofa," West volunteered gruffly. He was still recovering from his earlier outburst. It'd take him a few rounds with a punching bag to release his simmering anger. "You can take my bed, Pinkie."

"What do you say, Zander?" Vixen pushed.

"I'll order more turkey," Zander grumbled reluctantly.

Vixen clapped her hands together. "It's settled then."

This would certainly be a Christmas to remember.

———

Vixen bundled Mieko and me into a car, giving the driver very strict instructions to escort us to our apartments and bring us straight back.

"Where does she expect us to run to?" I scowled. "It's not like I have anywhere else to go."

"I think it's cute she's being protective."

I scoffed. "She only gives a shit about me now because she thinks she owes me something."

"I don't think that's true," Mieko said, thinking the best of everyone as usual. "What do you think is going to happen to Red?"

"That's up to Zander," I said, trying not to let my thoughts wander to what his judgment would be.

Zander wouldn't do anything to hurt him, right? Rocky made a mistake, but he didn't need to keep being punished. Once upon a time, revenge is all I thought about, but now? Things had changed.

"I'm sorry about what happened to you," Mieko whispered. "I know you don't want to talk about it. You don't have to. But, if you ever do, I'm right here."

"Thanks." I squeezed her hand, touched by her care. "And you know I'm here for you too."

"I know." She squeezed back, then frowned. "Do you think the Sevens are really okay with me staying for Christmas?"

"Vixen invited you," I pointed out, then winked. "You must be a pretty good lay."

"I don't want to mess things up with her." Mieko wrung her hands in her lap. "What if she thought last night was a mistake? Maybe she felt she had to invite me out of pity?"

"Trust me, Vixen wouldn't have invited you, if she didn't want you there," I said. Vixen had no shame and didn't give a shit about who she offended. "Last night must have been pretty special…"

"It was." Mieko blushed, then her face turned to horror as she yelped like someone had poked her in the eye. "What about presents? We don't have any presents!"

I rolled my eyes at her sudden hysteria. "You can't be serious right now…"

"We can't turn up with nothing," she wailed like Armageddon had descended. How come she wasn't bothered about sharing a ride with a serial killer but gift shopping tipped her over the edge? A giggle-snort escaped my lips. "What's so funny?"

The seriousness of her face only made me laugh more. I laughed so damn hard my shoulders shook, and I worried I'd pee on the seats. To anyone looking in, I must have resembled a demented clown on crack. Mieko soon joined me. Both of us laughed until fat tears rolled down our cheeks and our jaws ached.

"Pull over at the next gas station," I ordered the driver.

Between us, we had seven dollars and twenty-five cents. The Sevens may be used to lavish gifts, but this was our only option.

I'd never really celebrated Christmas before. In Evergreen, a cold slice of meat and lukewarm vegetables was the best you got. My only fond holiday memories were days spent with Rocky. Christmas in the Evergreen group home was usually quieter because the other kids spent time with distant family members. One year, Rocky smuggled a portable television upstairs into his room We watched Home Alone four times and ate so much chocolate we almost threw up.

When the car came to a halt outside the gas station, we bundled inside.

"What can we get?" Mieko asked, roaming the aisles in despair and attracting strange looks from other shoppers because of her hysterical tone. "All we can get is candy."

"Well, we'll get candy then," I said decisively.

After dwelling over choices of candy and spending twenty minutes annoying the cashier, he eventually caved and said he'd cover the cost of the bars where we fell short. Who said the Christmas spirit was dead, huh?

As we piled back into the car, Mieko looked down nervously at the assortment of snacks. "Should we wrap them?"

"I've got foil back at my apartment."

Who wouldn't want a wrapped up Twinkie as a gift?

After a quick stop at our apartments to collect our belongings and ten calls from Vixen to track our whereabouts, we finally arrived back at Lapland. The club was closed for the next few days, so the street was unusually quiet without music blaring.

Mieko pushed the door open, and her eyes widened. "Wow."

A long banquet table decorated with garlands, flickering candles, and fake snow had taken over the dance floor. Christmas trees of varying sizes decorated the different podiums. Lights twinkled through the cage bars, where dancers usually performed, catching the sparkly surfaces of the baubles strung across the ceiling. I blinked twice to check I wasn't imagining things. Had we stepped into a motherfucking grotto?

West's head poked around the side of the largest tree on the main stage. He was the only person tall enough to reach the topmost branches. He gestured down at the red Christmas sweater he was wearing, with a giant reindeer in the center. "Vix really takes the holidays seriously."

"I can tell," I murmured. How many balls of wool would have been needed to knit a sweater so large? "Who knew she'd traded her piercings and leather pants for pointed ears?"

"Where's the music, West?" Vixen screeched from behind the bar. If she worked in the North Pole workshop, the elves would unionize against her leadership. "You said you were putting it on ten minutes ago."

West cursed under his breath and disappeared behind the boughs. A few seconds later, 'Santa Baby' started playing. I mean, we *were* still in a strip club.

Mieko admired the table decorations, running her hands over the crackers, as Vixen joined us to lay the final touches. "It all looks amazing."

"There's not enough room for everyone to sit in the penthouse," Vixen replied nonchalantly. Although, the slight twitch of her lips hinted at her appreciating Mieko's compliment and trying her darnedest to hide it. "Can you help me hang the rest of the lights upstairs?"

"Sure!" Mieko jumped at the chance. Vixen's vagina must have done some weird Christmas voodoo on her. "Do you want to help, Candy?"

"You two go ahead," I insisted, not wanting to be a third wheel. "I'll hang out here."

Not that I had any company. Q sat alone in a booth, typing furiously away on his laptop. When he was in the zone, he wouldn't want to be disturbed. Meanwhile, West's obsessive tendencies extended to dressing the tree. I watched as he held up a ruler to measure the exact distance between baubles. There was no sign of Rocky or Zander. Had Rocky returned, or would he spend Christmas Eve roaming the streets?

"Candy," Zander's voice called to me from an open door, extinguishing any ounce of my festive cheer like a snowfall. "I need to see you in my office."

After our dramatic breakfast, something told me this conversation wouldn't go down well.

———

In his office, Zander gestured for me to sit down opposite him.

"I'm sure you know what I want to talk to you about," Zander said, watching me closely from across his desk. He'd changed and was wearing a black Christmas sweater with 'ho, ho, ho' over the front, which made him appear a lot less threatening than he intended. Vixen must have forced him into wearing it.

"Where's Red?" I asked.

"Out," Zander replied abruptly. His smoky gray eyes pierced mine, searching for answers he wouldn't find. There was also something else lurking in his eyes. Anger, perhaps? Finding out about Rocky and I's past had irritated him. "Red won't be coming back. Not unless you want him to."

"You're leaving it down to me?" My mouth fell open. Zander never relinquished control to anyone. Did he expect me to believe he'd suddenly had a personality transplant? I arched an eyebrow. "What's the catch?"

"No catch," he said. "Loyalty is everything in the Sevens. We can't change what Red did, but we can change the future. If you don't want him around, all you need to do is say the word. I can make him disappear."

"You'd kick him out?" My words came out in a furious burst as I slammed my clenched fists down on the wood. "After everything he's done for you?"

Ending Rocky's life used to be my sole motivator, but everything was different now. Even though Zander was on my side, his ability to turf Rocky out like garbage made my blood boil. Rocky was no fucking angel, but he'd been part of their gang for years. After hearing Nico's praise during our visit to Hammerville, I learned how Rocky helped to set up their growing business. Where the fuck was Zander's loyalty?

"You're a Seven now. Red wronged you, so the decision lies in your hands," Zander said with zero emotion. "Whatever you choose, know it is final. The Sevens don't give second chances."

Wasn't this what I'd been waiting for? It was my last chance to erase Rocky from my life for good. I tried killing him myself but failed. Now, I had the opportunity to stay in the Sevens and never see him again.

"How long have I got to decide?" I asked.

Zander cocked his head to the side, watching me closely. "How long do you need?"

Rocky had caused me unthinkable pain, but he was also the only person who I'd truly loved. The joy we had shared only made his betrayal more pronounced. He played a part in sending my life down the wrong path but, until then, he'd given me a reason to live.

My mouth started moving before I even realized what I was saying.

"He can stay," I blurted out.

No punishment would compare to the mental torture Rocky inflicted on himself every day. I knew how he felt. Whenever I looked at Q, my chest ached from the raw anguish of knowing I was the reason Crystal ended up dead.

"Noted." Zander nodded curtly. His shoulders slackened slightly. Despite his icy demeanor, he cared more than he let on about Rocky's fate. "But know there will be consequences for his actions."

"What will you do?"

He paused. "I'll think of something fitting to his crime."

"Well, whatever it is, keep me out of it," I huffed, crossing my arms over my chest. "I'm over all of your macho drama. You guys are worse than the dancers. First, Rocky punched West. Now—"

"He did, what?" Zander cut in sharply.

"It was nothing," I muttered. *Great job, Candy. Way to stick your stiletto in your mouth again.* "Just the usual homoerotic tussle. You don't see me tackling Mieko to the floor and trying to punch her in the tit, do you?"

Zander didn't look convinced. After this morning, how had I not learned my lesson? Zander didn't know everything that went on inside Lapland walls.

"And what do you think of macho guys, Candy?" Zander asked, steering the conversation in a new and dangerous direction. "What type of men do you like?"

Men like him.

Men like West.

Men like Rocky.

Wicked men who set my skin alight, and a twisted part of me fucking embraced it. Men who I should want to run from...

I swallowed hard. "I need to get back to decorating."

Zander looked at me in bemusement. "I didn't think you were into holiday celebrations."

"Says who?" I bluffed defiantly. "I *love* the holidays."

"Yet you didn't know it was Christmas Eve?"

Well, he had me there. *The bastard.* He saw straight through my lies.

"If you hadn't noticed, I've had a lot going on." I flicked my hair to make myself look bored with his conversation. "What's your excuse?"

"There are better ways to spend my time than dressing a tree." He looked me up and down hungrily. My cheeks flushed at the memory of what happened the last time I'd been in his office. Sitting down had only become bearable again. "I prefer undressing my presents."

"Enjoy sitting here alone, Zander," I said, rising from my chair.

"Don't you want to stay and keep me company?" he purred.

"I'm not another one of your girls, Zander," I snapped. My pussy wasn't a hose he could turn on with a flick of his wrist. "I'm not like Bella or the others."

"Oh, I know you're not." A panty-dropping smile spread over his face. "But you can't deny you want me, little one."

"The only present you'll be getting from me this Christmas is blue fucking balls." I flipped him off and stormed out.

The worst thing is, Zander was right. The more time we spent together, the less control I had over my actions. Being in his company was fucking intoxicating. Losing control left me open to being hurt, and worse? Zander wasn't the only man I felt drawn to. He, Rocky, and West had burrowed underneath my skin. Being around them felt like balancing on a cliff edge, so close to plummeting into jagged rocks below.

———

"Is Scrooge coming to join us?" Vixen asked as I returned to the main area.

"I doubt it," I said, surveying the club again in appreciation. Even the candy stripper pole looked like a purposeful Christmas accessory rather than an X-rated prop. "Who knew you had such an eye for interior design?"

"I always wanted to go to art college." Vixen shrugged wistfully. "This isn't my usual style."

"What kind of art do you normally do?" Mieko asked.

"I paint," Vixen replied, which only made Mieko look at her with even greater admiration.

"She's great," West chipped in. "Not that she ever lets people see her work..."

"Since when are you a fucking art critic?" she sneered. "You wouldn't know a damn Frida Kahlo if it hit you in the face."

"Isn't she the chick with the unibrow?" West asked.

"Exactly my fucking point, West. You're so—"

"Maybe you can show me your paintings sometime?" Mieko stepped in before Vixen could finish her sentence. Damn, she was brave. Who would try to stroke a dog after it'd bit off a stranger's arm?

"Sure," Vixen said, then coughed, trying to cover her keenness. "I mean, only if you'd like to see..."

"I'm almost done with the playlist, Vix," Q called over from his nook.

"Hey," West objected with a moody pout. "You put me in charge of the music. Isn't mine good enough now?"

"Hook it up, Cupid," Vixen ordered, then grinned mischievously. "None of us want to be listening to West's Spotify all night."

The Hulk looked outraged. "What's wrong with my music?"

Vixen snorted. "We're not all into the Spice Girls…"

"I only played Wannabe one time!" West's pout deepened. "So much for you being a fucking feminist."

Lapland's door opening sent a cold gust whistling through the building. Silence descended as Rocky stepped inside. West dropped his box of baubles with a crash and hurtled off the stage with the grace of a raging bull.

"West," I shouted, causing him to reluctantly halt by my side like I'd yanked him on a leash. "Don't."

West turned to face me. I saw the fury and disappointment in his eyes. The Sevens prided themselves on their closeness. Learning his brother hadn't been the person he'd thought had hit him hard. "How can you defend him after what he did, Pinkie?"

I put a hand gently on his arm and whispered, "Don't you have things in your past that you wish you didn't do?"

None of us had the right to act like self-righteous assholes. We'd all done things that could have had us locked up for the rest of our lives. We were all haunted by regrets, but didn't those mistakes make us who we are?

"Candy wants Red to stay." Zander's commanding voice echoed towards us, as he stepped out of the shadows. "If she wants to move past it, we must respect her decision."

Rocky blinked back tears of disbelief. "You really want me to stay, C?"

"It doesn't mean there will be no consequences," Zander cut in. "You will pay for what you've done."

"I understand." Rocky hung his head in shame, then turned to address me. "You know I'll do anything to make things right again with you, don't you?"

I nodded curtly, but couldn't meet his gaze. When I first returned to Lapland, Rocky appeared to be confident and outgoing. The longer I stayed, the more he turned into a ghost of his former self. My presence forced him to confront his feelings about what he'd done. Seeing him like this made me wonder whether it would have been kinder to kill him. This is the second time I'd saved his life, but what had it achieved? It only caused him more suffering.

"All of us have a past," I said, aware everyone's eyes were on me. "But it doesn't mean we have to punish ourselves forever. I don't want anyone's pity. I don't want you seeing me as a fucking victim. The only thing I want is to get Hiram out of my life for good, and I can't do it alone."

"We'll deal with Hiram together," Zander vowed.

"He will never take you away again, C," Rocky promised. "We won't let that happen."

"I'll fucking kill him if he tries," West growled, re-directing his anger away from Rocky to a better target.

"From now on, we trust no one outside these walls," Zander continued. "My father and Giles aren't the only ones mobilizing against us. Now, we have Hiram too. We will take them down together. All of us."

I looked at the faces around the room. We had all done fucked up shit but, for the first time since joining the Sevens, I finally felt like one of them. Alone, I was vulnerable. But together, with Mieko and Q? We were all in. *I* was all in. Heads would roll if anyone stood in our way.

West nodded in agreement, then turned to Rocky and held out his hand. Rocky took it and West pulled him into a man hug to slap him on the back. "Welcome home, brother."

Vixen cleared her throat to get our attention. "Now, before we take down all the motherfuckers, can we try to have a *nice* Christmas? For once, I'd like to have a few days without planning revenge."

"We can do that, right?" I aimed my stare at the Seven guys, then poured myself a glass of eggnog and raised it in the air. "Merry fucking Christmas, Vix."

———

The rest of the day passed in a weirdly wonderful blur. Zander served up a delicious meal, and we played drunken rounds of charades. We were so used to living in a world filled with darkness; it felt amazing to let loose for a change. Maybe Vixen would convert me to becoming a Christmas lover, after all...

"I'm callin' it a night," Q slurred, getting up from the table. The poor guy was a lightweight and had been trying to keep up with the guys. He'd be nursing a banging headache when he woke up. "See y'tomorrow."

"I'm feeling pretty tired too." Vixen yawned melodramatically, not fooling anyone. "I might head upstairs too..."

"Yeah," Mieko agreed, biting her lip. "I'm feeling kinda sleepy..."

"Sleepy, my fucking ass." I rolled my eyes. If I wasn't so happy for them, I'd have made retching noises. "You could at least try to be subtle about it."

"I don't know what you mean," Mieko stammered.

"Sweet dreams." West smirked, then added, "if you get any sleep."

"Go to hell, West," Vixen shouted, as she and Mieko stood to follow Q out. They had to put their arms around Q's shoulders to help guide him upstairs to the penthouse.

"Vix seems happy," Rocky remarked, as we heard the pair of them giggling in the distance. "I've not seen her like that for... well, ever."

How had she and Mieko not hooked up before now? They'd instantly clicked and had bounced off each other all afternoon. Their conflicting personalities complimented each other. Mieko's sweetness would help temper Vixen's fieriness, whilst Vixen's ball-breaking attitude could push Mieko out of her comfort zone.

"Why don't the four of us play a little game?" Zander suggested. He placed an empty bottle in the middle of the table. "Truth or dare."

"Come on, Zander." I sighed and rolled my eyes. "We're not teenagers."

"What's wrong?" he asked. "Too scared?"

My eyes narrowed. He knew how to get to me. "Spin the fucking bottle."

With a flick of his wrist, it spun in circles and slowly came to a stop in front of West.

"Easy!" West lounged back in his chair casually. "Dare."

Rocky rubbed his chin in thought, then grinned. "How about we get the tattoo gun out?"

"You bastard," West groaned, cupping his head in his hands. "Not again."

"What happened last time?" I asked.

West grimaced and stood to roll down his waistband. *Fuck*. His V-lines were out of this world. I pulled my eyes away to look at where he was pointing and snorted. A wonky inked heart on his hip bone with 'Red' scratched inside.

"How about we add a candy cane next to it?" Zander said. "You don't want to make your *fiancée* jealous."

"Perfect," Rocky said, nodding in agreement.

"Fuck it," West declared. There was no way he could talk them out of it. "Bring the gun."

Rocky vanished upstairs and returned with the case a few moments later.

"Why do you even have one of those?" I asked as Rocky busied himself with setting up the supplies in a booth.

"Vix used to tattoo," Rocky explained. "She got really good in juvie."

"Maybe we should ask her to do it then?" I questioned, thinking about what diseases West could contract. I'd been to enough decent tattoo shops to know sanitation was important. After leaving Hiram, I'd spent time on the road. I'd traded jewelry for cash and got inked along the way. Sure, I could have spent money on more sensible things, but you can't put a price on feeling like you belong in your body again.

All of them laughed. Hepatitis was the last thing on their minds when screwing over their friend was at stake.

"Come on, C," Rocky said, pouring black and red ink into tiny caps. "Where's the fun in that?"

All of us gathered around the machine as it buzzed to life like a bat outta hell. The sound instantly made my shoulders tense. For people who'd spent many hours in a tattooist's chair, the noise took you straight back there. Thank fuck Zander took me to an actual studio to get my new Seven tattoo last month. Anything was better than getting my skin permanently marked by a group of psychos. Thankfully, West's body was already covered in artwork and a tiny candy cane would blend into the background.

Rocky handed me the gun. "Here."

"You want me to do it?" I gasped as West rolled down his pants to reveal more of his deep muscle lines and a delicious snail trail, leading down to his… "I can't."

"Sure, you can," Rocky replied. "It's easy."

"Do we have any gloves?"

Rocky chuckled, while West lay down across the seats to get himself into prime position.

"Just get it over with, Pinkie," West growled.

I'd watched people tattoo me before. How hard could it be? I dipped the needle into the ink. The gun rattled the bones in my hand and sent vibrations up my arm. How could tattooists make such precise lines? West held his skin taut to expose a small spot of bare skin between other designs. I took a deep breath and pushed the needle into his skin. The first stroke made me jump.

Zander shook his head and tutted. "You can slit someone's throat but can't do a little tattoo?"

His taunting made me push the needle in harder.

"Not so deep," West complained.

My hand shook as I completed the outline, which was about the size of my little finger. I wasn't sure whether I was shaking because of marking West's skin or because I rested inches from The Hulk's massive cock. Eventually, I settled into a rhythm. After the black outline and striped lines, I enjoyed filling in the red. His body was my own freaking coloring book.

"There." I sat back triumphantly to admire my slightly wonky masterpiece with uneven color. "What do you think?"

In twenty minutes, I'd been marked on West's skin for life. He wasn't the first person to have a candy cane tattooed in my honor. When Crystal got her ink, it symbolized our friendship, but it sentenced her to death. Hopefully, this wouldn't seal West's fate, too.

"She's on you forever now, bro," Rocky teased, passing him a towel.

"Fucking great." West scowled in annoyance as he wiped up the stray ink. "Who's up next?"

We all returned to the banquet table, where Zander spun the bottle again.

Fuck... it landed on me.

"What'll it be?" Zander asked. "Truth or dare?"

"Truth."

With the tattoo gun lying around, there's no way I wanted to risk getting a penis in the middle of my forehead or a 'property of the Sevens' tramp stamp.

"I've got one for you." Zander's cool, no-bullshit tone sent a shiver down my spine. "Which one of us would you rather fuck?"

Oh, shit...

I faltered as his gray piercing eyes ran over my curves. I looked at West, whose expression remained as dark and unreadable as ever. Then Rocky, who balled his hands into fists on the table.

All three of them were criminals. They'd all done twisted and terrible things. Their damaged pasts had brought them together, and they formed a bond deeper than blood. They were a family. Brothers. They were also all devastatingly panty-meltingly gorgeous.

How could anyone choose between them?

First, there was Zander. The leader with no limits. If you went against him, you'd be dead. No questions asked. Zander had a ruthless efficiency and vicious streak that made the hairs on the back of my neck stand on end. He had the money, power, and connections to get whatever he wanted no matter the cost. While he got off on power, more depth hid beneath his angular jawline. Zander was a fierce protector and didn't trust easily. He'd gut anyone who crossed his family and if you were in, he'd never let you go...

Then there was West. The giant who could rip your legs off with his bare hands. When West saw red, violence was the only language he could understand. He was a powerhouse of brute force and would do whatever needed to be done for those he cared about. Underneath his thick biceps, West had a softer side too. As much as he liked to make out he was a monster, the big, scary beast protected an inner teddy bear. Even if he was too scared to show it or admit how he felt...

Finally, Rocky. The only person I'd ever truly loved who betrayed me in the worst way. Gang life and Redlake had changed him. Over the years, he'd seen and done things no one should ever have to do. This is not the life he'd have chosen for himself and he hated himself for it. His anger at the world made him an unpredictable loose cannon who could explode at any moment, but I still caught glimpses of the funny laid-back guy I fell for as a teenager. Would it be possible for him to find his way back, or was he too broken to fix?

"Tell us who you want to fuck, Candy," Zander repeated.

Why the fuck hadn't I chosen dare? Flashing my tits would have been easier.

"I can't choose," I said finally, refusing to look them in the eye. "All of you."

On their own, they were powerful, but together? They were unstoppable.

"At the same time?" A sly smile crept over Zander's face. "Maybe we could arrange that."

He looked pointedly down at my nipples poking through the thin fabric of my shirt. Goddammit. Why did my body have to betray me? I'm supposed to be a badass chick with no feelings; yet, the twins instantly perk up at the thought of having a... wait, what the fuck would it be called? A foursome? A gang bang? A four-way fuckathon?

I jumped up. "I'm going to bed."

Yep, an icy shower would stop my cock-hungry vagina from wanting to munch on a man meat sandwich. I ignored their laughter and raced upstairs. Alone.

"Merry fucking Christmas to you too," Zander called after me.

Now, I didn't *want* all of them... I fucking *needed* them.

CHAPTER

Ten

"It's Christmassssss!" A voice roared through the door like Noddy Holder. "Wake up!"

After my confession during our game last night, it was a relief to wake up in West's bed alone. The big man's mattress was as comfortable as a freaking cloud.

The light flicked on above me, causing me to shield my eyes and squint at the shadow looming in the doorway. "Vixen? Is that you?"

"Get the fuck up, Candy," she ordered, then continued to march down the corridor to screech at everyone to gather on the sofas. Aren't holidays *supposed* to be a time for relaxing?

"Okay, okay!" Rocky's cries of objection were drowned out by splashing water. Was waterboarding a fucked up Seven tradition? "Goddammit! I'm up!"

I jumped out of bed before Vixen got the chance to return and dragged myself to join the others, who had the same idea. I usually slept naked, but I was glad I'd decided to pack a tank top and shorts set. Rocky, still cursing, arrived with wet hair stuck to his forehead and a towel draped over his shoulder. There was always a casualty in a war.

I took a seat next to Q, who groaned and clutched his head. "Why did I agree to this again?"

Vixen scowled as she sat down, finally content after rounding us up like fucking sheep. "It's ten-thirty, asshole."

"I don't know what you're complaining about, Cupid." West glowered at him from the other end of the enormous sofa where he'd slept. The sight of him sprawled over the cushions without a shirt and in gray sweats made my stomach somersault. "You kept me awake with your snoring."

Zander didn't sit down with the rest of us. He busied himself in the kitchen, already chopping vegetables with ruthless precision. He knew his way around a blade. I'd never seen Zander without a suit before, but he suited his casual black T-shirt and jeans.

"We've already been awake for hours," Vixen declared smugly, slinging a protective arm around Mieko's shoulder. Mieko, unlike the rest of us, looked positively glowing in Vixen's oversized band T-shirt.

"I bet you have," Rocky chirped, unable to resist a cheap shot, making the rest of the guys snicker.

"Nice tattoo." Vixen raised an eyebrow at West, spotting the candy cane poking out of his waistband. She missed nothing. "It looks fresh."

"Truth or dare," Rocky confirmed, as West pouted and pulled his pants up to cover it.

"Fucking idiots." Vixen rolled her eyes, then rubbed her hands together and called over to Zander. "Is breakfast ready, Zander?"

"Of course," Zander replied, pulling a tray of mouthwatering pastries out of the oven and leaving them on the counter.

The prospect of food instantly perked up Q's mood, and he clambered over my legs to be the first to dive in.

"Aren't you joining us?" I called over to Zander, as we piled our plates.

"I'm not hungry," he said, without looking in my direction and staying focused on his preparation. It seemed criminal he'd got up early to make us an incredible feast, but not touch it himself.

"Save some space for later." Vixen glared at West, slapping his hand away as he reached for a fourth croissant. In response, he added another two to his mountain.

"Cut him some slack, Vix." Rocky elbowed her in the ribs. "It is Christmas..."

After we filled our plates, we returned to the living area where conversation broke out in smaller groups. I seized the opportunity to speak to Mieko, while Vixen and Rocky tried to steal food off West's plate. They'd be lucky to keep all of their fingers.

I lowered my voice. "So you had a good night, huh?"

"I keep thinking this whole thing is a dream," she whispered. I raised my brows, then she added hastily, "Not *that*. I mean, Christmas. It's never been a good time for me. Since my grandma died a few years ago, I've spent it alone. But, this? It almost feels like being with a proper family."

We watched as West almost stabbed Rocky in the hand for trying to steal a pain au chocolat he had his eyes on. Sure, this may not be a traditional family Christmas, but it's the closest I'd gotten to a normal holiday season. In the past, the day had only highlighted everything I didn't have.

"I'm glad you're here," I said. "Although, I still think you're mad for hooking up with the Ice Queen."

She smiled. "She's not as much of an Ice Queen as you think..."

I held up my hand to stop her. "Spare me the dirty details."

"Besides, what about you?" Mieko asked, wiggling her eyebrows suggestively. "What happened last night after we went to bed?"

"We played a stupid game," I mumbled.

Yeah, a stupid game where I admitted to wanting to fuck all three of the Seven guys. Hopefully, my admission would be brushed off as a result of drinking too much of Zander's amazing eggnog.

Mieko leaned in closer. "Don't think I haven't seen how they look at you."

"I don't know what you mean," I said unconvincingly.

"You'll have to face it eventually..."

Vixen plopped herself down next to Mieko. "What are you two whispering about over here?"

"Nothing," I interjected, shooting Mieko a glare to make sure she kept her mouth shut.

"This tastes amazing." She crammed a mouthful of food into her mouth, causing her cheeks to bulge like a cute squirrel. "Mmm!"

Thankfully, Vixen didn't notice. She was too busy waiting for everyone to finish their food, so she could move on to her next item on her Christmas morning agenda.

"Is everyone ready for presents now?" Vixen asked as Rocky finished the final crumb on his plate. A chorus of groans followed her question. "Cheer up, you miserable fuckers. Zander, you need to get over here, too."

Zander opened his mouth to object, but changed his mind after seeing the look on her face. He could see she was one step away from her entering full-on boss bitch mode.

"Okay," he agreed reluctantly, slowly lowering the knife. "I'll give you five minutes."

Vixen dove under their perfectly decorated tree to gather presents, as the rest of us stayed rooted to our comfy spots. She pulled out the badly wrapped foiled candy bars and held them up in the air.

"Who brought these?" she demanded.

"Let's do ours first," I said, biting the bullet. Mieko and I did what we could to source the gifts in haste.

"But they don't have labels," Vixen said, tossing them to me to distribute and throw at their intended recipients.

"Sweet." Rocky unwrapped his Snickers and started to scoff it straight away. "You remembered my favorite."

"Oh, was it?" I shrugged nonchalantly, pretending it was a fluke. How could I forget his penchant for Snickers when it used to be 99% of his diet? Considering his childhood malnutrition, it's a miracle he'd grown to be so tall and lean.

West winked at the sight of his Twinkie. "I'll eat anything."

Mieko bit her lip and mumbled apologetically, "It was a little last minute..."

"Don't worry, Reeses are my favorite." Vixen kissed Mieko on the cheek, making her light up brighter than Lapland's neon sign.

Zander discarded his candy to the side in distaste. I'd bet he wouldn't eat anything not made by a Belgian chocolatier.

I crossed my arms. "If you want something more extravagant, you need to pay your dancers better, Zander."

Before Zander could respond in his usual snarky fashion, West thrust an impeccably wrapped box into my hands. "Here. It's from all of us."

A lump formed in my throat. "Oh."

I ripped off the paper to find a box with a beautiful pocket knife nestled inside a sheaf. A sparkling ruby embedded in the hilt perfectly matched my ring. At the base of the knife, the number seven had been expertly engraved into the silver. When I lived in Blackthorne Towers, Hiram used to give me gifts. They usually took the form of expensive dresses, perfume, and shoes, but the knife? It seemed so... thoughtful. Hiram taught me caring about others was a weakness, but maybe he was wrong.

"Do you not like it?" Vixen watched me closely, then turned on the guys. "I told you I should have got the Jimmy Choos."

"No, this is perfect," I murmured. The blade was well-balanced and almost weightless. I'd never go anywhere without it. "I love it."

Vixen beamed. Who knew she had a beautiful smile underneath her resting bitch face? She proceeded to throw the guys their gifts. Their unwrapping process was total carnage. Shreds of paper flew over the place like a detonating pipe bomb.

Finally, there was only one box left under the tree. Vixen held it out for me. "Someone sent this for you."

My mouth went dry. From the black paper and silky silver bow, I knew instantly who my Secret Santa was. I took a deep breath. "It's from Hiram."

Zander jumped to his feet, dropping his new Rolex with a crash.

"Don't worry," Vixen said quickly. "I already had security check it out. It won't hurt her."

Everyone watched as I carefully opened it. A single black rose rested inside the tissue paper with a neatly written note.

These were always your favorites, Kitty.

They *used* to be my favorites. I *used* to be proud of who Hiram had turned me into. I *used* to be grateful for him showing me another way to live. I *used* to see myself in the black rose. Now, all I could see was something natural polluted by evil. Instead of admiring it, I wanted to destroy it. Just like I wanted to destroy him.

I ripped off the delicate flower head and let the petals flutter down at my feet.

"Are you okay, Candy?" Mieko asked, gently placing her hand on my arm.

"Never better," I said, slamming the box shut along with my memories.

Hiram had already taken so much from me. I wouldn't let him ruin my Christmas, too.

———

"You can come through now," Zander said, opening the door. He had exiled everyone in the dressing room for the last hour while he completed the finishing touches. It was a great opportunity for me, Mieko, and Vixen to dress Q, West, and Rocky in strange elvish hats and ears we'd found lying around.

We followed Zander to the main club area and banquet table.

My mouth fell open. "Holy crap, this looks..."

"Amazing." Mieko said, finishing my sentence.

I couldn't even find the words to describe how delicious everything looked. How had Zander made all of this? He must have a secret stash of house elves hidden in the underground tunnels.

Zander shrugged as if it was only a takeout from Taco Bell. He grabbed a plate and cutlery. "I'm eating in my office."

"No way, it's Christmas day," Vixen argued, but West caught her arm to stop her. She looked like she wanted to say more, but West shook his head quickly to silence her. Whatever look passed between them was enough to make her sigh and let Zander leave without resistance. What the fuck was his deal?

We all sat down around the table to eat.

"This is the best meal I've eaten in years," Q murmured, spilling gravy down his shirt. He had always been a slim guy, but he was the thinnest he'd ever been. Grief affected the body as much as the mind.

"Enjoy." Vixen grinned, spooning out green bean casserole and creamed potatoes onto her plate. "Save space for dessert."

CHAPTER
Eleven

Why was Zander still skulking around in his office?

After serving dinner, he'd avoided everyone for the rest of the day. He'd missed West's embarrassing attempts at miming out 'Finding Nemo' during charades, then Rocky's hilarious acting out of 'Legally Blonde'. With everyone else wallowing in a food coma watching 'It's A Wonderful Life' in the penthouse, I decided it was the perfect time to track the miserable fucker down.

"It's your funeral, Candy." Vixen wished me luck. "Zander is not a holiday person."

We'll see, I thought, as I stormed down the stairs to find him. I rapt hard on the door. What business couldn't wait a few hours to spend time with his fucking family? He didn't answer, so I burst through.

"I'm busy," he snarled as his eyes snapped up from a pile of papers.

"Are you always such a Grinch?" I clicked the door closed behind me. "You're missing all the fun."

"I'm not interested," he said flatly, then spun around on his chair slowly and opened a drawer in the cabinet behind him to rifle inside. "But while you're here, I have something for you..."

I frowned. "For me?"

He pulled out a thin leather box and slid it across the desk toward me. "Open it."

I did as he asked. A gorgeous silver necklace with a circular pendant nestled against crushed red velvet. I pulled it out gently to get a closer look. One side of the pendant was smooth, while someone had etched thin roman numerals into the other. I ran my fingers over them. 2… 3. . 1… 1… It's a good thing I paid attention during history class.

"What do the numbers mean?" I asked.

Zander was a womanizer, but, even he, didn't have time to fuck that many women.

"They add up to Seven," he replied. "It's platinum."

"Yeah, I can do the math," I muttered. What I wanted to know is why he hadn't saved the cash by getting the numeral for seven engraved. But I didn't feel bratty enough to ask — I mean, it must have cost a bomb.

"Thanks." I snapped the lid shut. I could understand them giving me a knife as a present, but this? Something felt off. "But I can't accept this."

"Don't be rude, little one. It's a gift." Zander's voice turned frosty. "Aren't you even going to try it on? Let me help you."

"Fine," I huffed. Reluctantly, I pulled my hair back as Zander joined me on my side of the desk. "I'll try it."

"This necklace will bring you luck," he said, gently slipping the cool chain around my neck. He could choke the life out of me if he wanted to. "Think of it as a present for passing your initiation and getting Cheeks on board. Now it's on, you can't take it off. Whatever happens."

I touched the strange necklace, which, unlike most things Zander owned, didn't seem brand new.

"What if it doesn't go with my outfit?" I joked.

"I mean it," Zander hissed, "never take it off. Promise me, little one. Whatever happens."

"Okay, fine. I promise." I rolled my eyes. Every time we were alone, it became strangely intense. Zander had a way of making me feel completely naked. I changed the subject to lighten the mood. "So, are you going to tell me why you're hiding away now?"

"I'm not hiding," he said. "I have work to do."

"Today?"

"What's wrong?" A small ghost of a smile lingered on his lips. "Missing me?"

"I'm just curious about what you're up to," I said, picking up a paper-weight and playing with it in my hands. "Vixen said you didn't like the holi-days. How come?"

"There's nothing to say. It's never been an occasion I've enjoyed celebrat-ing. You can imagine it used to be a big occasion in the Briarly household," he said wryly. "My father always felt Christmas had to have a special… impact. It's when he used to do his best work."

He didn't need to continue for me to know what he meant. Bryce waited until the happiest time of year to deploy his most twisted schemes and leave a young Zander alone to explore the dark corners of their creepy gothic home.

"I've never enjoyed Christmas either," I admitted. The season always felt like a special club I wasn't part of... until now.

"Red told me about what it was like at Evergreen."

"They were some of the better Christmases I've had..."

Like Bryce, Hiram thought killing over the holidays had a theatrical flair. As well as ruining family dinners, he used to enjoy mailing body parts out to victims' children. Horrified relatives had to explain Santa's elves had suddenly turned into psychopathic little monsters who killed their daddy.

"You don't mind Cupid being here, do you? I thought he might bring memories back," he probed, resting on the edge of his desk. "How well do you know each other?"

"He used to work for Hiram," I said, keeping my answer short and avoiding his gaze. "Our paths crossed from time to time."

"Why do I get the sense you're lying to me?"

"There are some things I don't want to talk about," I snapped. Although I'd suffered at Hiram's hands, Q had been punished the most. Losing your soulmate was a wound that would never heal. "You may know about my past, but you don't need to know all my secrets."

"I'll find them out, eventually. It's inevitable."

I folded my arms. "Why do you always act like everything's a game?"

"Isn't it?" He cocked his head to the side, studying my reaction. "I'm not the only one playing games here, Candy."

My mouth turned dry, and I stammered, "I don't know what you mean."

"You think you can play us all." Zander trailed his finger across my collarbone, then shot me a devastating smile. When Zander went on the charm offensive, I could see why girls dropped their panties for him. He knew all the right words to say, but I knew better. Underneath his smile lay a vicious predator. "Usually, I'd never let a girl come between me and my brothers, but you're not like the others."

Zander may have figured out that Rocky and I had a brief fling as teenagers from our reactions yesterday, but there's no way West had talked about what happened in Hammerville. He'd been the one who'd insisted we'd keep our mistake a secret.

"No, I'm not just *any* girl," I replied, staring back and mirroring his intensity. "I'm pretty fucking skilled with a knife."

"I've been thinking about it," Zander said. "How we're going to fix the problem."

"Oh?" The feel of my new knife tucked into my waistband gave me the extra reassurance I could get out alive if I needed to. "And what conclusions have you come to, Your Highness?"

Zander was the leader of the Sevens, but he was also a lone wolf. He didn't answer to anyone but himself. He should remember how he'd cleaned up the bodies of five men I killed before jumping to any conclusions I didn't like.

"You're a Seven right down to the blood running through your pretty veins, but you're poison." Zander stepped closer, leaving only inches between us. His breath tickled my neck as he whispered, "Until you, the brothers were united. But now? You'll destroy us from the inside if I don't act."

"What do you plan to do about it?" I spat, squaring my shoulders. "Kill me and cut me out of your gang because none of you can keep your hands to yourselves?"

"Not kill you." Zander laughed as his eyes glinted mischievously. "*Share* you."

"I'm not a piece of meat you can pass around," I said, my voice wavered slightly.

"You didn't seem to mind the idea last night," Zander went on. Shit, he must have been more sober during the game than I'd thought. "You're the one who gave me the idea."

"I'm a Seven," I said, regaining my assertiveness. "Not one of your groupie whores."

"Oh, I know." Zander put his hands on my hips and yanked me towards him. "I wanted to have you all to myself, but I can see it's going to cause us problems. The Sevens can't have secrets, and you're the little secret we've all been keeping. I'll be willing to share you with my brothers. On one condition."

"What condition?" I shot back sarcastically.

"Before sharing you with them, I get to have you all to myself."

I went to shove him, but he caught my wrists before they hit his chest. The spark from his touch sent a shiver down my spine. "Have you ever thought that maybe I don't want *you*?"

"Your body tells me otherwise." Zander shot a knowing glance at my hardened nipples. I may as well have a flaming 'please enter' flashing sign above my fucking head. "Do you think I haven't noticed how you are around West? How he squirms around you? How he tried not to look at you for weeks? Or, how about Red? How he looks like he's ready to throw himself in front of a bullet whenever you're around?"

My heart rate quickened, but I kept my legs and lips pressed shut. Zander always had a hidden agenda. How was I to know this wasn't another of his plans? He enjoyed asserting his dominance and, after seeing him in action in the tunnels of the Maven, I knew he enjoyed women. A lot. How did he expect me to believe anything he said was real?

"You're the only woman who hasn't been afraid to say to me what you think," Zander continued. "You want us to be done with keeping secrets, don't you? You wanted to be all in. Sharing you is the only way."

"Don't you think Red and West get a say in this?" I called his bluff.

West lost his shit over me drinking his coffee. He wasn't exactly the sharing type. Then, Rocky… with our history, I couldn't even imagine how he'd react.

"We all want you, little one." The heat radiating off Zander's body made my throat feel like it was closing, and I needed to gasp for air. "I know you want us, too. "

"I won't be another Bella," I hissed. "I'm not waiting at home while you go out and screw other people. I'm not your fucking toy, or anyone else's."

I knew what they were like. Unlike them, sex meant something to me. My body may melt like wax under Zander's touch, but I'd rather die than become a trademarked Seven personal Kleenex.

"You're not a toy to me, Candy." Zander stepped back and dropped his hands to his sides. "I would never hurt you. You may think I'm a monster, but I'd kill for you. I'm going to make sure we bury Hiram for what he put you through."

"Not if I get to him first," I muttered.

"Your problem is our problem," Zander said with fierce determination. "We'll finish him together, but I'll let you deliver the killer wound…"

I snorted. "Who knew chivalry wasn't dead?"

"It may surprise you to know I can be a gentleman when I want to be." Zander stroked my cheek with gentle tenderness. "You're a Seven girl, remember? *Our* Seven girl."

Our Seven girl. I liked how those words sounded on his lips. He took a step forward, his hands trailing up my thigh.

I slapped his hand away. "I thought you were supposed to be a gentleman."

"I can be." He grinned, making the rose on his cheek dance. He was the same as the flower. He looked fucking angelic on the outside but hid thorns that could tear you into pieces. "But I didn't say I was going to be."

"Admit it," Zander whispered. "You want me as much as I want you."

Zander was the most arrogant, head-fuckingly smart, calculated, and twisted… his lips crushed me, stealing all my oxygen and putting a stop to my traffic jam of thoughts. His tongue probed my mouth with an unquench-able hunger. It wasn't just a kiss. He was fucking stealing my soul every second his mouth was on mine.

He pulled away, giving me a chance to come up for air.

"Take off your dress, Candy," he growled. Something about his tone told me this wasn't a question.

I raised an eyebrow. "You think you can unwrap me like a present?"

Zander grinned wickedly. "Why don't you sit on my lap and see what happens?"

"What if I don't take it off?" I asked, swishing the hem of my dress.

He looked me up and down then said, "Then I'll bend you over my knee and spank you so hard you won't be able to sit down for a week."

My cheeks flushed as I undid the bow holding my dress together. It fastened at the waist like a kimono. Zander watched my every move. He looked at me like a bomb he wanted to dismantle. It wasn't a friendly look. It was the same look a lion gave a gazelle before it sunk its teeth into its neck and tore it apart.

I let the dress fall open to reveal my underwear and felt pleased I'd worn one of my only matching sets of lingerie. My black bra may have shrunk in the wash, but it made my tits look great. Who says you can't rock lingerie and black combat boots together?

"Lie back," Zander ordered.

"Wait, what...?"

Zander pushed everything off his desk with a crash. Papers fluttered to the floor, pens rolled away and a glass smashed. Even his fucking lamp cracked.

"On the desk," he said, walking me back until my ass perched on its edge.

His firm hand grabbed my hair and forced my lips to his in a kiss that made me forget my name. Zander's hands snaked their way up my back, and fingers expertly unhooked my strapless bra. I froze as he threw it at our feet.

Zander usually fucked supermodels. I was used to being paraded in front of a crowd in scantily clad clothes, but no one had seen me this exposed since I lost my virginity to Rocky.

"You're so fucking beautiful, little one," Zander breathed, sensing my hesitation as he caught one of my hard nipples between his fingers and a moan escaped me. "This is all about you."

His hands slipped down further, making my heart race. Once we crossed a line, there was no going back.

"Zander, I—"

"Shh." The corners of his mouth twitched upward in a devilish grin as he pressed a hand to my mouth. The fingers of his other hand brushed over the thin fabric of my panties. He could feel the slick wetness soaking through. There was no hiding how much my body craved him. His fingers slid over my panties and circled my clit in slow, torturous circles. "There's a good girl."

He slid my panties to the side to slip his fingers into my underwear. My wetness met his hands as two fingers slipped between my lips, teasing my entrance. I pushed my hips into his hand, but Zander only laughed and pulled out of my panties. He wanted to make me beg.

"You're a bastard, you know that?"

My whole body craved more. Needing to be touched more than I needed oxygen. My pussy pulsed and all the blood rushing to the heat between my legs could have set his fucking desk alight.

"I'll give you what you want." Zander licked my slick from his fingers. *Tasting me.* "But only if you agree to be ours. *Our* Seven girl."

Between my legs, his hard erection pressed against me in the promise of what was to come. All I had to say was a few words.

"I'm *a* Seven," I said, ignoring my vagina screaming in objection like the guy from the 'Save Britney' video. Why was my brain being so fucking selfish? "Isn't that enough for you?"

"Fucking you isn't about getting my cock wet." Zander stroked my inner thigh, making me struggle to stay standing. "As much as I want to fuck your sweet little pussy, this is about more. You're not like the others. I'm asking you to be *ours,* and only ours."

How is a girl to think straight while his magic fingers are playing a fucking symphony on their thighs?

"Your body already knows that you're mine," Zander purred. "But I can stop if—"

"No," I interrupted, more violently than I'd expected. "Don't stop."

"Then tell me what you want," Zander murmured into my neck, as he slipped his hand back into my panties and found my entrance.

My experiences made trusting someone impossible. But I was already a Seven and, as much as I tried to resist, I couldn't hide my attraction to Zander, West, and Rocky any longer.

"You," I whispered, finally relenting to his will. "*All* of you."

I gasped, my head rolling back, as Zander pushed two fingers deep inside me until I felt the cold edge of his gold ring digging against me. I gasped as he withdrew and twisted his fingers around, slipping inside to stroke my swollen G-spot.

I cried out. Being with him felt like a devastating inevitability. The moment my mind stopped resisting, my body took over. I wanted him. Every fucking inch of him. I reached to pull up his shirt, wanting to feel his skin, but Zander grabbed my wrist to stop me and tutted.

"Sit," he ordered.

He pushed me backward until my ass was firmly on his desk and forced my legs apart. He slid my panties off so fast I hadn't realized they were off until I saw them in his hands. I tried to close my legs, but Zander stood between them. He didn't give a fuck whether I felt exposed. He wanted me spread wide and open for him.

"Don't hide from me, little one." He looked down at my pussy like the big, bad wolf who wanted to devour me. "I love seeing how you're dripping for me."

My breathing quickened as Zander started to kiss down the length of my body. He took my nipples into his mouth, swirling his tongue over my tented peaks then caught them between his teeth and made me yelp. He grinned and continued to trace his tongue down my stomach.

"Your piercing is fucking hot," he murmured, pausing to admire my silver jewel belly bar. I bucked my hips in frustration, making him chuckle. I didn't want a fucking compliment. I wanted him to touch me. Zander sensed my impatience, but he didn't speed up. No, he was taking his sweet time and enjoying every fucking second. His tongue tickled my ribs, roughly kissing down my snake tattoo, which coiled to my hips.

Zander paused, looking up at me, and grinned. "I've been waiting to taste you from the moment I first saw you."

"Zander, please..." I begged. If he wasn't careful, I would drip all over his fucking desk.

He took to his knees, grabbed my hips with his hands, and pulled me towards him. Having a man like Zander bow down at my pussy like he was worshipping at an altar gave me a whole new sense of power. His tongue darted out, licking the length of my slit and spreading me open wider to taste my juices.

"You taste fucking incredible," he murmured, licking his lips, then burying his head between my legs.

I moaned, as his tongue found my clit and he applied soft pressure with his tongue. I wanted more. Hell, I fucking needed it. I ground against his face, as his tongue explored me like he was eating the best tasting ice cream. If Zander was skilled with his hands, holy fuck, his mouth was on another level. When Rocky and I were younger, we'd messed around, but neither of us knew what we were doing. But Zander had years of experience. He knew exactly what he was doing. He knew how to make a woman feel fucking incredible.

My legs shook with anticipation as my orgasm built. I held myself back, resisting the urge to tip over the edge of no return when Zander rose from his position. He undid the buttons on his shirt, but didn't take it off. His muscles flexed, as he unsheathed his belt, springing his cock to life.

It'd been five years since I'd last had sex, but I was no stranger to playing with toys. But this was not the same as using my cute pink rabbit... where was West's fucking ruler when you needed it? Eight inches? Nine? Hell, it could even be ten.

I eagerly reached out to feel his silky head.

"Be patient, little one," he promised, stepping closer and catching my hand. His cock felt hot against me as he parted my lips and slid himself up and down to coat his shaft. "You're doing so fucking well. Now, lay back and show me what I've been waiting for."

I lay back on his desk, legs spread, bearing my whole soul ready for the taking. Zander stood between them, grabbing my ankles and wrapping them around his neck. My flexibility from dancing around the pole was paying off now.

"I want to watch you while I fuck you," he purred. "I want to see all of you."

I gasped as his cock teased my entrance, rubbing against my wetness. I liked the feeling of him against me. We shouldn't be doing this. We shouldn't be mixing business with pleasure, but I wanted him. Damn, I wanted him more than I'd wanted anything, and I couldn't think of anything beyond this moment.

"You're so wet for me," he praised, as the head of his cock pushed into me. A twinge of pain followed, making me wince. "What's wrong, little one? I know you can take me. I can feel how ready you are."

I bit my lip as his cock slid deeper. Zander didn't need to know he was the second man I'd ever had sex with. *Holy shit.* I felt like I was being impaled. Was 'death by the sword' another way of saying killed by cock? As another inch slid in, my pussy started to open up and become accustomed to his girth. The pain was quickly replaced by the overarching feeling of full-ness. His cock seemed to pulsate as he pushed in, burying himself as far as he could go, with a smug smirk.

"You're mine now, Candy," he said, beginning to thrust harder. His eyes never left mine, watching my whole body jerk with each of his purposeful motions. "You're my fucking girl."

Screwing my boss had never been part of the plan, but I wanted him. So fucking badly. Zander bent forwards, arching his back. The position hits my clit and sweet spot at the perfect angle. My breathing grew more ragged. He'd kept me on the edge for so long that my body begged for release.

"I want you to come for me," Zander ordered, as he coaxed my orgasm to the point of no return. I didn't need him to ask me twice. I cried out as my pussy squeezed his cock, like it never wanted to let go, as pleasure erupted from my core. "Now, say my name. I want to hear you say it."

"Zander," I moaned, rolling my head back and bucking my hips against him. My orgasm rippled through my whole body like a fucking tsunami. "Fuck, Zander."

At that moment, the office door burst open.

Zander didn't stop. His hips slammed into me harder, like it was the last fuck of his life, and sent my moans into an uncontrollable fucking tailspin. It was like we were at the top of a rollercoaster and started hurtling to the ground with no chance of pulling the brakes.

"What the fuck?"

I heard the shock in Rocky's voice as I turned my head to see him and West standing in the doorway. Finding Zander balls-deep in me was not the sight they'd expected to be met with.

My body shuddered as I gasped in surprise. I was already coming hard and couldn't stop, even though we had an audience. Instead of wanting to push Zander off, my pussy clung to his cock. The adrenaline burst and the shock of knowing West and Rocky were watching only intensified the sensation. The rational part of my brain had shut down, and I couldn't restrain my moans because of how freaking amazing it felt. Zander continued to thrust, riding the wave of my climax, then bucked into me for a final time, shooting a burst of heat between my legs. He had no fucking performance anxiety.

"We'll come back later," West growled, looking at us in disgust.

I was trembling and tried to say something, but it was too late. He slammed the door closed behind them with such force it made the wall shake.

Holy fucking shit.

Zander grinned, as he pulled out of me and zipped up his pants. "I told you I'd make you mine."

From the look of satisfaction on his face, he knew exactly what he was doing and who was watching. I wouldn't be surprised if he'd somehow paged the two of them to arrive at the perfect time. He wanted to mark his fucking territory.

I sat upright and pulled the sides of my dress closed around me. "Did you plan this?"

My pleasure was turning into a raging fury. How could he be fucking casual about this? Didn't he care about the consequences? Or, about what West or Rocky would say? Shit, I didn't know whether I'd be able to look them in the face again…

"They all have to know who's boss," Zander replied with a shrug. "Besides, they'll get their turn with you, eventually."

"Fuck you," I spat, jumping up and shoving past him.

"Candy?" Zander called after me. He twirled my wet panties around his finger. "You're forgetting these."

I snatched them from him, feeling my cheeks heat and his cum drip down the inside of my leg. "Go to fucking hell, Zander."

CHAPTER

Twelve

After cleaning up in the bathroom, I couldn't put off seeing them forever — even though I'd rather flash my tits to a coach full of freaking nuns than face West and Rocky. *You can do this*, I psyched myself up. *You've killed people, remember? This is nothing.* Ripping off a bandaid quickly is always the best way, right?

As soon as I walked back into the club, Vixen rolled her eyes and Mieko shot me the same smirk I'd given her this morning. It was a lot less satisfying to be on the receiving end of it. Karma is a bitch.

"Where is everyone?" I asked, looking around nervously to check for obvious signs of damage after a West rage attack. So far, everything looked intact.

"Q had to leave and the others went for a drive," Vixen said with a devilish smile. "They weren't happy to find out Zander got the first slice of dessert."

My cheeks burned, but the twinkling lights disguised it. "They told you."

"Sure did, but I'm kinda disappointed..." Vixen sighed and slapped ten dollars into Mieko's outstretched hand. "My bet was on West."

"You two bet on it?"

"We all knew it was going to happen, eventually. I just didn't know which one you'd screw first." Vixen shrugged innocently. Why was I the only one who *hadn't* thought it was inevitable? "Hopefully it'll kill the sexual tension around here."

Mieko tucked her winnings into her bra and mimed 'I told you so'. I scowled back. They were fucking unbelievable.

"Do you want some pie?" Vixen asked, cutting out a large wedge of pecan goodness and sliding a bowl across the table to a vacant spot. "Do you want more cream, or are you good?"

"Real fucking mature, Vixen," I huffed but took a seat anyway. Dessert looked too delicious to resist and a girl needed a sugar boost to replenish after a mind-blowing orgasm. "At least we can get some before West devours it all."

Outside, the screech of tires caused Vixen to curse under her breath. "It's like he's psychic or something. How did he know I cut into the fucking pie? I've told West a thousand times not to slam on the brakes like that. He's not in a fucking race car."

Zander emerged from his office, bringing with him the festive cheer of a funeral march. The narrowing of his brows hinted whoever was outside was not a welcome visitor.

"We have company," Zander declared as someone started pounding on Lapland's door. "None of you move."

I ignored Zander and rose to my feet, ready to face our new arrival. He scowled in my direction. "What part of my orders didn't you understand?"

Zander may have given me my daily cost of vitamin D, but it didn't mean I would submit to his demands every time. I widened my eyes and fluttered my eyelashes innocently. "You didn't say please."

Vixen snickered. "It looks like you've finally met your match, Zander."

Zander glowered at her, pursing his lips, but didn't argue with me again. He opened the door to greet the gatecrasher. "To what do we owe this pleasure, *cousin*?"

"It's Christmas!" Giles's English drawl grated my eardrums like the sound of toenails being sanded to the bone. A visit from him was akin to expecting Father Christmas and being met by Darth fucking Vader. "I'm here to return something that belongs to you."

"Come in," Zander hissed. From his glacial tone, it's not the type of invitation you'd accept unless you wanted your pubes plucked out one hair at a time.

Vixen's chair screeched across the floor, and she stood protectively in front of Mieko to shield her from view. "What the fuck are you doing letting *him* in?"

I was about to agree with her when I noticed Giles wasn't alone. Cheeks trawled behind him with shackles around his ankles. His freshly bruised left eye was so swollen he couldn't open it, while the other had a spaced out appearance. How was he able to stand? He looked like a zombie.

"It's a shame none of you received an invitation to lunch at the manor. You missed out," Giles said dryly as I scowled at him. "It was quite the occasion."

"I'm sure it was," Zander replied unflinchingly, surveying Cheeks's disheveled appearance with distaste. "Father always enjoys playing with his food."

Blood congealing on Cheeks's chin and neck had left him with an unsightly crusty beard. His mouth slackened to reveal where the blood was coming from... a fleshy stump where his tongue used to be.

Mieko gasped, covering her mouth with her hands, at the sight of Cheeks's injuries. Although Vixen was squeamish, she didn't show it. She squeezed Mieko's shoulder to comfort her and gritted her teeth, waiting for Giles's next move. *The girl was doing me proud.*

"It looks like I arrived in time for pudding," Giles chirped. He cracked a smile and pulled out a chair at the table to make himself at home. "You don't mind, do you?"

"Of course not," Zander sneered, sitting across from him. Vixen and I followed his lead. *We'd humor him... for now.* "Candy, why don't you serve dessert?"

I scooped out a slither of pie and spat on it.

"Here." I slammed the bowl down in front of Giles. The glob of my spittle rested atop the cream like a garnish. *Eat shit, motherfucker.* "Enjoy."

"You're not as sweet as your name after all, are you?" Giles hissed, shoving it away. The bowl flew off the table, smashing on the floor and causing Mieko to flinch. *What a waste of pie...*

"Why don't you get to the fucking point already?" I snapped. "Say what you've come here to say, then get out of *our* fucking club."

"Can you imagine how surprised I was to find out what deal you made with Cheeks?" Giles laughed, tipping back and forth in his chair like a gleeful schoolboy. "All I had to do was offer money to get him to talk."

The double-crossing weasel rat bastard. I knew we couldn't trust him. At least Bryce had saved us the effort of keeping his mouth permanently shut. Cheeks would never be able to say another word again. The information he delivered to Zander before he blew his cover better have been worth the trouble...

"So?" Zander stretched out and yawned. "Do you expect me to be impressed?"

"Your father wanted me to deliver the Sevens a message," Giles said, his cheeks reddening in annoyance at Zander's attitude. *Damn, what I wouldn't give to leave an imprint of my boots across those plump rosy apples.* "He wants you to stop looking."

Stop looking? What did he mean?

"Couldn't you have written your message in a fucking Christmas card?" Vixen asked, balling her hands into fists in front of her.

"Only *family* makes the list," Giles rebutted, making Zander's jaw clench. "Besides, I also brought you a present. One I needed to deliver in person."

Giles stood and pulled a gun out of his jacket pocket, waving it around like a magic wand. Vixen acted fast. She grabbed Mieko and pulled her to the floor as Zander and I got to our feet, ready for whatever came next.

"Merry Christmas, cousin," Giles said in a sing-song voice, then pointed his gun at Cheeks and squeezed the trigger.

Mieko screamed as the bullet ripped through Cheeks's head, shattering his skull and obliterating his brain. His lifeless body landed on the floor with a thump.

Cheeks should have known better than to reveal he was working for us. Even if he'd offered to feed us false information on their behalf, the Briarlys would never have taken kindly to learning how he'd been a spy. They were happy to send him to the grave like an old dog they no longer had a use for. Delivering a fresh corpse was Bryce Briarly's idea of a perfect gift. How many similar performances had Zander witnessed as a child?

"Is that everything, Giles?" Zander asked, tapping his foot.

Giles's face fell. He didn't like discovering his message hadn't gotten the effect he'd hoped for. *Poor diddums.* What toys would he throw out of his pram next?

Before I could stop it, a manic laugh escaped my lips.

Giles turned on me. "What's so funny?"

"I was just wondering why Bryce didn't send one of his henchmen to deliver his *present*?" I lifted my chin in defiance. I knew exactly how to get a rise outta him. "Are you doing all the dirty work now? I thought you were higher up in the ranks?"

Sure, it's never a smart idea to goad someone with a loaded gun... but, how could I resist? The uppity motherfucker needed a reality check. Think of it as payback for ruining our Christmas. Giles had extinguished any festive spirit along with Cheeks's life.

"I could shoot someone else if you'd prefer. Who's next?" Giles leveled his gun, his hands shaking and less confident than before. He aimed it at Mieko, who yelped and looked close to vomiting. "How about her? You can always replace a whore."

"In your fucking dreams," I snarled, staring him down.

Giles pointed the gun at my head. "Are you volunteering?"

"I'd think carefully about what you do next, cousin," Zander warned. His menacing tone slashed through Giles's courage like a dagger, causing him to lower his weapon and the color to drain from his face.

"We were only playing," Giles dismissed, stashing the gun away. Where was his backbone? He could kill a defenseless man but knew he stood no chance if forced to face his cousin's wrath. "Weren't we, Candy?"

"The only game I can see being played around here is chicken—"

"Candy," Zander interrupted. "Enough."

"What?" I asked, twirling a strand of hair around my finger. "I'm only *playing* — right, Giles?"

"Where is your fiancé, anyway?" Giles asked, flaring his nostrils like a raging bull. "Isn't *he* the one who should be protecting you?"

"We're already cleaning up one body tonight," I hissed. "I don't mind adding another."

Giles's corpse wrapped up in a pretty bow and left on the manor steps would be a perfect way to end the day.

"Have we missed dessert?" West's voice from the other end of the club cut short our confrontation as he and Rocky crept in. For big guys, they sure knew how to move stealthily. West's eyes skimmed over Cheeks's corpse, but his expression darkened at the sight of the ruined pecan pie. "What happened?"

"Giles decided brains would be a perfect addition to dessert," I replied as West joined us and draped his arm over my shoulder. Now, spilling Giles's blood was the only thing I was hungry for.

"It's time for you to leave, Giles," Rocky said. Unlike the other guys, who could remain calm, Rocky's expression was murderous. He was a loose cannon ready to explode, and Giles could sense it. "I'll show you the fucking door."

"No need. I'll show myself out," Giles said. He kicked Cheeks's dead body as he passed. He didn't care whether the blood would stain his tan leather shoes. Everything, and everyone, was expendable to a Briarly. Vixen would be furious she'd have to replace the new floor… again. Giles paused as he reached the exit, then turned to wink at me over his shoulder. "I'll see you around soon, *Kitty*."

Adrenaline surged through my veins with a reawakened bloodthirsty clarity. I felt *her* rise to the surface. The Kitten was ready to fight. If Giles wanted to meet Kitty, then he wouldn't leave Lapland alive. It wouldn't take long to pounce and break his neck in a swift jerk. This pussy had sharp claws and wasn't afraid to bite.

I dove to attack, but West was faster. His arms wrapped around me like an Iron Maiden. I wrestled against him and tried to kick out, but he pinned my back against him to hold me still. There was nowhere I could go.

"Let me fucking go, West," I demanded, thrashing against him.

Giles laughed as Zander slammed the door on him. The others were talking, but I couldn't hear what they were saying. Their voices became a hum like background noise. All I could think about was how we were wasting precious time. Giles was getting away.

Through the rage induced fog, I could hear West's voice in my ear.

"Stop struggling," West whispered, which only fanned the rage burning inside me more. It spread faster than a forest fire at the peak of summer. "You're only making it worse."

West didn't understand what he was doing.

Giles knew about *me*.

About Hiram.

Why were we letting him go?

Cheeks may have been too stupid to see me for who I really was, but Giles had worked it out. Knowledge in the wrong hands would put all of us in greater danger. How long could my secrets stay buried if Bryce Briarly wanted to unearth them? Letting Giles walk away was like signing a death wish for the Sevens.

"Fine," I said, pretending to play his game. "I'll stop, okay?"

West laughed, holding onto me even tighter. "Nice try, Pinkie."

The fucker. As soon as the roar of Giles's car engine faded into the distance, West's grip loosened and I turned on him.

"You fucking idiot!" I pummeled my fists into his chest to take out some of my building frustration. "We should have killed him!"

"You're not thinking straight," Zander said.

"I'm the only one thinking straight," I exploded. "He knows. It makes us as good as dead, don't you get that?"

Zander shrugged and checked his watch. "He's known for a while."

"He's, what?" I blasted in outrage.

Rocky's eyes darted to West nervously. "You might want to hold her back again, bro."

"Don't you fucking dare," I hissed, dodging West's lunge, and pointing at Zander. "You'd better start talking."

"I think we're going to get out of your way," Vixen said, grabbing Mieko's hand. Smart fucking move. "Can we go to your place?"

Mieko nodded shakily. Anywhere would be better than staying at the club with a dead body or around me when I was about to lose my shit. Before the two of them left, Vixen called back, "Please don't kill anyone else, Candy. Remember, the clean-up crew charges triple over the holidays."

"I can't make any promises," I snapped. As soon as they left, I zeroed in on Zander again. "Well? Tell me everything you know. Real fucking fast."

I wanted to rip his head off his perfectly tattooed neck. Why did everyone I had sex with make me want to kill them afterward? Was my vagina cursed?

"The envelope Cheeks delivered contained information about you," Zander explained. "My father has been busy investigating our newest Seven member."

We'd been overly optimistic to believe Bryce wouldn't question West falling for a stripper. The only thing more infuriating than my identity being uncovered was how Zander had kept it a secret. Keeping it from me wasn't his call to make. It was *my* fucking life.

"Why didn't you say anything before?" I demanded, crossing my arms.

"Because I was handling it," he replied smoothly.

"Yeah, it sure looks like it," I said, gesturing at Cheeks's bloody remains. "What information was in the envelope?"

"Pictures were taken at a party on the night Giovanni Romano was murdered," Zander said. His calm, detached tone put me on edge. "Can you imagine how surprised my father was to see you serving drinks? Especially after hearing what Cheeks told him about the Raphael Jacobson video that mysteriously disappeared. It's a little too much of a coincidence, don't you think?"

He may have forced me to confront my past about how I used to work with Hiram, but I hadn't shared any details. All the Sevens needed to know was that I'd done bad things. Knowing any more would be too dangerous. For all of them. But Bryce's digging had left me with no choice. They were all going to find out what I'd done…

My mouth went dry. "How long have you known?"

"About how you had something to do with Raphael Jacobson's disappearance? Since the first time I saw the video," Zander replied. "Who do you think organized for all the copies to be wiped from Cheeks's hard drive before his arrest? Red got the dancers to erase their copies, and we made sure everything disappeared."

Hiram had been the one who'd arranged for Cheeks to be beaten to a pulp and arrested. I hadn't realized the Sevens were also working in the background to help cover my tracks. Back then, Zander barely acknowledged my existence. Why did he go out of his way to protect me?

"Why go through the effort to get rid of the video?" I asked. "You didn't even know me."

"I didn't want the Jacobsons sniffing around. It'd be bad for business," Zander said matter-of-factly. All he cared about was self-preservation. "It wasn't until later that I realized who killed him. After seeing what you did to my father's men, everything made sense. Then, seeing pictures of you at the Romano mansion—"

"Wait, hold up," Rocky interrupted, holding up his hand. "Let me get this straight. You killed Raphael Jacobson *and* Giovanni Romano?"

West stayed silent but studied my reaction closely. Judging by his tensed jaw and Rocky's incredulous expression, it seemed I wasn't the only person Zander had kept in the dark after learning this information.

"I told you I could take care of myself," I said flippantly. "Would you like a catalog of all the other people I've killed, too? If so, you better sit down because we'll be here a while."

"Holy shit, C…" Rocky ran a hand through his hair and looked at me with fresh eyes. I didn't know whether to be offended or flattered by his shock. "I mean, this is bad. Real fucking bad. I knew Hiram made you do things, but Romano's murder? That's—"

"A big fucking deal? Yes, I know." I snapped. "You remember I said I made a deal with Hiram? He let me go free in exchange for killing Romano."

"Why didn't you tell us?" Rocky asked.

"Why do you think?" I looked down and played with the ruby ring on my finger. My clammy hands made it slip around easily. "I didn't want to relive that part of my life, and I didn't want to put you at risk. Knowing who killed them implicates you all. It's dangerous."

"The Sevens don't run from danger," West said fiercely. "It doesn't matter who you killed before."

"It does, if Bryce is going to use it against us," I reminded him.

"What other evidence does Bryce have?" Rocky asked.

"That's everything," Zander said. "So far."

"A photo at a party proves nothing," West growled. "And the video with Jacobson? It's gone. Bryce has nothing."

"You might have gotten rid of the video with Raphael, but Hiram will still have copies," I pointed out. "He can expose me anytime he wants."

"But he won't do that, right?" Rocky said, biting his lip. "Not if he wants you back working for him. And… those pictures… you may have been at the party, but it doesn't mean you killed him."

"The Romanos aren't the kind of family who listens to reason," I said. "They shoot first, then ask questions later."

Whispers still circulated about Giovanni Romano's mysterious murder. While his son had taken over and started to work with Hiram, it hadn't stopped the Romano family from yearning for revenge. They wouldn't stop until they got it.

When I struck a deal for my freedom, Hiram never thought I'd be able to kill Giovanni Romano. Hell, men had tried and none of them lived to tell the tale. Hiram had underestimated the will of someone with nothing left to lose. With Crystal gone, death would have been more favorable than staying in Blackthorne Towers forever.

"We need to find out how Bryce got those photos," Rocky said. "Then we can—"

"This isn't your problem," I interrupted. No one else needed to be dragged into my past. I'd made those choices. It was down to me to deal with the consequences. "*We* don't have to do anything. This is my fucking mess."

"You don't get it, do you?" Rocky said. His gaze softened. "You're a fucking Seven, C. We're in this for life."

"A problem for you is a problem for all of us," West agreed. "We're in this together, so we'll deal with it. What's our next move, Zander?"

"We do nothing," Zander said like this was a test. "For now."

"What?" Rocky gasped. "You expect us to sit around and wait for the Romanos to come along and kill her?"

"They could try." I scoffed. If I could take down the ex-head of the Romano empire, henchmen shouldn't cause me any trouble.

"I know my father. If he was going to tip the Romanos off and send them the photographs, he'd have done it already," Zander said. "He is holding onto the information until he wants something. We don't know what that is yet. We need to play the long game."

"I don't like it." Rocky shook his head. "Can't we get back the evidence?"

"Stealing from them will start a war," West said, nipping in the bud any elaborate fantasies about storming the manor. "Zander's right."

Rocky's fists clenched. "But we can't do nothing."

"That's exactly what we'll do, Red," Zander ordered sharply. "If you want her to stay alive."

"If they find out and want me dead," I said, "they'll find me."

"No one is going to touch you," Zander replied. "You're *our* Seven girl, remember?"

The three men exchanged glances between themselves and nodded. I appreciated the sentiment, but the Sevens didn't know who they were up against. They may run a casino, strip club, and weed-dealing operation, but they were no match for the people who could come looking for me... *or Hiram.*

"I have other matters to attend to." Zander pulled out his cell to signal our conversation was over. "I'll be back later. West, I trust you have this under control?"

"Seriously?" I asked in disbelief. We were used to Zander disappearing with no explanation, but vanishing on Christmas day with a dead body in the middle of your club didn't seem like ideal timing. "You really have to go now?"

Zander ignored me to prompt West. "You know what to do."

"I'll call clean-up," West grunted. It wouldn't surprise me if he had them on speed dial...

"Can we talk, C?" Rocky asked. "It'd be better if we're out of the way."

"Sure." I shrugged. I'd never got my kicks from cleaning up the mess after a kill — well, not unless I could get creative with body disposal.

Before I could follow Rocky, Zander caught my arm.

"Remember what I said, little one," Zander said, then lowered his voice so only I could hear, "you are *our* girl now."

His dark, possessive stare pierced into my soul to let me know exactly who *he* thought I belonged to. I turned my back on him before he could see the blush spreading over my cheeks. Even a bullet through Cheeks's head and discovering the Briarlys were closing in on my secrets wouldn't let me forget the ache Zander left between my legs.

"Where are we going?"

I followed Rocky through the club, figuring we were heading for Zander's office or the dressing room. Instead, he led me to another door, which I'd always assumed was a storage closet.

"I want to show you something," he said, pulling out a key and twisting it in the lock. He pushed the door open to reveal another stairwell. Lapland was like a Russian nesting doll, filled with hidden openings, secret floors, and an underground bunker.

I raised my eyebrows. "Don't tell me this is your torture chamber?"

I was only half-joking. I knew better than most how such rooms existed in the homes of twisted psychopaths. Hiram's favorite place was his work-shop deep in the underbelly of Blackthorne Towers. I didn't want to think about how many people lost their lives there. Hundreds? Thousands? Anyone who messed with Hiram ended up dead, and those who were inno-cent? Sometimes he enjoyed killing simply for the fun of it.

"This is where I come to get away from it all," Rocky explained, leading the way up the narrow steps. Eventually, we came to another door which opened onto what looked like Lapland's roof. In the middle of it, he had set up two deck chairs. "It's nicer in the summer. Do you wanna sit down?"

"Sure," I agreed, plopping my ass down. My nipples felt like they were about to fall off, but it'd be preferable to sticking around while Cheeks's corpse got dragged out. "It's quiet up here."

Well, apart from the vans pulling up in the street below and hushed voices wrestling with a body bag.

"Doesn't it remind you of the old times?" Rocky asked, then added hastily, "The good times, I mean."

I eyed him suspiciously. "I guess so..."

After watching me moan over Zander's cock and learning I'd murdered the leader of an infamous crime family who could come after us, his laid-back casualness was the last thing I expected. Throwing me off of the roof would be a more natural reaction. Why wasn't he angry? Or maybe he was only pretending?

"What do you say?" Rocky pulled two freshly rolled joints out of his pocket and cocked his head to the side. "Just like the old days?"

I took one from him. "Thanks."

I hesitated, waiting until he lit up first.

"It's not laced with anything," he insisted, and I detected the hurt in his voice.

"I didn't say it was," I replied, balancing the joint between my lips.

"Here." Rocky held out his lighter, and I leaned forward to catch the end. I inhaled deeply.

Holy shit.

It was better than anything we'd ever smoked in Evergreen. I let the smoke fill my lungs, holding it until my chest felt like it would burst, before releasing it slowly back into the December air. The slightly fruity aftertaste lingered on my tongue. What better way to unwind after witnessing a murder?

"It's good shit, right?" He grinned, watching my reaction, and flicked ash to the side. "I grew it myself. It's our most popular strain. They call it 'Candy's Breath' on the streets. It tastes sweet but pulls a hell of a punch."

I spluttered. Who needs to be a celebrity with a make-up line when your ex names his homegrown bud after you?

"How did it get to this?" I asked, not sure whether I was talking about him growing weed, Cheeks's death, or how our lives had turned out so differently from what we'd envisioned.

"We never got out, did we?" Rocky said forlornly. We may be out of Evergreen, but being a Seven was no less complicated. Kids trying to steal a CD Walkman had been replaced by the Briarlys and Hiram, who cast an uncertain shadow over our futures. "We were set up to fail from the start."

"Do you remember how we used to talk about how things could be?" I asked as I watched the sunset in the distance. The weed had taken effect and relaxed my muscles and mind, allowing me to peel away a layer of armor I kept up constantly. "You wanting to go to college... me coming out to join you later..."

As teenagers, we fantasized about going away to study, taking road trips — hell, even traveling around the world hadn't seemed out of reach. We were stupid kids who dared to dream and should have known better. Why did we ever think our lives could have been ordinary?

"Sitting on the roof of a strip club and being members of the same gang was never part of the plan," Rocky said, shaking his head. "But we're together again now, right? Us against the world, like we always wanted."

The lights of Port Valentine sprawled ahead of us like a roadmap, and smoke swirled above our heads with unsaid words.

"Why aren't you mad?" I blurted out.

We both knew what I was talking about.

"It's funny." Rocky laughed, leaning back in his chair. "I always thought it was West who I had to worry about."

I spun to face him. "Wait, what?"

"We were fighting over you the night we went to the Smoker." Rocky took his final drag and crushed the roach underfoot. "And all along, it was Zander. Why him, C? West, I can understand, but Zander? You know he's a monster."

Zander *was* a monster. He hid his real feelings under the surface and had a twisted way of showing he cared about people. But if he did care, didn't that make him human?

"Why him?" Rocky pressed, pulling out his papers and tin to roll another joint between his fingers. His brows furrowed in confusion. "Zander is barely even a fucking human."

"It wasn't planned," I stammered, inwardly cringing at the memory of him and West walking in on me mid-orgasm. "It just happened, okay?"

"Do you want it to happen again?"

Good question. It's something I was still figuring out. I finished my joint before answering. When stoned, I could be more honest — not just with Rocky but with myself, too.

"I don't know," I replied eventually. Zander was the second man I'd had sex with. The thought of fucking him again terrified me, but not doing it seemed even worse. When I lost my virginity to Rocky, he'd been slow and gentle. He didn't want to hurt me and kept making sure I was okay. With Zander, it was different. He fucked me to make me his. The experience had been both amazing and soul-destroying. He wanted me to come undone, and I fucking had. "I'm sorry you had to see... what you did."

"I have one more question for you..." Rocky's voice trailed off as he changed the subject. He paused to light up and blow three perfect smoke rings into the breeze. "When we kissed, at the town hall, did it mean anything to you?"

If it wasn't for the incredibly potent pot, I'd have told him to fuck off. Instead, a small voice in the back of my head urged me to stay.

"It confused me," I answered.

He held his joint to my mouth for me to take a drag.

"Why?"

"For so long, I thought I hated you," I said. "And I did. I mean, I really fucking did... then, suddenly, I realized I didn't. At least not in the way I thought. Kissing you showed me that."

"For what it's worth, I'm glad you didn't kill me when you had the chance," he joked.

I laughed, then his expression turned serious. Was this when he revealed his plan to hurl me to my death?

"What happened with Zander doesn't change anything," Rocky said, staring into my eyes with a deep intensity. "It made me mad, but I'll never make the same mistake again. I let you go once, C. I'm never going to do it again."

"We don't need to talk about this now," I said wistfully as Candy's Breath worked her magic. I pulled my chair closer to him and rested my head on his shoulder. "Let's just sit here for a while, like the old times…"

The two of us looked over the skyline. Sitting on top of the world used to fill us with thoughts of possibility. Neither of us had the same feelings of hope now, but it didn't matter. Somehow, through everything, we'd found our way back to each other. It had to mean something, didn't it?

———

"Did you two have fun?" West asked coldly when Rocky and I returned to the penthouse. The dropping temperature and high wearing off made it impossible to stay on the roof any longer.

West's gigantic frame took up most of the sofa, as he flicked aggressively through the TV channels. It's a miracle he hadn't punched holes straight through the remote from the force he was using to push the tiny buttons.

Rocky cleared his throat. "I've got to water the plants."

He hurried out of the room, leaving West and me alone. No doubt he had a secret stash of marijuana growing somewhere in the building.

"Did you get cleaned up?" I asked. Goddammit, I should have smoked another joint before attempting to speak to The Hulk.

"Obviously." West's stormy blue eyes studied me closely, looking me up and down to undress me with his stare, then scowled. "I know how to cover *my* tracks."

"You're mad," I said. *Talk about stating the fucking obvious, Candy.* "Look, I didn't know the pictures from Romano's mansion would get out, okay?"

After Zander, West cared about how the Sevens were perceived more than anyone. He'd be furious about the Briarlys holding information over our necks like an axe.

"You think I'm mad about that? I don't give a shit about the Romano party or what you did there." West turned up the volume on the TV so our conversation wouldn't be overheard, then he rose to his feet and approached me. He lowered his voice and snarled, "I didn't think you joined the Sevens to be another one of Zander's whores."

His words hit me like blunt force trauma to the head. When I started working as a dancer in Lapland, insults were a regular part of my day. But I was a Seven now. West had no right to judge or put me in the same category as Zander's old groupies. He knew me better than that... or, at least, I thought he had.

"So, it's not okay for Zander to fuck me? But it's fine if you want to?" I snapped. Unlike my weed namesake, West was about to face a Candy fire-breathing dragon. I'd roast the bastard over my fucking flames like a slab of hunky meat. "You didn't seem to mind breaking any rules when we were in your car or at the motel. You were pretty happy then."

"That was different." West slammed me backward into the wall with his body. He was a hypocrite. Zander was possessive, but at least he owned it. "You screwed *him*, Candy!"

"You're jealous," I hissed.

I knew the damage that West could do, but I didn't want to diffuse the situation. I wanted to draw out the fucking beast and let it loose.

"You don't know what you're talking about."

"Oh, I think I do," I replied, narrowing my eyes and looking up at him through thick lashes. "I'm not one of your airhead playthings. I'm a fucking Seven, and it's about time you started treating me like it. You're only mad because Zander got to fuck me, and you didn't."

West's nostrils flared in fury, and a vein protruded in his forehead. His trembling arms rose into the air and punched a hole into the wall to the right of my face like a passing train.

"If I was going to fuck you," West spat, "I'd do it somewhere better than over a fucking desk."

He stalked away, slamming the penthouse door behind him. It didn't matter what bullshit Zander said about them wanting to share me. How could I get involved with all three Seven men and expect it not to end up in a fucking disaster when being in the same room with them felt like riding a testosterone-powered rollercoaster?

Joining the Sevens had caused nothing but trouble. If I hadn't moved to Port Valentine, Cheeks would still be alive, and Bryce Briarly wouldn't be using my past to trap the Sevens under his thumb. As soon as I got involved, everything seemed to fall apart.

"He'll calm down," Rocky said, appearing conveniently as West's footsteps faded away. I had a sneaking suspicion he'd waited for The Hulk to leave. "Give him time."

Rocky may feel indebted to forgive me for anything, but West didn't have the same obligation. Although, the thought of losing whatever connection I shared with West stung more than I cared to admit.

"Who says I give a shit about West?" I lied, flopping down on the sofa and hugging a bowl of chips. I stuffed a handful into my mouth. The munchies were setting in, and I knew the barbecue ones were West's favorite. I didn't like the flavor much, but I'd polish off the whole bowl before he returned out of spite. "He can do what the hell he likes."

We were supposed to be professionals. West should be able to keep his dick from poking into Seven business relationships. Then again, I recalled my searing rage when Penelope tried to smother him with her perky rack. My stomach churned at the thought of West finding solace in her bed. If West was a hypocrite, so was I...

"I know you, C," Rocky said, sitting down next to me. "You care about him."

"Since when did you turn into my fucking therapist? I'm done talking," I snapped. "We're gonna watch a movie."

Rocky held up his hands in surrender. "Suits me."

I'd already seen Die Hard a thousand times, but it provided a momentary distraction from my thoughts. As we reached the one hour mark, Zander and West's voices alerted us to their return.

Fuck.

I didn't look up from the screen when they entered.

"Space for two more?" Zander asked with a cheeky half-smile.

I kept my legs stretched out while Rocky shifted around to make extra room. Zander may have wanted to assert his dominance earlier, but I was not giving up my sofa territory for his arrogant ass. And, for all I cared, West could freeze his balls off on the fucking roof.

West settled on the furthest seat away from me and scowled at the barbecue chip crumbs. A sly grin spread over my face. It didn't go unnoticed. West clenched his fist and shot me a venomous look, like he wanted to ram it down my throat until I choked.

Nobody spoke for the rest of the movie, but I felt their eyes watching me. Why the hell had Vixen, Mieko, and Q left? Was sticking around while a crew cleaned up a body really *that* bad? They'd have helped to break up the awkward atmosphere.

As the credits rolled, Rocky dared to speak. "Are we going to talk about what happened earlier?"

"That depends," I said, glaring at West in accusation. "Can West have a conversation without punching another hole in the wall?"

West looked down at his lap like a naughty schoolboy. He needed to learn it wasn't cool to destroy property every time someone touched a nerve. "Take it out of my salary, Zander."

"Where have you been, anyway?" I turned to Zander, not expecting him to answer.

"I reached out to some of my associates to find out more about what Giles is up to and what my father is planning," Zander said. As he talked, I sat up straighter to listen. It was rare for him to share his thoughts, so I wanted to pay fucking attention. "Killing Cheeks for betraying my father's trust was logical, but revealing they know Candy's identity? It makes no sense."

"It's not Bryce's style." West nodded in agreement. "The fucker doesn't reveal what he knows until the final second."

"So, you think Giles screwed up?" I asked.

I'd been winding him up, so it's possible he'd given away more than he should have in retaliation. He was hot-headed and would defend his pride to the end, even if it meant showing his hand. Bryce had a lot of work to do if he expected Giles's pompous ass to become his successor.

"If my father doesn't know, it gives us an advantage," Zander said. A plan was forming in his dark, twisted mind. "Giles isn't stupid enough to let him know that he made a mistake."

"So? We still know they have the power to bring me down whenever they feel like it," I muttered.

"Bring *us* down," Rocky corrected, looking pointedly at me.

"The plan remains unchanged. We do nothing," Zander decided with an air of finality, "until I say otherwise."

"C'mon, Zander," Rocky objected, his voice rising. "There must be something else we can do?"

"You're already walking on thin fucking ice, Red," Zander warned, shooting him a frosty glare to silence him. Rocky had crossed a line by keeping secrets from him about our past, which Zander wouldn't let him forget easily. "Don't fucking question me. I make the rules. You all need to trust me."

Trust had nothing to do with it. Doing nothing may be Zander's plan, but being a sitting duck wasn't my style. Didn't he understand the Romanos would be out for my blood if they discovered I murdered Giovanni? They'd kill me, and everyone I'm associated with. I was a puppet dangling on a string until Bryce decided it was time to cut ties and drop me into the Romano wolf den.

If Zander wouldn't act, I'd have to figure it out on my own. I needed to get the damaging evidence from the Briarly Manor before Bryce could share or use the information as leverage. From the look on Rocky's face, I may have an accomplice...

"I'm gonna have an early night," I said, then narrowed my eyes at West. "Enjoy sleeping on the sofa."

My eyes snapped open. Another vivid horror scene filled with blood and entrails. What did normal people dream about? Whenever I was lucky enough to fall asleep, the nightmares were never far behind. During the day, my brain compartmentalized the trauma, but at night? My head turned into a fucking Halloween fun house.

A gentle knock and the bedroom door opening startled me. I sat upright, switching the bedside lamp on, and scowled at the gigantic figure loitering in the shadows. "Do you make a habit of sneaking up on girls when they're sleeping?"

"Hey, Pinkie." West ignored my snarky response and stepped inside, clicking the door shut behind him. "I couldn't sleep. I heard you—"

"What are you? The dream police?" I snapped, pulling the comforter up to my chin. I didn't want to talk about my sleep quality with a psychopath who pounded bricks like feather pillows. "I'm fine, okay?"

"About earlier..." West exhaled like it was causing him physical pain to speak. "I shouldn't have got up in your face or said what I did."

"Is this supposed to be an apology?" I snarled. "Because, if so, it's pretty fucking lame."

He grinned, and the orange glow of the light illuminated the scar on the side of his face. "I'm not good at apologies."

"Clearly."

"You were right, okay?" He sighed, shuffling from one foot to the other. "I was jealous. Seeing you with Zander made me want to kill him. My own brother. I acted out like a fucking idiot."

"Wait!" I called after him as he turned to leave. West paused as he reached to turn the handle. "You're not an idiot. Well, maybe a bit... but I get it, okay?"

"Go on," he urged, taking a step closer. If West could be honest with me, then maybe I could be open with him. "I'm listening."

"When I saw Penelope all over you, I wanted to rearrange her perfect fucking face," I admitted. The mattress dipped as he sat on the edge of the bed next to me.

"That's not the same," West said, staring into my eyes with a deep intensity. The big guy was hurting. "You *fucked* him while I watched."

"Look, it's complicated..."

"What's complicated?" he asked. "You picked *him*."

"I've not picked anyone," I said, too quickly, then took a deep breath to regain my cool. "I don't even know what's going on here, or how I feel. I know it's greedy and unfair. I don't want to play you off against each other, but things just happened."

"I thought we had something…" West's voice drifted off as he looked away. "When I want a girl, I want her to be all mine."

Zander was right about how one person could alter the dynamics of an entire group. For the Sevens to work together and bring down our enemies, we had to be on the same page. We couldn't let anything get between us… least of all, me.

"I understand." I nodded, gulping down the lump forming in my throat. "Whatever happened between us, we'll forget about it, okay?"

As I said the words, I knew I didn't want them to be true. West was the main reason I stepped into Lapland. Watching him release his monster drew me in. As I watched him, I saw someone who was like me. He made me want to learn more about the people who ran the joint. West's rejection stung like a bitch, but I had no right to feel sad. No one had forced me to spread my legs for Zander. I'd wanted his cock as much as he'd been willing to give it.

"But I realized something else today." West slid closer, narrowing the gap between us. "My brothers are my life. No one can get between us."

"I never wanted to—"

He reached out and pressed a finger to my lips. What was he going to do? Smother me to death? Choke me until I turned purple? No one would hear me gasping for air through the thick penthouse walls.

"You'll only get between us if I let you," he whispered. His rough touch gently skimmed over my cupid's bow. "There's no point in fighting it, Pinkie. We all want you, even if it means I might have to share you."

My mouth fell open, not comprehending what he was saying at first. "I thought you said—"

"The thought of not feeling your sweet lips on mine made me feel worse than watching Zander make you come," he said, his eyes lingering on my mouth as he grinned. "You look fucking beautiful when you come, by the way. Only next time, I want you to be saying *my* name."

"We should sleep." I cleared my throat and tried to ignore the heat between my legs, wanting to do anything *but* sleep. What else was I supposed to say? My sassy ass mouth had no response. Was I still dreaming? "It's late."

West tenderly kissed my forehead. Who'd have guessed he was the same man who had me pinned against a wall a few hours before? He was a gentle giant beneath his skull smasher facade.

"Do you want me to stay?" he asked.

"It's your room," I said, not sure what response he was hoping for. "You make the rules."

He pulled the blankets back and flicked the lamp off to plummet us into darkness. I moved to make room for him to slip into the warmth. It was a squeeze, even in a Californian King. I turned my back on him, thinking he would give me space. Instead, his body moved closer, curving around mine.

"Are you still tired?" West murmured into my hair as I froze in place.

"Uh-huh," I mumbled unconvincingly, as his hand slipped around my waist and stroked my stomach.

"There's always something that helps me sleep," he said, drawing swirls over my skin. "Wanna try it?"

"West, I—"

"Don't worry, Pinkie," he whispered. "I'm not going to touch you. Not yet."

He rolled me gently onto my back and placed his hand over mine. Unlike Zander, West's hands were lined with scars and rough skin. He was no stranger to hard work. He pushed my hand down, forcing my fingers to glide over my front until they reached the waistband of my pajama shorts. In the blackness, the sound of our shallow breathing was amplified.

"I told you. I'm not gonna touch you," West murmured.

He guided my fingers down further, slipping underneath the soft fabric. My heart hammered at the heat of West's skin against mine, but I didn't object. I stopped at the point of no return. I couldn't touch myself in front of him, could I?

West paused, sensing my reluctance. If I moved a little further, the tips of his giant fingers would rest between my legs as his hands dwarfed my own. He pulled back, sliding upwards, to stroke the back of my hand and wrist. For someone with the strength of a grizzly, he had a softer and more considerate side. He wanted to make sure I was comfortable.

"Make yourself feel good for me, Pinkie."

It didn't count if it was dark, right? My clit begged to be touched and welcomed my soft caress like an old friend. I teased her, gently circling to make my body beg for more. West could feel the rhythm of my motions, and I sunk my teeth into my lip to stop myself from sighing. The feel of his heavy, muscled arm resting on mine only added to the excitement building in my hot core.

"Does that feel good, Pinkie?" West purred.

"Yes." I breathed, squeezing my eyes shut and daring to explore myself more.

"Keep going," he urged. His cock pressed into my side as his fingers stroked the back of my hand in encouragement. "This is all about you."

I moaned as my fingers slipped between my lips and welcomed the wetness. I teased my entrance to mirror West's strokes and imagined it was him touching me. I slipped a finger inside, wondering how many it would take to fill me as much as his cock would.

"West..." I panted, slowly withdrawing my fingers from my pussy and hoping he would take their place.

Instead of taking my hint, he retreated and stroked my inner arm. "What is it, Pinkie?" he asked.

"I want you to touch me."

"I told you I'm not gonna touch you. Not yet." His voice came out in a low, gravelly rumble which sent tingles shooting up my thighs. "I want you to come all over your fingers for me."

West took my wrist in his grasp and pushed it back down between my legs. I explored my pussy with urgency this time, unable to hold back a moan as I stroked my clit.

"After my actions earlier, I'm not worthy of you," West said. His hardness left me under no illusion he wanted me, but his self-control was impressive. "When I have you for the first time, I'll claim you as my own. I'll worship every fucking inch of your body and bury my cock deep in your wet pussy. But tonight? It's all about you."

My breathing grew more ragged as I slid two fingers down my slit and into my wetness. West's grip guided my hands deeper, forcing me to fuck myself again and again. Each push rubbed against my clit and made my thighs tremble with longing.

This was not how I'd expected the night to end, but I couldn't stop now. I relished the hotness of his body against mine and fantasized about how good it would feel for him to roll on top of me. As well as West, I thought about how Zander pounded into me like a speeding truck and how kissing Rocky ignited a flickering inside me that I thought was lost forever. The Seven men would be the fucking death of me. How was a girl supposed to function surrounded by smoking hot men all the time?

"West," I cried out as my orgasm rolled in.

My legs tensed as an explosive burst rippled through my body. I rolled my hips onto my hand, wanting it to never end. I prolonged the sensation, teasing out my pleasure by applying and releasing pressure on my clit to enjoy the pulsing. I'd mastered the art of making orgasms last three times the length. When you used to spend a lot of time locked in a bedroom, it was one way to pass the time... but this was different.

The lights were off, but West had *seen* me as he'd made me come undone. The blackness allowed us to focus on the other sensations. The heat of our bodies. The swell of his cock against my ass. The sound of our breathing blurring into one. West may not have used his own hands to give me pleasure, but his guiding touch felt even more intimate. If I'd fallen apart in his arms now, what would happen when he touched me himself? I'd unravel and never be able to be put back together again.

"I knew you'd be moaning my name," West murmured triumphantly as I slid my hands out of my shorts. "Next time you come, it'll be all over my face."

Self-consciousness replaced my wild abandon as I snatched my hand away. In the throes of passion, I didn't think about anything other than chasing a release. My cheeks burned at the thought of what I'd just done. What did this mean for us? For the Sevens?

"I need a minute," I stammered, slipping out of his bed on wobbly legs and stumbling to his en suite.

I purposefully took my time and, when I returned, West's snoring greeted me. As I got in, he slung his arm around my shoulders and pulled me close, so I could hear the thud of his heart through his muscles.

"Sweet dreams, Pinkie," he whispered sleepily into my hair.

"Night, West," I replied as tiredness swept over me.

Fourteen

"Sleep well?" Zander raised an eyebrow as West and I emerged from his room simultaneously. Rocky didn't look up from his cereal. He was busy dunking fruit loops violently into the milk like he wanted to drown them… or someone else.

"He didn't touch me, okay?" I said defensively, grabbing a piece of toast from the rack on the counter. I mean, it was *technically* true. West may have lain next to me while I touched myself, but there wasn't even a freaking base for that. It was basically PG-13.

"Not all of us are like you, Zander," West said, making me choke on my mouthful.

After West's blow-up yesterday and our conversation last night, the atmosphere felt lighter in the penthouse. Sitting in a room together without one guy trying to assassinate another with dagger-like side glances was a sign of progress.

Zander poured himself a black coffee and cleared his throat like we were in a business meeting. "It's time we addressed the Candy situation."

"I'm not a fucking *situation*," I objected, crumbs flying everywhere. "And FYI, I'm also not a morning person. I'd think carefully about what you say next, asshole."

The three of them snickered.

"Rocky, West," Zander continued, addressing them like I wasn't even in the freaking room, "are we all in understanding?"

They nodded curtly.

"Hello! What understanding?" I pointed my toast at Zander like a weapon. "Why do I feel like I'm missing something here?"

"We've finalized our arrangement," Zander said, then caught West's eye. "Haven't we?"

"Yes," West growled.

"That's settled," Zander said, placing his cup down like a judge slamming a hammer in a courtroom.

My brows furrowed in confusion. "What arrangement?"

"We have all agreed to make you our Seven girl officially," Zander said. "We'll share you, little one. You're all fucking ours."

"Don't you think this should have been a conversation we all had together?" I asked, heat rising to my cheeks in anger. What the fuck had I signed myself up for? "Maybe I don't want any of you anymore."

Zander chuckled. Who was I kidding? What woman alive wouldn't start gushing at the thought of screwing one of the Sevens? Let alone having all three!

Rocky smiled slyly. "You've never been a good liar, C."

"Fuck off." I scowled at him, then glared at the others. "What else did you talk about when I wasn't around? Did you draw up a fucking schedule?"

"Would you like that, little one?" The mischievous glint in Zander's eyes returned. "One-on-one time with each of us? Or, how about a group session?"

As I looked at the three of them, West's neck tensed, and he sat up straighter in his chair. For a guy who didn't like sharing, he'd kept his cool... so far. He may be happy with Zander's proposal, but it would take him time to adjust.

"You said you couldn't choose between us," Zander continued, "now you don't have to."

"I'm not a hole in the fucking wall you can bone whenever you feel like it." I threw down my toast. "Is this how it's going to be, huh? Leaving me out of important conversations? I'm not being a Seven groupie."

"You would never be, C," Rocky said, the corners of his mouth quirked upwards in a smile. "We agreed you're the only girl we want and the only girl we'll have. There's no pressure on you, okay? And you don't have to do anything you don't want to. If you don't want any of us, that's fine, but we're not gonna be screwing anyone else."

There may be no pressure, but my head felt like it had been jammed inside a crock-pot. Would they really be happy leaving behind their bachelor lifestyle? It felt as ridiculous as the Pope deciding to become a rapper. Could I be enough for them?

"I need some time to process whatever 'this' is," I said. Suddenly, I felt very aware of how much of my skin was on display, and I pulled down the hem of my pajama shorts. I'd opted not to change before breakfast and now regretted it. "Is this really what you all want?"

I half-expected them to burst out laughing and claim it was their idea of a prank, but they didn't. They all nodded solemnly. Zander's eyes scanned my body possessively, visually marking me as his territory. Rocky remained straight-faced and serious. His inner determination to win me back meant he would do anything to get a second chance. West looked more apprehensive. Sharing a woman would be an adjustment for him, but he nodded with more ferocity than the other two. He wanted me to know that he would make it work.

"Being a Seven is a lifetime deal, remember? So is this," Zander said. "Take the time you need, but why keep fighting the inevitable when we all know you want it? We can all see how much your body wants us."

"You're such an ass, Zander," I hissed. His gaze lingered on my nipples pebbling beneath my top. I folded my arms across my chest to hide the twins from any further visual violation. "If I had a schedule, then you wouldn't be fucking on it right now."

West snorted, then added possessively, "This is why you're our Seven girl."

"Well, can your *Seven girl* have some pancakes?" I asked.

I couldn't decide whether I found the 'Seven girl' label a douchebag misogynistic move, or whether I liked how these men wanted me to be theirs and weren't afraid to own it.

Zander grabbed his spatula and headed to the kitchen like a knight going into battle. "Of course."

I blinked twice to make sure I wasn't imagining it. Nope, it was definitely happening. Who knew he could be so obliging? Maybe I was seeing another side to him... one he liked to keep hidden under layers of sexy ink.

"And that doesn't mean I'm agreeing to your arrangement either," I said hastily. I may have got myself caught in the middle of a tangled muscled mess, but I had to take advantage of the perks. "I want pancakes with no strings attached."

West and Rocky chuckled as Zander shot back, "Oh, little one... you're still acting like you have a choice."

"Ignore him," Rocky said, then lowered his voice and winked. "Zander's used to getting his way."

"Well, things are gonna change around here," I muttered, making West and Rocky laugh.

If they wanted me in their lives and beds, they needed to understand I wasn't the type of girl who'd worship their every move. I'd call their sexy asses out if they were acting like jerks every damn time. Could they handle a hot stab-happy mess with serious trust issues? Or, better question, could I handle them?

"What's so funny?" Zander called from behind the kitchen counter as he violently whipped up a fresh batch of batter.

I widened my eyes innocently and smiled. "Oh, nothing..."

———

After eating breakfast with the guys, I needed time alone to get my head around their proposal. There was no rule book to read about being the girl who three criminals share. How would our arrangement work? Managing one relationship was complicated enough, but juggling three simultaneously? I had years of experience in seducing men for extortion but fell short in the romance department.

When Rocky broke my heart, I vowed to never let it happen again. I built armor to protect myself. Why let anyone in and give them the power to hurt me? The Sevens changed that. Those fuckers were pulling my guard down, piece by piece.

Despite my resistance, I was coming to the realization that Zander was right. I had no choice. Rocky, West, and Zander had gotten under my skin. No matter how hard I tried, it was impossible to fight my instincts. I didn't need an arrangement or a fucking label to tell me what my gut already knew. I was theirs, and they were all fucking mine.

"I can come with you?" Rocky offered as I gathered my belongings.

"I told you already, I'll be fine," I said, slinging my bag over my shoulder and heading out of the penthouse.

"Are you sure?" Rocky pressed.

He followed me out onto the street, where Zander and West were already waiting to say goodbye. I didn't need a fucking farewell party; I was only going home until my shift later that night. Like Rocky, West and Zander didn't look pleased about my departure, either. West donned his signature sulky pout, and Zander's arms were crossed.

After an eventful Christmas in Lapland, returning to my grotty apartment would be a jolt back to reality and provide a break from the growing sexual tension. The only appointment I had this evening was with my pink vibrating pet rabbit.

I raised an eyebrow at West as a bullet-proof Lexus pulled up at my feet. "I thought you'd called a cab?"

"We're not letting you get into a car with a stranger," West said with the seriousness of a bodyguard being tasked to protect the President. "Our best driver will take you wherever you wanna go. He'll be permanently stationed with you from now on."

"I don't need a fucking escort." I jabbed my finger into his chest, then remembered how Giles and Bryce were digging into my past. I could take care of myself, but it *would* be nice not to worry about having to fight my way out of a cab. I sighed and added reluctantly, "I guess it beats waiting in the cold for an Uber..."

West shot me an 'I told you so' look.

"We'll see you tonight," Zander said, opening the car door and undressing me with hungry eyes. We hadn't been alone together since we'd fucked in his office, but the thought of it happening again kept slipping into my consciousness when I least expected it. When he served my pancakes, I couldn't even look at him without thinking of how good he'd looked with his head between my legs. As soon as my mind strayed to what happened between us, Zander sensed it. Was he psychic? A dark grin spread over his face like a promise of what was to come the next time he got me alone. "Our girl can take care of herself."

"Damn right I can," I said, slamming the door shut and leaving them behind as the car takes off.

As soon as I arrived back at my apartment and turned the key in the lock, I knew something was wrong. I got the same feeling whenever a creep who'd been checking me out all night slid a drink across the bar. My skin crawled, and every instinct told me to run.

I reached for my new knife and tried to push the door open, but the wood is met with resistance. I forced it open with my shoulder until I created a big enough gap to slip inside.

Well, shit... this was the complete opposite of a home makeover.

"Hello?" I called out, brandishing my blade.

There was no response. Whoever had broken in had either already left or had hidden somewhere. Where could a person conceal themselves amongst the mess?

It looked like a small tornado had ripped through my apartment and destroyed everything in its path. The sofa was upturned, and cushions slashed open, spilling out their stuffing like entrails. My tiny adjoining kitchen was no better. The blocked sink was overflowing and flooding onto the floor while the cabinet doors had been torn off.

"Anyone here?" I asked, fairly confident the culprits had made themselves scarce.

I picked my way over the rubbish to enter my bedroom and survey the damage. The entire contents of my wardrobe had been shredded into piles. Hell, they'd even transformed the freaking curtains into strings. I wrinkled my nose at a suspicious-looking stain and smell coming from the mattress. Casual vandalism was small fry and didn't bother me... but something else did.

Above my bed, a gigantic pink graffiti outline of a cat had been sprayed over the wall. You couldn't miss it. Someone wanted to send me a message.

It was too messy to be Hiram's style. If Hiram wanted to trash your place, he'd set fire to the whole fucking block — not make a shit sandwich outta your sheets. No, this was an amateur scare job. The last words a British asshole said to me sprung to my mind instantly.

'See you soon, Kitty.'

Behind me, something stirred.

"Giles." West's deep growl over my shoulder confirmed my suspicions as he reached out to place his hand on my arm. I grabbed his wrist and twisted it, making him yelp. Hey, at least it confirmed I hadn't started hearing voices in my head.

"You should know better than to sneak up on me."

"Noted," he muttered as I dropped my hold on him. He pouted, massaging his wrist. The big guy could dish it out but didn't know how to take it.

"How the fuck did you get here so fast, anyway?" I asked, peering around him to check whether the others had arrived, but it looked like West had come alone. Surely, it couldn't be a coincidence? He'd appeared out of fucking nowhere like a superhero.

West held up his hands and started backing away slowly. "I may, or may not, have installed a hidden camera in your apartment."

"You did, what?" I spluttered. It's a good thing he was out of stomping range. Otherwise, I'd have crushed his toes under my heel. "Where? When?!"

He strolled casually through to my main living area and pointed to a spot above the TV, where a crack ran down the side of the wall. "I installed it the last time I was here."

I racked my brain to remember. He'd only ever been over once, before our trip to the junkyard, months ago. How many hours had he spent spying on me while I'd been curled up with a tub of ice cream? We were not in nineteen-fucking-eighty-four.

"You've been watching me all this time. Why? I wasn't even a Seven then!" I balled my fists and shoved his muscled chest as a fresh swell of rage rose inside me. For a guy the size of a house, he could be sneaky. "What am I to you, huh? Your personal reality TV show? Did you get bored with watching the Real Housewives?"

I wasn't only mad with him, but with myself. How hadn't I noticed before? If this had gotten past me, I'd let myself get too comfortable. Being comfortable meant making mistakes and getting sloppy. It couldn't happen again.

"It's not like that," West said, catching my wrists before I could push him again. "You attract trouble, Candy. When Cheeks got locked up, I wanted to make sure you'd be safe."

I couldn't decide whether to be horrified or flattered The Hulk cared about what happened to me enough to set up a live stream to my fucking sofa.

"Why go through the effort of installing a covert surveillance system when you didn't use it when it mattered?" I said, gesturing wildly at the ruins around us. "Couldn't you have stopped all of this?"

"I didn't realize someone had cut the feed until after you left Lapland. I didn't check it over the holidays," West mumbled, looking at his feet and finally having the decency to look ashamed of himself. He'd fucked up, and he knew it. "The last thing the footage showed was three guys wearing bala-clavas. The fuckers cut the power, which messed with our signal. Zander's looking into it. We're working on the theory that Giles paid a group of local kids to do it."

At least something good had come from the break-in. West's private cable channel had got taken off-air.

"Figures," I said, rolling my eyes. Giles, like his uncle, wasn't above using easily influenced kids to do his bidding. "Now, you've seen I'm alive. Are you here to help me clean up, or what? It's the least you could do."

West laughed in disbelief. "Did you think we'd let you stay here after this? I'm here to bring you and, what's left of your things, home."

"Home?" My mouth fell open in shock. "You want me to move into the penthouse?"

Spending the festive period in Lapland with the Sevens was one thing, but moving in with them permanently? It was a big step…

"You're a Seven, so it makes sense that you live with us," West said, with a casual shrug. From the way he was acting, you'd have thought he'd asked me to go out bowling. "It would have happened, eventually. I want you somewhere I can keep my eye on you."

"But where will I sleep?" I stammered as my mind worked quickly to count the number of bedrooms in the penthouse. There was nowhere for me to go. A twinge between my legs reminded me that there was one obvious solution… no, Candy! We may have made an arrangement, but a girl needed her space — especially if she had to juggle three Seven men. "There's not enough room."

"It's taken care of," West answered. "Vixen is giving up her walk-in closet."

"I bet she'll fucking love that…" I muttered sarcastically, imagining her reaction to giving up storage would be akin to an earthquake. I'd never seen inside her closet but knew she had a vast collection of leathers she liked to store correctly.

"It's small," West said, "but it's nicer than—"

"Than this place?" I finished his sentence and placed my hands on my hips in defiance. "I could sleep in my car."

"That piece of junk? I've already sent it to scrap." West laughed as I sent him a scathing look, then his expression turned deadpan, and he took a step forward. He leaned in closer, running his knuckle over my cheek. "Look, Pinkie. We can either do this the easy way or the hard way. If you don't come with me, I'll carry you out. It's your choice."

"I can walk myself," I hissed, turning my back on him and marching out empty-handed.

I may be stubborn and not want to bend to West's will, but what choice did I have? Getting Zander to make me pancakes every morning was better than dealing with my headache of an apartment. There was no point in trying to salvage any of my belongings either. Giles's stooges had done a thorough job of trashing everything I owned.

My nuisance neighbor poked her head out of her apartment across the hall. "What's all this noise about?"

"Mind your own fucking business," I spat, flipping her off as I passed. "I'm moving out."

Starting over with nothing didn't scare me. I'd done it before. But moving in with three monsters who I either wanted to strangle or jump their bones? That was fucking terrifying.

———

I refused to speak to West on the journey to Lapland. I may have gone with him willingly, but it didn't mean I was happy about being coerced under the threat of violence.

Vixen was waiting for us to return. She stood outside the sparkly entrance with a pile of cigarette butts at her feet. She'd been chain-smoking, something she only did when she got stressed.

"After you," West said, holding the car door open for me. I scowled as I got out without thanking him. Who was he kidding? He was no gentleman.

As my heel hit the sidewalk, Vixen hurtled forward like a cannonball. I clenched my fists to gear up for a fight. Instead, she threw her arms around me in a tight hug.

"I came home as soon as I heard," Vixen said, squeezing me harder than a boa constrictor. "I'm sorry about your place."

"It's fine." I patted her awkwardly on the back. What had Mieko's magic vagina done to her? The old Vixen would have electrocuted anyone who got within an inch of touching her. "It's not like anyone died."

Vixen flinched and pulled away. I guess it was too soon to be making jokes after Cheeks's murder…

"Where's the rest of Candy's stuff?" Vixen snapped at West like a concierge addressing a porter. "You can carry them upstairs."

"There was nothing worth saving," I answered.

"When we found out what happened, we figured you might need new clothes, and it's a good thing we did. Zander's gone shopping with Mieko to get you some," Vixen said, then scowled bitterly. "He didn't trust me with his platinum."

I bit my tongue to stop myself from saying it may not have been a bad thing. I didn't want a full closet of fetish club gear.

"Or, maybe Zander didn't want you going on a spending spree of your own, because you had to give up your walk-in?" West teased. "Didn't you say you wanted compensation?"

"You try finding storage solutions at the last minute." Vixen shot him a venomous glare. "Do I look like Marie-fucking-Kondo?"

"If you don't want me to stay," I said, "I can find somewhere else."

Now, I was on the receiving end of Vixen's 'shut the hell up, if you don't want me to rip off your nipples' look.

"This is your home now. I'll show you to your new room," Vixen insisted fiercely. She grabbed my arm and pulled me inside before I could say any more, or try to talk her out of it. I followed her up to the penthouse as she chatted about her conditions for sharing. "I'm happy for you to have the walk-in, but I draw the line at sharing a bathroom. My nails are too expensive to be picking your long pink hairs outta the drain."

"Sure," I agreed, as West snorted behind me. It blew my mind that not sharing a bathroom was an option some people had. Growing up in Evergreen meant you were lucky to shower with hot water.

"Good luck, Pinkie," West chirped, disappearing into his room, which only made me more anxious. For all I knew, Vixen could be luring me away to be sacrificed.

"We rarely have guests, so the main bathroom can be yours," Vixen said, pointing at a sign on the door with my name on it. Her refusing to share a bathroom was no fucking joke. "Through here…"

I followed her into her bedroom. Instead of resembling a gothic playboy mansion, it looked more like an art studio. She'd decorated tastefully; abstract paintings hung on the walls, candles burned on every spare surface, and the lingering smell of incense gave the air a mystical quality. Off of her main suite was a door to her bathroom and another which, I presumed, led to my new box room.

"Go on." She gave me a push in encouragement. "There are no monsters in there."

My jaw dropped as I stepped inside.

Holy shit.

My new room was only slightly smaller than hers. An enormous bed with powder pink bedding and a sweeping overhead canopy sat in the middle. Around it, shelving and a beautiful Hollywood-style dressing table lined the walls. How had they had the time to pull this together?

I turned to Vixen in disbelief. "This used to be your closet?"

"Well, duh!" Vixen rolled her eyes. "I haven't had time to clear all of my stuff out yet."

"You can keep it here," I said. "I wouldn't be able to fill half this room, even if I went shopping every day for the rest of the year."

Vixen flopped down on my new bed and kicked off her New Rock boots. "Are you ready for the rest of the rules?"

"There's more?" I groaned, collapsing next to her.

"Rule one, no smoking in the room," she counted the points off on her tombstone painted talons, "rule two, you can borrow whatever you like as long as you put it back where you found it."

"Anything else?" I asked sarcastically.

"I'd rather you didn't fuck the guys when I'm in the next room," she said, then a sly smile crept over her face. How the hell did she find out about our conversation this morning? On second thoughts, I didn't even want to know. "Although, I don't think that's gonna be a problem when everyone else is down the hall."

Rocky's head poked around the door to interrupt our conversation. "How are you settling in?"

"Hey!" My voice came out three octaves higher than usual. He'd spared me from having to talk to Vixen about whatever was going on between me and the guys. I ignored her growing smirk, which told me this wasn't the end of our conversation. "Yep, all good here."

"Candy's settling in fine, no thanks to you," Vixen said. "Where the fuck were you when I needed help with moving my latex?"

"What can I say?" he replied. "Business called."

She threw a pillow, *my* new pillow, at him. "Smoking pot does not count as business."

"I need to sample the goods to check the quality." His lopsided grin made my stomach flip. "Do you need any help with unpacking, C?"

"Sure, now, he turns into the knight in shining armor," Vixen grumbled under her breath.

"I have nothing to unpack," I said. "Nothing was worth keeping."

My ruby ring, pendant necklace from Zander, and the knife in my back pocket were the only items I owned of any value. I wasn't dumb enough to let them out of my sight for a second.

Rocky's expression turned stony. "Giles is a fucker."

Strangely enough, Giles may have done me a favor. I'd be glad not to have to deal with my neighbor nagging about noise or worrying about getting fried by dodgy electrics whenever I wanted to curl my hair.

"You should be grateful you're not related to the asshole," Vixen said.

"Oh, I am," Rocky said, then pulled a clumsily wrapped package from behind his back. "I got you a moving gift. I've been saving it for a special occasion."

I took it from him, turning it over suspiciously in my hands, then ripped it open. I gasped at the CD Walkman. *It couldn't be, could it?* I ran my fingers over the familiar smooth plastic. The stickers had faded after all these years, but it was the same one. *My one.*

"Did you travel back to the nineties or lose your fucking mind?" Vixen asked, making it clear what she thought of his gift. "How much green did you smoke, Red?"

Rocky ignored her, giving me his undivided attention. "Now you have something else worth keeping."

"You kept it all this time?" I murmured, feeling the grooves where I'd etched my initials into it with a compass during math class.

Music brought me salvation when I lived in the Evergreen group home. As a teenager, I spent hours listening to CDs when everyone had already moved onto iPods. The Walkman had been my gateway to another world. A way for me to dance, dream and wish for better things.

"Of course I did," Rocky said, burying his hands in his pockets and looking bashful. "I wouldn't let them take it off me — even in Redlake, the guards let me have it. I hoped I'd be able to give it back to you one day."

"Thanks." I sniffed and looked away, hoping he wouldn't see the tears forming in my eyes. The Walkman wasn't only a way to play CDs. It was a symbol. A symbol of Rocky showing he remembered. A symbol of his words being true. After all the shit he'd gone through, he could have given up and tossed it into the trash with our memories. Instead, he dared to hope we'd find each other again. "It's perfect."

Rocky's eyes sought mine and held my gaze for a few seconds. We shared a look of understanding and promise. We couldn't change what happened in the past, but he'd proved himself. Together, we'd find a way to move past our mistakes.

"Welcome home, C," he said.

Being 'home' was a strange concept when you'd grown up in a world where you felt like you'd never truly belonged. Coming to live with the Sevens scared me, but it didn't make me want to run. Who knows? Maybe it meant I'd finally found what I was looking for...

"You two are so fucking weird." Vixen frowned and shook her head, breaking our moment. Her face lit up at the sound of approaching footsteps. "They're back."

A second later, Mieko stumbled into my room with bags stacked up her arms. She wouldn't need to hit the gym anytime soon. Carrying them looked like a fucking workout. Zander followed close behind her, holding even more boxes.

"Did you buy the whole freaking store?" I asked, surveying the mountain of goods they laid on the floor.

"Mieko seemed to feel bad about spending money, so I helped," Zander replied. "I only want the best for our Seven girl."

Hiram always had an ulterior motive when he used to buy me clothes. He wanted me to look the part for whatever twisted job was coming up next, but it was different with Zander. His thoughtfulness and desire to look after me made me feel warm and fuzzy. As an independent, kick-ass woman, it was something I had no fucking idea how to deal with...

I pushed my emotions aside and picked out a dress from the closest bag, which looked like it'd be fit for a red carpet event. "When will I get a chance to wear *this* in Port Valentine?"

When I didn't know how to react, resorting to my usual snarky self was the only way.

"I'm sure you'll find the occasion," Zander said, then turned to the others. "Why don't we leave Candy to unpack? We'll need to get ready for tonight."

"Tonight?" My head jerked upright. "What's happening?"

"We're going to the Golden Gloves," Rocky said. The Golden Gloves is Port Valentine's underground cage fighting ring, most famous for the number of men who died in it. "I've been drafted in at the last minute."

"You fight?" I spluttered, thinking I'd misheard him. "At the Golden Gloves?"

When we were younger, Rocky never used his fists unless he had to. Being locked in Redlake and joining the Sevens must have changed him more than I knew...

"You didn't know?" Vixen let out a low whistle. "Red's a fucking legend. You should have seen him in juvie."

"I want you all to be there," Rocky said. "I need cheerleaders."

I scowled. "If you want me to be peppy with pompoms, you have another thing coming..."

"You're coming too, Mimi," Vixen said.

Mimi? If the two of them weren't so damn cute and happy, I'd have barfed over my new shoes.

"What's the dress code?" Mieko asked nervously.

"Whatever it is, I'm sure I have something you could borrow," I said. There was no way she was getting out of it.

"It's boiling in there, so wear something short," Vixen said, then considered it further, "but with a crotch."

Why couldn't a woman go into a crowded place without worrying about sweaty hands trying to slip under their skirt? If any asshole dared to touch me, or the girls, I'd rip off their fingers with my canines.

"Don't worry, little one," Zander said, turning to me with a playful grin. "No one will touch you when I'm around."

I rolled my eyes. He never missed an opportunity to step into his role as the alpha. "Save it, Zander."

"It'll be a fun night," Rocky said, cracking his knuckles and shooting me a mischievous smile. "You'll see."

CHAPTER

Fifteen

Our limo pulled into the Golden Gloves parking lot. The boxing gym looked like it'd been around since the dawn of time. People queued around the building, raising bottles of beer, throwing smack talk and betting on who would bleed out when the bell rang. I recognized many of Lapland's regular customers and members of the Sevens security team waiting in line. A real charming crowd.

Rocky was somewhere inside, preparing for his fight. Could he handle himself around thugs who fought for a living? He usually made use of his green fingers, not fists in boxing gloves.

"Have you ever seen Fight Club?" Vixen asked, holding the door open for me and Mieko to get out of the car. "This is the real fucking deal."

Zander, already waiting outside, beckoned us forward. "This way."

He greeted a pair of beautiful women, who hung on his every word. While they competed for his attention, he watched me out of the corner of his eye, searching for a reaction. Being treated like royalty would do nothing for his ego, and the bastard wanted to make me jealous. A woman took his arm, and I stepped forward. I wanted to bash the bitch's head against the ground for touching my man.

"I won't be needing an escort tonight," Zander said, carefully removing her hand. He held out his arm for me to take. Her face fell like she'd been diagnosed with gonorrhea as I linked my arm through his. *Good fucking riddance.* I'd rather have made a show of running my fingers through his hair, but we had to be careful. Everyone in Port Valentine believed I was engaged to West, and it was easier to keep it that way… for now.

"It's like we're celebrities," Mieko murmured as we sauntered to the front of the queue.

Vixen snorted. "You expect the star treatment when you hire half the staff as dealers or clean-up crew."

A few daring men wolf-whistled as we passed, which Zander silenced with one deadly glare. Vixen and Mieko looked incredible; their outfits reflected their contrasting personalities. Vixen wore leather pants with a fishnet halter top, while Mieko had borrowed a gorgeous sparkly playsuit, which looked way better on her than it ever would on me. I'd ignored Vixen's advice and opted to wear a skintight black Bardot dress. Why should I have to cover up because of assholes who couldn't keep their hands to themselves? Besides, my sharp stiletto heels could easily pierce a scrotum.

Zander approached the beefy guy guarding the entrance, who nodded to let us pass. As we did, the guard bent down to whisper in Zander's ear.

"What did he say?" I asked as Zander turned to look at me wearing his 'I want to rip someone apart limb by limb' expression.

"Giles is here."

That only meant one thing... trouble.

Inside, the Golden Gloves smelled like stale sweat, iron and alcohol. Uncomfortable folding seats had been crammed around the ring, and groups congregated in the back. The crowds parted for us to make our way through. Even though the chairs were ass-numbing, they were reserved for a privileged minority.

People came here looking to settle scores. They wouldn't fight clean. It'd be hard, fast, and dirty. I understood why West had elected to stay behind and look after the club. If West lost self-control at a place like this, someone would end up dead by the end of the night... and it wouldn't be him.

Zander led us to the ringside, where our seats were waiting. Mieko was right. It felt like we'd got a front-row ticket to the most anticipated premiere of the year. We were close enough to smell the sweat of the fighters, but far enough away to be out of blood splatter range.

I turned to Mieko on my left. "Is this your first proper date?"

"I guess it is," she said, shooting Vixen an adoring stare on her other side.

The referee climbed into the ring. Beside him, a half-naked girl paced with a sign to declare the night was starting and winked at the hecklers.

"Are you ready for the fun to begin?" Zander purred in my ear as his hand rested casually on my knee. We were sandwiched so close together, no one would be able to see. His touch on my bare skin sent hot tingles up my thighs, but I kept my legs pressed firmly together. I knew how skilled his fingers were, but right now? I was playing the role of West's fiancée, and we needed to keep it that way.

I grinned back at him. "I was born ready."

Adrenaline fizzed in the air, ramping up the crowd's energy and engaging their 'fight or fuck' response. Humans liked to think we were more civilized than our ancestors, but we couldn't hide from our innate drives: sex and violence. Places like the Golden Gloves drew out our most primal, raw and deadly urges.

Two opponents staggered into the ring. From the chanting and symbols on their chests, I guessed they were from two opposing gangs. I'd seen how this situation went down before. Whoever won would gain a slice of turf and the respect of their group, but the losers would become hungry for vengeance. Whatever the outcome, lives would be lost.

The shorter of the men wasted no time. He charged at his opponent and landed a punch with a thwack. The crowd jumped to their feet and cheered as his head spun. His opponent staggered from the blow, but only for a second. He recovered and advanced for revenge by smashing his fist into the jaw of his enemy. Teeth flew out of his mouth and landed at our feet with a ping. It was weird not to be the person knocking them out for a change.

"Want a souvenir, Candy?" Zander asked.

"I don't keep trophies," I said, talking about more than what was happening in front of us. Some serial killers got their kicks by collecting mementos, but I was smarter than that. Why take anything that could lead back to you?

Zander leaned in to whisper, "Do you think you could do better?"

"Well, duh." I flicked my hair over my shoulder. "Of course, I fucking could, and you know it."

The fight didn't last long. It only took three minutes for the loser to collapse in a bloody heap. This wasn't just any ring. Here, nothing was off the table. There was only one rule: fight until your opponent can't fight anymore.

Zander caught the eye of a man, who brought us beers in glass bottles. They didn't serve drinks in plastic by principle. Why would they? Any extra bloodshed in the crowd was seen as a bonus between rounds.

I saw Vixen nudge her head out of the corner of my eye. "Spawn of the devil incoming at four o'clock."

Zander gripped my leg tighter. "It was only a matter of time."

"Front row, I see?" I ground my teeth at the sound of Giles's irritating drawl. He swanned in front of us, flanked by two cronies. Why did he think wearing a white suit to a fight was a good idea? Clearly, he wasn't worried about anyone hurting him. The spineless bastard was too afraid to come to the Golden Gloves without reinforcements. We may not be able to touch him without causing an outright war with the Briarlys, but some of the locals may not be afraid to throw a punch his way. I'd like to see his suit with a new red splattered accent. "I hear there is a last-minute change to the schedule."

"Don't tell me you're going in the ring?" I feigned surprise, knowing he wouldn't last ten seconds. I'd be able to take the motherfucker down quicker than he could say 'God save the Queen'.

"It looks like Kitty has claws. I hope Red has your enthusiasm," Giles taunted. "He's up against the Rhino."

The Rhino? I didn't think we were in a zoo.

"The Rhino?" Vixen blanched, the color draining from her face. "Since when? That wasn't the fucking plan."

"Things can change quickly, Vixie," Giles said, with a wicked glint in his piggy eyes. A change of plan was easy to orchestrate when you were being bankrolled by the deep pockets of Uncle Bryce. "Enjoy the show."

"Oh, we will," I spat as he walked away.

Zander rose from his seat. His jaw set in furious determination. "There's someone I need to speak to," he growled, then stormed into the crowd while Vixen shifted around in her seat like she'd caught crabs.

"Someone's gonna lose their job over this," Vixen muttered, shaking her head. "Anyone with loyalty to the Sevens would know better than taking a bribe from Giles, especially one like this."

"What's so bad about the Rhino?" I asked.

"You'll know when you see him," she said, squeezing Mieko's hand so hard her knuckles turned white. "Red's a good fighter, but the Rhino? He's a fucking animal."

A few seconds later, Zander returned with a thunderous expression. He was not a person who took kindly to being double-crossed. Who needs enemies when your family is obsessed with trying to screw you over? Before I could ask him whether he'd sourced who had accepted a dirty bribe, Mieko squeaked at the sight of a man entering the ring.

"He's the Rhino?" she asked shakily, her lip trembling.

"See what I mean now?" Vixen said.

The Rhino looked like he weighed as much as a small transportation truck. His skin was thick and leathery, covered in scars from stab wounds and bullet holes from head to toe. I don't know how many steroids he'd pumped through his veins, but it looked like he could crush two cars between his hands. He might be the only person who could rival The Hulk...

"You've got to be fucking kidding!" I looked at Zander incredulously. "You're going to let him fight *that*?"

"Red's made his choice. He wants to fight," Zander replied nonchalantly with a dismissive wave of his hand. He'd been more bothered about finding out someone accepted Giles's bribe. Didn't he care that Rocky was going up against a guy who looked like a scary creature from a fairytale? "I have money riding on this now."

Was he out of his fucking mind? I appreciated his confidence but, being a gambler myself, I didn't favor Rocky's odds.

Vixen echoed my concerns aloud. "You'll be spending more on a hospital bed when the Rhino's through with him."

Suddenly, a night to unwind had turned into something darker. There was a lot more at stake than dignity or wiping the smirk off of Giles's face. Rocky had to fight to stay alive.

"It's starting," Zander said, sitting up straighter.

A hush fell over the crowd as Rocky entered the ring shirtless. His torso revealed scars I'd never seen before. Unlike West and Zander, who were covered in ink, Rocky's only visible tattoo was the number seven in the center of his chest. He was built like a surfer, tall and toned. Someone like West wouldn't look out of place in the Golden Gloves, but Rocky? The Rhino could snap his spine like a twig.

"I don't know if I can watch," Mieko mumbled, covering her eyes and peeking out through her fingers.

Seeing Rocky stand next to the Rhino was like looking at a bus and a kid's bicycle. Everyone knows it only takes a second for a bike to become mangled under bigger wheels.

"It'll be fine," I reassured her, trying my best to keep my voice steady.

If anything happened to Rocky, Giles would pay. I'd make sure of it. Hadn't the Briarlys learned their lesson after what happened when their henchmen and Razor groupies tried to take us down? How many more men could they afford to lose?

The bell hadn't rung to start the fight, but the Rhino was ready to go. He stomped towards Rocky, each step making the ring vibrate. The blank stare in his eyes would be enough to make anyone run, but Rocky didn't move. His eyes found mine in the crowd, and he grinned. What the fuck was going through his head? I was already planning on avenging his death and the crazy bastard was smiling?

Dinging signaled the start of the fight, and the Rhino lunged. Rocky was quick on his feet. He effortlessly dodged the punch, ducking under the Rhino's muscled bicep. After a few more thwarted attempts, the Rhino was panting and his cheeks were reddening in fury. The Rhino ran at Rocky, who managed to spin out of his reach and trip him over in the process.

"Are you going to fight or dance, Twinkle Toes?" the Rhino grunted as he heaved himself to his feet.

"Catch me, if you can," Rocky replied unflinchingly, which only angered the Rhino more.

Rocky moved in the ring like he was part of a strange ballet. He didn't fight with force but with skill like a trained athlete. The Rhino's aimless slings were no match for Rocky's slick motions. I was impressed. With each of Rocky's misses, the crowd grew restless. The Rhino was a big name and, so far, they were not getting the bloodbath they'd been promised.

Rocky approached us ringside, as the Rhino struggled to get up off his ass for the third time in a row.

"I'm glad you came, C," Rocky said, leaning against the ropes and making me smile. He wasn't even out of breath. Where the fuck had he got his moves and nerves of steel?

Before I had time to respond, the Rhino was up quicker than we'd expected. Rocky's momentary lapse in attention meant he was *just* a second too slow to avoid a right hook delivered to his shoulder.

The audience clapped and cheered. *This* is what they'd paid money for. I expected Rocky's confidence to get knocked by the blow, but he shrugged it off and bounced back on his feet. His level of casual confidence had sent lesser men to the hospital with brain injuries. Did he have a fucking suicide wish? As the Rhino tried to swing again, Rocky tripped him over, and he dropped with a bang.

"Do you think you can concentrate on not getting your ass beat?" I asked as Rocky approached us again.

"Keep your eyes on the fucking game," Vixen shrieked.

The Rhino staggered backward to prepare to make another dive to the delight of hollering fans.

"If I finish him," Rocky said, his soft brown eyes met mine, "I'll do it for you, C."

"Do it," I urged, sensing he was holding back. I wanted to see what he could do and end the fucker. "Give me a fucking show."

"Don't encourage him," Vixen wailed. "He'll be lucky to get out of the ring alive."

Or, maybe I'd given him the best chance he had. I knew he wouldn't want to let me down.

The Rhino charged with a vengeance. Rocky narrowly avoided another punch but got caught by the Rhino's knee cracking into his middle. Rocky fell to the floor, clutching his stomach, and curled into a ball. It must have hurt like a motherfucker.

The Rhino grinned triumphantly, wanting to take advantage of the opportunity. He kicked Rocky in the back, but Rocky didn't move. The Rhino didn't relent. I edged closer in my seat to get a better view.

"Sit back," Zander urged, but I couldn't.

Vomit rose in my throat. I asked him to give me a show, but not like this. *This wasn't supposed to happen.* How could I have thought Rocky could take on someone like the Rhino and get away unscathed?

"Can't we do something?" I asked, wincing as another kick drove into Rocky's side.

"Red knows what he's doing," Zander replied coolly, seemingly unperturbed by his friend getting beaten to death.

From where I was sitting, the only thing it looked like Rocky knew how to do was to take a beating without passing out.

"Be patient," Zander murmured.

The Rhino took a few steps back, gearing up for a body slam. The weight of the beast would turn Rocky into nothing but a bloody pancake. I couldn't let him get crushed by a steamroller and do nothing.

I stood to my feet. "No!"

As the Rhino leaped into the air, Rocky rolled away at the last second. The Rhino slammed into the ground, and Rocky jumped on top of him. How had he sustained such an ass-kicking and recovered so fast? Rocky raised his fist and slammed it into the Rhino's head, causing his nose to explode. Rocky didn't stop, though. He kept going, like a crazed animal, pummeling the Rhino's face until his eyelids fluttered shut.

"We have a winner," the referee called, racing over to check the Rhino's pulse. The audience waited with bated breath, followed by a disappointed sigh at finding out he was still breathing. I didn't care whether the Rhino had a pulse. The only thing that mattered was Rocky being okay.

"Now do you believe me when I said he could handle it?" Zander said smugly.

The crowd cheered and stamped as Rocky punched the air in victory. Vixen and Mieko jumped up and down clapping, but I struggled to join their celebrations. Not after thinking I was about to lose him...

Rocky stepped out of the ring, slightly unsteady on his feet, but I wouldn't let him off so easily. He stretched his arms out, expecting me to walk into them. Instead, I punched him square in the chest. I may not have as much power as the Rhino, but my fist hit an already blossoming bruise.

"Ouch." He rubbed the painful spot. "What did you do that for? I won, didn't I?"

I wanted to scream at him for putting everyone through that. For what could have happened. For what we could have lost. But I didn't say anything. I simply glowered at him and debated whether he could take another punch.

"Were you worried about me, C?" Rocky teased. "I had him all along."

Zander slapped him on the back. "Good job, Red."

"Well done," Mieko stammered, still looking a little queasy despite his victory.

"Congratulations, Red," Giles said, creeping up behind us. Zander grabbed my wrist before I could spin around and twist his tiny balls off like screwcaps. I gritted my teeth, hoping we wouldn't have to suffer through his presence for long. Giles pulled an envelope addressed to Zander out of his pocket and thrust it forward begrudgingly. "Here's an invitation from your father to the Briarly New Year Ball. All of your waifs and strays are welcome."

"How generous," Zander replied coldly, snatching it from him. "We'll see you there."

Giles nodded curtly and turned on his heel. If he didn't have Rocky's loss to gloat over, what was the point in him sticking around?

"We aren't seriously going, are we?" Vixen groaned.

"And miss a chance to find out why my father is summoning us?" Zander furrowed his brow. "This is the first invitation we've had in years. It's no accident."

"I think Zander's right, Vix," I said, already formulating a plan for how I could use the visit to my advantage. If we were going to Briarly Manor, I could slip away to try and find the evidence they were holding over us.

"Why don't we get out of here?" Rocky suggested, draping his sweaty arm around my shoulder and casting a worried glance at the jostling spectators. Fights were breaking out, and it'd only be a matter of time before we got caught up in the brawl. "It can get ugly fast."

"Fine," I agreed, shrugging him off, "but if you touch me again before you shower, I'll give you a black eye."

"But I thought you were my cheerleader, C?"

I narrowed my eyes. "I wouldn't be seen dead waving pompoms."

He smirked. "You'd look pretty cute in a cheerleader outfit, though…"

"Gross. Can you keep your dick in your pants until we leave?" Vixen interrupted, shutting Rocky down. "Let's get the hell outta here before I heave."

We shoved our way through the crowds and into the parking lot, where a driver was waiting.

"I know a place we can go for drinks," Zander said, getting into the limo. "We have a win to celebrate."

"Count us in," Vixen said, clambering after him with Mieko.

I held back. Mixing alcohol with the lingering adrenaline in my system would only lead to more trouble we didn't need.

"Why don't you drive me back, C?" Rocky asked, sensing my reluctance. "I can't leave my car here overnight."

It was a bad neighborhood, and the only reason his car hadn't been stolen yet was because people knew the Sevens were nearby. If we abandoned it until morning, it'd be free fucking game.

"Fine, but only because it'll annoy West," I said. West hadn't let me behind the wheel of any of the Seven cars since we'd burned one of his babies. How was it fair that a small incident got me blacklisted from the entire garage? "But I'm not your fucking chauffeur, okay?"

"We'll see you back at Lapland then," Vixen called through the lowered window, then winked. "Don't wait up."

The three of them sped away into the night as Rocky threw me the keys to his red shiny beauty. "You think you can handle my Mercedes?"

"Hell yeah," I said, or at least I thought so...

———

"I can see why West doesn't let you drive anymore," Rocky said as I narrowly avoided taking out the wing mirror of a parked car. It's not my fault it's a narrow street, and I was sat next to an asshole who'd just evaded death.

"It beats letting someone behind the wheel with a concussion," I pointed out, slamming my foot on the gas to make us jolt forward.

He flinched. "You're still mad about it, huh?"

"Where did you learn to fight?"

"They didn't print all the reasons why Redlake got shut down in the papers," Rocky said, keeping his eyes fixed on the road ahead. "I may not have got any qualifications when I was there, but I got a different type of schooling. The safety of inmates wasn't exactly high on the list of their priorities. They were more interested in cashing in on boxing."

"They made you fight?"

"Trust me, being a fighter made you one of the lucky ones," Rocky said. "Winning gave you privileges. I was coached by one of the best."

"Those fuckers got someone to coach you?"

"Hell no!" Rocky laughed bitterly. "They'd rather we were untrained. It was more fun for them to bet on which of us would die, but I made a friend in Redlake. Do you remember reading about Oliver Filey?"

The name sounded familiar, then it came flooding back. Oliver's face had appeared in the news. He was a promising boxing star who was killed in his cell by other inmates. They blamed it on gang violence and no one questioned it. His death acted as the catalyst for the riots which broke out and eventually led to Redlake being shut down for good. It wasn't until it closed that stories of abuse circulated and the state paid to silence survivors.

"You knew him well?" I asked gently.

We pulled into the Seven garage down the road from the club, but neither of us made any effort to move as I turned off the engine.

"Ollie was my bunkmate," Rocky said, his voice thick with emotion. "What those reporters said about his death was all bullshit. He died in the warden's fucked up games. No one in there was stupid enough to jump Filey. Hell, he was one of the good guys."

"I'm sorry about what happened to your friend," I said, reaching out to take his hand, "and I'm sorry about what happened to you there."

"I don't like talking about it." Rocky took a deep breath to regain his composure as he blinked angry tears away. "It brings it all back, y'know?"

I got that. When Hiram kidnapped me, I'd spent my first weeks in Blackthorne Towers locked in a dungeon cell without natural light. Therapists talked about how looking back at your past helps you to move forward, but I've never found solace in revisiting the dark times. Why would I ever want to relive my personal hell?

"You don't have to talk about it," I said. "All that matters is you got out."

"At least I got something good out of my time there," he said wryly. "I know how to fight now."

"You scared me tonight," I admitted. Seeing him helpless at the Rhino's mercy was terrifying and left me wondering whether he'd ever get up again.

Rocky nudged me in the ribs playfully. His cheeky grin reminded me of the playful side he used to have but didn't come out as often anymore. "Maybe you won't underestimate me next time?"

"You can't blame me," I said scornfully. "The last time you got in a fight, I had to step in and kill five guys to save your sorry ass."

"You'll never let me live it down, will you? I got ambushed in the dark." His defense argument fell on deaf ears. "You're not the only one who can fight their own battles. Remember, you don't have to fight everything on your own. I said, I'd be here for you, and I meant it."

"Even if it means going against orders?" I whispered. If Zander ever found out about this conversation, we'd both have to face the consequences.

"I'm listening…"

"What if I wanted to get the photographs back from the Briarlys at the ball?" I asked. "Would you help me?"

This was a test of Rocky's loyalty — not to the Sevens, but to me. Actions spoke louder than words, and I was giving him a chance to prove he meant what he'd promised. I didn't know what our plan was going to be, or what our actions could set in motion, but it would be dangerous. If we got it wrong, we'd be putting the Sevens at stake.

His face set in serious determination as he answered with zero hesitation, "For you, I'd do anything."

"How do I know I can trust you?" I asked, studying his face for any sign that he was lying.

"Let me prove it," he said, keeping his eyes locked on mine.

"Okay." I nodded. A look of agreement passed between us. "I'll let you try."

It transported me back to a simpler time, when it was the two of us against the world. We may be part of the Sevens now, but we were also C and Rocky. Once upon a time, we'd been the only person the other could depend upon. The only constant in our fucked up world.

I may be a fool for trusting him, but he knew how it felt to be powerless. I refused to leave our destiny in the hands of Port Valentine's rich overlords. Zander and West grew up with connections. They focused on what was good for the gang, but neither had to claw their way up the ranks from nothing. Rocky had to earn his position. He knew it was important to take matters into his own hands. When he hadn't, he lost me.

"I won't let you down again, C," he said.

His burning stare and set jaw told me he was telling the truth. I believed him. Suddenly, I realized how close we were... and how he was a half-naked, sweaty, delicious mess. Letting Rocky into my life and heart again was a risk. One I didn't know whether I could come back from for a second time but after tonight? I couldn't fight it any longer.

Rocky opened his mouth to speak again but, before he could, I leaned in to crush my lips against his own.

His hands immediately cradled my face like he held the entire world in his palms. Sure, we'd kissed before... but never like this. When his lips explored mine, he cracked open a small part of me I thought I'd never get back.

He pulled away breathlessly. "I need to shower, or you'll give me a black eye. Remember?"

"I like you like this," I murmured as my eyes trailed down to see the outline of his hard cock through his silky red shorts.

"I don't think you understood me, C," he said. His fingers slid over my thigh, feeling the raised skin of my scar underneath my dagger tattoo. He continued upwards, dipping into my soft inner thigh and stroking my delicate skin. "It was an invitation. West is working all night, and the others won't be back for a few hours..."

My heart hammered. Who could refuse an offer like that? Plus, I wouldn't want to see West's face if he found cum stains on the car seats.

We only made it out of the garage when Rocky pushed me against the brick wall outside. His hand ran through my hair then grabbed it in a hold, pulling my face towards him and coaxing my mouth open with his tongue. Neither of us cared about someone walking past to find West's fiancée kissing the hell outta his friend. We were like horny teenagers again, not able to get enough of each other, and stopping was out of the question.

"If we don't go inside, I'm gonna have to fuck you out here," he murmured.

I caught his lip between my teeth, making him groan, then pulled away.

"It'd be just like our first time," I said breathlessly, tracing my fingers down over his chest and stroking his Seven tattoo. I'd lost my virginity to Rocky on the roof of an abandoned warehouse. It'd been the only place we could go to have privacy.

The sounds of footsteps and giggling growing louder made him grab my hand.

"Come on," he urged, tugging me down the alley towards Lapland's side entrance and into the empty kitchen.

As soon as the door closed behind us, Rocky's mouth was on mine again with a desperate eagerness. He cupped my ass, guiding my hips towards him until we were pressed together. I didn't stop for air. I kissed him back with ferocity and enjoyed the salty taste of his skin.

"Fuck, C," he moaned as I trailed my fingers gently over his back. His muscles were pronounced and defined, but they'd be sore after taking a beating. "I want you so bad."

I squealed as I caught a glass with my elbow and sent it smashing to the floor. Way to ruin the fucking moment...

"You've left me with no choice," Rocky growled. In a slick motion, he threw me over his shoulder.

"You're hurt," I objected as he threw open the door to the club. "Come on, Rocky. What if people see?"

He grinned, already two steps ahead. "I'll say you twisted your ankle in those ridiculous heels."

As Rocky carried me across the dance floor, I caught sight of West behind the bar. His eyes met mine with burning fury, then he turned away to serve a customer. Was he going to be okay with this? The Hulk was green with fucking jealousy.

"You can put me down now," I insisted as we reached the staircase to the penthouse.

"No way," Rocky said, continuing onwards to his room. "I'm a gentleman."

He took me into his room, which boasted a massive sound system and TV. The lingering smell of weed hung in the air, but not in an unpleasant way. He placed me down gently on his bed.

"So, this is your room..." I said, looking around.

My burning passion had been replaced by something else. Nerves. It took me back to the last time I'd been intimate with Rocky. I was sixteen and had no idea what I was doing.

He sat down by my side, taking my hand in his. "If we're going too fast for you, we can slow things down?"

"No," I said quickly, then tried to play it cool. "I mean, no..."

"It's just me, C," he said, softly stroking my cheek. "Can I kiss you?"

I nodded. Rocky leaned forward, allowing his soft lips to graze mine, and pulled me close. I clung to him, remembering my fear of thinking he was about to die. I parted my lips to greet his tongue. The years that had passed without each other melted away as I climbed onto his lap, craving closeness. He was smeared in blood and sweat, but none of it mattered. This was our reality. Relationships weren't neat and simple; they were raw and imperfect. They challenged and pushed us until we broke, then had the power to fix us again.

Rocky's fingers found the zip at the back of my dress and undid it slowly, running his hand over my back as the fabric came undone. I took a deep breath and pulled my dress over my head, leaving myself vulnerable and open.

"You're so fucking beautiful," he murmured, his voice low and husky with desire. His finger slipped under my bra strap to stroke my shoulder, then I pushed him backward.

I liked the feeling of his body being trapped between my thighs. When we were younger, I let Rocky take the lead, but I wanted to feel in control this time around. His body felt familiar but new, like the same landscape but in a different season. There was so much we had to learn about each other and he stretched beneath me like a new territory to explore. I took the time to run my fingers over the scars covering his chest and arms like a roadmap.

I slipped my hand down further, stroking his hard cock over his shorts. Instead of being even, it felt...

"You're pierced?" I gulped as I slid over the smooth metal balls adorning his shaft.

"Do you wanna see?" he asked.

I nodded and shuffled to allow him to slip his cock out of his shorts. A six-rung Jacob's ladder glittered against his thick brown cock. The two balls nearest his head were bigger than the others, presumably to maximize pleasure and sensation. The ladder ran up to an impressive silver ring at the top of his shaft.

Shit, would *fucking* it hurt? Or worse, get hooked inside and rip me apart? Everyone has read horror stories online about something like that happening after not being able to sleep and falling into an internet black hole. I stripped for strangers on a pole and didn't get nervous, but this was different.

"Don't worry," Rocky said in a soothing voice. "I'll be gentle."

While his cock looked like something from a futuristic movie that would set off metal detectors in an airport, it was fucking *hot*.

"You're forgetting I'm in control here," I said.

Before we did anything else, I needed a closer inspection of robocock. I slid down his body, admiring the tense muscles hiding underneath his hazel skin. He moaned as I traced the tip of my tongue along his V-lines, salty with a hint of iron. He kept his hair trim and short, and it tickled my face as I moved down to face his reverse Prince Albert. Who knew royalty would be so pleased to see me?

I locked my fingers around his base, having to use two hands, and licked up his silky shaft, feeling the cool raised metal against the flat of my tongue. His cock twitched underneath me, craving more. I paused at his swollen head, gently playing with the ring and flicking it back and forth with the tip of my tongue.

"Candy, you feel so fucking good," he moaned as I bent forward to seal my mouth around his dick. I took his cock deeper, enjoying the feel of his piercings and imagining how they'd feel inside me. They'd bring a whole host of new sensations.

Giving head wasn't something I thought I'd enjoy doing, with the memories I had of tearing cocks off whenever one stared me in the face. But I loved giving him pleasure and feeling his body writhe underneath me. He grabbed a fistful of my hair as I sucked on him gently, pushing him to the back of my throat until he was panting. His thighs tightened as his balls clenched, but I wasn't giving him a release... not yet. I paused, then slowly withdrew my mouth with a pop and slid my tongue over his tip to lick a drop of his pre-cum.

"I want to taste you," he demanded, pulling me up and into a kiss. At the same time, he expertly unhooked my bra and threw it to the side. His hands found my nipples and gently squeezed them between his thumb and forefinger, sending tingles shooting down my body.

I pulled away, propping myself up on my elbows. The last time he saw me naked, I'd been an A-cup. "You don't think they're too... big?"

"I think you're perfect. All of you. You were then, and you are now," he said in a gravelly voice. "Now, are you going to keep torturing me, or are you going to sit on my face and let me worship you like the fucking queen you are?"

I'd never been interested in becoming a monarch before, but damn. Now, I could see why having a throne would have some perks.

I slipped off my panties, and his eyes trailed down to my wet slit, groaning appreciatively. Any self-consciousness or hesitation I had evaporated as a primal groan erupted from the back of his throat. "You're driving me fucking crazy, C."

I used the headboard to balance my weight, as his palms grabbed my ass to lower my pussy onto his face. His soft stubble gently tickled my thighs, and his tongue slipped in between my lips to taste my wetness. He moaned, sending vibrations up my legs, and devoured me like I was the first meal he'd eaten in weeks. He licked upwards and I tipped my hips, allowing his tongue to probe my clit and making me gasp. It's a good thing the music was loud downstairs…

Rocky's hand snaked up to my breasts to tease my nipples as his wet tongue rediscovered my entrance. It darted in and out of me in hot hard strokes. My thighs clenched around his head. He looked right at home there, like he could lick me all night long.

"Fuck," I moaned, closing my eyes and rocking my hips to allow the flat of his tongue to knead my clit. Warm arousal dripped out of me, coating his face as he hungrily lapped it up.

My heart rate quickened as he drew me closer to climax. But I wanted more... I wanted to feel his pierced cock tease me and tip me over the edge of no return. Taking his Robocock was not something I would shy away from.

"Hey," Rocky objected in a growl as I rose to my knees to get my pussy out of his grasp. "I wasn't finished."

"Neither was I," I said, meeting his gaze and sliding down his body.

"I want to make sure I don't hurt you," he said, reaching over to grab a bottle of lube from his bedside table. He smeared his cock until it was glistening like a freshly polished statue.

I rolled my eyes. "As if I'm not wet enough..."

"Are you sure you—"

His sentence turned into a moan as I slid my wet heat over his dick. I lowered myself onto him gently. I expected his piercings to feel like being impaled on a bumpy tree stump, instead, it was smoother than I expected. The nubs provided extra sensation, like a ribbed dildo, but nothing I couldn't handle. If anything, it turned me on more.

I sunk my pussy down, taking him as deep as he could go, then rolled my hips. The angle and how we fit together meant one of the metal balls rubbed against my G-Spot, bringing me closer to release. Meanwhile, Rocky's thumb found my clit as we locked eyes. Neither of us looked away. His pupils seared into my soul, and everything else around us fell away. I wasn't the virgin he'd fucked all those years ago. Our bodies had changed, *we* had changed, but it still felt just as good to be together again.

Intense pleasure built from the tip of my toes to my flushing cheeks, causing my whole body to tense like we'd reached the peak point of a roller-coaster and were about to plummet fifty feet below.

"You feel so fucking good," Rocky groaned.

I cried out as my pussy clamped down on his dick like it never wanted to let go. An orgasm shook through me and drowned him in a gush of wetness. Rocky didn't stop though, his fingers continued to work their magic until a second ripple descended over the first, like waves crashing over the beach. I collapsed onto him, breathless, as his hands held me in place and fucked me from beneath, grinding into me.

"Fuck, C," he gasped as his hips bucked into me for a final time and came hard. I rolled off him, trembling and panting, completely incapable of moving.

"I never thought I'd get to do that again," Rocky murmured, propping his head on his elbow and tucking a rogue hair behind my ear while looking down at me.

"No one is more surprised than me," I breathed.

"Are you glad you didn't kill me now?"

I laughed. "I guess not killing you has had its upsides…"

"I've missed you so damn much," he said. "And we will get the evidence back from the Briarlys whatever it takes."

"Shh." I pressed a finger to his lips to silence him. "Not here."

"If you want to shut me up, there are other ways to do it," he said with a wink.

I'd never had a proper home before, but being in Rocky's arms felt like I was returning to a place where I'd always felt safe. The problem was, I couldn't decide whether the feeling of comfort trumped my deep-rooted fear of worrying it would be snatched away…

CHAPTER
Sixteen

The day of the Briarly New Year Ball had finally arrived. Rocky and I had stolen a few conversations on the roof about our plan, but it'd been hard to find time when we had to focus on running the club, a poker game, and him dealing with a moldy plant outbreak. We would have to wing it.

Thankfully, Rocky knew his way around Briarly Manor and had a few ideas about where Bryce may be keeping evidence of my involvement in Giovanni Romano's death hidden. It would be his job to find it while I created a diversion. All we had to do was get through the dinner first. It couldn't be too difficult, right?

"You've been quiet today." Vixen poked her head into my bedroom as I finished getting ready. "Everything okay, or do I need to be worried about finding body parts under your bed?"

"PMS," I lied, to avoid answering any more questions. "Mood swings."

She snorted. "I don't think you can blame those on PMS."

I shot her an 'I'm not in the mood to be fucked with' look. "Do you want something, or are you just being a pain in my ass?"

"I wanted your opinion." She stepped inside and did a twirl. It was a black-tie occasion, but Vixen was wearing jeans so ripped they showed more skin than denim and a leather crop top. "What do you think?"

"Bryce will love it," I said, rolling my eyes sarcastically and adding, "like a severe case of genital warts."

"Perfect." She smiled in satisfaction and made herself comfortable on my bed. "Did you know this is the first time they've invited me? Bryce puts on his bullshit ball every fucking year. Maybe he's going senile in his old age..."

Somehow, I doubted it. Bryce would have a motivation for wanting all of us there. Whatever it was, it better not interfere with Rocky and I's plans. Finding the photographs of me in the Romano mansion was our number one priority.

"What's his deal with you, anyway?" I asked. Bryce hated Zander, but still acknowledged his existence. Hell, he even pretended to be pleasant to West. Vixen was his flesh and blood, but he treated her like a deadly contagious disease. "Did you burn down his summer house as a kid or something?"

"If only." She scoffed, her eyes blazing. Whatever grudge Bryce held against her ran deep, and the feeling was mutual. "Although, I'd happily strike a match under the manor and watch it burn if Zander would let me."

"The car's waiting," Rocky called through to us from the corridor. "Zander and West are meeting us there."

Vixen pulled a hip flask out of her back pocket and drained it. "It's motherfucking showtime."

After spending the night with Rocky, I hadn't seen a lot of Zander or West. They'd both gone to Hammerville three days ago to sort out a crisis at Seven Sins. Even though we'd all come to an arrangement, the three of them reuniting made my palms sweat — especially after seeing West's reaction to Rocky carrying me through the club when we returned from the Golden Gloves. Sharing didn't come naturally to him.

"Rocky, can you help me reach something?" I called, pretending to be helpless, then turned to Vixen. "We'll see you outside."

"Suit yourself," she said, swaying slightly as she swaggered out. Keeping a drunk Vixen under control at the manor would be like trying to pin a firework to the ground and telling it not to explode in your face.

"How can I be of assistance?" Rocky asked, in an awful attempt at a British accent, and made a goofy bow. He wore a black tux and had even fastened his top buttons. Fitting in would be important if he didn't want to draw any extra attention to himself when sneaking around the manor.

I pointed at the patent red leather clutch on the top shelf and asked loudly, "Can you get it down for me?"

The bag would go perfectly with my black satin dress, which made me feel like a million dollars. It had thin spaghetti straps and a cowl neck which showed off the pendant necklace Zander gave me for Christmas, which I hadn't taken off since.

Rocky retrieved my purse with ease, then grinned mischievously as he blatantly checked me out. "Is this just an excuse to get me alone? We can be late to the party, if you want..."

"You wish," I said as my cheeks heated under his scrutiny. *Don't get distracted, Candy.* I waited until I heard the penthouse door click behind Vixen, then lowered my voice. "Are you ready?"

His teasing demeanor vanished. He knew instantly what I meant and nodded. "We're getting the fucking evidence."

If our plan didn't go smoothly, monitoring Vixen wouldn't be the only mess we had to control...

———

Despite Rocky's attempt to wrestle bottles of champagne from Vixen in the limo, she was wasted by the time we reached Briarly Manor.

"Should we send her back with the car?" Rocky asked. "Zander is going to flip..."

"I can hear you," Vixen replied indignantly. "I'll be fine."

"It's your funeral," I muttered as the limo came to a stop by West and Zander, who were awaiting our arrival.

They both looked ridiculously handsome in their black pressed suits. I couldn't help feeling a smug swell of pride at knowing those men were all fucking *mine.*

The manor itself was as imposing as I remembered. If Vixen ever lit the place up, the whole skyline would be ablaze for miles. I'd enjoy watching it burn to the ground almost as much as seeing the Briarly empire turn to ash.

West opened the limo door and extended his hand for me to take. His fingers eclipsing mine sent a sizzling spark of desire racing through me. Goddamn you, body. I needed to concentrate on my real reason for being here, not my vagina's uncontrollable urge to pounce on the Seven men.

"You look... incredible," West admired. His Adam's apple bobbed as his gaze lingered on the slice of skin peeking through my dress. My gown was floor-length but had a slit down the right side, opening the fabric to expose my upper thigh with every step.

"Thanks," I said, smiling coyly. "You don't look too bad yourself."

"What are you wearing?" Zander hissed at Vixen, who practically fell out of the limo after me and Rocky. He turned to Rocky in accusation. "Why did you let her come like this?"

"I'm not a fucking child, Zander," she said, getting up in his face. "Last time I checked, we live in a free fucking country."

Zander beckoned over a server standing nearby, who carried a tray of champagne flutes. "She drinks water all evening. Nothing else."

"Killjoy." Vixen pouted and slung her arm around the server's shoulder. He looked like he wanted to run or cry... or both. She squeezed the poor guy's cheek between her fingers. "You'll give me a drink, won't you? Don't listen to nasty Zander."

"She drinks water," Zander spat through gritted teeth. "Or, you'll have me to deal with."

"Shall we go in?" I asked West, nudging my head in the opposite direction and leading him away. I wasn't going to be Vixen's babysitter. She was Zander's problem. "How was the Seven Sins?"

"As expected," he replied, staying as tight-lipped as ever. Even if he wanted to talk, he'd give no details now. "Are you ready to mix with Bryce's nearest and dearest?"

"You mean the lowest of the low," I corrected in hushed tones as we mounted the sweeping steps to the manor.

"What does that make us?" West asked.

"The bottom of the fucking barrel."

West chuckled. I lost my footing and almost stumbled, but his strong arms were there to steady me. I'd need him to lean on if I didn't want to break my ankles.

"Don't worry," he said. Seven-inch heels were ridiculous, even for me, but they looked gorgeous. They were red and shiny, with a golden snake wrapped around the pointed heel. "I'll catch you if you fall."

"You better," I said, then added under my breath, "because I'm sure the hyenas will be ready to close in and destroy my carcass."

As soon as we strolled into the grand foyer, Bryce hurried over to greet us with a fake ass smile. He had fewer wrinkles than the last time I'd seen him, so he must have invested in Botox or a face-lift for the occasion. New year, new him.

"I see you all made it," Bryce commented as his eyes rested disapprovingly on Vixen's brawling figure in the distance. "And you've all dressed for the occasion."

"Your messenger didn't mention a dress code," I said defensively, noticing Giles standing a few feet away and smirking out of the corner of my eye.

"No matter," Bryce said, waving his hand dismissively, and greeting me with a kiss on both cheeks. His attitude would only antagonize Vixen more. She needed to sober up before facing him, otherwise she could get us all kicked out. "How are your wedding plans coming along?"

"We're in no rush," West replied gruffly.

"Pity," Bryce said with a dramatic sigh. "One never knows what is around the corner."

I bit my tongue to stop myself from adding how it was hard to plan for a day when he and Giles kept trying to get a Seven killed every few months. If

Zander's father had his way, there would be no wedding or guests left alive to attend.

"Great things take time to plan," Zander said, appearing out of nowhere. "You taught me that, father."

Bryce's eyes were cold as he regarded his son with indifference.

"What a shame none of the valuable lessons stuck," Bryce replied dryly as Giles strode over to join us. He wore a ridiculous pale blue suit and a pink shirt, which made him look like a candy wrapper. "Giles has always been a better learner."

Giles puffed out his chest like a peacock at the compliment. Bryce may have the business acumen and ruthlessness to have built an empire, but it wouldn't last if he trusted a moron to stand at the helm when he was gone. Bryce should know better.

"I'm going to take our newest Seven member on a tour of the manor," Zander said. "She didn't get a look at the family art collection on her last visit — did you, Candy?"

"Sadly not," I said quickly, masking my surprise and going along with Zander's suggestion. Who knows what he had up his sleeve? "It was *such* a disappointment."

Bryce eyed me suspiciously. "I didn't realize you were a fan of art?"

"Oh, very much," I gushed. Well, if you counted graffiti and tattoos. "Zander has been telling me about the pieces you have here."

"We have quite a collection," Bryce said proudly, not missing an opportunity to inflate his ego. "They have been passed down through the generations. Some from the town's original founder, can you believe?"

I'd never understand why people paid immense sums of money for crusty old relics that didn't even look great. Bryce lapped up the prestige that came from owning such a collection. He wanted what others couldn't have.

"I'll show you now," Zander insisted, taking my arm.

"I can't wait to see." I feigned a smile, then made a show of kissing West on the cheek and whispered, "Look after Vixen, okay?"

With Zander throwing in a curveball tour, someone had to take care of her to free up Rocky's time. How could he search for evidence when he was busy trying to stop Vixen from turning an expensive vase into a hat?

West glowered, unimpressed by his new responsibility. "I'll try."

Eyes followed us as Zander and I ascended the staircase. Whatever Zander wanted to show me must be important. Otherwise, he wouldn't leave the others unattended with Bryce, Giles, and a circle of their closest friends.

The Briarly family had resided in the manor for decades, but it didn't seem like a home anyone lived in. Everything was staged from the obscure marble statues to the furniture positioned with an interior designer's eye. The manor was nothing more than a mausoleum to the Briarly wealth.

"Are you going to tell me what the deal is?" I asked as Zander escorted me down a winding corridor.

"Maybe I wanted to get you alone?" he said in a husky tone.

"Puh-lease." I scoffed. His sexy voice wouldn't work on me. "I know you, Zander. You always have a reason for everything you do."

"Perhaps I wanted to show you the place where I was brought up?" he suggested. I wasn't buying it. Since when was he the sentimental type? He took us through large wooden double doors into a square room that resembled a museum exhibit. Canvases hung on the walls showing sullen faces from times gone by. "This is the Briarly family personal collection. The rest are downstairs in the library."

"Don't you feel you're being watched in here?" I asked. My heels hitting the floor left an eery echo as I examined the art. "There are so many eyes everywhere..."

"On the contrary, it's one of the few places I don't feel like my father is standing over my shoulder," Zander said, looking around at the paintings of his ancestors. Many of them had the same piercing gray stare. "When I was a kid, I used to make up stories about them. About how they would be better than the father I knew."

Zander talking about his past was a big fucking deal. I didn't want to push him too hard as soon as he'd started to open up, but I wanted to be someone who he could confide in. I wanted to get to know the *real* Zander.

"What do you know about them?" I questioned, seeing his brow furrow, deep in thought. "Were they better than Bryce?"

"Fuck no." Zander shook his head, his lips pressed into a thin line. "The Briarly family has always been the same, but I didn't know that then."

I came to a painting of a young boy who must have been around three or four. He looked like a cherub with his blonde, perfect ringlets and rosy cheeks, but the serious expression on his face made me uneasy. Behind him, two figures rested a hand ominously on each of his shoulders.

I pointed at the youngster. "Is that you?"

"Yes," Zander said, tucking his hands in his pockets and coming over to join me.

I recognized Bryce from the painting. He looked younger, similar to how Zander looked now, but with a sharper nose and more menacing stare. The face of the woman on Zander's other side was painted over. My heart sank at the blur of colors obscuring where she used to be like someone had reached into the image and blended the oils together. A few strokes of a brush had erased her from the painting, but it couldn't erase her from existence.

"What happened to your mom?" I whispered, fearing I already knew the answer, but unsure whether Zander would be willing to tell me more.

"My father doesn't want to be reminded of the woman who wronged him," Zander said, running his fingers over the ruined image. He swallowed hard as if he was fighting inner demons. "She's dead, not that I have any proof. They never found her body. My father knows how to make people disappear."

"Zander... I'm... I'm so sorry," I said, placing my hand gently on his arm. Sorry didn't seem enough, but it's all I had. We stood in silence, lost in our minds. I'd never known who my parents were after being dumped on the doorstep of Evergreen as a baby. I used to think it was a curse, but after meeting the Briarly family, it made me realize that it may have been a blessing. "What was she like?"

"She was kind," Zander said, donning a rare smile. "She taught me to cook and filled this place with laughter. She was beautiful, too. You've seen her, remember? The painting you tracked down at the junkyard that we put for auction was the last trace of her after he erased her from existence. He destroyed everything else after she disappeared."

I exhaled slowly, looking at the painting of a younger Zander and thinking about how he didn't know then what his life would grow to become.

"How did you find out about the painting?" I asked.

"My mom had a lover," Zander explained matter-of-factly. "I didn't blame her. My father was a violent man and was never around, so she fell in love with someone else. He was an artist. I have no proof, but I believe my father killed them both when he found out about their affair. When I was older and conducted my own investigations, I found out they had declared his death a suicide. But my father didn't know my mother's lover had kept some of his earlier art in a storage facility. It took me months, but I tracked down his old paintings."

Suicide my ass. Bryce got to him. If he killed his wife, then he would want to destroy everything and anyone associated with her.

"How old were you when she... disappeared?"

"Fifteen," he said, averting his eyes from the painting. I could see behind his neutral expression to the hurt he was holding onto inside. A pain you pushed to the back of your consciousness because it was too hard to process. "When I was away at school, she used to call me every week. The calls suddenly stopped. I'd hoped she'd come to her senses and left him, but I knew something bad happened when I came back home for the summer. She was gone, and so was everything she'd ever touched. I knew then... what he'd done."

Getting kidnapped by Hiram as a teenager showed me the darkest side of human nature, but how would it have felt to have been shown that by your own father? How did a teenager ever come to terms with the fact their dad had killed their mom? I can't even imagine how someone, especially at a young age, could deal with that...

"He's a monster," I spat as my shoulders trembled with anger. "How can you even stand to be here? In this house? In this town? Knowing what he's done."

"He's still my father," Zander said bitterly, his eyes darkened, "and, as long as I play along, he won't break our deal."

I gasped in shock. "Your deal?"

What deal could they have possibly made to stop Zander from cutting his father's throat? He loved his mom. What was more important than giving her the vengeance she deserved?

"Do you want to know why he hates Vixen so much?" Zander paced back and forth. He was speaking words, but only for my benefit, as he allowed his mind to stray to a dark place. "Why he can't stand for her to be around? He couldn't erase her from existence. He would have if I hadn't found out about his plans."

"I'm not sure I'm following," I said, frowning. "What does this have to do with your mom?"

"Keep up, Candy," Zander snapped in annoyance. Under normal circumstances, I'd have retaliated with a snarky response, but I knew his anger wasn't directed at me. Reliving a horrific event brought raw emotions to the surface. "An affair wasn't all my mother was hiding. When my father found out she had birthed a child with another man and kept it hidden from him for years, how do you think he took the news? He didn't want his reputation being muddied by a bastard child."

"Vixen's your half-sister?" My jaw dropped as realization set in, then my heart twisted with dread. "What deal did you make?"

"He allowed Vixen to live in exchange for my silence on her birth and signing over my inheritance and any stake I had in the Briarly empire," Zander said, turning away so I couldn't see his face. "He didn't think I'd take the deal, but he was wrong."

I'd always assumed Zander had been another spoiled rich boy growing up, but I was wrong. So fucking wrong. Zander's revelations fueled my hatred for Bryce even more. He'd been willing to kill an innocent child because he didn't want her tainting the Briarly fucking bloodline.

"To explain why a teenager fell under my care, we decided it was easier to say she was my cousin," Zander went on. "When I first tracked down Vixen, she was already in juvie. It turned out she'd known about me all her life. My mom used to see her when she could, but not enough, and her dad struggled to make ends meet with his art. She had to fend for herself, whilst

I was away at school and on holidays to fucking ski resorts. She had nothing, and I had everything."

Zander's shoulders slumped as soon as he'd finished talking as if retelling the story had drained all of his energy.

I didn't know a lot about Zander and Vixen's mom, but I knew what kind of man Bryce was. She must have been incredibly brave to conceal a pregnancy and hide a child without him finding out for so many years. When he killed her, had Bryce even considered how it would leave two children without a mother? Worse, he'd left Zander to pick up the broken pieces.

"You can't blame yourself," I said, reaching out to take Zander's hand to bring him some kind of comfort. I wasn't good at this kinda thing. I'd rather run from emotions than face them, but I wanted to be there for him. I needed to be. Zander's eyes met mine, and my gaze softened as I saw the guilt written all over his face. I could understand now why he was so protective of Vixen and how he seemed older than his years. "There's nothing you could have done for her. You were only a kid."

Zander shrugged and dropped my hand like youth was no excuse.

"Why did you come back to Port Valentine?" I asked gently. "Why not stay in Hammerville after you started over? You and West had Seven Sins. You could have stayed there."

"I'm here because I want to make my father pay for what he did." Zander's voice was as hard and cutting as a razor's edge. His words were a fucking promise, and he'd do anything to make Bryce suffer. "I had a hundred dollars when my father cut me off, but I still have my name. I may not have an inheritance, but being a Briarly still means something here. I play along with his games knowing, one day, he'll slip up. And, when he does, I'll be there. Ready to take him down."

Zander took the phrase 'keep your friends close, but your enemies closer' to the next level. I don't know how he could breathe the same air as Bryce without wanting to rip his heart out. Zander was playing the long game, which explained his obsessive control freak tendencies. It was easier to take down an institution when you were on the inside. When he made his move, I'd fucking be there alongside the rest of the Sevens. We'd do whatever it took for him and Vixen to get justice for their mom, and all the other lives Bryce had mercilessly ruined over the years.

"I'll help you," I said fiercely, realizing I would do whatever it takes for him and the other Sevens. They were all I had, and I'd protect them with my fucking life.

"I know you will, little one," Zander said with affection, tucking a stray hair behind my ear. "You're already helping more than you know."

"Why didn't you tell me all this sooner?" I probed. "Why now?"

"I needed to be sure you were one of us," he replied. Like me, Zander didn't trust easily. Him sharing his past showed I'd finally earned his confidence. He was breaking down his barriers and letting me get to know the real him. "Now, I know you are. You were made to be a Seven, little one."

"I'm all fucking in," I confirmed, flashing him my number seven tattoo and reminding him of the lifelong commitment I'd made to them.

"There's something else I need from you too," Zander said, closing the gap between us to ensnare me in his delicious scent. Fresh citrus bergamot with musky undertones brought back memories of him pressed against me. "I need you to give me your word you won't speak about this to anyone outside of the Sevens. Not ever."

My body tingled with the anticipation I get before a kill, but I reluctantly suppressed my urge to serve Bryce's head on a silver platter. If Zander and Vixen could restrain themselves, then I could too. I made a zipping motion with my hands. "My lips are sealed."

Zander ran a finger over my lips, leaving a blazing hot trail behind. His eyes looked at me like he wanted to draw me into his darkness, consume me and never let me go. His gaze flickered to my mouth like he was contemplating what he was going to do next, then dropped his hand abruptly, like I'd scorched him.

"There's something else I want to show you," Zander said, turning on his heel.

I had to race to keep up with him. His head swiveled around as he scanned the area for any sign of movement. Why did I get the sense we were doing something wrong? During my time with Hiram, I developed a knack for remembering building floor plans. As we pressed into the depths of the manor, its layout was becoming clearer in my mind. Who knows? Maybe it'd come in handy...

"This used to be my room." Zander paused outside a door. I thought we'd go inside, but he continued on. "I only stayed here in the summer when my father couldn't enroll me on an overseas summer program. Austria, England, Germany, France... I traveled all over."

After what I'd learned about his childhood, spending vacations in Europe would beat staying at home with his father.

"Come through," Zander said, hurrying forward and looking over his shoulder before opening a door that led into a room lined with books. It was too small to be a library but too big for an office, and there was no desk. "In here."

I looked around as he closed the door behind us. "What is this place?"

Zander grabbed my arms, pushing me backwards and pinning them to my sides against the door, meaning no one else could walk in. He showered gentle kisses up my neck until he reached my ear, then whispered, "I want you to listen very carefully. To the left of this room is a door which is always locked. It's an old servants' entrance. It leads downstairs into their old quarters and onto the manor grounds."

"Why are you—"

Zander cut my question off with a kiss. He took my breath away as his lips pressed against mine, consuming me in a frenzied heat like he wanted to seal away secrets in our embrace. Secrets that I didn't understand.

"No more questions," he murmured, catching my lip in his teeth and nipping it gently. "Just remember what I've told you, okay? You never know when you might need it."

I nodded breathlessly, unsure what relevance this had to anything, but unable to shake the feeling that what he'd told me was important. If his kiss hadn't rendered me incapable of any logical thought, I'd have pressed him more.

"We need to get back to the others," he said, straightening his tie, and looked down at my necklace with a smile. "It suits you."

I stroked the pendant, warm against my skin, and cleared my throat. "I keep my word."

"I know you do." He held out his arm for me to take. "That's only one reason why we're lucky to call you our girl."

I cleared my throat and fluffed up my hair, hoping my flushed cheeks wouldn't rouse any attention when we went back to the party.

———

Zander and I returned to the foyer, where West stood at the side of the crowd eating a tray of canapés. He towered over everyone else and growled at someone who looked like they wanted to take a snack from him. I couldn't see the others anywhere.

"I thought you were looking after Vixen?" I asked, rejoining West. "Where are the others?"

"I've been busy," West said, wiping crumbs off his jacket and gesturing at the stack of empty trays. "Rocky has everything under control."

Zander looked on edge. After finding out how much Bryce had once wanted Vixen dead, I'm shocked he hadn't put her on a fucking leash and installed a tracker in her arm.

Before we could find them, Bryce made his way toward me. I flashed him a smile like a shark baring its teeth before it ripped its prey in two.

"What did you think of the art, Candy?" Bryce asked.

"You have quite the collection," I said, trying to keep my tone level and control my urge to snap his neck.

Over his shoulder, people parted for a drunken figure to stagger through. How the fuck had Vixen gotten into such a mess? Rocky was supposed to be sobering her up. Zander's jaw clenched as she stumbled over to join us. It was the first invitation to the Briarly New Year Ball she'd received, but it would be her last. Maybe that had been her intention all along?

"What a great party," Vixen slurred, attempting to poke Bryce in the chest, but missing. "All paid for with blood money. Isn't that right, Uncle Bryce?"

Bryce's nostrils flared in fury as other guests tutted and looked down their pretentious noses in disgust at her. I wanted to force their heads into Lapland's urinals until they licked them clean. Vixen was twice the person they'd ever be.

"I'm going to take Vix for some air." Rocky appeared at her side to steer her away before she said something else to anger Bryce further. "We'll be back by dinner."

"We won't wait," Bryce spat through gritted teeth.

As Rocky passed, he caught my eye and winked. Enabling Vixen to get so drunk had been no accident. Looking after her was the perfect excuse. What better time to slip away to steal the photographs? All I needed to do was keep Bryce occupied until he returned.

Before we had time to recover from Vixen's outburst, Bryce beckoned Giles and his female companion over.

"Have you met Giles's new girlfriend?" Bryce asked. "I think you may have gone to school together, Zander."

A fresh swell of anger grew in my chest, and West slipped his arm around my waist to hold me tight. I'm not sure whether it was for my benefit, or his. The giggling bitch on Giles's arm would make staying in this room of fuckwits even more unbearable.

Zander regarded the woman coldly, with no emotion. "It's been too long, Penelope."

"Not long enough," I muttered under my breath.

I'd last seen Penelope Cole in a motel room where she tried to fuck my *fiancé* in front of me. Her history with the Sevens went way back. She knew what West had done in school as a teenager, and even though she'd been paid to keep quiet about him almost killing a kid in a fight, I didn't like the thought of her knowing our business.

"I met Giles through work," Penelope simpered, stroking Giles's arm, but allowing her gaze to rest on West for a few seconds too long.

I wanted to rip off her ridiculous false eyelashes and skin her eyelids with a peeler, so she couldn't look at him ever again.

"Easy," West whispered soothingly into my hair.

He was fucking delusional if he thought it would calm me down. He wasn't the one having to watch a gold-digger undress him with her eyes like he was a slab of delicious meat. The Hulk was *mine*, and the bitch needed to keep her dirty paws off.

"I'm the new property manager for Giles's development," Penelope announced with a sense of self-importance as if she'd secured a presidency. "Have you heard about it?"

"I didn't know you were interested in property, Giles," I hissed, unable to stop myself, "considering your habit of trashing it."

As much as I hated my dingy apartment, I hadn't forgotten how he'd carelessly ruined everything I owned.

"Some places are beyond saving," Giles said, flashing me a snide smile. "There is nothing to do but start from the ground up."

"The work starts next month," Penelope gushed. "At Bayside Heights. The entire estate is going to be ripped down and turned into luxury apartments. You're familiar with Bayside Heights — aren't you, West?"

The name meant nothing to me, but West tensed. Penelope was goading him. She was only doing this to make him pay for rejecting her. From her smug expression, her revelation was getting the reaction she'd hoped for.

"It's going to be real estate gold," Giles declared, rubbing his hands together gleefully. "A whole new generation for Port Valentine."

"What about the people who live in the Heights?" West cut in. His irritation crackled through the air like thunder. "What's going to happen to them?"

"What about them?" Giles laughed, clinking his glass with Penelope's. "They'll get their eviction notice two weeks before."

"But those are people's fucking homes," West snarled, lowering his voice to a threatening rumble. "You know there's nowhere else for them to go."

Giles waved his hand nonchalantly. "They're not the type of people I'd want in *my* neighborhood."

Unsurprisingly, the unfeeling bastard knew nothing about what it was like to have a place you feel safe snatched from you.

"I can give you a discount on a new apartment if you'd like?" Penelope purred, running her tongue over her lips and not looking away from West. "I'm sure you'd be *very* comfortable there."

"See? That's my girl. She never stops working." Giles slapped her ass in encouragement, oblivious to how she was offering herself as part of the fixtures and fittings.

"Thanks for the offer," I snapped, narrowing my eyes at Penelope like a lion locking in on its prey. "But I think we'd need something bigger than an apartment. We wouldn't want to keep the neighbors awake at night — would we, West?"

Penelope winced. If she thought her dating Giles would make West crawl back, she was wrong. Flaunting our relationship in front of her was a better form of torture than tearing off her fake nails and extensions.

"Oh, look…" Penelope mock-whispered in Giles's ear, loud enough for everyone to hear, and pointed at the entrance. "It looks like the trash is back."

Vixen and Rocky had returned. I studied Rocky's face, as he inclined his chin in a nod so subtle only I noticed. I don't know how he'd done it, but our mission had been accomplished. His guess for where Bryce might have kept the evidence must have been correct.

"What is *she* doing here?" Vixen demanded, putting her hands on her hips. Her lip curled as she looked at Giles and Penelope's linked hands.

"Be nice," Rocky encouraged.

"What's wrong, Giles?" Vixen taunted, undeterred by Rocky's polite request. "Can't find a girlfriend of your own? You're going through all of the Seven's sloppy seconds."

I disguised my laughter in a cough as Giles's cheeks reddened in anger. The ring of the dinner bell conveniently diffused any confrontation. If this is how things were before the entrees were served, I'm not sure we'd make it until the main course.

"Let's take our seats, shall we?" Bryce said, leading the way to the dining hall.

All we had to do was get through the rest of the evening without someone finding out Rocky had taken the photographs.

———

The giant dining hall boasted a long banquet table, which could seat forty people. Candelabras cast the plum walls and guests in a flickering orange glow. Embossed name cards in front of the place settings indicated where we should sit. Whoever was in charge of the seating chart needed firing.

The Sevens were sandwiched between a group of men who looked like ancient mummies resurrected for the occasion, and Bryce, Giles, and Penelope. Bryce's older associates said very little. He seemed to prefer to surround himself with people who had no opinions of their own and mindlessly did his bidding.

When everyone was seated, servers brought out the first course and laid the plates down like a perfectly timed synchronized dive. I couldn't pronounce the name of the dish, but it contained figs and something floral which made my tongue taste like bad perfume. Whatever it was, I finished it in two bites. Why was it that the more zeros on the price tag, the less you got to eat?

"What was it that attracted you to Giles?" Vixen asked, ignoring her food and focusing her attention on Penelope. If looks could kill, West's ex would already be six feet under. "His lack of charm or his bank balance?"

"I told you we shouldn't have invited everyone, Uncle," Giles said, cutting his food into tiny pieces. "Not everyone was brought up to act civilized. It's all about the blood."

"Now, now. Let's all get along nicely!" Bryce raised a hand to silence the bickering, then grinned. "At least until after dessert."

The atmosphere was fraught. Zander's glare burned into his father like he was afraid something bad would happen if he looked away. Rocky tried to talk to Vixen about music, but she ignored him and glared at Penelope, who was trying to eat Giles's face while making eyes at West. West didn't look in her direction; he was too busy finishing Vixen and Zander's plates. Neither of them had touched their food.

"When do you think we can leave?" I murmured in West's ear, making a show of walking my fingers seductively up his arm.

"Whenever Bryce tells us why we're really here," he muttered as the plates were taken away.

I laughed loudly like he'd told a funny joke, causing Penelope to scowl. She wasn't the only bitch who knew how to play games.

Shortly after, the servers reappeared with the main course. An expensive cut of steak which was smaller than my palm. It had nothing on Big Al's in Hammerville.

"I'm a vegetarian," Vixen declared.

"Since when?" Rocky asked in disbelief.

She pushed her plate away. "Since now."

"I'll find out whether the chef can bring you an alternative?" the server offered. From the furious look on Bryce's face, he wouldn't be hired for a Briarly function again.

"Don't bother," Vixen said, folding her napkin and fanning herself with it. "I've lost my appetite."

Next to her, Rocky devoured his meal like an alien who'd never experienced human food before and couldn't get enough of it.

Penelope shot him a look of disdain as some of his food flew off his fork in her direction. "We're surrounded by savages, Giles."

I fought the urge to giggle. If Rocky heard her, he didn't give a shit. It spurred him on more. He ran his tongue down the side of his knife to lick up every drop. After growing up not knowing when you were next going to eat, it was a hard habit to break.

Aside from the classical music playing in the background, the room ate in silence. I struggled to enjoy the taste of the food when I was imagining tearing through Penelope's tongue with each chew.

"Are you going to keep us waiting all night, father?" Zander asked, dropping his cutlery and causing everyone to stare. "When are you planning to tell us why you summoned the Sevens here?"

"Did you forget one of my rules?" Bryce tutted, dabbing his mouth and clicking his fingers for the servers to clear the empty plates. "We never talk business at the table."

"I'm growing impatient," Zander snarled.

"We all are," West growled in agreement. His hand tightened around his fork, making me wonder whether he'd morph the metal out of shape.

"You don't have to stay," Giles said, turning to West and speaking slowly like he was talking to a child. "You're here as the muscle, not the brains. Why don't you leave the business talk to the real men at the table?"

"Are you counting yourself as a real man?" I spluttered, then laughed maniacally before turning deadpan. "If you were a real man, your new girlfriend wouldn't be panting over every cock in sight."

"That's rich coming from the Seven's personal whore," Giles hissed.

"Say another word to her and I'll break your jaw," West warned. His body shook like he was ready to dive over the table and carve Giles up. There would be something satisfying about seeing him strung up with an apple in his mouth like a pig.

"See?" Giles smirked. "What did I say? All muscle and no brains. You're nothing but a monkey doing my cousin's bidding."

I stood up, slamming my hands on the table and making everything rattle. "Say that again and *I* will break your fucking jaw."

"Does every dinner have to devolve into a brawl?" Bryce asked, leaning back in his chair and sipping a glass of wine. The bastard wasn't fooling anyone. This was the type of shit he lived for. "Can't we enjoy a peaceful meal?"

"Why don't we skip the bullshit and you get to the fucking point?" I snarled, unable to hold back my anger.

"I see they did not teach you manners at Blackthorne Towers," Bryce said without losing his cool.

How dare he bring that up?

"They taught me a lot more than manners," I sneered.

West was on his feet. He grabbed my arm to hold me back as rage seared through my veins. I wanted to rip off the tablecloth, smother Bryce with it, then set fire to his corpse along with the whole freaking manor.

Rocky clenched his fists under the table. Vixen was too drunk to realize what was happening, and Zander? His expression remained emotionless. Why wasn't he bothered? Surely, throwing my past in my face was a sign of Bryce escalating the threat against us.

"West, Candy. Why don't you go back to the club and check everything is in order?" Zander addressed us coldly. "The three of us can handle it from here."

I glared at him. Why did I suddenly feel like we were the ones who had done something wrong? He was treating us like naughty children who couldn't behave. It wasn't our fault *his* family was filled with the world's biggest assholes. He may be content to sit back and play the long game, but I wouldn't let the gruesome twosome speak to us like that How could he even bear to sit in the same room as them, knowing what they'd done?

"If I'm staying, I need more fucking wine," Vixen slurred, gesturing for the server to top her up. Luckily for her, Zander was too busy staring me down to notice. It wouldn't be long before she passed out at the table.

"It's probably for the best you two leave," Bryce agreed.

"Fine," I said, knocking over my chair. If Zander was going to treat me like a moody teenager, I'd fucking act like it. "We didn't want to stay at your shitty ball, anyway."

"See you around, West," Penelope said, wiggling her fingers in farewell.

"You'd better hope you don't," I snarled, then grabbed what was left of my glass of wine and drained it. Zander may want me to go, but he didn't say I couldn't take my sweet fucking time. I licked my lips, staining them red. "You may be a psycho bitch, *Penny*. But you have nothing on me. If you come near him again, you'll have me to deal with."

Penelope gulped. Maybe she'd finally get the message this time?

"Out," Zander ordered, pointing at the door. "Now."

"Thank you for dinner, Bryce," I said in my most sarcastic tone and slammed my glass down. "The pleasure was all mine."

I took West's hand and swung my hips as we left. My ass looked killer in this dress, and Zander needed to remember who he'd sent away. Making an impression when you entered any room was important, but everyone knew a good exit made a lasting impact. *Always leave them wanting more.*

West and I were like high schoolers who'd got kicked out of prom for sneaking vodka into the punch bowl or smoking pot under the bleachers.

"How do you feel about having a little fun?" I asked as we burst out of the manor. Just because our evening got cut short, it didn't mean our night had to end yet.

West looked at me like I was crazy. Hell, maybe I was... but I knew he'd bite. He was every bit as crazy as me, and I already had a plan. A smile danced over my red lips. "You know how to hot-wire a car, right?"

I nudged my head towards Giles's classic Cadillac. There was no question it was his from the personalized plate. Who else would leave it in the most prominent spot to show off their success to the other guests? The piece of metal on wheels costs more than a normal person's freaking house. Giles may have money in his bank account, but dollars couldn't buy class. He was practically begging for someone to take it away. It's about time someone taught the asshole a lesson.

"Obviously," West said. It was a stupid question. Of course, he knew how to hot-wire a car. He was a guy who treated waxing cars with the same attention to detail as a Korean skincare regime. "You want to go for a joyride?"

"Maybe." I sauntered over to Giles's car and ran my hand over the shiny hood. "But we're not just gonna steal it, we're gonna destroy it."

West smirked. He needed no more persuasion. "It's a good thing Giles is into vintage motors, and I know where the Briarly tool shed is..."

With all of Bryce's staff inside assisting with the elaborate dinner service, it was easy for us to scale around the side of the building and for West to force his way into a small outbuilding, where the manor's gardener stored his supplies. Next, all West needed was five minutes with a screwdriver and a hammer...

"You sure know your way around an engine," I said, slipping into the passenger seat as Giles's car whirred to life.

"Are you ready?" he asked, raising his eyebrows in anticipation.

"You said you used to be a racer," I said, then winked. "Let's relive your glory days."

West slammed his foot on the gas and we sped down the drive, leaving a trail of dust and destruction in our wake. I stuck my hand out of the window and gave the manor a middle finger as we zoomed past the CCTV cameras monitoring the entrance.

Fuck you, Giles.

We wouldn't make it far before he realized his precious toy was missing, but that made it even more fun. If Giles couldn't play nice, then he shouldn't play at all. I laughed, keeping the window open and letting the wind whip my hair into a frenzy.

"You're a bad influence," West said, but he couldn't hide the wide grin spreading over his face as our speed climbed and we weaved through the empty roads like we were competing in the Grand Prix.

My purse vibrated in my lap. I glanced at my cell, then switched it off. Zander could wait. He was the one who had wanted us to leave, remember? We didn't need a lecture. If he thought we'd come rushing back at his beck and call, he was wrong.

"I thought you couldn't destroy cars?" I asked.

"I can make some exceptions," West replied. "Giles is one of them."

"You know everything he says is bullshit, right?"

Giles may think West had nothing more to offer than muscle, but I knew better. West was smart. One of the best poker players I'd ever seen. He was also the glue that held the Sevens together. A fierce protector who would do anything for those he loved.

"He can say what the fuck he wants about me," West said. His jaw clenched as he gripped the wheel tighter. "But no one speaks to you like that."

"How chivalrous..."

"I mean it, Candy." West sped up. "I'll fucking kill him if he talks to you like that again."

The car screamed in objection as we hit three figures. It was a beautiful vehicle, but no one had pushed it this hard before. I couldn't hear anything but the roar in my ears, which sounded like a train about to derail. I wanted to wreck the car, but not while we were inside it.

"Pull over," I shouted. West didn't listen. He was too busy chasing the adrenaline rush, no matter the consequences. "I said, pull the fuck over."

West swerved suddenly, and we hurtled off the concrete down a bank. Our seat belts held us in place, but my teeth rattled as we flew down the uneven terrain. As we neared the bottom of the incline, he slammed the brakes, jolting us to a halt. After taking a second to check we were both alive, my hand was on the door handle, and I jumped out before West took us on another death-defying ride.

"What's wrong, Pinkie?" West asked, following me out. The wild look in his eyes told me the beast was coming out to play. "Too extreme for you? You're the one who asked me to race the car."

"And now, I'm asking you to destroy it," I said. My voice shook, but I refused to admit he'd scared me shitless. "Any ideas?"

West roared like a wild beast and smashed his foot into the side of the car, kicking a huge dent in the door. The metal crunching told me it wouldn't be long until the car wasn't the only thing damaged.

"C'mon, West," I said, standing in front of him before he could take out his repressed anger again. "You'll break your leg."

"Get out of my way," he snarled.

He'd already tipped past the point of no return.

"Make me," I challenged. I didn't move an inch. "I know you won't hurt me."

"You don't know a thing about me," he said, advancing towards me and pinning my body against the cool metal. He leaned down, his hot breath tickling my cheeks. "We're all alone in the middle of nowhere. This is where I bring men to die. This is a place where people disappear and never come back."

"You know, West," I said, raising my eyebrows in amusement, "I don't think you're as scary as you think you are."

"And you're not the bitch you pretend to be," he whispered in my ear, making the hairs on my arms stand on end. "You pretend not to give a shit about anyone or anything, but I see the real you. The parts you want to stay buried. The pain you want to pretend doesn't exist. You care about people, Pinkie, even if you won't admit it."

"What about the parts of yourself you keep buried, West?" I fired back, ignoring his assessment and how scarily accurate he was. "How does it feel to have to hold back every urge inside your body to stop you from losing control?"

"I'm a fucking monster," he warned, "and the sooner you see that the better."

"Show me," I said, raising my chin in defiance. I knew how to deal with the dark side of West. I could channel darkness, and right now? I wanted it to consume me. I didn't want to think about Giles's reaction when he found out we took his car, how Zander would be furious, or what Bryce would do when he realized we stole from him. I needed West to take my worries away in a way only he could. "I want to see your monster."

I couldn't decide what I wanted to see more: the depraved animal who had the power to slay anyone on sight or the growing bulge in his pants that looked like it'd tear me in two.

"You don't know what you're asking..."

"What's wrong, West? Not man enough?" I taunted, cocking my head to the side, knowing this would rile him. "You said you're a monster, so fucking prove it."

Bingo. A low rumble erupted from the back of his throat as the beast's attention turned to me. His hands closed around my throat, squeezing until I was gasping for air. His vicious streak was coming out, and all of his previous concerns for my safety vanished. He pulled my face close to his but didn't kiss me. He enjoyed feeling my pulse constrict under his grasp.

"This is what you want, huh?" West murmured menacingly. His pupils dilated — big black saucers eclipsed his blue irises.

My eyes watered, and my breathing quickened as I nodded. This is what I'd asked for, and there was nowhere to run.

West loosened his hold, making me go dizzy as the blood rushed back to my head, and fuzzy dots eclipsed my vision. Meanwhile, he grabbed my hips and forced me to turn around. The spear in his pants jabbed into my back like an enticing promise of what was to come as he threw me forward over the hood, still warm from the overworked engine, and held me down.

He tore the back of my dress open to reveal my legs and ass in an explosion of passion, spiking my excitement. Before I knew what was happening, he ripped my panties off, allowing the cool night breeze to tickle my pussy. Above us, the headlights of cars from the highway rushed past. All anyone had to do was look over the edge of the grassy verge to see us, but I didn't care. His urgent desperation to have me only heightened my desire. We were too far gone. We couldn't stop now.

West spat roughly onto his hand and forced my legs apart, exposing me in the most vulnerable way for the best access. His wet fingers found my heat, but he wasn't gentle. He forced his way inside me, and I cried out. No one could hear my cries here.

"I'll fucking destroy you, Pinkie," West growled.

His fingers fucked my pussy in hard, brutal strokes. The beast wanted to take everything he could from me by using my body for his gain. He was raw, real, and unrestrained. This was a version of West he never let loose, and I was the only person he could share it with. It's what I'd been waiting for since the first time I saw him.

"Do it," I begged.

His fingers withdrew, and he unbuckled his belt. A few seconds later, he unsheathed his cock. His head found my entrance, rubbing against it, then plunged in as far as he could go. I gasped, rooted to the spot as my insides stretched to accommodate him. My hips slammed into the hood with each of his deep thrusts. I tried to shift to adjust my position, but West held me down, using me like a rag doll and continuing to pound into me mercilessly. The beast took what it needed and gave me what I desperately craved.

"Is this what you wanted?" West grabbed a fistful of my hair and jerked my head back as his balls slapped violently against me. My ass throbbed, and I'd be bruised in the morning, but he wasn't done… far from it, and I was loving every second. "Have you seen enough?"

"More," I pleaded as he released his grip on my hair. His inhibitions were shedding, which only made me desire him more. I'd lusted after him for so fucking long but never wanted to admit it, but now that it was happening? I didn't want it to end. "Show me more."

He grunted, slamming me forwards until my cheek was pressed against the car. Looking to the left, all I could see was darkness. It consumed me, just like West.

"You're gonna regret asking that," he murmured, then cleared his throat.

His spit dripped down my ass as his fingers explored me in places where no one had ever touched me before. Ass play was new to me. I tensed, trying to shuffle away, but West was too strong. His wet thumb circled my asshole, and a giggle escaped my lips. No one said it tickled.

My laughter only infuriated him. He pushed his thumb into my ass and continued to pound into me from above. Initially, it burned, but as his thumb pushed deeper, I got used to the weird but arousing sensation. He built up speed, fucking both holes with the same aggressive vigor.

"You like being our Seven girl, huh?" he growled. "You like being fucked by all of us?"

"Harder, West," I begged as the car shuddered from the force. It felt like I was being taken from behind by a fucking truck, but my pussy welcomed it. I needed it. I've needed *him* for so long. "Fuck!"

West roared like a wild animal, then slammed into me one final time. He grunted as his hot cum spilled into me, flooding my insides with warmth. He pulled out and murmured, "Shit…"

No one could tame West's monster, but I'd happily volunteer to take it out of the cage again. I knew how to handle his darkness. He'd given me everything he had and, now I'd seen the side of him he tried to repress, I never wanted to let him go.

I turned to face him, slightly unsteady on my feet and aching all over in the best possible way. A sheen of sweat covered West's skin from the exertion, but the beast was gone. He had fucked it out of himself. Instead, West's eyes were wide with horror, like he'd seen a ghost.

"Are you... are you okay?" he asked. His eyes searched me for damage and lingered on the tattered bottom half of my dress, swallowing hard. "Did I... did I hurt you?"

My hips would be bruised tomorrow, but it'd be a welcome reminder of how his body had ripped through mine like a hurricane. I traced a finger up my thigh to collect his cum dripping between my legs, then popped it into my mouth to suck it clean. "I told you I could handle it."

Did that answer his question?

West's eyes widened, then a half-smile spread over his face.

"Get in the car, Pinkie," he ordered, his voice deep and husky.

"Why?" I asked as he opened the door to the backseats. "Are you gonna try to kill us again?"

"Maybe later." He grinned, pulling me to the open door. His hand cradled my head as I ducked down, then he pushed me backward. "But, first, I always clean up my mess."

Well, duh. He was a clean freak... but this time, it took on a whole new meaning. West climbed in after me as I backed up, enjoying the chase and teasing him. His gaze trailed down my body, but I kept my legs pressed shut and slid out of his reach, pressing my back against the car window opposite him. I felt behind me for the handle. It was locked.

"You can't escape me," The Hulk said, his patience wearing thin. He grabbed my legs, pulling my knees over his shoulders and pushing my crotch into his face like he was bobbing for a freaking apple. "This cunt is mine."

Most guys were afraid of their cum, but West didn't flinch. His mouth eagerly dove between my legs. He parted my lips, then fucked my pussy with his tongue, savoring the taste and making me writhe uncontrollably beneath him.

"I could eat your pussy all night long," he murmured, his hot breath tickling my inner thighs.

"Then fucking eat it," I demanded, pushing his head back down and grinding onto him. He'd taken what he wanted from me, and now it was his turn to oblige.

West didn't disappoint. Damn, he approached the task like his life depended on it. The sound of him murmuring in appreciation between lapping up my wetness turned me on even more. His tongue glided over my clit. He took it into his mouth, sucking softly, and sending vibrations shooting through my whole body.

Suddenly, he caught my clit gently between his teeth. My back arched with the change of sensation, and I cried out as an unexpected toe-curling orgasm rattled through me. I dug my nails into his shoulder, clinging on, as West latched onto my clit, teasing out every drop of pleasure.

"It's too much." I shuddered as the rising peak left me a shaking puddle of mess.

"You're not done yet, baby," West said, sliding his tongue down to lick up my juices and his cum seeping out. He spat on his fingers before pushing one inside me. Then two. His hands were so gigantic that two of his inked fingers were wider than an average man's cock. They made a squelching noise as they slid in and out. "You're so wet, Pinkie."

He stroked my G-spot, massaging it gently, then returning to kiss my inner lips before returning to pay my clit more attention. My legs clamped down around him to lock him in place, as the pleasure built inside my pussy and begged to explode. I thought I'd already got off the pleasure train, but boy was I wrong. West didn't stop. His determination to get me off only turned me on more. He kept licking and probing my insides with a hungry enthusiasm until I couldn't take it anymore…

"Fuck," I screamed.

My pussy squeezed around him, and hot liquid gushed down his hands onto the seat. My head rolled back, and I closed my eyes as I embraced the orgasm enveloping my body in blissful pleasure. I forgot where we were. How we'd got here. Nothing else mattered other than this fucking feeling. If you asked me my name, I wouldn't be able to tell you.

As soon as I returned to my body, I realized I was soaked. What the fuck was that? I'd never been so wet before. Is this what squirting was? West groaned into my pussy, licking it up. Whatever it was, he seemed to love it.

"Now you're officially *our* Seven girl," West said, sitting up to wipe his chin with the back of his hand. He had to slouch to stop his head from hitting the roof. "Damn, you have no idea how long I wanted to do that."

"How long?" I asked breathlessly, unable to move from my position for fear I'd pass out. My thighs shook uncontrollably like the aftershocks of an earthquake.

"Since the moment your smart mouth whipped my ass in poker and didn't give a damn about what anyone else thought of her," West said. "I was so used to getting my own way, but you? You came in and fucked everything up."

"What did you call me again? A gutter trash whore?" I asked, raising an eyebrow. "Maybe you have a better poker face than I thought…"

"Just because I had to have you, it didn't mean I had to like you," West snapped, then leaned back, deep in thought. "When I watched you dance in blood on the stage, it made me realize you were as fucked up as the rest of us. When we kissed that night after the Maven, I broke Zander's orders for the first time, and I didn't care. You were like a fucking poison. It didn't matter how many girls I tried to screw to get you out of my head. You were the only one I could think of. Yours is the only face I could cum to, and I fucking hated you for it."

Knowing that The Hulk had felt as drawn to me as I had to him only deepened our connection. Our lust had been forbidden, but we'd fought our desire for too long.

"And now?" I slid closer, running my hand over his chest to feel the tense muscles underneath his shirt. "Do you still hate me?"

"Now, you're still driving me insane." West cupped my chin in his hands and forced me to look up at him. His pupils dilated as he maintained eye contact and drew me into his world, where I could get lost forever. "You've seen the monster that lives in me first-hand. You didn't run from it. You trusted me not to hurt you when I could rip you apart."

"I knew you wouldn't."

"How could you know that when I didn't even know myself?" he said, dropping his hold on me and looking away. The car windows were steamed up, so there were no other distractions. He couldn't avoid this. "Tonight... I lost control... I could have really hurt you."

"But you didn't," I reminded him. "You may have darkness living inside you, but so do I. Instead of keeping it chained up, maybe you should let it out sometimes?"

His eyes trailed down to my pebbled nipples and swallowed hard. "Are you volunteering?"

"Maybe," I whispered, then kissed him, tasting myself on his tongue. Whenever we kissed, it made me ravenous. A hunger that could never be satiated when he was around. My pussy ached, but I still wanted more. Where the Sevens were concerned, there were no limits. Is this how normal people felt when they cared about someone? Like they were an addiction, and nothing ever seemed to be enough? I sunk my teeth into his lip to draw blood, then sucked it off. "Your monster and mine can be friends."

"You're crazy." West shook his head. He ran a finger over his lip to collect the blood, then held it out. I licked it off slowly, mesmerizing him like a hypnotist's pendulum. "You're all fucking ours. We're never letting you go."

"Don't make promises you can't keep, West."

"I'm not planning on breaking it," he growled. My eyes flickered to his lap, where his cock was as hard as a rock. He chuckled, following my gaze, then sighed. "What I wouldn't give to make your tight pussy gush for me again."

"I've never done that before," I confessed, a blush creeping over my cheeks. His fingers had been in my ass, and he'd made me squirt all over his chin, but now I was embarrassed?

"It was fucking hot," West said. "I like knowing you were so wet for me that you couldn't control yourself. Wait until I tell Zander and Rocky..."

"Hey." I nudged him in the ribs. "Just because we have an arrangement doesn't mean we have to share everything."

"So, I can't even tell them how fucking good you taste?"

I cleared my throat. If we kept talking like this, Giles would find us before we destroyed his car. In the distance, fireworks showered the night sky in pretty colors and sparkles. I'd forgotten changing a calendar was an occasion people celebrated. A new year had never made a difference to me before but, with the Sevens by my side, maybe this one would be different...

My heart and soul had been crushed under Hiram's regime, but slowly, the Seven men were helping to put me back together and rediscover who I really am.

"Happy New Year, Pinkie," West said, grinning wickedly. "Way to start it with a bang."

"We may be in another year, but there's no excuse for dad jokes." I rolled my eyes. He looked way too pleased with himself for that comment. "Now, are we gonna ditch this ride or not?"

Before we could be the dazzling 'new year, new me' versions of ourselves, we had to get rid of last year's problems.

"I have a plan," he said, getting out and hopping into the driver's seat. "Belt up."

I wasn't convinced the engine would start after West pushed the car to its limit earlier, but it didn't object. Just like me, the car couldn't resist his magic touch. My heart hammered in my chest, and I hoped we wouldn't have to get out anytime soon. I needed longer for my legs to recover and not feel like they were made from Jell-O.

We took quiet roads, snaking around the edges of Port Valentine until we arrived in an area I was unfamiliar with. There were three high-rise apartment blocks, a worn basketball court, and other tired surrounding buildings. It was a place where society put people they wanted to forget about — just like Evergreen, where I'd grown up.

"Where are we?" I asked as we parked. So far, no one had followed us, but the sun would come up soon. A Cadillac was hardly inconspicuous in this neighborhood.

"This is Bayside Heights," West said. "The place Giles wants to knock down. Here, put this on."

He handed me his suit jacket to wear. It dwarfed me, but at least it covered up my ass and ripped dress. He got out, and I followed. A group of teens played basketball nearby and listened to rap music. Overhead, pot plants lined the modest balconies. It may not be a wealthy neighborhood, but it was a place where people were trying to make themselves a home and a decent living. A place where parents wanted their children to do well and had to work damn hard to provide for them.

"What are we doing here?" I questioned. While seeing what buildings Giles intended to turn to rubble was interesting, it wasn't the time for a tour. Driving around in a hot vehicle wouldn't do us, or the residents, any favors.

"Fixing our problem," West replied.

Before he could explain, a young kid from the court sprinted over. He must have been around twelve years old, wore an oversized cap, and almost tripped over his laces to get to us.

"West," the kid panted. "Have you brought anything today?"

"Not today, kiddo." West ruffled his hair fondly. "Next time, though. Is your brother around?"

"He's over there." The kid pointed, racing off at a hundred miles per hour again, and his voice trailed after him. "I'll get him."

A few minutes later, an older kid swaggered over. He was in his late teens, but looked older and had the attitude to match.

"Is this your new girl I've been hearing about?" The kid looked at me suspiciously. He may be young, but I could tell he had a shrewd eye. He knew better than to trust outsiders. I liked him straight away.

"Sure is. Candy, this is Jacob. He and his family do odd jobs for me," West said. I smiled, and Jacob grunted back in acknowledgment. It's the best I'd get. West turned back to Jacob and asked, "Is your uncle still around?"

"It's a sweet ride." Jacob walked around the car and let out a low whistle. His eyes narrowed. "How much for the job?"

"As long as it's off my hands, you'd be helping me out," West said.

"I'm no charity," Jacob said, crossing his arms. This is what happens when you grow up hustling. You learn quickly that nothing good ever comes for free. It's better not to owe anyone anything.

"Fine, we'll split three ways. You, your uncle, and me." West grumbled. He didn't need the money, but it was worth compromising for Jacob's pride. "We got a deal?"

Jacob nodded curtly. "Done."

"It needs moving fast," West said. "People are looking for it."

Jacob asked no more questions. A second later, he jumped behind the wheel. We watched as he drove to a row of garages down the block. A few moments later, the car vanished from view.

I stared after him and frowned. "Is he even old enough to have a license?"

"The kid is a better driver than you," West said, making me scowl. "Jacob and his uncle can flip the car. It'll look completely different when they're done with it. Jacob's parents died a few years back. Their uncle does what he can, but it's tough. For them, and most of the other kids around here."

"You seem to know them well," I said.

"This is where I grew up." West looked around wistfully, then threaded my fingers through his. "Come inside. I want to show you something."

He led us into the nearest block. The hallway was cramped and the air stale, but it pleasantly surprised me to see the lift still worked. We stepped inside and took the squeaky ride up to the fifth floor, while I wondered whether we were about to plunge to our death.

"This is where my father lived," West explained, as we climbed upwards. "When he died, his lease got passed to me."

The lift pinged at our stop and West took me through a dimly lit corridor. It was narrow and the ceilings were low, making him look like a giant. At its end, West ducked down to feel around underneath a doormat for a key.

"Home sweet home," he said, unlocking the nearest door and letting us into an apartment. "After you."

Inside, it was basic but spotlessly clean. Apart from cans of beer, a TV, a sofa, and a side table, there was no other furniture or signs of life. It was the opposite of the flashy penthouse in Lapland, where the Sevens lived.

"Do you come here often?" I asked.

"Here and there." He shrugged. "It's another place to come to when I want space. The club can get... intense."

While there are many benefits to living above Lapland, I understood the appeal of having a place to escape when things got too much. This was his refuge amongst the chaos, and I felt special he'd chosen to share it with me.

"I help around the Heights, where I can too," he said. I followed him over to the window, where we made sure Jacob had hidden Giles's car from sight. The kid was good. "I try to get the kids here to make better choices. It's too easy to fall into the wrong crowd. This is one of the places where the Razors and other gangs come to recruit. "

"I get it. They're easy pickings for those fuckers," I muttered. "What will happen to them if this place gets bulldozed?"

"The only other places they'll be able to afford are outside town. If you think it's bad here, it's fucking anarchy on the fringe. The Razors—"

"Run riot?" I finished his sentence.

After watching a new member of the Razors bleed out on Lapland's floor, I didn't want to see any other kids suffer the same fate.

"Exactly," West said, strolling over to the fridge and grabbing a bottle of beer. He held one out for me, but I shook my head. He cracked open his and drained it.

When Rocky and I lived in Evergreen, he joined a local gang. He wanted money, and selling drugs was the only way for him to make enough to go to college. It was supposed to be a way of financing our future. Instead, his decision had devastating consequences for both of us. If he hadn't joined the gang, would Hiram have seen me that night? Would things have been different?

"Is there anything we can do to help?" I asked. I couldn't change the past, but I could help make the future a little less bleak for others. I knew what happened to vulnerable kids. How easy they were to exploit.

"Stopping the development would help." West laughed hollowly. His eyes narrowed. "But that'll never happen. The Briarlys have allies everywhere — even tying ourselves to the building before they blast it down wouldn't be enough to stop their plans."

They'd probably see crushing us in the process as a massive bonus.

"But there must be something," I said, surprising myself with the passion of my conviction. Hell, it'd been a while since I'd felt strongly about something that didn't involve spilling blood or revenge. The passion to make a difference got stamped out of you after you realized bad things happened to good people, no matter what you tried to do. Had West's tongue fucked with my brain chemistry?

"This isn't a battle we can win." West sighed in defeat, then checked his cell and frowned. "Zander has called a meeting. We have to go back."

"Do we really have to go so soon?" I asked, running my hand down his chest and lingering on his waistband. "Doesn't this place have a shower?"

"You'll be lucky to get hot water," he said, then winked. "Besides, I want you to walk back into the club smelling of me."

"I'm not a piece of territory, you know." I scowled. "My leg is not a fucking tree you can piss all over."

He roared with laughter. "I can't say anyone has ever said that to me before."

When he smiled, small crinkles appeared around his eyes which I hadn't noticed before. I concentrated hard to keep my sulky pout firmly in place. There's no way the bastard was ever going to find out his smile was contagious and gave me butterflies.

"Do you enjoy showing off all of your conquests?" I said, then paused after seeing the mischievous twinkle in his eyes that matched his silver canine. "Don't answer that."

"Is the girl with no feelings getting jealous?"

"You wish," I lied.

"You know, I've never given a girl a ring before..."

"Am I supposed to be flattered that I'm your first fake engagement?"

He grabbed me by the waist and pulled me close. My heart sped up, remembering how his hands held me down as his cock pounded into me.

"Fake or not," West said, sweeping a loose hair off my cheek, "you're the only girl I'd want to wear that ring."

I turned away before he could catch my smile. "Let's go before Zander sends his minions out looking for us."

West may think he was a monster but, beneath it all, he was a teddy bear.

We hitched a ride back to Lapland with a kid from Bayside Heights. West tipped him a hundred bucks for his trouble, making the kid's face light up brighter than a neon sign.

"Zander is going to be furious about the car," I muttered as we made our way through the empty club.

New Year was usually a busy time for Lapland, but we'd made a lucrative deal with the manager of the Smoker. He had hired all of our dancers for the evening for their burlesque-themed celebrations. We had tasked Mieko with making sure they behaved. It worked out perfectly with the rest of us attending the Briarly event.

"Maybe," West said, grinning. "But it was worth it."

The ache between my legs agreed, but I shushed him. We were like naughty teenagers sneaking home after curfew...

The first thing I saw upon entering the penthouse was Vixen sprawled over the sofa like a limp piece of lettuce. A bucket rested on the floor in front of her and a large glass of water perched precariously on the arm, close to toppling over.

"Are you okay, Vix?" I asked. "You look like death."

"I *feel* like fucking death, too," she croaked like a zombie coming back to life after being killed one too many times. "Do you have to talk so loud? I blame Red. It's his fault for giving me all those shots."

"Let's not pretend you didn't force them down yourself," I said, catching Rocky's eye from across the room. He sat on the floor next to Vixen's bucket, presumably on hand to throw it under her face if she retched. We were getting into dangerous territory. The last thing we wanted was for anyone to wonder how she'd gotten so drunk after Zander cut off her supply.

"Where's Zander?" West asked, looking around. "I thought we were having a meeting?"

"He's coming soon," Vixen said, then clutched her head and groaned, sinking back into the cushions.

"What did we miss?" I asked Rocky.

"Vixen throwing up over Bryce's new Bengali rug was the highlight of the evening," Rocky said with a smirk. "Well, until Giles noticed his car was missing."

"Oh, really?" I feigned shock. "What a shame."

Vixen raised a sharp eyebrow in our direction. Even when recovering from alcohol poisoning, she had the radar of a bat. "What do you two know about that?"

"Nothing," West declared. He sat down on the opposite end of the corner sofa to Vixen and pulled me onto his lap. "Nothing at all."

Rocky laughed. If West wrapping his arms around me bothered him, he didn't show it. I didn't know how this whole sharing thing would go down, but I couldn't help feeling guilty. I didn't want to rub it in his face. I'd be furious if another girl came within an inch of him.

Rocky shook his head and said, "I haven't seen Giles so mad since—"

"What's that smell?" Vixen interrupted, wrinkling up her nose and staring pointedly at me like I was a walking cum rag. "You smell like a fucking—"

"I'm going to shower," I said, jumping up before she could finish her sentence. West chuckled. The big man loved claiming his territory.

By the time I cleaned the smell of steamy car sex off me and re-joined the others, Zander had returned. I expected him to launch into a lecture. Instead, his expression remained impassive as he sipped his drink.

"You shouldn't have taken his car," Zander said, keeping his tone light as I sat down next to West.

West slung his arm over my shoulder and pulled me close. He didn't seem to mind that I'd chosen to wear his T-shirt. I had a whole wardrobe filled with new skimpy clothes, but I opted for comfort. There was something nice about wearing the guy's clothes.

"Karma is a bitch. Maybe *he* shouldn't have been such an asshole?" I retorted huffily, then decided changing the subject was the smartest course of action. "What did Bryce want to talk to the Sevens about, anyway?"

Before they sent us away from the table, Bryce was building up to the climax of the evening. He invited the Sevens to his ball for a reason, and I wanted to know what it was.

"That's why I've called this meeting," Zander said. "He made us an offer."

"And?" I flicked my wet hair over my shoulder impatiently, showering West in water. "What was his offer?"

"He wants us to join forces," Zander continued. "He thinks it'd be best to combine all of our assets. He feels having two Briarlys in the same town is giving mixed messages. He wants us to be partners."

"He's gotta be joking," West growled.

"Okay, I'm done." Vixen threw her arms in the air and rose to her feet. "I'm going to bed, where none of you fuckers can disturb me."

"Why would he do that?" I hissed, dropping my voice until I heard Vixen's door slam. "What did you say?"

"I didn't give him an answer," Zander said with a shrug. "Not yet."

"Joining forces doesn't make sense," I said. Bryce had more wealth, power, and influence in Port Valentine than the Sevens. *Why would they want to team up with us?* Sure, we had the Seven Sins casino, a decent weed-growing operation, and a strip club, as well as doing extra jobs on the side, but it was small fry compared to the Briarly empire. "There must be a reason."

The way I saw it, there were only two possible reasons why Bryce would want to merge. Either the Briarlys were burning through cash quicker than they were making it or, the more likely option, they were looking for a fall guy for something else they were planning.

"In case you haven't noticed, my father isn't exactly transparent," Zander said, rubbing his chin. "He gave us a few days to think about it."

"You're not seriously considering it though, are you?" I asked. "I know it'd be easier to take him down from the inside, but—"

"Of course I'm not considering it," Zander snarled, cutting me off. "I'd rather die than work with my father, but I am going to find out why he put forward the proposal. One way or another."

"What can we do?" West pressed.

Zander tapped his foot impatiently. "I'm working on some leads."

"Care to share, or are we always the last to know?" I snapped.

West squeezed my knee in warning. Fuck his warning. Zander may be our boss but, if he wanted me to be *their* girl, he had to get used to me saying what was on my mind.

Zander's stare burned through me as his eyes narrowed. "Maybe I'm working out who I can trust."

"What's that supposed to mean?" I hissed, trying my hardest not to raise my voice. After opening up to me about his mom, I thought we'd got past the point of keeping secrets from each other. "If you have a problem, why don't you just come out and fucking say it?"

"Why should I trust you if you go against my orders?" Zander said, holding up a USB stick and dangling it from his fingers. From the way Rocky squirmed in his chair, I knew exactly what it was. *Shit.* "I have my sources within the manor, and Red's disappearance didn't go unnoticed. Neither did his attempts to cover it up or lie about it."

Well, I suppose Zander finding out on his own was better than Rocky throwing me under a bus. I wasn't going to apologize for doing what was right. The Briarlys owned a lot of shit, but I wouldn't let them own *me*. We'd taken back what was rightfully ours. Didn't he understand why we had to do it?

West frowned, completely oblivious. "What's going on?"

I ignored West's question, not taking my eyes off Zander. "We wouldn't have had to steal the photographs if you agreed to help."

"I told you I was working on it." Zander slammed his glass down on the table, all of his prior calmness gone. "You realize you have made things worse, don't you? When he notices it's missing, he'll know who to blame. The only good thing to come from your covert operation is access to my father's computer, which gives us a few days to find out what he's working on."

I looked at Rocky, who'd sunk back into the sofa and tried to make himself invisible. "What's he talking about?"

"I may have had some help from Q on the tech side," Rocky said. "He showed me how to clone a drive."

"So, let me get this straight…" I said, turning back to Zander. I bit my lip and pretended to be deep in thought. "You're mad at us for not telling you, but it turns out us breaking the rules was a good thing?"

"It gives us a chance to get ahead and find leverage before he finds out what you've done," Zander said, his expression darkened as he rolled up his sleeves, "but breaking my rules is *never* a good thing."

"If your rules made sense, I wouldn't have had to break them," I spat.

"Being a Seven is about trust and loyalty." Zander rose to his feet, his lip curling. West tightened his grip on my leg. "You need to learn that when I say I'm handling it, it means I'm handling it. If we don't have trust, we have nothing. We are nothing."

"So, I have trust issues!" I threw my hands in the air. "What are you going to do about it? Kick me out?"

"You still don't understand, little one," Zander said. "You can't *leave* the Sevens. When you're in, you're in. But disobeying has consequences and you need to learn to trust us."

"Trust is something to be *earned*," I insisted.

He may have been brought up in a world where everything could be traded, but my trust could not be negotiated. Trusting someone was about more than words.

Zander's gaze lingered on my lips. "Then, let us earn it."

I rolled my eyes and tried to ignore how his probing stare set every nerve in my body on fire. "You say that like it's easy..."

It's not like there's a magic pill to take to trust someone. Sure, I'd let the Seven men into my life more than anyone else in years. I'd shared my body with them. I'd learned things about each of them, but did I fully trust them? I wanted to, but a part of me was still holding back.

"It is easy." Zander pulled a blindfold out of his jacket pocket. What kind of person carried something like that around with them? Most guys carried around condoms, not softcore bondage accessories! "You want me to teach you how to trust us? Keep the blindfold on for the next thirty minutes."

"Really?" I scoffed. "You think me not being able to see will change things?"

"Humor me," Zander said.

"Fine," I relented, standing and snatching the blindfold from his hands. I never shied away from a challenge. "Who is going to tie me?"

"Let me," Rocky said, standing and gently placing the soft black fabric over my eyes. He paused. "Are you sure about this, C?"

"Just fucking tie it, Rocky," I snapped, wanting to prove myself.

He was careful and methodical so as not to catch my hair. He bound me tightly, forcing my eyes to close, and descending my world into darkness. "There."

"Our girl needs to be taught a lesson in trust," Zander purred. "Start the timer, West."

Footsteps circled me. Without my sight, all of my other senses were heightened. The heat of a figure closed in from behind, pressing their muscles against me and gently stroking my hair. Then another in front, sliding warm hands under my shirt to stroke my stomach.

"This is really how you build trust, huh? This is just an excuse to—"

Before I could say 'see me naked', lips pressed against mine hungrily. *Rocky.* I recognized his soft, but aggressive kiss. He kissed me like it would be our last, sweeping me away in the passion and fear that this moment could slip through our fingers.

"What happened to you?" Rocky murmured. His fingers ran over my hips, where the skin was tender. I suspected bruises were already blossoming from being bent over the hood of Giles's car. It didn't take him long to put two and two together. "You did this? You hurt her?"

"Do you think I'd still be standing here if I did?" West spat in reply behind me. The Hulk had a point. "She enjoyed every minute of it."

"How do we expect to bring down our enemies when we're working against each other?" Zander snapped at them from somewhere in front of me, he sounded close by. "How can she trust us if we can't trust each other?"

Rocky mumbled a few curse words under his breath.

"We're brothers until the end," Zander said. "And Candy? She's our Seven girl."

"You all know I'm still standing here, right?" I said. "I told you already, I'm not some piece of property."

"No, you're *our* property," Zander corrected. His breath tickled my cheek as he pulled West's T-shirt over my head. "You'll see..."

Strong hands from behind helped him slide the fabric from my body, leaving me half-naked in nothing but a pair of panties.

"We'll show you how to trust us," Zander whispered in my ear. "There's just one final thing..."

He pulled my hands together behind my back and bound my wrists with silky fabric. The bind was tight enough to completely restrict my motion but still allowed my blood to flow... *just.*

"Hey," I objected, my voice a pitch higher. "This wasn't part of the deal."

"No one is going to hurt you," Rocky murmured, brushing his lips against mine.

For someone who valued control above everything, submitting was scary. It was different when it was me and Zander alone in his office. When I'd stretched out over his desk, I'd voluntarily offered myself to him to prove I wasn't afraid but submitting to all of them at once? I was vulnerable and, even though I couldn't see, it felt like a giant spotlight was shining down over my head.

"You need to let go," Zander said.

I opened my mouth to argue, but Rocky's kiss swallowed me whole. A different pair of firm hands ran down the length of my body from behind. My bound hands rested on a large bulge. *West.* Wherever we were, he'd always have my back and make me feel safe.

I was so wrapped up in our kiss; I yelped a moan of surprise as Rocky's hand slipped into my panties, while West yanked them down to expose me. Suddenly, I was glad of the blindfold as I stepped out of them like a cater-pillar shedding its skin.

A second later, muscular arms scooped me up like I weighed nothing. From the smokey cologne, I knew it was Zander. He cradled my naked body and carried me to another room, where he placed me down carefully on a bed, trapping my arms under me. The luxurious satin sheets felt incredible against my bare skin.

"Look at our girl," Zander admired. "She's all fucking ours."

The sound of belts unbuckling, unzipping, and fabric falling to the carpet made me gulp. I was completely at the Seven's mercy.

The mattress dipped as bodies joined me, and the kissing began again. Someone different this time. *West.* His giant hands cupped my face, then slipped down my neck and squeezed my nipple between his thumb and finger. At the same time, another body coaxed my legs apart, spreading me wide open. Rough kisses ran up my inner thighs, nibbling and biting until I could feel hot breath against my pussy. I couldn't keep track of what was happening; all the sensations blurred into one to heighten my pleasure. I moaned as a tongue dove into my wet pool and slid up to my clit.

"She tastes so fucking good," Rocky groaned as West continued to play with my nipples and send bursts of pleasure rippling through my body.

My senses were overpowered, melting away any lingering self-consciousness I had.

"Let me taste her," Zander ordered.

Rocky pulled back momentarily, and West broke away from our kiss. Did he want to watch? A second later, two fingers ran down the length of my slit, then teased my entrance. Zander pushed in deep and slow, allowing my wetness to coat him down to the knuckles, then withdrew. I heard the small pop of his fingers leaving his mouth.

"Delicious," Zander said. I could hear the smile in his tone. If I didn't feel so overwhelmed, then I may have blushed.

Rocky replaced Zander's fingers as he returned to eat my pussy with even greater enthusiasm. His tongue plunged in and out of me, while West stroked and caressed my breasts, leaving a trail of kisses in his wake. I moaned, gyrating my hips into Rocky's face as West took my nipple into his mouth and sucked gently. That, and the rhythmic licking against my clit, felt like an inferno had ignited and I couldn't stop it. Every inch of my skin was ablaze with their touch.

Then, just as quickly, they both stopped and pulled away.

"Hey," I objected, breathless and panting. "You can't just stop like that."

"Isn't our girl so beautiful?" Zander praised; he sounded far away like he was watching from a distance. "Why don't you give her what she wants, West?"

A moment later, a heavy body rolled on top of me.

"I'll take care of you, princess," West whispered. His hands slipped under my ass and rolled us over, so I was straddling him. His cock dug into me, hard and swollen from longing. When we'd fucked outside, I hadn't felt his body against mine. Now, it's all I could fucking feel. His muscled body lay in my wake. My breasts pushed against him, our skin covered in a slick sheen of sweat. The beast may have taken from me, but it was my turn to take from him.

I arched my hips, sliding my wet pussy over him. The heat from his erection warmed my lips as his soft head pressed into my clit. I ground against him, using him for my pleasure. West growled in lust, squeezing my ass hard. Him wanting me so badly was the biggest turn on.

"What a view," Zander purred as West spread my ass wide and reminded me we weren't alone. Knowing the others were watching made me soaked and even hotter for them. "Make her feel good, West."

"Are you ready?" West asked as his cock rubbed against my entrance. For someone not keen on the idea of sharing, he was coping pretty well. Maybe that's why Zander was letting him claim me first?

"Yes," I moaned. *I mean, hell fucking yes — I'd do anything, yes!*

West guided my pussy down onto his cock. I perched above, my thighs burning as I stretched to accommodate him.

"Do you like him fucking you, little one?" Zander asked, his words short and breathy. The sound of his hand pumping up and down his shaft made me grin. Knowing Zander was pleasuring himself made me want to give him a show to remember.

"Sit up, C," Rocky encouraged. "I want to see you."

I did as he asked, inhaling deeply, as I straddled West, and every inch of him sunk deeper. How was there enough room for him to fit? It felt like I was being impaled to my belly button.

"Put your arms out," Rocky asked in a gravelly voice. I held them out, following the sound of his voice. He took my wrists and untied my binds. "You're going to need them."

West wasn't happy with Rocky's interruption and growled. His hips bucked violently and made me fall forwards. The big man wanted my attention, but he had to be taught a lesson. Even though I was wearing a blindfold, West needed to remember that I was the one in control. I slid up his shaft, almost to the tip. He groaned, trying to pull me back down, but I resisted. I circled my hips, dancing around his head until he almost fell out, then suddenly plunged his cock in deeper and made him gasp. I enjoyed the power and how fucking crazy it made him, hoping it had the same effect on the others.

As I turned my head, a pierced dick hit me straight in the nose.

"Ouch." I laughed, then felt around in the dark for robocock.

Bingo. I took it in my hands.

"C—" Rocky began, then gasped.

"Shh," I murmured, looking up in the direction where I thought he was kneeling, hoping he could hear how thick my voice was with desire for him. For them all. "I want to taste you, Rocky."

He guided his cock to my mouth, sliding the pierced end over my lips until I opened to welcome him. The balls of his piercings slid along my tongue as I licked along his length like an ice pop. If Zander enjoyed watching West fuck me, what would he think of this? I heard a grunt from behind us. The boss approved.

"Shit," Rocky moaned as West's thrusting forced his cock further down my throat. "Your mouth feels incredible, C."

Rocky's hands grabbed my hair, pulling it into a rough ponytail, then pushed my head down his length to the rhythm of West's thrusts. The two of them were using my body, but they were working as a team to make sure I was comfortable. What could be more freaking hot?

I gagged as Rocky's Prince Albert hit my tonsils, coating him with my spit. His hips shuddered, holding me there. While the last time we had sex was gentle and loving, he was also an animal too. What guy didn't want a girl to choke on his dick?

"Have you ever been fucked in the ass before, little one?" Zander asked.

I tried to answer, but my mouth was full. I almost choked on Rocky as he yanked my head away, leaving a trail of spit dripping down my chin.

"N-n-n-no," I stammered breathlessly.

Hell, I'd basically been a virgin before coming to the club. Being fucked by two men at once was a lot to handle, but three?

"It's okay. Be a good girl and lean forward," Zander soothed. I stretched out over West, burying him, as two powerful hands spread my ass further apart. "We'll be gentle with you."

West didn't move as Zander's hot spit dripped down my ass. I expected him to stroke me, like West, but squeaked as the tip of his nose tickled me and his tongue darted out to probe my entrance, tasting me where no one else had before.

"Fuck, she likes that," West said, as the sensation sent vibrations to my pussy and made me quiver. They had overwhelmed my senses, making fireworks explode in my brain and suspending me in a state of pure ecstasy. Nearby, Rocky let out a groan as I heard him touching himself. "Don't you, Pinkie?"

I couldn't talk. Words wouldn't come out, but I arched my back in agreement, hoping spreading myself wider to give Zander a better angle would answer West's question. Zander wanted me to trust them fully. He wanted me to give myself to them, and for them to give themselves to me to fully bind our bond. If we did this together, there was no going back.

Zander paused, withdrawing his tongue to stroke me with his finger and slip it inside gently. I let out a moan as my thighs clenched around West's torso.

"See?" Zander said, pumping his finger in and out of my ass. "I knew you'd like it."

As Zander eased another finger into me, West's hand found my clit and caressed it softly. I pushed myself down onto his hand, sliding against it to increase the friction.

"Rocky?" I groaned, reaching out blindly for his cock.

It wouldn't be fair to leave him out, right? I wanted to feel him. I *needed* to feel all three of them filling me at the same time. Rocky took the hint and positioned himself to give me better access. I clutched onto his muscular thighs, feeling upwards until I found his balls, gently cupping them, and taking him into my mouth. I moaned over his shaft, making his cock twitch and a fat drop of pre-cum spill over my tongue. He was close, but I wanted this to last. I slowed down, running my tongue over every little piercing playfully.

"She's ready," Zander announced, withdrawing his fingers and squirting something cold over me. I tensed as something bigger rubbed against my ass. He sensed my hesitation, slathering what must be more lube over the two of us. The sheets would need burning after this.

"Don't worry," West murmured to reassure me. "I'll stay still."

I stayed frozen in place as Zander's cock edged his way into my ass. After the initial squeeze, he eased deeper, giving me an inch at a time. I took it slowly, fearing he was about to rip my asshole in two, but the tight pain gave way to another feeling... it felt *fucking good.* Zander grunted as he started to slide back and forth easier.

"She's so wet for us," West murmured, thrusting to match Zander's pace. "Do you like being fucked by all three of us?"

"Uh-huh," I gargled back onto Rocky's cock, making him groan.

"She was made to be our Seven girl," Zander said. "She fits us perfectly."

Could he and West feel each other inside me? They must be able to. For me, it felt like there was nothing but a thin wall separating them as their cocks slid together. Double-penetration felt fucking incredible. As well as their motions, the friction of their dicks against each other flooded my body with new sensations. As Zander pushed in further, and West's shaft rubbed against my G-Spot, Rocky plunged to the back of my throat, making my eyes water.

"That's it, baby," West encouraged. "Drench me with your pussy."

Before I even realized what was happening, Zander thrust into my ass and I tightened around them both. It was all too much. The heat, the friction, the overwhelming fullness... *fuck.* My insides felt like they were imploding as an orgasm ripped through my body. I was so stuffed, there was nowhere for the release to go, amplifying the feeling tenfold. My whole body shook, but six firm hands held me in place as they continued to rock me into oblivion. Rocky's cock muffled my screams, as Zander teased new feelings out of me I didn't think possible.

"Fuck," Rocky growled out. His hips shuddered as I sucked on him hard.

He couldn't hang on any longer, spraying the back of my mouth with his salty cum. I swallowed it down, sliding my tongue over his head to make sure I got it all before releasing him.

"We're not finished with you yet, little one," Zander purred as Rocky pulled out of me and I took a gasp of air. "You're going to take until we tell you it's time to stop."

"Zander, I-I-I..." My voice trailed off and turned into moans as he and West continued to fuck me. "Fuck!"

I didn't think my body could take any more, but the two of them sliding against each other caused a new strange wave of pleasure. An intense, almost ticklish feeling built up from my toes and fizzed through my limbs as their cocks defiled me.

I cried out as they tipped me over the edge again. I expected my orgasm to be over quickly, but it wasn't. It kept on going and going. Wearing a blindfold made no fucking difference. Bliss blinded me. I couldn't hear or think... all I could feel were them. Crashes of pleasure rippled through me, and I cried out again and again. I'd read about full-body orgasms before and thought they were bullshit, but now I knew I was wrong...

Zander's thrusts sped up as my ass latched around him. His breathing grew more shallow as his hands gripped my cheeks tight, and he blew his load.

"You feel fucking incredible," West breathed as Zander pulled out.

Now, he had me all to himself and didn't hold back. With a final push, he exploded and filled me with his warmth all over again. He put his arms around me and brought me closer. I was a shaking mess. I couldn't move, even if I wanted to. The three Seven men had ravished me.

Beep. Beep. Beep!

"What the hell is that?" West growled.

"The timer's up," Zander replied.

Holy fucking shit.

Rocky undid my blindfold to reveal West grinning underneath me like a sweaty Cheshire cat. I may not have been able to see what was happening and, if it wasn't for the cum dripping down my thighs and out of my ass, I wouldn't have believed it either.

I looked around at the enormous bed we were lying on. I'd never been inside this room before, so it must be Zander's.

"Well?" Zander asked.

I rolled off West to look at him. He was busy buttoning up his shirt, but his cock was still out on display like it was for sale in a store window. No amount of money could buy such a high level of confidence. The guy looked like a fucking Greek statue someone had graffitied over.

"Well, what?" I raised an eyebrow. "Do you want me to score your performance?"

I'd give them all a ten, not that I'd let them know that. There was always room for improvement, right?

Zander scowled. He needed to lighten up. "Have we proved to you we can be trusted now?"

I paused, considering his question. They could have done anything to me without my sight and use of my hands. "It's helped."

Zander looked down at me in disbelief. "What more can we do?"

"That," I said, grinning wickedly. "Again and again."

"She's definitely our girl." West laughed as his cock sprung back into action again. Hell, we'd fucked earlier and now again... his stamina was insane. As good as screwing him again would be, even I had limits — if I wanted to walk again tomorrow.

"Are you, Candy?" Zander asked, his cool gray eyes burning into mine. "Our girl?"

Even though I'd thought about their offer a lot, I'd not officially given them my answer. He, Rocky, and West stared at me. Waiting. Fuck knows how the three of us would work. It'd make everything more complicated, but if they were happy to give it a try, then so was I. Sure, the mind-blowing sex helped. But Zander's trust exercise had proved to me I wasn't afraid to be vulnerable around them. These were men I could trust. Men who made me feel safe.

"Yes, fine," I relented. "Whatever this weird as fuck arrangement is, I'm in."

I sat up and looked for something to cover myself with. Rocky was already waiting and handed me his shirt. West growled, he preferred me to wear his clothes, but I was teaching him how to share.

"Even though I'm in, I'm sleeping in my own bed tonight, okay?" I declared, getting up shakily to my feet. There's no way my vagina could cope with any more action tonight. She needed time to recover with a hot water bottle and binge-worthy Netflix series. "I'll see you all in the morning."

Their eyes watched me leave.

I may be their girl, but the Seven men? They were all fucking mine.

After being railed by three guys in the early hours, I planned to stay in bed until lunchtime. I needed time to recover and wrap my head around what happened. Not just how incredible the sex was, because it was out of this freaking world, but how *right* it had felt. I'd questioned how being in a relationship with all three of them would work. Now, I couldn't imagine being with one over another. There was no other way; the Seven guys were a package deal.

My thoughts were rudely interrupted by Vixen bursting into my bedroom like a runaway train hurtling down the freaking alps. "Get up."

"What's wrong?" I sat up and checked the clock. It was almost noon. Why the hell was she up so early? I expected her to be confined to bed and nursing her hangover. Had I accidentally used her shower without asking? Or worse, had she overheard our sexcapades last night and wanted me out of her closet for good?

"Get the fuck out of bed. Now!" Vixen screeched. She looked like she'd snorted ten lines of cocaine from the way her eyes were wide, like saucers.

This was bad.

Really fucking bad.

Even with a gun held to her head, I'd never seen Vixen so rattled. A crazy banshee had possessed her body.

Something was wrong.

"What is it?" I asked.

"It's West," she said, her voice breaking. My mind ran through the possibilities; each of them worse than the last, but none as bad as the words that came out of her mouth next. "He's been shot."

I had to be with him. I threw my comforter to the floor and jolted upright as a spike of adrenaline surged through me. My body went into autopilot as my limbs moved of their own accord. I slipped my feet into the nearest set of sneakers. "Where is he?"

Rocky's shirt hung lifeless and limp around my thighs, but there was no time to change. We needed to get him. *Fast.*

"He's on his way to the hospital," Vixen said. A tear slipped down her cheek, but she sniffed, refusing to break down. She knew she had to get her shit together. West's life was on the fucking line. "We can meet the ambulance there. Zander and Red are already on their way."

We raced through the penthouse and down the stairs. I took two at a time, cursing my legs for not being able to move any faster. Why did I have to get fucked by three guys the night before? My aching thighs burned in resistance, but I pushed on.

Outside the club, Vixen threw keys into my hands. Her face paled like she was going to be sick.

"Can you drive?" she asked, gesturing towards the closest car. West's prized SUV. "I... I don't think I can."

I nodded and jumped inside. My body somehow went through the motions of turning the key in the ignition while I was screaming internally. As soon as Vixen shut the car door behind her, I slammed my foot on the gas. The rubber wailed against the concrete as we hurtled away. I'd passed the hospital on my old commute, so I knew where to go.

"Who did it?" I asked. "Who shot him?"

Would West forgive me for wrecking his car if it meant we got to the hospital faster? West was usually the speed demon, but it was my turn to channel my inner racer.

"I don't know... I don't know anything..." she stammered, still in shock and clinging to her seat. "It's bad... real bad."

We needed to get to him.

Vixen continued to blather in broken sentences, but I couldn't comprehend what she was saying. All I could focus on was getting to the hospital. I wove between lanes and cut in front of people, ignoring the beeping horns following us. Memories of Crystal bleeding to death on the sidewalk flashed through my mind. A few seconds could make all the difference. Did they get to him in time?

"Blood everywhere... ambulance..." Vixen kept talking, but my thoughts were a complete scramble.

Please don't let him die.

I kept repeating it over and over like a mantra.

If there was a God, perhaps they would listen? Not that my prayers did any good for Crystal. Willpower wasn't enough to start a heart beating again.

Please don't let him die.

None of this made any sense. Who? Why? Where? Was he shot because we stole Giles's car? Surely even Giles wouldn't be so petty, especially when Bryce was waiting on our answer about whether he and the Sevens could join forces. Then again, Giles's last temper tantrum resulted in Cheeks being shot dead, so attacking West didn't seem like a stretch.

"There," Vixen yelled, pointing at a sign by the next turn to make sure I didn't miss it. I swung a sharp right towards the hospital, making Vixen scream.

Please don't let him die.

My bruised hips reminded me of how alive West had been a few hours before. He was the strongest of all the Seven men. My big strong Hulk. How could this have happened?

We're nearly there, West...

In some stroke of luck, we made it to the hospital without crashing. I maneuvered into the nearest parking spot. We flew out of the car, leaving the keys dangling in the ignition and the doors wide open. Someone could steal the fucking car for all I cared. A car was replaceable, but The Hulk wasn't.

We sprinted through the hospital doors. Our feet hit the ground. One after the other.

"This way." Vixen grabbed my arm and pulled me along like baggage in an airport. She seemed to know where she was going as we rushed past the sea of gowns, trolleys, and faces. Everything streamed by in a blur.

Please don't let him die.

Rocky and Zander stood at the end of the hall, talking in hushed serious tones with a doctor wearing bloody overalls. *West's blood.* In my previous line of work, I'd never been squeamish, but my stomach turned at the sight of it. I knew a fatal amount of blood loss when I saw it.

"He's in surgery." I heard the doctor say as Vixen and I neared. "We're doing all we can... touch and go... internal bleeding... bad condition..."

Zander listened to the doctor intently, only glancing away briefly to acknowledge our presence. Rocky tried to put his arm around my shoulder, but I shook him off. The only person who could make this better was bleeding out through the wall on the operating table. A hug didn't solve anything.

"What happened?" I gasped, finally daring to take a breath and realizing my chest was heaving for air.

"He was over in Bayside Heights," Zander explained. "If a kid didn't follow a blood trail, West would have bled out at the scene. No one saw anything or who pulled the trigger."

Bayside Heights. Jacob. The car. *The fucking car.* West will have gone over there to check our deal had gone smoothly. Someone had to have followed him. Whoever used West as target practice would pay.

Stealing the car had been my stupid idea. It was my fault. I'd been so hellbent on annoying Giles that I hadn't thought about the consequences. We may not have any proof Giles was behind West's shooting, but I was ready to decapitate the bastard and mount his head on a pole if I found out he was responsible. No one would be able to stop me. Until then, there was nothing I could do but wait, and it was fucking infuriating.

"Will he be okay?" Vixen asked as her bottom lip wobbled. "How long will he be in surgery?"

"However long it takes to dig out the bullet lodged in his thigh. It hit his femoral artery," Zander replied bluntly. How could he be so fucking casual? If I wasn't imagining West staggering through empty streets alone and injured, I'd have swung for him.

A familiar face raced towards us. Mieko's wet hair was scraped back in a ponytail as if she'd jumped straight out of a shower.

"I came as soon as I could," Mieko said, pulling Vixen into her arms. "Have you heard any more news?"

"Not yet," Vixen said, falling into her embrace. "You didn't have to come here, Mimi."

"Of course, I did," Mieko said, smoothing down Vixen's hair. The look of tenderness passing between them was almost too much to bear.

"He'll be okay, C," Rocky murmured. Although, from the way he was biting his lip in concern, he didn't seem to believe his own words.

"You don't know that," I snapped. "Nobody does."

"You need to calm down, C," Rocky said in his best attempt at a comforting tone.

"Calm down? He could fucking die," I blasted, clenching my hands into fists and digging my nails into my palms. "How can you stay so fucking calm?"

He and Zander exchanged a 'she's losing her shit' look, making me want to rip their heads off. Why were they looking at me like *I* was crazy? How were they keeping it together? Images of pools of blood and broken bodies were all I could see. Even the world's strongest man wasn't immune to having an artery ripped open.

"I'll get you all some coffee," Mieko said, sensing it may be a good time to leave us alone for a few minutes. She squeezed my shoulder as she passed, but I couldn't meet her pitying eyes. I didn't want her sympathy. Sympathy didn't heal bullet holes.

Please don't die, West. Please.

———

Minutes stretched into hours.

I clutched the cold polystyrene cup, coffee untouched, in my hands.

Doctors moved around us in a frenzy of activity. Hospital machines beeped. Wheels ran up and down the corridors. The smell of disinfectant and cooked canned food lingered, but it couldn't disguise the scent of death lurking around every corner. Hospitals were designed to make people better, but not everyone made it out of their walls with a pulse.

Vixen and Mieko sat away from us, whispering in a corner. Rocky paced and kept trying to assure everyone that West would be fine, but his attempts to lift our spirits diminished with every second West remained in surgery. Zander's initial cool exterior was starting to break. He stared at the clock in brooding silence, only breaking off occasionally for a controlled angry outburst.

"Whoever did this will pay," Zander muttered to himself.

For once, revenge wasn't the first thing on my mind. Sure, it was a close second, but before I wished someone dead, I needed to know he would live.

Please don't let him die.

A doctor burst through the door, and we all jumped to our feet. His expression was difficult to read and somber. The face of a man who was used to being the bearer of bad news.

"How is he?" Vixen asked.

"Stable," the doctor confirmed. "He's lucky someone found him when they did. Not many people survive after losing so much blood. We need to keep monitoring his condition, but he's through the worst."

He was going to be okay.

Relief swelled inside me, flooding through my body like rain falling after a long drought. Vixen's shoulders slackened as the weight of her worry lifted, and Mieko pulled her closer into an embrace. Rocky mumbled 'I knew it' under his breath, while Zander simply nodded in acknowledgment, processing the news in his quiet way.

"When can we see him?" I pressed, having to stop myself from barging past to be at West's side. "Can we go now?"

"Not yet," the doctor said. "I'll send someone to fetch you when he's somewhere more comfortable."

Zander thanked him, but I couldn't relax. Not yet. It didn't matter what the doctor said. I had to see West with my own eyes to know he would pull through. Life had a cruel way of twisting you in the gut when you thought you were safe and through the worst.

"I need to get some air," Vixen stammered. We'd all been on an emotional rollercoaster. It'd take time to work through the shock. "And more coffee."

"I'll go with you," Mieko insisted, taking her hand and leading her away.

They may have only recently started dating, but they'd already been through more challenges than most married couples. From burning bodies to seeing Cheeks get shot, it brought them closer together. Hopefully, like Mieko and Vixen, my guys and I would come out of this ordeal stronger.

"I'm going nowhere," I said, returning to my seat and crossing my arms stubbornly. "Not until I've seen him."

Rocky sat next to me and slipped his fingers through mine. "I'll stay with you."

I managed a small smile and squeezed his fingers back. Sometimes it takes almost losing someone to realize how much they mean to you. Not just West. All the guys, Vixen, Mieko, and Q. Maybe we were, in our own fucked up way, the real family I'd always wanted...

————

Rocky didn't let go of my hand until the doctor returned half an hour later.

"You can see him now," the doctor said. "But only two at a time."

"Let Candy and Vixen go first," Zander said.

The doctor took us into West's private room. I'd waited for this moment all day, but now that it had arrived, I didn't know what to do with myself. I awkwardly shuffled in after Vixen. Inside, West was hooked up to a host of beeping machines and drips hung out of his arms. He looked like he'd fallen into a deep sleep.

"Can he... hear us?" I asked the doctor as Vixen and I sat at his bedside.

"He's out cold," the doctor replied, writing notes on a clipboard and nodding in satisfaction. "We had to give him extra tranquilizers to, um... keep him under... I'll leave you both to it."

As soon as the drugs wore off, I'm sure West would be ripping the wires out of his arms and discharging himself. It was strange. Usually, our lives were filled with constant threats and movement. It didn't feel right to stop and... just sit. Shouldn't we be doing more to make whoever did this pay?

I took West's hand. You did that in hospitals, right? He may not know I was there, but it wasn't for his sake. I needed to feel his skin, his warmth, the blood pumping through his veins, to really believe he would pull through.

"You care about him, don't you?" Vixen asked softly, taking West's other hand.

"He's a Seven," I snapped, watching West's eyes flicker underneath his lids. "Of course, I fucking care."

"That's not what I meant," Vixen said. "I mean, you *really* care about them. All of them."

I let my hair fall over my face. "I mean, I guess..."

"Look, I'm no expert and I don't even want to know what kind of arrangement you guys have going on," she continued. "But I do know I've never seen the guys like this before. There's not been another girl around since you came into the picture, and the penthouse used to be like a freaking revolving door. When you first arrived, I thought you were another fake ass bitch."

"Are you supposed to be trying to make me feel better? Because it's not working—"

"If you'll let me finish," Vixen talked over me, sighing dramatically, then picking up where she left off. "What I'm *trying* to say is, whatever the hell is going on, I'm glad they have you. You have our backs."

"Didn't a tattoo prove that to you already?" I muttered sarcastically. Or, maybe she'd expected a spare kidney to symbolize my loyalty...

"Having a tattoo doesn't prove you're a Seven," Vixen said. "Being a Seven is about family. No one could fake the reaction you had this morning. I know you're all in."

Mieko had seen past Vixen's bullshit when I thought there was nothing more to her than being a snarky slave driver. She hid a sensitive side underneath her badass bitch persona, and her words meant a lot. Vixen knew who I was. She knew about all the mistakes I'd made, the horrible things I'd done, but it didn't matter. She accepted me, anyway. They all did. I had spent years fending for myself but, with them, I didn't have to be alone anymore. Finally, I belonged.

"Since when are you going soft?" I asked, quickly wiping my eyes before she could see and never let me live it down. I wasn't used to this type of affection. West being shot had turned me into a pile of mush. "Mieko must be getting to you."

She scowled, but her eyes lit up at the mention of Mieko's name. After the worst day, it was a small glimmer of sunshine amongst the darkness.

"I've never met someone like her before," Vixen admitted. "She's..."

"Too nice for you?" I scoffed, helping her out. "If you hurt her, you'll have me to deal with."

"If I hurt her, I'd want you to," she said earnestly then bit her lip. "I've never really... felt... like this about someone before."

"Have you told her how you feel?"

"Have you told *them* how you feel?" she rebutted and raised an eyebrow. "What do you think?"

For people like us who tried their darndest not to show vulnerability, prying off your toenails would be easier than admitting you had emotions.

"Well, don't wait too long to tell her," I said, dismissing her question and stroking the back of West's hand. "Not everyone would be able to put up with your bitch ass."

"Says the psycho who has all three of the Seven guys on a fucking leash."

"I'll need more than a leash to keep them in check," I mumbled. If getting shot is what happened when I wasn't around, I didn't want to let any of them out of my sight again. West stirred in his sleep; he looked so... helpless. "He *will* be okay, right?"

"He's strong," she said fiercely. "He'll pull through, and he has you now. He won't want to leave you in the hands of Zander and Rocky for long."

She had a point there...

———

We'd been in the hospital for eight hours, but I had no intention of leaving.

"You need to eat," Mieko urged. She'd been looking after everyone all day and refused to leave Vixen's side. "Come with me and Vix to the cafeteria?"

"I'm not hungry," I snapped, then my stomach rumbled to give me away. "I mean, I wouldn't hate it if you brought me a sandwich."

She hid her smile, then nodded curtly. "Of course."

The two of them hurried away, leaving me alone in the corridor. The doctors had insisted we give West time to rest, but I was already itching to be back at his side. As soon as Zander found out West was out of surgery, he and Rocky returned to Lapland to try to work out who was responsible for West's attack. Although, you didn't need to be Scooby Doo to work out that fucking mystery...

Before the guys left, Zander insisted on enlisting two henchmen to guard West's room and keep an eye on me. As if I needed a babysitter. Not that Zander listened. He ignored my arguments about not needing extra protection, and the men stood outside West's door like a pair of oversized angry thumbs. I made a mental note to ask West whether shaving their heads was part of their job description when he recovered.

My head snapped up from my lap as the click-clack of heels grew closer. *What the fuck was she doing here?*

Penelope swished towards me in a fog of Chanel Number 5 with a Birkin on her arm and a lavish bouquet in hand. She had some nerve showing her face after what her new boyfriend had done. West didn't need fucking flowers.

I gritted my teeth and stood up, waving aside the two henchmen who tried to make a human wall between us. I could protect myself better than either of those jerks could.

"What do you want?" I spat, squaring my shoulders.

"I brought flowers," she chirped. She shot me a perfect white dazzling smile, which was too straight and shiny to be trusted. "They're from the whole Briarly family."

"Were you saving these to put on his grave?" I snarled, snatching them from her and throwing them straight in a trash can. For all I knew, they'd be laced with poison. They'd already tried to kill him once – what was stopping them from trying again?

"Can I go in and see him?" Penelope asked, craning her neck to get a look through the blinds.

"Over my dead body," I growled. "He's still breathing, and we'd like to keep it that way."

Penelope looked me up and down like she was considering whether she could make a dash around me. I may be a foot shorter than her, but I was a thousand times deadlier. "I didn't realize you were his guard dog."

I stood my ground, planting my hands on my hips. "I'm not a bitch you want to mess with today, Penelope. I suggest you leave unless you want to be lying in the next fucking hospital bed."

"Fine, but before I leave, there is one more thing," Penelope said, narrowing her eyes. If she thought playing the high school mean girl act would turn me into an insecure wreck, she was freaking delusional. "I'm also here to deliver a message. For you."

"I'm not fucking interested in anything you have to say."

"I think you'll be interested in this," she said. Penelope took a step closer, almost gassing me with the amount of perfume she'd layered on. "Someone told me something was taken from the mansion last night... and I'm not talking about a set of wheels."

The evidence from my time in the Romano mansion. Rocky cloning Bryce's hard drive. *They knew.*

"Oh, really?" I looked down to check my chipped nails. Speaking to her was more boring than watching cleaning commercials on repeat. "Maybe the mansion should consider improving its security?"

"You think you're so clever, don't you?" Penelope hissed. When she was angry, her whole face contorted and twisted, making her resemble a gremlin over a Victoria's Secret model. "But the Briarlys don't take kindly to things being taken from them."

"So, you've come here to threaten me?" I laughed. Puh-lease. If they wanted to intimidate us, they shouldn't have sent Barbie to do it. "Isn't coming to gloat over what your new boyfriend did to West enough?"

"Giles didn't do this!" Penelope gasped as her eyes widened. "He wouldn't."

"If you think that, you don't know him or Bryce at all," I said. I considered telling her about how Giles blew Cheeks's brains out over the Christmas table and ruined a perfectly good pecan pie, but decided against it. She'd learn who he was the hard way. "You should get out while you still can."

Giles may be a spineless coward who didn't mind shooting a defenseless man, but Bryce was pure walking evil. If someone stole from him, he wouldn't hesitate to do whatever it took to get revenge. Including shooting West.

"You want me out the way so you can keep West all to yourself," Penelope said. "You're threatened by me."

I resisted the urge to laugh. The Sevens were facing many threats, but Penelope? She was nothing more than a stupid bitch who believed the world revolved around her and that every man would drop at her feet. Looks could only carry a person so far.

"I thought you were here to deliver a message?" I reminded her, taking a step forward and making her flinch. "Why don't you spit it out before Vixen comes back and rips your fucking tongue out?"

She winced at the mention of Vixen's name and said, "Bryce wants to meet with you tonight to discuss his proposition. Alone."

"Why me?" I asked, cocking my head to the side. There had to be an ulterior motive. "Zander is the boss. His word is final."

"For some reason, Bryce thinks you may be able to influence him," she said, then couldn't resist adding, "although... I can't see the appeal myself."

I grinned smugly. "West can."

Her face turned to stone. "If you don't come tonight, Bryce said there will be consequences."

Where had I heard that line before? Like father, like son.

"Did you think blackmail would work?" I threw my head back and laughed, then stopped suddenly. "I'm not going anywhere."

"Has West ever told you about what happened when we were at school together?" Penelope changed the subject. "How a student was hospitalized after a 'nasty fall'?"

The bitch just didn't quit. Her attempts at scaring me hadn't worked, so she wanted to use West's past to get me to do what she wanted. West told me about how Bryce had paid off the school, and his classmates, to cover up what happened after he'd lost control in a fight. Who would believe her all these years later? Why would anyone care now?

"I know you received a sizable amount of money to keep your mouth shut," I said. "Remember?"

"Not everything is about money." Her eyes darted towards the door of West's room. She gave off seriously obsessed stalker vibes. This was about more than getting me to meet with Bryce. It'd become personal. She couldn't hide how much she wanted West back, and if she couldn't have him? She didn't want anyone else to. "The boy West hurt came from a powerful family. I'm sure they'd like to know how an out of control scholarship kid cracked their son's skull and how his rich friend's daddy covered it up. The guy was in a coma for two years. He never recovered. Brain damage for life. It'd have been easier if he was dead."

West hadn't told me any specific details about what happened the first time he lost control, but I knew he agonized over it and regretted his actions every day. Penelope may be calling my bluff, but I didn't want West to have to wake up and relive his biggest mistake again.

"You wouldn't fucking dare," I snarled, wanting to grab her by the hair and smash her face into the wall until she needed reconstructive surgery.

"Do you want to take the risk?" She leaned in to slip a piece of paper into my hand with an address written on it. "Be there tonight, or else."

I heard Vixen before I saw her. "What is *she* doing here?"

I crushed the paper into a ball as Vixen stomped towards us like an angry rhino ready to trample whoever stood in her path.

"I was in the area," Penelope replied, flicking her glossy hair over her shoulder. "I wanted to see how he was doing."

"Or finish what my bastard cousin started," Vixen cut in, her spit sprayed over Penelope's perfectly made up face.

Mieko caught Vixen's arm to hold her back. "Not here," Mieko whispered, trying to calm her down. She was the only thing standing between Vixen and Penelope's expensive weave.

"Why not? We're in the best possible place," Vixen replied. Her body trembled, torn between following her instincts and not wanting to disappoint Mieko. "They won't have far to move her when I'm finished."

Penelope cackled, sensing she was on borrowed time. "Don't worry, I'm leaving."

Penelope sauntered away, catching my eye as she passed.

"What else did she say?" Vixen questioned.

I shrugged, gesturing at the discarded flowers. "Same old bullshit..."

No one else had to know the real reason Penelope came by. Loyalty and trust were what the Sevens valued most, but which did they value more? Was keeping a secret from them worth it to protect West?

CHAPTER

Twenty

"I told you, we'll let you know if anything changes," I said for the tenth time, finally breathing a sigh of relief as Vixen relented and agreed to go back to Lapland. After sitting in the hospital all day, Penelope's visit, and the food not being up to her standards, Vixen's sulky mood was driving me insane.

"I would not wanna be Mieko right now," Rocky muttered under his breath.

"She has the patience of a saint," I agreed.

Rocky had been glued to my side since he'd returned from wherever he and Zander disappeared to earlier. His lips were firmly sealed about what the two of them had been up to and discovered in the hours since they'd left the hospital. I would have forced him to tell me if I hadn't been keeping a secret of my own. This made us even.

"Let's hope Mieko's patience holds out long enough for Vixen to track down a cheeseburger," he said.

I snickered as a gentle knock on the door of West's room broke up our chat. Although Zander hadn't returned to visit, he'd pulled some strings from a distance. He arranged for West to be moved to a larger room with greater visitor privileges. As well as that, he'd gained remote access to the CCTV stream for West's room and the adjoining corridor. Thankfully, Penelope showed up before Zander started spying on our asses.

West's bed was already surrounded by cards, enough grapes to feed an army, and other pointless shit people sent when you were sick. People always give more gifts when you scare the living shit out of them.

A nurse stepped inside. Her cheeks reddened as her words came out in short nervous bursts. "Only one of you can stay for the night. Well, one and the... erm... guards outside."

I spotted one of our henchmen peering through the door as her blush deepened. It seemed even nurses weren't immune from the allure of a bad boy. Who knew a goon could have attracted her attention? West's nurse was in her mid-forties and a real sweetheart. I wanted to tell her to run while she had the chance, but if she was tough enough to deliver injections then who knows? She may be down for dealing with the grisly shit they did daily.

"I'll stay," I said definitively. Well, maybe not for the *whole* night...

The shred of paper Penelope gave me was burning a hole in my panties. What harm would it do to talk to Bryce, anyway? Staying with West for the night would grant me the perfect opportunity. There was no chance in hell I'd be capable of slipping in and out with Rocky around, and Zander's cameras would only be able to follow me so far.

Rocky frowned, wrestling with contradicting thoughts. "I don't like the thought of you being here on your own."

"I can take care of myself," I reminded him. Had he forgotten I'd murdered Raphael Jacobson and Giovanni Romano? "Security is right outside, remember? It's not like I'll be left alone."

Zander's strict instructions meant West would not be left unprotected for a second. If someone came back to finish what they started, then they'd be ready and waiting.

"I still don't like it," Rocky huffed.

"I'm not made of glass," I snapped. "I don't need you watching over my shoulder all the fucking time."

"Someone tried to kill West today," Rocky said. As if I needed a reminder. "Is it so bad that I want to look out for you? I want to make sure you're safe."

"You want me to start trusting you, don't you? Wasn't that the whole point of last night?" I reminded him. "You need to stop treating me like someone who needs saving. I need you to trust me, Rocky."

Did I feel bad for manipulating him? Sure, a little... but it was for the greater good. I was acting in the Seven's best interests and, if I could put a stop to Penelope airing West's past and find out what Bryce wanted, it'd be worth it. After all, my stupidity was the reason why West ended up in the hospital and that guilt was on me.

Penelope may be stupid enough to believe the Briarlys had nothing to do with West's shooting, but I knew better. It couldn't be a coincidence it happened the day after I'd recruited Rocky to steal evidence from Bryce and persuaded West to help steal Giles's car. If we hadn't taken the damn car,

West would never have been in Bayside Heights. I owed it to him to fix things.

"If it's so dangerous here, don't you think Zander would be hanging around?" I asked to emphasize my point. "I'll be fine, okay?"

"Alright!" Rocky sighed and raised his hands in defeat. "But it doesn't mean I like it."

The nurse popped her head around the door again and tapped her watch. "It's time to go."

"Call me later," Rocky said gruffly, planting a kiss on my forehead.

"Sure," I promised. Well, if I wasn't neck-deep in Briarly drama...

I watched Rocky disappear from view. With the others gone, the beeping of machines seemed to get louder. Each beep was a welcome confirmation that West's heart was still breathing. I took West's hand in mine and stroked the rough skin on his palms.

"I'm sorry," I murmured. My recklessness had gotten us into this mess, so I had to get us out. "But I'm gonna fix this."

I wouldn't let Penelope punish West for his past mistakes. He'd already suffered enough. If meeting Bryce would prevent his secrets from being unearthed, I'd do whatever needed to be done for my Hulk.

Getting out of the hospital undetected was simple. All I had to do was slink to the bathroom at the same time one of the henchmen went to take a leak and the swooning nurse batted her eyelashes at the other. Zander seriously needed to review his security detail. If it wasn't for knowing someone would be monitoring through the cameras, I wouldn't have dared to leave West unattended.

After memorizing the address and flushing the evidence, all I had to do was shimmy out of the window and hop into the nearest cab. Vixen had taken West's car back to Lapland, and a quick flash of my seven tattoo would be enough to scare any driver in Port Valentine to take me anywhere without cash. I would already be on my way to the meet-up location before anyone noticed I was missing.

I may not know where I was heading, or what Bryce wanted to talk about, but I knew I was heading straight into the lion's den... and my instincts told me it wouldn't be pretty.

"Are you sure we're in the right place?" the cab driver asked nervously. We'd driven twenty minutes out of Port Valentine, and he looked like he wanted to speed away as quickly as possible.

I didn't blame him. Places like this were perfect for nefarious business dealings. We'd pulled up outside a disused factory in the middle of nowhere. There were no other signs of civilization for miles, so no risk of members of the public strolling by. No one would hear you scream this far out. Was coming here alone really a good idea?

"Yep, this is it," I said, mustering my confidence and climbing out. "Thanks for the ride."

I made my way toward the well-maintained iron gates bordering the property. A sign whoever owned it wanted to keep people out... or in. Thankfully, I didn't need to pick any locks. They were open, and I stepped straight through.

I headed into the central courtyard area. Orange flickering lights mounted on crumbling walls cast an ominous atmosphere. As I got closer, two figures came into view: men with guns guarding an entrance to the old building.

Bingo.

If Bryce thought two gorillas on steroids would frighten me, he was mistaken. If anything, they should be afraid to be out here with someone like me.

"Are you lost, little girl?" A figure called over, repositioning his gun to draw attention to it. Puh-lease, him showing off his weapon was as welcome as an unsolicited dick pic. "This isn't somewhere you should be wandering around at night."

"Bad things can happen to pretty girls with faces like yours," his colleague cooed. Stupid fuck. Didn't he know some monsters had pink hair and cute nails that could squeeze his balls until they popped? "Why don't you tell us your name?"

"Cut the bullshit," I snapped unfalteringly. Their faces fell. "You know exactly who I am. Bryce is expecting me. Are you going to open the door, or do you want me to tell him you've been keeping his guest waiting?"

"Watch your step," one snarled, moving to let me pass and following close behind.

"I don't need a fucking escort," I spat, swirling around to face him as his gun dug into my back. "And if your gun touches me again, I'll make sure it's the last thing you ever do, asshole."

His face screwed up into a snarl, but he took a step back as I entered the building into a vast windowless room. The steel walls, cold temperature, and rusty hooks hanging from the ceiling indicated it may have once been a meat production facility. Although, if Bryce owned it, I'd guess animals weren't the only creatures slaughtered here.

A red chesterfield sofa looked out of place in the center of the sterile surroundings, like a throne in the middle of a walk-in freezer. Bryce and Giles lounged across it with drinks in hand. As well as the guards who'd followed me inside, four men were positioned in each corner of the room, watching from the shadows. Should I be flattered that Bryce decided this level of security was necessary?

My eyes sought out the escape routes. Aside from the door I'd come through, the only other exit was a second door at the opposite end, which led deeper into the complex.

"You came." Bryce stood to greet me. His voice echoed around the space. "I knew you would."

"You say that like I had a choice," I said sarcastically, putting my hands on my hips. "Why don't you spare me the fucking formalities and tell me why you brought me here?"

"I'm an English man," Giles piped up. How could I forget when I constantly fantasized about smothering him with a Union Jack flag? "We still believe in good manners and old-fashioned Briarly hospitality."

"Yeah, just like you believe in shooting an innocent man and leaving him to die," I said, throwing him a withering look. "Your psycho stalker girlfriend wasn't happy that you almost killed the man she's obsessed with."

"You bitch—" Giles began, rising to his feet.

Bryce coughed to intervene, making Giles sit straight back down again.

"That's right," I mocked. "Sit down like a good boy, and let the adults talk."

Giles's face flushed in anger, but Bryce raised his hand to stop him from retaliating and motioned for a guard to advance. I stood straighter, ready to act. Instead of attacking, the guard pulled a chair from the darkness. The legs grating across the blood-stained concrete made the hairs on the back of my neck stand on end.

"Why don't you join us for a drink, Candy?" Bryce offered. "You are our guest."

"I'm not thirsty."

Well, not for drinks, anyway... but I wouldn't say no to cutting Giles open.

"Suit yourself, but take a seat," Bryce said, motioning towards the chair that his guard had set down opposite them. "It'll be much more comfortable."

I'd rather sit on a cactus, but I wanted to get our meeting over with. Bryce thrived on drama, and I didn't want to give him the satisfaction of getting another rise out of me.

"Gladly," I snarled, sitting down and surveying the room with interest. "Nice place you have here. But it's not quite the manor you're used to."

Bryce ignored my comment and clicked his fingers for his men to bring him a martini. "Are you sure we can't tempt you?"

"Positive."

Bryce shook his glass, swirling the liquid around the sides, then took a long sip. I balled my hands into small fists in my lap. He was testing my fucking patience.

After a long pause, Bryce cleared his throat. "Well, Candy... it seems you took something that belonged to us. I am willing to overlook your lapse in judgment if an agreement can be made. I'm looking for a new partnership to support our new endeavors."

Bryce's cordial demeanor contradicted the brutal edge of his stare. A cut-throat merciless psychopath lay beneath Bryce's smooth businessman exterior. His eyes may be the same color as Zander's, but they couldn't be more different.

When I looked into Zander's eyes, I saw a fire burning. Zander may be fucked up, but he cared about those he loved in his twisted possessive way. He'd shown me his softer side when he talked about his mother and how far he'd gone to protect Vixen. Zander was capable of feeling. Why else would he have sacrificed his inheritance for a half-sister he'd never met? Bryce was the opposite. There was nothing but emptiness in his rotten core. Bryce had killed the only woman he'd truly loved because he didn't want her to be with someone else. He was more deadly than I'd first given him credit for.

"Do you really think the Sevens would work with you, after everything you've done?" I sneered, narrowing my eyes and wishing my stare was enough to disintegrate him into nothingness. "Zander may be considering your proposal, but I think we all know what he's going to say. If you think I'd be able to convince him otherwise, then you don't know your son at all. Zander would never partner with you. Ever."

Bryce threw back his head and laughed.

"I didn't realize I'd said a fucking joke," I hissed.

This only spurred him on further. Giles joined in, clutching his stomach, and they laughed maniacally like they were riding the high of a mushroom trip. What was going on?

Bryce's laughter slowed. "Oh, Candy," he said, shaking his head in pity. "I wasn't talking about Zander."

Behind him, the second door creaked open, and a shadowy figure stepped out.

"Hello, Kitten." Hiram's voice sent a shiver racing down my spine. "I've been waiting for you."

———

Adrenaline surged through my limbs as I jumped to my feet. My heart pounded in my throat like a tennis ball trying to force its way out of my mouth. I'd kill every motherfucker in a mile radius and hang their cocks to the overhead hooks if that's what it took to get away.

One of Bryce's men dove forward to contain me. I dodged his lunge, then swung a punch and made contact with his nose. It snapped under my knuckles. He staggered backward as another advanced to take his place. I took him out just as quickly. I drove my knee into his balls and delivered an uppercut to his chin to knock him out cold. A stream of them kept coming. Too many of them.

I thrashed around, but they descended like a swarm of angry bees. Hands grabbed my arms, forcing them behind my back to hold me in place. My chest heaved from the exertion as I looked up to face him.

Hiram.

Footsteps reverberated off the steel walls as he swaggered over with the arrogance of a celebrity on a red carpet. He arched an eyebrow in amusement. "Are you ready to put your claws away, Kitten?"

I gritted my teeth, trying to keep my shit together. "Tell them to put me the fuck down."

Bryce looked at Hiram for approval, who nodded in agreement. He knew I wouldn't be stupid enough to continue fighting outnumbered. As talented as I was in combat, I couldn't tire myself out too soon. I needed to bide my time until it counted. In the meantime, I'd have to use my brain.

"Retreat," Bryce ordered his men. They let me go and doubled back like obedient robots.

I readjusted my clothes, wiping my bloody hands on my shirt, and smoothing down my hair.

"What is this?" I demanded. "An ambush?"

"Why don't you sit down, so we can continue our conversation?" Bryce suggested. The sadistic bastard was enjoying every second.

I took a seat — not because I wanted to comply with Bryce, but because I needed to reassess the situation. There were ten guards, not including the two lying unconscious, along with Giles, Bryce, and Hiram. I had two escape routes, both blocked by Bryce's men, with no way of knowing how many reinforcements were hiding elsewhere in the building. Hiram's eyes burned into me from where he stood next to Bryce, knowing what I was thinking.

Shit.

"When I discovered the photographs of you at the Romano mansion, we conducted some research of our own," Bryce said, gesturing with his arms as he talked like he was performing a magic trick. "Zander would never have agreed to work with me, but inviting you to the manor bought me more time to find who would be interested in a real partnership... for a price. After learning what you stole from me, I knew I had to act."

Hiram smiled. He circled my chair, then stopped. His leather-gloved hand reached out to stroke my cheek. I shrunk away from his touch but knew better than to break his wrist. "You didn't think I'd let you leave me forever, did you, Kitty?"

"Fuck you," I spat. "I'm not going anywhere."

"You're coming back home with me," Hiram said. He smiled, which made Giles reccil like he'd seen a ghost. "Or your *fiancé* won't be the only one of your new playmates in the hospital."

"You shot him," I murmured, more to myself than to anyone in particular. History had repeated itself all over again. First, Crystal… then, West. Where would it end?

"Did you think I'd waste *my* time killing him? You know how much I love treasure hunts. If I killed him, his body parts would be strewn so far over the country he'd never be found. " Hiram shook his head like ending West's life was beneath him, making me hate him more than ever. He turned to address the Briarlys, who cowered under his furious stare. "Unfortunately, I didn't realize I was doing business with *amateurs*."

"I had assurance that he was dead," Giles stuttered, turning an uneasy shade of green and confirming my suspicions about his involvement. If he wasn't wearing black trousers, we'd see stains spreading through the fabric.

In Port Valentine, Giles sat on his plush lily pad, like a slimy toad, picking off easy targets like flies. Next to Hiram, everyone could see Giles for the coward he really was. Hiram swam in the darkest depths of the ocean. He was a Great White that could tear you apart before you saw it coming… if you were lucky.

"Let's hope your men are better with business than they are at killing, Briarly," Hiram sneered. His disapproval was clear. "You'd better pray your new development makes the profit you claim it will because my men never miss."

"It will," Giles stammered. "Investing in Bayside Heights will triple your money. It'll be all profit."

The Briarly fortune must be drying up if they were looking for external investors, and even Bryce looked nervous at Giles's sales pitch. Was he having doubts over the success of Giles's new venture when Hiram's threat hung over their heads like a guillotine? The bastard only had himself to blame. Bryce was already heading straight to hell, but making a deal with Hiram would get him there much faster.

"Plus, you have the girl," Giles continued, almost pleading. His desperation and desire to impress only made him look more pathetic. "We brought her here like you asked."

My whole body shook as rage tore through me. If my stare could fire lasers, I'd have burned holes straight through his empty skull. "You wanted me to come here tonight, so you could get a fucking investment?"

Before he could respond, an explosion of gunshots firing outside caused the guards to disperse and Giles to drop to the floor in fear like the little bitch he is.

"It seems we have company," Bryce said wryly, looking down at Giles's trembling body in disapproval.

Hiram shrugged like an annoying mosquito was buzzing around his head. Gunshots were simply a nuisance.

Seconds later, the door flew open. Zander stepped inside like a sexy tattooed knight in a suit. He kicked a corpse out of his way like a piece of trash. Rocky followed close behind him, looking around with wild eyes like an animal unleashed. His gaze sought me out immediately, and relief flickered over his face to see I was okay, but something else lurked behind his brown eyes... *hurt.* I'd tricked him into leaving me alone at the hospital. I'd betrayed his trust.

"Excuse us," Zander snarled, narrowing his eyes at his father. "I see we're late to the party."

The guards didn't know what to do. They stood hesitantly, pointing their guns at the intruders and awaiting Bryce's instructions. Zander and Rocky may have killed two of their colleagues, but Zander was also a Briarly.

"Zander." Bryce stood, motioning for his men to lower their weapons. He drew himself up to full height like a parent getting ready to scold a young child. "To what do we owe this pleasure?"

"I heard you were trying to *sell* a member of the Sevens," Zander confronted him as he and Rocky made their way toward us. Zander wasn't a little kid Bryce could bully anymore. He was taller, stronger, and more imposing than his father.

"Not *sell*," Bryce corrected, "we are here to make a *delivery*."

"And what about the money from the Bayside Heights development?" I cut in, blowing up his argument. "It sure sounds like selling to me."

"The Sevens don't belong to you, father," Zander spat, ignoring my input. He hadn't looked in my direction since they'd burst in. "It's not your deal to make."

I tried to read Zander's expression, but there was nothing but emptiness behind his chiseled jaw. How did they know where to find me? I'd been careful to cover my tracks: flushing the note, leaving my phone behind, hitching a cab...

"You're too late, Zander," Bryce said. "You have to learn that not everything goes your way. Candy came here tonight willingly."

Hiram's hand rested on my chair possessively. He may be content surveying the unfolding altercation between the Briarlys, but he wanted to make sure everyone knew I belonged to him.

"Her coming here isn't a fucking agreement to be traded. Candy is one of us," Rocky snarled. The veins in his neck throbbed in fury as he glared at Hiram. "She's not going anywhere."

If Zander and Rocky stood in Hiram's way, he wouldn't hesitate to kill them. They may have come to save me, but their valiant rescue was nothing but a fucking suicide mission!

"The deal's already been made," Giles rebutted, then smirked. Thinking he was on the winning side had made him miraculously rediscover his vocal cords. "We have a contract."

Zander narrowed his eyes. "You're wrong—"

"Zander, don't," I interrupted, aware of Hiram's looming presence breathing down my neck. I don't know what the hell he was going to come out with next, but I knew Hiram better than anyone. Resisting his wishes meant death. West would already be dead if Giles's idiot henchman had done their jobs right. I couldn't let them die because of me. Not here. Not like this. "I'll go with him."

"Shut the fuck up, Candy," Zander growled, finally looking at me for the first time. His gaze darkened. "You don't know what you're talking about."

"Yes, I do," I insisted. My voice sounded stronger than I felt as I implored him and Rocky with pleading eyes. Couldn't they see why I was doing this? It was for the Sevens. For them. To keep them safe. "I'll go with him, but I have one condition."

"I said, sh—"

"Let her speak," Hiram roared, cutting Zander off. Everyone else in the room was irrelevant to him. He didn't care about making money from Giles's development in Port Valentine. The whole thing was a ploy to get him what he wanted... me. Hiram's voice softened, as he turned his attention back to what I was saying. "I'm intrigued. Go on, Kitten. I'm listening."

I took a deep breath to brace myself for what I knew I had to do.

"I'll return to Blackthorne Towers and void our contract *if* the Bayside Heights development doesn't go ahead."

Even though I'd be leaving my new family, I wanted to be damn sure that Bryce and Giles wouldn't profit from it.

"No! That's fucking insane, C!" Rocky shouted, reliving his worst nightmares all over again. We'd been here before. He looked at Zander in desperation. "You can't stand by and let this happen, Zander. Are you even hearing what she's saying?"

"Perfectly." Zander said in a short clipped tone. Surely, he could see I was protecting them? "Candy has chosen where her loyalty lies."

Relief flooded through me. Zander understood. He knew why I had to do this. He knew I'd chosen where my loyalty lies. With him. With the Sevens.

It had been inevitable that Hiram would find me. He was an obsessive collector of people, and I was his prized possession. It didn't matter how far I ran, he would never be far away. As long as he lived, danger would stalk me. With me gone and the Briarly empire floundering, maybe the Sevens would be safe? Maybe they could even take down Zander's father for good like they'd always wanted. Zander must know it was the only way.

During my time with the Sevens, they'd taught me how to trust again. They'd seen past my bullshit to the real me. I'd let them into my life, my body... and my heart. They'd shown me how it felt to be part of something. How life wasn't for living alone. The Sevens gave me a fucking family, and now? I had to prove my loyalty to them, even if it meant having to lose them forever...

When Crystal died, I vowed never to let another innocent life be lost because of me. Returning to Blackthorne Towers would be hell, but it would be easier to live with than the knowledge everyone I'd ever cared about had, or would, die at Hiram's hands. The only solace I had was knowing my departure would have a lasting impact — at least the kids at Bayside Heights could keep their homes, and I'd be wiping the smug smirk from Giles's face. I may be signing myself up for a life filled with hatred and ruin, but those kids didn't need to have the same fate. Maybe there was still hope for them...

"Done," Hiram said, stroking my cheek. Zander's gray eyes blackened like the sky before a storm. I'm not sure what angered him more: Hiram agreeing to my deal or him touching me. "Consider it a homecoming gift."

"But we had a deal," Giles burst out like a petulant child whose toys had been taken away as Bryce pursed his lips, seething under the surface. "You can't back out of it now!"

"Actually..." Zander stepped forward and held out his hand. A slow smile spread over his face. The smile of a twisted psychopath who'd murder a whole family while they slept. "*We* had a deal."

Hiram shook it. "It's been a pleasure doing business with you."

Wait, what?

I blinked, making sure I wasn't imagining Hiram and Zander shaking hands and conversing like old friends who'd won a game of fucking base-ball. I pinched my arm to wake myself from whatever nightmare I'd fallen into, but the image didn't go away.

The walls closed in around me, suffocating me in my disbelief. I wanted to be sick. I wanted to scream. I wanted to stand up and claw Zander's eyes out... but I couldn't move. Everything I thought I knew came crashing down around me.

"You did this?" Rocky's voice shook in horror as he began to compre-hend what was happening, turning to his boss in disbelief. "Zander?"

Zander arriving unannounced was no fucking accident. He'd known where I was going all along. He'd planned this. Hiram had told him.

"I make the rules, Red," Zander snarled, then addressed Bryce. "You see, father. I am the one who controls the Sevens, and the money Hiram promised you? It's all mine. It always was."

"But... the development..." Giles mumbled, his mouth opening and closing in disbelief.

"The development was never going to happen," Zander sneered, then laughed. Goosebumps spread over my arms. How hadn't I seen it before? I knew he was ruthless, but I'd thought he had another side to him. A caring side. Was everything a lie? "Hiram and I came to an understanding. The development was just a little fun on my part. Hiram agreed to play along. I wanted to get your hopes up, then crush them. Think of it as a warm-up for what I'm going to do to the rest of your dying empire. Your hold on Port Valentine will be over."

Bryce's lip curled as he wrestled with what to say next. He hadn't seen this coming. Zander smiled like all of his birthdays had come at once. Who was this person? Where was the guy who'd talked to me about his mom? Where was the guy who said I was unlike any girl he'd ever met? Where was the man who said they'd do anything to protect me?

All these months, he'd been busy brainwashing me. Making me think I was safe... making me think *he* could be trusted. When, all along, he'd been plotting how to make the most out of me. All he'd ever wanted was to make his father pay. I was nothing more than a vessel for his fucking revenge.

I'd thought being a Seven meant something. Why did he keep me around for so long? Did he enjoy fucking me while knowing what he was planning? Did knowing he was going to ruin my life make him hard, while I cried out his name, and thought I'd finally found someone worth fighting for? I used to think Hiram was the worst person to walk the earth, but Zander had proved me wrong.

"You're a fucking traitor!" I screamed, finding my voice again. I leaped out of the chair, but Hiram wrapped his arms around me, holding me tightly until I couldn't move. "What happened to loyalty being everything?"

"Some opportunities are too good to miss," Zander replied with an impassive shrug. "We all know who you are. Don't pretend you wouldn't have done the same."

"Never," I shrieked, battling with Hiram to be free of his grasp, but not going anywhere.

Zander looked at me in disgust. I recognized his expression. It's how he used to regard Bella and other women he'd grown tired of. Was that all I was to him? A hole to fuck until the time was right?

"Oh, Kitten..." Hiram purred in my ear. "Don't tell me you didn't suspect something like this happening? Did you really think he cared about you? I tried to warn you."

How didn't I see this coming? Zander broke my guard down. He'd pushed past all my resistance until I let him in. The blindfold trust exercise was probably another way for him to throw me off the scent of what was about to happen. I'd been a naïve fucking idiot to have believed anything he said. I'd thought Rocky's betrayal was bad when I was a teenager, but this? It was worse. So much worse. At least Rocky felt he had no choice. He'd handed me over to Hiram because he thought he was saving my life, but Zander? He knew exactly what he was doing.

"No hard feelings, Kitten?" Zander said, having the fucking nerve to smile.

I roared as fury erupted from me in a burst. I'd chosen to go with Hiram to save their lives, but now? All I wanted was to wring Zander's inked neck. He'd used me. Entrapped me. Lied to me. Violated my trust. His hatred for screwing over his father had come at the expense of subjecting me to a life of hell, but he wanted no hard fucking feelings?

"Come on, Kitty. You were happy to make a deal yourself, remember? What difference does it make?" Hiram said, stroking my arm. "I'll still honor your proposal and make sure a development on Bayside Heights never happens if it makes you feel better."

"That was before I knew you had no intention of ever investing in Bayside Heights," I shrieked. My stare burned into Zander, as I pointed my finger, wishing I was close enough to blind him. "*You* were playing me this whole time. You were playing all of us. Me, Bryce, and Giles... like you always do."

"My poor Kitty," Hiram whispered. "It looks like you got out of practice during our time apart."

"This isn't happening. You're not taking her, Hiram. Not again," Rocky snarled. He'd been watching our confrontation in stunned silence, but he'd heard enough. He pulled a gun from his waistband and aimed it at Hiram's head. Without hesitation, he squeezed the trigger. Then, nothing... a small click. This isn't what he'd expected to happen. His brow furrowed as he checked the chamber, then realization dawned on him. Rocky turned on Zander, his face contorted in vicious fury. "You took out the fucking bullets?"

You couldn't fake a reaction like Rocky's. He hadn't known what Zander was planning, but what about the others? West? Vixen? I'd like to think Zander had been working alone, but how could I be sure?

"Let her go, Red," Zander commanded. "I'm your boss. You do as I say."

"No!" Rocky yelled. "Candy's not going anywhere. She belongs here. With us... with *me*."

"I'm getting rather tired of you getting in my way," Hiram drawled, clicking his tongue in impatience. "If I remember correctly, you were happy to give her to me before."

Hiram knew how to get into people's heads. He could find your most shameful secret and force you to confront your demons. Rocky's jaw clenched. He knew what mistakes he'd made and would stop at nothing to make sure they didn't happen again. He'd tried to kill Hiram, but it wasn't enough... Zander had made sure of that.

"We're better off without her, Red." Zander's words tore through me like a knife, cutting straight down into my core and ripping me in two. "She was never a Seven."

"If you want to take her, you'll have to kill me first," Rocky growled, his eyes met mine. I saw the boy I used to love. The person who would do anything to protect me. "I'm not leaving you, C. I *fucking* love you."

His words made my heart sing, but they were also fucking stupid. Without bullets, his gun was about as useful as a water pistol. How did he expect this to end?

Hiram pulled a gun out of his jacket and sighed, pointing the barrel straight at Rocky. "If that's the way it has to be..."

Whatever lie I had been living in Lapland, at least some of it had been real. Rocky hadn't turned against me, and that was enough for me to hold onto... which is why I had to do this.

Before Hiram could squeeze the trigger, I snatched the gun from him. I took the cool metal into my hands and fired once. The surprise on Rocky's face made my heart ache, but it was the only way. The only way he'd let me go. I had to do it. He left me with no choice.

The bullet flew through the air in slow motion. It headed straight for Rocky's shoulder as I'd intended, but he was moving...

Shit, he was fucking moving!

I hadn't meant to... I didn't mean...

My body shook from the release as Rocky's wide eyes met mine for a split second. They were filled with shock, hurt... betrayal. It's a look that would be burned into my memory forever. He staggered on his feet, looking down at his chest in confusion, then dropped to the concrete.

"No!" Zander yelled, diving to his knees and ripping off his jacket to stem the bleeding as Hiram hooted with laughter.

The Briarlys stayed frozen in place and watched the scene unfold. Both of them were too terrified to move. Neither of them wanted to be on the receiving end of another of my bullets.

"Welcome back, Kitty," Hiram said, putting his hand firmly on my arm to steer me away. I could hear the smile in his voice. "Let's go home."

I allowed Hiram to guide me. I couldn't think rationally. A jumble of thoughts raced through my head, and my ears were still ringing from the bang of the gunshot. A shot I'd fired to save the only man who'd ever loved me, but that had torn through his chest and broken his heart in the process.

"Before we go, why don't we leave a parting gift behind?" Hiram suggested. He brutally yanked the ruby ring off of my finger, almost breaking it, to sever my connection to the Sevens. "You won't be needing this anymore."

The sparkling jewel hit the floor and was instantly lost in the red pool spilling from under Rocky's body.

Zander's hands were covered… the blood… there was so much of it…

I'd shot Rocky to save his life, but as his blood continued to flow, I realized I may have killed him.

BOOK THREE

What's the point of playing nice when you're born to be bad?

Ash is all that remains of my hopes to leave my old life behind. Bittersweet memories and betrayal have ignited a vicious fury that burns through my veins like poison.

Vengeance consumes my every moment, and I won't stop. Not until I'm holding a bleeding heart in my fist and staring at a chest emptier than my own.

I'm ready to unleash the darkness. Even if it destroys me and everyone I've ever cared about.

Maybe it's time I embraced my destiny...

"You know I have to do this, Kitten." Hiram's voice came from above. "It's the only way."

Chains locked my wrists and ankles in place. They were pointless. We both knew I wouldn't resist. No, the restraints weren't *just* about physically immobilizing me. Hiram needed to satisfy his sick fucking desire to control another human being. To control *me*.

"I understand," I mumbled, avoiding looking in his direction and keeping my gaze fixed on the gray, blood-flecked ceiling. I'd survived five years in Blackthorne Towers with Hiram before. Acceptance and obedience were easier.

Goosebumps raced over my skin from the chill of the metal table beneath me. The temperature didn't bother me. My mind was already far away from my body, thinking about the life I left behind… and the betrayal I couldn't stop reliving.

Hiram grabbed my chin with a blood-stained butcher glove and jerked my head upward to face the boning knife. He rotated it, making the shiny edge glint off the glaring white light. I swallowed hard, causing a wide grin to spread over Hiram's face.

"There's no need to be afraid," he purred, wrongly interpreting my reaction as fear. "I'll make it quick."

Bullshit. When Hiram took victims to his workshop in the depths of Blackthorne Towers, he made the experience last. This was his dungeon playroom, and I was his favorite toy.

Hiram's blade didn't scare me, though. Neither did what he was about to do with it. What made me shiver was having the blood of his victims smeared over my face. His hands had brought hundreds of lives to an end. Some of them deserved to die, but others begged for mercy because their only error was being in the wrong place at the wrong time. When Hiram decided you were going to die, there was nothing you could do to stop it.

Hiram forced my head to the right, brutally slamming my cheek against the table with a thud to pin me in place. He swept my hair off my neck and danced the blade over my skin, leaving a stinging trail behind.

I didn't make a sound. I welcomed it. Hell, I *wanted* it! Pain is exactly what I deserved. Hiram may have thought he was delivering a punishment, but he was doing me a favor. I deserved to be punished for my stupidity.

"Ready or not," Hiram said.

I needed to wipe my time in Port Valentine from existence. I wanted it gone. The memories. The Sevens. They were not part of me. Not anymore.

"Do it," I spat.

Hiram's fingers gripped my throat, almost cutting off my airway. My eyes watered as he made the first slice. He scraped the skin from my body easier than spreading butter on a piece of toast. The sound of flesh splitting filled my ears as warm liquid slid down my neck. Pain was better than remembering.

Fuzzy dots obscured my vision as I fought for breath. My lungs burned for oxygen, and heavy darkness hovered close by, begging to swallow me whole. I hoped it would.

Just as I started losing consciousness, Hiram released his hold. I returned to my body and the nightmare I hoped I'd wake up from. *Fuck.*

"You were always mine," Hiram said. He ran the flat of the knife over his tongue, savoring the taste of my blood. In his other hand, he held up the patch of skin like a trophy. It was the size of a postage stamp with an inked outline of the number seven. "Now you're mine again."

Why couldn't erasing the Sevens from my life be as simple as getting a tattoo removed? Removing my mark of loyalty didn't strip away the memories. Memories I couldn't trust. How much of my time with the Sevens had been real? Was everything a lie?

The hole in my neck didn't come close to the crippling ache in my chest. Watching Zander shake hands with Hiram ruined me, but shooting Rocky desecrated my fucking soul. I may have pulled the trigger, but Zander was equally to blame. He removed the bullets from Rocky's gun, and his meticulous plans hadn't taken into account how far Rocky was willing to go to protect me.

Had Vixen or West played a part in Zander's scheming? Either way, it didn't matter. I'd broken a Seven rule by shooting Rocky. None of them would ever forgive me. With my track record, they'd never accept that I hadn't meant to hurt him — well, not *really* hurt him. A bullet to the shoulder should have subdued him. Why did he have to move in the final second? He could be lying in a morgue now, and it was all my fault.

"Why don't we do something special with this?" Hiram suggested, examining the skin with satisfaction. He wasn't finished yet. "What do you think, Kitten? It'll make a perfect gift."

He carried it to his workbench on the opposite side of the room, leaving my wound open as blood soaked into my hair. He positioned his tools in the perfect position for me to watch. How considerate.

Hiram hummed as he carefully placed my skin on a piece of paper and pulled out a needle and thread to carefully sew it down like a fucking cross stitch. The Sevens were violent killers, but they had nothing on Hiram's depravity. As well as being a psychopathic serial murderer, he was a creative genius.

"How does it look?" Hiram prompted, holding up his work like we were kindergarteners playing show and tell. I didn't answer so he moved it closer, waving it inches from my face. "Well?"

"Perfect," I said through gritted teeth.

"Everyone will know you're mine again."

My stomach churned as he stashed his art inside an envelope, licking it shut and smearing remnants of my blood over the seal. He turned the envelope around to show the name of the addressee: *Zander Briarly*.

Seeing his name in ink made my blood boil. I bet the bastard would frame Hiram's gift and hang it on his office wall like a proud parent displaying their kids' drawings on the fridge. Whenever anyone asked about it, Zander would gloat about how he tricked the Kitten into his bed and fooled her into trusting him. Rocky warned me Zander was a monster, but I didn't listen. I *hated* him. More than Hiram. More than anyone else in the world. More than I hated Rocky all those years ago.

"Why send it?" I asked, trying to keep my voice steady. The blood loss was making me light-headed, but I couldn't pass out on Hiram's watch. If I did, I risked waking up without an ear. "I'm home now, aren't I?"

"Call it a reminder," Hiram said; his face darkened as a storm rolled over his features. "Now that I have what I want, I can't allow the past to go unpunished."

He wasn't talking about me. Hiram may have made a deal with Zander for my safe return, but he wouldn't forget how I'd sworn allegiance to someone else.

One way or another, he would make sure Zander Briarly was going to fucking pay. We both would.

CHAPTER

One

TWO MONTHS LATER...

"You don't seem like yourself today, Kitten," Hiram remarked, pursing his lips in disapproval from his high-backed chair that resembled a throne.

What did he expect me to say? I was cramping like a bitch and soaking through jumbo tampons every few hours during a monster period. Cut a girl a fucking break. Instead, I replied, "I'm fine."

We were in the sitting room of his penthouse suite in Blackthorne Towers with the Blackbird. Despite its luxurious appearance, none of the furniture was comfortable. No matter how hard I tried to relax on the leather sofa, it twisted my back out of joint. A faux fireplace cast strange shadows across the room, while mounted animal heads on the walls watched me.

"Why don't we talk about the good old days?" the Blackbird suggested from the opposite end of the sofa. He flashed his yellowing teeth in a smile. His dislike for me had amplified since my return, and his beady eyes followed me whenever I moved. The fucker didn't trust me as much as I didn't trust him. "How about one of my favorite stories? The one about how Giovanni Romano's son wanted his father dead?"

I scowled. He and Hiram enjoyed taunting me about my recent defection. After leaving the warehouse in Port Valentine, Hiram took great pleasure in informing me there was no value to the photographs Bryce Briarly found of the guests at the Romano mansion on the night Giovanni died. All my worries about the Romano family coming to kill me, and the Sevens, had been pointless. Despite the rumors, those running the Romano empire didn't have an interest in finding out who killed their ex-leader. After he died, Giovanni Romano's eldest son partnered with Hiram. If I hadn't killed Romano, his children would have.

"You know what else is funny?" I snapped. "Me making you choke on your own fucking cock."

The Blackbird's brows lowered as he leaned back in a sulky silence, and Hiram cackled.

"The threat of violence always cheers her up," Hiram said fondly, making the Blackbird's frown deepen.

Hiram was wrong. Nothing cheered me up anymore. The Blackbird's joke only reminded me of how naive I'd been. While I worried about the Sevens and my past catching up with us, I was blind to what Zander was doing right under my fucking nose.

Transitioning fully back into the Kitten was an ongoing battle. When Candy broke into a thousand pieces, the Kitten rose to the surface to take her place. She'd always been there, waiting to return and rule like a fucking queen. But emotions were hard to seal off completely. As much as I tried to lock them away, they resurged when I least expected them.

"What reports do you have from Port Valentine?" Hiram asked, changing the subject.

He enjoyed keeping up with the latest news. After getting me back, I thought he would want to leave the past behind. Instead, spending more time in the area made him want to expand his reach into the godforsaken town. He saw potential in its lawlessness, which made it harder to forget what happened there, and the people I left behind.

"Red is still in the hospital," the Blackbird said. "My sources say they'll turn off the machines any day now."

"The sooner the better," Hiram said, rubbing his hands together. "Don't you agree, Kitten?"

"Of course," I replied.

It would have been easier if Rocky died in the warehouse that night. Hearing about him clinging to life only prolonged the inevitable. It gave me a tiny shred of hope and stopped me from letting go of the little humanity I had left. Having hope was dangerous. Hope usually came to nothing but disappointment.

Whenever I slept, I relived the moment the gun fired like a torturous dream version of *Groundhog Day*. My time with the Sevens was built on a lie, but *he* thought I was worth saving. Rocky fought for us in those last moments.

"I'm surprised," the Blackbird continued, daring to challenge me and forgetting his place. "You seemed rather fond of the Seven men when I visited you."

"You know nothing," I hissed, pushing away the memories of days spent in Lapland with people I thought I could trust and had started to love.

My chest ached like I'd been sucker-punched as I stopped myself from remembering. I didn't want to think about them. I couldn't. A world I thought was real had been shattered. My focus had to be on the present. Being with Hiram gave me a purpose and status.

'We're better off without her, Red.'

I used to think Hiram was the worst human to walk the earth, but Zander Briarly was pure evil and rotten to the core. He tricked me into trusting him and joining his gang. He infiltrated his way into my life, my bed, and my fucking heart. He played me to get what he always wanted. A fat paycheck from Hiram and revenge on his father.

'She was never a Seven.'

Zander used me like a cheap piece of ass... and I let him. As for the other Sevens, I knew Rocky loved me. He proved it when he was willing to die to stop Hiram from taking me, but what about West? As much as I could hope the big man who made me melt hadn't plotted against me, how could I be sure? I mean, he did install a surveillance system in my old apartment. Maybe he lied and was spying on me for Hiram. How could I ever trust my judgment again when I'd been so fucking wrong?

"Why are you still wearing that necklace, Kitty?" the Blackbird asked, pulling me out of my reverie.

His smart mouth had grown bolder during my months away. He needed a friendly reminder of who the real authority was around here. He may be the guy who skulked around in the shadows to gather intelligence, but he didn't get his hands dirty.

"I'll rip through your weedy spinal cord if you question my loyalty again," I warned, my hands jumping to the pendant Zander gifted me. "And this necklace? Call it an incentive. I'll be burying it with the body of Zander Briarly."

With any luck, I'd choke him with it. Zander messed with the wrong girl.

"Patience," Hiram said, waving his hand. "We do not need to kill him. Not yet. He still has some use to me."

Maybe Hiram knew as soon as I was done with Zander, he'd be next on my list. What other reasons did I have to live other than taking down everyone who wronged me? The only person who ever truly cared about me was hooked up to life support. There was nothing left to lose.

———

Hiram didn't trust me to be alone for long periods, so I lived in his suite. Even with my own room, there was no privacy. The red blinking camera light in the corner reminded me that he was always watching. Although, after spending time as a teenager locked in the dungeon, I couldn't complain.

Hiram didn't need to worry about me escaping, though. Where the hell would I go? Back to Port Valentine to settle old scores and torch Lapland? Start afresh somewhere new in the knowledge he would be close behind? The bitter irony of history repeating itself was the universe's way of saying this is where I was supposed to be.

Being back in Blackthorne Towers also afforded me the luxury of having eyes on my enemies. The Blackbird's regular updates about the Sevens kept me in the loop about what they were doing. It gave me time to form a plan without worrying about making rent or looking out for someone trying to hunt me down.

My new cell rang, vibrating wildly on my bedside table. The only person who knew the number was Hiram. He'd installed tracking software to monitor every tap of my fingers. I felt like a kid whose Catholic parents were desperately trying to stop their horny teen from accessing porn.

I answered after two rings, as per his orders. "Hiram?"

He may not trust me to go outside yet, but he liked to keep me busy. Every day, he'd call to summon me to his workshop. He never rang at the same time. His calls were a test and he was trying to catch me out, but I hadn't missed one yet.

"Did you dress as I told you?" he demanded, referencing the note he'd slid under my bedroom door before he left.

"Of course," I replied. "Ready for a special occasion."

I wore a green body-con dress that hugged my curves and made me feel like a sexy Tinker Bell. My hair was blow-dried into tousled waves and paired with a silver smokey eye and a pink, glossy lip. Understated, but sexy.

"Perfect," he purred. I could almost hear the twisted smile spreading over his face in his tone. "The code today is your birth year."

"I'm on my way," I said, hanging up.

Going to Hiram's workshop was the worst part of my new routine. My return from Port Valentine had reignited his enthusiasm for my so-called 'education'. He'd taken my leaving as a personal insult and relished every opportunity to test my loyalty, giving me the scars to prove it.

My first lesson had been on obedience. It involved letting him burn me without moving or making a sound. In another, he forced me to use a blunt pen knife to cut a dismembered leg into fifteen pieces — the damn thing took hours, and my hands were blistered after sawing through the bones. Hiram believed all of our practice was preparing me to be his protégé, but it only gave me more reasons to hate him.

"Let's get this over with…" I mumbled to myself as I left the penthouse to join him in the darkness below.

A guard, already waiting, escorted me to the elevator where another was ready to take over. Walking unattended was not an option.

He bowed his head to greet me. "Good evening, Kitten."

The Blackbird may have gotten more brazen, but at least some of Hiram's employees still showed me respect.

When I lived in the Towers as a teenager, it felt strange for grown men to treat me like royalty. Naively, I thought they must have felt sorry for me after what I endured at my Keeper's hands. It wasn't until a few years later that I learned the real reason why… they feared me, and the person they knew I'd become.

I shot the guard a small smile in reply. He shuddered in response. Maybe I truly was the heartless monster I saw every time I looked in the mirror. A few months ago, my heart softened for the first time in years. Now, it was as hard as fucking nails. Either that or I no longer had one.

After riding the elevator down the floors, I arrived in the dungeon. I tried to ignore the rattle of chains and groans coming from the hunched figures in the cells as I continued along the corridor to a locked door. I punched in my birth year and it chirped in confirmation. Hiram's workshop was only accessible through his fingerprint or a code that changed every few hours, which only he knew. Most people who saw inside never made it out again.

Unlike usual, there were no cries for help when the door creaked open. Hiram stood alone amongst his tools and grinned as I entered. What was he planning? After asking me to dress up, I assumed we'd have company.

"I've got a surprise for you," Hiram said. He gestured toward a red box carefully placed on his operating table and tied with a silky bow. "Look inside."

I took a few steps closer, gritting my teeth and closing off my nostrils to prepare for the worst. Limbs, rats, worms, spiders... I wouldn't put anything past him. The general rule is, the better dressed the package, the more unpleasant its contents are likely to be.

I lifted the lid and frowned. "What is it?"

I gingerly prodded the white fabric folded in the box. So far, no movement. A lump formed in my throat as I pulled the heavy garment out, and my mouth fell open.

It couldn't be… could it?

My heart plummeted to the pit of my stomach.

"You seemed so keen to get married a few months ago," Hiram said, confirming my worst suspicions. Months ago, Hiram visited me in Port Valentine and confronted me in the Smoker. I'd introduced him to West as my fiancé. The bastard wasn't about to let it go. "I wanted to arrange it myself."

"Wh-what?" I stammered. My stomach churned in dread as the dress slipped from my fingers onto the concrete floor.

Hiram tutted, bending down quickly to pick it up. "We don't want it getting covered in blood now, do we?"

He held it up to display the dress in all its glory with a smug smirk. A severed head would have been a more welcome sight than *this.*

"Do you like it?" he asked. "It's not like you to be speechless."

It's a miracle I was still standing. He'd been waiting for the opportune moment to drop this bombshell and took great pleasure in watching my soul implode.

"I thought you'd be happy." Hiram frowned. "This is a treat for all of your good behavior."

"Playing dress-up?" I asked, finding my voice again and praying this was a twisted joke.

"Oh no, better than that." Hiram's eyes twinkled with glee, relishing pulling the strings like the world was his fucking puppet show. "The real thing. Think of it as an arranged marriage."

"Who?" I croaked.

"I picked him out myself," Hiram said. He neatly folded the wedding dress and put it back in the box. "It'll be the perfect match."

This was the worst idea he'd ever had. I knew the type of people Hiram rubbed shoulders with. Any potential suitors were not likely to resemble a hot guy from *The Bachelor.* He would want someone compliant. Someone who wouldn't dare to question his authority. A person who could follow orders and have their tongue so far up his ass that they'd be licking his intestines.

"There must be another way," I said, desperately trying to appeal to any humanity he had left. "Give me a new target to kill, a bank to rob... anything else!"

"Don't be ungrateful, Kitten," he snarled as his face contorted in pure fury. His pulsing temple was a sure sign I tested his patience. "You didn't think things could go back to how they were before, did you?"

"But I came home. I agreed to."

His hand struck me hard across the face, sending me staggering backward.

"You left," Hiram hissed. "Things change."

"Please," I whispered, clutching my stinging cheek. "Can't we go back to how things were before?"

Hiram advanced, drawing himself up to full height. I winced, expecting him to strike me again. Instead, he grabbed my chin and forced me to stare into his black, soulless pupils.

"Never beg me for anything again," Hiram warned, making my skin prickle. "You're going to do as I say. You're going to put your new white dress on or I'll order the guards to do it for you."

Was all of this another way for him to psychologically torture me? My engagement to West may not have been real, but Hiram wanted to ruin all my happy memories.

"Fine," I relented, shaking slightly.

Hiram turned his back for me to change.

I unzipped my green dress and let it fall to the floor.

I would not say 'yes' to this fucking dress.

The gown was made from a thick fabric which made it hard to move. The bodice was adorned with sparkling sequins and my cleavage spilled over the top. To some, it would look like a fairytale gown, but to me? I felt fucking ridiculous. How would anyone take me seriously in a puffy skirt that could house a small army underneath? It was also heavy. Dragging it down the aisle would be like pulling a tractor tire. Maybe that was the point? It'd make it harder to be a runaway bride...

"Well?" Hiram clicked his tongue impatiently, his back still turned. "Is it on?"

"Yes..." My voice trailed off as he spun around.

It was a princess dress, but it made me feel like a royal prisoner.

"Don't ever think about running," Hiram warned, stepping close like he could read my thoughts. He pulled a knife from his sleeve and held it to my throat. The cool blade teased my artery. "Remember what happened last time you disobeyed my orders? People die. What was her name? Crystal?"

I flinched, then mentally kicked myself for showing him he'd bothered me. It only played into his hands.

Hiram laughed. It echoed around the cold concrete walls. "Don't tell me you're still mad about that whore?"

My friendship with Crystal made my last stay in Blackthorne Towers bearable. Hiram bought her to 'service' his men and, over time, we struck up an unlikely bond. She dreamt of becoming a make-up artist. After helping me get ready for my work as the Kitten, I persuaded Hiram to promote her as my stylist. I wanted to do her a favor, but, if I hadn't, she might still be alive today...

I wasn't the only person who cared about Crystal. While working for

Hiram, Crystal met Q. They fell madly in love, and Q had the tech skills to make them both disappear. When they made plans to run away together, we were all stupid enough to believe happily ever afters might be possible...

Before Crystal and Q were due to leave, we snuck to a tattoo parlor to get ink to commemorate our friendship. She got a candy cane. I got a small diamond. We were careful, but it didn't stop Hiram from finding out. The night Q and Crystal planned to skip town turned from a fairytale to a bloody disaster with a single bullet. A hit Hiram ordered. Our friendship ended Crystal's life and changed mine forever.

You need to stay focused on the present, Candy. My survival instincts kicked in. Hiram arranging my marriage would be as good as signing a death warrant. *Stay focused.*

"Did you want me to come home only to marry me off?" I asked. None of this made sense. If he'd wanted me back for so long, why give me away? "What about the work I do? You know I can help you."

"You have no choice, Kitten," Hiram spat, continuing to hold the knife to my throat. "You know better than to disobey."

He flicked the blade downward with a swipe of his wrist and slashed my collarbone. The red petals of my rose tattoos cried bloody tears that Hiram caught with his finger and smeared across my skin before they stained the white fabric. The way things were going, I'd be a corpse bride.

"You're my property," Hiram said. "I do what I want with my property."

I took a deep breath to regain my composure. If I wanted to survive, I needed to treat this like any other job. As long as Hiram and Zander's hearts were still beating, then I had to live, even if it meant marrying whatever chump he'd lined up.

"Do you remember how I used to keep you hidden away from all but my closest associates? They never saw your face. But this time is going to be different," Hiram continued, sliding the flat edge of the blade over my carotid artery. "It's about time everyone in the underworld met the Kitten, don't you think?"

Years ago, it would have been a privilege to be introduced to Hiram's wider circle but now? It was a living nightmare.

"We don't want your dress getting ruined," Hiram said, tucking his blade away. He pulled a silk handkerchief from his pocket and dabbed at the blood dripping down my chest.

I wanted to scream at the top of my lungs, to squeeze his throat so tightly that his evil eyes popped out of their sockets... but I met his stare with a blank glare of indifference.

"Of course not," I agreed.

"My *arrangement* will be in everyone's best interests," Hiram said. Of course, this union would fulfill one of his many political ends. "The groom is happy to have you as a bride."

"I hope he isn't expecting a happy one," I muttered under my breath. "Because I won't be fucking smiling."

"Even better." Hiram said with an approving smirk. "Don't all weddings come with drama?"

Other people watched trash TV to satiate their morbid fascination, but Hiram? People were nothing but his playthings.

He held out his arm for me to take like a proud father. "It's time."

I reluctantly took it. I didn't know what Hiram was planning or why, but someone who had killed my friend over a tattoo would never allow me to marry someone else unless he had a good reason.

"Whatever happens today changes nothing, Kitten," Hiram said, leading us from the workshop. "It doesn't matter who you are married to, you will always be mine."

———

A huddle of Hiram's cronies stood awaiting our arrival in the lobby of Blackthorne Towers. It looked like he'd planned the operation with greater precision than the most expensive wedding planner. Amongst our entourage, the Blackbird caught my eye. His lips curled into a grin as he soaked in my unhappiness like an energy-zapping vampire.

"Shame about the color of the dress," the Blackbird remarked.

I shot him my death stare. "Say something like that again, and I'll show you why they invented the word 'Bridezilla'."

Smothering him in the meringue skirt would be a breeze. Damn, I could even use it to conceal his body, too. The Blackbird edged closer to a muscled guard for protection like the cowardly piece of shit he was.

"Ready, Kitten?" Hiram asked, his fingers digging into my arm.

"As I'll ever be," I murmured through gritted teeth.

When Hiram set his mind to something, there was no way to change it. He steered me out of the front door and straight into a waiting car before I could take a gulp of fresh air. He left nothing to chance. High-security prisoners getting escorted to jail were given more freedom.

Heading to your wedding was a moment people waited for all of their lives. The journey should be filled with nerves, excitement, and racing pulses... instead, the atmosphere was more depressing than a funeral march.

"Is security really necessary?" I asked, looking out of the window to see a fleet of Hiram's men surrounding us on bikes and cars.

"Nothing will spoil my Kitty's special day," Hiram purred.

What did he seriously expect to happen? The twisted son of a bitch was enjoying every moment of my discomfort.

I crossed my arms over my chest and leaned back in a huffed silence as a numb acceptance took over. I may have no choice over who I was marrying, but I'd make damn sure the only thing my *groom* would kiss was my fucking fist.

We didn't speak again until the car came to an abrupt halt. A tiny part of me still hoped this was another of Hiram's sick jokes, but rolling up outside an old church extinguished any suspicions. Seeing the stained glass windows slammed me back to reality like a kick to the gut.

My mouth fell open. "A church?"

"The priest was very grateful for my generous donation," Hiram replied with a casual shrug. If the devil could bribe a man of God, then there was no hope for the rest of us.

Maybe I'd be lucky and the wedding wouldn't go ahead? The guests should ignite in flames the second they step over the threshold. A wedding was meant to be the best day of your life, not a sordid occasion that swapped bullets for bouquets and vows for death threats. Who needs a wedding registry when your guests could give you the best drugs and arms in the state?

Guests filed into the church, and I squinted to get a better view of their faces. I recognized many of them from working with Hiram over the years. Someone needed to blow up the church and purge the fuckers.

"Come on, Kitten," Hiram urged, turning the door handle and stepping out of the car. He turned back to me and extended his hand. "You don't want to keep him waiting."

Grudgingly, I shuffled out. A nearby guard thrust a bouquet of black roses into my hands, then turned to Hiram. He bowed his head as he handed over a matching boutonnière. Every last detail had been meticulously plotted.

Fuck.

This was happening.

This was happening.

I counted to stop myself from spiraling into the pit of emotions rising from my core.

500...

Don't show them your weakness, Candy.

493...

Do what he wants.

486...

After fastening the flower to his jacket, Hiram looked at me with a deep intensity that made me squirm.

"You look beautiful, Kitty," he said, tucking a stray strand of hair behind my ear. His eyes misted over, then, just as fast, his jaw clenched. His voice lowered into a menacing growl, "Don't even think about doing anything stupid."

472...

Suddenly, a conversation I had with Crystal years before came to mind. After a night working at one of Hiram's parties, she'd returned with a black eye and busted lip. During that period, bloodlust ruled my senses. I couldn't understand why she hadn't fought back. Sure, she was petite. But Crystal had grown up on the streets, and the crazy bitch could fight like a wildcat.

"Candy," she'd said after I demanded to know why she didn't defend herself, *"you have to pick your battles. If he thinks he's won, then he won't see it coming next time."*

This is what I had to do now.

Let Hiram win... this time.

Not fighting back didn't make me weak. I tried to channel Crystal's bravery and turn myself into a fucking warrior. It'd make me come back stronger, even if it meant I'd be leaving with a ring on my finger...

"What are we waiting for?" I asked, holding my head high and throwing my shoulders back. "You want me to get married, so let's fucking do this."

We made our way up the church path in silence. Guards circled the perimeter, working under strict instructions to kill any wedding crashers. Was Hiram worried about someone showing up? Would the Sevens have heard about my wedding? Would they even care?

STOP IT, CANDY!

The three Seven men were part of my old life. A life I'd never get back. A life I traded to protect them only to find out it was all a fucking lie. Now, I had to face the unknown and whoever was waiting at the end of the aisle.

The church door wailed as Hiram pushed it open, and we stepped inside. The guests rose from their seats as haunting music filled the vast space.

Do not think of it as an aisle. Think of it as a motherfucking catwalk.

Hiram held my arm and guided me. Even though my dress had its own gravitational pull, I felt naked without any weapons. How was it fair that I was the only unarmed person at my fucking wedding?

The aisle seemed to stretch on forever. Leering guests cheered as I passed, but my eyes were fixed on the figure waiting for me. The groom kept his back turned, not that he needed to worry about bad luck, it was already a fucking guarantee. Besides, his unfashionable powder blue suit was begging for me to tear it to shreds and not in a 'can't wait to rip your clothes off' kinda way. Behind him, a priest stood clutching the Bible and muttering prayers under his breath. Hopefully, one of them was for me ..

The music halted, and my soon-to-be husband turned to face me for the first time. This was the moment Hiram had been waiting for. The moment I fully understood how much he wanted to punish me.

"I believe you two have already met," Hiram said as all the air drained out of my lungs.

Giles Briarly stared back at me wearing his token shit-eating grin because, today, I was about to become his wife.

CHAPTER

Two

"Hello, Kitten," Giles drawled in his annoying British accent. His eyes slid down my body and landed on my chest. "Have you missed me?"

"Like a hole in the head," I hissed, spinning to face Hiram. My eyes burned through him in furious accusation while he remained emotionless and regarded us with cold indifference. "Giles fucking Briarly? You can't be serious."

"Oh, I am," Hiram replied, narrowing his eyes. "Deadly."

It made sense he'd pick a suitor with no backbone, but Giles? Sure, he'd roll over to satisfy Hiram's whims, but only because he didn't have a fucking spine. Why would he choose *him*? There must be better choices.

I last saw Giles and Bryce in the warehouse on the night I left Port Valentine. We left Giles trembling on the floor with no investment and the Briarly empire hurtling towards financial ruin. What had changed since then? What was Hiram's end game?

"Don't tell me you're disappointed?" Giles cocked his head to the side. Disappointed was the understatement of the fucking millennium. Death row would be preferable to spending a lifetime with a sack of shit like him. "We all want the same thing, Kitty."

"You don't look suicidal to me," I snapped, loud enough for our wedding guests to hear. They were watching our every move. It was only fair we gave them a show, right?

Laughter burst from the pews. Giles shifted uncomfortably, loosening his tie as a flush crept up his neck. He wasn't used to mixing with criminals like Hiram's nearest and dearest. His social scene usually involved drinking champagne while schmoozing royalty and politicians.

"Careful, Kitty…" Hiram warned, digging his fingers into my arm and leaning in closer, so no one else could hear what he said next, "or this won't be a wedding, it'll be a funeral."

Would a coffin be so bad? At least shutting the casket would block out the smug face of my soon-to-be husband.

Hiram stood straighter and released his hold on my arm. He kissed my cheek stiffly, making me shiver. He'd never shown me any real affection before, and I couldn't decide whether it was genuine or for the benefit of the audience. Whatever his motive, it put me even more on edge.

"Remember what I said," Hiram said. "Play nice."

This is just another act, Candy.

All you have to do is get into character.

You've played roles before…

Giles winked. "I don't mind it rough."

"Really?" I mocked, grinning, and slowly ran my tongue over my teeth. The watching crowd cheered along in encouragement. They knew the Kitten's reputation for her special methods. "Neither do I."

Giles's Adam's apple bobbed wildly up and down as he turned an unsightly shade of green, clashing with his awful suit. Everyone said you had to kiss a few frogs to find a prince, but they didn't mean it in a literal fucking sense. Hadn't I suffered enough?

"Off with his head," a voice shouted, followed by more threats of violence from people we'd never met before. "Slit… cut… rip…"

"What's wrong, Giles?" I teased, twirling a strand of hair around my finger. "Not the kind of rough you had in mind?"

Despite his lousy macho charade, Giles was out of his depth. Hiram may be forcing me to marry, but I still had power. It was my freaking wedding, and watching Giles squirm would be my present.

The priest's eyes darted nervously between us. His shifting gaze hinted at his growing regret of accepting a generous donation. "Are you ready for the ceremony to begin?"

"I'm ready for it to fucking end," I replied without hesitation.

There were a few whistles and claps from the back of the church. Everyone loved it when the Kitten's claws came out. Hiram's laughter boomed above the rest. He always appreciated it whenever I carried out a job with theatrical flair. Entertaining the crowd would gain me his favor and let me distance myself from reality.

"Look, she's playing hard to get," the Blackbird said above the heckling. "But we all know Kitty has got a soft spot for Briarly men."

"Let's get this over with, shall we?" I snarled, choosing to ignore the Blackbird for fear of giving the frail priest a heart attack at what I wanted to threaten.

The priest nodded, taking a giant inhale to brace himself.

Giles held out his sweaty palm. I frowned, looking at it in confusion. What did he expect me to do with *that*? I scowled and slapped him away with a vicious swipe of my bouquet.

Giles yelped, pulling it back quickly and cradling his scratched fingers like a newborn. "Ouch."

I rolled my eyes. What a crybaby. Hiram may not have allowed me to carry sharp weapons, but I could make use of anything at my disposal. Roses may look pretty, but those thorny fuckers could slice you open.

"What's wrong?" I asked, shooting him my best look of innocent surprise. "Want me to kiss it better?"

A bead of sweat dripped down Giles's forehead as his blush deepened. If he thought marrying me would be the ultimate 'fuck you' to his cousin, then he underestimated what he was getting into. Back in Port Valentine, Giles knew me as Candy, but here? I was the Kitten. Hiram's merciless protégé. I made grown men fall to their knees and weep.

"Let's start," the priest stammered, his hands gripping tighter onto the Bible in his grasp. Puh-lease. It was too late to pray to God for protection. He should have thought harder before he agreed to host a wedding for Hiram.

The priest talked fast, stumbling over every other word. I zoned out as he rambled on. Blah-fucking-blah. What did it matter, anyway? None of this was real. His words *meant* nothing.

Growing up, I was never the type of girl to fantasize about my dream wedding or practice my signature using the surname of my crush in high school. But I believed in marrying for love, and my nuptials couldn't be further from that. I was stuck with a sleazy ginger asshole who was trying not to crap his pants in a church filled with bloodthirsty delinquents — definitely not scrapbook material.

The priest cleared his throat as we reached the pivotal part of the ceremony. "It's time for your vows."

Vows? More like empty fucking promises. When I joined the Sevens, Zander promised we would be bound for life. Vows were made to be broken.

"Do you have the rings?" the priest asked.

Giles pulled simple silver bands from his pockets, coating them in sweat and handing them over. Gross.

"Erm… Kitten…" The priest looked at Hiram, who nodded in approval. Using my pet name was an unorthodox request, but Hiram would have provided him with strict instructions to follow. Orders the priest was too terrified to break, even if it meant facing the wrath of God. The priest handed me a ring as Giles held out a quivering hand. "Do you take Giles Edward Briarly to be your husband?"

I took a deep breath. I didn't need to turn around to know Hiram's eyes burned into my back.

"Yes," I said, my voice dripping with bitter resentment as the words rolled off my tongue. I pushed the ring onto Giles's finger with enough force to try and deglove him. "I do."

"Giles." The priest addressed him. "Do you take… the Kitten… to be your wife?"

"I-I-I do," Giles stammered.

Before he got the chance, I snatched the ring from him and put it on myself. A simple silver band. Lifeless. Impersonal. Un-fucking-wanted. Just like our marriage. Although, it wasn't all bad…

Seeing Giles waiting at the end of the aisle filled me with sickening fury and dread, but our so-called 'union' could be used to my advantage. Hiram's twisted plan was my ticket to a confrontation with Zander. A meeting he would never get out of alive. Giles and Zander were cousins, but their bitter rivalry had gone on for years. Zander wouldn't miss an opportunity to brag to his cousin about how he'd been the first to fuck his new wife.

My cheeks heated at the memory of Zander's touch. Zander had betrayed and used me, but my body couldn't seem to forget how good he made me feel. Not just Zander, but West and Rocky, too. How was it fair that I couldn't shake the memories, no matter how hard I tried? And why, in the middle of my fucking wedding, did my mind stray to how incredible it was to have all three Seven men filling me at once? Hiram was a master at brainwashing his subjects, but Zander was better. Mind-blowing orgasms blinded me to his deception… and I hated myself for how much I enjoyed it.

The priest's voice brought me back to the present moment.

"I now declare you husband and wife," the priest declared. "You may kiss the bride."

Giles lurched forwards quicker than a vulture descending on its prey. As soon as his sticky upper lip grazed mine, I sunk my teeth into him as hard as I could. What better way to start wedded bliss, right?

"Fuck!" Giles staggered back. "What was that for?"

"Let me give you some advice, *husband*," I snarled, wiping my mouth and smearing lipstick across the back of my hand. "If you ever try to touch me again, I will bite your tiny cock right off, chew it up, then run it over with a fucking truck. Got that?"

The crowd applauded. Hiram, still clapping, rose from his seat. While Giles tried to stem the bleeding with his sleeve, I turned my back on him and marched out of the church. Hiram followed close behind like my fucking shadow.

"You did well, Kitten," Hiram said, catching up with me.

"I did what you asked," I snapped. "What next?"

Hiram nodded his head towards a car screeching to a halt outside the gates. "We celebrate."

I paced through the church grounds to get to our ride, not giving a shit that the hem of my dress was dragging through the dirt.

"Hey," a breathy voice called after us. I didn't stop. "Wait up."

"This car is for the Kitten and me." Hiram stopped and held up his hand to stop Giles from following. "You can drive with… one of our guests."

Hiram's driver opened the car door and, as I turned, I caught a glimpse of Giles over my shoulder. His face was whiter than my fucking dress. Hadn't he learned his lesson after Hiram screwed him out of the Bayside Heights development?

Hiram slid into the seat next to me. Neither of us said a word as the car pulled away. Leaving Giles whimpering at the mercy of Hiram's army of crooks was the highlight of my day so far. The bastard only had himself to blame.

"That wasn't too painful now, was it?" Hiram asked.

"It beats having a tattoo cut out," I replied sarcastically.

Hiram's expression darkened, his brows lowering. "Everything I do is for your own good, Kitty. This is another one of my lessons."

"I prefer the ones that involve acid baths," I muttered.

"Think of it as a learning opportunity," Hiram said, drumming his fingers against his knee. "You know I want to expand my operations to Port Valentine. It has real potential."

"Potential?" I crossed my arms. "Couldn't you have expanded without forcing a ring on my finger?"

This wasn't about money. Hiram had enough cash to buy a private island and spend the rest of his days sipping Piña Coladas on a beautiful beach. Expanding into Port Valentine was about power. He couldn't let the Sevens get away with taking me from him. It infuriated him to know I'd slipped from his control into their influence. Getting me back wasn't enough. He needed to destroy them.

"Of course, I *could* have," Hiram said with a shrug, then smiled. "But where is the fun in that? I need you on the inside, and Giles has connections."

Connections? Pfft. Giles may know the relics in Port Valentine, but the old Briarly empire was crumbling down around him and Bryce. After receiving a payment from Hiram for my safe return, Zander would be able to expand and take them down.

"If you want to expand your operations to Port Valentine, then Giles isn't the partner you want," I said. The guy turned into a nervous wreck whenever he faced real danger. "He'll be of no use to you. He's a fucking liability."

Bryce Briarly may have primed Giles to take over the Briarly business, but he wasn't cut out for the job. He knew nothing about what it took to earn your place or the hunger in your belly from having to fight your way to the top.

"I don't want a partner." Hiram chuckled to himself. "Can't you see, Kitty? Giles is perfect because he's disposable."

"So you've lied to him," I summarized. "What does he think he's getting out of your 'arrangement'?"

"Lied? No, I'm only giving him what I promised," Hiram said, then counted the points on his fingers. "Money... resource... *revenge.*"

"What makes you think Giles believes you after what happened last time?" I raised my eyebrows. "Don't you think he'll see it coming if you plan to double-cross him?"

"The Briarlys and I have the same goals," Hiram said. "Giles and your new uncle-in-law see the benefits of working together. What happened with the Sevens? It's water under the bridge. They see the value I can bring and what I can do for them... for now, at least."

Hiram's promises wouldn't last. When the Briarlys least expected it, Hiram would tear them down.

I rolled my eyes. "And here I was thinking I'd be the Briarly heir."

"Oh, but you will," Hiram said, his eyes lighting up. "If something happened to Bryce and Giles, a wife would be a natural successor. We use them to build an empire, then take it for ourselves."

Well, shit...

There were many things I could criticize about Hiram, but his twisted logic wasn't one of them. If Giles and Bryce weren't such assholes, I might even feel sorry for them.

"As I said, today changes nothing," Hiram said. "You will always be mine. Wherever you go. Whoever you marry. You belong to me."

A piece of paper in the eyes of the law was meaningless, but Hiram's word was as real as a chain tied around your ankle. He was ready to drag you underwater until you hit the bottom of the fucking ocean and drowned.

———

Our wedding party was taking place in a private club that had hosted many of Hiram's intimate gatherings in the past. The place was a cross between a whore house and a circus, where drugs were passed around like candy. By the time we showed up, extra guests had arrived. Those who weren't hell-bent on letting loose like it was 3am instead of 3pm were sitting in dark corners scheming far worse plans.

"What do you think, Kitty?" Hiram asked as we got out of the car and headed into the flashing lights. "Does it remind you of your early days?"

Yeah, days where I'd spend my evenings lurking around in bars to seduce a target, then rob or kill him… or both. After so long locked in the confines of Blackthorne Towers, I relished the outings and embraced the responsibility. I knew about the terrible things my marks had done, and it gave me great pleasure to obliterate them from existence.

As we entered the club, an older man in a perfectly tailored navy suit swanned over to greet us. He shook Hiram's hand and exchanged greetings, but I didn't look in his direction.

"Kitty, what a long time it's been," Bryce Briarly said, finally turning to me. From the smug smirk on his face, I sensed he was proud of his nephew for finally earning them an invitation to a criminal A-list event. "Forgive me for missing the ceremony. I couldn't make it in time."

I narrowed my eyes. "You weren't missed."

Bryce may have gotten screwed over by his son in his attempt to make a deal with Hiram, but I hadn't forgotten how he'd been the one to lure me to that warehouse and planned to use me to make a profit. Being a monster runs in the family.

"How about we let bygones be bygones?" Bryce suggested. "After all, you're part of the family now."

"I will never be part of your family," I spat.

The Briarly bloodline was nothing but pure poison.

"Having a reunion, are we?" Giles swaggered over to join us, puffing his chest out like a peacock. Judging by his saucer-like pupils, it was no mystery as to why he'd gotten over his bout of stage fright at the church. He may be embracing the attention, but he was too stupid to realize he was the butt of everyone's jokes.

I raised an eyebrow. "You couldn't wait to start on the coke, huh?"

Giles pulled a large bag of white powder out of his pocket and waved it around like a toy airplane. "It was a wedding gift."

"Rule number one." Hiram snatched the drugs out of his hand. On the streets, shit that pure could be cut to make more than the cost of the wedding. "Don't snort the merchandise."

Giles's cheeks reddened in anger, but Bryce's stern look and quick head shake stopped him from objecting. He knew better than his nephew.

"See?" I said pointedly to Hiram. "*This* is what happens when you bring in amateurs."

Before anyone could say more, the girlfriend of the State's biggest hallucinogenic dealer staggered across to congratulate us. She wore heels that looked like tiny gnomes and stroked my meringue skirt like it was a fluffy cat.

"Your dress is amazing," she admired. "It's so soft. Look at all the pretty patterns. It looks like a rainbow."

I tugged my dress out of her grasp. She didn't notice and continued to stroke the air. Wouldn't it be nice to see the world through her technicolor lens?

"I'm gonna step outside," I muttered, needing to get away from the bustle.

"But you've only just arrived," Bryce said, then gestured to Giles. "Don't you want to celebrate with your new husband?"

"*Celebrate*?" I snorted. "I've already spent enough time with the Briarlys to last a fucking lifetime."

"Kitten was taken by surprise today," Hiram cut in to smooth over the situation. "Give her time."

I shouldered past them to get to the exit.

"Don't wander too far," Hiram called after me.

As if I could. There was no way to escape when the entire block was crawling with his best guards. Plus, it was pretty hard to be inconspicuous when you resembled a tiered cake.

I continued onwards, pushing against the flow of people rushing into the venue and meeting their good wishes with a scowl. I'd gotten married as Hiram asked. I had zero intention of being the life and soul of the fucking party, too.

"Kitten!" A tall, dark, handsome man blocked my path. He was in his mid-thirties and wore a black suit with a crisp white shirt that looked expensive, despite him undoing the top two buttons to look casual. He outstretched his arms in greeting, taking up the narrow corridor leading outside and giving me no choice but to stop. "I'm glad we get to meet at last."

I'd never met him before, but he didn't need to introduce himself. The resemblance to his father was apparent. His father who I killed.

"Juliano Romano, but you can me Jules," the man said. He grinned to reveal sparkling white teeth and held out his hand for me to shake like we were attending a business meeting. "It's a pleasure."

My immediate reaction was to knee him in the balls. Running into a member of the Romano family was a moment I'd been running from for years. Before learning from Hiram and the Blackbird that Giovanni Romano's son was already plotting his demise, I'd done everything to keep my involvement in his death a secret, from playing mind games with Cheeks to asking Rocky to steal photographs from Briarly manor.

I shook his hand, but Jules tightened his grip around my palm. He yanked me forward and pulled me into a hug. His cologne smelled spicy and expensive, the kind that would linger on your clothes long after he'd gone.

"Thanks for saving me a job," he whispered, sending a chill down my spine as he patted my back. By killing his father, I allowed him to take over the family business without getting his hands dirty. "Tell me, did he suffer?"

I pulled away and hesitated as Jules watched me intently. I mean, how did you go about explaining to someone how you murdered their father?

"He got what he deserved," I said finally.

Giovanni Romano had a whole career under his belt that was built upon, amongst other nefarious deeds, the exploitation of women. It was only fitting that he got taken down by someone who he viewed as an inferior species.

"I hope you enjoyed yourself," Jules said. Most women's panties would melt at a flash of his gorgeous smile, but it hid a darker side, and my inner voice was screaming to get away. "My father was a lucky man for yours to be the last face he ever saw. Let's hope your husband will take good care of you. I'm sure there will be other men happy to take you off his hands."

Romano Junior must have developed the same sadistic appetite as his daddy. His father was a twisted motherfucker, but Juliano? With his looks and charm, he had the potential to be even worse.

"Have you met my husband yet?" I asked, ignoring his comments. He and Giles were both misogynistic assholes, so they'd have plenty to bond over. "I'm sure he'd love to make your acquaintance."

"Enjoy your evening, Kitten." Jules winked. "The drinks are on me tonight. I owe you."

What good did taking out the bad guys achieve? There would always be someone new to take their place.

———

A guard nodded his head in my direction as I stepped into the cool breeze outside the club. "Congratulations."

Hiram's security team was stationed at every potential escape route. For once, I didn't care that they were watching me. Anything was better than being surrounded by pounding bass, half-naked women, and people I hoped never to see again.

"Where are you going?" another guard asked as I headed for the parking lot.

"I'm taking a fucking walk," I snarled. "Do you have a problem with that, or do you want me to tell Hiram you're trying to ruin my big day?"

He pressed his lips together, not pushing me any further.

After walking around the parking lot and checking out the rows of sports cars, I started a lap of the building. Scoping out a location was always a habit of mine. As I neared a corner, a low, hushed voice talked quickly around the other side. Whoever was hiding out back didn't want to be overheard.

"He's losing his touch," the Blackbird murmured. "Letting *her* come back here. Arranging a fucking wedding. It shows how weak he is."

I pushed myself flat against the wall and tried to flatten my skirts down, holding my breath. I hadn't gained my nickname 'Kitten' by standing out. Slinking around unnoticed until the perfect moment to pounce was my greatest talent, but doing it in a wedding dress was harder.

"I know, I know, I understand..." the Blackbird said. I peeked around the edge of the wall to see him holding his cell away from his ear. I couldn't hear whoever was on the other end of the line, but they must be pretty fucking unhappy to be shouting. The Blackbird sighed as the caller's rant came to a close. "I've got to get back inside, but I'll keep you posted."

I stepped out of the shadows. "Having fun?"

The Blackbird's eyes widened as he stashed the phone into his pocket. A flash of fear crossed over his features before his expression transformed into his usual blank mask. He would already be racing through the possibilities. *How long had she been standing there? How much did she hear?* Mobilizing against Hiram was a fatal offense. The question was, who was he speaking to and what was he planning?

"Why are you hiding out here?" he asked, opting to play it safe and not address what was really on his mind. "You should be getting back inside. Your new husband will be missing you."

"Why don't we rejoin the party together?" I suggested. A wicked smile spread over my face. I could smell fear oozing out of his pores. "Unless you have any more calls to make?"

His eyes narrowed, but he said no more. The Blackbird would have to be nicer to me in the future... if he wanted me to keep my mouth shut.

———

When will the night end?

I threw another shot of tequila onto the floor. This may be my wedding party, but alcohol and being stuck in a room with the most dangerous people in the country didn't mix.

Hiram's icy hand on the small of my back made me jump. "Are you having fun, Kitty?"

"The best fucking day of my life," I grumbled, gesturing around at the fact I was standing alone at the corner of the bar and avoiding any attempts at conversation. Thankfully, after hours of partying, people were too busy dancing, fucking, or riding a high to bother me.

"There is one thing that will make today better," Hiram said. Like me, he was perfectly sober. He enjoyed fine wine but always kept a sharp mind in the company of others. "I have to give you my wedding present."

Hiram's presents were not likely to be a pair of vintage Jimmy Choo shoes or a designer handbag. He'd once gifted me the severed head of a guy who groped me. Another time, he gave me a stolen necklace he'd ripped from the neck of a woman before he slit her throat.

"I couldn't help myself," Hiram said, unperturbed by my silence and lack of enthusiasm. His joy made my stomach lurch. Anything that made a sadistic psychopath smile wasn't a good sign. "Come outside."

We weren't the only ones heading out. The wedding party dutifully followed behind us and spilled into the parking lot. Apart from a few orgies happening in the back of cars, there were no bound victims or misshapen trash bags around.

"Look up," Hiram ordered.

As I did, a firework screamed into the night sky. Red and yellow shots of light lit up the entire horizon, showering it with sparkles.

"That's not my only gift," Hiram said as the sky turned black again. "I've just received a call."

"Oh?" I asked, bored and disinterested.

"The call confirmed what we've both been waiting for," he said. "Red Marshall is dead."

"What?" I stammered, turning to face Hiram and hoping I'd misheard amidst the noise. "What did you say?"

Another firework exploded above, illuminating us in a blue glow.

"Red Marshall is dead."

My knees turned to jelly. The tiny shred of hope I held in my core shattered with a bang. Two fireworks hurtled over our heads and left burning trails behind them. Like Rocky and me, they were heading straight for destruction. The two of us fell in love as kids. We'd made stupid choices along the way but, somehow, we found our way back together. His final act on earth had been trying to protect me. He told me he loved me, and how had I repaid him? I pulled the fucking trigger. The fireworks exploded and, with them, my heart fragmented into a thousand pieces.

It didn't matter that I didn't intend to kill him. Death was irreversible, and nothing could change how it was my bullet that ripped through his chest. A bullet that ended his life.

With him gone, the Sevens would be out for my blood. I was no better than any of the monsters standing around me. This is where I belonged.

"Let's go inside, Kitty," Hiram said. I hadn't realized everyone else had gone back into the club, and the display was over. There was no way back. "It's time to cut the cake."

Rocky was dead… and I killed him.

CHAPTER

Three

Sun shining through the windows signaled the start of a new day, but I'd already been awake for hours. After the firework display, the rest of the evening passed in a blur. I played the role of Hiram's dutiful protégé, but my thoughts were so far away it didn't even cross my mind to slice Giles's hand when he insisted we cut the extravagant vanilla sponge.

All I could see was his face. Rocky's face. I couldn't stop replaying the moment he fell to the floor like a video caught in a never-ending loop. Blood spilled from his body, and my face stared back at me in the crimson puddle, haunted by regret.

I thought I knew pain, but nothing compared to the deep ache in my chest that was crushing me from the inside out. It'd been hard enough to know he'd hate me for shooting him, but never having the chance to apologize or explain? The pain was agonizing and all-consuming. It swallowed me in a black hole I'd never be able to claw my way out of.

Rocky wasn't the only one who died yesterday. My hope was slaughtered alongside the last part of me with any goodness left. Now, I was nothing but *this*. A monster who killed her chance at happiness.

I deserved to suffer. Rocky's blood was on my hands, and it was time for me to succumb to my fate. But I wasn't the only person to blame for his death. If Zander hadn't lied, we'd never have been put in a position where Rocky had to stand between me and Hiram. Spending my life with Hiram and marrying Giles was my punishment, but what about Zander? He needed to pay for his choices. Rocky went to his grave thinking I'd turned my back on him, but Zander would go to his wishing he never turned his back on me.

"Fuck," I cursed as loud knocking erupted on the door.

I hauled myself into a sitting position. My limbs were heavy and moving drained the little energy I had. All I wanted was to curl back into a ball again and hide from the world. A world I didn't know how to live in knowing Rocky wasn't in it.

"Get up, Kitten," Hiram ordered, entering my bedroom without an invitation. As usual, he wore a pressed suit and tie. It's all he owned. "We have a guest joining us for breakfast."

"I'm not hungry," I mumbled, pulling my knees up to my chest and pretending to cough. "I don't feel good."

Hiram's eyes narrowed. He saw through my act quicker than a porn actress faking an orgasm to cut the shoot early.

"Don't keep us waiting, Kitten," he hissed. "You have five minutes, or I will drag you out myself."

He stormed away, and Giles's laugh belted down the corridor like an unwelcome alarm. After returning to Blackthorne Towers after the wedding, I'd not expected to see Giles again so soon. Our union was a sham, so I assumed he'd only appear when Hiram called. We never ate together in the morning, so Hiram must be using the meeting as a way to lull Giles into a false sense of security. He made people comfortable before snatching everything away from them.

I dragged myself out of bed, threw on leggings and a tank top, then made my way to the kitchen at the end of the hall. The smell of Hiram's chef-prepared food spread over the table made my stomach churn.

"I was beginning to think you weren't going to be joining us," Giles said, already busy piling his plate high.

I scowled and poured myself a cup of strong black coffee. My hands shook as I resisted the urge to throw the boiling liquid in his face and sat in a chair opposite the two of them.

Hiram's brow furrowed. "You're not eating."

"I told you, I'm not hungry," I replied, crossing my arms and zeroing in on Giles. "What do *you* want?"

"To see my wife, of course," Giles replied, dabbing his face with a napkin and leaving behind a crumb of toast on his upper lip. "I brought you a present."

I wrinkled my nose at his toast wart and snapped, "I don't like surprises."

Especially ones from assholes like him.

"You'll like this one," Hiram said.

Yep, now I was certain that it wouldn't be good.

"An associate delivered this to me this morning," Giles said.

He slid a white envelope across the table.

I eyed it suspiciously but didn't move. "What is it?"

"Open it," Hiram encouraged. "You'll see."

I snatched it up and tore through the paper. My eyes scanned over the words written on the thick white card. Hiram and Giles watched on. Waiting. Waiting for me to fuck up. I bit my tongue and took a deep breath, keeping my poker face intact. I couldn't show emotion. Not here.

"So, what?" I threw the invitation down and leaned back. "Do you expect me to care?"

"Don't you want to pay your respects, Kitty?" Hiram asked. He flashed his sparkling white teeth in a smile filled with evil and malice, making my skin prickle. "We can put an old chapter to a close."

"I guess," I replied, shrugging. Underneath the table, my nails dug into my palms. He wanted to watch me squirm. "Who needs to go on a honeymoon when there is a funeral to attend?"

Rocky's funeral.

"I couldn't agree more," Hiram said. He seemed satisfied with my reaction, or lack of it. "Besides, a visit to Briarly Manor could be helpful."

"The wake is happening at the manor?" I asked, grabbing the invitation again. I'd skimmed over the sentences but hadn't paid attention to the finer details. I turned to face Giles. "Your uncle helped plan this?"

Giles's cheeks flushed, and he dropped his cutlery with a crash. His hands clenched into fists as he wrestled to keep his composure. His piggy eyes flitted between me and Hiram. What was I missing?

After a strained silence, Giles finally cleared his throat and found his voice again. "You haven't heard?"

"Heard, what?" I demanded.

"I'll leave you to catch up." Hiram smirked and rose from his seat. "We can debrief later."

As far as I was aware, I hadn't missed any of the Blackbird's updates about what was happening in Port Valentine. From what he said, the Sevens had been splitting their time between staying with Rocky at the hospital and keeping Lapland running as normal.

"Well?" I arched my eyebrow at Giles, who suddenly decided he couldn't break eye contact with the mounted antelope head on the wall. "Are you gonna fill in the fucking blanks?"

He murmured something under his breath, but I couldn't make it out. Giles usually enjoyed being the loudest dick swinger in the room, so his sudden shift was out of character.

"Well?" I clicked my tongue impatiently, but still nothing. He knew how to test me. I had better things to do than sit around in his company, like wallowing in my fucking misery. "Are you going to tell me, or should I call Hiram in again?"

Giles's eyes widened in fear and he muttered, "The money's gone."

"The money?" I pressed as he shuffled around in his seat like he'd caught crabs. "What do you mean?"

"The Briarly fortune," Giles said, more loudly this time. He finally mustered the courage to meet my stare. "All the money's gone. They took everything. The Sevens took it all, even the manor."

It didn't make sense. How does a family with a seemingly unlimited bank balance fall destitute in a matter of weeks?

"How is that even possible?" I asked.

Zander may have been scheming his father's demise, but he was no magician. Dollars can't disappear in a puff of smoke. I'd been to Briarly Manor and attended their extravagant parties. I'd walked the lavishly decorated halls and sipped wine alongside Bryce's devout followers. Centuries of wealth don't just vanish overnight.

"My uncle made some bad investment decisions," Giles explained, hanging his head. "Everything was going to be fine... until you came along."

"*Me*?" I scoffed. Of course, it was easier to blame someone else than take responsibility for their own fucking mistakes. "I don't remember putting a gun to Bryce Briarly's head and telling him to put his money in the wrong places."

"The Bayside Heights development was our last chance," Giles insisted. His desperate tone matched the crazed look in his eyes. The look of a man who'd lost everything. "We could have made it all back. We *would* have. But Zander snatched the deal from under us, and you made sure Bayside Heights would never be built on again. After that, we had no choice but to sell the manor. Zander bought it... the manor... the money... he has no right. It was rightfully mine. All of it."

Zander used to spend hours holed up in his office making plans for the future. Since finding out about what Bryce did to his mother, he'd been waiting until his father was in a vulnerable position to take him down. By using me as a pawn in his games, I'd given Zander everything he always wanted.

"Zander didn't do all of it alone," I reminded him, leaning across the table. Giles had partnered up with someone who'd been part of taking everything away from him. "Why would you strike a deal with Hiram? Why marry me?"

"Because we want the same thing. Hiram wants to gain control of Port Valentine and, to do that, we need the Sevens gone. We can do it together. I'm going to take back what is mine, and marrying you was Hiram's collateral to show how serious I was," Giles said. For a split second, I *almost* pitied him. He and Bryce were so desperate to get their old lives back they were overestimating Hiram's generosity. He'd never have their best interests at heart. As soon as Hiram helped them get their fortune back, he'd swoop in to take it all. "You didn't think that I wanted to marry a stripper slut, did you?"

His words dashed any of my sympathy. Taking everything from them all over again would be a sweet victory. Zander and his Briarly bloodline wouldn't be an institution in Port Valentine for much longer. It was time to make way for new traditions.

"You think I'm a slut?" I laughed. "You dated Penelope, remember? The bitch's legs open and close more than a freezer in a fucking mortuary."

"Don't call her that." Giles slammed his fist on the table. His cheeks turned the same color as a strawberry Slurpee. "She's not like that."

"Have I touched a nerve?" I asked, putting my index finger to my chin and pretending to think hard. "Where is she now? Let me guess, she ran as soon as the money was gone?"

"You don't know what you're talking about," Giles hissed, then changed the subject. "What about my cousin? Don't you want to get back at him for what he did?"

"Are you forgetting you and your uncle tried to do the same thing?"

"But we weren't screwing you," he sneered, bringing out the vicious side hiding underneath his bravado. "Everyone knows you were the Sevens' personal whore."

"Think carefully about what you say next," I warned, shooting him a glacial stare and rising from my chair. "You're in *my* territory now, and I have nothing to lose. If Hiram hears you've upset me, he'll cut off your balls and use them as earmuffs."

Giles paled, and his eyes darted around the room. If we were going to be seeing more of each other, maybe I'd be able to teach him how to treat a woman like she was more than a second-rate fucking citizen.

"What I'm trying to say is that we want the same thing," Giles said, trying to reason with me. Like any good politician, he spoke out of his asshole and spouted bullshit to smooth things over. "Taking down my cousin is within both of our interests, isn't it? I'll help you and Hiram get what you want."

Giles and I may hate each other, but he was right. We'd finally found common ground.

"We have a funeral to attend," I said curtly. "Get your black suit ready, and I'll see you in two days."

He gulped and nodded.

I'd make sure our appearance at Rocky's funeral was one the Sevens would never forget.

———

The dress code instructions were specific. Wear black. Who made it an unspoken rule that mourners had to wear black, anyway? Regardless, I was breaking it. This wasn't an *ordinary* funeral. This was Rocky's, and I needed to make a statement, not only to stand out, but because it's what *he* would have wanted.

I picked a bright red dress that hugged my curves. The neckline was low and the necklace Zander gifted me nestled between my cleavage. With it, I wore gorgeous black thigh-high boots. I'd stand out like a flashing neon warning sign. Hiram thought I picked it to pay homage to Rocky's violent death, but I had my reasons. Red was Rocky's chosen gang name and the color of the shorts he wore when he fought at the Golden Gloves. It would be our final secret.

I stared at my reflection in the mirror. After spending hours getting ready, I barely recognized the person looking back. My pink hair had faded to a faint pastel hue which was most noticeable under the sunlight. Hiram wanted my hair blonde, but my stubborn strands clung to the rosy color no matter how many times I shampooed. I leaned forward to examine my black circles. After hours of meticulous makeup application, they were hidden. Just like the feelings I had to shut away.

"Shit," I cursed as my cell buzzed on the dresser.

That was my cue.

A guard was already stationed outside of my bedroom. I strolled ahead of him, throwing my shoulders back and swaying my hips like I was about to attend the party of the year. We walked through Hiram's penthouse suite and into the elevator. It chimed as we came to our stop.

It was time.

Hiram and Giles waited for me by the entrance to Blackthorne Towers. Dawn had just broken, but we needed to leave early to make the funeral on time.

"Do you understand what you're there to do?" Hiram asked, looking between us. While he was sending guards to accompany us on the journey, Hiram wouldn't be traveling with us. "You will follow the plan. No distractions."

"We've got it," I said flippantly, then counted the points off of my freshly painted nails. "Go to the funeral, head to the wake, stir shit up, help Giles find his goddamn ornament, and get outta there."

Hiram looked uneasy. I couldn't have him back out now that we were so close…

"It'll be easy," I bragged. "When haven't I delivered?"

We went through the plan yesterday. As well as making an appearance to shock the Sevens, we had another reason to go to Port Valentine. Giles wanted to retrieve an object of value hidden in the manor — something he and Bryce could use to subsidize their lifestyles.

"Remember, I'll be watching," Hiram said. "I'll be joining you at the manor after I've taken care of a few things."

Yeah, as soon as he finished with the newest prisoner in the basement…

"We don't need a babysitter," I muttered. He shot me a warning glare, so I quickly added, "We'll see you then."

Hiram turned to Giles with a face of stone. "If anything happens, I will hold you responsible. Don't let her out of your sight."

"I-I-I won't," Giles stammered.

Hiram nodded in satisfaction and stepped aside to let us out of the building. As I passed, Hiram caught my arm.

"I mean it, Kitty," he hissed. "No distractions."

"We've got it," I repeated with a smile.

He released his hold, and I strolled out. I took a second to breathe in the fresh air. It'd beat having to share the same oxygen as Giles on the ride over.

Giles held open the door to the waiting bulletproof Range Rover Sentinel. "You look… nice."

"Spare me the fucking compliments, Giles," I snapped, cutting him off and sliding into the backseat. His presence and fake ass remarks only made me more annoyed at the thought of having to spend the day with him. "Save them for when you're licking Hiram's ass."

Giles slipped in next to me.

"Are you ready to go, Kitten?" our driver asked, paying no attention to Giles. He knew who was really in charge.

"Yes," I replied. Well, as ready as you could ever be to gatecrash the funeral of someone you killed.

"I almost forgot," Giles said, ruffling around in his jacket pocket, "I have something for you."

"You can keep your gifts," I snapped. "You need the money more than I do."

Giles scowled as he presented a small jewelry box. "Hiram thought it was a good idea."

A ring with a huge diamond was nestled inside. It was flashier than the wedding bands we exchanged at the ceremony. Diamonds weren't my favorite stone. With their ridiculous price tag and bloody history, I didn't get the hype.

"Fine," I retorted, sliding the ring on and holding it out in front of me. It fitted perfectly but didn't feel natural. The rock weighed my hand down like a freaking anchor. "I'm sure the Sevens will love it."

"How do you feel about seeing the Sevens again?" Giles asked, spraying me with spit as he said the 'Sevens' aloud.

I shot him a twisted smile. "The real question is, how are they going to feel about seeing *us*?"

We may be going to Port Valentine to help Giles find an old family relic, but that wasn't the only thing I was looking forward to. Zander was guaranteed to be there. I wanted to take the traitorous bastard out. He'd ripped my heart out, and I was going to do the same.

———

"Are you sure we shouldn't get out now?" Giles whined for the thousandth time.

We'd been sat in the car outside the cemetery for an hour, and he'd done nothing but moan like a fucking toddler. Next time, I'd bring along a pacifier.

"Have you listened to a word I've been saying?" I snapped. "We have to make an entrance."

Hell, I'd love nothing more than to escape being trapped in a confined space with the British asshole, but we had to wait for the perfect moment. We needed to take everyone off-guard. We'd parked across the street, giving us the best view of the attendees waiting outside the chapel for the proceedings to begin. We weren't alone. Hiram's henchmen were prowling the area disguised as joggers and dog walkers. Hiram didn't trust us enough to work unsupervised.

So far, none of the main players had arrived.

"Come on," Giles moaned. Without Hiram around, he was turning into a total diva. "How much longer?"

I waved my hand to shut him up and jabbed a finger at an approaching vehicle. "Look."

It was starting.

Even though the car had tinted windows, I instinctively ducked as a hearse rolled by. Seeing a coffin surrounded by flowers made everything more real. Rocky's body was in there... only a pane of glass away. The closest I'd ever be to him again.

Giles watched me closely. "Are you... you know, okay?"

What kind of question was that? We were on a fucking job, not a therapy retreat to talk about our emotions. He had to get his shit together.

"I've never been better," I snarled.

Two cars followed the hearse. Both of them were part of the Sevens' fleet. I'd been waiting for this moment since I rejoined Hiram. Seeing all the

Sevens together in one place. A lump formed in my throat as my brain corrected itself. Well, the ones who were left...

We watched as the hearse and cars came to a stop. Vixen and Mieko got out of the first car, together hand-in-hand. Vixen's hair was dyed black all over and didn't have her usual wild streaks. Her mascara dripped down her face and made her look like a gothic model.

Mieko looked even more concerned than usual. Her eyes flitted nervously around the milling crowd. She whispered a few words in Vixen's ear, and I imagined she was reassuring her that everything would be okay. For selfish reasons, I secretly hoped the two of them wouldn't still be together. I didn't want to hurt them — especially Mieko — but I wouldn't hesitate if they stood in my way.

West stepped out of the second car. I'd forgotten how ruggedly attractive he was. The last time I saw him, he was lying in a hospital bed rigged up to machines. He'd made a perfect recovery and looked more muscular and angry than ever. His sunglasses and black suit made him look like a special agent.

How did I think that a guy like him could seriously have been interested in me?

West paused for a second and turned back to the car. He held out his hand, and a woman practically skipped out after him.

"Bastard," Giles yelled, making a lunge for the door handle. Thankfully, Hiram had been smart enough to give the driver orders to lock us in until I said so. We couldn't have Giles storming out and ruining everything. "I'll fucking kill him."

Penelope smirked as she took West's arm. From the look on her face, you'd think she was arriving at a film premiere with a celebrity, not a gang member who was getting ready to bury his brother. Numbness swept through me at the sight of them together. They were both gorgeous and looked like they belonged together, but it didn't stop a wave of anger from rising inside me. I wanted to claw her fucking eyes out.

"Get your shit together," I hissed, not sure whether I was trying to convince Giles or myself more. "This isn't about her. We have a job to do. We're here for a reason."

Giles's chest heaved. "But—"

"No fucking buts," I interrupted. "If you can't keep your head together, you're not going anywhere. You're not about to ruin this."

Giles slumped back in his seat and crossed his arms. "Fine..."

His moody schoolboy act didn't fool me. Unrest bubbled under his expensive tweed suit. He wouldn't be able to control himself if he got the chance to speak to Penelope, which I could use to my advantage later.

"I mean it, Giles," I warned. "I'll take you out if you get in my fucking way."

As the two couples greeted the mourners, I kept my gaze fixed on the Sevens' cars and waited for the final figure to emerge. Then, nothing. The cars drove away.

"Where's Zander?" Giles asked, voicing my own confusion.

Good fucking question.

———

We waited for everyone to go inside, allowing time for the service to begin. Seeing Penelope in West's arms ignited a fire under Giles's balls. His impulsiveness and questionable judgment were a concern, but I had my own shit to worry about. Seeing West with his bitch of an ex left a bitter taste in my mouth, and I needed to bottle up those feelings before both of us were compromised.

"When can we go in?" Giles asked. "It won't last long. There can't be that many nice things to say about him."

I bit my tongue to stop myself from saying if it was *his* funeral, it'd already be over by now.

There were plenty of nice things I could say about Rocky. I knew him better than anyone. We'd come from the same background and understood each other on a level others didn't get. I'd have talked about how he used to look out for me, about how kind and funny he was, about how he'd do anything to right his mistakes, and would risk his life to protect the people he loved... and how stupid he was to believe there was anything redeemable about me.

A walkie-talkie crackled over the car radio.

"That's the signal," I said, putting my game face on. Hiram had posted an undercover guy on the inside to alert us when we should enter. I'd been against the idea but, without it, I don't know whether I'd have been able to muster the courage to get out of the car. "It's time."

"Finally," Giles said as the driver unlocked the doors and we stepped out.

I held out my hand and allowed him to slip his sweaty fingers through mine. If Rocky was watching, he'd be shaking his head. I could almost hear his voice in my head saying, *'Do you even know what you're doing, C?'* and then he'd light a spliff to brighten the mood.

We paced to the chapel in determined silence. When we arrived, we exchanged a look of mutual understanding. We may be here for different reasons, but we both agreed on something. Zander was going to fucking pay.

"Let's do this," I spat through gritted teeth.

I threw the door open with a bang that caused every head in the building to swivel around. Rocky's coffin was directly in front of us. It was a relief to see the casket was closed, but I avoided looking at it. Soon, he'd be nothing but embers. The only thing I'd have left of him were our memories and, one day, even they would fade. I couldn't process that now though, all I could do was smile and step inside.

My heel hitting the stone floor echoed through the rafters. There was a collective intake of breath, then complete chaos broke out. Just as I'd been hoping for.

Vixen's toe-curling shriek broke the silence. "You bitch."

"It looks like we made it in time for the best part," I said, hating myself for what I had to do.

I'm sorry, Rocky. I pleaded to his spirit, in case he was listening. *This is what I have to do.*

Vixen jumped up from her seat in the front row and started sprinting toward me. West was faster. He caught her, wrapping his tree-trunk-like arms around her waist to hold her back as she screamed like a banshee.

"You murderer," she screeched, trying to kick West away. The black make-up smudged around her eyes which made her look like a psycho zombie against her chalky complexion. "I'll fucking kill you."

"Don't speak to my wife like that," Giles piped up. "We came to pay our respects—"

"Your wife?" Penelope's high-pitched shrill voice cut in, making me wince. "You married *her*?"

I'd almost forgotten Giles was standing by my side, but everyone suddenly acknowledged his presence. West's expression turned furious and his momentary lapse in concentration was all it took for Vixen to knee him in the groin and wriggle herself free.

She barreled forward. I didn't move as she crashed into me and knocked me to the ground, bearing her talons like weapons. A searing pain spread over my face as her claws sank into my cheek. I didn't blame her for being angry. If the situation was reversed, I'd be going for fatal wounds over a catfight. I would let her get in a few more swipes before she forced me to break her arm. It's what Rocky would have wanted.

"You're the reason Red is dead," she shouted as tears streamed down her cheeks. "You should never have come into our fucking lives."

Vixen tried to throw a punch, but I rolled away to dodge her fist. I'd tried to teach Vixen how to defend herself when we lived together, but I never thought to tell her she actually had to *see* when aiming.

Before she got the chance to try again, Mieko and West hauled her off of me. I stood, fluffing up my hair and smoothing down my dress as if nothing happened.

"How can you even look at yourself?" Vixen hissed. "He trusted you and you fucking shot him. You just couldn't wait to get back to your old life, could you?"

"Maybe it's best you leave, Candy," Mieko whispered.

I *could* try to explain to them what happened. I *could* apologize and say I never meant to hurt him, but I wouldn't. What difference would it make? It wouldn't bring him back. It was easier if she hated me. If they all hated me.

"You shouldn't have come," West said, looking straight through me like a ghost. His eyes were empty. Hollow. A shell of the person I thought I knew.

His cold indifference shocked me. Where was his fire? Where was the beast who lived inside him? It would have been better if he tried to kill me or thrown insults my way. Anything would be better than *this*. He met me with nothing but emptiness like I was a fucking stranger. Had I meant so little to him?

"At least we bothered to show up," Giles said. "Where is my cousin today?"

"That is none of your concern, Briarly," West growled.

"Why don't we all catch up at the after party?" Giles suggested. "It was an open invitation, after all."

"We'll see you there," I said before they could answer, then turned on my heel and flipped my hair so hard that I almost gave myself whiplash. The motion covered up the disappointment I needed to hide. West didn't let me down, I did. I'd been stupid to think I belonged with the Sevens, and I was paying the price.

There was no turning back. The battle lines were officially drawn, and I wouldn't leave Port Valentine without Zander's head.

My cell rang as soon as we stormed from the chapel. Hiram wanted answers. I picked up and said, "Part one is done. We're on our way."

Causing a scene was the first step. If Vixen's reaction was anything to go by, then the wake would devolve into full-blown chaos — especially if Zander was around. His not attending Rocky's funeral confirmed everything I knew to be true. Didn't West and Vixen see through Zander's bullshit? He only cared about himself. The egotistical psychopath couldn't spare an hour out of his day to pay his fucking respects.

"I'll see you at the manor," Hiram snapped, hanging up.

Returning to Port Valentine was surreal. A few months ago, I thought of this town as a home and the Sevens as my family. But, now, being here was a painful reminder of something I would never have or get again. It would be a day of retribution, and I was here for answers.

After allowing the funeral-goers a head-start, our drive to Briarly Manor seemed to take forever. Giles made the ride even more unbearable by muttering unimaginative death threats against West under his breath. If he was going to make threats, couldn't he try to be a little more creative? Besides, he shouldn't be surprised. I'd already warned him what she was like after watching Penelope throw herself at West every time they were in the same room.

I decided to talk, hoping it might reduce the chances of him doing something stupid. "So, you really cared about her, huh?"

Giles didn't see past her smooth skin, long legs, and bouncy hair. He should be happy he'd gotten a lucky escape from that bitch of a gold digger.

"No," he said, too quickly. "It doesn't matter."

"She's not worth it," I said.

"Doesn't it bother you seeing the two of them all over each other?" he asked. "You were engaged."

Pfft, my engagement to West was no different from my new marriage. Phony. I followed Zander's orders because I stupidly bought into his and the Sevens' vow of unbreakable loyalty. In reality, Zander's real motivation was to get what he wanted, whatever the consequences.

"The only thing I care about is getting revenge for what he did to me," I said, trying to scrub the image of West and Penelope from my mind. It shouldn't bother me. It couldn't. "The sooner you learn to stop caring, the better."

The truth is, a tiny part of me *did* care. I expected to see West in full-on beast mode, not showing off a fucking she-devil on his arm. Penelope wasted no time in looking to reassert her status after Giles lost his fortune. I thought West knew better. What happened to him saying he'd never go back? That there was nothing between them? Maybe I never knew him at all...

Giles scowled as we pulled into the driveway of Briarly Manor. "Look at all their cars on *my* land."

I looked past the parking lot to the grand building. If Hiram's plan worked, this would be my palace one day. I'd take everything from each of the Briarlys and rule my own fucking kingdom.

"I'll key them on our way out," I promised. West's cars meant everything to him. Every scratch would be a slash on his heart. "We'll call it a parting gift."

Rocky's wake attracted a large crowd. It seemed like more of a party than an occasion where someone had just died. People never turned down the chance of free food and booze. Fucking freeloaders.

The Sevens' security team didn't stop us from climbing the manor steps. The manor was different in the daylight. Instead of feeling foreboding, like on my previous visits, there was a new warmness to the place... until I saw two figures who made my blood run cold.

"Here they are!" Hiram beckoned for us to join him and Zander in the doorway. He frowned as we got closer, admiring the scratch on my cheek. "What happened to your face, Kitty?"

Zander's gray, piercing eyes regarded me with zero emotion like we'd never met before. I don't know what I expected. A flicker of recognition? A glimpse of the person I thought I knew? But, like West, there was nothing. Zander tucked his tattooed hands, laden with silver rings, into the pockets of his black suit in boredom. He'd gotten new ink on his face since we last saw each other. A number seven inked into his temple. The tattoo taunted me. He may claim loyalty to the Sevens meant everything, but where was his loyalty to me when it counted?

"Not everyone was pleased to see me," I replied to Hiram's question while keeping my stare fixed on Zander.

Hiram's lip curled. "Don't you have your people under control, Zander?"

"I can only apologize, Hiram," Zander said in an icy tone, extending his hand. "You and your associates are always welcome in our home."

The bastard didn't even acknowledge me. At least Vixen had a reaction. She felt *something*. How could this be the same man who fucked me and made my body come alive with a few touches? Zander was a walking ice statue, not someone I'd lived with and lost my anal virginity to.

Hiram grasped Zander's hand with a firm shake. He may want to take Port Valentine from the Sevens, but he had to play nice for now. "We all wanted to pay our respects."

"I'm sure you'll be keen to see the improvements we've made to the manor, cousin," Zander said, addressing Giles with a smug smirk I wanted to wipe off. "Come inside."

Holy crap...

Giles's jaw dropped. The manor was almost unrecognizable as the same building. Bright and modern decor replaced its older interior. Chandeliers, oak paneling, and ancient art had been swapped for abstract contemporary pieces and glass lights that looked like they were melting. If it wasn't for Zander's deal with Hiram helping to bankroll the transformation, I'd have been impressed.

"What do you think, Giles?" Zander probed.

Giles's fingers curled into tight fists. He was a traditionalist, and this was his idea of a nightmare. Thankfully, we were spared a Giles temper tantrum as Penelope and West approached.

"You have a nerve showing yourself here," Penelope hissed in my direction. "Have you come to gloat?"

"It looks like you have," I rebutted. "You seem to be the only person looking happy on the day of a fucking funeral. How long did it take you to jump on West's cock after Rocky died?"

Hiram chuckled, putting his hand on my arm. "Be nice, Kitten."

"How could you have married *her*?" Penelope asked Giles in an almost pleading tone. "She has zero fucking class."

"You should be thanking me, Penny," I snarled. "Now, you've got everything you've always wanted."

West wrapped his arm around Penelope's shoulder to hold her back. "Leave it, Penny. She's not worth it."

His words hurt like a metal crowbar to the head, but I kept my expression neutral. He'd made his choice and deserved everything that came to him.

"You're right," Penelope said, flicking her hair over her shoulder dramatically like a cheerleader in a movie. She was a walking freaking cliché. "Why don't we go up to your room, West? I need to rest."

I clenched my jaw to stop myself from saying something I'd regret.

"I've converted your old room, Giles," West said, then smirked. "It's very… comfortable."

That was all it took for Giles to explode. He dove at West like an angry hornet being released from the nest. Unfortunately for Giles, he rebounded straight off of West's pecs like they were a bounce house.

Hiram caught Giles by the collar and heaved him back. Giles paled as Hiram whispered something in his ear. He had high expectations and did not appreciate being let down. West laughed as he and Penelope took off in the opposite direction.

"It's an open bar, right?" I asked Zander. "Where are the drinks?"

Zander didn't answer and hailed over a server. Had he seriously called someone over because he didn't want to address me himself? It seemed like having staff was the only thing he wanted to keep from his father's old system. Zander's ego was like a fucking goldfish, and the manor was giving it room to grow.

"How can I help you, miss?" the server asked.

"Where are the fucking drinks?" I spat, feeling my anger rise.

"Enjoy your evening, Hiram," Zander said, continuing to ignore me. He'd never been great at customer service, but this was an all time low. "I'm sure we'll see each other soon."

"I'll show you to the bar," the server said. "Would you three like to follow me?"

I wasn't interested in having a drink, but I followed the server. I'd seek Zander out again when I was away from Hiram's scrutiny. We went into the old library. Bookshelves still lined the walls, but they'd turned the room into a private bar, which looked like an exclusive member's club. The bar at the back was better stocked than the one in Lapland. Plush seats and comfy sofas gave it a cozy feel, and they even had a foosball table. It was easy to imagine the Sevens kicking back in here, joking and making toasts about how easy it was to screw me over.

In the corner of the room, I spotted Mieko standing alone. She kept glancing in my direction, then looking away. As Hiram continued to chastise

Giles for losing control, I caught her eye. Mieko nudged her head in the direction of the next room and walked out.

Could she be beckoning me over, or was this another ruse so Vixen could finish what she started?

"If you'll excuse me," I said. Either way, I wanted to find out. "I'm going to the bathroom."

Hiram's brow furrowed, but I was already heading out before he could question me. I may be walking into a trap, but it was worth it to speak to Mieko. Even if it was just to say goodbye...

———

As soon as I entered the next room, Mieko threw her arms around my neck. Her sudden outburst of affection was unexpected and stunned me to the spot.

"Candy!" She squeezed me tightly. "I've missed you."

I pulled away and did a quick scan of the space to see if Vixen was about to taser me.

"I'm sorry about what happened at the chapel," Mieko continued. Her eyes were swimming with tears, but she blinked them away "I tried to talk Vix out of it. I said to her that there must be more to it. That you wouldn't do what they said you did."

"You're wrong," I said bluntly. "I did it, Mieko. I killed him. I fucking shot him, okay? There's no more to say."

"But you loved him. I know you did," she said, her voice softened. "Why did you do it, Candy?"

There were many things I could say. Many things I *wanted* to say. I did it to protect him. I wanted to make sure that he went on living and didn't die because of me. Instead, I told her what I wanted everyone to believe. The truth changed nothing. Mieko wanted to believe the best in people, but it was too dangerous for her to see any good in me. Everyone who does ends up dead. Look at what happened to Crystal and Rocky. It was better for Mieko to be scared and hate me like the others.

"I shot him because he was in my way," I said. "I'm not who you think I am. Vixen was right about everything. You should go before she finds out you're speaking to me. It's not safe."

I'd already messed up Vixen's life by killing her best friend. I didn't want to get in the middle of her relationship and screw that up, too.

Mieko looked around to check no one else was in earshot and whispered, "There's something you need to know—"

"Care to introduce me to your friend, Kitty?" Hiram's voice behind us made me jump.

He looked at Mieko like he was sizing her up for a meal. I recognized that look. I saw it on the night he met me.

Think fast, Candy.

"She's no one," I said dismissively. "Just another whore from Zander's club."

This was for her own good.

"Don't be unkind, Kitty," Hiram purred in his most charming voice. He knew something was off. "Why don't you introduce us?"

"She's just leaving," I said, shooting Mieko my scary 'don't you dare fucking argue' look. "Weren't you?"

"Actually, I wasn't," Mieko said, not moving an inch. Did she have a suicide wish? Mieko knew about my past and what Hiram was capable of. What the fuck was she thinking? "I'm Mieko."

"Hiram," he said, extending his hand. She took it, and he brought hers up to his mouth to kiss it. "It's a pleasure."

Fuck, no! No, no, no!

Hiram possessed a sixth sense for finding a weakness in others. He harnessed people's insecurity for his own gain. Mieko had been through a lot of shit. She'd come from an abusive home and spent her life doing what she could to get back on track. Hiram didn't only sense weakness, but people who had inner strength. He liked a challenge.

I knew how this situation played out. At the start, Hiram would charm you. He'd ask questions about your life to find out your story. He makes you feel like your voice is the most important one. He pretends to care when all he does is analyze and measure you up to see whether he could put you to use.

"We should get back to the party, Hiram," I said, my voice a pitch higher than usual, "before Giles does something stupid."

"I'm sure you can handle your husband without my help," Hiram said, dismissing me with a wave. "I would like to get to know my new friend better."

I sent Mieko a pleading look, hoping she'd be able to read my signals.

Get as far away from here as you can. Run and don't look back.

Instead, she giggled. It sounded unnatural coming out of her mouth, like how dancers in the club would simper to get a few extra bucks out of a client. I don't know what she was doing, but she didn't understand how much danger she was putting herself in.

Hiram taking an interest in someone was like being taken under the wing of the Grim fucking Reaper. If he decided he wanted you, then there was no escaping the inevitable. He couldn't have Mieko. I wouldn't let it happen.

"I was just about to look at the Briarlys' new paintings. Would you like to see them?" she suggested, her voice shaking a little. Goddammit, why couldn't she have put a little more oomph into her words? Hiram would find her timid nervous manner enthralling. "I mean, you don't have to if—"

"I would love to," Hiram insisted, reaching out to grasp Mieko's arm. She winced at his touch but didn't try to push him away. "Ignore Kitty. She can get a little jealous."

"I think I'll join you," I said through gritted teeth.

"You need to get back to babysitting, remember?" Hiram said with a twisted grin. *Fuck!* He could tell from the look on my face that I cared about her, and it only made him more excited. Everything was a game to him. "I'll join you again soon."

I watched as he and Mieko headed into another room. With Hiram distracted by Mieko, it would be the perfect time to track down Zander, but this wasn't just about me anymore. The question is, did I care more about ending Zander's life or Hiram ruining Mieko's? The decision was easy.

I returned to the bar to see Giles and Penelope bickering in hushed tones, but none of the Sevens were around.

Where the fuck were they?

I made a snap decision. This was a huge manor, and Vixen liked to avoid people. The bedrooms seemed like a good place to start my search. I may not be Vixen's favorite person, but I had to find her. I don't know what dangerous game Mieko was playing, but Hiram was not the type of man you wanted to take an interest in your girlfriend.

———

I remembered the floor plan from my last visit and raced to the staircase. Zander had shown me where his old bedroom was, so it seemed like a logical place to begin. Maybe they had adopted that part of the building as their new living quarters?

"Vixen?" I called out as I paced along the corridor. "Vixen?"

Nothing.

Why did they have to move to the fucking manor? In huge places, you needed a megaphone to be heard from one side to the other. I couldn't shout the place down without drawing Hiram's attention.

I tried a few of the doors. All of them were locked.

Fuckety-fuck-fuck-FUCK!

As I hurried along, one of the doors flew open, and a strong arm yanked me inside, almost knocking me off my feet. The door shut behind us, and I looked up to see West staring menacingly down.

"Mother fu—"

West pressed one of his hands against my mouth and pushed me back, pinning my body against the wood. My heart pounded. The narrow space between us didn't leave enough room to pull the knife out of my bra without slicing a nipple off. What was he planning to do?

"Listen carefully to what I'm about to say," West growled. His blue stare burned into me with a deep intensity. "Do you remember what Zander told you last time you came here?"

I didn't have time for cryptic riddles. Mieko and Hiram were roaming around together somewhere on the floors below. He needed to help me.

I tried to speak, but West pushed his hand down over my face, almost smothering me with his giant fingers to drown out the sound.

"I'm going to move my hand," West murmured, "but you have to promise not to scream."

He pulled his hand away.

"I need to see Vixen," I panted. "Now."

"Have you listened to a single fucking word I've said?" West hissed, his jaw setting in fury. "Do you remember how to get to the servant's entrance?"

"Of course I do," I snapped, but none of that was relevant now. We were losing time. "Mieko is downstairs with Hiram. You need to get him away from her. I know you hate me, but you need to help her. Right fucking now."

I reached behind to feel for the door handle, but West caught my wrist.

"Leave Hiram to us." West's brow set in a determined line as his grip on me tightened. "But you have to listen to me, Pinkie. There's no time to explain. You need to do exactly as I say. You need to fucking trust me, okay?"

My mouth went dry at his use of my old pet name.

"Look at what happened the last time I trusted the Sevens," I hissed. "How can I trust a single thing that comes out of your mouth?"

West looked pointedly down at my chest. "You're still wearing your necklace."

"As a reminder of the biggest mistake I made," I spat.

"You came to kill him, didn't you?" West sighed. "You came to kill Zander."

I don't bother denying it. What's the point?

"Did you come to kill me, too?" West pressed. "What about Vixen and Mieko?"

I crossed my arms. "Only if you get in my way."

West laughed, the fine lines around his eyes crinkling. "You haven't changed at all."

"We're wasting time, West," I said. "You need to tell me where the fuck Vixen is, or do I have to use force?"

West's eyes darkened as his beast rose to the surface. In a flash, his hands wrapped around my throat. The last time I played with the beast, he'd fucked me so hard he left bruises... but this time was different. He knew I planned to kill Zander. What was stopping him from choking the life outta me with his bare hands?

"I said, leave Hiram to me," West snarled.

My heart rate quickened as he squeezed, causing the blood to rush to my cheeks. I spoke in short, breathless bursts. "How are you going to explain killing me to Hiram?"

His face was so close to mine that his hot breath tickled my cheeks. "You think I'm going to kill you?"

Suddenly, his lips crashed against mine in a brutal assault. The smell and heat of his body enveloped me as his erection pressed hard into my stomach. I kept my lips sealed shut, but the tightening of his hands on my throat made me gasp for air. West took advantage of the opportunity, forcing his tongue into my mouth to take what the beast wanted. To taste me.

After a few seconds, he stopped and pulled away, leaving my mouth feeling like it'd been set on fire. His hands dropped to his sides. Guilt and disbelief were written all over his face, dumbfounded at his lack of control. I don't know what the hell happened, but if he wanted to fuck with my head, then he succeeded.

"It looks like you haven't changed either," I said, massaging my neck. When Hiram saw the marks he left, there would be another fucking funeral.

"Fuck," West groaned. His tone shifted to pleading desperation as his words got caught in the back of his throat. "For once in your stubborn fucking life, you need to listen to what I'm saying. I'll handle Hiram but you need to go."

"Go?" I repeated. West had always been on the edge of unstable, but Rocky's death must have tipped him over. "Go where?"

"Remember what Zander told you," West said as he opened the door to let me out of the room. "Please, Candy. Leave Hiram to me. I'll make sure Mieko is safe, but you need to go. Now!"

I burst out and fled. My feet ran before my thoughts could catch up. West's footsteps thudded away in the opposite direction. Why did he kiss me? Why didn't he kill me when he had the chance? As much as my head screamed to go back downstairs and accept my fate, I trusted West when he said that he would protect Mieko. He had no reason to lie about that, but he *did* have a reason to lure me to a secret part of the manor. Whatever it was, I wanted to find out. He may be sending me into a trap, but I needed to satisfy my curiosity. Plus, if Zander was waiting, I'd be ready to face him.

I opened the door to the old servant's entrance that Zander showed me months before. The vacant room was filled with nothing but boxes.

"Hello?" I called out.

No answer.

What the fuck was this place?

I pressed on, noticing an adjoining door leading to a staircase. I descended, going deeper into the belly of the manor until I came to the bottom, where a steel door blocked my path. I thumped my fist against it, but the metal didn't budge. There was a security keypad to my right, reminding me of the bunker in Lapland's basement.

I tried 6-9-6-9. A Lapland classic. It lit up red. No entry.

Why would West tell me to come here if I couldn't get through?

None of this made sense.

Hold up! A random thought came to me. I never understood the meaning of the numerals engraved on the pendant Zander gave me. They added up to seven, but it made no sense to use four digits. Until now. My hands shook as I pressed 2-3-1-1. *It couldn't be, could it?*

The keypad flashed green. After several mechanical clicks, the door swung open like the beginning of a bad horror movie. There could be a bomb ready to detonate, but I didn't turn back. Danger sucked me in like a hurricane. I pulled out the tiny, but lethal, blade from my bra and brandished it. Sure, it wouldn't hold up against an explosion, but there was no harm in being prepared.

I took a deep breath before stepping to the other side. Then, nothing. Stillness. It must have once functioned as a kitchen, but layers of dust now coated every surface. Clearly, Vixen hadn't included it in her massive renovation.

Something wasn't right.

Daylight filtered through onto the wooden floor from the gap underneath the door. I remembered how Zander said the servant's quarters led outside. Through the wall, a car engine roared to life.

I should know better.

I should turn back.

That's what any sensible person would have done, right?

A nagging feeling in my gut willed me to follow the noise. Whatever lay outside couldn't be worse than what I was running from. I'd come to Rocky's funeral to confront Zander and help Giles steal an old treasure, not play hide and fucking seek. Yet I was right where West wanted me to be, seeking answers to the questions that kept me up at night.

I took a deep breath and turned the handle, expecting to be welcomed by the barrel of a gun prodding into my forehead. Instead, a figure lounged against the running car. He'd pulled a black hoodie up to hide his face and wore sunglasses. His casual way of leaning looked so familiar... so...

The knife slipped through my fingers. "Rocky?"

"What's wrong, C?" Rocky asked, taking off his glasses and grinning. "You look like you've seen a ghost."

Five

Some people claim you see visions when you're about to die. You could glide down a dark tunnel, be reunited with dead loved ones, or watch moments from your life whizz by like a movie. I always thought it was bullshit, but maybe I was wrong? Someone could have blown my brains out the moment I stepped outside.

"Are you..." I stammered as I tried to find the words. There's no right way to ask someone if you've lost your fucking mind. "Are you really... *here*?"

Rocky wiggled his eyebrows playfully. "What do you think?"

He could have come back to haunt me. I cautiously approached. I mean, he *looked* real. As real as everyone else I'd seen today, anyway. Shadows moved across his face as the sun hit him at a weird angle. Ghosts didn't have shadows, did they? The cheeky twinkle in his eyes wasn't glassy or vacant like the stares of dead bodies frozen in place.

Shaking, I reached out at the apparition and poked him in the chest. I expected my finger to disappear through him like they did in the cartoons, but it didn't. He felt solid, but was that really proof? Stories could have been wrong about spirits all along.

I poked him again. I shook my head, backing away.

"This can't be real," I murmured in disbelief. He should be nothing but a pile of ash — not a solid-feeling idiot with a smirk on his face. "You can't be real."

"If I wasn't real," Rocky said, stepping forward, "would I be able to do this?"

His arms closed around me, pulling my body into a tight embrace. I breathed in his scent. Earthy. A hint of peppermint. Fresh laundry. Warmth radiated from his skin, and the rhythm of his beating heart pumped through his clothes. A heart that should have stopped beating. How was this even possible? I watched him bleed out over the concrete after I pulled the trigger.

"But the funeral... the coffin..." I babbled as my shaking hands traced the strong muscles in his back. "You're dead."

"Not yet," he replied, reluctantly pulling away and glancing over my shoulder nervously. "But I will be if we don't get the hell outta here."

"Where will—"

"You'll see," Rocky interrupted. "Why don't you get in the car before you pass out? Do you have a cell?"

I was too dumbfounded to argue as he took control of the situation. He searched my purse, found my phone, and abandoned it in the dirt, then walked me around to the passenger side of the waiting vehicle. It was one thing to hallucinate a person, but surely a ghost couldn't drive a freaking car? Let alone a white and black striped Dodge Viper.

My rational brain kicked in as Rocky walked around to get in the car. I lowered the window. Before he could get a proper look at them, I pulled the rings off my wedding finger and hurled them out. Giles or Hiram could have implanted the jewelry with some kind of tracker.

"Ready now?" Rocky asked in bemusement, shutting the door behind him.

I nodded as he turned the key in the ignition, and we sped away from the manor.

I paid no attention to where we were going. I was too busy staring and taking in every single feature of him. The familiar scar on his chin from a football injury. How his hair had grown out and flopped at an adorable angle, which made it look like he just rolled out of bed. How his stubble made him look older, but he still somehow kept his boyish good looks. Dead people could fart, but they couldn't grow body hair, right?

"How long are you gonna keep looking at me like that?" Rocky asked, tearing his gaze from the road to glance at me. He bit his lip, something he only did when he was figuring out what to say next. "You're creeping me out, C."

"What do you expect?" I demanded. I was sitting across from someone I thought I'd never see again. "I went to your funeral today. I'm the one who killed you, remember?"

"*Almost* killed me," Rocky corrected smugly. "I have another scar to thank you for, by the way. Can you aim for somewhere less painful the next time you try to shoot me?"

"It was your fault for moving at the last minute," I scolded. "I'd never have... hey! If you've been alive all this time, then where the fuck have you been hiding?"

"Can't you go back to staring at me in silence again?" Rocky groaned.

"Do you even realize how it's felt to think you were dead?" A fresh swell of anger grew in my chest. "How long were you going to let me believe I was a murderer?"

Rocky snickered.

"You know what I mean," I snapped. Well, I guess being a killer was nothing new. "How did you pull it off?"

Thinking I killed him had almost destroyed me. How had he fooled everyone, including the Blackbird? Had this been Zander's plan all along? He'd given me the necklace months ago.

"I promise I'll explain everything later," Rocky said, putting an end to my questions. "When we're somewhere safe."

Fear quickly replaced my shock as the gravity of the situation sunk in. Hiram was back at Briarly Manor. What was he going to do when he found out? He'd have realized I was gone by now. "What about Hi—"

"He's not going to hurt you again, C," Rocky interrupted, gripping the wheel so tightly his knuckles turned white. "I won't let him."

I looked through the back window to check for any chasing cars on the horizon. There was nothing yet, but it didn't mean they wouldn't be coming. "Where are we going?"

"You'll see," Rocky replied mysteriously. "Don't worry, I've got every-thing covered."

I exhaled deeply, trying to calm my erratic breathing. When Hiram found us, my life wouldn't be worth living, and Rocky would be dead. For real, this time.

"Why are you helping me?" I asked as nausea stalked the pit of my stom-ach. If someone fired a bullet into my chest, I wouldn't welcome them back with open arms. I'd be out for their entrails like an omega on heat. "Aren't you mad? I fucking shot you."

"I've had a lot of time to think," Rocky said calmly. "I get why you did it, C."

I blinked. "You do?"

"I've been in the same position, remember?" he said. "If you didn't shoot me, then Hiram would have. I know whose hands I'd rather die at."

"Rocky... I'm... I'm..." My voice broke, but I kept going. I never thought I'd get the chance to tell him this, and my words came out in a breathy rush like I was scared the opportunity would slip through my fingers. "I'm sorry. I know words aren't enough, but I need you to know that. I never meant for you to get hurt. You moved, and then... I was trying to protect you."

"So was I." Rocky reached over to put his hand over mine and squeezed it before putting his back on the wheel. "I made a promise to you, and I intend to keep it, even if it means dying."

"No more dying," I said, sniffing and wiping away my tears. I couldn't take it. Not again. The relief was indescribable and my body felt almost weightless.

"I'll try," he joked.

"I mean it," I insisted, my tone serious. "Next time, don't try to play the knight in shining armor. I can't save your ass a third time."

"I think I preferred it when you were groveling," he teased, slipping back into our usual playful banter. "But I'm gonna make everything up to you. Do you remember when I promised to take you on an adventure?"

I did. When we were teenagers, our favorite place to go was an abandoned warehouse. We sat on the edge of its roof and dangled our legs off the sides without fear of falling. One night, we were sharing the last of a spliff and staring up at the stars.

Rocky had turned to ask me a question, "Where would you go if you could go anywhere?"

"Somewhere where I can be free," I'd said after taking time to think. "A place with no rules and nothing standing in my way. I'd like to go somewhere where I could be anything I want to be."

"So, you wanna go on an adventure?" he'd said, blowing smoke rings into the air. "We'll go together. I promise we'll go somewhere where we'd never want to look back."

I'd laughed and called him an idiot, but the conversation stayed with me. Back then, everything felt so *possible*. All these years later, it's a memory I kept coming back to — especially when I believed his life was hanging in the balance.

"This isn't exactly the type of adventure I meant." I scowled. "Faking your death and forcing me into a car is abduction."

Rocky chuckled. "I wondered how long it'd take you to go back to your normal self."

"I'm getting driven around by a freaking corpse," I said, looking out the window at the interstate rushing past. "Nothing about this is normal."

"It may not be normal," he said, "but I keep my promises. You wanted an adventure, and that's what we're going to do. We've reached our first stop."

He turned to pull up at an abandoned rest stop, where a white van was waiting.

"Time to go, C," Rocky said, yanking up his hood and putting on his sunglasses. He didn't want the world to know he'd been resurrected from the dead yet.

The driver of the van followed our lead. He approached us, and Rocky slipped him a roll of cash for a set of keys without exchanging words.

"Since when are you so good at this shit?" I asked, following Rocky into the white van.

Switching vehicles was smart. It'd throw any followers off our trail… for a while, at least.

He arched an eyebrow. "Are you impressed?"

"*Impressed*?" I laughed, then it turned into a snort, and I clapped my hands over my mouth in shock. When was the last time I laughed like that? I tried to recover and play it cool. "As soon as I get over the novelty of you being alive, I might just have to kill you again."

Rocky smiled, making his face light up, and draped an arm over the back of my seat as we rejoined the highway.

"It's us against the world, C."

———

The sun broke over the horizon like a split egg yolk, casting an orange glow over the purple sky. The beautiful view took my breath away.

"Are we going to stop?" I asked, fighting back a yawn.

After days of no sleep, tiredness was finally catching up with me. We'd been driving all day and switching vehicles every hundred miles. Hiram following in pursuit was still on my mind, but even the fear of his fury didn't dampen my happiness at seeing Rocky again.

"Soon," he promised. "Very soon."

"Are you going to tell me where we're going yet?"

It'd been hours since we passed a town or city. Were we going to hide in a mountain cabin? Start a new life on a patch of farmland where there was no internet connection?

"You'll see," he said. "It's a surprise."

"I've had enough surprises today," I grumbled, pouting and crossing my arms. "Like you coming back from the fucking dead."

Rocky's eyes sparkled, making my heart somersault. Damn, the way the setting sun almost made him look like an angel.

He pointed. "Look over there."

I dragged my eyes away from him to see what he was looking at.

My mouth fell open. "You have got to be fucking kidding me."

A helicopter waited in a field ahead. Despite my persistent efforts, Rocky hadn't given me an explanation about what happened since we last saw each other. Our escape had been meticulously planned. There's no way he pulled it off alone. He was good, but not *this* good. There was only one person who was.

After my encounter with West and the keypad code on the necklace, I already figured out they were involved. But it didn't mean I could forget the past. Did this make up for what Zander had done, or how he'd kept everything from me?

I pushed thoughts of Zander away as Rocky pulled on the brakes. He hopped out and raced around the car to hold the door open for me like a true gentleman. Right now, Rocky was my priority. Experiencing the crippling pain of losing someone, then the dizzying euphoria of finding them again, was an emotional rollercoaster. I'd been given a chance most people never got. I couldn't take it for granted. I wanted to cling to the moment like my life depended on it and never let it go.

"How is this for a surprise?" he teased.

I punched him playfully on the shoulder as I got out.

"Not bad," I replied as the helicopter blades whirred deafeningly to life.

Who was I kidding? This was the best day of my entire life. We were once two kids who'd come from the wrong side of the tracks. How was it possible we were stepping straight into a scene from a billionaire romance novel?

"Hey." Rocky paused and frowned. He caught a tear falling down my cheek before I could stop it. "Are you okay?"

"It's just the wind," I lied, turning away and hoping my hair whipping around my face would hide them. "I'm fine."

"Are you ready to do this?" he shouted over the high winds and held out his hand.

I sniffed, slipping my fingers through his. Hell, who cares where we were going? We were together again. It's all that mattered. We abandoned the car on the roadside and trudged over the boggy grass.

"Shit," I cursed, wrenching my foot upwards like it was caught in a puddle of syrup. Heeled boots were impossible. The damn things sank into the mud with each step.

Rocky yelled something, but I couldn't hear him over the sound of the helicopter.

"What?" I shouted.

He shook his head, then sprang into action. He swept me off my feet and up into his arms like I weighed nothing. I held onto him as he unsteadily moved through the terrain. He gritted his teeth, battling against his recovering body and instinct to hold me.

He almost lost his footing, making me squeal. "Don't fucking drop me."

"Never," he promised. "I've got you, C."

My shoulders slackened. If I was with him, nothing else mattered.

Rocky was alive.

He was fucking alive!

The pilot was waiting for us. He opened the door for us to climb into the back and handed us headsets to wear, to protect our hearing and as a way of communicating with each other. I'd never been on a big airplane before, let alone a small chunk of floating metal. The pilot checked we were strapped in and headsets were on like we were about to go on a fairground ride and gave a nod. What use would the seatbelts be when we were plummeting to our deaths?

"I promised you an adventure," Rocky said through the microphone as the pilot performed his final checks.

"Ready for take off," the pilot said.

My heart dropped into my stomach as we rose from the ground, and my hand jumped to Rocky's thigh. I wasn't scared of facing scary gangsters, but heights? Well, they turned me into a nervous wreck. I squeezed my eyes shut, not wanting to look down.

"It'll be fine, C," Rocky reassured me, putting his hand over mine and stroking my skin. "Just look out the window. Enjoy it."

I gulped, opening one eye to watch the field and car disappear underneath the clouds. I looked over at Rocky, who was grinning from ear to ear like a kid visiting Disney World for the first time.

"Do you like it?" Rocky asked. "What do you think?"

I opened both eyes. Towns and cities became tiny specks of light below. Up here, nothing else mattered. The Sevens. Hiram. Above the clouds, we were untouchable. We were on top of the fucking world, and even better? We were free.

"It's beautiful," I breathed eventually, completely in awe as my fears fell away.

Before long, the pilot's voice crackled over the air. "We're starting the descent."

"But we're in the middle of nowhere," I said, peering down. Apart from a small lit runway, there were no other lights for miles around. I'm not sure what I'd been expecting. A helipad or secret underground Batman cave, maybe? Here, there was nothing. "Are you sure?"

"We've still got one final journey," Rocky said, pointing through the glass at a yellow metallic blob.

I scrunched up my nose as we got close enough for me to see the shiny Lambo waiting. "It's not exactly inconspicuous."

"Live a little." Rocky laughed at his joke. "What's the fun of running away if you can't do it in style? This is the first time I've been out in months. I'm not gonna stop until you're safe."

CHAPTER
Six

R ocky's voice sounded far away. "Wake up, C."

Was I still dreaming? I expected to wake up in Hiram's penthouse in Blackthorne Towers. Resigned to my fate in a world where Rocky was dead, and I followed Hiram's orders.

Rocky nudged me gently, making my eyes snap open like he'd jabbed my ass with a cattle prod. *How could I have fallen asleep?* I reached for my knife, patting down my sides, then felt panic rise in my chest as I realized I left it behind at Briarly Manor.

"It's fine," Rocky said, catching my arm. "You're safe, okay?"

My shoulders sagged in relief as Rocky's deep brown eyes watched me closely, wide with concern. His stare may be filled with worry, but it was also full of life. You know the feeling you get when you wake up and think you're late for work, then realize you have the day off? It was like that, but a million times better — like if you were to throw in pizza, plus a string of multiple orgasms.

"What's wrong?" I asked, taking a deep breath to calm my racing heart and mentally curse myself for letting exhaustion take over. "Why have we stopped?"

"Because we're here."

Rocky opened the car door to get out.

"Here?" I looked around wildly. "Where the fuck is *here*?"

We were at the edge of a mooring where a lone white yacht waited. The moonlight cast flickering shadows off the water, making the boat glitter. I gulped, pushing away my *Pirates of the Caribbean* fantasies. I was no boating expert, but this was no Black Pearl. It looked like a loaded tycoon's perfect holiday location or somewhere where you'd see celebrities hiding from the paparazzi.

"Come on, C," Rocky said, already striding down to the small wooden strip, swinging his arms with purpose. "We gotta go."

I stumbled after him, abandoning the car. "Is the boat *ours*?"

"You bet," Rocky said with a grin. He waited for me to catch up and wrapped his arm around my shoulders. He frowned at the goosebumps blossoming over my skin and took off his hoodie. "Put this on."

"But you don't even know how to steer a boat," I said, pulling his warm hoodie tightly around me. As nice as it was, a hoodie wouldn't keep me afloat when a yacht was sinking. Rocky knew how to grow weed and fight, but he wasn't a sailor.

"I may not be able to sail, but we know someone who can," he said, then smirked as he led us to the passerelle.

Lights lit up the side of the yacht, and my stomach lurched quicker than an anchor plummeting into the ocean as a shadowy figure emerged onto the deck. I craned my neck to get a closer look, but the mooring was dimly lit. Could this be another trap?

"You said you wanted an adventure," Rocky said, pointing upwards as lights on the top deck turned on.

A man approached the silver railings and waved.

I gasped. "Q?"

I tore myself away from Rocky's grasp and ran to greet him. After leaving Port Valentine, I wasn't sure whether I'd ever see him again. Q's clothes hung off him, and a navy cap contained his unruly hair. Even though the lines on his face seemed more pronounced, there was a new sparkle in his eyes. He was pleased to see me.

"It's Captain to you," Q said. He pulled his hands awkwardly out of his pockets to hug me. "It's good to see you again, Candy."

"Why didn't I get that kind of reaction when you saw me?" Rocky grumbled, trudging after me. "I was supposed to be dead..."

"That reaction is something I'd have paid to see." Q chuckled, then his expression turned somber as he checked his watch. "We need to go before the wind picks up."

"Since when can you steer a boat?" I demanded, planting my hands on my hips. "I thought it was only money you could move offshore."

"How do you think I stayed off Hiram's radar for so long?" Q raised his eyebrows. Damn, now it made sense why Hiram had no luck tracking him down. At sea, he was virtually untraceable. Q turned to Rocky. "I'll leave you to show Candy around."

Rocky saluted. "Aye, aye, Captain."

Q disappeared into the nearby cabin which had the word 'Crystal' painted across the side. A lump formed in my throat at the realization this had been Q's plan for him and Crystal. This is where he'd wanted them to spend their lives together. She'd have loved it. The top deck was gorgeous. It had a private bar, sun loungers, and a small pool; everything you need to try and forget about any drama happening on land.

"What do you think?" Rocky asked, spinning around. "Is this enough of an adventure for you? Pretty epic, huh?"

"I mean..." I struggled to find the words. "I don't know how you pulled it off. Are you—"

"Shh." He pressed a finger to my lips. "We'll talk about it tomorrow. For now, can we just enjoy it? Everything is *almost* perfect."

I cocked my head to the side. "Almost?"

Rocky didn't answer. Instead, he stepped forward and kissed me, making me forget about all the questions I wanted him to answer. It was the kiss of a lifetime. A kiss you'd never forget. A kiss that penetrated your soul and rocked your fucking core so hard it left you trembling. Rocky cupped my face in his hands, pulling me close as his tongue danced against mine. His lips erased my tiredness, replacing it with burning lust, desperation, and something else...

He pulled away, leaving me breathless and my body screaming for more.

"I've been waiting weeks to kiss you," he murmured, stroking my cheek. He traced a finger over the outline of my tingling lips. "I'm sorry, C. So fucking sorry that I couldn't have done more to stop you from going back there."

"You said we'd talk about it in the morning," I reminded him. My voice came out low and sultry, thick with lust. "Right now, the only thing I care about is that you're here."

My logical thoughts still hadn't caught up. I didn't need any of this to make sense yet. Hell, I didn't even want to try and figure out how we'd got here. All I wanted was to feel him again. To taste him. To get lost in his scent. I fucking needed him more than anything.

My hands slid under his shirt, over his taut muscles, then up to his chest. My palm glided over his new raised scar, then rested on his steady heartbeat, confirming none of this was a dream.

"But—"

I locked eyes with him as a fierce, primal desire took over. "I'm done talking."

It wasn't a request. It was an order.

Rocky was here. *This* was real. We were together again, and my body responded to his presence like an addict seeking a fix. My all-consuming need blinded me to reason. Words were not enough. I needed to have *him*.

Needed to feel him. Every perfect fucking inch of him. I wanted him to bury himself inside me and never let me go again. This is a moment I never thought I'd get again, and I wanted to devour it. Devour *him.*

Rocky growled, taking the hint. He wove his hands through my hair, and our lips met again. We kissed like these were the last minutes of our lives, and the entire world was crumbling around us. The yacht pulled away from the harbor with a jolt, pushing Rocky into me and the hard bulge in his pants against the ache between my legs.

The salty breeze was cool, but the heat of his body felt like the glow of a fire. It drew me closer, making me want to bask in it. Rocky's hands trailed down, stroking the curve of my lower back, then traveling further down to my ass.

"You're alive," I murmured as his fingers slipped down my upper thighs and underneath the fabric of my dress, leaving a burning trail behind.

I wanted more.

He yanked my dress up, and I let out a strangled moan.

More!

The noise of the yacht cutting through the waves masked the sound. The further we got from shore, the more it felt like we were suspended in a place where nothing else mattered but how good his touch felt.

"And I'm yours," Rocky groaned. "All fucking yours."

He grabbed my ass to hoist me into his arms, and I wrapped my legs around him. Damn, he was hard. So fucking hard. Rocky carried me over to a deck chair and laid me down. Goddammit, why had I worn a curve-hugging dress? There was no time to wrestle out of it. Rocky didn't care. His pupils dilated as his gaze swept appreciatively down my body and lingered on my black lace panties. This is not the kind of action I expected to be getting when I put them on this morning. Black was the color I wore whenever I planned to kill. Everyone knows sexy underwear makes a girl feel invincible.

"Fuck, C," Rocky breathed. His Adam's apple bobbed up and down as he swallowed hard. "You're so beautiful."

I cast a quick look at the cabin. Q had drawn the blinds to the deck. Thank fuck, because I couldn't wait.

I spread my legs wider, knowing he was watching my every move. I slid my panties to the side to reveal my pussy, already glistening wet and ready for him. His hypnotic brown eyes couldn't look away, mesmerized as I slid my finger down into the pool of wetness I desperately wanted him to explore.

"Rocky," I said, making him tear his eyes back to my face like I was pulling him out of a trance. "Fuck me."

"Here?" His voice came out in a low rumble. "Are you sure?"

"Uh-huh." I slid my panties off and let them fall to the deck in confirmation.

Rocky took off his belt, letting it drop with a clang. His hard cock strained underneath his pants, begging to be unleashed. The sound of his zipper sent an electric bolt up my thighs. Damn! I gasped as his cock sprung free. I'd forgotten how big he was. The metal balls of his piercings and ring caught the moonlight reminding me of an armored soldier gearing to face battle. Robocock could conquer me anytime.

"Are you sure about this?" Rocky asked.

I slid forward, balancing on the edge of the deck chair to face his cock. I licked his shaft from the base to the tip, then paused to look up and smile.

"Does that answer your question?" I asked, running my tongue over my lips. What more did he need to hear to hurry the fuck up and fill me already?

Rocky groaned, pushing me back and climbing on top. I half-expected the chair to collapse under our weight, but it held firm. Not that it would have mattered. What we'd started now couldn't be stopped.

Rocky kissed me, holding himself up with one hand as he used the other to slip between my legs. He caressed my pussy, teasing me gently, and smearing my slick over his fingers, but I needed more. Fuck, I needed it now. I pushed my hips against him impatiently, catching his hand at an angle that forced his finger inside of me.

"You're so wet, C," he murmured as I thrust myself against him to rub my clit against his palm. He added an extra finger, pushing as deep as they could go. But it wasn't enough... I needed everything.

"Fuck me, Rocky," I pleaded, hooking my legs around his middle to draw him closer.

For the first time in my life, I was ready to skip foreplay. I needed him to *fill* me. I wanted him to fuck away all the dark thoughts I'd had about him over the last month. I wanted to give him everything and let him fucking take it.

The barbell on the tip of his cock rubbed against my warm entrance. The cold smooth surface of the metal only added to the mix of sensations, making me moan. His cock teased, circling my heat, like a predator sizing up its prey. I may be dripping wet, but it'd been a while since I'd taken something *that* big.

He edged in, one inch at a time, as my pussy opened to fit his girth. The overwhelming feeling of fullness sent tingles racing to my toes. My thighs clenched tightly around him, but I didn't dare move.

"You're so fucking tight, C," Rocky breathed, thrusting until his soft hair tickled against my smooth skin.

As he rocked back and forth, his cock slid easier in and out as my pussy got used to his girth. I tipped my hips up to meet his, matching the rhythm, to increase the dizzying friction against my swollen clit.

Rocky groaned into my ear. "You feel so fucking good."

I dug my nails into his peachy ass in agreement, encouraging him. He responded instantly, picking up his pace and thrusting with a more urgent force. His Jacob's ladder rungs stroked my insides with every probing inch, creating a build-up of pleasure that felt so good I forgot where we were. Even this wasn't enough, though. I wanted him to bury himself so deep inside me that he left fucking scars. I tore at his back, making him pound harder.

Uncontrollable moans escaped my mouth, but Rocky silenced them with his. He caught my lip between his teeth, gently nibbling it, then thrust deep and held himself there.

"Don't stop," I gasped as he slowly started to withdraw.

"Oh, I won't." He grinned, only stopping momentarily to scan my body with his eyes. "I'm just taking in the view."

He slipped back into my wetness. One of his piercings slid against my g-spot and made my vision blur. He had my body under his control. The mounting pressure made my pussy hang onto his cock like it was life itself. He anchored me to reality. A reality I thought I lost.

I squeezed my legs around him, wanting to be as close as physics would allow, as our moving bodies matched the roll of the waves. I needed to erase every crushing thought of what life looked like without him. We were one with each other and the whole fucking ocean like the universe was trying to tell us that this moment was meant to happen. He was here and wasn't going anywhere.

The sudden friction of his piercing against me made me cry out. He muffled my cries with hungry kisses, making me melt into pure bliss. The night may be cold, but his touch set every inch of me alight.

Rocky slowed down; his calculated strokes only drove me crazier. I couldn't hang onto it forever, though. I craved release, and as he slipped torturously into me, my body surrendered.

"Rocky!"

A sudden burst of slippery heat coated his shaft, showing him exactly how much I needed this. *Needed* him. He growled like an animal as I clawed his back and cried out his name. It was all he needed to hear. His hips tensed as he grunted and sprayed my insides with his cum.

Our chests heaved as he stopped, propping himself up on his elbows. His forehead was covered in a sheen of salty sweat, and his piercing gaze met mine. He looked at me like I was the only girl in the fucking world.

"I love you, C."

At first, I thought I imagined it. The sound of the waves, an incredible orgasm, and our heavy breathing could have made my mind go wild. But then he said it again, "I love you."

I stared back blankly. My body may have separated from my brain for those wondrous minutes, but I was firmly back inside my head again. Sure, he'd said he loved me once before, back in the warehouse before Hiram took me. It was different now. Hearing those words rendered my usually snarky mouth speechless.

Why wasn't there a rule book for this kinda thing?

What the fuck is wrong with you, Candy? I'd spent the last month wishing we could be together. Now that it had happened, I'd frozen like a mannequin who had cum dripping down her thighs.

Love. Is that what this *thing* between us really was? We always managed to find our way back together — even his 'death' hadn't kept us apart.

"It's okay," Rocky said, planting a tender kiss on my forehead. "You don't have to say it back. Not yet."

"Rocky, I—" My stammers turned to nothing.

He tenderly brushed a strand of hair out of my face. "I'll wait forever for you, C."

Saying those three words aloud wasn't the problem. It was realizing that I might feel that way about another human and succumbing to the dread that came with it. When you cared about someone, it normally ended with getting hurt. Everyone knows that.

Rocky stood up, tucking his cock back into his pants and looking around sheepishly. "Cupid is going to kill us for screwing on the deck."

I snapped my shaking legs closed as he held out his hand for me to take.

"Why don't I show you below deck, huh?" he said. "It's been a long day."

———

I don't know whether I was dizzy from sex or the day's events finally taking their toll, but I struggled to pay attention as Rocky waltzed me through the yacht on a tour.

The ceilings were low, but the bright white walls and lights made it feel like less of a tin can. He pointed out the doors to different rooms as we walked. Kitchen. Bedrooms. Living room. I wouldn't be able to remember any of them in the morning.

"This is your room," he said, coming to the end of a corridor and standing awkwardly like he wasn't sure what to do next.

In the movies, there's always a weird moment at the end of a date when someone will ask the other in for a coffee. What did you do when you'd already fucked and didn't need an extra caffeine hit?

"My room?" I ached an eyebrow. After doing my best goldfish impression after he told me how he felt, I needed to take charge of the situation. "Are you not staying with me?"

"I didn't want to be presumptuous," he said, then added with eagerness, "but I'll stay if you want me to."

I rolled my eyes. "Sure, but I'll need something to sleep in and," I paused, looking down at my thighs and what looked like an art project gone wrong, "I need to clean myself up."

He cleared his throat and pointed at the door opposite. "The bathroom's in there, and while you're, um… I'll find you something to wear."

I laughed at his bashfulness as I slipped into the bathroom and he hurried away down the corridor. It was modern with clean lines and looked like it'd been recently renovated. I took a second to look at my reflection in the mirror. My cheeks were flushed with a natural glow I hadn't seen in weeks. Maybe sex was a miracle cure for everything?

A few seconds later, Rocky knocked on the door. "C?"

I poked my head out to see him holding a T-shirt like a Prince holding out Cinderella's slipper.

"Since when were you a fan?" I asked, taking it from him and seeing the unmistakable Ash and the Basilisks logo on the front. Not that I was complaining. They were fucking kick ass, but I didn't think heavy metal was his thing. When we were younger, Rocky only listened to R&B and hip-hop.

"They're okay," he said with a casual shrug, trying to play it cool. "Vixen made me listen to them and got me the shirt."

"Whatever you say," I replied with a chuckle, then shut the door on him before he ruined the image I had of him headbanging in a mosh pit.

After cleaning up and changing into Rocky's shirt, I joined him in my new room. Compared to the Blackthorne Towers penthouse I left behind, it was the size of a shoe box, but it was cozy, and Rocky sprawled over the length of the bed, already tucked under the covers like a caterpillar.

He pulled back the quilt for me to slip inside his cocoon, swallowing me in his delicious scent. The smell of safety. The smell of home. His strong arms pulled me into a warm embrace.

"I'm never letting you go again, C," he murmured.

Good, because I didn't want him to.

CHAPTER
Seven

Waking up in Rocky's arms on a yacht in the middle of the ocean couldn't be further from what I expected to be doing today. My original plans would have involved mounting Zander's head above a fireplace, but this? It was better, despite the hundreds of questions I still had. Although Zander's head would make it a definite improvement…

"How long have you been awake?" I asked, turning to face Rocky, who looked like he'd been up for hours. He was only wearing boxers and one of his legs poked casually out of the covers.

"Not long," he replied, shuffling closer and trailing a finger up my thigh. "What are you thinking?"

"About how the fuck I ended up on a boat with someone I thought was dead. You know, maybe you should—"

"I've got a better idea."

He pushed me onto my back, letting me sink into the mattress as he coaxed my knees apart and slipped his hand up my inner thighs, caressing my sensitive skin.

"Rocky, we should talk about—"

"But do we really have to talk now?" He cut me off and rolled on top of me. For a toned guy, Rocky was heavier than he looked and the weight of him made me breathless. He stroked my cheek with the back of his fingers, sending a shiver of desire racing down my spine.

"You're just avoiding my questions."

"Maybe," he replied with a mischievous grin that made it impossible for me to be mad. He leaned back onto his knees to pull my tee over my head.

After losing my panties to the wind last night, I was naked underneath. "But some things are more important than talking."

My body agreed as he began to kiss down my neck, leaving delicate kisses on my collarbone and traveling down my body.

"Rocky, we really need to talk," I began unconvincingly, my voice turned into a whimper as his tongue flicked over my peaked nipple. He took my nipple into his mouth, sucking and cupping my breasts, then caught it between his teeth to make me moan.

Well, shit… this was certainly one way to avoid talking.

Rocky continued to slide further down my body. His soft floppy hair almost tickled as he gently kissed down my chest, stomach, and waist. My heart rate sped up as his breath tickled my pussy lips, but he didn't touch me. Instead, he kneaded my inner thighs, kissing and nibbling them until I writhed around.

"Rocky…" I murmured.

"Tell me what you want, C," he said as his fingertips danced along my skin.

"I want you to taste me."

There was no point in trying to get him to talk when his other offer was so tempting. He slid one finger between my lips teasingly, only touching enough to get a shiny trail of wetness on the tip of his finger. He put it in his mouth and licked it clean. "Like this?"

Rocky was a joker, but my sexual frustration was now through the fucking roof.

"No," I said, reaching to put my hands behind his head, and lacing my fingers through his hair. "Like this."

I pushed his face into my pussy, and his mouth responded hungrily. My legs trembled as his tongue glided along my lips, pink and swollen from desire. His tongue swirled around and penetrated my wetness, lapping it up. My head tipped back, holding him in place as I ground my hips against his mouth. Was there any better way to wake up in the morning?

His attention turned to my clit, he probed and licked, eager to please and only focused on my pleasure. With Q somewhere on the boat, I bit my lip to stop myself from crying out as I quivered under his touch and released my hold on his head. Rocky wasn't letting me go anywhere though. His two strong hands grasped my hips to pin me in place. He moaned, like someone who'd been ravenous and finally had the chance to feast. His moans sent vibrations racing through my limbs, causing me to grab the quilt in my fists.

He knew exactly what he was doing. The fucker wanted me to scream the yacht down.

My voice shook. "Rocky, I—"

I gasped as he slipped two fingers inside me easily, using them and his tongue to bring me closer to the edge. He curled his fingers slightly, applying a firm grip. The feeling was overpowering. Like a can of shaken pop, my pussy was going to explode.

I grabbed the quilt and forced it into my mouth to drown out a scream as an orgasm rattled my core. My muscles clenched around his fingers, soaking him in a way that had only happened once before with West. Did this mean I was officially a squirter now? I couldn't see Rocky's face as I bit down and let waves of pure ecstasy roll over me until my knees were weak. Would I ever be able to walk again?

A knock on the door made both of us jump, and Rocky reluctantly pulled away.

"Are you awake?" Q called through.

"Um… yeah," I stammered back, my eyes darted to the door to check it was locked. Phew.

"I've made breakfast if you're hungry," Q said.

"We'll be out soon," Rocky replied, wiping his mouth with a grin. As Q's footsteps treaded away, he added, "Not that I'm hungry anymore."

I fought back a blush. The mention of food made my stomach grumble loudly. After an orgasm, a girl needed to refuel.

Rocky laughed. "Let's get you some food."

"Shit," I murmured. "I have no clothes."

Running away last minute was great in principle, but it didn't take into account the practicalities. In the middle of the sea, I couldn't exactly drive to the store.

"I'd rather you didn't wear anything," Rocky said.

"We're not the only two people on the boat," I reminded him.

"Fine!" He sighed dramatically. "You can borrow one of my shirts. I like you in my clothes."

That'd have to do… for now.

———

"Did you have fun last night?" Q asked as we joined him in the dining room. He sat drinking a cup of orange juice with a smirk on his face.

"Don't you have a boat to be steering?" I grumbled, collapsing into a chair next to him.

"We're anchored," he replied, then turned to Rocky. "They'll be here soon."

My head swung around to look at Rocky in accusation. "Who will?"

He scratched his ear and squirmed in his seat, shifting his gaze to anywhere but me.

"You haven't told her yet?" Q let out a low sigh and shock his head. He wasn't stupid. "Looks like it's gonna be your funeral... again."

"Told me, what?" I asked.

"I was going to tell you, but there's never been a right time," Rocky insisted. "We've been busy."

"You'll never be 'busy' again unless you tell me what the fuck is going on," I snarled. With Q around, there was no chance for him to distract me with incredible cral. "You better start talking. Fast."

"I don't want you to get mad," Rocky said, wringing his hands. Whenever anyone says that it's because they *know* what they're going to say will make you lose your shit. "We're not the only ones getting aboard."

"Who?" I snapped. Although, I think I already knew the answer.

Rocky didn't reply. He looked guiltier than when he got caught stealing candy from the store as a kid.

"Is this why you've been avoiding all my questions?" I pressed.

"You won't have long to find out." Q stood up and cleared his throat. He nudged his head upward and reached out to grab a pair of binoculars that were lying on the table.

I got there first. I snatched the binoculars and stormed to the deck before they could follow me. It was a crisp, still morning with little wind. A thin slice of land was visible in the distance, but it was too far away to make out any discerning features. I preferred looking in the opposite direction, where there was nothing but an endless stretch of undisturbed blue. I turned back to face the land and saw something out of place. A speedboat appeared on the horizon, ripping its way through the waves.

I looked through the binoculars and adjusted the lenses for a better look. A skipper accompanied a small group, and I recognized the figures aboard. *Mieko. Vixen. West... and Zander.* My heart rate quickened. There was nowhere to run. I was stuck and my safe place was about to be invaded by my fucking enemy.

I hadn't realized Q and Rocky were standing behind me until Rocky placed his hand on the small of my back.

"I know you want answers," he said gently, "and you'll get them. As soon as the Sevens are back together."

I snorted in disgust. "Back together?"

Q and Rocky exchanged 'I told you so' looks between themselves, which poured gasoline on my burning fury. We weren't a band who'd broken up and were going to have a reunion concert. There was no such thing as being back together when Zander's actions had already ripped the Sevens apart. Why didn't Rocky see that? All Zander did was make false promises and keep everyone else in the dark about his plans. There was no fucking 'togetherness'. Being a Seven meant *nothing.*

"Give Zander a chance, C," Rocky said. "Hear what he has to say."

"I don't owe *him* anything. I'm not a Seven anymore," I hissed. To prove my point, I pushed my hair out of the way to reveal the raw skin where my tattoo used to be. "Remember?"

Rocky's shoulders tensed, and his eyes flared in anger. He'd never been a good liar, so this was news to him. His voice shook as he asked, "Hiram did that to you?"

"See?" I laughed bitterly. "It's just something else your precious Zander hasn't told you."

"I-I-I didn't know," Rocky stammered, hanging his head. "I've been out of town since you left. Zander arranged it. We've not had much contact."

"Go figure," I snapped. Zander liked keeping secrets, and I knew Hiram arranged for Zander's 'gift' to be delivered by hand. If he hid this from Rocky, what else was he hiding? "Where have you been, anyway? A fucking doomsday bunker? Zander knew what Hiram did to me. If he cared, why didn't he do something about it?"

"C—"

I held up my hand and didn't give him the chance to speak. He could save his fucking excuses. I continued, "While you've been hiding, other people have had real shit going on. Can't you see that Zander has you all working as puppets for him? Our lives are just fucking games to him. He let me go back with *him.*"

"You don't know him like I do," Rocky said. "And I'm no one's puppet. Everything I did was for you, so we could be together. We've all made sacrifices, even Zander."

"Zander Briarly makes no sacrifices," I spat. Rocky may be blind to Zander's flaws, but I saw them perfectly. I knew who Zander was. A soulless monster. "He'd sacrifice anything and everyone to get what he wants. You're a fucking fool to think otherwise."

Q cleared his throat to break up our argument and pointed across the water. Our new arrivals were close enough that I didn't need to look through the binoculars to see them.

"I'm going to get ready to help them board," Q said, then addressed me directly. "And Candy? Please don't spill blood on my boat."

I glowered back. "I can't make any promises."

"Why don't you take her downstairs until they arrive, Red?" Q suggested.

Rocky nodded. He tried to put his arm around my waist, but I shoved him away. We may have shared a magical evening, but we couldn't live in a dream world forever. Reality was about to hit us with the force of a fucking iceberg. My walls were up, and my fight or flight response was overcome with the urge to hold Zander's head underwater until he stopped breathing.

"I don't need a fucking chaperone," I hissed. "I can walk by myself."

I stormed away and threw the binoculars in a fit of rage. They narrowly missed Rocky's shins as he paced after me.

"Don't be like that, C. I know it doesn't make sense yet, but we'll explain everything soon." Rocky said. "Give Zander one chance to explain. When you hear him out, you'll feel differently. He did this for us."

"You're fucking delusional," I sneered. My inner bitch rose to the surface, and I couldn't hold her back. "If you believe Zander did anything for us, you're not as smart as I thought you were."

"We did it because we love you, Candy," he said. Words that felt like fireworks last night tasted like ash in my mouth in the light of day. Good things didn't last. "*I love you.*"

"If this is what love is," I said, "then I don't want it."

Rocky flinched like I'd slapped him. He reached out, but I caught his wrist.

"Don't touch me." I dropped his wrist with zero emotion. "If you don't want to die for real, then you should stay out of my fucking way."

The Sevens were arriving, and there was nothing I could do to stop it.

———

I paced back and forth as I heard the upheaval of the others arriving above us. Rocky was torn between wanting to greet the Sevens and making sure I didn't kill anyone. Through the porthole, we watched the speed boat zoom away. They were here.

I grinned maniacally. "Looks like it's showtime."

I grabbed the nearest life ring. We were close enough to shore that I could swim to safety, but I wasn't about to take any chances.

"What do you need that for?" Rocky asked.

"You may trust the Sevens," I said. "But I don't."

Shit was about to go down faster than the Titanic.

I stomped away, climbing the stairs up to the deck two at a time.

Rocky groaned, following in pursuit. "Don't do anything stupid, C."

"Or, what?" I challenged, whirling around to face him on the final step. "You're the one who said you wanted to go on an adventure. Isn't a little excitement what you wanted?"

Being stuck on a floating vessel with these monsters was not how I anticipated our trip to go. But I'd be damned if I was about to show our new arrivals any sign of weakness. I may have dropped my knife back at Briarly Manor, but my bare hands were my most lethal weapon.

Up on the deck, the Sevens and Mieko were gathered around Q.

"Were you followed?" Q asked. His eyes scoured the skyline as if he were expecting to be ambushed at any moment. "Did anyone see you?"

"We shook them off." West shrugged casually. "For a criminal master-mind, I expected more."

"Don't underestimate Hiram," Q said. He knew better than anyone what atrocities Hiram was capable of.

West smirked like the arrogant asshole he was. "He's no match for us."

"We would have got here last night if it wasn't for someone tailing Mieko and me. The motherfucker had to sleep at some point…" Vixen's voice trailed off as I caught her attention. Her eyes flicked down to the ring in my hand, and she cocked her head to the side, grinning. "Nice choice of accessory."

The others all turned to face me. Despite her queasy expression and unsteady legs, Mieko beamed. West's expression remained neutral, but his stare raked over my body with a burning intensity, like he was searching for something. Either that, or he was trying to figure out whose T-shirt I was wearing. Zander barely acknowledged me. He continued to lean casually against the railing, only looking at me for a few seconds before his gray eyes returned to the stretch of the shore they left behind.

"Orange looks good on me," I snapped at Vixen defensively. Carrying the bright life ring may not make me look the most intimidating, but I'd be having the last laugh. "And it'll look even nicer when someone is begging for me to throw it over."

"No one is going overboard," Rocky said, placing a firm hand on my shoulder. I may not have a gun to shoot him if he stood in my way again, but I wouldn't hesitate to break his wrist.

"It looks like isolation has turned you into a killjoy, Red," West teased.

"You shouldn't joke about it," Mieko chastised. In my absence, she must have spent more time with the guys; she'd never have been so outspoken before. Maybe Vixen's opinionated nature was rubbing off on her. "It's not funny. None of it is."

"Lighten up, Saint Mieko." West rolled his eyes and ruffled her hair play-fully like she was his kid sister. "Everything worked out how it was supposed to, right?"

"Easy for you to say," Mieko said, then flinched. "You're not the one who had to hang out with Hiram."

"Hang on!" My mind replayed what happened at Rocky's 'funeral'. Mieko had insisted on showing Hiram the artwork, which gave me time to slip away. "You being friendly with Hiram at the manor was all an act? A distraction?"

"I did what had to be done. It turns out my acting skills aren't bad,"

Mieko said. "I guess all my time spent playing up to the customers for tips paid off."

I ignored Mieko. Instead, I turned my attention to the others and glared at the three of them. Hiram wasn't someone you could play games with. He wouldn't forget Mieko's role in helping me get away... and someone would have to pay for it.

"You fuckers used her as bait?" I exploded. "Do you even realize what danger you put her in?"

"Do you really think I'd leave her alone?" Vixen wrapped a protective arm around Mieko's waist and kissed her cheek. "I wouldn't let anyone touch a hair on her fucking head."

"Mieko was under our protection the whole time," Zander confirmed, waving it off with a dismissive flick of his wrist without looking at me. "She was perfectly safe."

"Your protection means nothing," I said, clenching my fists. "You don't know the meaning of the word. I'm surprised you didn't auction Mieko off to Hiram, too."

"Everything I do is to protect the Sevens," Zander said. He took a few steps towards me. His gray eyes were stormy but looked over my shoulder, and his voice was cold with zero feeling. "You may not believe me now, but you'll see how my actions were the only way. I owe you an explanation."

The only way my fucking ass. Whatever garbage explanation he'd spent the last two months polishing wouldn't be enough to justify what I'd been subjected to in Blackthorne Towers.

"Why don't we all go downstairs?" Mieko said, looking nervously at my life ring. She was the only one who realized my earlier overboard threats weren't entirely fantasy. "We can talk there... you know, away from the water."

"Good idea," Q said. As always, he wanted to avoid confrontation. "We need to get moving. Candy, why don't you hear what Za—"

"I don't want to hear *his* explanation," I said, realizing I sounded like a moody teenager but not giving a damn.

"Please, C," Rocky pleaded. "You need to hear him out. You can trust me—"

"Says the guy who was supposed to be dead twenty-four hours ago and who kept me in the dark to get me on this boat,' I said, bursting the happy bubble of our recent reunion.

"Red didn't tell you sooner because we all agreed we'd wait until we were together," Zander said. "You need to hear us out. That's an order."

"An order?" I clutched my chest and laughed. "I don't answer to you. I'm not a Seven anymore."

"A tattoo doesn't change anything." Zander's jaw hardened in a firm line like he was biting down on his back teeth. "The Sevens are a lifetime deal. Leaving isn't an option."

"Just watch me," I snarled. "Maybe you should have left me with Hiram. At least then I wouldn't be trapped on a floating fucking dingy with a group of people who are so happy to screw over people they claim to care about."

"It's not a dingy," Q mumbled under his breath, but I was too angry to care about bruising his ego.

"You're worse than Hiram," I said, staring Zander down. "At least Hiram doesn't pretend to be something he's not. He's a monster, and he owns it. But he has one thing you don't. He has fucking loyalty and when he says something, he means it. Your word means *nothing*."

Zander let my insults ricochet off him like bullets off steel, while Mieko's look of wide-eyed pity only fuels my anger more. I didn't need pity from her or anyone. What I needed was for Zander to be punished.

"Are you finished?" Zander asked, meeting my eyes properly for the first time since the day I shot Rocky in the warehouse.

"Finished?" I took a step closer. I wouldn't be finished until I ended *him*. I racked my brain to remember the rules about murder in international waters. I wasn't sure about the legalities, but it'd be worth the risk. "I've not even fucking started."

"We're not the only ones with explaining to do," West said, stepping in. He raised an eyebrow. "Have you told Red about your new husband, Pinkie?"

"You're married?" Rocky's head whipped around so quickly that he almost snapped his neck. "What? A husband? Who?"

I ignored Rocky's questions. My marriage to Giles wasn't worth wasting my breath on. It was a union of arranged convenience. It'd never have happened if Zander hadn't handed me over.

"Nice try, West," I said. His deflection wouldn't change anything. Besides, he was hardly one to talk after asking the skank of the century to be his funeral date. I raised my eyebrows and pretended to look around. "Where's your girlfriend, anyway? I didn't think she'd be one to miss out on a boating trip."

The muscles in West's arms tensed as he balled his gigantic hands into fists. "You don't know what you're talking about."

"Was Penelope in on Zander's plan, too?" I asked, goading him. "Were the two of you working together, waiting until you could get your slice of the cut? Did fucking me sweeten the deal?"

Having sex with the Sevens had meant something to me. For West to have jumped into bed with Penelope the moment I disappeared showed how little I meant to him.

"Be careful, Finkie," West growled through gritted teeth. "Don't fucking push me."

"I bet Penelope wouldn't be happy to hear what you did at the funeral," I continued, ignoring his warning. Judging by everyone else's confused expressions, West mustn't have told them about how he pinned me against the door and kissed me. "You can't control yourself, can you? I used to think what we had was special, but you'll just fuck anything that moves."

West's face reddened.

"What're you gonna do, big man?" I challenged him, wanting to push until he snapped. "Throw me overboard?"

"Don't," Zander ordered. He put a hand on West's shoulder for him to stand down. "That's enough."

"That's right, West," I said, shooting him a sarcastic smile. "Do as your *master* says."

Vixen shook her head. "You can be a real bitch, Candy."

My lip curled into a snarl. "It takes one to know one."

"I said, enough," Zander intervened. The menacing edge to his tone sent a shiver racing down my spine. "You have no idea about the sacrifices we've made to get you here, Candy."

"Do you expect me to be flattered?" I laughed hysterically, then stopped abruptly. "Did you think a helicopter ride and a cruise would magically erase what happened? If so, you never knew me at all."

I turned and stormed away. We may be stuck here, but we didn't need to spend any time together.

———

My chest heaved up and down from the exertion as I slammed the door to my room closed. Seeing all the guys lined up together lit my blood on fire with anger and something else stronger... *hurt*.

A soft knock on my door caught my attention.

"Candy? It's me," Mieko called through. "Can I come in?"

"Go away," I said, grabbing the nearest pillow and squeezing it hard, pretending it was Zander's neck. "I don't want to talk."

"Tough shit," Vixen responded with the tact of a rhino and threw the door wide open. "You don't get a choice, and there's nowhere for you to run."

"If you're thinking of clawing me again," I warned, "I won't go easy on you this time."

"I didn't think you'd be so easy to take down," Vixen replied, then held up her hands after I shot her a death stare. "I had to make it look convincing."

"Only because I let you," I snapped. "If I'd known Rocky was still alive, you wouldn't have gotten close."

"Maybe we should go, Vix." Mieko bit her lip and tugged at her girl-friend's arm. At least one of them was sensible. "Can't you see she's upset?"

"I'm not upset," I hissed. "I'm angry, and if I were you, then I'd get the fuck out."

My comment only made Mieko look even more worried.

"No, we're not leaving you alone until you hear us out," Vixen said, bounding onto the edge of the bed next to me. Was she outta her mind? "You have a right to know what happened."

"I'm not interested."

"I get it. Trust me, I do," Vixen said. Get it? How could she? She wasn't forced by Hiram to saw through bones with a blunt pen knife until her palms blistered. "Zander is a fucking asshole. When he told me what happened, I moved out of the club for two weeks and melted all his cooking utensils."

"His cooking utensils? Really?" My voice dripped with sarcasm. "Well, as long as he can't make pancakes, then all is forgiven."

"He loves them as much as West loves his cars," Vixen pointed out.

"What Vix is trying to say," Mieko intervened smoothly, "is that Zander tracked her down and forced her to hear him out. It changed things."

"Zander should never have made a deal with Hiram," Vixen said. "But it was the only way."

"There is always another way."

"You were never supposed to stay with Hiram for long," Vixen explained. She hung her head, giving the impression she was being sincere. "Why else would Zander have given you the necklace or shown you the way out? Rocky getting shot added an extra complication. He had to change the original plan."

"How does that make Zander betraying me any better?" I hissed, narrowing my eyes. While he'd been plotting, he'd also been fucking me and screwing with my head. "He still planned it."

"Maybe we should leave Candy alone?" Mieko suggested. "Give her time to process it?"

"No," Vixen said, not moving an inch. She softened her voice. "Look, you don't know what Bryce has done. How much we needed to get him back. Zander has waited his whole life to do this. If you knew—"

"You can save me his fucking sob story," I interrupted. "I know what Bryce did to *your* mom."

"What?" Vixen's face paled. "He told you?"

At our last visit to Briarly Manor, Zander disclosed the Sevens' biggest secret. He and Vixen were half-siblings, and he believed Bryce arranged for their mother and Vixen's father to be killed. Bryce Briarly was a jealous psychopath who murdered two innocent people because he didn't like to share or play second best.

"What Bryce did was terrible," I said. "But it doesn't make what Zander did right. It makes him as bad as his father."

Vixen opened her mouth to object, but Mieko sent her a warning look to stop her.

"Zander didn't do this for revenge," Mieko said cautiously. "By absorbing the Briarly estate, Zander could get enough resources to do what he really wants."

"And what's that?" I muttered, feeling anger build inside me like a simmering cooking pot. "A fancy new mansion and a hundred new cars? What does a monster like Zander Briarly *really* want?"

Suddenly, the cabin door flew open. What was the point of a closed fucking door if everyone just ignored it? Zander stood in the doorframe, flanked by West and Rocky. The three of them had been eavesdropping on our conversation.

"You asked what I really want," Zander said. His eyes met mine with shining determination. "I want to kill Hiram, and now? We can."

"You're lying," I spat.

Zander was a master manipulator. This is what he did. If he was going to try to spin everything around to make *him* look like the good guy, I'd rather blow a hole in the side of the yacht and sink us all than hear another word he had to say.

"All of this was for you," Rocky confirmed, his tone pleading, thinking Zander's revelation would instantly make everything better. Unless Zander's newfound wealth was enough to build a fucking time machine, his hopes were about to get crushed.

"There was no other way," Zander said. "We stood no chance against Hiram's empire alone but, with my father's assets, we can take him down."

I looked from Rocky to West, then to Vixen and Mieko. "You all knew about this?"

"If I'd known what he was planning, it'd never have happened," West growled. He looked at Zander like he wanted to rip his head off, making his denial seem almost plausible. Before West could say more, Rocky elbowed him sharply in the ribs, causing him to re-direct his anger. "Now we have a chance to rip Hiram's throat out, we're gonna take it."

"Why do you care, West?" I asked. "Haven't you got Penny to worry about?"

West's jaw clenched. "If you think I could ever be with her, then Hiram really has destroyed you."

He turned his back on me and stormed away. A crash came from down the corridor. Typical. As per, the big man was taking out his anger on something nearby. His words left a dull ache in my chest, but I didn't have time to think about what he'd said properly.

"You're our Seven girl, little one," Zander spoke again. "You can't escape it. You're bound to us."

"You severed any ties I had to the Sevens the moment you went back on everything you stood for," I said, looking at him with pure hatred. My body shook as I resisted the urge to fly across the cabin and finish him. It's what he deserved. "You're a hypocrite."

Rocky stepped in, sensing I was close to exploding. "Come on, C."

"No," I shouted, cutting him off and making Mieko yelp in surprise. "Get the fuck out of my room. All of you!"

Everyone looked to Zander and, with a swift nod, he gestured for the others to leave.

Mieko placed her hand on my shoulder as she left. "We'll see you later, Candy."

"It's not like I have a choice," I muttered under my breath. I'd swapped one prison for another.

The others filed away obediently like dogs on a leash. If Zander asked them to jump off the boat, they'd ask how fucking high. Why don't they just carve a golden statue out of him already?

Zander paused at the door.

"You're a Seven, Candy," Zander said. His tone wasn't forceful or demanding. It was softer with a hint of something else that I couldn't place. "We did this for you."

He looked like he wanted to say more, but I wouldn't give him the chance. I slammed the door in his face, leaving me with nothing but my conflicting thoughts and the sound of crashing waves. Even if what Zander said was true, how could we ever come back from this?

"If you've come to speak to me, then you can fuck off," I yelled at the persistent rapping at my door. Why couldn't they take the hint already? I'd made it as clear as a polished diamond that I wanted to be left alone. "I don't want to hear it."

I pressed my back against the cabin wall and hugged my knees against my chest.

"Um…" The person on the other side of the door hesitated. From their reluctance, it seemed they didn't want to be there any more than I wanted them to be. "It's Q. The Captain of the dingy."

Well, shit. My earlier outburst had offended him, too. *Way to fucking go, Candy.* It wasn't his fault the Sevens had entangled me in a huge shit storm. Q gingerly pushed the door open, cautiously peering inside like a whack-a-mole daring to rear his head. If it was any of the others, except for Mieko, I'd have happily punched it back where it came from.

I took a deep breath. "What do you want?"

"We're going to eat soon," Q said, daring to edge closer. "Do you want to join us?"

"Seriously? You know me better than that." I raised one perfectly arched eyebrow. "Why don't you tell me the reason you're here, Q?"

Q shifted his weight from one foot to the other. "I don't want to get involved…"

"Don't then," I snapped, despite sensing a 'but' coming my way. "You can shut the door on your way out."

"You're not making this easy for me, kid," Q said, running an exasperated hand through his wavy hair.

"Don't tell me Zander has bullied you into speaking to me?" I rolled my eyes. "Save it, okay? I've already heard enough."

Q clicked the door shut and gestured to the edge of the bed. "Can I sit down?"

"It's your yacht, you can sit where you want."

"I'm not here for them, Candy," Q said after a long pause. "I'm here for *you*, and I know better than any Seven what life is like inside Blackthorne Towers."

Q flinched as he said the words 'Blackthorne Towers'. He may not have lived in the building, but he used to be a regular visitor. He knew a prolonged stay there makes an asylum for the criminally insane seem like a freaking summer camp.

"I don't want your pity." I swallowed the lump in my throat and focused on my anger instead. "Seeing Mieko's puppy-dog eyes is bad enough."

"She cares about you," Q said. "They all do."

I snorted.

Q ignored me and kept talking, "None of us know what you've been through, but I know what Hiram is capable of. I know what type of life he lives, and I want you to know that I'm here. If you ever need someone to talk to."

"Thanks, but no thanks," I dismissed. "I'm more of a fists over therapy type."

"You've always been tough. Tougher than you look," he observed with a sad smile, reminding me of the first time we met in Blackthorne Towers. During the early weeks of my first stay, he'd been the only person to show me kindness in a world filled with darkness. "But you don't have to do everything alone."

"I'm the only person I can depend on."

"Do you want my opinion?" Q asked.

"No," I grumbled, "but I can tell you're going to give it, anyway."

"For what it's worth, I think Zander thought he was doing the right thing," Q said, then held a hand up as he saw my mouth open. "There's still no excuse for him doing what he did. I told him all along that he should have told you what he was planning."

"So, you knew?" I turned on him. Zander's plan would have been hard to orchestrate alone. How could he have managed to keep the Sevens in the dark, but not Q? "If you didn't agree with him, then why help him?"

Zander betraying me was one thing, but Q was supposed to be one of the good guys.

"Hiram was going to come for you. He was getting closer," Q said. "I helped him because I wanted to get you out... for good."

"And because you want to take Hiram down more than anyone," I hissed. Hiram killed the love of his life. He'd do anything to get vengeance. "You had your own agenda, Q. Don't pretend this was all for me."

"I didn't know exactly what Zander was going to do until after you were gone, but I already offered him the yacht. I never wanted to take Hiram down at your expense," Q said, then his voice dropped to a whisper. "It's not what Crystal would have wanted."

"What do you think she'd say if she was here?" I asked, wanting more than anything to see my old friend again.

"I don't know." Q shrugged, tears filling his eyes as his mouth twitched up at the corners. It didn't matter how much time had passed, a love like theirs was timeless. "But I know you don't realize what you have until you lose it. I saw how happy you were last night to get a second chance with Red. If I got a second chance with Crystal, I wouldn't waste it."

"It's not that simple," I mumbled.

Rocky and I hadn't spoken properly since the others arrived. He should have told me the whole truth the moment we left the manor, but he wasn't entirely responsible. I wasn't stupid. I knew that something was going on, but I didn't want to face it. I was so wrapped up in an imaginary fairytale that I followed him blindly to avoid reality.

"Nothing worth fighting for is ever easy, especially in a world like ours," Q said gently. "When a chance at happiness comes along, you need to snatch it before it disappears or it'll get stolen from you."

"Rocky told me he loved me last night," I said, the words spilling out uncontrollably. "I know Zander kept him in the dark, but how can he still stand with him? How are you meant to get over someone screwing you over and making you relive the worst nightmare of your life? Why are they all so blinded by him? Love isn't always enough."

"What did you say when Red told you he loved you?" Q asked

"I didn't know what to say, so I said nothing."

"And do you love him?"

Hiram once made me read a manual on how to chop up a body, but no one ever taught me how healthy relationships should work. It wasn't as simple as fiction made you believe. Real love was messy, like an explosion of paint over a canvas. No one prepares you for how painful it is or how it can tear your soul apart.

"I'm not... good... at this," I said, avoiding answering his question. "Can you love someone and hate them at the same time?"

"I can't tell you what to feel, but I can tell you Red isn't the only man on this ship who cares about you," Q said. "The Sevens were not the same without you gone. They put on a face for the world, but I saw through it."

"Then why doesn't Zander suck it up and apologize?" I blasted, then went on to answer my question. "Because it'd mean him having to admit he felt something, which he doesn't because he isn't even human."

"I can't tell you what Zander's thinking, but I do know what it's like to be hurting when you lose someone," Q said. "Would you accept an apology?"

Hell fucking no…

"Exactly," Q declared triumphantly, reading my thoughts. Maybe he had a sixth sense after all. "But if revenge was the only thing you cared about, then you'd have killed them all as soon as they got on board."

"They outnumbered me."

"Both of us know being outnumbered has never stopped you before," he said. "Even if you don't want to admit it to yourself, you still care."

"You don't *know* that."

"Call it a hunch," Q said. "The way I see it, you have two choices. You can either hide away down here forever or face them again."

Q got up to leave. The only thing worse than being near Zander was letting him think I'd been beaten. No one could keep me down. Not Hiram, not the Sevens… no one.

"One more thing," Q said over his shoulder. "Vixen brought you a suitcase of clothes. I'll leave it outside if you decide to join us."

Trust Vixen to care about appearances after our world has been torn apart.

"Q?" I called after him. My mind was already made up. "Don't start without me."

———

I climbed the stairs to the deck, mentally preparing with every step. As much as I hated to admit it, Q had a point. Our conversation didn't change my opinion of Zander's actions. They were still the douchiest move of the century, but I had to know more. I needed to understand how Zander's twisted mind worked and how he planned everything down to the last detail.

I held my head high as I entered. The Sevens, Mieko, and Q were already sitting around a large table that hadn't been there earlier. Candles were lit and twinkling fairy lights had been strung up around the railings. If it wasn't for my instinct to stab most of my fellow diners with their forks, the scene would make a perfect romantic backdrop.

When he saw me, Rocky's mouth fell open wide enough for a cruise ship to sail through. To his right, Vixen rolled her eyes and said, "Put your tongue back in your head, Red."

"Wow," Rocky murmured, keeping his eyes on me. "You look… incredible."

Hell yeah, I did. Out of the endless skimpy outfits Vixen crammed into the suitcase, I selected a blush pink mesh dress with a hint of sparkle. The top half consisted of a boned corset with built-in balconette cups that pushed my boobs up perfectly. It also spared me from wearing a peek-a-boo bra which provided as much support as a shoelace. Vixen favored style over function when it came to lingerie.

West turned his head to follow Rocky's gaze. He almost choked on his beer, then hastily downed his drink to disguise it. Zander didn't even bother moving, keeping his back turned away.

I moved to take the final vacant seat between Mieko and Q, making the fabric shimmer with each swish of my hips. Despite hugging my curves like plastic wrap, the dress had enough stretch to stop me from waddling around like I was trying to prevent anal prolapse. Why did designers make tight clothes without movement in mind?

"I knew that dress would look good on you," Vixen admired smugly. "What did I say, Mieko?"

"You nailed it," Mieko agreed, leaning over to kiss her fondly on the cheek. "As always."

"Quit it, you guys." Rocky made a fake retching noise. "Some of us are about to eat."

His attempt at lightening the mood failed dismally. A few months ago, we would have slipped back into easy conversation, but the atmosphere was tense as my chair screeched across the wooden boards below.

"I didn't know whether you'd be joining us," Zander said from across the table. Why did I have to be opposite him? "Are you hungry?"

Zander may be a traitor, but he sure knew his way around the kitchen. In the middle of the table, a stack of cooked steaks and a variety of bowls filled with delicious food made my mouth water.

"Starving," I replied without any enthusiasm.

I had to act civil until I got answers… and finished my meal.

"How do you like your steak?" Zander asked.

I picked up my cutlery, squeezing it tightly. "The bloodier, the better."

"I'd expect no less," Zander replied, putting a steak on a plate and pushing it towards me.

Everyone drew a breath as if they were expecting me to fly into a fit of blind rage.

Q squeezed my shoulder in encouragement. "I'm glad you came."

Zander continued to serve up food while everyone sat in silence. West shuffled his chair an extra few inches away. After my outburst about Penelope, he was purposefully avoiding looking in my direction. Maybe I'd been too quick to judge, and his feelings were hurt... but what did he expect me to think? How could I not second guess everything after what Zander did?

Despite the heaters on deck, the cool breeze chilled my skin. Apart from a thin shawl, Vixen hadn't considered I might need to dress for something that wasn't fit for a club or a freaking movie premiere.

"Are you cold?" Rocky asked, picking up on it instantly. He hadn't taken his eyes off me since I sat down. Without my prompting, he started to take off his sweater. "You can have mine."

"No," I snapped, causing him to halt. His wounded expression almost made me feel bad, but not bad enough to accept his offer. I didn't need him, or anyone else, to act as a knight in shining armor — even if it meant freezing my nipples off. "I'm fine."

"This looks amazing," Q said as Zander passed him a plate.

"Are we going to sit around and pretend to play happy families?" I asked.

You'd need a fucking chainsaw to cut through the tension at the table.

"I don't know," Zander replied calmly. "Are we?"

"Play nice," Q whispered under his breath.

I stabbed at my steak and started carving it in two.

"I'd like to propose a toast," Zander said, raising his glass. My glass stayed untouched as the others held up their own. "To homecoming."

It didn't feel like a celebratory dinner. It felt more like a waiting room full of patients waiting to hear bad news. This was no time for celebrations, and here? I was anywhere *but* home. I didn't have a fucking home anymore. I shoveled a forkful into my mouth to forget the... *Mother of everything holy.* The steak tasted out of this world, but I kept my face impassive. Manipulating me through food was just another one of Zander's ploys.

Nobody spoke for the rest of the meal. My skin prickled as the others watched me, but I didn't look up from my plate. Didn't they know I preferred to work on a full stomach? With West's reputation for flipping tables, I wasn't going to ask any difficult questions yet. It'd be a criminal offense to waste anything. After I finished eating, I dabbed my mouth with a napkin. I wanted to talk business.

"Why don't you fill me in on what I missed when I was gone?" I said, sliding my empty plate away and crossing my arms. "It seems like a lot has changed in two months."

Vixen, Mieko, and Q exchanged nervous looks. West scowled, refusing to look at me, and Rocky bit his lip in concern for what was going to happen next.

"My father is destitute. With Hiram's money, we bought the manor and still have cash in the bank," Zander said. He drummed his fingers on the table to an irregular beat. "We have the money and the connections to take down Hiram once and for all. I meant what I said earlier. Now is the time. We're ready and, this time, we're going to kill him."

"I don't *want* your help with Hiram," I spat.

"You may not want it," Zander said, "but you know you can't do it alone."

"So, you want me to forget everything you've done?" I asked. "You went behind my back and auctioned me off like a fucking painting. Did you even think about what life was like for me? After all the time we spent together, didn't it ever occur to you to let me in on your plan?"

"If you'd have known, it wouldn't have worked," Zander replied. "Hiram would have seen through your lies. We needed him to believe you hated us."

Rocky coughed, and Zander loosened his collar then corrected himself, "*I* needed Hiram to believe you hated us. He couldn't have seen it coming otherwise it would never have worked."

"Well done." I narrowed my eyes at him. "Your plan worked, and I don't even need to pretend to hate you."

"Hiram couldn't have seen it coming," Zander repeated. Although, I wasn't sure whether it was for his benefit or mine. "It's the only way we were able to get you back."

"What about now? Hiram will know you've played him," I pointed out. "He may have made a deal to give you all the cash you asked for, but did you think he would let you go without punishment? I joined your gang. That's reason enough for him to want you dead. He used you to get me back, and now he's coming to take you down. You have no idea about the hell he is about to bring down on your head."

They didn't need to know the full story about Hiram's plans, or how he arranged my marriage to Giles to make sure I was the Briarly successor. Some things were better kept a secret. Zander kept secrets, so why couldn't I? I didn't owe him anything.

"We can handle Hiram," Rocky said with determination.

"You mean, just like the time you 'handled' a group of Bryce's cronies?" I scoffed, reminding him of the time he got jumped and only made it out alive because I'd chosen to spare him. "You don't understand what you're taking on."

"I've been planning this from the moment you joined the Sevens. We *will* do this, Candy," Zander said, leaning across the table. "Think about it. A future without Hiram. Don't you want that?"

What a stupid fucking question. Of course I *wanted* Hiram dead. But this wasn't a high school football game or a gang of untrained kids running the streets who didn't know better. Hiram was a big fucking deal. The Sevens were no match for him.

"What you're talking about is impossible." I shook my head. "It's one thing trying to kill someone who doesn't know you're coming, but Hiram is already out for your blood. He wants to take over Port Valentine, and he will. You can't beat him. None of you can."

"Don't underestimate what we can do, or the lengths we're willing to go to get what we want," West growled under his breath, but loud enough that we could hear. He was talking about more than Hiram. Sure, I'd jumped to conclusions about him hooking back up with his crazy ex. But what had he expected me to think after seeing her draped over him like a fucking coat?

"Sometimes wanting something isn't enough," I replied coldly.

Zander rolled up his sleeves to expose some of his inked forearms. My mind lapsed momentarily, taking in his taut muscles, then averted my gaze to his face.

His lips twitched up at the corners. "How about a compromise?"

Vixen gasped like he admitted to wanting to join a monastery. Compromising wasn't part of Zander's vocabulary. He was lucky to get a second of my attention after sending me back to Blackthorne Towers, but his offer piqued my curiosity.

"Go on." I straightened in my seat. "I'm listening."

"Stay with us until we kill Hiram," Zander said. "Then you can choose to stay or leave."

Rocky's eyes widened and West's knuckles clenched, but Vixen was first to spring into action.

"No," Vixen objected. "The Sevens are a lifetime deal. There's not an opt-out clause."

"I don't like it." Rocky shook his head, then looked at West to back him up. "West?"

West said nothing, sitting in a sulky silence and watching everything unfold. What was The Hulk thinking?

"It's Candy's choice," Zander barked, slamming his fists down on the table. "I make the rules. What I say is final."

I leaned back, stretching my arms out in front of me and mulling over my options. I checked my nails, giving the illusion that I didn't care at all. "If I choose to leave, you won't stop me?"

"If she goes, then I'll go with her," Rocky said defiantly.

"Silence, Red," Zander snarled. "This has nothing to do with you."

"It's everything to do with me," Rocky said, standing his ground. The last time he stood up to Zander ended with a bullet in his chest. "I wasn't the only one who didn't know what you were planning, and I took a fucking bullet because of it."

Zander's compromise was turning into a revolution. The Sevens were once a strong united front. Now, they were falling apart like an unstoppable series of tumbling dominoes.

"This is exactly why you didn't know, Red," Zander said. "Because, if you had, it would never have been believable."

"Zander's right," Q admitted. He liked to stay quiet and out of Seven business but also wanted to keep the peace. "Hiram would have known something was off if you weren't willing to fight. He'd have killed you all."

Rocky cursed under his breath, knowing Q was right but being too stubborn to admit it.

Zander turned his attention back to me. "What do you say, Candy?"

"I have a counter offer," I replied.

Hiram taught me how to negotiate. Never accept the first offer.

Zander tipped his head to the side. "I'm listening."

"Your deal applies to all of the Sevens," I said. "We stay together to take Hiram down. After that, if they want out, they get to leave. If you don't accept my offer, I'll walk as soon as I step off this boat. You can't keep me here forever."

My offer wasn't just about what Rocky had said. It was about bringing Zander's controlling reign to an end. My proposal may go against everything the Sevens stood for, but Zander already broke our bond. He'd broken his own rules, and it was his turn to face the consequences. If we made it out alive and he is left alone, then so fucking be it. At least everyone would have the choice.

Vixen opened her mouth to argue, but Zander spoke over her. He didn't even take a second to think.

"Deal," he said, extending his hand for me to shake, "*if* we play by my rules until then."

"Done," I replied, rising from my chair. "But I'm not shaking your fucking hand."

I walked away swinging my hips. My ass looked great in this dress, so the guys better get a good look because I was on borrowed time. If we took Hiram down, I'd be outta there. The real question was whether I'd be leaving alone if and when the time came…

CHAPTER
Nine

"Candy?" Rocky pushed the door open to the cabin I'd claimed as my own. On a boat filled with inked men I wanted to throttle, I needed a place to breathe freely. Rocky edged the door open and put one foot inside after not being met with initial resistance. What did he expect? A fucking barricade? "Can I come in?"

I glared at his sneaker, already invading my territory. "Why ask when you're already fucking inside?"

He gulped at my deadpan facial expression and clicked the door closed behind him. After having a funeral, any normal person would want to try to avoid any life-threatening situations.

Rocky buried his hands in the pockets of his sweats sheepishly. "You're still mad at me."

Well, at least he didn't completely lack perception.

"So?" I fired back, then reclined back into the pillows. "But I'm not going to shoot you again… well, not yet anyway."

"It's good to know you care so much." He clamped his lips together like he was trying not to laugh which only infuriated me more. "But I was actually coming to see whether you shredded my T-shirt."

"Don't flatter yourself," I snapped. No matter what I thought of him, I wouldn't do that to Ash and her guys. They were musical fucking geniuses.

"If you do plan on shooting me, maybe you should improve your aim next time?" Rocky teased. His smartass comments wouldn't magically erase how he'd kept his mouth shut about the Seven's sudden arrival, even if he'd shown his loyalty to me at dinner. "Can I sit down?"

He didn't wait for an answer and sat on the edge of the bed, wringing his hands.

"I should have told you the full plan at the manor." He looked down at his lap guiltily. "It wasn't fair to keep you in the dark."

"No, it wasn't."

"We'd agreed to tell you together, but I still should have said something." Rocky sighed and ran his fingers through his hair. "I guess a part of me used our agreement as an excuse. I was scared to tell you, okay? Damn, C... I wanted you to come with me so bad. I didn't want you to say no and, after seeing you again, all I wanted was for us to have one perfect night."

"You should have learned by now that nothing is ever perfect." I blew out a breath in a dramatic huff. "Not in our world."

"Did you really mean what you said to Zander?" he asked. "Will you stay with us until Hiram is dead?"

I must have been batshit crazy to make any kind of deal with Zander, but I saw no other way around it. It was a win-win situation and, for the first time since knowing the Sevens, I had all the fucking power.

"Unlike other people, I keep my word when I say it."

"I meant what I said up there," he said, shuffling closer. "If you leave, I'll leave with you."

"The Sevens are your family," I replied dismissively. "I'm not going to make you choose."

"There is no choice," Rocky said. "I also meant what I said last night."

I played dumb. Rocky dropping the L-bomb had been playing on my mind, but I tried not to think about it. Especially when I didn't know how I felt. When I thought I'd killed him, it felt like a massive fucking hole had blasted straight through my heart. Was the inexplicable pain love? And, if it was, was that something I wanted?

"The Sevens are my family," Rocky continued, daring to reach out and take my hand. His eyes met mine with a burning intensity that took my breath away. "But you are the one I love. I know what life is like without you. Even for them, I couldn't live like that. Not again."

"You might not have to," I said, breaking eye contact and shaking my hand out of his grasp to cross my arms over my chest. "If we're trying to take down Hiram, we'll be lucky to get out alive."

Our blissful reunion yesterday had turned into a nightmare. My feelings were raw, my thoughts a mess, and I had no fucking idea how to process everything. At least in Blackthorne Towers, I knew my place and where I stood. Here? I knew nothing. How could I come to terms with knowing someone I trusted had betrayed me because they believed it was for the greater good? Plus, adding into the mix a pouty ass Hulk and your childhood sweetheart coming back from the dead was enough to fuck with anyone's head.

"Hey," Vixen's voice boomed and interrupted our conversation, sparing us from having to talk about the future. A future Rocky and I might never have. "Leave Candy alone, Red. We are having a girls' night, and no assholes are allowed."

"I'll take that as my cue to leave," Rocky said, getting up then pausing. He turned to wink at me over his shoulder. "Have fun."

Yeah, like painting my nails and having a pillow fight were going to help…

I scowled as he opened the door and squeezed past Vixen, who waved around a bottle of Russian vodka. Behind her, Mieko grinned apologetically and screwed up her nose to say, 'sorry, I couldn't stop her'. There's no arguing with Vixen when she sets her mind to something.

"You can either sit on your own all night or drink enough vodka to sink this fucking boat," Vixen addressed me with the command of a drill sergeant. "What's it going to be?"

"We have chocolate," Mieko said with a bright smile. "And ice cream."

I may not be happy to be on board, but Mieko knew my guilty pleasures and how I couldn't resist a sugar bribe.

"I'll also drag you by your fucking hair if I have to," Vixen threatened.

"Most girls' nights don't start with the threat of scalping," I muttered sarcastically.

"What Vixen means," Mieko said, putting her hand on Vixen's arm to silence her, "is we've missed you."

Vixen shrugged like she didn't give a shit, but the way her stare burned into me said otherwise. "Are you coming or what?"

"Fine." I rolled my eyes. It couldn't be any worse than when the three of us had to burn a body. "But only because you have ice cream."

Since my arrival, I hadn't explored the yacht properly as I'd either been on the deck or… in bed. Following Vixen through the narrow corridor made me appreciate how vast its insides were. The carpets were plush, the walls lined with sleek white paneling, and the paintings added sharp pops of color. Q must have skimmed a heap of cash to afford a boat like this.

"Red and West are sharing," Vixen explained, pointing at a door as we passed. "You should see West trying to squeeze on the top bunk."

I snickered at the thought of the big man crammed onto a bunk bed. It'd be a miracle if Rocky didn't get squashed by a falling bed as he slept. We went into the living area. It resembled a villain headquarters in a James Bond movie. A large white leather sofa and two chairs took up most of the space, along with a wooden mini-bar and a massive fold-down projector. A zebra shag rug, silver candelabras, and a chandelier-type light fitting gave the room an added sleek vibe.

"What do you think?" Vixen extended her arms and twirled around. "It's insane, right?"

I nodded. "I've never seen anything like this before."

Growing up in a group home, the lavish lifestyles of the rich and famous were something I only saw on the covers of glossy magazines I didn't have the money to buy.

Q appeared behind us, and Vixen spun around to face him.

"No men allowed," she shrieked.

"But it's my boat," Q objected. Yeah, like a small technicality would stop a control freak bitch from getting her way.

"And I'm the one who has spent the last month turning it into something that doesn't resemble a dingy man cave," Vixen pointed out, propping her hands on her hips in a power pose. "Beat it."

"Fine," Q grumbled reluctantly, shuffling back down the corridor like a kid being sent back to bed.

I frowned in confusion. "You've been preparing this place for a month?"

"It's the least we could do while we were waiting until Rocky was strong enough for the plan to work," Mieko explained, jumping onto the sofa and patting the seat next to her for me to sit down. "Vixen wanted everything to be perfect. She planned it all."

I didn't want to imagine how neurotic Vixen had been about interior design between renovating a boat and Briarly manor at the same time. So far, it's the only solace I could think of for me being stuck in Blackthorne Towers.

"Shame she didn't pack me something more comfortable to wear." I collapsed down next to Mieko. After our meal, I changed out of the gorgeous dress into a skimpy crop top and skirt. "All I've got is a bag of lingerie. If we're planning on killing Hiram, I'll need more than a lifetime supply of crotchless panties."

"You know, it was getting really quiet around here without you bitching all the time," Vixen said with a grin. She opened the vodka and took a swig from the bottle. "We need ice."

She disappeared down the corridor, presumably to wherever the kitchen was, to leave the two of us alone.

"She may not act like it, but she has missed her roommate," Mieko said, then smiled shyly. "And I've really missed my friend."

"I've missed you, too."

Mieko chewed her lip and played with her hair as her expression darkened. "I couldn't stop thinking about you and what was happening. I wanted to do more. I—"

Under the artificial lighting, the dark circles around her eyes were more pronounced. Mieko had always been slim, but she'd lost a lot of weight, making her seem smaller and more fragile. I'd been so wrapped up in myself, I hadn't taken time to appreciate how I wasn't the only one who'd suffered over the last two months. When you were living in survival mode, there was no time to think about others. But looking at Mieko made me want to pull her into a hug and tell her everything would be okay.

"Hey!" I cut her off before she could fall into a downward spiral. None of this was her fault. "There's nothing more you could have done. You got this place ready and distracted Hiram so I could get away, which was a stupid fucking idea, by the way."

Mieko shivered and pulled her cardigan tighter around her shoulders. "He's a monster."

"You didn't have to do that for me."

"I wanted to," she said fiercely. Her delicate appearance hid her strong spirit. "It was my idea."

I swallowed down the lump in my throat. She'd put herself on the line for me. Loyalty was hard to find in a world filled with superficial trends and people ready to stab you in the back. No matter what happened with the Sevens, I had a true friend in Mieko.

"Thanks," I murmured.

"You'd have done the same for me," she said softly.

I smiled, sniffing away the tears threatening to fall.

Vixen returned with ice-filled glasses and looked at us in confusion. "What did I miss?"

I took a deep breath to regain my composure and held out my hand for a glass. "We just decided to have a night where we don't talk about anything that's happened in the last month — right, Mieko?"

She nodded.

I couldn't keep blaming her and Vixen for what Zander did. They'd been as clueless about his planning as me. Neither of them had forced him to become a scheming snake. It's who he was. My anger needed to stay focused on those who deserved it. I couldn't let my fury at Zander poison my other relationships, especially when they were also victims who risked their lives to help me.

Vixen poured out a generous measure for each of us, then held her glass up. "To kicking ass!"

Optimism was for fools, but I drained the shot anyway.

Mieko noticed my dubious expression. "Everything will be okay, Candy."

I couldn't tell whether she was saying it for her benefit or mine. Either way, I shot her a tight-lipped grin that didn't meet my eyes.

"Why don't we watch a movie?" Vixen suggested, picking up the television remote. After scrolling through, it appeared she'd already downloaded enough films to last an average person a lifetime. The pointer landed on *Jaws*. "How about this? Seems fitting, don't you think?"

I did, but not for the same reasons. Whatever was swimming in the depths below our feet didn't scare me as much as the creatures walking on land. Hiram wasn't a small town punk. His teeth were razor fucking sharp, and it'd take more than clinking glasses to take him down.

"I'll get the ice cream and snacks," Mieko said, jumping up. "Popcorn or chocolate?"

"Bring them both," Vixen replied, sliding into the spot she'd vacated and slapping her playfully on the ass.

I made a retching noise as Mieko giggled and hurried away.

For tonight, I'd pretend this was a 'normal' slumber party and try to forget how we were floating on a yacht in the middle of an ocean with a crime lord on our tail. Hiram had taken me back once before, but my departure at the funeral would be an unforgivable offense in his eyes. A cat only had nine lives, and maybe he'd decide it was time to put the Kitten down.

My thoughts strayed from the movie as I drank the rest of the vodka. I may have agreed to stay with Sevens for the time being and they may be willing to stand up to Hiram, but how many of them would be left when this was all over?

CHAPTER
Ten

After a night of watching horror movies and feasting on junk food, Mieko and Vixen returned to their cabin, but I wasn't ready to go to bed. I needed to clear my head first.

Watching a movie about a predatory hunter only made me realize how we weren't so different. I headed up to the empty deck. The bright crescent moon illuminated the waves in a ghostly glow, and the wind stung my cheeks. I wandered over to the metal railings and clutched onto them, peering over the side to look into the dark waters below. Who knew what creatures swam beneath us? Humans hadn't been able to explore the ocean bed. For all we know, alien civilizations could be partying down there around the clock.

A low, gravelly voice came from behind me. "You shouldn't be out here alone at night."

"And you shouldn't sneak up on people," I snapped, especially when someone was in the middle of thinking about weird sea alien species.

"It's not safe," West warned, stepping out of the shadows. How long had he been watching me? "Especially without your life ring."

My earlier accessory choice hadn't been lost on him.

I scowled. "What's your excuse?"

"I couldn't sleep," he replied. "I thought I'd take a walk."

"Well, this space is occupied." I turned my back on him and stared back at the waves. It was nice to be away from the city, the constant pollution, the gangs, and the guns. I wasn't about to let The Hulk ruin my peaceful tranquility. "Unless you want to go for a midnight swim, go and skulk around somewhere else."

West took no notice. He came to join me, looming above like an imposing brick wall, blocking out the moonlight. His inked muscles seemed to suck away some of the available air. He didn't take up space. Space made room for him.

"Want to know a secret?" West asked.

I kept my mouth shut. After he'd spent dinner avoiding looking in my direction, he could shove his mind games straight up his ass.

"I can't swim," West admitted. "Never could. If you want to throw me off, there's nothing I could do."

"Maybe you should have kept that secret to yourself," I said. "Don't you think a boat filled with serial killers in the middle of the ocean isn't the best place for you to be?"

I imagined his massive body rolling over the side. It'd crash into the water, sending spray flying high, and then sink like a block of concrete. It wouldn't take long. No one would ever know.

"I can tell you're thinking about it. Whenever you're plotting, you get this look of deep concentration," West said, reading me like we were playing a game of poker. "Do you want to throw me off? How long are you going to keep taking out your anger on everyone else because of what Zander did?"

"You don't know what I'm thinking or what I want," I snarled.

"Then try me. What do you want?" West asked, turning to face me. "If you want me to take it to a watery grave, you know what you've got to do."

I flicked my hair over my shoulder and inclined my chin to stare into his stormy blue eyes. Like the ocean, unpredictability stirred behind his black pupils, and chaos glared right back.

"I don't owe you anything, West," I said.

West laughed chillingly, then his lip curled. "Not even a thank you?"

I blinked. "A fucking thank you? You expect me to be grateful that you all left me to rot in Blackthorne Towers for eight weeks? Do you even realize what it was like there?"

"What about Red?" he rebutted, disregarding my points. "You put him in the hospital, Pinkie. We didn't have to go back for you. We could have left you to rot there forever."

"If you didn't want me to come back, then why help?" I snarled, feeling my inner bitch rise to the surface and take over. "I'm sure Penelope will keep your bed warm."

"Do you realize how much of a selfish brat you sound?" West spat. His knuckles turned stark white as he gripped the railings tightly, making his forearms bulge like he was resisting the urge to wrap his hands around my neck. "Do you think I liked asking Penelope to come to Red's funeral as a cover-up? It was the first time I'd seen her in weeks. No one is begging you to stay. You accepted Zander's deal for a reason. Why don't you be honest with yourself for a fucking second?"

My chest tightened. The sound of the water and engine filled my eardrums as I gulped air to steady myself.

"You could be lying about Penelope. Lying is something the Sevens are good at," I sneered. "Give me one reason why I should believe a single word coming out of your mouth."

"Because Zander told me what you did at the warehouse the night Hiram took you. He told me about how you tried to stop the Bayside Heights development. You wouldn't have done it if all of this meant nothing. I can see through your bullshit," West said, stepping closer. His body was inches away. "I know you, Candy. You pretend not to care about anyone or anything, but you do, and it makes you so fucking angry that you don't know what to do with yourself."

"What do you want to hear, West?" I snarled. Unexpected tears stung the back of my eyes, but I didn't dare blink. I wouldn't let him see weakness. I couldn't. "Do you want to hear about how I was stupid enough to believe I'd finally found a real family? A real home? But then it all turned out to be a fucking lie."

"Zander was telling the truth," West said. His tense features softened as he edged closer. "His plan had always been to protect you, but it backfired because *you* were trying to protect us. Protect *me*. Protect *Red*. Damn, you were even willing to sacrifice yourself for the kids at Bayside you don't even know."

"So, now you're blaming *me*?"

"Never," West murmured, brushing a tear off my cheek and making me jerk backward. "When I woke up in the hospital and found out you were gone, I discharged myself. I got as far as the State line, then Zander caught up and explained why we had to do it. How we could never keep you safe until Hiram's heart stops. This was the only way to break the fucking cycle and let us look after you like we should have all along."

"I may have made a deal with Zander," I said, "but what makes you think I'll want to stay?"

"Because you're our Seven girl," West replied with zero hesitation. "Because we're selfish assholes, and *we* want to keep you. *I* want to keep you, and I'm not letting you go again. Ever."

West may have uncontrollable anger issues and a beast inside him who was hungry for blood, but he had a softer side. His gaze was filled with a furious intensity like he'd jump in front of a moving train to stop it from hitting me. How was I to deal with the whiplash of emotions? I couldn't decide whether the warm fuzzy feeling made me happy or unnerved, in the same way watching Anakin Skywalker babysitting would do.

I turned away from him to pull myself together. Anyone could tell a person what they wanted to hear. Talk is cheap, actions are what counts.

"I can't trust you," I said.

"Then don't," West said, grabbing my arm and spinning me around so I couldn't run. "Let us earn your trust back. You're our Seven queen, and we're going to bring you Hiram's head on a silver fucking platter."

"If anyone is going to take Hiram down," I said, "it's going to be me."

"Then we'll help you."

"For how long? You'll help until Zander decides something different?" I mocked. "What if he changes his mind? He makes the fucking rules. He has power over you. Red and Vixen. You'll do anything he says."

West laughed. The moonlight lit up the scar on his face and his smile lines as he continued, clutching his stomach.

"What's so funny?" I demanded, popping my hand on my hip and cocking my head to the side.

West shook his head. "You really have no idea, do you?"

"What are you talking about?"

"Zander won't change his mind. There's only one person who has power over Zander," West said, then paused for a few seconds that seemed to stretch into minutes. "That's you."

"Bullshit."

Zander had everything in his life under militant control. He calculated every action and how he could capitalize on it. All he answered to were his selfish desires. Pfft. I had no fucking power over him. If I had, he should have known striking a deal with Hiram would ruin our relationship for good.

"You haven't known Zander as long as I have," West said. "I've known him my whole fucking life. You're the only person he's ever compromised with. Ever."

"Maybe everyone else is just shit at negotiating?" I said. "Unlike most people, I'm not scared of him."

Looking at Zander was no worse than looking in a mirror. The darkness didn't scare me. It's where I'd spent most of my life.

"Your fearlessness gets you into a lot of trouble." His voice was smooth but with the hard edge of an underlying threat. "You're a fucking anomaly."

"If you're calling me a freak, don't expect me to throw you a fucking life raft when you fall overboard."

"See? This is what I mean." West edged closer again. "You don't care what you say. You show no fear."

"That's because you don't scare me," I said without flinching. "None of you do."

West moved quickly. He spun me around and used his body to block me in, pinning me against the railing. The coldness ebbed through the thin layer of my skirt as the metal dug into my lower stomach, but the feel of his hot body pressing into my ass scared me more than the icy water.

"All it'd take is one push," he whispered menacingly into my ear.

"Go on. What are you waiting for?" I goaded. West's pathetic attempt to scare me was almost comical. It took all of my self-restraint not to bite back a sassy remark about how this wasn't exactly the Kate and Leo moment most girls dreamed of. "Fucking do it."

West's warm breath heated my skin. "What will it take to make you break?"

"Haven't you heard?" I jerked my head in an up and back motion, making contact with West's jaw. "I'm already broken."

West staggered backward, spitting blood from his mouth. Q would be mad about the red stains on his deck, but what option did I have? Not retaliate after being provoked? Instead of charging at me, West slowly clapped his hands together.

"See?" West said, smiling and continuing to applaud. "This is why you're one of us."

"A liar and manipulator like Zander?" I snarled. "I'm nothing like him."

"Tell that to the congressmen you scammed," West said. "Or how about the men you tricked into hotel rooms to meet a bloody end? You're no better than him. Or how about how you turned a gun on a Seven? I assume you shot Red so Hiram wouldn't?"

"You don't know what you're talking about," I hissed.

"Did you really want to kill Red?"

"No, I—" My voice faltered, realizing he'd caught me in a trap and hating myself for being the cause of his smug fucking smirk.

"Tell me, Candy. How is what you did to Red any different from what Zander did to you?" he asked. "Everything we've done, no matter how fucked up, has been to protect each other. To protect *you*. The Sevens aren't afraid to make tough choices, which is why you had to squeeze the trigger and why Zander had to do what he did. We do what has to be done."

"Nothing *had* to be done," I shouted, my voice carried away in the wind.

"Stop acting like an innocent fucking princess, because I know exactly who you are and what you're capable of," West said. His deep voice hinted at darker intentions. I recognized the tone from the night he bent me over the hood of Giles's stolen car. "You're a fucking Seven. Through and through. You can't deny it forever. You know it. You can fucking feel it in your bones, and in the blood pulsing through your sweet veins. You're part of us, whether you want to be or not."

My cheeks flushed in anger. "Go to hell, West."

I wanted to jump across the deck and unscrew his neck from his shoulders like a bottle cap because, deep down, I agreed with his point. Sometimes the hardest decisions to make were the only way, even if they came with a cost.

"Touched a nerve, have I?" West taunted, wiping his mouth and smearing blood over the back of his hand.

I sprung into action and hurtled towards him. I had no plan for what was about to happen next, but I raised my fist to make contact with his face. West caught it in his palm like a tennis ball.

"You're a fucking asshole," I spat.

"Maybe. But it doesn't change the fact that you're a Seven, and you fucking know it." West said, gripping my hand so hard I was afraid my bones would break. I tried to headbutt him again, but he dropped his hold and backtracked. My movements were guided by raw emotion. They were clumsy and erratic, but West treated the unsteady floor like a karate dojo. He expertly deflected my attempts, then wrapped his arms around my torso. His arms crushed my ribs, leaving me gasping for air. "If I let you go, will you promise to stop fighting?"

"Never."

He laughed, letting go and allowing me to catch a breath before grabbing my waist to pull me into his chest.

"Good," he said. "Because I've fucking missed you."

West's mouth descended on mine, and my body reacted involuntarily. Instead of lashing out to get away, I responded hungrily, tasting his blood on my tongue. The metallic taste ignited a primal instinct in my core. I don't know what I wanted to do more: kill him or fuck him. I caught his lip between my teeth, sucking his blood, as he groaned.

West knew how to draw the worst out of me, just like I knew how to bring the worst out of him. His giant hands lifted me, allowing me to wrap my legs around his waist.

"I'm not leaving you alone," he growled possessively. "You're coming with me."

Somehow West managed to navigate his way down the dark staircase. I yelped as I thought we were about to fall, then he pressed his lips against mine to silence me, crushing my breasts against his hard pecs. He backed up, carrying me to my cabin.

Inside, he threw me on the bed and shut the door behind us. When he turned around, his hungry blue eyes sought me out in the darkness. He resembled a giant wolf, circling its prey before it got ready to dive in and rip out its throat. He licked his lips like he was thinking about how good his next meal would taste.

The tiny cabin window let in a sliver of moonlight as I slid up the bed. He may be eyeing me up like a fucking entree, but I wouldn't make it easy for him. He wasn't the only predator in the room.

West grinned. "So, you wanna play games?"

"Bring it," I snarled.

West took off his shirt. His beautiful inked torso came alive in the silver glow. The black and gray images swirling over his defined muscles stunned me to the spot. He joined me on the bed, his weight tipping the mattress forward and pushing me towards him. He didn't waste the opportunity.

His giant hands grabbed me firmly by the waist and forced my knees apart with his elbows, then pulled me down the smooth, silky fabric until I lay at his mercy. He leaned down, dwarfing me under his broad shoulders, and put his arms on either side of my head.

"You don't stand a fucking chance, Pinkie," he said, running his tongue down the side of my neck until he reached the soft flesh at the point where it met my shoulder. He nipped the tender spot between his teeth, making me moan, then sat up. Trying to shuffle away wouldn't help. There was nowhere to go. He read my mind and growled, "You're not going anywhere."

He ripped the front of my crop top open. I hadn't worn a bra, and my nipples stood hard at his attention. *Fuck.* They didn't know what was good for them. While he was distracted by the twins, I reached out for the dresser, where I knew there was a pair of scissors. I'd left them out earlier. A girl never knew when she might need a blade.

West laughed coldly. "Do you think those are going to help you?"

He may think he was in control, but he was wrong. I hated my body for wanting him, but I couldn't stop it. If I was going to have him, it needed to be on my fucking terms.

"Strip," I ordered, pointing the scissors at him like a loaded gun. "Unless you want me to make a scarf out of your intestines."

West looked down at my hands and chuckled, but he didn't hesitate. He backed away, taking his sweet time to drop his pants. I swallowed as he took off his boxers. When we last had sex, I never got to see his cock, only feel it, but goddamn. His tattoos didn't only extend to his body. Ink wrapped around his hard shaft in a beautiful pattern that made his dick look like a missile. A missile straight from hell.

"Are you gonna put down the scissors now?" he asked, standing stark naked with his hands on his hips. He looked like a fallen angel, and he fucking knew it.

"No," I replied as my cheeks flushed. Thank fuck it was dark. "I want you to lie down."

West complied. The cabin was small, but West's presence made it seem like a dollhouse. As soon as he was on his back, I rolled over, climbing on top to straddle him. It was like mounting a freaking tree. I had him right where I wanted him. He was my prey now.

I pulled the zip on my skirt that ran down the entire length of the fabric and let the tatters of my top fall from my shoulders, watching his pupils dilate at seeing me in nothing but panties and getting a kick out of the effect I had on him. I wanted him to beg. I leaned forward, stopping when my lips were close enough to feel his breath on my face but not quite touching. West had taken from me, so it was my turn to take from him.

He groaned as I slipped down his body, tweaking his nipple piercing. I'd been so distracted by his incredible body and tattoos that I'd never noticed it before. His skin smelled familiar, a sexy mix of sandalwood, leather, and a hint of salt from the sea breeze.

His hands reached to touch my ass.

"No," I snapped, reacting instinctively and making a cut across his skin.

Panic rose in my chest. What was he going to do? Maybe this would tip his beast over the edge. I expected him to get mad or throw me off, but he surprised me. He dropped his hands to his sides and moaned. "Shit, Pinkie..."

As the blood pooled, I slid my tongue over it, tasting him and making his cock twitch, relishing the power I had. His erection rubbed against my panties, causing friction against my clit that made me want to jump his freaking bones, but I wouldn't... not yet.

Instead, I continued to explore. I trailed the tip of my tongue down his carved abs and delicious V-shaped hips. He growled, but he didn't try to touch me again. He knew better.

Holy fucking shit.

I came face-to-face with his cock. The ink had a life of its own under his throbbing skin, begging for me to touch it.

I stopped, looking up at him through heavy eyelids. "Do you want me to suck your cock, West?"

West growled in agreement and grabbed my hair, making me pull back.

"I didn't say you could touch me," I reminded him, cutting his inner thigh.

"Fuck, Pinkie!" West dropped his hands and sunk deeper into the mattress. It was fucking wild to have a mountain of a man acting like putty under my shiny red nails. "You're killing me here."

I grinned as I licked along his cut, then ran my tongue over my lips. I wanted to tease him. I wanted to make him fucking suffer. How long would it take for him to unleash the beast?

I turned my attention back to his cock. The mini monster pulsed with desire, and a drop of pre-cum showed how much he wanted this. I tasted him on the tip of my tongue and made his hips jerk. Cum didn't taste as sweet as ice cream, but it was *his*.

I held his hot silky base in my free hand and wrapped my mouth around his tip, sucking gently. If he knew about the other acts I committed in this position, he wouldn't be as keen on me blowing his trophy-winning schlong. One wrong move from him, and I could pierce his balls with the scissors.

I took him slowly to the back of my throat. My jaw would ache from having to stretch around his girth, but it'd be worth it. My spit dripped down his dick as I breathed funny and almost choked from lack of air. Damn, I needed to get my gag reflex under control. West, Zander, and Rocky may have all fucked me at the same time, but the whole sex thing was still relatively new to me.

West grunted in pleasure as my tongue ran over his veins. "Fuck, Pinkie..."

He tugged my hair into a rough ponytail and forced me down further while he thrust upwards to hit the back of my throat, pistoning his hips unable to control himself. I threw the scissors to the side. I needed two hands to tame the monster. I used my mouth and hands to pleasure him, making him pant. From his heaving chest and groans, the big man was close.

"Fuck!" With a thrust of his hips, West came. He sprayed my mouth like he was trying to extinguish a fucking fire with his dick. Had he been storing it up for weeks?

I pulled away, spit trailing from his cock to my chin, and grinned at the sweaty mess he'd become.

His skin was covered in a sheen of sweat, but he didn't take any time to recover. He sat up and took my face in his hands. His mouth assaulted mine in a frenzy. He didn't give a shit that the metallic taste of his blood and cum made me taste like a salty cocktail. His rough kiss was filled with intention... and promise.

He slipped his hands under my ass and threw me down at his side, then pinned my arms above my head. The fingers on one of his hands wrapped around both of my wrists to restrict my motion, and the weight of his thighs on either side of my body trapped me in place.

"Do you think we're done?" He grinned wickedly. "We're just getting started."

West ducked to retrieve my dropped scissors. *Fuck.* A flush crept over my chest as I drew a sharp intake of breath.

"You've had your fun, Pinkie," West said, his eyes shining with desire as he held the blade to my neck. "It's my turn now."

"This isn't a fucking game, West," I snarled.

"Maybe not," West replied, parting my legs with his thigh. He looked down with a smirk, making me squirm under his scrutiny. "But your panties are soaked for me."

He removed the blade from my pulsing neck and slid the cool metal teasingly down the center of my body. He didn't make me bleed but left a ghostly white trail behind until he reached my underwear. My breathing hitched up a notch as the scissors cut through the thin fabric easily. He slashed through the lace, slicing the sides away. Vixen would be pissed if she ever found out he turned expensive lingerie into party streamers.

"West—"

He pressed the scissors back to my throat, applying pressure with the point. "Don't fight me, Pinkie."

I swallowed hard as he tore the remnants of my underwear away with his spare hand and tossed them aside. His cock stiffened, ready for action again.

"Do you always force girls to fuck you by holding a blade to their throat?" I taunted, knowing this would anger him.

"Only when they like it," West replied. His fingers dipped between my legs and slid between my pussy lips, making me gasp. "And you can't deny that you like it, Pinkie. I can feel how wet you are."

A whimper escaped my lips as he slid a finger inside me. He smirked, pleased to evoke a reaction and prove his point. My hands were free, so I could fight him off... but I didn't want to. We had started a chain reaction that I was powerless to stop

"You're so fucking tight," West murmured appreciatively.

His finger fucked me in slow torturous strokes as his thumb stroked my clit to the same rhythm. As he pushed in a second finger, the scissors dug deeper into my neck and broke the skin, causing blood to drip down. West's hot mouth was on it instantly. The stinging sensation and his tongue lapping against me only amplified the pleasure of him exploring my heat.

"You taste so good." West's whisper against my neck made me tremble. "You're the only girl I want to do this with. The only girl who can make me hard and whose pussy makes my cock feel like it's gonna burst."

"More," I gasped. "Give me... more."

"More?" West climbed on top of me, sinking me into another world. He angled his hips like he was about to launch a rocket. "Do you want me to fill you, Pinkie?"

"Uh-huh," I moaned. If he didn't, I'd cum all over his fingers.

The pressure on my neck lessened, so I dared to move my hands. I stroked down his back, then dug my nails into his skin in encouragement. What the hell was he waiting for?

"If I fill you," he said, sliding the flat of the scissors down my cheek, "will you gush on me again, baby?"

I blushed at the memory of how I wrecked the seats in Giles's sports car. Until then, I thought that squirting was a myth.

"Well?" West prompted as his tattooed cock rubbed against my wet pussy, turning me on more. "Are you going to give me what I want?"

He wanted me to succumb. He wanted me to give in and beg, but I wouldn't. This wasn't about what he wanted. This was all about me. His beast couldn't rule me. I sunk my teeth into his shoulder, making him curse and his hips buck, giving my pussy more of the delicious friction she craved.

"So, you don't want to play nice?" West purred. He tossed the scissors away and moved both of his hands to the headboard, casting me in a dark shadow. "I'll need both hands for what I'm going to do to you."

West may think he'd won, but when he flipped me onto my front and his giant hands yanked my hips upward to force me to my knees, I knew who the real winner was. He was going to take me. His hand forced my head back down on the mattress, keeping my ass pointed in his direction. I stretched my arms out in front, knowing it would give him the best view.

He spread my ass cheeks to get a good entrance then thrust into my pussy with an urgent force, making my whole body rock. I tried to resist, pushing my ass back against him, but this only drove him crazier. He grabbed my hips and slammed into me, making my toes curl and moan uncontrollably.

"Gush for me, baby," West ordered.

I didn't need him to ask. I couldn't hold in the feeling any longer. My back arched as I came undone. My vision blurred in pure bliss as every thrust hit a new wave of pleasure and drenched his cock in my wetness.

"I missed this," West said as he slid out of me, then rolled me over to face him. His gaze was soft and adoring, totally different from the unbridled beast who'd fucked my brains out seconds before. "And I missed you."

My post-orgasm bliss clouded my judgment as I whispered back, "I missed you too."

CHAPTER
Eleven

Goddammit. Why was my pussy possessed by a cock-hungry demon? The universe has it out for me. Unlike downing too many tequila shots, fucking West left me with a thumping ache between my legs instead of my head.

Waking up with his heavy inked arm draped over my naked body almost made me forget how I ended up on the boat in the first place and what I'd endured over the last few months.

Before West's eyes opened, I crawled out of bed and put on an oversized tee. Sometimes words aren't enough, and our bodies take action. We'd got lost in the moment. But where the hell did it leave us? What did last night mean to him? Did I even want to know? After Rocky declared his love for me, I wasn't ready to face another emotional conversation. The Sevens had to focus on what was important... killing Hiram.

"Looks like you should be thanking me for the crotchless panties after all..." Vixen smirked knowingly as I entered the living room. It didn't seem like a good time to mention the panties were completely destroyed. She lounged over a chair, wrapped in a black dressing gown, and cradled a strong cup of coffee. She had a sparkle in her eyes like an evil villain, which I'd grown to love but also hate when she directed it at me. "We sleep next to your room, remember?"

"What are you doing up so early, anyway?" I snapped, swishing my hair over my face to hide my coloring cheeks. So much for trying to keep it a secret. The sooner we got off the sea, the better. It was bad enough when I used to share a room with her, let alone being stuck on a yacht where every thrust could be felt like a mini tsunami. "Shouldn't you be sleeping?"

"I'm planning a party tonight," Vixen said. Her skin was positively glowing. "I want everyone to be there."

"From where I'm standing, there doesn't seem like we have much to celebrate," I grumbled. "Have you forgotten that we're on a suicide mission?"

She waved her hand dismissively and jumped up from her comfortable spot.

"I'm going back to bed," she said, sauntering away with a huge smile and a spring in her step. Anything that made Vixen smile couldn't be a good thing, right? She halted, then turned to add over her shoulder, "Suicide mission or not, we're having a fucking party."

I rolled my eyes and headed into the kitchen, expecting it to be empty. Instead, Zander was preparing food on the counter. He wore a crisp black shirt with loosened top buttons and pressed gray trousers. Did the guy ever sleep?

"Morning." Zander's eyes strayed from the chopping board to look me over, lingering on my bare legs. "How did you sleep?"

His tone was neutral and unreadable. If he heard West and me making waves in the next cabin, he didn't show it. Regardless, I wasn't about to join him in playing fucking house. I may have agreed to stay with the Sevens until Hiram was dead, but we didn't make a clause that required me to act civil or talk to him.

I spied a blueberry muffin on the side and snatched it, taking a huge bite.

"Fine," I snapped back with my mouth full, spraying crumbs everywhere. Screw manners. I was no fucking lady.

"How is West this morning?"

Shit. The bastard heard everything. Good fucking riddance. It would serve as a reminder of something he would never get again.

"Lucky to be alive," I said, not flinching and changing the subject. If he wanted to put me under the microscope, I'd put him on a slide to make him squirm like the lowlife bacteria he was. "Tell me, was it part of your plan for Hiram to arrange for him to be shot?"

After hearing Zander's explanations, I could wrap my head around how he screwed me over to get Hiram's money and ruin his father. That made sense, but could it have been a coincidence that West was shot on the night Hiram came to town? He removed the one person who might physically stand a chance against Hiram from the equation.

A storm rolled across Zander's features.

"Hiram arranged it with *your husband* on his own," Zander spat through gritted teeth. "West knows that. Hiram changed our plans last minute. The exchange was never meant to happen like that. Do you really think I'd have let you go to the warehouse alone?"

"I see right through you, Zander," I scoffed. I may not be a lady, but he was no fucking gentleman. He cared about no one but himself. "You can't hide who you are. Everyone else might not see it yet, but they will. And when they do, they'll leave you, too."

"Maybe they will," he said, stepping closer until he was inches away. The warmth radiating from his skin was suffocating. "But I'd do it all again for you, little one."

"Go to hell," I snarled, turning around and stomping away.

"Where are you going to go?" Zander called after me. "You can't run from me forever."

"Try me!"

Zander had a point, though. The Hulk had taken over my bed, and the only place to go for space was the Captain's cabin on the top deck. It's a good thing my time as the Kitten prepared me for keeping a low profile because I needed to spend the day avoiding all the Seven men.

———

After West got up at noon, I gave Vixen strict instructions to make sure no one disturbed me, then locked myself in my cabin like Rapunzel for the rest of the day.

Mieko slipped her Kindle under the door to keep me company, already pre-loaded with some of my favorite classics. I finished *The Strange Case of Dr. Jekyll and Mr. Hyde* and got halfway through *Pride and Prejudice* before losing concentration because the room smelled like a sex den. Lizzie wouldn't have the problem of her sheets smelling like dirty, bloody sex with an inked Adonis. Even alone, I couldn't avoid them!

Whether I liked it or not, I had to attend Vixen's party. Music had been playing for the last half an hour, and Vixen wouldn't stay patient for much longer. Would it be awkward seeing the guys together? When we used to live together in Lapland, it was simple. Their agreement to share me had been a mind fuck, but at least we were on the same page. Now, I didn't know whether we were even in the same fucking dimension.

I picked out a soft green silk dress to wear. It swished around past my ass and had long sleeves that hugged my wrists. The luxurious fabric tied around my waist to accentuate my figure and left a plunging neckline similar to the fit of a blazer. After not topping up my fiery pink hair, it faded to a baby pink hue. I ruffled it up at the roots to give it a 'just out of bed' look.

Go, Candy. I pushed myself. *If anyone should miss out on the party, it should be Zander.*

I made my way to join the others. When I arrived, everyone gathered on the deck. A delicious assortment of snacks and drinks was laid on a table. From the empty platters and West re-filling his plate, it looked like he'd already made a considerable dent in the mountain of food. Next to him, Q and Rocky were engaged in a comical heated debate about something. Mieko and Vixen were watching, laughing at them, and trying not to get involved. Zander stood alone, sipping a glass of wine. I could feel his eyes on me as soon as I stepped out, but I avoided his gaze, pretending he was nothing more than another deck chair.

"You took your fucking time," Vixen remarked as soon as she saw me, but her tone was light. Mieko nudged her in the ribs, and Vixen cleared her throat. "Now that we're all here..." She threw me a pointed glare. "We have an announcement to make."

Mieko took her hand and squeezed it. It was sweet that they were in love and everything, but couldn't they cut the rest of us a break? They were the perfect example of what a healthy relationship looked like. It was nothing like the explosive reaction that happened between West and me last night when we wanted to kill each other.

"What is it?" Rocky asked as they took a long and dramatic pause for effect.

"We're getting married!" Mieko squealed, her voice high-pitched and giddy. She was practically floating on air as she held up her hand to show us the dainty silver band with a flat surface and the letter 'V' engraved.

"Pretty neat, huh?" Vixen said, holding up an identical band with an 'M' on it. Among the array of other rings she wore, it blended in.

"Marriage?" Zander's shoulders tensed. "Now?"

"It's legal!" Vixen stuck her chin up high. Not that legality was an issue the Sevens usually had a problem with. "Nothing is stopping us, and why not now? Life is too fucking short. If we're all gonna die soon, why wait another day?"

"We wanted to wait until everyone was together again to tell you," Mieko said, her eyes glistening with happy tears. I didn't know whether to be pleased they wanted me there to make the announcement or guilty they'd put their happiness on hold on my account. "Vix asked me on the day of the funeral."

Rocky was first to barrel over and pull the two of them into a big bear hug. "Congratulations, guys!"

Q followed close behind. Although he was smiling, it was intermingled with sadness. For him, it was another painful reminder of how he lost the love of his life.

"Congrats," West said, raising a glass in their direction. "Welcome to the family, Mimi."

Zander didn't move or say anything. His expression stayed blank, like a sexy fucking mannequin.

"Candy?" Vixen turned to me. "What do you think?"

Shit. I hadn't realized I'd been standing gawping at them.

"I think you owe me for introducing you," I said. "And if you hurt her, you'll have me to answer to."

As well as being my best friend, I almost saw Mieko as a little sister. She'd come so far in the time we'd known each other. She went from being a dancer who tried to stay in the shadows and was afraid to say the word 'sex' aloud to helping with my escape and getting engaged to the Ice Queen.

I didn't believe in soul mates. I thought all of that was bullshit. Even if they did exist, what were the chances of two people finding each other among six billion other assholes? But Vixen and Mieko made a perfectly complementary pair. Vixen's no-bullshit attitude and Mieko's caring nature didn't sound like it'd work on paper, like fried chicken and waffles, but they did.

West poured a glass of champagne and walked over to join me. His fingers brushed against mine as I took the glass, sending a tingle up my arm, but I didn't meet his gaze.

"Maybe you should give them tips for the big day?" West suggested under his breath. If it wasn't for the mischievous glint in his eyes, I'd have smashed my knee into his balls. Instead, I rolled my eyes and shoved him hard. As usual, it hurt me more than him.

No one had properly addressed my sham wedding to Giles yet, and I wanted to avoid the subject. I had a reputation to uphold, and marrying that loser was like Beyoncé hooking up with Bob Ross.

While everyone fussed around Vixen and Mieko, Zander left the throng of the group. He went over to the railings, gripping them with white knuckles, and looked moodily across the ocean. He was an emotional vampire. Why did he have to drain all the happiness out of a good situation?

"How did you propose?" Q asked. As much as he liked to pretend he was always doing sketchy shit on the computer, I could have sworn I once saw him watching a trashy marriage reality show.

Vixen shrugged like it was nothing, but she looked practically ethereal. Her porcelain skin had an almost sparkly quality, and she wore bright red lipstick for the announcement. She never usually wore a shade lighter than plum. That's how you knew it was true love.

"I guess I just came out with it," Vixen said. "There's some truth in the bullshit people say. When you know, you know."

Underneath the layers of black eyeshadow, there was more to Vixen than being a control freak bitch. She wore her cold exterior like a Seven badge of honor, but she had a soft center hiding, and Mieko drew it out of her.

"Is that really you, Vix?" Rocky teased. "Have you been body-snatched?"

"If any of you tell anyone I said that, then I'll fucking bury you before Hiram does," Vixen said, then shot him a devilish smile. A sight that would make most normal men wet their pants.

"Now you're back!" Rocky said, wiping his brow. "Your secret's safe with us."

For the first time since the Sevens boarded, the atmosphere felt lighter. It *almost* reminded me of how things were before, despite Zander's brooding in the corner like a toddler. It was hard to stay angry when Mieko and Vixen's happiness was contagious — even if their glowing cheeks forced me to face how screwed up my love life was. I had no idea what was going on between the guys and me. Rocky said he loved me, West fucked all the hate out of me, and Zander... well, that was another story.

"I'm so glad you're here!" Mieko hurried to my side. I did the customary picking up her hand to examine the ring like I'd seen people do in movies. It looked even more perfect up close, an understated but personal design. "I still can't believe it. It doesn't feel real, you know?"

"You deserve it more than anyone else I know," I said, meaning every word.

They'd both had tough lives. Bryce murdered Vixen's parents in cold-blooded revenge, and Mieko's dad was a walking monster. They deserved to have someone to come home to at the end of a long night serving drunk customers in Lapland.

"I didn't want anyone else to find out before you," Mieko said, lowering her voice. "If it wasn't for you, I wouldn't have had the courage to speak to her."

"Looks like we have two Cupids around tonight," I said.

"I didn't think you were a romantic, C," Rocky said, eavesdropping and raising one eyebrow in my direction.

"Who wants a glass of the good stuff?" Q asked, brandishing a bottle of vintage champagne, hidden at the bottom of the deck bar. He popped the cork, and Mieko swerved to avoid being blinded.

Zander cut off the cheers with his abrupt, steely tone. His lips curled into a vicious snarl. "I have some business to take care of."

He stormed away and disappeared below deck. Vixen's face fell as he left. She wouldn't admit it, but her brother's approval meant a lot. She wanted to have a special night, and, regardless of how I felt about him, it was a time for everyone to be together. I would not let him ruin this for them. But, first, I raised a toast to the happy couple. An alcohol jacket would help me confront the one person I wanted to avoid.

CHAPTER

Twelve

As Vixen lined up the second row of tequila shots, I made the excuse of going to the bathroom with an ulterior motive. While everyone was partying, they wouldn't be paying attention to what was happening below deck. Zander was alone, and we needed to talk.

Through the process of elimination, I figured out which room was his. There was nowhere to hide on a yacht. Fuck knocking. He'd lost the right to common courtesy. I pushed the door to his room wide open, expecting him to be hunched over his desk, not... *THWACK!*

Zander kneeled in front of a long mirror with his back turned. His eyes were closed, and he hung his head, oblivious to my presence. His torso was fully exposed. Deep red scars — old and new — covered his back, making it look like a pack of she-devils attacked him with freshly manicured claws. He raised the whip in his hand again, then drove it down onto his spine with a vicious swish of the wrist.

THWACK!

His body jolted from the force as it struck, but Zander didn't make a sound. The slight scrunching of his nose was the only sign he was in any pain. A trail of blood seeped from the laceration over his ghostly pale skin. When we had sex, I never saw him without a shirt. I knew why now.

Tattoos wrapped around his chest and arms, meeting at his sternum to form an ornate skull, but his back was completely bare. Scars are difficult to ink over. Judging by the faint white lines, some of the scars had to be years old.

I cleared my throat to alert him to my arrival and stepped inside, shutting the door behind me. Zander didn't move, but his eyes snapped open and met mine in my mirrored reflection. They were devoid of emotion. Empty and cold. It was the first time we'd been alone since the warehouse. He didn't look surprised to find me staring at him. Instead, he raised the whip in the air again.

"Don't!" I cried out.

Zander lowered his hand and rose from his position. He turned to face me, and the blank look in his eyes was even worse in the flesh than in the mirror.

"Didn't I teach you to knock?" he asked.

My mouth felt like it'd been stuffed with hundreds of cotton balls. Zander held the whip forward and pushed it into my hands. His fingers curled around mine, forcing me to grip the handle tightly.

"Do it," he requested.

"I won't," I replied. As much as I'd like to inflict serious bodily harm, I wouldn't do it on his fucking terms.

"It wasn't a request." Zander returned to his previous position on his knees. He leaned forward, curving his spine as an invitation. Nausea stalked my stomach. In this pose, he was vulnerable. I could snap his neck, and he'd be utterly defenseless. "You agreed to follow my orders."

He wasn't begging. His tone was matter-of-fact like it was an inevitability.

I kept my voice level. "I don't want to."

"What you want doesn't matter. It didn't matter to me before, so why should it matter now?" Zander snapped. "Do it."

I raised the whip and slapped it gently on his back, making light contact. It was more of a brush than a slap. I'd been dreaming of ways to make him pay, but this isn't how I imagined having my revenge.

"Is that really the best you can do?" Zander snarled. "Remember what I did to you, Candy."

I raised it again and hit harder this time. The leather made a satisfying crack as it caught his shoulder blade. An angry red mark appeared quickly in its place. The first time Zander called me into his office in Lapland, he bent me over his desk and spanked me. He made his mark on me, and this was my turn. Zander had always been the one in control. He was the leader, the person everyone submitted to, but he was handing over the power to me.

"You're not even trying!" Zander blasted. His face contorted with fury as he caught my gaze in the mirror, then he shot me a twisted smile. "Do you want to know what I'm thinking about? I'm thinking about how much I enjoyed your sweet, tight pussy, knowing that I was planning to give you to Hiram. Every time we fucked, I knew what I was going to do."

Anger rose in my chest, blinding all my senses as the Kitten rose to the surface. She remembered what Zander had done, and she enjoyed making bad men pay.

I hit him again. And again. And again. I didn't stop. I couldn't. The urge to make him suffer was overwhelming. It was too strong...

THWACK!

Returning to Blackthorne Towers was something I could deal with, but knowing someone I trusted was behind it ruined me all over again. All the anger I'd been holding came out like a volcanic eruption.

THWACK!

I'd shared my body with him! Hell, I even let my guard down enough to believe that being part of the Sevens was like belonging to a real fucking family.

THWACK!

Why did I fall for his act? Zander built our connection on a web of deceit. How could I have seen a future with him? I cared about my loyalty to the Sevens so much that I'd been willing to trade my freedom.

I raised my hand again.

STOP!

A small voice in the back of my head whispered into my monster's ear. It was a quiet murmur but loud enough to bring me out of my frenzy. Whenever I killed, I went into a hypnotic state. Hiram's training had desensitized me from seeing the horror.

I took a step back.

Blood and large welts from where the skin hadn't broken covered Zander's back. His breathing came in short, gasping bursts, but he hadn't moved or objected during my attack. He allowed me to keep going. The whip fell from my shaking fingers and hit the floor with a bang.

"Why?" I stammered.

"It's what I deserve, Candy." Zander stood up. Every movement must have been agony, but he didn't flinch. He spoke quietly and inclined his head. "Every action has consequences, remember?"

I thought his mantra about consequences only applied to other people. Since when did he hold himself to the same cruel standards? He grabbed a clean shirt and headed into his adjoining en-suite. His jaw clenched in determination. No matter how much pain he was in, he refused to show it.

"You can go," he dismissed.

"No." The word came out before I could stop myself, and I followed him into the bathroom. "Let me help you."

"You want to stay?" He frowned in confusion. "Why?"

I ran the faucet and ignored his question because I didn't know the answer. I'd not caused him enough harm to warrant missing my best friend's engagement party, but I couldn't leave him. Not like this.

"Turn around and stay still." I held up a warm washcloth and signaled for him to rotate, hoping he didn't sense my hesitation. I wasn't the nurturing type. My usual clean-up jobs involved cutting up body parts. It was easier to work with a corpse who couldn't complain. Zander's shoulders tensed as I dabbed his skin. "What part of 'stay still' don't you understand?"

"Why do you want to stay, Candy?" he asked again.

"I'm not in the mood to party," I lied, continuing to clean him up as noisy water bounced off the basin. We didn't speak again until I asked gently, "When did it start? Those aren't fresh scars."

"I was five years old the first time my father used the belt," Zander said, surprising me by answering the question. "Pain is punishment, and I deserve to be punished for what I did. I went against the Seven code and everything we stand for."

I already knew Bryce was a total fucking monster, but this only made me hate him more. Who could do that to a fucking child? Apart from when he told me about what happened to his mother, Zander never let anyone know what he was thinking. He lived like each day was a battle. He gave orders to his soldiers and wore his armor, but he let no one see the war he waged against himself beneath.

"Zander—"

"I don't want or need your pity," he snarled.

"I'm not giving it," I snapped back. "If I wanted to hurt you, I could come up with more imaginative ways to do it."

"You're missing the point," Zander said, clenching his fists as I scrubbed a wound roughly. "This isn't just about pain. Pain is my release, but I could take a hundred more lashes, and it still wouldn't be enough for what I did."

I looked at his scars and bloody back, struggling to see anything else. "If it's not about pain, what is it about?"

"Control," Zander replied. "Until you came into our lives, I controlled everything: the Sevens, our business, how I inflict my punishments. I made a deal with Hiram for the future of the gang because it was the only way I could see our lives without him in it, but it didn't turn out how I hoped. I was wrong."

Zander admitting he was wrong was almost as unlikely as being able to kill Hiram and walk out alive.

"Why didn't you tell me about your plans?"

"To make it more convincing," he replied.

Bullshit. I wrung the cloth and watched his blood swirl down the plughole. "We both know I'm a good enough actress to have pulled it off," I said. "That's no excuse, and you fucking know it. There's more to it."

A long silence stretched out.

"Because I wanted to be the one to save you," Zander whispered. "You were never meant to be with him for more than a few hours. A day, at the most. I arranged for you to be intercepted, but everything changed. I misjudged what you and Red were willing to do for each other. It changed everything. The only hope I held onto was knowing I'd shown you the way out of Briarly Manor in case of an emergency. I had to find a way to get you there."

"Hang on, let me get this straight, you put my life at risk because you wanted to be a fucking savior?" I threw down the cloth, abandoning my role as a nurse. "You're unbelievable!"

"I underestimated your loyalty to us," he said, his voice thickening with emotion as he turned to face me. "I let you down. All of you."

I put my hands on my hips. "Is this your attempt at saying sorry?"

"I'm not going to insult you by apologizing," Zander replied. Maybe he understood me more than I thought. "Words won't change the past or what I've done. I know what I did was unforgivable."

"Then why didn't you leave me with him?" My nostrils flared. "Why bring me here if you knew I'd hate you for it?"

"My destiny is already sealed, but yours isn't," he said, a far-off look flitted over his face as he stared past me. "I've spent my whole life trying to be nothing like my father. But after what I did to you, I'm no better. I can't escape it."

His chin dipped, allowing me to see the vulnerabilities he hid from the world. *Don't feel sorry for him, Candy!* I cursed myself. *This is the time to agree and crush him!*

But I couldn't. The man before me gave me a glimpse of the person he used to be. A boy who loved his mom and sacrificed his future for a half-sister he didn't know. That's not something you'd do if you didn't have a heart... even if it was buried under a steely and ruthless exterior.

"If you were like your father, you wouldn't have given me the choice to leave," I reminded him gently.

Bryce killed people who stepped out of line. He would rather they die than leave him behind or go against his orders.

Zander grabbed my arm. His sudden touch scorched my skin like his fingertips were made of flames, but he didn't let go.

"After we kill Hiram, I want you to leave," he said. His eyes burned into mine with a deep intensity that made me dizzy. "I want you to get as far away from the Sevens as you can. I'll give you all the money you need."

"You'll pay me to disappear?" My voice shook. If it's what I wanted, why did my chest ache? "Why go through all this effort only to send me away?"

"This isn't the life I want for you," he murmured. "If you are around us for too long, we'll destroy you. *I'll* destroy you."

"You can't play God with people's lives, Zander!" I blurted out. "You need to put away your fucking violin and face the music."

"I'm Briarly blood, Candy," Zander said. For the first time, I thought I saw fear flicker across his face. His shoulders slumped in resolve. "It's who I am."

A hysterical laugh burst out of me. Zander's jaw clenched as he put his hard mask back on. He narrowed his eyes. "What's so funny?"

"You are Zander fucking Briarly," I said. "History will only repeat itself if you keep acting like an asshole."

He brushed my comments away. "Being a Briarly only ends one way. I'm toxic. My whole family is. We're rotten to the fucking core, and, as soon as we kill Hiram, I want you to run and never look back."

"What about Vixen?" I asked. "Is she toxic too?"

"Briarly blood doesn't run through Vixen's veins," Zander snarled. "She still has a fucking chance."

Zander may come from a family of psychopaths, but DNA doesn't dictate our actions. We all have a choice. If Zander couldn't see that, it was already too late.

"Your problems don't lie in your genetics," I said. "You think pushing people away will help, but it won't. Your problem is that you can't see *you* are the one running. Why did you walk out of the party?"

Zander grabbed a black shirt hooked on the bathroom door. He pulled it on roughly. The fabric rubbing against his wounds must have hurt like a bitch, but he didn't wince.

"Because I want her to be happy." His cheeks flushed in anger. "I'm not going to ruin her life, too."

"She wants you there!" I insisted. "You're her fucking brother!"

Zander ignored me and continued to talk. It was hard to tell whether he was talking to me or himself. "Vixen has found something that I'll never have."

"Cry me a fucking river! You have it all, Zander." I scoffed. He had the looks, money, Briarly Manor, and more power than most people could dream of. "You got revenge on your father. Isn't that what you always wanted?"

"It used to be," he replied, looking at me like he was trying to suck the soul from my body.

I averted my eyes. Could I be feeling sorry for Zander Briarly? Like him, I believed happiness was something reserved for other people.

"Look at what I did to you," Zander pointed out, stepping closer. The bathroom was small, and there was no room to slip around him. "Someone who does things like that doesn't deserve to find what Vixen and Mieko have. I will spend the rest of my life killing and taking over my father's legacy. No good will ever come from me."

"Nothing is inevitable," I said, my voice a few octaves higher than usual. "I'm living proof of it. You can keep feeling sorry for yourself and complaining about your daddy or do the fucking work. You can be the man you want to be or let your father win."

His eyes widened in surprise. "Even after everything I've done, you still believe that?"

I shrugged. Some people were past redemption, like the men I killed without guilt because they had zero humanity left, but Zander? He inflicted pain to cope with emotions. Wasn't that a sign of someone who felt remorse?

Despite the shit Bryce put him through, Zander turned his back on his father's ways and started out on his own. When West's father died, Zander used his influence to help a friend. He looked after Vixen when she had no one else and gave Rocky a safe place to call home. His psyche may be shrouded in darkness, but he had a light inside him too.

"You should have killed me tonight," Zander said. "I wouldn't have blamed you."

"I could have," I replied, flicking my hair over my shoulder. "But I can't take down Hiram alone. Besides, it would have been too easy."

I didn't want to mention that I knew how it felt to think I had Seven blood on my hands and didn't want to go through that again.

"My words may not count for a lot, but I need you to know I meant everything I said tonight," he said. His serious expression sucked all the air out of my lungs "I saw my plan as the only way. I wanted you to be safe from him forever, Candy. Since the moment you walked into Lapland, you tore apart all my rules. When I saw who you really were, I knew you had to be mine. *Ours.* And I'd do anything to keep it that way."

"Zander—"

"Shh, little one." He pressed a finger to my lips. "If I don't say it now, I never will. You have to know."

My heart pounded. Was this the moment he wrapped his hands around my throat? Was Hiram on his way to collect me? Would Hiram and the Blackbird be boarding the yacht?

"I don't deserve your heart, nor will I ever ask for it," Zander said. He stroked my cheekbone with two fingers, making my legs feel like they were about to collapse. "But you have mine. Whether you choose to stay or leave, I want you to know that you have mine."

I stepped back and stumbled, catching myself before I fell into the toilet. I needed to get back on the pole to work on my balance.

"You're cleaned up now."

It's all I could manage to say as Zander moved to let me pass. He strode over to his cabin door and held it open. Words didn't change anything, did they? Zander said that himself, but it was hard to ignore a strange fluttering sensation in my chest. Zander confessed his love for me, but could it be possible *I* loved him back? Could I love all three of the Seven men?

"You should go," he said, back to his usual business-like demeanor. "You don't want to miss any more of the party."

I didn't argue. My lips stayed clamped together like they were sealed with superglue. Somehow, I made it to the door without tripping again.

"Goodnight, Candy."

He shut the door, leaving me staring at the wood and wondering whether Vixen had slipped me something stronger than tequila. Zander had shown me parts of himself he kept hidden. Whoever said the number seven was lucky was wrong…

Thirteen

I put on my best fake smile and returned to the party, but the initial sparkle to the evening had vanished. I couldn't get rid of the image of Zander's bloody back from my mind. What was wrong with me? I'd killed people. My days of being squeamish were long over. No, it was why I stopped myself that was terrifying… and what it meant.

Rocky's eyes lit up as I rejoined them. He strolled over and wrapped an arm around my shoulder. "Where have you been hiding? Everything okay?"

"Seasickness," I lied.

"You know what helps with seasickness?" Rocky pulled a bag of weed out of his pocket and wiggled his eyebrows. He'd never go anywhere without a stash. "Candy's Breath."

I smiled thinly. Getting stoned would only heighten my paranoia. "Maybe another time."

"Suit yourself." Rocky shrugged, pulling out his papers to roll. He nodded at the chairs on the far side of the deck. "I'll be over there if you change your mind."

West lurked nearby, shamelessly listening in on our conversation. A cheeky grin spread over his face, making his scars dance. "You seemed okay with the rocky waves last night, Pinkie."

Could the fucker be any more obvious?

"Well, I'm not today," I snapped.

Rocky looked between us, then realization dawned on him and his mouth fell open. "You two—"

"We're not talking about it," I interrupted, shutting him down.

Our situation was weird enough without them comparing notes. I didn't need everyone to know that my vagina had her own fucking ideas about what was good for me… and they started and ended with the Sevens.

"Shame," West said. He leaned in to whisper in my ear, knowing Rocky was watching on. "I was hoping for a repeat performance."

He was fucking unbelievable.

"The only thing you're getting is blue fucking balls," I said, wiping the smug smirk off his face.

I'd forgotten how fragile The Hulk's ego could be. Rocky, on the other hand, found it hilarious. He snorted and slapped West on the back as he passed him. "Nice try, bro."

West pouted the way he always did when he didn't get his way or something irked him.

"What's Red laughing so hard at?" Vixen asked, coming over to join us with Mieko and Q as Rocky passed them to light up at the opposite end of the yacht.

"Nothing," I replied quickly, putting an end to the conversation and steering it back to safe waters. "Tonight is all about you."

"Tell that to Zander," Vixen grumbled.

She tried to pretend she didn't care, but the hurt was visible in her eyes. As much as I wanted to say more and explain what Zander shared with me, I stayed silent. If he believed he was a curse, how could anyone convince him otherwise?

Mieko placed a hand gently on my arm. "Are you sure you're feeling alright?"

Q frowned. "You look pale."

"Seasickness," I repeated.

Before they could press me, Vixen squealed as West scooped her up into his arms and started doing bench presses with her like she was a kettlebell. Goddammit, if this was his attempt to show me what I'd be missing, it was working. His perfectly defined muscled arms could carry a small car.

I rolled my eyes. "Does the macho act ever get old?"

In response, West threw Vixen into the air like a circus performer. Mieko's hand flew to her mouth.

"Don't worry," West said, winking in Mieko's direction and catching Vixen perfectly. They were like a cheerleading double-act. "I'm not gonna drop her."

Mieko wasn't convinced. She didn't exhale fully until Vixen returned to her feet and did a small bow for the hollering Rocky and Q.

"You know what, I think I might call it a night. I don't feel so good," I said, unable to bring myself to fake a smile. "Sorry, I know it's your special night and all."

"I'm just glad you could be here," Mieko said, then winced as West and Vixen started on another routine. "I think West has the entertainment covered."

"I'll walk you back to your room if you like?" Rocky called over from behind a haze of smoke.

"I'm capable of walking myself," I replied, then hugged Mieko. "Congratulations again."

I *should* go back to my room like I said I would, but I knew I wouldn't...

I couldn't stop thinking about what Zander said. His words were like an annoying song I couldn't shake off. The fucker knew how to get under my skin more than anyone, and I couldn't decide what annoyed me more: him telling me I had his heart or how a part of me liked it.

I went straight to his cabin. My fists hammered on his door before I could change my mind. He answered immediately. Looking at him, you'd never be able to guess that his back was bleeding and covered in lashings.

Zander leaned in the door frame, raising an eyebrow. "Back so soon?"

I didn't wait for an invitation and barged past.

"You can't just come out with things like that," I exploded as he shut the door behind me. "You mess with people's heads, Zander. It's what you do. I didn't say anything earlier, but..."

Words continued to tumble out of my mouth, but they made no sense. I intended to be controlled and poised during our confrontation, but I was a babbling freaking mess. Zander's eyes glittered in mild bemusement, which only infuriated me more.

"You don't feel anything," I finally declared. "You're not capable of it."

Zander stretched his arms out. The motion would have aggravated his wounds and torn his lacerations open wider, but he showed no sign of discomfort. The marks I etched into his skin matched those he carved into my fucking heart that night at the warehouse. The night that changed everything.

"It doesn't matter whether you believe me or not," Zander replied. "But I needed you to know."

I fucking hated him. Not just for what he did to me, but for how he made me *feel*. His words were gasoline, setting fire to all of my logical reasoning and burning me from the inside out.

My body shook with anger. "I hate you."

"Why are you here then?" Zander asked. "You left a party to speak to me. There must be a reason why you came back."

I hadn't planned ahead. What had I been hoping to achieve? All I knew was I couldn't enjoy a party knowing he was alone and thinking he was doomed to have the same miserable life as his father.

"I don't know," I admitted.

"Did you come to finish what you started?" Zander suggested. "I don't blame you. If you want to kill me, I won't resist. I won't even make a sound."

"Shut up, Zander."

He obliged and bowed his head. He closed his eyes, waiting in silence. Instead of delivering a fatal blow, my lips brushed against his cheek. My heart raced at his familiar smell. Smoke, leather, bergamot, and a hint of citrus.

Zander's head jerked up, his eyes wide in shock. "Wha—"

Before he could say more, I put my hands on his cheeks and pulled his mouth down to meet mine. His lips responded hesitantly like he suspected the punchline of a joke was still to come. Maybe he thought I was delivering the kiss of death? It wouldn't be the first time I seduced a man before killing him.

A few moments later, Zander broke away, and my hands fell to my sides. His gray eyes probed my soul, searching for a reason why this was happening. I stared straight back, unblinking.

"Is this really what you want?" Zander whispered, stroking his lips with his finger as if he couldn't believe what happened. If his were anything like mine, they'd feel on fire. I may have made out with a viper, but poison didn't scare me. My soul was already too far gone.

"Just kiss me before I change my fucking mind," I growled.

He held my face in his hands as if it were made from china and kissed me. His tongue cautiously explored my mouth, parting my lips like they were breakable flower petals. When we'd fucked before, it'd been rough and primal, but this was different. The night blew apart a hidden barrier between us. All of our hard edges had fallen away to leave the shattered remnants of two hopelessly broken people looking for a way to put themselves back together.

"I don't fucking deserve you," he murmured, caressing my hair.

"No," I replied, sliding my hands up his chest. "You don't."

I wasn't stupid. Zander didn't deserve me after what he did. He deserved to be buried in a shallow grave and left to rot, but my body craved him. His hands trailing down my back sent a lightning bolt between my legs. Instead of polluting my veins with venom, his touch acted as an antidote to a disease I never realized I had. After tasting him, I couldn't stop.

Zander showed me who he really was. He was the badass, ruthless leader of the Sevens, but he was also twisted and fucked up like me. He held those he loved to high standards and himself to higher ones. He favored loyalty above all else, no matter the cost. For the first time since we met, he wasn't hiding anything. I could see the real Zander Briarly.

Before moving to Port Valentine, I would have slit his throat and delighted in rolling around in his blood, but things were different now. I recognized myself in Zander. He allowed me to see the shadowy depths of his mind, and it didn't make me want to run... not anymore.

The Sevens were under Zander's control, but West had been right. Zander was under *my* control. If I had Zander, they were all mine, and things would never be the same again. For any of us.

Zander stroked my back and pulled me into his embrace like he was afraid I'd change my mind and wanted to grasp the moment before it was stolen. He untied the knot holding my dress together at the front and gently slipped the fabric away, letting it fall. He didn't say anything, but his eyes looked for permission as his warm hands paused at my bra clasp. I nodded.

When Rocky and I reunited, our emotions took over. After learning he was alive, I wrapped my legs around him and never wanted to let him go. With West, our heightened emotions came out in a passionate and violent frenzy when our twisted monsters collided. With Zander, I didn't know how to feel...

I'd always hate Zander for what he did, but not in a way that made me want to claw his eyeballs out. I pitied him without feeling sorry for him. My head was a mess, and my feelings were deep and complex. They made no fucking sense, and I didn't have time to thrash it out over a therapist's couch.

I reached for the bottom of Zander's shirt, then stopped. I didn't want to hurt him. He sensed my reluctance and took it off himself.

"And the rest," I ordered.

Zander undressed and stood naked before me. I swallowed hard as my skin heated, feeling like a virgin all over again. My eyes scanned over his strong shoulders, tattoos, the scars across his chest, then...

"Zander..." My voice shook as I looked at his ribs where the name 'Candy' was inscribed. From the clear lines, the ink was fresh. "You did that... for me?"

"I meant what I said, Candy," Zander purred. He took my hand and held it against his chest, letting me feel the beating of a heart I didn't think he possessed. "Whether you want it or not, my heart is yours. *I* am all fucking yours."

"I-I-I—" I stammered like an idiot, not sure what to say. Was this the proof I'd been waiting for that he'd been telling the truth?

"You are the only person who has seen the real me," Zander said. "I did what I did because I wanted you to be ours forever, little one. But I was wrong, and I'm going to prove myself to you."

I arched an eyebrow. "Since when does Zander Briarly need to prove himself to anyone?"

"You're different," he replied, stepping closer, but not close enough for his hard cock to brush against me. "And whatever happens, you will always be my Seven girl. My *only* Seven girl."

Zander reached out to stroke my shoulder blade, sending tingles racing down my body.

"I'll prove I'm worthy of you, little one," Zander said fiercely. He grabbed my hips suddenly and pushed me back onto his bed. "If you'll let me."

His words were still whirring through my mind as Zander parted my legs. His lips grazed the tops of my knees, and his hair tickled my skin as he pushed my legs apart. He hooked his hands under my thighs and gripped my hips, pulling my pussy onto his face. Vixen's crotchless panties weren't a total bust.

I whimpered as his hot tongue licked along my wet slit. "Zander..."

"I've missed the taste of you, little one," Zander said. He pushed his tongue into me, making me gasp, then pulled away. I looked down to see him grinning and licking his lips. "You taste so fucking good."

We should stop, the sensible part of my brain reasoned, it would only complicate everything further. *But don't you want to believe him?* Another small voice piped up. *What if he is telling the truth? If he wants to worship you, why don't you let him?* You're already going straight to hell, and the devil gives damn good head.

I pushed his head down, locking him in place. He ate me out with the same calculated focus as an athlete going for gold, murmuring in appreciation and sending vibrations pulsing through my limbs. A sizzling heat spread from between my legs over my entire body, making my chest feel like it was about to burst wide open like everything I'd been holding onto was going to crack and explode like an escaped firework.

"I want you to come for me," Zander said, sliding his finger inside me and stroking my g-spot, causing the pressure to build. "I want to taste your sweet juices all over my tongue."

"No!" I gasped suddenly, sitting upright. I couldn't come... not like this. "I want to feel your cock."

Zander slid up my body, the weight of his muscles bearing down on top of me.

"Do you want this?" he asked as his erection rubbed against my thighs teasingly.

If I did, there was no going back...

"Yes," I breathed, pushing my hips against him as his cock rubbed against my wetness, slathering him in it. I reached down to grab the base of his shaft and angle it inside me. A girl could only take teasing for so long until she needed to be filled. "I want this."

Zander thrusted deep, making me moan.

"You're so wet, little one," Zander murmured gruffly. "Your pussy was made for me."

He leaned down and kissed me. There was an added depth to his kiss and touch. His tongue consumed me with lust as he fucked me with a slow and meaningful tenderness. This wasn't a quick bang after a wild party. Our connection was buzzing with a supercharged intensity I couldn't begin to explain. The emotion was both exciting and terrifying.

My climax hovered on the edge. I craved the release, but I resisted succumbing to him. Fighting my orgasm made me want to scream as his tongue danced with mine, coaxing my reluctance away. How could fucking someone who'd caused me so much pain bring such toe-curling pleasure?

Zander pulled away from our kiss.

"I'm all yours, Candy," he said. His gray eyes weren't cold and unfeeling. That one look showed me he'd burn the whole fucking world down if I asked him to.

He sensed my hips shift and thighs tense beneath him and sped up, then sank his teeth into my neck like he was trying to claim me. The sudden burst of pain made me cry out, catapulting me over the edge. Everything fell apart as I came undone.

My body couldn't stop the feeling anymore. Every thought and emotion I was holding onto unleashed, and an incredible orgasm rippled through me in waves. I wrapped my arms around Zander's neck, drawing his body closer as his cock pushed as deep as it could go, wanting to draw every ounce of pleasure from me until I had nothing left to give.

It was more than an orgasm. It smashed down all the guards I'd put up against him and made me surrender to the desires I wished I didn't have. It went against all of my instincts, but I was powerless to stop it. Whatever connection I shared with the Sevens transcended all reason.

Zander's breathing grew ragged. With an aggressive buck of hips, he groaned and blew his load. He didn't withdraw right away. He stroked my face and caught a tear I didn't realize I shed.

"I won't let anyone hurt you again, little one," Zander promised. "Do you understand?"

I nodded as he kissed my forehead gently and rolled off of me.

"I will never deserve your forgiveness," Zander said, standing up. I pressed my lips together to stop myself from recoiling at the sight of the wounds I'd inflicted on his back. "But I will do anything to try to earn it if you'll let me."

I took a deep breath. "I'm still here, aren't I? That has to mean something."

Zander nodded curtly, but his lips twitched at the corners like he was holding back a smile. He hurried to the bathroom to bring me back a warm cloth to clean up with. By the time he returned, I'd already put my dress back on.

His face fell. "You're welcome to stay the night."

"I think it's best if I sleep alone," I insisted, already heading for the door.

"I understand." Zander bowed his head. "Sweet dreams, little one."

Even if I could move on from what happened, I'd never be able to forget it. Some things couldn't be erased. At the same time, I couldn't deny how being back with the Sevens felt right. When I returned to Blackthorne Towers, everything about it felt wrong. From being surrounded by Hiram and his cronies to the way the building felt.

Being with the Sevens felt like coming home, but we had a long way to go. It's hard to imagine a future when you don't know whether your heart will still be beating, but screwing Zander didn't change the deal I'd made. If we were still breathing by the end of this, the Sevens would have a decision to make.

Would we stay together, or would we part? The more time I spent with them, the harder it would be to leave.

CHAPTER

Fourteen

The Sevens and Mieko gathered on the deck to eat breakfast while Q remained in the Captain's cabin. As everyone was nursing hangovers after a wild night, I was hoping to avoid any awkward questions.

The guys and I would have to talk about what happened between us eventually. Before Zander made a so-called 'deal' with Hiram, the Sevens agreed to share me, but is that still what they wanted? More importantly, is that what *I* wanted? Sure, we had mind-blowing sex... but could I trust them beyond their magic fingers and cocks? From experience, I knew when the real world came knocking, it never led to sunshine and fucking rainbows.

Before my ass could get comfortable at the table, a loud ringing caused everyone to spin and face West. He whipped his phone out of his pocket and frowned. How did his cell work out here? I knew Q had a radio in case we sank, but this was the first time since arriving that the outside world had tried to contact us.

Zander's jaw set. "Who is it?" he demanded sharply.

I sat up straighter.

"An unknown number. Our security guys are the only ones who have it," West replied, then picked up and growled, "You better have a damn good reason for calling."

West muttered a few curse words under his breath, holding the phone away from his face. His muscles tensed like he was clutching a bomb. His hand shook as he held the phone out and turned to me. "It's for you."

"Me?" My eyes widened, fearing the worst. "Who is it?"

"Your *husband*," West spat through gritted teeth. "He won't speak to anyone but you."

I snatched the cell from him. Out on the ocean, I'd *almost* forgotten about the English sleazeball.

"What the fuck do you want?" I snarled down the line, my voice simmering with underlying hatred. There's no way I could work in a call center.

"That's not how a lady should address their husband," Giles's nasal tone mocked, "even if you are a runaway bride."

Whoever said distance makes the heart grow fonder was talking bullshit or had never met someone like Giles fucking Briarly.

"Our wedding was bullshit, and you know it," I snapped. "If you don't start talking in the next ten seconds, you'll never hear from me again."

Zander watched on, casually sipping his coffee like he couldn't give any less of a shit. On the other side of the table, West's face reddened with each passing second as he used every ounce of his self-control to not rip the cell straight outta my hands. Rocky couldn't stay still. He got up and paced the deck like an animal ready to hunt while Vixen stroked Mieko's shoulder, and both of them hung off my every word. We all knew we were entering a war, and the battle lines were being drawn.

"Don't be like that, sweetheart," Giles drawled. Any man who talked down to a woman by calling them 'darling' or 'sweetheart' needed their testicles used as a pincushion. "I'm calling because I wanted you to be the first to hear the news."

"I'm losing patience, Giles." I clicked my tongue. "Cut to the fucking point already, or I'll show you just how much of a *sweetheart* I can be."

Giles laughed. He enjoyed dragging out our conversation like a call girl hoping to scrape a few extra cents. It would be different if we were talking in person. People squealed fast when they had a pair of pliers held against their toe nails.

"I'm sitting outside Briarly Manor now," Giles said. In the background, the distant screech of sirens grew steadily closer.

My stomach lurched in dread. "What have you done, Giles?"

Vixen motioned for me to put the call on speaker, but the line was starting to crackle, and I batted her away with my hand.

"Me?" Giles taunted. Of course, *he* would never get his own hands dirty. "*I* have done nothing."

"I'm not going to ask a second time," I warned.

"The Sevens may have taken my wife, but they are not taking *my* destiny too," Giles sneered. It was hard to hear him over the static and commotion. The sirens almost drowned out his voice completely, but I made out the last line, "Your new love nest will be ash by the time you return to Port Valentine."

I ended the call. *Holy fucking shit.* Giles may be a pathetic excuse for a human being, but he knew how to stage a performance. Giving him a reaction would only have fanned the flames. Besides, I was more of a 'show' not 'tell' type of girl. He'd know exactly how I felt when we next came face-to-face.

"Well?" Vixen slammed her palms on the table. "What is it? What did he want?"

"It's the manor," I said. I liked to deliver bad news like ripping off a bandaid. The quicker the better. "Giles burned it down."

"Are you sure he's not joking around?" Mieko stammered.

I shook my head. It'd be a good hoax to lure us to Port Valentine, but I detected the overwhelming smugness in Giles's tone. I wanted to stuff fifty scones down his throat until he stopped breathing.

Rocky slumped back. "Shit..."

He pulled a weed baggy and papers out of his pocket. His fingers moved quickly and rolled a joint expertly. Q poked his head out of the Captain's cabin, but after seeing our somber expressions, he ducked back in again.

I'd fantasized about being the one to strike the match and watch the manor burn, but never like this. Zander had spent his life wanting to get away from the building that was a prison to him as a child. Regaining ownership of the building was a way of reclaiming it and righting the wrongs of the past — not to mention all the time and dollars Vixen spent upgrading its interiors.

"We need to go back," Zander said.

Vixen nodded in agreement. "Before Giles burns everything else we own."

"I'll increase the security at the club and in Seven Sins," West said, already dialing. "I'll order them to shoot on sight."

"Giles wasn't working alone," I said. "Hiram's behind this too."

Burning the manor sent a clear message. Hiram wanted to destroy the future he planned for me. He'd intended for me to become the Briarly heir by succeeding Giles and killing Zander. After I abandoned him again, he wanted to make sure I'd have no fucking future at all. This was only the beginning.

West slammed his fists down on the table, making it rattle. "I'm going to kill that motherfucker."

"You can take Giles," I said. My muscles tightened with purpose. "But Hiram is all mine."

"We're going to do this together," Zander said. "All of us."

Mieko and Vixen looked at me and Zander curiously, sensing a shift between us, but didn't ask any questions.

Rocky took a long drag of his joint and slowly released the sweet-smelling smoke out of his lungs. "It's settled then. We're going home."

We needed to armor the fuck up because we were heading straight into a war.

———

"We'll arrive at the nearest port in an hour," Q said. "The helicopters are already waiting."

"That's not soon enough," Zander snarled, checking his watch. "I knew we should have installed a helipad on the deck."

"Quit being such a diva," Vixen snapped as Q scurried away. "Cupid's only trying to help."

"Why don't we pack our bags?" Mieko suggested, taking Vixen's arm and steering her away from confrontation.

Arguing with each other wouldn't help. The atmosphere had changed on the yacht since Giles called. We all knew that we couldn't stay on board forever, but we'd not expected an iceberg to get in our way so soon, especially like this.

"You need to calm down, Zander," I said as Mieko led Vixen away.

West and Rocky had already gone downstairs to collect their belongings, and it left the two of us alone.

"I'll do what I want," he snarled. His posture was rigid and tense. If he didn't chill the fuck out, it'd take days to massage out those knots. "My manor is gone."

"Your manor?" I raised one eyebrow. "Or the Sevens' manor?"

"Same thing," he replied, pacing up and down, mumbling under his breath. I hadn't seen him so rattled before. "I can understand why Giles would want to burn the place down, but what's in it for Hiram?"

"He's sending me a message," I answered. I bit my lip, debating whether to tell him about Hiram's plan. *Fuck it.* It's not like it mattered now the manor would soon be a pile of rubble. "If Rocky hadn't miraculously come back to life, it would have been *my* fucking manor on paper."

"The marriage… of course… that makes sense." Zander stopped walking and turned to face me. Was that hurt in his eyes? "Why didn't you say anything?"

I scoffed. "Because we hadn't done any real talking until last night," I reminded him, then rolled my eyes. "It doesn't matter anyway. The only reason I wanted the manor was to screw you over."

He grinned mischievously, despite his anger. "Does that mean you're done with trying to screw me over?"

"We're on the same side for now," I replied. After last night, I had no idea where we stood. "That's what matters."

"I'll make them pay for this," Zander vowed. His gray eyes darkened like the sky before a storm.

"I always thought you hated the manor?"

"I do, but I hate my father more," he said, then redirected his anger to his cousin. "Giles is going to regret this. All of it: the manor and marrying you. He won't get away with it, Candy."

"None of them will," I said. "*We* will make them suffer. All of them."

Zander took my hand and kissed it. "That's a fucking promise."

Q cleared his throat behind us, making me jump and pull my hand away.

"There's someone on the radio asking for you, Zander," Q said, shuffling awkwardly on his feet. "Something about bad weather causing delays."

Zander nodded and stormed through to accept the call.

Q lingered and nudged his head at Zander's retreating figure. "So, you took my advice, kid?"

"That's none of your business." I scowled. "And I'm not a kid anymore."

"Maybe not, but that doesn't mean I'll stop looking out for you," he said, ruffling my hair playfully. "I'm happy for you, though. All of you. When you find something good, don't let it go."

I smiled sweetly. "If you touch my hair again, I'll cut your hand off."

Q chuckled and headed back to steer the yacht. It was so fancy it had cruise control, but he still liked to manually steer.

"Q?" I called after him, my voice softening. "Thanks for… you know."

I was a fiercely independent woman who didn't need to take advice from anyone but her gut, but Q's advice helped. If it hadn't been for him talking about Crystal and second chances, I don't know whether all of the Sevens would still be alive to return to Port Valentine.

Q grinned back. "Anytime, kid."

Even though being a Seven again was a temporary arrangement, it went against everything Hiram taught me. But, no matter how hard I tried, I couldn't ignore the magnetism drawing us together. It was unavoidable. My heart was caught in the surf with nowhere to go but under. Would I come up for air or drown?

———

We stood in silence and watched as the shoreline came into focus. Frizzy hair from the spraying water was the least of my concerns. Two small boats cut across the choppy waves in our direction. I assumed we'd be pulling into a harbor, but it looked like these would be our escorts back to land.

I turned to Q and frowned. "You're not coming with us?"

We'd already put him in enough danger, but I'd grown used to his presence. He was basically an honorary member of the Sevens, and I enjoyed his company — not that I'd ever tell him that.

"It'll be easier if I stay out of town for a while. I can work from here," Q said. "I'll be back when I can."

"Take care of yourself, Cupid," Rocky said, slapping him on the back. "We'll see you on the other side."

As I watched the others say their farewells, I realized they believed this could be the last time they saw each other. I couldn't let that happen, not on my fucking watch. Hiram had already taken years of my life. He would not take anything else from me, especially people I'd grown to care about.

I was last to say goodbye.

"I'm not going to say goodbye," I said, meeting his eyes with fierce determination and hoping he felt it. "We'll see you again soon."

"You bet you will," Q said, pulling me into a hug before I could stop him. He whispered in my ear, "If anyone can take him down, you can. Do it for Crystal."

I squeezed him tightly and blinked back tears. "I will."

He pulled away with shiny eyes and nodded. "Safe travels."

Leaving the yacht and traveling back to land on the small boats felt like we were leaving a dream world behind — even the clouds seemed to grow darker. Being on the sea may have no rules, but where we were heading was its like the Wild fucking West.

"I'll miss him," Mieko said wistfully, watching the 'Crystal' take off in the opposite direction.

"We all will," I replied. "But he's gotta do what he has to do."

Just like we did.

"Ready for your second helicopter ride, C?" Rocky asked as we returned to solid ground.

"Do we all have to go in one?" Mieko asked, overhearing our conversation. "I thought some of us would be going back by car."

Rocky laughed, nudging her shoulder playfully. "You're not scared of heights, are you?"

Her paling face answered his question before her mouth had a chance to move.

"I don't think helicopters crash that often," he teased. "Not unless you count—"

Vixen sent him a threatening glare and made a cutting motion with her hand across her neck behind Mieko's back.

"It'll be fine," I reassured her, linking my arm through hers.

The journey home wouldn't be as terrifying as what lay in wait for us on the other side...

————

"Finally," Vixen declared as the neon lights came into view.

"You're telling me," I muttered.

Mieko rolled her eyes, but I sensed she was relieved to be getting out of the cramped space too. After a helicopter ride, we had to drive for hours back to Port Valentine in a black bulletproof mini-bus. It was okay for Zander and West, who were sitting up front, but I'd have thrown Vixen and Rocky's bodies down a ditch off the highway if I had to sit behind them for another hour. They were worse than kids asking 'are we there yet?' every ten miles. Next time, I'd insist we travel in separate cars or bring them a fucking coloring book to pass the time.

From the outside, Lapland looked no different. The familiarness of its seedy exterior and flickering pink light were almost comforting. This is where it had all begun. I hadn't known it then, but stepping my heels over the threshold changed the course of my entire life.

Outside Lapland's entrance, a group of the Sevens' best security guys lined up shoulder-to-shoulder like soldiers expecting our arrival.

"Home sweet home," West murmured as we parked up.

He got out and handed the keys to one of our men. Who needs to park their own car when you have a freaking entourage to do it for you? That kind of luxury is something I'd never get used to.

"Glad to be back, Candy?" Mieko asked as I followed her out and filed into the club after the others.

"It's like I've never been away," I said.

Nothing had changed inside. It had the same sparkly floor, dim lighting, and sticky velvet booths crawling with clients hoping to cop a feel. The dancers were already in full swing. Long legs, swinging hair, and perky tits filled the club from wall to wall.

Every head turned to look at us. After twelve hours of traveling, the Sevens were officially back in town and ready to take their rightful throne. A glass slipped through one of the dancer's fingers and landed with a smash. Her face paled like she'd seen a ghost... *oh, shit.*

I nudged Rocky in the ribs. "You know you're supposed to be dead, right?"

"Oh, that." He chuckled and shrugged, then made a comical bow to our staring audience. "Turns out the coroner didn't check my pulse properly."

There were a few nervous laughs as people were unsure how to act.

What was the point in forcing Rocky into hiding now I'd returned to the Sevens? Hiram would find out sooner or later. Besides, no one would be brave enough to probe him about his miraculous resurrection.

"What're you staring at, huh?" Vixen snarled, pointing at the ogling group of shot girls. "Get back to fucking work."

The girls squeaked in response, more terrified of Vixen than being faced with a supposed dead man. Taking less than two seconds to fall back into control freak bitch mode must be a new world record. Vixen may come across as a tough boss, but she did try to look out for the girls and wouldn't let anyone touch a single hair on their heads. Although, not many dancers met her high standards.

"Do you see this?" Vixen asked. She picked up three discarded glasses, and her eyes darted around the room to track down the dancer who'd been brave enough to stand in during our absence. "Have they forgotten our fucking standards?"

"Maybe we should have a drink first?" Mieko suggested. For someone who used to be scared of Vixen, she now seemed immune from her explosive outbursts. A cheeky grin spread over Mieko's face. "We should celebrate Rocky coming back to life."

Before Vixen got the chance to respond, a man approached us.

"Are you Zander Briarly?" he asked.

From his clipped tone, ironed shirt, the clear liquid in his glass, and the way he didn't eyeball the topless women handing out drinks, he could either be gay or a cop. Or both.

The man held out a badge for inspection.

Bingo.

I sure could teach plainclothes officers a thing or two about blending into their surroundings. This guy needed to up his game.

Zander barely glanced at his badge. He looked the officer up and down coldly. "You're new."

The cop flinched under Zander's appraisal. Having a badge didn't mean he had the courage to face a man like Zander. West edged closer, drawing himself to full height and cracking his knuckles menacingly. I made a mental note to tell him to stop doing that. Looking cool was not worth the risk of joint damage, but I'd let him have this one for dramatic effect.

The officer loosened his collar and gulped. A glance at West's balled fists was enough for him to lose any of his existing confidence. Being confronted by Zander was terrifying enough, but The Hulk? That was another matter.

"Can we have a moment to talk?" the officer stammered.

"Whatever you have to say, you can say here," Zander said. "It's late to be making a house call on this side of town."

"We've been trying to contact you," he said. "It's about Briarly Manor. There was an incident this morning."

"We are aware."

The officer's mouth opened and shut as if he wanted to talk but couldn't form the words.

"The fire crew is finishing their investigations, but you'll be able to visit in the morning," he said, finally finding his voice again. "The area will be cordoned off because it's unsafe."

"How bad is the damage?" Rocky piped up.

Out of all three guys, Rocky looked the most approachable. Perhaps it was the fact he wasn't covered in tattoos or because he was wearing a loose T-shirt and sweatpants? Appearances were deceiving, though. Rocky was our dark horse, and, after seeing him in the ring, he was probably the most skilled fighter in hand-to-hand combat.

The cop scratched his neck nervously. "It's better you see it for yourselves."

His shit-scared expression told us all we needed to know. If Giles had Hiram's help, it would have been a thorough job.

"We'll be there tomorrow," Zander said. "Will that be all?"

"There's one more thing…"

The officer reached inside his jacket. At the same time, Zander's hand slipped behind his back to rest on the gun tucked into his waistband. How long had he been carrying that?

"Your cousin asked me to deliver this note to you personally," the officer said, holding out an envelope.

Zander snatched it from his shaking hands. "Do you often do deliveries for my cousin?"

Zander's icy tone took the cop by surprise. He must be new in town, otherwise, he'd know about the ongoing feud between Zander and Giles, which had been brewing for decades.

"No," he spluttered. "This is the first time."

"For your sake, I hope it's the last," Zander said, then cocked his head. "If you're picking sides, make sure you pick the right one."

West nodded at two henchmen loitering in the shadows. They advanced forwards and stood on either side of the officer.

"They'll see you out," West growled.

"That really won't be necessary…"

West shot him a smile, making him shiver. "I insist."

"Call it good old-fashioned hospitality. Have a good evening, officer." I blew him a kiss. "Drive safe now, won't you?"

The officer paled further and scampered into the night without looking in my direction. He wasn't as dumb as I first thought. It's funny how others can instinctively sense when they are amidst a predator. The poor guy's flight or fight response must be in overdrive.

"Want me to blow up the cop's truck, boss?" West asked. His muscles jumped under his shirt, itching for a fight. Biding time wasn't one of his monster's strengths. "Say the word, and it'll be done."

"Not today," Zander replied, causing The Hulk to pout. "He's not important enough, but Candy made sure he'll be checking his brakes before he leaves."

The threat of violence can be even more effective than its demonstration. Paranoia fucks with people's heads, and if someone was going to side with Giles, they'd get what was coming to them.

"Well?" Vixen demanded, eying the envelope pointedly. "Are you going to open it?"

Zander carefully unpeeled the seal and pulled out a notecard. He held it out for us to see. It was blank. A plain old white page.

Rocky frowned. "Has he written in invisible ink or something?"

Everyone looked at him like he was mad.

"It was just a suggestion," he huffed, crossing his arms.

"We're not in a fucking mystery novel," Vixen grumbled.

"Why would he send the cop here for no reason?" West asked.

"He wanted us to know that he's watching," I replied.

"Let him fucking watch," West said, scanning the crowds in the club. Someone had tipped Giles off about our arrival. Was it someone from our security team, or had a conversation been overheard? Either way, it meant we couldn't trust anyone. "He won't see us coming when we make our move."

"Before you get into the ring with Giles, can we talk about the manor?" Vixen said, then addressed Zander directly. "Are we really going to wait until the morning to go by?"

"We're going to play by their rules," Zander said with an air of finality. "For now."

Doing anything law enforcement requested rubbed me the wrong way. If conforming was a class at school, I'd have failed, but Zander made a good point. We'd all barely slept, and it'd be hard to assess the damage in the dark.

"In that case, there's only one thing we can do." Vixen threw her hands up in the air. "Let's hit the fucking bar."

"Yeah, because a hangover is the only thing that won't make tomorrow morning even worse," Rocky muttered sarcastically.

A pounding headache may be the only thing that'd help distract her from her renovations being turned into smoldering ash.

"I don't see you having any better ideas, Red," she snarled.

Mieko concealed a yawn behind her hand but said, "I'm in."

"Me too," I said, showing female solidarity.

The journey back had been exhausting, but I knew I wouldn't be able to sleep. Partying was our best alternative.

Zander's lip curled in disapproval. "I'll be in my office. We leave at nine sharp tomorrow morning. Be ready."

"Whatever." Vixen rolled her eyes and grabbed Mieko's hand. "Let's go."

Before following, I hung back with the guys. I caught Zander's arm. "Are you sure you can't stick around?"

"What's wrong, little one?" The corners of his mouth turned upward in a sly smile. "Don't want me too far away?"

I scowled. "You need to get over your fucking ego."

West smirked. "Looks like the old Candy is back."

"She never left," Zander said, running a hand down my cheek and sending shivers down my spine. "She's always been *our* Seven girl."

Rocky raised an eyebrow. "You guys made up too?"

"Not exactly," I snapped, hoping the strobe light hid my heated cheeks. "We came to an... agreement... for now. Nothing is final, and I'm not *your* fucking girl, Zander. Things can't just go back to how they were before. Things have changed."

"Have they?" Zander stepped closer. His body was inches away from mine, and the heat from his skin made my head spin. "You may not want to accept it yet, but we'll wait. You may not be fully ours, but we are yours."

On the yacht, the three of us had never been alone. Mieko, Vixen, and Q were always around to extinguish underlying tension. Being back in Port Valentine felt different. We were surrounded by other people, but it felt like we were the only four people in the room, and they were all looking at me like a meal.

"And we always will be," Rocky confirmed, wrapping his strong arm possessively around my waist.

I hesitated, not sure whether to push Rocky away. He sensed my shift and held on even tighter.

"But what about the others?" I asked.

We'd never flaunted our status in the club before, and the dancers were watching our every move. Hooking up with Zander, West, and Red is something many of them aspired to. They collected notches on their bedposts like Girl Scout badges. Scarlett, a long-serving dancer who had a raging she-boner over West, looked over at us with bulging eyes. *Take a picture, bitch. It'll last longer.*

"Let them stare," West replied, brushing a rogue hair out of my eyes. "We have nothing to hide."

"We'll make the world burn for you, little one," Zander said. "But it's up to you whether you stay a Seven at the end of it. Whatever happens now doesn't change our deal."

You're in control of the situation, Candy. I reminded myself. *You have a way out if you want it.* If that was true, then why did I suddenly feel so powerless?

"Can we pretend no decisions have to be made for now?" I sighed, putting an end to my racing thoughts. "Let's just run with this. I need a fucking drink..."

"Now, if you'll excuse me, Red." West shouldered Rocky out of the way. "Our lady said she wants a drink."

I squealed as West threw me over his shoulder. If Hiram had his way, we'd all be dead soon. Was there any harm in living a little?

Fifteen

West's voice rattled through my soul. "It's time to rise, sleeping beauties."

The bastard may as well have crashed a cymbal over my head. My eyes flickered, then snapped shut again as he threw open the curtains and blinded me with the morning sun.

I groaned. "But we've just gone to bed."

"Whose fault is that?" West asked pointedly, raising one of his eyebrows in accusation.

Memories from last night came flooding back: twirling around poles and making new cocktails with drinks that don't mix well together. Whoever had the idea of combining rum and vodka deserved to have pins stuck into their eyes. Shit… the more I thought about it, the surer I became that it was me.

Vixen lay on a nearby armchair while Mieko stirred underneath a pile of blankets near my feet. We passed out on the sofas after belting out '90s classic tunes. CCTV cameras better not have audio recording because I'd have to kill people if they ever got out. I have a badass reputation to uphold.

"Fuck off, West," Vixen croaked.

Suddenly, Mieko jumped from her resting spot under the blankets and dashed through the room, holding a hand over her mouth.

I looked at the paper cups in West's hands. "They better be ours."

"Of course," he said, passing them over with a grin.

How come he was able to wake up early and stop at a coffee shop? Zander was a grumpy ass and holed himself in his office all night, but West and Rocky joined in with our celebrations. Although I had a fuzzy recollection of them bailing when we started playing Britney on repeat. Their loss.

"Are they ready to go?" Rocky asked, entering the living room. The guys smirked at each other knowingly, but I didn't have the energy to respond with a snarky line. They'd be smug for the rest of the day. "Zander is already waiting outside."

"Don't fucking rush me, Red," Vixen warned.

"What about you, C?" Rocky asked. "Regretting hitting the bar too hard?"

His 'I told you so' look made me jump up in anger and spill burning coffee over my tits.

"I'm fine," I insisted. "I'll be ready."

My steaming nipples didn't fool anyone. The only thing I was ready for was to be wrapped in a blanket with a hot guy, or three, and a marathon run of trash TV with junk food. Instead, I'd have to settle for a burned manor.

———

After getting ready in record time, I was starting to feel more alive, despite my pounding head. I fared better than Vixen, who wore huge diva sunglasses covering half her face. She looked ready to murder anyone who spoke above a whisper.

Unfortunately, Mieko couldn't go further than two steps from the bathroom without retching. She made a fatal decision to match her fiancée drink-for-drink, and even a copious amount of caffeine wouldn't be enough to make her borderline functional.

"Zander is not going to be happy," Rocky murmured as we stepped outside the club to see two cars waiting.

Zander tapped his watch. "You're late."

"The manor won't burn down any more in the next five fucking minutes." Vixen scowled. "Chill out already."

Zander ignored her and opened the door to a black sports car, which looked like a panther in mechanical form. In the same way that dogs resembled their human owners, Zander was like his car: smooth and fucking deadly.

"You'll ride with me, Candy," he ordered, opening the passenger side door. "Get in."

I slid in without arguing and hoped he'd go easy on the gas. I already had a reputation for ruining cars after using one of West's favorites to dispose of a body. He still hadn't gotten over it.

The engine purred to life, and we pulled away as the others followed behind.

"How are you feeling about seeing the manor?" I asked.

Zander's eyes stayed fixed ahead. He didn't say a word.

"Fine," I huffed after a long pause. "I'll take the hint."

Riding in silence didn't bother me. If anything, it was better for my hangover. Plus, it'd beat the carnage that would be going on in the Jeep behind us when Vixen heard the roar of West's engine.

I lowered the window and closed my eyes, enjoying the cool breeze hitting my face. A brisk wind and icy shower were the best ways to bring you back to life after a rough night.

Minutes ticked by. Finally, we started to climb the hill to the manor. The smell of a dying bonfire hung in the air and grew stronger the closer we got. I closed the window to block it out, but it'd already made its way inside. The smell lingered like a dark history that couldn't be brushed away.

I gulped as we came to a stop. The last time I visited the manor was after Rocky's funeral. It wasn't recognizable as the same building and had been reduced to a half-charred mound of rubble. The harsh smell of gasoline stung my nostrils and burned the back of my throat. This was not an amateur pyromaniac's job — it was professional. Whoever did it wanted to make sure nothing was salvageable. Judging by the impressive holes blown out of the sides of the building, controlled explosives had been used to bring it down. When they lit the place up, the sky would have been illuminated for miles around.

Zander stalked out of the car without saying a word. I followed quickly, having to take two steps for each of his long strides. His face remained emotionless as he stopped to regard the damage. For a place that used to be a hub of social activity, there was nothing but an eerie silence around us.

"Zander?" I asked gently. "Are you—"

He didn't let me finish my sentence. He hurried over to the police tape that cordoned off the scene and ducked underneath. No amount of yellow warning signs would hold him back.

"Fuck," I whispered as I got closer.

Huge holes where windows used to be meant you could see from one side of the ruins to the other. The heat of the fire must have blown the glass clean out of its frames, and crushed shards coated the ground, crunching under our feet like a layer of diamonds. Flames had ravaged the building, consuming it from the inside out. The upper floors collapsed into a mountain of remains. A lifetime of memories reduced to scraps of burnt fabric, ash, timber, and broken pieces. Briarly Manor, home to Port Valentine's oldest family, had been wiped out.

Zander kicked a chunk of debris. "I've wanted to see this place burn for as long as I can remember."

"And how do you feel now?"

"My mother loved it here," he said, walking around the edge of the charred remnants of his former home. "As much as she hated my father, she still liked this place."

Until now, he hadn't realized what memories the manor held for him. It only amplified my hatred for Giles more. Vixen's voice pierced through the clearing and broke the moment.

"Holy shit…" she gasped, holding a shaking hand to her mouth.

The others trekked over to join us, but no one said another word. We stood together like we were the only survivors at the end of the world.

The manor had once been a home, a prison, and a dream for some. It had been an institution in its own right, and now? It was over. The Briarly reign had ended, and a new history was about to be written. But what part would the Sevens play? It was anyone's game, and people were playing to win.

I don't know how long passed before West cleared his throat. He turned and gestured at the cop cars approaching. "We have company."

It wasn't one car, but a whole fucking fleet. They raced up the road like they were ready to stop a bank heist and turned on their wailing sirens to make a point.

Rocky scratched his chin and voiced what everyone was thinking, "Why are there so many of them?"

"I swear to fucking God I'll kill someone if they don't turn the sirens off," Vixen said, holding her head.

The first cop car's brakes screeched as it came to a halt. An officer holding a megaphone jumped out. "Back away from the building," he ordered. "This is a crime scene."

Another officer jumped out of the second car and ran over to snatch the megaphone from his hands, motioning for his colleague to cut it out.

Vixen sighed in relief. "Thank fuck for that."

"It doesn't look like all the cops in town have been infiltrated by Giles," West said, nodding at the more superior officer in mutual understanding. "Some of them still know their place."

"Are we gonna hear them out?" I asked, already itching to leave. Being around law enforcement made me twitchy. Zander didn't reply and started walking. "I guess we'll follow your lead then."

Behind the row of cop cars, white vans climbed the hill. Forensics. Why so many reinforcements? This didn't seem like the standard procedure for a case of arson. Anyone with a nose could smell the gasoline from miles away.

"Sorry for the entrance," the cop said apologetically as we approached, then glared at his co-worker. "Some of us didn't realize who it was."

"This is my fucking land," Zander replied coldly, making the officer who acted out of turn shiver. "Make sure he falls in line."

"I will, sir." The cop nodded. "But I have to tell you, there have been new developments."

"Developments?" Zander asked sharply.

"Well…" The cop's voice trailed off like he was scared of breaking the news.

"Why are they here?" West asked, motioning at the procession of approaching vans. "What's going on?"

"A body was found," the cop said. "This is now an active murder investigation."

"A murder investigation?" Vixen's mouth fell open. "But we're all here?"

Zander's shoulders tensed. "How old were the remains?"

I knew what he was thinking. We all knew Bryce murdered his and Vixen's mother. They never found her body. Was it possible that she'd been buried in the walls of Briarly Manor for all these years?

"They were… fresh." The cop grimaced. "Whoever was inside died in the fire."

"Do you have an ID yet?" West pressed.

"Not yet," he replied, scrunching his nose. "The body is in pathology now. We're having to check dental."

Whoever it was had died a terrible death, but who the hell was it? And why were they snooping in the manor when we were out of town? Hiram's men were too well-trained to trap themselves inside. We knew Giles was in the area, so it ruled him out. But what about Bryce? It's not a stretch to imagine he could have returned to the manor to steal a long-forgotten treasure. After all, it's something Giles and I initially planned to do on the day of Rocky's funeral.

"We'll be in touch as soon as we've made an identification," the officer said. "We understand you were all away at the time of the fire, but we still have to take statements. I'll make it quick. It's just formality."

Vixen paled, swaying on her feet. "I think I'm going to be—"

Rocky grabbed her hair just in time for her to vomit over the officer's shiny shoes.

"My cousin is in shock," Zander said. "You can take our statements at the club later today."

"Of course." He nodded obediently. If the new decoration on his shoes and the disgusting smell of acidic tequila bothered him, he didn't show it. "I will see to it personally."

Giles may have wanted to send us a message through a rookie cop to show he had his claws in local law enforcement, but he was still an outsider. Zander was the true heir to the Briarly line in everyone's eyes. That still held credence… for now, anyway.

———

After getting through the police statements in less than ten minutes, we huddled together in a velvet booth. Despite my lack of sleep, adrenaline coursed through my veins. We expected there to be a body count at the end of this war, but not this fast.

"I still can't believe it," Mieko whispered.

Rocky slapped down a bottle of whiskey and poured generous measures. "Hair of the dog?"

Vixen pushed it away. "Are you trying to make me sick again?"

Zander sipped his drink silently. He hadn't spoken since the police left. His arms were crossed, and his face closed off like an impassable wall.

West checked his phone, and his lip curled. "We have a visitor."

He spun his cell around to show CCTV footage of the street outside. Ahead of our return from the yacht, he'd ordered his guys to update the security systems in Lapland and the Seven Sins casino. The new system gave him full access to the camera feeds at the club, casino, garages, and his apartment in Bayside Heights.

On the screen, we watched as Giles sauntered over to Lapland's entrance. He wore a perfectly pressed suit and looked like a wannabe gangster, surrounded by a four-man entourage. I recognized their faces as Hiram's lower rank goons. It was laughable that Giles believed Hiram valued him enough to give him proper protection. Anyone half-trained would be able to kill them with their hands tied.

"Do we let our men take him out?" West asked, his eyes lighting up.

"No," Zander said. "Let him in."

West pouted and grudgingly sent a text to the security guards at the entrance. They would frisk each person down before they set foot in the club. Giles was too smart to show up with a weapon, though. The fucker was here to do what he did best. Gloat.

We filed out of the booth.

"You need to tell your men to be less handsy next time," Giles said, entering and readjusting his jacket. "A little birdie told me you visited the manor this morning. What did you think?"

"I'll show you, you fucking bastard," West growled.

I grabbed his wrist to stop him from doing something stupid, despite every instinct in my body begging me to do the same. We had to be calculated. West retaliating would play straight into his, and Hiram's, hands.

"It's nice to see you again, Candy," Giles said coldly, his gaze lingering on my fingers holding West back. "But it looks like you may have broken your vows."

"Don't," I warned as Rocky and West tensed.

Giles's henchmen stepped forward. A fight is what they wanted, but we didn't need to waste time spilling the blood of people who weren't important. We had to hit Hiram where it would hurt the most, and he wouldn't even know the names of the goons he hired to look after Giles. They were nothing.

"Although I can't say I'm surprised. What did I expect when I married a stripper whore like you?" Giles taunted. "Hiram is disappointed."

"Our vows aren't the only thing I'll break," I spat.

"Why are you here, cousin?" Zander asked.

Giles paced around the club, running his hand over the bar top to inspect it for dust. "I wanted to pass on my commiserations, of course."

"More like you wanted to brag about how good a job you did," I corrected him, narrowing my eyes.

"It's rare you give compliments, my darling wife," Giles mocked scathingly.

West wrapped his arms around my waist, rooting me to the spot.

"Don't," he hissed in my ear. Goddammit, karma was a bitch. Next time he wanted to attack someone, maybe I'd let him if it meant him not having to restrain me in return.

Zander's ringing phone stopped us all in our tracks. Giles continued to talk and blow more smoke up his own ass, but none of us listened. We all knew what call Zander was waiting for. His brows furrowed, stopping only to say 'yes' and 'no', then ended the call.

"You seem proud of yourself, cousin," Zander said as soon as he hung up. "But I wonder whether anyone checked if the manor was empty before torching it down?"

Giles's smug grin faltered momentarily. He hadn't expected the conversation to go this way.

"That was the pathologist's office," Zander continued, holding up his cell. "The manor wasn't empty when you burned it down."

"You're lying," Giles said, but his voice was an octave higher than usual like someone was sinking their nails into his scrote.

"What have I got to gain by lying? My manor is gone," Zander replied. "They've identified the body."

"Who?" Vixen asked.

Zander didn't take his eyes off Giles. I didn't think it was possible for the cousins to hate each other any more than they did, but resentment sizzled in the air.

"Penelope Cole."

Giles's rosy cheeks turned a ghostly white. A shade I'd only seen on cadavers. It wasn't a surprise Penelope would try to leech off the Sevens. I bet she'd caught word they were out of town and wanted to make quick cash. Her family fortune was crumbling, and after dropping Giles and failing to seduce West, she had nothing and no man to rely on.

"You're making it up," Giles stammered.

"Did you think Hiram would send his best men to do your dirty work?" I asked, looking at Giles in disgust. "Do you think his men are the type to check whether a building is empty before blowing it apart?"

"I don't believe you," Giles said. His tone was riddled with desperation like he wanted to convince himself. "Any of you."

"Listen closer, cousin. Because that's not all," Zander hissed. "Penelope was pregnant."

Pregnant?

Mieko gasped in horror, and Vixen turned on West. "You didn't....?"

"Of course fucking not," West spat. "I wouldn't touch her. The only time I saw her was at Red's fucking funeral, which means..."

West's voice trailed off. As the realization dawned on Giles, he looked like he wanted to throw himself into a fucking fire. I remembered how devastated he was when we attended the funeral together. It crushed him to see Penelope sidling up to West. He loved her, and now? She was gone, and so was his unborn child.

"You're lying," Giles screamed, his voice shook and shoulders trembled. "It's what you want me to think! Just like you did with Red."

"If you don't believe me, call the pathologist yourself," Zander said with no ounce of sympathy. "They'll tell you the same thing I did."

Giles pushed aside his security and fled. He thought burning down the manor would be the ultimate act of revenge, but it cost him the most important people in his life. He couldn't fix this mistake with his Uncle's help. Death was irreversible, and there was no worse punishment than him having to live with the consequences of his actions for the rest of his miserable and pathetic existence.

———

It's funny how the death of someone you hated can still get under your skin. Penelope was a gold-digging bitch I'd have been happy to scalp on many occasions, but she didn't deserve to die like that. Motherhood could have been the making of her, but we'd never know.

Since we heard the news, a strange, unsettling feeling swept over Lapland. West had been sitting alone at the bar drinking for an hour. I pulled up a stool next to him. Emotional conversations weren't usually my jam, but I had to say something.

I cleared my throat and asked, "Are you... you know ...okay?"

What a stupid fucking question. Of course he's not.

He drained his glass and slammed it down, then poured another.

"I'd feel better if I could put Giles in the ground," he replied.

West hated the person Penelope became, but he used to care about her once. They had a shared history. They'd known each other since boarding school. Penelope used West's feelings for money and crushed his heart, but, before all that, she must have been bearable for him to fall for her.

"Why do you think she was at the manor?" I asked.

"Money," he replied without hesitation. "It's what she always wanted."

She must have been desperate. Maybe that's why she jumped at the opportunity to be West's guest at Rocky's funeral? Sure, she had feelings for West for years, but there could have been more to it. After finding out she was pregnant and Giles was destitute, she needed to fill his place quickly. Was she planning to seduce West? Would she have told Giles about the baby? There were many questions we'd never get the answer to.

"I guess that's one thing she and Giles had in common," I replied wryly. "He's already got the worst punishment."

"Don't tell me you're feeling sorry for that murdering bastard?" West snarled.

"Hell fucking no," I said. "But having to live with knowing what you did? That's worse than jail. I know what it's like to lose someone and think it's your fault, remember?"

"What happened with Red was different," West muttered. "You thought you were saving him when you shot him."

"That didn't make a difference when I thought I killed him," I replied. "Having to live with that *feeling* for the rest of your life is worse than any beating you could give him."

West swirled the bourbon around in his glass, almost sloshing it over the sides. "You think Giles loved her, huh?"

"Yup," I said, popping the p. It'd be easier if he hadn't as he wouldn't be stuck in his own personal hell forever. "He had it bad."

"Penny wasn't always a bitch," West said. "When she was younger, she was different."

"Will you miss her?" I asked, bracing myself for him throwing the glass.

"The person she turned into? No." West shook his head, taking me by surprise and keeping his cool. "The person I used to care about was dead years ago, but dying like that with a kid? It's not right."

"We'll make them pay for it." I put my hand on his inked forearm and stroked his prominent veins, bulging from his clenched hand. "Giles didn't do this alone. He may have been behind it, but Hiram will have pulled the strings like a puppet master."

West drained the rest of his glass and slammed it down. A crack appeared down its side from the force. "We'll kill him."

"I'll drink to that," I said, grabbing the bottle and taking a slug. I looked around the empty club. The others had gone upstairs. We settled into a thoughtful silence, then I asked, "Is this where you thought you'd end up?"

"Exactly in the same position as my pa working for a Briarly?" West laughed coldly, taking the bottle from me to take a swig, then wiping his mouth with the back of his hand. "No fucking way."

"Would you do things differently if you could go back in time?"

West's brows drew together in deep concentration. "No," he said finally. "Would you?"

"Sometimes I feel like all I do is bring destruction," I admitted. The news of Penelope's death and alcohol was not a good combination. It forced me to confront feelings I usually ignored. "It's like I'm cursed or something. Bad things follow me wherever I go."

Fate had it out for me from the beginning. After I was born, someone dumped me on the doorstep of a group home. Whoever my mother was could probably tell I'd bring trouble and wanted to save herself the hassle. Despite growing up in Evergreen, I tried to keep my head down throughout school, but it made no difference. The devil came into my life and sealed my fate.

"Hey!" West put his thumb under my chin and tipped my head up to face him. "This isn't your fault."

"Quit the bullshit, West," I snapped. "We both know this wouldn't have happened if I didn't leave Hiram in the first place. If I never set foot in Lapland, none of you would be in this fucking mess."

Why can't you keep your mouth shut, Candy? Hiram taught you how emotions get you killed, but I couldn't stop myself.

"You're all risking your lives, don't you get that?" I continued. "Since I came to Port Valentine, your lives have been a fucking train wreck."

"What would have happened if you stayed at Blackthorne Towers?" West asked. "Could you keep killing on command for the rest of your life? That shit doesn't last forever."

"I never thought that far ahead," I said. Getting from one day to the next was a small achievement. "There's only one way out for people who don't follow Hiram's orders. A future is something I never had to think about."

"You'd better think about it now, Pinkie," West said. "Because we won't let anything happen to you."

"But what if something happens to *you*?" I could still see the image of Rocky bleeding out on the warehouse floor like it was happening in front of us. What if West was next? Or Mieko? Or Vixen? Or even Zander? "How am I supposed to feel knowing you died because of me?"

The last few days had been a total head fuck. Being around the guys again made me *feel,* and I couldn't control it. The Sevens cracked open a small box hidden in my chest with a crowbar, and its insides were spilling out.

"Nothing is going to happen to us," West said fiercely. "I'll make sure of it. The Sevens are a family. If someone comes for one of us, they come for us all."

If only words were enough to keep Hiram at bay. If he wanted to take us out, he could do it with a click of his fingers. It wouldn't be long before the fire came to our door, and none of us would see it coming...

"We're shutting the club tonight, so I'm going to stay at Mieko's apartment," Vixen said, popping her head around my door. I'd reclaimed her closet as my room again. "I'll see you in the morning, okay?"

After being away, it felt strange to be back in the penthouse. Thankfully, Vixen decided she wanted to buy everything new when renovating Briarly Manor — otherwise, we'd have had nothing left. The furniture and rooms hadn't changed, but everything else had.

I glanced up at her from my spot on the bed, where I hadn't moved since leaving West to drown his sorrows at the bar this afternoon.

"See you tomorrow," I replied with a small wave.

"You might want to change out of pajamas," she said pointedly.

"Who are you? The fashion police?" They were the most comfortable things in existence, and, until we had a plan for killing Hiram, I would be living in full comfort. "Just leave already."

"The guys are planning a…" She quickly checked over her shoulder, then mimed 'surprise'. "Have fun."

"Way to go, Vix," I muttered. "Remind me to never trust you with a secret."

"You're welcome, bitch," she said, blowing me a kiss.

———

A knock came on my door half an hour later.

"C?" Rocky stepped inside without waiting for an answer. "Are you hungry?"

"Why knock if you're just gonna charge in?" I asked, but my rumbling stomach answered his question.

"We've made food," Rocky said with the tone of an excitable puppy.

I arched one eyebrow. "We?"

He looked sheepish. "Well, I mean, I helped..."

I laughed and followed him through to the living area.

"What the hell is this?" My mouth dropped as I took in the scene. "A fucking intervention?"

Lit candles gave the room a romantic glow, and pretty flowers in a vase made the table look like a restaurant. Zander's head was in the oven, checking that something wasn't burning, and West held out a bottle of wine like a butler. What had they done with the scary Seven men who Port Valentine feared?

"We've had a rough few days," Rocky said, pulling out a chair for me. "We wanted to do something special for you. Why don't we call it *our* first proper date?"

I was too dumbfounded to do anything but sit my ass down. Were group dates even a thing? Thousands of articles had been written about first dates, but I'd never read one involving three guys. That made my chances of fucking up three times higher.

My mouth went dry. "I don't know if it's the best time for a date night," I stammered.

"Doesn't something bad happening make you realize how important it is to live for now?" Rocky said. Damn, for the joker of the group, that shit was profound. "It's a perfect time."

I turned to The Hulk. "This was your idea, wasn't it?"

He shrugged and poured me a glass of wine, then took the seat on my left. The big guy would never admit it, but underneath his muscles, he was a true romantic.

"Our food is almost ready," Zander called over.

Dates were nerve-wracking enough, let alone when they were with three gorgeous Greek God lookalikes. I'd never been on a proper date before, well, not unless you counted the times I seduced marks before killing them.

"What are we having?" I asked, trying my hardest to keep my cool and not freak the fuck out.

"Your favorite," Zander said. "I'll break the culinary rules this once and have breakfast food for dinner."

"You know, I never thought I'd go on a date with you, Zander," Rocky teased, sitting opposite me. "But I'm definitely starting to see the perks."

Zander shot him daggers. "This isn't for you, Red."

Rocky rolled his eyes and winked, but he'd lightened the mood. Had he sensed my nerves and wanted to put me at ease?

"That's not all," West said. He pulled out a jewelry box and placed it in front of me. "I had it made before we boarded the boat."

I opened it to see a ruby necklace that looked strangely familiar.

"I used the stone from your old ring," he explained quickly. "May I?"

I nodded shakily, speechless, and turned to him, pulling my hair to the side. West carefully put the delicate chain around my neck. The beautiful stone felt cold against my skin, but West's fingers warmed me as he fastened it. It was one of the most thoughtful gifts I'd ever received, along with the pendant with the secret code that Zander gave me last Christmas. I didn't wear the pendant anymore but kept it stored away... it served its purpose. My new necklace was a symbol of how things had changed and how we'd come back together to create something different, but equally as beautiful.

"It's perfect," I said, reaching to feel the gem, then added, "but you shouldn't have. All of you. I mean, I don't even know where we stand. It's all..."

"Too much?" Rocky interrupted with a grin. "I thought you'd say that."

"There's no pressure," West said. His giant hand squeezed my thigh under the table. "We wanted to show you that we care. Don't overthink it."

"I'm..." A blush spread over my cheeks. "Look, I'm new to this, okay?"

"Don't you count the times I took you to a fast-food joint when we were kids as a date?" Rocky gasped in fake surprise and clutched his chest. "I'm wounded."

"That was one time, and it wasn't a date." I rolled my eyes. His goofball ways were exactly what I needed right now. "We were just two friends hanging out, remember?"

Putting together enough loose change to share a milkshake and fries didn't count. It'd been a shock when Rocky kissed me for the first time. He was a cool jock, and I didn't get why he was interested in someone like me. The quiet, weird kid who sat alone in the lunchroom.

"They were dates to me," he said. "Why do you think I kept asking you to hang out?"

"Evergreen had shit food," I replied, "and you were always hungry."

"Ouch, dude." West threw his head back and roared with laughter. "You had no game."

"If those didn't count, then let us make up for it tonight," Rocky said, his eyes glittering mischievously. "How many girls would kill to be waited on by the three Sevens?"

"Too many," I replied grudgingly. All the dancers were practically panting at the sight of them when we arrived back. "But if they knew the truth about you all, they'd run."

West raised his glass. "Touché."

"Although, I must warn you," I said, making them all stare — even Zander stopped dishing up to hang on my every word, "the only other dates I've been on ended in someone dying or being blackmailed."

Zander grinned. "We'll take our chances."

He carried over a stacked plate of waffles topped with fresh berries, brownie pieces, and vanilla ice cream, all drizzled in chocolate sauce. The most delicious things on one plate. Why had Vixen convinced me to change out of pajamas if she knew what I'd be eating? My denim hot pants wouldn't give me the stretch I needed.

"If you keep cooking like this, you're pretty safe," I said. "For now."

"Fuck..." Rocky sighed, taking his first bite. "This is good shit, Zander."

Zander ignored him, waiting for my reaction. West had already cleared one waffle in thirty seconds flat and was going in for another.

Holy fucking shit.

I resisted the urge to moan. It tasted even better than it looked.

Zander grinned, looking at me expectantly. "Well?"

I shrugged noncommittally. "It'll do."

"That means I'll have to do better next time," he promised.

"Who says there will be a next time?" I asked.

"That's your choice," Zander said, then smirked. "But I'll make it worth your while."

He liked a challenge, and flirting in front of the others didn't phase him.

"So, about Hiram—" Rocky began.

"We're not talking about that tonight." Zander silenced him, dropping his fork with a bang. "No business talk at the table."

"But don't you feel weird?" I asked. "Should we be enjoying ourselves after everything that's happened?"

"Red was right about what he said earlier. Bad things make you realize what's important," West said. "We deserve to have a night off and celebrate our girl coming home."

"Without her wanting to kill Zander," Rocky chipped in, making West choke on a mouthful as Zander sent him a frosty glare.

"Who says I don't want to kill Zander?" I teased.

"If the rocking boat was anything to go by..." West's voice trailed off, and my cheeks pinked. My disappearance from the engagement party hadn't gone unnoticed by everyone.

"We're all together again," Zander said with an air of finality. "That's all that matters."

A few days ago, we'd been on a yacht. Before that, I thought Rocky was dead and wanted Zander to join him. Someday soon, Hiram would be coming and we had to be ready. But maybe the guys were right...

We shouldn't waste a fucking minute.

It didn't take us long to eat as we were all starving. Zander eyed my empty plate as I ran my fingers around the edges to mop up the extra sauce.

"Did you enjoy my cooking?" he asked.

I popped my finger in my mouth as an answer and watched his pupils dilate. I may be outnumbered by dicks, but I had all the freaking power. This is why men worked so hard to keep women oppressed. They feared what would happen in a world where we had control.

"What's up next?" West cleared his throat. "A game of poker?"

"A smoke?" Rocky suggested.

"How about we let Candy decide?" Zander said.

All eyes fell on me.

"Why don't we clean up before Vixen decides to castrate you all?" I suggested.

Zander grinned and reclined in his chair. "The cook never cleans up."

"Fine, I'll wash," Rocky groaned and stood, starting to gather our dishes. When he reached the kitchen, he threw West a towel. "You can dry."

I frowned. "Don't you have a dishwasher?"

"It's broken," Rocky replied.

Is this how ordinary people lived? Eating a nice meal and washing up together? While it may be someone else's idea of normal, it was another universe compared to what we were used to.

I jumped up. "I'll help."

"No!" the guys cried in unison like I'd declared a lifetime vow of celibacy.

"I'm all for smashing gender constructs, but there's nothing wrong with me helping," I said, flipping my hair over my shoulder. "I don't need you to do everything for me."

Zander rose and blocked my path to the sink. West and Rocky's eyes watched us closely, unsure of what Zander's next move would be.

"Then tell us, little one..." Zander purred, stroking my cheek. "What *can* we do for you?"

My heart thumped hard in my chest.

Has it suddenly gotten warm in here?

Zander didn't wait for an answer and leaned in closer. "How about this?"

He brushed his lips against mine. I pulled away to steal a glance at the others before Zander could sweep me away. The sink was almost over-flowing with bubbles, and West had balled the towel into a fist in his hand.

I looked at the three of them through fluttering eyelashes. "Fuck the dishes."

I didn't want to use tonight to forget about the past. I wanted to use it to *remember* all the feelings I had for the Seven men. I needed to explore our connections. Hell, I needed to explore *them*. Soapy hands or not, I needed to get lost until our problems fell away.

"You heard our girl," Zander said, nodding at the other two. "It's time for dessert."

By dessert, he meant me.

West and Rocky didn't need any extra encouragement.

"Where are you going, little one?" Zander asked, grabbing my wrist as I turned to leave the kitchen. A wicked grin spread over his face and the flickering glow of the candles illuminated his rose and Seven face tattoo. "We're not finished yet."

"I thought—" I began.

Had he gotten rid of his giant bed since the last time I was here?

"Shh." He put a finger to my parted lips. "This night is about us giving you what you want wherever *we* want."

I swallowed hard as my heartbeat quickened. The Seven men surrounded me. Their eyes were full and hungry, swallowing me in their gazes and making it clear that their intentions were anything but holy.

Zander kissed my forehead, making me frown in confusion at his sudden display of tenderness. Why wasn't he ripping off my clothes? He leaned in and lowered his voice, "I'm going to watch as they pleasure you until you're screaming our name, little one..."

Zander took a step back, and West took his place. The Hulk had made an effort. He was freshly shaved and wearing a white shirt with the first two buttons undone. The fabric strained under his muscles, allowing me to see the outline of his ink underneath, like the beast he kept hidden within.

West wrapped his hands around my waist and pulled me into his embrace with none of the gentleness Zander possessed, making me forget we weren't the only ones in the room. West wanted me, and he wanted me right fucking now. His mouth assaulted mine as he yanked me closer to him, pressing my tits into his chest as he stood back against the kitchen counter.

Another figure stepped behind me. I could smell Rocky and feel his soft, floppy hair tickling my shoulder as he left gentle kisses along my skin. His hands slid up the back of my thighs, igniting excitement.

From the front, West's hands moved from my waist to the bottom of my crop top. He didn't ask for permission as he pulled it up. I raised my arms as he peeled it off and let my breasts spring free from the tight spandex.

"You're so goddamn beautiful," West murmured, looking down at me.

"She is," Rocky agreed as he unfastened my black bra and let it fall to the floor.

West's eyes widened as his fingers stroked my peaked nipples. They were sensitive to his touch, and I yelped as he squeezed them between his thumb and forefinger.

Meanwhile, Rocky's hands slipped around my waist to find the button of my hot pants. As he played with the zipper, West growled and shot him a filthy look over my shoulder.

"Hey," Rocky objected. "I didn't mean to touch you, man."

"This isn't about you two," Zander's voice said from behind us. "This is all about her."

I giggled. "How did he feel, Rocky?" I teased.

"You'll find out in a minute when I'm fucking you," West murmured, sending a wave of desire rippling through me as he pushed his hardness against my body in a promise of what was to come.

Rocky tugged my pants down to show off my G-string.

"What an ass," he admired. "You're missing out on this view, West."

"I'm enjoying the view right where I am," West replied, continuing to play with my nipples as he kissed me again.

Rocky's touching stopped, making me question whether he was afraid to keep going after The Hulk's possessive remarks, but then he planted his hands firmly on my hips and forced me to stick my ass out further.

"Holy shit..." Rocky said in a low, gravelly pitch, as he stepped back to check me out from behind.

"She's perfect," Zander purred.

My cheeks heated at the thought of their eyes watching me but kissing West kept me distracted. Making out with him could make me forget the day of the week.

A second later, I gasped as Rocky grasped my ass and spread my cheeks. A second later, his tongue was eagerly exploring me. The sensation of him licking my asshole made my legs tremble. On paper, I didn't think it was something I'd enjoy, but damn. I couldn't help myself. I pushed my ass onto his face, forcing his tongue to work harder.

With his free hand, Rocky slipped between my thighs to stroke my pussy. He slid between my lips but didn't penetrate me. He wanted to tease and stroke my clit, making me moan against West.

"Do you like what he's doing to you, Pinkie?" West asked.

"Uh-huh," I moaned as Rocky's finger finally slipped into me, soaking him with my wetness.

I wanted West to feel as good as I did. I trailed my hands down his torso, undoing his buttons as I went until his shirt was open and his chest exposed. I kept going down and stroked his giant cock through his pants, feeling it twitch at my touch. It gave me a kick to have that effect on a mountain of a man.

I undid his pants, shuffling them down, to release his inky cock and take his shaft in my small hands. I looked down and spat on it, aiming perfectly, and covering him, allowing my hands to slide up and down him easily.

Rocky finger fucked my pussy more aggressively as he took to his feet. The sound of clothes hitting the floor behind me hinted at what was to come, so it wasn't a surprise when his piercings rubbed against my heat a second later. Being the filling of a man meat sandwich wasn't so bad…

"Do you want Red to fuck you, little one?" Zander asked.

Behind Rocky, I couldn't see where Zander was standing, but wherever it was, I'm sure he could see everything that was going on.

"Yes," I sighed, craving his cock more than the chocolate waffles I ate earlier.

Rocky groaned as he slid easily inside me. West gathered my hair in a loose ponytail and yanked my face up to look into his eyes. His jaw was tense, and I couldn't tell whether it was from passion or jealousy at feeling Rocky's thrusts push my hips into him.

"Does that feel good, Pinkie?" West asked. "Do you like being our Seven slut?"

Usually being called a slut was something I'd knee a guy in the balls for, but it was hot coming out of his mouth.

"Yes," I said, then cried out as Rocky's hips bucked harder.

"Good." West grinned with satisfaction. "Then you won't mind sucking my cock at the same time."

He pushed my head down to his cock, and I took him into my mouth. It was hard to keep my balance while being railed from behind, so I couldn't use my hands. I put them on either side of West in front of me and gripped the kitchen counter, so I didn't fall.

West's hands in my hair controlled my pace. He guided my face up and down his cock then shoved it down my throat so violently that it made me gag. Then again, and again. He was so huge he could choke someone to death by throat fucking them for too long.

"Be careful, West," Zander warned, his tone harsh as my eyes watered and tears dripped down my face.

"Sorry, Pinkie," West replied gruffly. "Your mouth feels so fucking good I can't control myself."

I didn't mind. Knowing I could get him to lose control gave me a twisted sense of power, but he eased up and loosened his grip, moving me in slower motions.

"Shit, Candy…" Rocky groaned from behind. "You'll make me cum."

"You're not coming until our girl does," Zander said. "We take care of her first."

"Why don't we swap, West?" Rocky panted. "If I keep going, I'm not gonna be able to stop."

He reluctantly pulled out as West wrenched me off his cock and kissed me roughly. His hands wrapped around my throat.

"Are you ready for us to ruin you?" he asked as he squeezed tightly. "I want both of them to watch as I make you cum so hard you'll forget where we are."

West's pants were off in a matter of seconds, and he picked me up like I weighed nothing. His arms swept under my knees, angling my pussy towards his cock and leaving my feet dangling like a rag doll. His hands spanned over my entire rib cage as he held me tight. I rested my hands on his shoulders, thinking it would give me some support or control, but all the power was in West's arms. My body was his to take.

His cock slid into me, and he bounced my body off him. Each thrust made my breasts go crazy, and even the watchful eyes of Zander and Rocky didn't stop me from crying out. When we had sex together before, it'd been a team effort, but they were getting to see West's monster ruin me firsthand. I loved the feeling of being used by him and from the wild look in West's eyes, he was enjoying it too.

West grunted as I threw my head back, letting my hair tumble past my waist, and cried out his name. I'm a strong woman who knows how to take care of herself, but West made me feel protected. He was a house of a man who could hold me in his arms and fuck me like I was his entire fucking universe.

I turned my head to the side to see Zander and Rocky. Zander watched with hooded eyes, still fully dressed, while Rocky's mouth hung open and it looked like he wrestled with the urge to touch himself.

"Clear the island," West ordered.

Rocky knocked everything to the floor with a sweep of his arm as West carried me over. His cock stayed buried inside me as he laid me back. The marble chilled my skin, making me feel like a specialty dish being served at a restaurant.

Rocky joined us. He spat on his fingers and rubbed my clit as West continued to fuck me. Any previous reservations West had about Rocky accidentally rubbing his cock must have vanished. The two of them were working as a team to get me off, and who was I to disappoint? My orgasm took me off-guard.

"Fuck," I screamed as my pussy squeezed West, and a flush spread over my chest.

Rocky didn't slow. He continued to rub my wet clit until a second explosion rippled through me, bigger than the first. My legs trembled, my vision wavered, and dizzying ecstasy took me to another level of euphoria. If God existed, she had to be a woman to have invented such pleasure.

West's breathing grew shallow. I expected him to cum, but he pulled out.

Rocky stepped out of my grasp and let West rub his cock up and down my pussy, sliding himself between my lips, and tapping against my clit to make me writhe.

I panted, looking up at the two of them with wide eyes and down at their cocks with desire. My chest heaved from the exertion, but I sat up and reached for their cocks. I paused, looking over at Zander.

"Pleasure them, little one," he ordered. "I want to watch."

I dipped my hand between my legs, using the wetness to coat Rocky's cock, then did the same for West. I couldn't reach them with my mouth from this position, but I got to see how their bodies responded to me. Rocky's thighs shook, and West's abs twitched as I worked my hands over them to the same rhythm.

I looked past them to Zander who was smiling in satisfaction. I didn't look away from him until Rocky grunted. A bead of pre-cum signaled he was about to explode. I slid off the island and onto my knees in front of him, still working West, and put my mouth around him.

"Fuck, C," Rocky growled as his hips bucked and he finished in my mouth. I swallowed it down, then turned my attention back to West.

I opened my mouth wide, licking his hardness while staring up at him through my thick lashes. He groaned, and came, not taking his eyes off my open mouth and his cum filling it.

When he finished, I licked my lips and stood to my feet.

Zander raised an eyebrow. "Did you enjoy your dessert?"

I rolled my eyes and approached him. He was still fully clothed in his suit, making me wonder whether he hadn't joined in because he enjoyed watching or because he didn't want the others to see the fresh scars on his back.

"Aren't you hungry, Zander?" I asked, trailing a finger down his shirt.

"I am always hungry for you," he replied, then dropped his voice so the others wouldn't hear, "and watching you fuck them will only make me crazier for you next time."

"How about we shower and watch a movie?" Rocky suggested.

"I'm down," West said, swaggering out of the room butt-naked with all the confidence in the world.

What better way to end our evening?

CHAPTER

Seventeen

Waking up in a bed filled with muscled limbs is not the worst way to start the day. My aching thighs remind me of what happened the night before and how it wasn't a dream. A dynamic shifted last night. As terrifying as it was to admit it, our weird four-way date made me feel closer to them again, *almost* like I could trust them. None of us know what the future holds, but working together was the only way we'd make it through.

"Pinkie?" West stirred next to me, stretching his arms out and pulling me close.

I shuffled out of his reach and slid out of bed.

The guys drew the line at sleeping in a bed together. They didn't mind when their cocks touched while sharing me, but falling asleep under the same blanket was a step too far for them. After yesterday's news, West needed me the most.

He pouted and asked, "Where are you going?"

"Can't you smell that?" I asked, sniffing the air and sighing at the smell of sizzling bacon. "I'm not missing Zander's breakfast."

West groaned into his pillow as he looked me up and down hungrily. His eyes lingered on my pebbled nipples. "You look good in my clothes."

A tent was pitching under the comforter. *Look away, Candy!* If I didn't get up, I knew I'd risk staying in bed with West all day when we had to plan our next steps.

"Thanks," I replied sheepishly, even though I thought I looked like a House Elf in his giant T-shirt.

"Are you sure you don't want to join me?" he asked again.

My mouth opened and closed, but a knock on the door spared me from having to answer.

"Are you guys up?" Rocky called through. "We've got a delivery."

"A delivery?" West sat upright and jumped out of bed at double speed, giving me a good view of his massive swinging package. He hastily put on clothes and opened the door. "What is it?"

"Zander's waiting," Rocky replied. I detected an edge to his voice. "Vixen and Mieko have just gotten back."

We followed him down the corridor into the kitchen where Zander was frowning at an envelope in his hands. Mieko and Vixen were sitting at the breakfast bar opposite him, waiting for our arrival.

A wax seal embedded with a family crest kept the envelope shut. West took one look at it and his expression darkened. "What does Bryce want?"

"Hasn't he heard of using a cell phone?" I muttered sarcastically.

Who still used the archaic means of letters to deliver messages? If he thought it made him look like a supervillain, it had the opposite effect.

Zander tore the letter open. His eyes scanned it quickly and they narrowed. "He wants to meet," Zander said. "He's been out of town with associates, but he's back now… and he heard about the manor."

Briarly Manor may have been a permanent fixture in Zander's life, but it was more than that to Bryce. It was everything he'd worked hard to maintain. It was his reputation and family legacy. Something he'd killed for and would have done anything to protect.

"Meet?" Vixen pressed. "Where?"

"He doesn't want to meet me," Zander said, his lips pressed into a thin line. "He wants to meet you."

"Me?" Vixen almost fell backward off her stool. "Why?"

"He requests you, and you alone," he said. "Expressly says he doesn't want any other Seven there."

Mieko stroked Vixen's knee to calm her, but she was already reeling.

"But why? The fucker's spent my whole life pretending I don't exist." She shook her head furiously. "What could he say to me that he wouldn't want to say to you?"

"I know my father," Zander said. "There is always a reason behind his actions."

"She's not going," Rocky said decisively, and West nodded in agreement. "It could be a trap."

Mieko chewed her bottom lip nervously. "I don't like it either."

"He wants to meet today at noon in a restaurant," Zander said. He checked his Rolex. "We've got an hour."

"Don't you want to see what he wants?" I asked. Bryce wasn't the kind of person to reach out, and I couldn't deny my curiosity at his invitation.

Vixen was more likely to be asked to visit the White House than Bryce inviting her somewhere. He had to have an agenda.

"Of course I do," Zander snapped. "But this is about safety."

"What if she didn't go alone?" I suggested as a plan started to form in my mind. "I'm not technically a Seven anymore, right?"

"No," West and Rocky said in unison, shooting down my idea.

"I want to go," Vixen said suddenly. "The bastard spent my life ignoring me. If he wants to speak, then I damn well want to hear what he has to say."

"Are you sure, Vix?" Mieko asked, taking her hand. "I don't want anything to happen to you."

"We'll take security with us," Vixen said, then turned to me. "Nothing will happen with Candy there."

"I'll kill him if he touches her," I confirmed.

"I don't like it," Zander replied, pacing back and forth. "We'll have to scope out the venue, take security, and we can wait outside the restaurant. I'm not heading into an ambush."

"Do what you need to do to make it safe, Zander," Vixen said, standing up. "But I'm going to speak to him."

———

It was impressive how many security checks Zander could perform in a short amount of time. Security was stationed around the block and at every exit of the restaurant, plus they had completed a thorough sweep of the interiors to check for bombs buried in the cushioned booths. He even set up a drone to monitor the neighborhood for any suspicious activity which may warrant cutting the meeting short.

"Are you ready for this?" I asked Vixen as we stood outside a small Italian restaurant. It looked unassuming from the street. Not exactly the type of place where I imagined Bryce ate often from the lack of caviar on the menu.

"As I'll ever be," she said, glancing over her shoulder at Zander and West, who watched us like hawks from across the street. They needed to chill the fuck out. I had the situation under control. Nothing would happen to Vixen when I was around.

I pushed the door open, and a bell tinkled above it to announce our arrival. "Let's fucking do this then."

Bryce sat alone in the empty restaurant at a table in the center. My eyes scanned the area for anything suspicious, but nothing looked out of place.

"I'm glad you made it. It has been too long," Bryce said. His gaze flicked to me in distaste. "And I see you're not alone."

"I'm not a Seven anymore, remember?" I sneered back.

"Why don't you both take a seat?" He gestured to the spare chairs opposite him, surprising me by not chastising us for bending his rules. "The food here is really something."

The cheerful background music playing juxtaposed the tense atmosphere. Vixen's chair legs squealed against the freshly cleaned floor.

"To what do we owe this pleasure, Uncle?" Vixen spat.

He smiled and picked up the bottle of red wine in the middle of the table to pour us generous glasses. "Is it a crime to want to see my family?"

"*Family*?" Vixen demanded. Her shoulders shook in anger. "Why don't you get to the fucking point? We're not here to mess around and, with one click of my fingers, Zander's men will blow your head clean off."

He may not want to speak to his son, but he was smart enough to know we wouldn't come unprotected.

"That's exactly why I asked you here," Bryce said, sipping his wine casually. "I have something to ask you. A favor."

"What makes you think we will do anything for you?" Vixen snarled.

"Because I have something you want," Bryce replied. He leaned over the table towards us and dropped his voice. "Something you have always wanted to know."

His attempts at being friendly were foolish. Did he think we were born yesterday? Dangling an imaginary carrot under our noses may tempt a naive rabbit, but I was a fucking wolf.

I crossed my arms. "What's the favor?"

"My son may want nothing to do with me, but I don't want to see my fortune go to my traitorous nephew."

I smirked. "Didn't you enjoy his fireworks display?"

Fury flashed over Bryce's angular features. He would have been handsome in his younger days, but he had long past his prime. Since I saw him at the wedding, he'd lost weight. His eyes were sunken and more lines filled his forehead, making it look like he hadn't slept in weeks. Losing his luxurious life would have made it difficult to keep up with regular Botox injections.

"Briarly Manor was our family legacy," Bryce snarled. "He destroyed it out of petulance."

"What's wrong, Bryce?" I cocked my head to the side, a grin dancing over my lips. "Not used to your old lapdog having a new owner?"

Giles may have followed Bryce's orders once, but he jumped ship as soon as a more promising offer arose. They may share blood, but Giles wanted more power than Bryce could give. Something Hiram had promised him.

"Giles took it too far," Bryce said, slamming his glass down on the table.

Puh-lease. It was hard to take 'too far' seriously from a man who ordered his wife to be killed because he couldn't stand to be second best. Karma has a way of biting you in the fucking balls.

"Why invite me here?" Vixen asked. "I'm not your fucking therapist."

I laughed as Bryce's lip curled. He was used to people licking his shoes clean. Being spoken to like that by a badass punk woman was a confronting experience for him, and I lived for it.

"I want to finalize my will," Bryce said.

A waitress came over to our table. "Do you want to order?"

Vixen stared at Bryce as she replied, "How about a hot plate of stop wasting our fucking time and I'm not buying your bullshit?"

The waitress nervously checked the menu board to confirm she'd not forgotten the daily specials.

"Umm…" she hesitated. "We have carbonara?"

"No thanks," I said, nudging Vixen in the ribs. "We're not hungry, right Vix?"

The waitress didn't wait for confirmation. She scuttled away with her notepad in hand as Bryce drummed his fingers on the table.

"Have you gone senile in your old age?" Vixen asked. "Or have you forgotten how you've lost everything? We bought the manor from you, remember? A will means nothing when you're penniless."

"Giles lost a lot of the Briarly fortune in his pathetic development schemes, but do you think I was stupid enough to give him complete control?" Bryce tutted. "I may have lost the manor, but I have contingency plans offshore."

"So?" Vixen's chin jutted out in defiance. "What's that got to do with me?"

"I want to name you as a successor to my estate."

"Me? I don't want your fucking blood money," Vixen spat. "And neither does Zander. We don't want anything from you. The Sevens built their empire on their own, and we'd rather die than accept any charity from you."

"Why don't you think about it?" Bryce suggested. "Don't you feel this is what you deserve after your childhood? You grew up without a mother and father having to fend for yourself on the streets like a rat, while Zander languished in luxury. Why not agree to be my successor?"

"I'd rather die than take a cent of your dirty money." The spray from her vicious words hit Bryce in the face. "You may be doing this to get back at Giles, but there is nothing you can do to get me or Zander to sign. Give Giles all your money for all we care. We have something worth more than all of your dollars, we have fucking principles."

"I thought you'd jump at the opportunity," Bryce said. "I'm offering you everything you ever wanted. You've always wanted to be recognized as a Briarly, and now you will finally get your chance."

Vixen's tough shell cracked for a moment as her jaw went slack. A second later, she gritted her teeth and went into psycho bitch attack mode.

"I would rather die than be recognized as a Briarly," Vixen hissed, standing to her feet. "Zander has always been right about you. You're a fucking monster and you always have been. I don't know what my mom ever saw in you."

She paused, letting her words sink in, then spat in Bryce's wine. She turned on her heel and stormed away. Her giant New Rock boots could have caused a small earthquake from the force she stomped out, but I didn't follow her… not yet.

"How long does she have to think about it?" I asked.

Vixen didn't want to accept Bryce's offer. But, with the manor gone, an extra windfall wouldn't be all bad. Call it reimbursement for all the years of private education she was robbed of.

"The sooner the better. A few weeks, a month at most," Bryce said, bending down to retrieve his briefcase. He placed it on the table and took a contract out of it. "All she needs to do is sign the contract in the presence of a lawyer and it's done."

"Why now?" I asked. "Why do you care about settling your estate? What's in it for you?"

Bryce sighed deeply. He usually played the part of a showman, but I could see him for what he was. A tired, exhausted, old man who knew his time at the top was ending.

"I'm dying, Candy," he said, meeting my gaze. All the money and power in the world couldn't make you immortal or immune to the perils of an ordinary man. "Cancer. They don't know how much time I have left, but it won't be long. Is it so hard to believe a dying man wants to do the right thing?"

He didn't know the meaning of right and wrong.

"Don't expect me to feel sorry for you."

"I never asked for your pity," he said. "But I am asking for your help."

"Help?" I scoffed. "Why would I ever help you?"

Did he have amnesia, too? He was intent on signing me up for a lifetime of hell with Hiram a few months ago. If he was hanging off the edge of a cliff, I'd happily kick his hands away.

"I want to keep the Briarly legacy alive."

"Haven't you ever thought it'd be better for the old legacy to die with you?" I snarled. "The Sevens are the future for Port Valentine now."

Anything Bryce built was something we'd want to take down. Any association with him would be a lasting reminder of all the shit he'd put everyone through.

"If Vixen doesn't sign the contract, Giles will get everything," he said. "I don't know whether that would be in anyone's interests, do you?"

He pushed the contract across the table.

"Go to hell, Bryce." I snatched up the paper and scrunched it into a ball in my first. "Giles already has Hiram's backing. Your money doesn't mean shit. If Giles gets your money, all I have to do is kill him to make it mine, or have you forgotten we're married?"

"Maybe there is another incentive I can give you?" Bryce suggested.

"We're done here," I said, standing up and throwing the paper on the floor. "Whatever you're offering, we're not interested."

"If you help, I'll tell them where their mother is buried," he called after me. I stopped in my tracks, and he continued, "If you don't, I'll take that secret to the grave. We wouldn't want that, would we?"

Just when I thought Bryce couldn't get any more manipulative, he knocked it out of the park. Even cancer hadn't been able to stamp the evil out of him. The man was rotten to the core and would stoop to the lowest of the low to get what he wanted.

"How do I know you're not lying?" I asked, turning around.

He pulled out a new contract and tapped it with his fingers. "Doesn't a dying man's word count for something?"

"Not when it's you."

"How would you ever forgive yourself if you robbed them of the closure they've been desperately seeking all these years?"

I was stuck between a rock and a hard place. I didn't know whether to believe a word coming out of his mouth, but he was also right. If there was the smallest chance Bryce would honor his word, then it was a risk worth taking.

"If I get her to sign the contract to be your successor, you'll tell us where she's buried," I said, snatching the contract and stashing it in my purse. "And we want to know the truth about what you did. Do we have a deal?"

"I have one more condition," he said.

"You know I could stop that ticking clock whenever I want, right?" I shot him my most fierce glare. "I don't think you're in a position to be nego-tiating."

"Call it a last dying wish," he said. "Don't tell the others about my cancer."

"Why?" I mocked. "Do you think they'll be sad? Because I promise you they won't be."

"I have my reasons," Bryce said. "If word gets back to me that they know or anyone finds out, I'll take my secrets to the grave."

"You know you're going straight to hell, right?"

"The best people always do," he replied smugly. "I can see what my son sees in you. You have spirit, Candy. He needs someone like you. Someone with spirit."

"If having 'spirit' is what you call controlling the urge to put an old man out of his misery, then yes, I have it in spades," I snapped. "And I don't need your fucking approval."

"You'd better get her to sign quickly." His voice followed me as I hurried from the restaurant. "Who knows how long I have left?"

I didn't look back, but the contract in my purse felt like it was burning a hole straight through the leather. The last time I kept a secret for the good of the Sevens, it had ended in me shooting Rocky and being escorted back to Blackthorne Towers. What had past mistakes taught me? I should go back to the club and tell them everything. Maybe they'd even agree with me, but I knew I wouldn't. I didn't want to take the chance.

Zander and Vixen needed closure, and I was going to make sure they'd get it — even if that meant tricking Vixen into signing a piece of paper.

———

Since our return from the restaurant, I successfully rebutted any questions about what happened after Vixen left. Everyone bought my story of how we'd argued over what happened the night in the warehouse.

Seeing Bryce hadn't only gotten under my skin. Vixen was barking orders at everyone like a shift at the strip club was as important as running a heart surgery. I snuck to the dressing room for some respite from her constant shrieking. The dancers would arrive soon, and Mieko sat at one of the dressing tables. She carefully pinned her black and purple hair into victory curls.

"What's the occasion?" I asked. "You look amazing."

She wore a stunning black and gold flapper dress reminiscent of the *Gatsby* era that showed off her toned legs.

"I'm taking Vixen out for a date to one of her favorite bars," she said, then winced at the sound of Vixen's shouting carrying down the corridor. "A change of scenery will be good for her."

"Thank fuck for that." I flopped down in the seat next to her. "I don't think we'll be left with any dancers by the end of the night if she keeps going."

Mieko rolled her eyes. "You know what she's like when she's stressed."

"A raging bitch boss?"

"I was going to say, misunderstood," Mieko said; only she could make her fiancée's mood swings sound like they were a gentle breeze instead of a house-destroying hurricane.

"Your rose-tinted glasses are making you forget about all of the times you used to hide in the costume cupboard to avoid her on shift," I pointed out.

"That wasn't because I was scared *of* her." Mieko laughed. "That's because I was scared of *talking* to her."

"Most people would kill to get that kind of money."

"Her mind is made up," Mieko said. She applied a matte plum lipstick and rubbed her lips together. "She doesn't see the cash. Taking money from him would be like saying she was okay with everything he'd done."

I took a deep breath. "What if I told you that there was more to it than just cash?"

Bryce had given specific orders to not tell anyone what was going on, but Mieko wasn't a Seven. She planned to marry into the Seven family but she hadn't been initiated into the gang or gotten a tattoo. Mieko may be the best chance I had at getting Vixen and Zander the answers they needed. She'd be the only other person who would understand.

Mieko eyed me suspiciously and raised her eyebrows. "What are you getting at?"

I poked my head out of the dressing room. The corridor was empty and, thankfully, the DJ was in the middle of a sound test so music was blaring. By my calculations, we had five minutes before the next shift started.

"There's something I need to tell you," I said, locking the door behind us to ensure we wouldn't be disturbed. "There's more to Bryce's offer than Vixen knows..."

After I finished explaining, Mieko leaned back in her chair. One of her curls escaped as she shook her head in disbelief.

"Bryce is unbelievable," she murmured. "So, what do we do now? If we told the Sevens what he said, then Vixen may agree to sign. Bryce would never know if everyone kept quiet."

That's the first thing I'd thought too, but the longer I considered it... the surer I was that it wouldn't work.

"It wouldn't change Zander's mind," I said confidently. "His hatred for his father rules above all else, even the truth."

Zander was stubborn to a fault. His burning curiosity to find out what happened to his mother would never cave to his father's demands. He vowed never to show a sign of weakness from the moment he left home.

"What about only telling Vixen, then?" she asked. "I know she would want to know what really happened."

"That's the problem," I said. "If Vix went behind Zander's back, he'd never forgive her. How would she explain all the cash? They'd be divided. At a time like this, we need to be on the same side. Otherwise, we don't stand a chance against Hiram."

"But what will Zander say when he finds out that *you* went behind his back?" Mieko wrung her hands anxiously in her lap. "You're meant to be following his rules, aren't you?"

I had agreed to follow his orders until Hiram was dead, but I'm not the kind of girl who falls in line when some things are more important. Zander had betrayed me before for something he believed to be right. How is what I'm doing any different?

"Rules are made to be broken," I said. "It's a risk I'm willing to take to get them the truth."

"I think you're right," she said. Mieko understood the dilemma we were in. Vixen had become like a sister to me, and Mieko loved her as much as I... well, as much as I *cared* about Zander. "I'd never forgive myself if we didn't help her get the answers she's been looking for. I know what not knowing has been doing to her all these years..."

"How can we get her signature in the presence of a fucking lawyer without her knowing?" I asked.

Mieko paused, then said, "I think I have an idea."

"I don't want this to come between you," I said quickly.

"I want to help, Candy," Mieko said, her voice strong and determined. Her decision was made. "I want to get the woman I love answers, and if she ends up hating me for it, then so be it, but we can't do nothing. Give me the contract, and I'll do the rest."

I passed her the paper, and she tucked it inside her purse for safekeeping. When I first met Mieko, she reminded me of a wide-eyed doe. She was too afraid to stand up for herself or what she believed in. Her inner strength had now come to the surface and she would do whatever it takes for someone she loved.

"What's your plan?" I asked.

"She has to sign so many delivery notes on a Thursday. She wouldn't even notice if I..." Mieko played with her hair, "distracted... her. If a lawyer happened to be dropping off the delivery, she wouldn't even have to know."

"Since when are you a mastermind?"

"I've learned a thing or two over the past few months." Mieko shrugged, then looked at me earnestly. "Do you think we're doing the right thing?"

"Honestly? I don't know," I admitted. Who even knew what the right thing was anymore? "Zander may be too stubborn to back down and accept cash, but if this is the only chance they'll get to find out what happened to their mom, I'll take the consequences."

Mieko played with her engagement ring and smiled, but it didn't meet her eyes. "Let's hope she still wants to marry me after this."

———

After waving Mieko and Vixen off on their date night, Zander pulled me aside as I returned to the dance floor. Since our meeting with Bryce, I'd tried to avoid him, and my mind was still whirring through the plans that Mieko and I had set in motion. There was no time to question whether we were doing the right thing or not.

"You've been avoiding me," Zander said, creeping up behind me. His breath on my neck sent a shiver down my spine.

I turned to face him and planted my hands on my hips. "Is it a crime to want some space?"

"What else did my father say after Vixen left?" Zander pressed. "You said you argued, but did he say anything else?"

"You know, just the usual Bryce being an asshole," I lied. "He reminded me about how much he loved my wedding to your charming cousin. Your father never misses an opportunity to gloat."

"He didn't say more about why he wanted Vixen to be his heir?" Zander continued.

I shook my head. "It looks like he's finally losing it."

"But he hates Vixen," he pondered aloud. "Why name her?"

"Because he knows you wouldn't accept it, and he wants to get back at Giles," I said. "And because he cared about that fucking manor more than anything else, including his own family."

Zander frowned, still deep in thought. Behind his gorgeous face, his mind was working overtime.

"His ego is bruised," I went on. "This is his way to punish Giles for stepping out of line. What better way to do that than offer what he has to one of the people Giles hates most?"

He still looked skeptical but nodded. "Perhaps."

"Maybe she should take the money?" I suggested. Although I already knew what his answer would be, it didn't stop me from hoping for a positive response. If we didn't have to trick Vixen into signing, it'd be easier for everyone. "Surely, it's the least Bryce could do after all he's done over the years?"

Zander's expression turned stony. "We will take nothing from him. Ever. I built the Sevens from nothing, and my father will never be part of that."

I'd get nowhere trying to persuade Zander with my charm. His problems with his father ran too deep. Some cracks couldn't be healed. Even if Zander knew why I wanted Vixen to take Bryce's money — finding out the truth about their mom after all these years — he was too proud to let that be a justification. I could only hope he and Vixen would understand the reasons behind me and Mieko's intentions when they learned the truth.

"What have you been up to?" I asked, steering the subject away from dangerous territory. "You've been spending a lot of time in your office."

"I reached out to some of my associates in law enforcement," he said. "Penelope's body has been released to her family. They received a generous payment to keep the cause of her death a secret. The coroner reported it as a suicide."

Yet again, money was enough to conceal a crime. From the stories I heard, Penelope's parents pinned their hopes on her marrying rich to correct their carelessness with money. She'd finally given them what they wanted in her death. Did they care about their bank balance more than getting justice for their only child? If it was someone I cared about, I'd make sure someone paid in blood.

"That's typical of Giles," I muttered. "Thinking that money can fix everything."

"Giles didn't pay Penelope's family off," Zander said. "I did."

"What?" I couldn't be hearing this right. "Are you out of your fucking mind?"

"Before I explain, there's someone I want you to meet," he said, taking my arm. "Follow me."

West and Rocky were already waiting outside Zander's office. From their tense expressions, they were bracing themselves to face whoever was inside.

"Don't freak out, C," Rocky said.

Didn't he know that whenever anyone tells you not to freak out it usually means you'll be tipped to the edge of a mental breakdown in seconds?

"I want you to remember he's a guest, little one..."

I wrestled my arm out of Zander's grip and turned on him, "And I want you to quit treating me like a fucking child."

I threw the door to his office open to see a familiar figure sitting at Zander's desk. He grinned with the smug air of someone who owned the fucking place.

"Hello, Kitten," the Blackbird said.

West's huge presence loomed behind me while Zander and Rocky were poised at my sides.

"One of you better start talking," I growled. I was already thinking about how I'd immobilize them to get to the asshole smirking at me in *our* club. "Or else."

The Blackbird was Hiram's right-hand man. Why was he sitting in Zander's office sipping a drink like he was on vacation? I wanted him to leave in a fucking body bag. This was our space, and he'd compromised it. He had to go.

"Are you pleased to see me, Kitten?" The Blackbird's yellowing grin made me want to turn into a crazy dentist and rip his teeth straight out of his gums. "The last time I saw you must have been your wedding. You did make a dashing bride."

"Sit down, Candy," Zander instructed as he pulled out a chair.

I kicked it aside.

"He is not leaving this room breathing," I snarled.

All I saw was a threat ready to take out. The Blackbird sat up straight and adjusted his sleeves nervously. He'd seen me at my worst. He could taunt me all he liked, but he knew what I was capable of and didn't want to be the person standing in my way.

"Told you, bro." West chuckled. "Less than thirty seconds for a death threat. You owe me twenty dollars."

Rocky grumbled and rummaged around in his pocket for a bill.

How could I dispose of the Blackbird's body without a trace? Staging his death as an accident would be best. When Q disappeared, Hiram thrived off tracking him. The Blackbird was an even more valuable asset, so he wouldn't stop until he found out what happened to him. We'd have to make the corpse easy enough to find, but not too easy to make him think it was laid out waiting.

"Remember what I said, Candy," Zander warned, oblivious to my thoughts. "He's *our* guest."

"I didn't invite him," I pointed out, baring my teeth.

"Careful, you're making me feel unwelcome," the Blackbird said. "But you've never had good manners, have you?"

West cracked his knuckles. "Speak to her like that again and I'll cut off your tongue, then feed it to you."

At least one of the Sevens was speaking my language.

"Protective. How sweet," the Blackbird said. Despite his unwavering voice, his eyes darted to the door and his escape route. A person couldn't hide subconscious fears no matter how hard they tried. "Your protection won't save her when Hiram comes knocking, will it?"

"Does he know?" I demanded.

My body was on edge, primed to pounce at any moment.

"That you're back in town?" the Blackbird asked. "Of course, but he's not ready to make a house call yet."

"So what are you doing here?" I crossed my arms. "Keeping tabs on me?"

"I invited him," Zander said smoothly. "We have an understanding."

I turned on Zander and jabbed my finger into his chest. "Do you even know who he is?"

He hadn't invited the fucking tooth fairy over for a tea party. He had allowed someone with the knowledge and connections to bring the Sevens to their knees into our safe haven.

"We've known each other for a while," Zander replied. He glanced at the Blackbird with disgust. The same way you'd regard someone who smelled bad on a cramped subway when there was nowhere for you to move. He clearly didn't like him but tolerated him.

I poked Zander again. "How long?"

The Blackbird was like a shadow. He never stayed in one place for too long. Hiram was the only person to know where he was at all times. How had Zander tracked him down? It wasn't as easy as stalking him on social media.

"We met at the auction," the Blackbird said. "Don't you remember?"

I cast my mind back. The auction had been my first official outing as a Seven. The Blackbird attended briefly, but I never saw Zander speak to him. Had he managed to corner him without my knowing?

"I'll give you one chance to tell me what the fuck you're doing here," I said, glaring at the Blackbird. "Or else these will be the last walls you'll see."

"Always so feisty..." The Blackbird shook his head. "It wasn't always that way, was it Kitten? You didn't have claws at the beginning, but you've grown into them now."

"You may be a guest in our club, but it won't stop me from crushing your skull," West threatened. At least he would have my back when it came to disposing of the Blackbird's body. "I won't warn you again."

"Suit yourself." The Blackbird held up his hands in surrender. "The auction house was the start of a… mutual understanding."

"I knew we couldn't take down Hiram from the outside," Zander stepped in. "I had to find someone on the inside who wanted the same thing we did. To see Hiram pay."

"He's been at the top for too long," the Blackbird said. "It's time someone else takes over."

I burst out laughing. "And you think *you* can do that?"

The Blackbird was a creep, but he didn't inspire the same level of fear Hiram did. He was a follower, not a leader.

"Hiram has become blind sighted," the Blackbird continued and ignored my comments. "He's neglected parts of the business. I have connections and know people who would be happy to take his place."

"So, you're looking for someone to take him out, then you'll auction off his services to the highest bidder?" I asked.

"He's losing his touch," the Blackbird said with a shrug. "People are ready for a change."

Hiram's most loyal servant wouldn't turn his back on him so fast. I held my chin up high and said, "I don't buy it."

"How do you think you were really able to slip away so easily at your lover's funeral?" the Blackbird asked. "Do you think that Hiram's security would be that sloppy? Times are changing, Kitten."

My blood boiled. Following my return to Blackthorne Towers, the Blackbird watched on from the shadows while I had lessons with Hiram. He never said anything other than demeaning remarks and attempted to make my life more miserable.

"You used to report back to Hiram about what was going on in Port Valentine," I said.

"Keep up, Kitty." The Blackbird clicked his tongue impatiently. "I only told him what we wanted him to hear. If he caught word the Sevens were preparing a luxury yacht, do you think it'd have still been floating when you left?"

"Did you tell everyone here what was happening at the Towers?" I pressed. My shoulders shook in anger. "Why didn't you tell me that you were working with the Sevens?"

"And blow my cover?" He laughed coldly. "You should know better than that. Living a double life is your area of expertise, after all."

"So is being able to skin your scrote without you losing consciousness," I snarled.

West snorted in amusement, reminding me that the Blackbird wasn't the only person in the room who had questions to answer.

"Why didn't you tell me who you were working with?" I asked Zander. "You could have slipped it into a conversation, or were you planning on keeping me in the dark? Like you did last time."

Zander flinched.

"That was upon my request," the Blackbird answered. "After Hiram's reprogramming, I had to be certain you were on the right side before exposing myself. You made your intentions clear the last time I saw you."

"So, you waited to see whether everyone came back off the boat?"

The Blackbird shrugged. "If you wanted to kill them, I knew everyone wouldn't be sailing back."

"What's the plan now?" I said. "That's why you're here, right? To tell us what we're gonna do next?"

"You've never been patient, Kitty." The Blackbird talked down to me like a toddler. "It's something Hiram always liked about you: your volatility, but it's also your biggest weakness. There are people in Hiram's ranks who feel the same way I do, but change takes time. You can't knock down a tower of cards from the top, you have to disrupt the foundations first."

My preferred approach would involve sticking dynamite underneath his whole rotten empire and blowing it up, but the Blackbird lived cautiously. He was a snake, lying in wait and readying to strike at the opportune moment.

"And you expect us to do nothing in the meantime?" Rocky wrapped his arm around my waist, sensing my rising fury. "If we do nothing, we'll die anyway."

"Dethroning Hiram is part of a collective movement," the Blackbird said. His words sounded like the same bullshit you'd hear in a presidential debate. "You won't be able to do it without my help. If you move too soon, you'll fail. The timing has to be right."

How long would it be until they came to burn us to ashes while we slept?

"I don't like this as much as you do, C," Rocky whispered. "But he's the best chance we have."

Did Rocky have a point? While I didn't trust the Blackbird, he would never do anything to put his neck on the line. If the Blackbird sensed Hiram was starting to crumble, he'd have already latched onto a potential replacement. He'd be all over them like a bloodhound, especially if it meant bene-fiting himself.

I narrowed my eyes at the Blackbird, wishing my stare would turn him into a mushy pile of goop that I could ditch in a dumpster. "How do we know that you're not double-crossing us?"

"You don't," the Blackbird replied. "But if I'm telling the truth and on your side, my coming here should tell you everything you need to know about how serious I am."

The Blackbird stood up and brushed down his suit, which didn't help with the creases. Had he never heard of an iron? If we killed Hiram and he was true to his word, I might have to treat him to one.

"I'll be in touch soon," Zander said briskly.

"Good to do business with you," the Blackbird gushed in an almost simpering voice, then nodded at me and muttered sarcastically, "It's always a pleasure, Kitten."

"Easy, Pinkie..." West murmured as the Blackbird left unharmed and breathing, contrary to all the images swimming through my head.

Grudgingly, I had to concede that the Blackbird had a point. As much as I hated relying on anyone else, I was no amateur. We were fools to think we could take Hiram down alone, and having an ally on the inside would help. But, even if the Sevens may actually have a shot at this, I wouldn't allow myself to hope. The Blackbird may be gone, but I wasn't finished with Zander yet.

"I need to speak to Zander," I said, crossing my arms. "Alone."

"Good luck, man." Rocky clapped him on the back. "I'll call the clean-up crew if we don't see you in an hour."

"Do it," I said, then smiled sweetly. "But there might be nothing left of him by then."

West smirked. "Damn, our girl's good."

They closed the door behind them and left us alone.

"Well?" Zander asked. He sat on the edge of his desk, so I didn't have to strain my neck to stare into his eyes. They sparkled, sensing a challenge. "Give me your worst."

"You should have told me," I replied. "If you've been talking to the Blackbird for months, how has it never crossed your mind to mention it to me?"

Whenever it felt like we were finally making progress with building trust, something else happened to set us back.

"We had an agreement."

"Didn't you think I had a right to know the full story about how you managed to pull off my great escape?"

You're a hypocrite, a voice in the back of my head reminded me. I was no better than him after what I'd been plotting with Mieko only half an hour before.

"Everything I've done has been for you. I saw an opportunity at the auction," he explained. "With the Blackbird on our side, I saw a way to keep you safe."

"Did he tell you what was happening when I was in Blackthorne Towers?" I asked. "About all the things Hiram made me do?"

"He let us know you were alive, but no more than that." Zander's jaw tensed. "Hiram's gift was enough explanation for me to know what was happening."

"I don't trust him," I huffed. "You don't know him in the same way I do. The Blackbird only cares about one thing: himself. He will screw us over in the blink of a fucking eye if he gets a better offer."

"In this world, there are two types of people: the Sevens and everyone else. We can only trust each other, but the Blackbird has his uses. He needs us as much as we need him, and you know that we need someone on the inside."

I pouted, feeling like a sulky teenager but refusing to admit he was right. "That doesn't mean I have to like it."

"No, it doesn't." Zander agreed, putting his hands around my waist and pulling me close. "But you agreed to play by my rules. Remember?"

"Or what?" I challenged.

He stroked up my sides to feel my curves. His presence was intoxicating, and another feeling started to replace my anger.

"Do you recall what happened the first time you disagreed with me?" Zander asked.

His lips grazed over mine teasingly. It was impossible to stay mad when he drew primal energy from me like it was his superpower. I tugged on his bottom lip with my teeth, then let him go.

My voice came out lower and more sultry than I expected before I could stop it. "Why don't you remind me?"

Zander spun me around, pushing my thighs against the wooden desk and my ass against his suit. I could feel the warmth of his cock through his pants, hard and ready. He wrapped his arms around my middle like we were starting a slow dance. His breath tickled my skin as he brushed my hair out of the way and kissed my neck. "Gladly."

He suddenly stepped back and pushed me down aggressively. I used my hands to steady myself as he pulled up my skirt and murmured in appreciation at the sight of my pink lacy panties. After being a voyeur last night, Zander was ready to make his mark on me again. But he didn't touch me straight away. He waited. The anticipation only turned me on more.

"Look how wet your pussy is for me, little one," Zander purred. He was careful not to touch me as he pulled my panties down. "Do you enjoy my punishments?"

"No," I lied, but reclined out across the desk in encouragement like a cat begging to be stroked by its master.

"You're lying," he said. His hand reached out to rub my ass with his hand then delivered a smack, making my body jolt. He stroked the stinging spot gently. He had a natural talent for balancing pain and pleasure. He paused, then walked away, leaving me bent over the desk as he sat down opposite me in his chair wearing a smirk. "I'm expecting a business call."

"A call?" My cheeks flushed, and I straightened up, feeling my frustration rise. "You've got to be fucking kidding me."

Zander had teased me once before, pushing me to the point of orgasm and then dismissing me. That was before I became a Seven, but times had changed. If I wanted his cock, then I was gonna get it. He said he was mine… so it was my turn to take.

I smiled and batted my eyelashes, trailing my finger along the top of his desk as I moved around to the other side. "I guess we'll have to be quick then…"

I didn't work in a strip club for nothing. I slid onto his lap, facing away from him, and ground my ass against him, making sure to sway my hips and press down to drive him wild. Zander groaned. He may be the king of teasing, but I was the motherfucking queen.

"Candy…" he warned.

"What?" I asked innocently, standing up and running my hand down his buttoned shirt, bending over to give him a great view of my cleavage. I unzipped his pants and tugged them down to release his cock. "I said I'd make it quick."

I slid onto his lap to straddle him. Thankfully, his office chair resembled a throne, so there was plenty of space for my knees to squeeze in either side of him. I wrapped my arms around his neck and pulled his face close to mine, getting lost in his dark gray eyes that don't look away from me.

We stared at each other for thirty seconds, neither of us saying a word. The look in his eyes told me everything I needed to know. I saw the pain. The suffering. The vulnerable child who was forced to become a man early. To make hard decisions and continue to be haunted by them. I may be broken, but so was Zander.

"You're perfect," Zander murmured, then a force of nature came over his body as he yanked my hair and pulled me into a kiss like he wanted to steal my fucking soul.

I gasped. Without panties, his cock rubbed up and down my lips, coating his shaft in my wetness.

"Fuck!" I was breathless and carried away in the moment as I knelt upward, reaching down to grab him and take what I needed.

I slid down onto his cock and moaned into his mouth. My pussy stretched to make room for him, making me gasp as he plunged deeper. Two fucked up souls becoming one. Zander sank his teeth into my shoulder, and I rode him furiously like we only had two minutes before we had to break apart. His hands grasped my ass cheeks hard, guiding me up and down, as his breathing grew heavier.

I slid upward, then stopped, letting him fall out of me. Anger flashed over his face.

"What's wrong?" I batted my eyelashes as I climbed off his lap, trying to stand up straight despite my shaky knees. I perched my ass on the desk in front of him and spread my legs to give him a good view. Zander watched, entranced, as I slid my hand down my front until my fingers stroked my wetness. I maintained eye contact with him as I stroked my clit and arched an eyebrow. "I thought you had a call to make?"

I moaned, sliding two fingers inside myself. I wasn't only teasing Zander but myself. It felt good, but damn! I missed his beautiful nine incher, but how much more of my teasing could he take?

Watching my fingers glide in and out made him see red. He grabbed my knees and pushed my thighs wider apart, then stood up. A drop of pre cum glistened from the tip of his erection, chasing the pleasure I denied.

"The call can wait," he said, angling his cock and thrusting into my pussy with purpose.

"Yes," I cried out as he pounded into me and gave me what we both craved. I wrapped my legs around his middle and threw my head back as he fucked a toe-curling orgasm out of me.

A flood of my wetness coated his cock, and Zander groaned. "Fuck, little one… if I keep going like this, I'll—"

"Come for me, Zander," I ordered, digging my nails into his ass cheeks. He wasn't the only one who could leave his mark.

He'd once made me come on demand. It was his turn now. Zander didn't hesitate. His body shuddered, and he grunted as he filled me. His shoulders shook from the release, and it gave me a proud sense of satisfaction to know the power of my words.

"See?" I whispered into his ear. "I told you I'd make it quick."

"Someone looks pleased with themselves," Rocky said, grinning knowingly as Zander and I returned to the bustling club to sit with him at the bar.

Were we giving off a post-sex glow other people could see?

"We're fine," I said stubbornly.

"A gentleman never tells, right?" Rocky joked, nudging Zander in the ribs.

He was too busy to pay any attention to Rocky kidding around. Zander scanned the crowd. Mieko had just finished a performance on the main stage and climbed off the pole to meet Vixen. The two of them came over to join us.

"Did you see her?" Vixen gushed. "Wasn't she great?"

Mieko shrugged like it was nothing, but her eyes lit up at the compliment. They launched into a new conversation about the best songs to strip to, while Zander stayed quiet. Suddenly, he tensed at my side.

"Why has West brought a kid in here?" Zander growled, nudging his head toward The Hulk standing near the entrance.

"It could shut us down," Vixen said, already springing into action. "If it's one of our runners, they know not to come when we're open..."

She was over to West in a flash. We watched as she argued with him, but West didn't relent. His firm hand stayed on the kid's shoulder. What was he thinking? The kid mustn't be older than fourteen and clutched a large box to his chest as if his life depended on it. The boy struggled to balance the package in his arms as West steered him through the club and into the back, nudging his head at us as he went.

"My office," Zander said. His lips pressed into a grim line. "All of us. Now."

He stormed after West like a demon ready to suck his life away as Rocky, Vixen, Mieko and I followed, shouldering past any customer who stood in our path.

"What's going on?" Zander turned on West as soon as we were inside.

"The kid has a delivery to make," West replied, then looked down at the boy. "Tell them what you told me."

The kid's face turned white like he was about to throw up. "A strange man came to Bayside. He had a package he wanted one of us to deliver. He said I had to deliver it..." He pointed at me. "... to *her* personally."

"How much did he pay you to drop this off?" West pressed.

"A hundred dollars," the kid replied with a sense of pride. That was big bucks when you were low on cash. "He picked me out of all the others at the Heights because I had a bike."

"I'll take it from here," I said, taking the parcel from his shaking hands. His shoulders slackened in relief in the knowledge that he delivered it safely. It would have taken two hours to cycle it over from the edge of town. My stomach sank as I read the label attached to the parcel: 'For my Kitten'. I turned to the child, still oblivious to the potential danger he'd brought to our door. "It's time you get outta here, kid."

West handed him a business card. "Call me if the guy comes back to Bayside again, yeah? I'll give you two hundred dollars. A car is waiting outside to drive you home."

"Thanks." The kid beamed and stashed the card in his worn jacket. "I will."

"What do you think it is?" Vixen asked as soon as the boy left, peering at the package with suspicion like she expected it to blow any second.

"Whatever it is, it's not gonna be good," I said. Presents from Hiram never were. I put the package on the desk and pulled a knife out of my bra. I looked at Zander for approval. Hiram wouldn't kill me with a bomb. If he wanted me dead, he'd do it by his own hand. "May I?"

Zander nodded. My blade cut through the tape holding it together, making a ripping noise. Inside, a nondescript polystyrene box nestled ominously. I'd seen those types of boxes before.

"You might want to look away, Mieko," I said, bracing myself for what I knew was to come.

I took a deep breath and opened the lid.

An object lay atop a layer of ice. It took me a second to comprehend what I was seeing.

Fuck, no...

My knees buckled as I stared into Q's glassy eyes. A pirate hat balanced precariously on his decapitated head. Hiram had a sick sense of humor.

Rocky grabbed my shoulders before my legs gave way, and Zander slammed the lid closed. It was already too late. Q was dead. And, just like Crystal, it was all my fault.

———

"How is she doing?" Mieko asked Rocky.

Puh-lease, did they think I couldn't hear them? They may talk in hushed tones, but they were standing right outside my bedroom door. I kept my eyes squeezed shut and pretended to sleep, pulling the comforter up around my ears to shelter myself from the world.

"The same," Rocky replied. He sounded as tired as I felt. "It's been two days, but she's not been eating. She's not been sleeping either, even though she's been doing a good job of faking it."

Damn, I thought he'd been buying it. What else was I supposed to do when it felt like someone had flicked a 'shutdown' button on my body? My limbs felt like bricks and moving was like wading through a sea of maple syrup. I was sinking fast. The harder I tried to fight it, the more difficult it got.

It's not like I'd never seen a decapitated head before. I'd seen many — hell, I'd helped Hiram mount a few, but never a friend. Watching Crystal die broke my heart, but seeing the brutal way Q met his end made my stomach heave. He would still be alive if he hadn't helped me escape from Hiram.

"Give her these," Mieko said. She twisted the cap off something. "They'll help her sleep."

If my eyes were open, I'd have rolled them. Why do they think I haven't touched proper food and have been living on packs of chips and candy bars? I noticed how they'd been trying to slip sleeping pills into my meals. They had the best intentions, but none of them understood that sleep was what I needed to avoid.

Seeing Q's head in my imagination was dreadful enough, but reliving the moment in my dreams would be like tearing open a freshly stitched wound. I couldn't face that... not yet.

Staying numb and trapping all my emotions inside helped me survive before. If I let my emotions out, I'd erupt like a fucking volcano, and I'd take the whole town down with me.

"I'll take over from here." West's comforting low growl joined in their conversation. "You look beat, Red."

The guys were taking shifts to check on me, but Rocky had stayed at my side for the longest. He read out random stories from the internet, played music, and cradled me as I held tears back. But I still hadn't been able to murmur more than a few words.

"Try to make her take these," Rocky said, presumably handing him over the pills.

West snorted. "I don't have a fucking death wish."

"I'll stay if you—"

"I'll try," West promised. "Get some sleep, man."

The door creaked open, and the mattress sagged as West climbed into bed next to me.

"You can quit pretending now," he muttered.

Him too? My acting abilities needed serious work. I opened one eye suspiciously. "How did you know?"

He pulled my body close. He was more a ladle than a big spoon. "You usually snore when you're really sleeping."

I jabbed him with my sharp elbow. "Fuck you."

"That's the most you've said in two days," he said. "Red's right though. You need to sleep at some point. You can't stay awake forever."

"Try me."

"I'm not going anywhere," he said. "I'll be right here with you."

"I can't," I snapped, trying to shuffle away from him, but he held on tight. "You wouldn't understand."

"Maybe I can?" He traced swirling patterns up and down my arm. "Do you remember the story I told you about what happened when I was in high school?"

I stayed silent. During a boxing game, he'd almost killed another student when he lost control during a fight. He caused enough damage for the poor kid to be hospitalized for life, and it still haunted him.

"I used to get the worst nightmares," West continued. "I'd wake up screaming. The months after it happened were the worst. Sometimes it'd get so bad I'd destroy an entire room in minutes. Me and Zander used to share a dorm then, and I made him tie me down before I slept. It worked... sometimes."

There was a long pause before West started talking again, letting his story hang in the air. I understood better than anyone how it felt to be left with conflicting feelings.

He went on, "When I slept, all I could see was his face. The look of surprise in his eyes as he fell. When I hit him that final time, I knew it was bad. It's like a piece of him disappeared when he hit the floor. I relived it over and over again, but there was nothing I could do to change it. No matter what scenario played out in my head, it didn't change."

"Do you still have them?" I whispered. "The nightmares?"

"Sometimes."

"It was an accident." I turned around to face him and saw the guilt etched on his face. "You didn't mean for it to happen."

"I know, but it still did," he said, stroking my hair. "But what happened to Cupid is different. Hiram did this. He is the only one to blame."

"But he died trying to help us." The lump in my throat grew bigger like I'd swallowed a golf ball whole. "He died because he tried to help *me*. First, there was Crystal, and now…"

"Listen to me." West grabbed my chin and forced me to look at him. "This is all on Hiram. All of it. *He* is the one that did this, and he's going to pay."

"He didn't deserve to die like that, West." My voice was thick and heavy, but I refused to cry. "He was a good person. When Hiram first took me, Q was the only person who looked out for me. If he hadn't helped us, then—"

"Cupid knew what he was getting himself into when he agreed to help," West interrupted. "He's been running from Hiram for a long time."

"I know what Hiram does to people, West." I shuddered. "I've watched him and seen people's last moments. If I sleep, I'll be taken back to his workshop. I don't want to see him there. I…'

Just thinking about the workshop brought back its sterile, meaty smell. I knew every inch of that godforsaken room. I'd laid on the metal table, where Hiram liked to carve bodies like hunks of meat, and stood on the sidelines. Faceless strangers screamed and begged for their lives while I watched on with indifference.

In the beginning, I tried to look away. That changed when Hiram tied me to a chair and forced me to watch. I never made the mistake of looking away again. Once he desensitized me to the gore, I helped. I passed him tools and instruments like a dental nurse, not thinking about how I was an accessory to murder. I was a teenager who was desperate to please because I knew it was better than the alternative.

Hiram would call our time together 'lessons'. He trained me in every aspect of the business, from the best way to extract teeth to the most efficient way to dissolve bones. The workshop was Hiram's happy place. He rejoiced in it and wanted me to get the same pleasure he did. For a time, I did, and that was the worst part of it all…

"You don't understand the things I've done, West. I've done awful, terrible things." I sniffed. "I'm scared that if I sleep and see Q in that place, all I'll see is anger. If I get angry, I'll lose myself again. I don't want the darkness to take over."

Hiram had once succeeded at inhibiting any ounce of humanity I had left. My life revolved around making him happy, and I'd do whatever it took to make him proud no matter what. He made me feel special to be chosen, and no other adult had made me feel like that before. Evergreen kids never got praise or affection. For a few years, I was a different person. I was the Kitten. Whenever I looked in the mirror, I saw myself in the image of what Hiram wanted me to be, and I'd do anything to live up to his hopes. I may know my mind, but evil still lives within me.

"I won't let that happen," West said, squeezing my shoulder in reassurance. "You have us now. We're here to remind you who you are and help you find your way back if you get lost. But we need you to rest."

"I don't know if I can…"

West stroked the scar on my neck where my tattoo used to be.

"I know you can," he said. "You're safe here. Nothing is going to happen to you in my arms. We need you, Candy. All of us. We can't do this without you."

"I'm scared," I confessed in a whisper. "I'm scared of what I'll do when I feel, West."

"I know, baby." His homely smell enveloped my senses, and his warmth protected my shivering frame. "But you're strong. You can face this."

"Can I?" I asked. "Everything I touch and everyone I care about gets ripped away. What if I lose control? What if I lose *myself*?"

"I'm not going anywhere," he said. "And you're not doing this alone. You have all of us. and I can help you. I can help you direct the pain and channel it into something bigger. Something powerful. Something you can control."

"How?"

He took a deep breath. "I'm going to take you into the ring with me."

"But you said you'd never go in the ring again…"

After what happened when he was in school, Vixen once told me he'd promised to never step into one again.

His blue eyes met mine. "We'll face our fears together."

"You'd really dc that for me?" I asked.

"I'd do anything for you," he promised. "But first, you need to sleep."

I sighed. "Hand me the fucking pills."

If West could face his fear for me, I would do this for him. Or, at least I thought I could…

CHAPTER

Twenty

I 'm back on the yacht. Thick gray clouds roll in overhead. I look for something to pull around my bare shoulders.

"Looking for something?"

Hiram's cold cackle rings out over the ocean waves, but I see nothing. He is everywhere and nowhere at the same time.

A scuffle ensues behind me.

I spin around.

"What were you expecting, Kitty?" Hiram asks. "For me to let you go?"

Q dangles over the railings. He tries to resist, but Hiram's grip on him is too strong. He screams for help, but I can't move. Hiram holds his favorite machete in his other hand.

I want to run, but my legs don't work. I'm rooted to the spot. I open my mouth to yell, but nothing comes out. I look down and realize blood has soaked through my dress. It's everywhere: down my chin, arms, hair, between my toes...

I reach for my mouth. There is nothing there.

"What's wrong, Kitty?" Hiram laughs like a maniac. He pulls a fleshy lump from his pocket and throws it overboard. "Cat got your tongue?"

Q's terrified empty stare pierces my own. His eyes plead for help. He opens his mouth to speak, but Hiram slams the machete into his neck. Not once. Twice. Three times. It takes four strikes to sever his head from his body.

Hiram turns to me, holding Q's head by his sandy hair, and throws it into the waves as Q's body falls at his feet. A sea of red coats the yacht deck, which Q had once taken pride in.

Hiram advances and says, "I'm coming for you next, Kitten."

———

"C?" Rocky could be on another planet judging by how far away his voice sounded. "Can you hear me? Her eyelids just fluttered."

"How many pills did you give her, West?" Zander scolded. "She's been out for twenty hours."

West mumbled a response, but it was too difficult to make out.

My eyes snapped open, and I sat up so quickly it made me dizzy. To an onlooker, I could have come out of a fucking exorcism. My heart pounded hard, like it wanted to escape my ribcage.

Rocky jumped out of his skin and almost fell off the bed. "Holy shit!"

The Seven men were sitting around me, their faces filled with concern. The blankets are damp underneath my body and stick to my cold skin. Gross.

"Candy?" Zander checked the pulse on my neck. "Can you hear me?"

I could, but all I cared about is the fierce determination flooding my veins at a hundred miles per hour. In my dreams, I was powerless to act, but I'd awoken ready.

The pain I repressed had bubbled to the surface. During my sleep, I saw all the memories I kept locked away: Crystal bleeding out on the sidewalk, Hiram's workshop of horrors, Giles waiting at the end of the aisle, the polystyrene box… Hiram was a dead man walking.

"Is she okay?" Rocky ran his hands through his hair. "She's freaking me the fuck out."

"Candy?" West asked sharply. "Say something."

I knew what I had to do. Nothing would get in my way.

"We need to go to the ring," I said. "Now."

"But you haven't eaten in hours," Rocky reminded me. "Don't you want to eat first?"

"We'll eat on the way," I snapped, jumping out of bed. I didn't give a shit about how awful I smelled. "This can't wait."

"I'll get the car," West said.

He understood my desire. He recognized the look in me that I'd seen so many times in him. I prided myself on self-control, but I needed to unleash *my* beast. Hiram picked the wrong Evergreen kid to mess with all those years ago. I would use everything he taught me against him. But before I did, I needed to release some anger. To win, we had to be smart. I couldn't think straight with the darkness clawing at my sides, begging for revenge.

"Do you want us to come along?" Rocky asked, biting his lip.

"This is something we have to do alone," West replied definitively.

Rocky opened his mouth to argue, but Zander shot him a look that advised him otherwise.

"Are you sure you can handle this, West?" Zander asked.

West nodded once. "I have it under control."

"Then go," Zander ordered.

He'd seen West in the same trance-like state and understood what had to be done.

———

Half an hour later, we pulled into the parking lot of the Golden Gloves. My whole body buzzed like I'd downed ten Jägerbomb's in a sitting.

West turned off the engine. "Are you sure you're okay to—"

"Quit the excuses, West." I held up the empty paper bag from the cheeseburger I devoured on the drive. "Let's fucking go."

"We have the place to ourselves," West said, taking keys out of his pocket and twirling them around his fingers. I didn't question how he'd arranged it so fast. It didn't matter. "We won't be disturbed tonight."

The lights in the gym flickered on as we stepped inside. The place smelled of stale sweat, blood, and tears — just what I needed. I headed straight for the ring. West grabbed my arm to hold me back. "Not yet."

"What're you doing?" I spat. "I need to fight."

"And I need you to be in control," West said, putting his hands on either side of my neck. He didn't hold on tight like he was trying to hold me back, but his touch was filled with concern. "At the moment, you don't have control of your anger. You need to find the balance before we fight."

"Why?" I snarled. "Are you scared I'll hurt you?"

"Just hear me out," he reasoned, stroking the top of my arms gently and leaning closer. "I want you to scream."

I blinked hard. "You're fucking joking, right?"

"We're doing this my way, Candy," West said. His grip tightened on my arms, and he slammed me back into the concrete wall. He wasn't messing around. "I don't want you to break my fucking neck as soon as we step in there, and I don't want to hurt you."

I shoved him off me. "How will screaming help?"

He grinned, making me want to punch him. "Try it."

"Fine." I threw my hands up and opened my mouth to let out a pathetic excuse for a scream, hardly raising my voice. "Happy now, West?"

"Do it again." His eyes narrowed. "You're not even trying."

I tried again, slightly louder this time.

"Is that all you've got?" he sneered. "I want you to let out everything in your nightmares. I want you to fucking scream. Let the whole fucking town hear you howl."

So I did.

I took a deep breath and let my lungs roar. The fury bursting from the back of my throat sounded like a wild animal, and it echoed around the empty space. I kept going until I was red-faced and shaking, tears running down my cheeks. West was right. It felt fucking good.

"Better?" he asked.

I nodded and wiped my eyes. Instead of running on adrenaline and being guided by pure bloodlust, my rational brain kicked in to remind me that this wasn't just about me. I'd tried to storm into the ring without thinking about how it was West's biggest fear.

"It's something I used to do when things got too much," West murmured, a troubled expression causing his eyebrows to knit together.

"Are you sure you still want to do this?" I asked, looking up at the ring. "We don't have to get into it. We can fight here."

"I'll do anything for you," West said with a ferocity that would not take no for an answer. "But first, let's expel some of that energy."

"Why?" I teased. "Scared I'll take you out?"

"That's fighting talk, Pinkie," he said. "But let's see how you do against a punchbag first, huh?"

I followed him to the training area. He hugged a bag to his chest, holding it in place.

I wiggled my eyebrows. "Ready?"

He grinned. "Do your worst."

When I landed a punch, he didn't wince.

"Not bad," he commented with a slight shrug. "More."

I imagined the bag was Hiram's smug face and kept going until I was breathless. My mind was back in control. In this state, I'd be able to rule my monster, and not let it rule me. The Kitten may be part of who I am, but she isn't *all* I am. I could summon her to the surface without becoming another person entirely.

West nodded in approval. "You're ready now."

He took off his shirt. Seeing his muscles under the stark light allowed me to see the raised scars over his chest that were easily hidden in the darkness. Maybe I should be the one who was afraid?

West went into the ring first. If it bothered him, he didn't show it. His focus was entirely on me. He extended his hand, and I ducked under the ropes to join him. He sauntered to the other end of the ring. He may avoid boxing, but he looked like a born fighter in his gym shorts as he clicked his neck on either side.

"Give it your best shot," he said. "Don't hold back."

I ran at him, but he was quicker. The fucker dodged out of my way and bounced off the sides. It'd be a challenge for anyone, let alone someone of my build, to take West out, but I was no quitter.

"You're going to have to do better than that," West mocked. "First on the ground for five seconds wins."

If I couldn't win with brute strength alone, I'd have to be faster and think out of the box. I growled as he grabbed my hips and pulled my body close to his.

"We're supposed to be fighting," I reminded him as his rough hands slipped under my tank top.

"Fighting isn't the only way to release anger," he said like a wise gang Yoda. "Maybe we should lose control together more often."

I balanced on my toes, tipping my face up to kiss him. But, as I did, I grabbed his arm and twisted it at the perfect angle. With one more jerk, it'd snap.

West cried out in pain. "Ouch."

"Nice try." I winked and released my hold as he massaged his arm. "But I don't give up that easily."

West's eyes lit up. "If you wanna play dirty…"

We separated again, circling each other. Neither of us wanted to make the first move, but we were not relenting.

"Show me what you're made of," I challenged.

He launched forward with the power of a raging bull. He wrapped his muscular arms around my waist and pinned me to him, then threw us backward in a full body slam. I landed on top of him with a whack. His rock hard abs were not as comfortable as a mattress. When we were down, he pivoted fast and flipped me over. His broad shoulders cast my world into darkness as he rolled on top. The weight of him bearing down made me short of breath.

"Is this what you wanted to see?" he asked, putting his hands around my throat. He leaned in closer. "Don't lock your feelings up again, Candy. You need to learn to control them. That power is what's going to make us win."

A slow clap echoed around the studio, making both of us jump. West's head turned sharply to the left. Judging by West's gritted teeth, our visitor was not welcome.

"It looks like I missed quite the show."

West fixed his dark stare on the intruder. "What're you doing here?" he snarled.

The Blackbird stepped out of the shadows and swaggered across the gym. How long had he stood watching us? He could have been there the whole time. He was so slippery, even his shadow struggled to stay attached.

West should have known better than to get distracted when fury still raced through my bloodstream. I slid out from underneath West's body before he realized.

"Candy," West called out, moving a second too late to stop me.

I may have the ability to control the Kitten, but the Blackbird's smug face made me abandon all reason. We were in a fucking war, and I was ready to go straight into battle. I didn't care that the Blackbird was a double agent working with us. He would have known Hiram was hunting Q down. Why didn't he say anything? His silence aided my friend's death, and I wouldn't allow it to go unpunished.

"I didn't think you'd be so pleased to see me," the Blackbird said, completely unaware he was now talking to the Kitten. If he knew about the delivery we received, the fucker would already be running.

"Oh, but I am," I replied in a sickly sweet voice. "Did I forget to say that Q sends his regards?"

The Blackbird's face fell as he pieced two and two together. Fear flickered over his face as he loosened his tie. He'd been stupid to come here alone. He'd gotten too comfortable. He may be in Zander's pocket, but I wasn't on Zander's fucking leash.

"I don't know what you've heard," the Blackbird said. I could smell his panic as he started to back away and almost tripped over his feet. Trying to escape was laughable. He was going nowhere until he answered my questions.

The Blackbird reached for the door and inched it open, but I was right behind him. As his fingers closed around the door's edges, I kicked into it and jammed two of his fingers in the gap. The sickening sound of his bones snapping gave me a sense of satisfaction. Playing with West had whetted my appetite, but confronting the Blackbird was like going to an all you can eat buffet after a fast. The Kitten was ravenous.

"Going somewhere?" I mocked. I grabbed him by the scruff of his collar and dragged him back. Real men didn't run. "I want to speak to you about a present Hiram delivered the other day. Q's fucking head."

The keys to the Golden Gloves were still in the lock. I twisted them to seal us inside and threw them out of his reach.

Tears filled the Blackbird's eyes as he rocked his hand like a newborn baby. "I didn't know he sent it to you."

I narrowed my eyes at him. "But you knew what he was planning, didn't you?"

"We're on the same side, Kitty," the Blackbird whined. "We're friends, remember? You can't hurt me. Think of what Zander would say."

"Zander isn't here," I said with a smile. "And I don't answer to him, Hiram, or anyone. Don't you know that by now?"

The Blackbird's bottom lip quivered. "What do you want?"

"I want you to answer my fucking questions," I screamed. My voice echoed around the gym, making the Blackbird shudder. "You knew what Hiram was planning, didn't you?"

"I knew he was looking for him," he mumbled. His eyes darted around the room and landed on West. "West, she's crazy. You understand, don't you?"

West didn't respond. He watched on from the sidelines. He was as angry as I was about what Hiram did to Q. How far would he let me go before he stepped in?

"Bullshit." My fist slammed into the Blackbird's ribs. He doubled over, clutching his stomach and gasping for air. "You know everything Hiram is up to. You are his intelligence guy. You had to know he was tracking Q down and getting close. The real question is, how would he have found out without someone feeding him that information?"

"I-I-I don't know," he croaked.

"We can do this the easy way or the hard way," I reasoned. "You know exactly what I'll do to get answers."

"Kitt—Candy! Please!"

I curled my lip in disgust. The Kitten didn't listen to men who begged. She didn't listen to anyone. I punched him square in the jaw, knocking his thin and wiry frame down like a coat hanger being bent out of shape. My knuckles would be bruised and bleeding by morning, but it'd be worth it.

"Don't fucking lie to me, Blackbird," I snarled. "You told him where to find Q, didn't you?"

"No," he lied, grabbing my leg and pleading like the pathetic sack of shit he was. "I said nothing."

"You're lying." I raised my sneaker, readying to stamp on his ribs again and make sure they were broken.

"Wait!" The Blackbird held up his hands. "I didn't have any choice."

"You could have given us a warning," I said, lowering my foot. "But you didn't. Why?"

"There's nothing I could do," the Blackbird said as blood from my earlier hit dripped down his chin. He started choking, then burst into a coughing fit like a cat trying to hack up a furball. It resulted in him spitting a tooth out with a clink against the floor. His face paled. "Hiram knew you were on a boat. I had to give him something. I had to throw him off the trail. Give him something else to focus on while we get ready to make our next move."

"You're wrong," I hissed, grabbing a tuft of his greasy hair and yanking his face upwards. He winced as he looked into my eyes. "You could have tipped us off. We could have warned Q, but you said nothing. You let Hiram murder him."

"Hiram would have killed him anyway," the Blackbird blathered on, but

I didn't listen. Words meant nothing. They couldn't bring back the dead. "Just like he'll kill you. You can't hurt me, Kitten. You need my help. You need me."

"We need nothing from you," I snarled, releasing my hold on his head. He collapsed into a heap, breathing in relief. "We can take him down without your help."

"Hiram made you, Kitten," the Blackbird said. "He will destroy you if you're not careful about who you trust."

I didn't let him say another word. I kicked him in the side with all of my strength. The bastard grabbed my ankle with his sweaty fingers, knocking me off balance and making me fall. The next few moments seemed to play out in slow motion. As I got to my knees, the Blackbird rolled onto his back and used his good hand to reach into his suit jacket.

West appeared out of nowhere, catching the Blackbird's wrist and crushing it with his monster grip until the Blackbird dropped the weapon.

West's eyes were black. His monster had been unleashed, and I was hardly keeping mine together. We were out of control, and no one was here to stop us.

"No one turns a gun on my girl," West growled.

"Come on, West," the Blackbird whimpered. "All of this is a misunderstanding. We can work it out like men, can't we?"

"The only misunderstanding—" West's voice came out in a deep and threatening rumble. He grabbed the Blackbird by his jacket and pulled him onto his feet. "—was trusting you."

"What about Zander?" the Blackbird pleaded desperately. West lifted the Blackbird into the air, carrying all of his weight like he was a toy until the tips of his shoes brushed against the concrete. "He won't be happy if you hurt me."

"You should know better than to believe everyone follows orders," West snarled. From the crazy look in his eyes, he'd already surrendered. Usually, I could bring him back from the edge to make him regain control, but I was too far gone. I didn't want to stop him.

"Hold him still," I ordered West, wiping myself down and wearing a manic smile.

"Please," the Blackbird begged. He flailed around like a freshly caught fish, but West didn't let go. He grasped him by the shoulders and spun the Blackbird to face me. "You don't need to hurt me. I'm sorry, okay? I should have told you."

"Talk is cheap," I hissed, getting up in the Blackbird's face. I could smell the fear on his acrid breath as tears streamed down his cheeks. I put one hand on his chin and the other on his shoulder then smiled. "This is for Q."

I twisted his head in a slick motion. His neck cracked then his head lolled forward like a scarecrow. West let his corpse fall to the ground with a thump. The Blackbird's eyes were still wide open, capturing his final moment of disbelief. Like Hiram, he underestimated what I was prepared to do to get justice for those I loved.

I brushed my hands together and scowled as I looked down at my top. Maybe I should feel remorseful, but all I could think about was how I'd never get out the bloodstains.

West showed no reaction as I snapped the Blackbird's neck, but he stepped towards me now. Blood dripped from his knuckles, and a layer of sweat made his perfect body glisten.

"This isn't what I planned to happen," he murmured.

That was the understatement of the fucking century. Self-control had a time and a place. I had learned something, though. West showed me exactly how committed he was to our mission. We may both be monsters, but we were in this together.

He looked at me hungrily. "Are you thinking what I am?"

My lips crashed into his and he responded with the same vigor. Every muscle in my body would soon ache from exhaustion, but the adrenaline burst made me want West more than I'd ever wanted anything.

Blood smeared over our skin, and our sweat mixed together as our monsters devoured each other. I clawed at his skin as his hands grabbed my ass and hoisted me into the air.

"You're fucking perfect," he growled as I squeezed my thighs around him, "and so fucking deadly."

I pulled my top over my head, needing to feel his hot skin against mine. Every inch of me was on fire, begging to be touched. He carried me back toward the ring, but we didn't make it that far. He slammed my back into the ring wall as I pushed my hand down and pulled his cock out of his shorts. He dropped me as if I burned him.

"Get naked for me, Candy," he ordered while stripping off himself.

I stepped out of my shorts and panties, wearing nothing but my sneakers and the Blackbird's blood. My tattoos got an extra burst of color from the red flecks.

"Fuck," West growled.

He grabbed my waist and flipped me upside down. His cock slapped me in the face, and my legs rested on his shoulders. I opened my mouth to ask him what the fuck he was doing when his tongue licked along the length of my pussy and started to eat me out furiously.

I turned my attention to his cock and tried to fit in as much as I could while clinging tightly to his back — not because I was afraid of him dropping me, but because I wanted to take him deeper. The angle made it easier for him to slide down my throat. West's groans against my pussy made my whole body vibrate with pleasure. His muscled arms supported my back as his hands slipped upward to squeeze my ass so tightly it'd leave bruises.

The blood rushing to my head had started to make me dizzy, but it also heightened the euphoric sensation as his tongue explored me more. When West twirled me around and put me back on two feet, my knees were already quaking like I'd had a string of multiple orgasms. We were lost and consumed in a moment that neither of us wanted to end.

Somehow, I regained my balance enough to crawl into the ring, leaving a trail of blood behind me. West followed like a beast tracking its prey, his eyelids heavy with lust and blinded by everything but his desire.

His voice sounded gravelly, "You are everything, Candy."

I stopped in the center of the ring and stay seated, then spread my legs for him. His eyes widened, looking from my face to my pussy.

"Prove it," I demanded.

West descended, climbing on top of me, in the same position as before the Blackbird rudely interrupted us. His hands closed around my throat as he grunted and thrust into me hard. His pace quickened, and my nails clawed his back, drawing blood and wanting to get under his skin. A place usually filled with the sound of panting and punches was replaced by my moans and his hips pounding into me mercilessly.

"You're perfect," he groaned as his grip tightened around my neck. "You know that?"

He choked me until my face flushed. I fought for air, and my eyes started to water, but I knew I could take it. I wanted him to do his worst. My pussy tightened around him then West released his grip. My soul felt like it was returning to my body after an astral experience as a blissful explosion burst from my core.

"West," I cried out his name as he fucked my orgasm out of me until my legs trembled, and I felt like I'd never walk again.

When he sensed I couldn't take it anymore, he let loose. His body shuddered from the force as he roared like a beast and came deep inside me.

"Fuck..." I gasped, my chest heaving.

He rolled off, and the two of us lay in silence. Red smears surrounded our naked bodies like bloody snow angels.

West turned his face towards me. "That was..."

"Incredible?" I offered.

"I fucking lo—"

West's cell ringing from the other end of the gym shattered our peaceful world and stopped him from dropping a bomb I didn't know how to respond to. The more time I spent with the Sevens, the surer I became that my feelings were fueled by more than bloodthirsty revenge. But *feeling* something was different to vocalizing it. If I said how I felt aloud, it would make it real and, if I admitted love was real, it would make it even harder to lose. After being burned before, how could I put myself in that vulnerable position again?

"Shit..." West clumsily got up and staggered towards the noise. As he passed, he looked sheepishly down at the corpse, then back at me. He scrubbed his face with his hand. "It's Zander."

"You'd better tell him there's been a..." I paused to think of the right word. "Misunderstanding."

CHAPTER
Twenty~One

Zander's face twisted in fury as he assessed the scene, pacing back and forth like a troubled detective from a cop show. He scowled as he looked at the ring. Sure, it was a forensic nightmare, but it would have been worse if he arrived to see West balls deep in me. That would have impressed him even less than the blood spatters over the floor.

He glared at West, who lounged against the wall. "I thought you said you could handle her."

"Her?" I jumped down his throat. "I have a fucking name, and that bastard was asking for it."

"Killing him was not part of our plan," Zander snarled, shooting me an icy look.

"So?" I shrugged and checked my nails. After the scuffle, they were now chipped. Brilliant. Another thing we had to thank the Blackbird for. "Plans change."

"Clearly." Zander's lips pursed into a thin disapproving line, then turned to West, "How does a lesson in self-control end in a murder?"

"I'm not going to apologize for protecting our girl," West said. "The slimy fuck pulled out a gun. What would you have done?"

Zander clenched his fists. He didn't reply because he'd have done the same thing without hesitation.

"The Blackbird knew what Hiram was planning to do to Q," I said. "He told him about the fucking yacht. That was never part of your plan. Who says he wouldn't have turned on us? You should be grateful for what we did."

"Grateful?" Zander laughed. "This is another mess I have to clean up because *both* of you couldn't control yourselves. Did he pull out a gun unprovoked?"

I rolled my eyes. "What does it matter?"

I'd already decided before the Blackbird tried to draw his gun that I wouldn't let him leave the Golden Gloves alive. Why did Zander care about the details? Knowing wouldn't restart the bastard's pulse.

"Don't pretend you did it for the Sevens," Zander seethed. "You did this for revenge."

"Wrong again, Zander," I said. "I didn't do it for me. I did it for Q."

"You were reckless," Zander sneered, spitting out his words. "You murdered our only fucking informant."

"The Blackbird wasn't an asset," I replied dismissively. "He was a liability, and he needed to be taken out."

Zander's shoulders shook in anger, letting his usual calm exterior slip for a moment. "That wasn't your call to make."

"If he hadn't crashed our party, this would never have happened." I batted my eyelashes innocently. "He served himself up on a plate."

"Why was he here?" Zander asked sharply. "He's not someone who shows up out of nowhere."

I stayed silent. The Blackbird only managed to say a few sentences before I'd gone psycho on his ass. Perhaps I *should* have done a little interrogation before breaking his neck, but I wanted to get to the fun part.

"See? Reckless!" Zander shook his head. "Whatever he was here for, we'll never find out now."

"I'll call in the crew to clean the place up," West said, picking up his cell and starting to dial. "It'll be done in an hour."

"Not yet." Zander held up his hand to stop him. "We can't have this getting out. Right now, we trust no one but each other. We need to plan our next move and control the damage. This needs to be kept quiet."

"What do we do now? Throw him off a cliff?" I grinned wickedly. "Or are we feeling an acid bath?"

"*You* are doing nothing," Zander said, pointing a finger at me. "You've already done enough for one night."

I pouted. "You ruin all the fun."

West coughed to disguise a laugh. I may be able to get away with mocking Zander, but he didn't want to push his luck further. Zander's ringing cell caused us all to freeze. He answered and his expression darkened as he listened to whoever was on the end of the line. "We're on the way."

West frowned, sensing his mood shift. "What is it?"

"We have another pressing situation to deal with," Zander said. "Giles has shown up at Lapland and is refusing to leave without speaking to his darling wife."

"I'll make sure he never leaves," I muttered under my breath. I'd already killed the Blackbird — what was another body to dispose of?

Zander grabbed my arm, his fingers squeezing tightly. "You will keep your mouth shut and fall into fucking line for once. We can't afford any more mistakes."

"What about the body?" West asked, casting a look at the Blackbird's corpse. "We need to get rid of it."

"Use the tunnels and take it to the bunker," Zander said. "We'll dispose of it later when we decide what to do with it. When it's gone, get the crew to clean up what's left behind. They don't need to know who died here."

"You want me to put him in my trunk?" West pouted. "I've just redone the upholstery."

"You know the rules," Zander hissed. "You were sloppy, and you have to deal with the consequences."

He knew how to sting people where it hurt. West's cars were like his children and no amount of bleach would remove the lingering smell of death. That car would be heading straight for the graveyard along with the Blackbird.

"What about me?" I asked, putting my hands on my hips. "I am still here, you know."

"You're coming with me," Zander said. "Now get in my car before Giles has the chance to burn another one of our places down."

"Do you expect me to walk into the club like this?" I gestured down at my bloody clothes. "In case you haven't noticed, it's not Halloween."

Zander sighed begrudgingly and pointed to a door at the other end of the room. "Shower first. I have spare clothes in my trunk."

"Who knew you'd come so prepared?" I teased. "Did you used to be a Boy Scout?"

West chuckled.

"You have five minutes, Candy," Zander warned through gritted teeth. Jeez, he needed to lighten up a little. "Go."

"I think you may have met your match, boss," West murmured as he lifted the Blackbird over his shoulder like a sack of potatoes.

"I preferred it when she was pretending to sleep," Zander muttered.

I turned back to look at them and grinned. "Didn't you already know? I'm your worst fucking nightmare."

———

Zander sped through the empty streets of Port Valentine above the speed limit. We passed abandoned buildings, groups of drug addicts huddling in dark corners, and party-goers staggering in heels looking for a good time.

I fought back a shiver. After the hose down from hell in the Golden Gloves showers, my wet hair stuck to my face, but Zander didn't offer to turn on the car's heating. He was intent on punishing me as much as possible. His 'spare clothes' involved nothing but boxers and a suit jacket, which buttoned just above my nipples. Thankfully, androgynous fashion was all the rage.

"Still pissed at me, huh?" I asked, pulling the blazer tighter around my shaking frame.

"What did you expect?" Zander gripped the wheel tighter, making the ink over his knuckles appear more pronounced against his skin. "An award?"

I crossed my arms in a moody sulk. "You hated that bastard as much as I did."

"Of course I hated him," Zander hissed. I held onto my seat as he swerved aggressively to avoid hitting a drunk. Any normal person would freak out, but not Zander. He didn't flinch. His gray eyes remained fixed on the road ahead as he talked, "But we have to be calculated if we're playing to win. The Blackbird was our only link to Hiram's inner circle. Now, it's gone."

"We can take Hiram down without the Blackbird's help," I insisted, although my voice wavered. My adrenaline had started to wear off, and doubt was creeping in. If I said something enough times, it helped, right? Fake it until you make it wasn't a popular phrase for no reason. "The Sevens don't need anyone else to do their dirty work. You said it yourself, we are the only ones we can trust."

"That depends on whether you can work as part of a team," Zander said. "You're not the only one who has something to lose, and it's up to me to keep everyone alive."

My vendetta may have clouded my better judgments, but I didn't regret killing the Blackbird after finding out the part he played in Q's death. He deserved to die... but maybe I *should* have waited until after Hiram was dead to kill him.

"So, I screwed up tonight. Shit happens," I said. "I'm only human."

"You're a human who seems intent on trying to kill yourself. You're your own worst enemy." Zander slammed his foot on the gas, throwing me backward in my seat. "I'm not going to stand by and let you die on my fucking watch."

"I'm not your problem, Zander." I raised my voice to be heard over the engine's roar. "You don't have to worry about me."

"I'm not losing you, Candy," Zander growled. He tore his gaze away from the road for a second, and I saw emotion stir in his eyes. "I, *we*, have lost enough already."

The Sevens had been surrounded by death for their entire lives. We loved more ghosts than people. The funerals, the glassy eyes, the blood... we'd lived amongst it for so long that it was hard to see a way out. The only light to guide us through was each other. If one of us was extinguished, we'd never be able to see properly again.

"We're not going to lose anyone else," I whispered, curling my hands into fists and digging my nails into my palms.

"If you're not working with me, you're working against us," Zander said. "No one can take on the world alone."

"Are you always so fucking righteous?" I blew out air in exasperation. "You're just as bad. You try to do everything alone."

He smiled sadly. "And remember how that turned out last time..."

We settled into a silence, lost in our thoughts.

"Candy?" Zander asked after a while.

"What?" I huffed.

"Can you trust me enough to follow my rules from now on?"

I watched the streetlights rush by. Playing by his rules and trusting him were two different things entirely.

"I'll try," I replied. Well, except for trying to secure Vixen as Bryce's heir, but Zander didn't need to know about that. I'd planned that *before* this happened. "But I can't make any promises, okay?"

"Good," Zander said. We stopped outside Lapland but didn't get out of the car straight away. His gray eyes found mine in the darkness. "So, tell me, how did it feel when you killed him?"

Killing people used to be a routine part of my day, like brushing my teeth in the morning, but my life was different now. When I first left Hiram, I convinced myself that my Kitten persona was the work of Hiram's conditioning. I blamed him for bringing it out of me. For changing me into something abhorrent. It was easier to blame him for the parts of myself I didn't want to face. But I knew the truth, and the night had forced me to accept what I'd always known. The Kitten has always been inside me.

I'd killed the Blackbird because I *wanted* to. His walking into the Golden Gloves was akin to waving a fat slice of chocolate fudge cake in front of someone on a diet. I'd been the judge, jury, and executioner, and it felt...

"Powerful," I admitted. "I liked it. Does that make me a psychopath?"

Zander laughed. The first real laugh I'd heard from him in a while. "Aren't we all psychopaths here?"

"Maybe," I replied. Was that why we were all drawn to each other? We were all equally fucked up and broken, like misshapen puzzle pieces that miraculously became whole when we were together. "Or maybe some people just deserve to die."

"Like Hiram," Zander said. His jaw clenched and any trace of a smile vanished. His tattooed neck and face almost made it look like he was wearing a mask. "If we're going to finish him, then we need to play the game carefully from now on. You're the only one with the knowledge to beat him."

"It won't be long until he shows up," I said, half-expecting to see him lurking in the shadows like the boogeyman as soon as we stepped outside. "He will come looking for the Blackbird soon."

"Then we'll have to be ready," Zander said. "And in the meantime, we won't kill anyone else."

I smirked. "Does this mean I'm forgiven?"

"I have a specific punishment in mind." Zander shot me a twisted grin. He could do anything he wanted with a smile like that and leave me begging for more. "But it'll have to wait."

"Fine." I grimaced, remembering Giles was waiting for us. "Let's see what my *husband* wants."

———

The night was already in full swing inside Lapland. A dancer was in the middle of her performance and drawing in the crowds with her tassel twirling abilities. Zander took my arm, and people parted for us to pass. They knew better than to stand in his way.

"Nice jacket." Vixen looked me up and down as we approached her, then wrinkled her nose at my hair. She was sitting at the bar while Mieko was busy serving customers behind it. "But why do you look like a drowned rat?"

After the night I'd had, looking like a drowned rat was almost a compliment.

"It's a long story." I waved my hand. One that I didn't have the energy or time to go into. "We'll explain later."

Zander rolled up his shirt sleeves. "Where's Giles?"

"Red's with him in the office," Vixen said, her expression turned stony. "We had to put him somewhere before he drained the bar dry and scared away the customers. A sniveling trainwreck was killing our vibe."

"Do you and Mieko have everything under control here?" Zander asked, looking to them both for confirmation.

"Of course," she said flippantly. "We're expecting a late liquor drop. Fuck knows why the guy couldn't have brought it earlier..."

After my earlier conversation with Mieko, something told me this late delivery was no accident. This could be her plan to get Vixen's signature on the dotted line. But I had another problem to contend with and had to trust Mieko would handle it.

I followed Zander through to the back and threaded my fingers through his possessively to mark my territory. Gorgeous strippers and shot girls fluttered their eyelashes at him as we passed. Did they have to make it so goddamn obvious? Zander didn't notice.

"What do you think Giles wants?" I asked.

"What he always wants," Zander replied, "to make a scene and my life more difficult."

Rocky stood outside Zander's office guarding the door.

"Where's West?" Rocky frowned, looking behind us. "I thought you'd all come back together."

"He's busy." I shot Rocky a look that hopefully said: 'busy stashing the body of our only informant in the doomsday bunker under our feet'. "Is he in there?"

Rocky stepped aside for us to pass. "Unfortunately…"

The smell of liquor burned my nostrils as we filed in. Vixen was right. Giles looked like he'd crawled off a sinking boat that got hit by a monsoon. The person in front of us was not the same smartass rich guy I had the displeasure of becoming accustomed to. His pressed designer suits and expensive cologne were long gone; his clothes were stained and looked slept in. Thankfully, the overpowering vodka fumes masked the more offensive odor of something that had crawled under his armpits and died there.

Giles staggered to his feet as soon as he saw me, almost knocking over a desk lamp and chair.

"Candy," he slurred, squinting at me through his bloodshot eyes. "I've been waiting for you."

"You can stay on that side of the fucking table," I spat, wanting to keep him as far away as possible. "Why are you here, Giles? You're not welcome."

"He says he has information," Rocky said, grimacing as he steered Giles back to the chair and pushed him roughly back into it. "Sit the fuck down before you break anything else."

I made a mental note to ensure Rocky sanitized his hands before touching me again.

"I needed to see you after what happened," Giles said.

"If you came here for sympathy, you've come to the wrong fucking place." I surveyed him in disgust. "You burned our fucking house down, remember?"

"I didn't mean it," Giles wailed. He held his head in his hands, mumbling to himself, then looked up with crazy eyes. "The fire. I never knew. I just wanted to… show you…"

"Show us, what?" I pressed. "How to light a can of gasoline? You wanted to destroy something because you couldn't have it."

His face crumpled like a wrinkled goblin, making him age ten years. His mouth contorted in physical pain and ugly tears left streaks down his dirty cheeks. Being able to sob like a baby and still make me want to punch him in the face was a rare trait to find in a person. If he thought crying would make me pity him, he was out of his fucking mind.

"I wanted to apol-ap-apolo-apologize." Giles sniveled loudly, wiping his snotty nose with his grubby shirt. "I didn't mean—"

"It's a little too late for that, don't you think? It's not us that you need to be asking forgiveness from," I replied coldly. "Your apology doesn't change anything. Words are not going to bring them back."

Giles started babbling to himself and rocking in the chair. "The men he sent... they said they'd checked... I sat and watched when... I didn't know..."

It's a good thing West was busy stashing the Blackbird's body in the bunker. He wouldn't have been able to contain himself while Giles hosted a pity party. One murder was enough for us to have to cover up for an evening.

"Red said you came here because you had information," I said. I tapped my foot impatiently. We had to get rid of the Blackbird's body. If he had nothing useful to say, we needed to throw him back in the gutter where he belonged. "Why don't you spit it out?"

"Hiram is coming to town," Giles said. "Tonight."

Zander, Rocky, and I exchanged glances. We couldn't trust a word Giles said, but what did he have to gain by lying? He wasn't a good enough actor to fake being this wasted.

"Where?" Zander slammed his palms down on the desk, making Giles yelp like he'd been slapped. "Where is he going? Here?"

Giles shook his head and grappled around in his pocket for his phone. He pulled it out after several fumbling attempts. "The Maven."

Zander snatched it from his fingers and scrolled through the messages to see for himself. His eyebrows lowered in confusion. "But there's no party scheduled."

The Maven only opened a few nights a year. If there was an event happening, Zander would know about it.

"It's an exclusive party. Your father is hosting it," Giles explained as his nose continued to run down his face. "I've seen the guest list."

"How do we know you're not setting us up?" I snarled. "It's not the first time you've helped lure me to an ambush."

"I want to make it right," Giles said. "I want to help after—"

His blubbering made the rest of the sentence incomprehensible. He'd already lost the woman he loved and a family he'd never have. What else did he have to lose?

Zander pocketed Giles's cell. "We're keeping it."

"Take it," Giles wailed, throwing his hands up hysterically. "Take everything. I've got nothing left anymore."

Giles rose from his seat and made a pathetic attempt at walking, like a toddler trying to take their first steps in the snow.

"Where do you think you're going?" Zander grabbed him by the collar to stop him and hissed in his ear, "You're not going anywhere. If you're lying, I want you to be in a place where I can make you pay."

"What're we gonna do with him?" Rocky asked, patting Giles down to make sure he didn't have another phone or any weapons on him. He grimaced as he checked inside Giles's dirty, but empty, socks. "Do you want to leave him here?"

"Take him to the bunker," Zander ordered with a smile. "He'll have company there."

I glanced over at Zander, questioning what the hell he was thinking. He ignored my side-eye and said, "It'll serve as a reminder of what will happen if he has lied to a Seven."

Rocky grabbed Giles by the shoulders and steered him out. It wasn't difficult to direct someone who couldn't stand without assistance. Giles's cries disappeared down the corridor, leaving Zander and me alone. They'd get a nasty surprise when they arrived in the bunker.

"Well?" I asked. Knowing Hiram was in town gave me a new burst of energy. "Are we going to act?"

Zander didn't reply straight away. He paced the length of his office as he considered the possibilities.

"You said we wanted to end this," Zander said, stopping abruptly in his tracks. "So let's end it. We need to act before Hiram finds out about the Blackbird. Tell Mieko and Vixen to look after the club, then meet me out front in ten."

I nodded curtly. "Consider it done."

———

After I gave Vixen and Mieko a quick rundown of where we were heading, Vixen shook her head.

"No," she said definitively. "You're not going without us."

"Vix, it's not safe for you," I tried to explain.

"It's not your decision to make," she hissed. She looked like she wanted to tear my head straight off my body and stormed over to the DJ booth. A second later, she cut the music. The crowd cried in objection.

"What is she doing?" Zander asked. He appeared at my side out of nowhere.

"Beats me," I muttered back as Mieko shrugged, equally confused by her crazy fiancée's actions.

Vixen snatched the microphone from the DJ. "The cops are on their way, motherfuckers," she shrieked. "Now get the fuck out. Go!"

I don't think I'd ever seen people move so damn fast. The dance floor cleared in a few minutes as everyone raced to the exit. Topless dancers fell out of private booths with money stuck inside their panties, followed by red-faced guys zipping up their flies. Customers abandoned half-empty drinks, afraid of what other substances cops would find in their pockets.

After the last customer staggered out, Vixen slammed the door shut.

"You are not going without us," she blasted. "No fucking way."

"This isn't a negotiation. It's too dangerous for you and Mieko," Zander said firmly. "I'm ordering you to stay here."

"The Sevens are all for one and one for all." Vixen stomped over to him and jabbed her talon into his chest. "If one goes down, we all fucking go down. Together."

"Where is everyone?" Rocky and West strolled into the club, looking mystified as to why everyone had vaporized.

"I closed up early," Vixen snarled. "We all have somewhere we need to be."

West raised his eyebrows. "We?"

Rocky must have filled him in after dumping Giles in the bunker. Conversing with the Blackbird's corpse would help sober him up, not that he'd get any responses.

"Yes, *we*," she replied indignantly. She looked at West's muscled arms, still streaked with the Blackbird's blood like war paint. "It looks like someone started the party early."

"Zander is right, Vix," I said, brushing over her observation and trying not to sound patronizing. "I don't want you two getting involved in this. It's not your fight."

"If it's your fight, it's our fight." Mieko stepped forward. Everyone turned to stare at her in stunned silence. Her quiet voice was filled with heavy conviction. "We're coming whether you like it or not. Arguing about it is just wasting time."

Damn, when did the shy stripper with doe-like eyes turn into such a fucking badass?

"We'll come prepared," Vixen said, lifting her shirt to reveal a gun tucked under her waistband. She nodded to Mieko, who hitched up her dress to reveal a taser slipped into her garter. "I also have pepper spray."

My mouth fell open. "Since when do you carry all that?"

Mieko smiled and winked. "We learned from the best."

"Fine," Zander snapped. He knew he was fighting a losing battle. "But you stay out of the way, and if there's any sign of trouble, you leave — understood?"

"I think that trouble is going to be a given," Vixen muttered sarcastically, but Zander's threatening glare made her relent. "Fine, that's a deal. We'll leave if things get too heavy, okay?"

I looked around at every face in the room, each set with determination and hunger in their eyes. We were heading into the unknown. None of us knew what we were about to face, but we were going in together. The Sevens. United.

"West will sort out our weapons." Zander nodded at him. "You all have five minutes to get ready, then get in the limo waiting outside. We'll go through the plan on the way."

Who needed an army tank when a stretch limo would do?

I dashed to the costume closet to change. If I was going to kill Hiram tonight, I had to look the fucking part. A red dress, leather jacket, and boots combo were perfect. I pulled my hair into a high ponytail. There's nothing worse than hair getting in your face when you're in the middle of a fight.

As I zipped up the knee-high black boots, my cell vibrated on the dresser. I glanced at the text flashing over the screen: *'I will be at the Maven tonight. Meet me there with the contract'*.

Bryce.

Little did he know we were already planning to gatecrash.

"Are you almost ready?" Mieko popped her head in to check on me, holding a small blade in her hand. "West told me to give you this."

"I'm fine," I insisted, not wanting to carry a knife. "Is Vixen around?"

"She's already outside," Mieko said. "She didn't want Zander to change his mind..."

"Good," I said, then showed her the text. "Are we ready to go? Is it done?"

She scanned the message and nodded. "I'll handle it."

"But—"

She pulled me into a hug and whispered in my ear, "You can't face Hiram and sort out Bryce, too. Leave Bryce to me. I'll do this for Vix."

"She's lucky to have you," I said, hugging her back.

"Let's go," West's growl interrupted our moment. "Everyone's waiting."

My expression hardened in determination. "Let's fucking do this."

I may not know what tonight had in store but, one thing is for sure, I was going into it with the best people at my side. In a way, that was the biggest battle already won.

Twenty-Two

W est cut through the barbed wire to create a Hulk-sized hole, making the space in the fence larger than your average door.

Zander had loosened the top buttons of his shirt to reveal more of the gorgeous ink cradling his neck. He stood next to the gap and inclined his head in a bow. "Ladies, first."

"What a gentleman," I mocked, strolling through first. A loose wire caught on my leg, slicing it open, but I didn't mind. The pain made me want to push on and would remind me that I was alive. Mieko and Vixen followed me.

"Wait," Rocky hesitated before he went next, "before we go, shouldn't we say something?"

We all knew what he meant. The last time Hiram cornered us, Rocky almost died. We had to expect the unexpected. We needed to be ready for anything, but it didn't mean we had time to stand around and say a fucking eulogy.

"We don't need to say anything," I fired back, giving no one the chance to question themselves. "We're the fucking Sevens. We'll go in together, and we'll all come out together."

One shake of confidence could bring everything slamming to the ground. We had no options. We *were* going to do this. We had to.

"Too fucking right," West growled, shoving Rocky forward and following him through. "We'll find Hiram and kill him. Easy."

After the bloodshed in the Golden Gloves, West's monster buzzed underneath his skin, craving release. He'd held himself back with the Blackbird. It gave him a taste, but he wanted a full fucking meal. Confronting Hiram at the Maven wouldn't be an easy task. If a brawl broke out, it would be easy for him to slip away undetected.

We stormed through the rows of shipping containers with our heads held high like we owned the fucking night. The darkness was ours. I'd never worked as part of a team before, and the energy was magnetic. We were six different bodies moving as a single entity. We made the shadows our own.

Mieko's bouncy strides and gorgeous sparkling dress made her look like she'd stepped straight off the stage of a 1930s cruise ship. The purse swinging off her wrist held the contract to give to Bryce, and the hidden taser stashed in her garter gave me the confidence she could pull this off. Blood may freak her out, but she'd have no problem frying an asshole's pubes.

Vixen wrapped her arm around Mieko's waist. Her heavy New Rock boots could crush bones if she stamped down hard enough. Her full leather outfit and black lipstick made her look like a sexy Grim Reaper. She'd do anything to protect her family.

Rocky laced his fingers through mine. He caught my eye and flashed a cheeky smile. Even though we were heading into war, he carried himself with his usual casual demeanor. Looking at him, you'd think he'd come straight from the gym in his gray slacks, sneakers, and black T-shirt. Despite his relaxed candor, his hand gripped mine tightly. Hiram's death would free me from him forever, but his death was about more than that to Rocky. Hiram embodied everything that had gone wrong in his life. After me, he wanted Hiram to meet his end more than anyone.

On my other side, West's soulless stare scanned the yard for any threats. The dead look in his eyes was more terrifying than the sight of his blood-spattered arms and neck. A few hours ago, we'd fucked in a puddle of blood. Now, he wanted to fucking bathe in it.

Zander walked a few steps ahead of the rest of us. As usual, he wore a tailored black suit. The dim lighting from the overhead lamps only stressed the ink that bloomed from his pressed clothes, giving the impression that a dark force had infiltrated his skin and taken hold of his body. Who knows? Maybe it had. Zander would stop at nothing to get what he wanted.

We neared the so-called VIP entrance to the Maven. The rusty shipping container looked in even worse shape than the last time I came, with even bigger indentations on the side and fire damage.

Zander's low voice was a whisper in the wind, but we heard him perfectly. "Is everyone clear on the plan?"

On the way, we decided what was going to happen when we went inside. We would split into pairs to give us the best chance of searching the area. I didn't like it, but the sprawling underground tunnels were vast, and we'd attract too much attention together. When we found Hiram, we'd give a signal, and then all hell would break loose. What could go wrong?

Rocky squeezed my hand and split to stand by Vixen's side. West loomed over Mieko's small figure as he held out his hand for her to take. We paired everyone to ensure maximum protection. Zander offered me his arm. He would not be letting me out of his sight.

Zander rapped on the metal side of the shipping container, and someone on the inside stirred. It had been months since I'd been here with Cheeks and so much had changed since then. Knowing the tunnels would soon flow with Hiram's blood would make our entrance even sweeter.

The door creaked open. A lone security guard looked us up and down with suspicion. Security was less of a concern when there was a private party taking place. We could work it to our advantage.

"Name?" the guard barked.

Zander stepped out of the shadows so the guy could get a long hard look at his face. Everyone in Port Valentine knew who the Briarlys were.

"I don't think that will be necessary," Zander purred. "Do you?"

The guard's brow furrowed. "Your father didn't put you on the list."

"I suggest you check again," Zander instructed smoothly with an air of entitlement that I'd find infuriating to be on the other end of.

As the guy looked at his clipboard, West lunged with the ferocity of a wild animal and slammed the guard's face into the wall. His nose exploded, and he dropped to the floor with a thud. His chest was still moving, but he'd have a monster headache tomorrow.

West kneeled to search the unconscious mound for weapons and stashed a gun in his waistband. The big man didn't need weapons to fight, but knowing there was one less gun on someone on the other side was a comforting thought.

We huddled around the trap door that led to the Maven below, and Zander gestured for the first pair to go. We'd agreed to enter in stages. It'd create too much of an impact for the entire gang to arrive together. This way, we could stay under Hiram's radar for longer.

Vixen and Rocky stepped over the unconscious guy and pulled up the hatch, unleashing the roar of the pumping bass.

"See you on the other side," Rocky said.

They headed down the metal staircase into the flashing strobe lights. My heart hammered, already counting down the seconds until we were next. Standing and waiting wasn't my style. Hiram was somewhere in the pit below, and time standing still was another moment wasted. But we had no alternative when the element of surprise was our biggest advantage.

Minutes passed, but they felt like hours.

"Next," Zander ordered.

West took a firm grip of Mieko's hand for them to step up. She inhaled deeply, but her confidence did not waver. She descended after West and didn't look back.

"How long do we have to wait?" I asked as we slammed the hatch down on them.

"We're going in another entrance," Zander replied coolly. "Through the tunnels."

I frowned. "But that wasn't part of the plan."

"Plans change."

I grabbed his arm to stop him from walking away. "But it'll waste time."

Time we didn't have.

"Trust me," Zander said softly. He wasn't using the voice he reserved for firing orders as a gang boss, but it was the tone he used when he admitted his feelings for me. "If Hiram has been watching and is expecting us to come down next, I will not let you walk straight into his hands."

"Fine," I conceded. "As long as it won't take long."

"It won't," he promised, leading us out of the container. Giving the others time to nail down Hiram's location had its advantages, but I hated leaving them to do the dirty work for me. I wanted to be among the chaos.

"How much further?" I asked, struggling to keep up with his long strides.

Zander didn't answer. We continued through the shipping yard until we reached a railing that stopped us from tumbling down a steep drop into black water that stretched ahead like a sea of tar. Once upon a time, many ships would have pulled in to unload, but empty containers were all that was left of the dead industry.

Zander turned right and kept on walking until we reached a rusty gate. He kicked it, making it burst open. The lock on it was so rusted it stood no chance against his foot. Beyond the gate, we followed a thin path until we came upon a stony staircase. The stairs were concealed from view from the yard, impossible to find if you didn't know what you were looking for.

"Seriously?" I raised an eyebrow.

The stairs were so crumbled and weathered they looked like they'd erode with any weight. Zander didn't flinch and started walking down them.

"Watch your step," he said. He stopped on the second stair and turned, holding out his hand.

I batted it away. "I'll be fine."

Well, I hoped so. Plummeting into the murky water wouldn't be an ideal way to spend an evening. The steps miraculously held out as we followed them down to a door embedded within the rock face. Had port workers used it as a control room? A large faded 'danger' sign warned trespassers away.

Zander took no notice. He pushed the heavy iron door open, making the rusty hinges groan. If the suicide staircase or warning sign wasn't enough to scare any sane person away, why lock the door? This must be a lesser-known entrance for it to have zero security.

Zander felt around on the side of the rocky wall for a switch and flicked it on. Emergency orange lights flickered to life down a long tunnel. Without them and with the door closed, we'd be in complete darkness. I wrinkled my nose at the smell of dank water. It must have flooded once, but the concrete below our feet was surprisingly dry.

"You sure know how to give a girl a grand entrance," I grumbled, trying not to flinch at the scratching noise of rats scuttling near our ankles. "How do you know about this place?"

From my last visit to the Maven, I knew that tunnels led away from the underground pit where the parties took place. Only someone who spent a lot of time here would know they existed.

"I'd heard rumors about this place," Zander explained. His voice reverberated off of the stone and gave it added depth. "My grandfather used this route for smuggling, or so my father says."

"Is it still used now?"

"My father prefers to do business above ground," Zander replied curtly. He paced along the tunnel, taking various turns left and right. The place was like a maze. "But I used to explore these tunnels when I was a kid. When my father cut me off, I slept here for a few weeks. Anywhere was better than the manor."

"You *slept* here?"

I couldn't imagine a kid who was used to a lavish lifestyle sleeping in dingy tunnels underneath a shipping yard.

"I did until West found out and let me couch surf at his dad's place," Zander said. I couldn't see his face but detected the slight smile in his tone. "Shortly after that, we moved to Hammerville and opened Seven Sins."

There was so much more to Zander than his suit, ruthless efficiency, and panty-igniting face tattoos. He may have grown up in privilege, but it'd spat him back out again, and he was forced to forge a new life for himself in the darkness.

I kicked a couple of empty beer bottles away, and Zander cleared his throat. "We're almost there."

The Maven lay at the rotten heart of Port Valentine's underground network. The surrounding tunnels were like veins, drawing us in with every step, along with the music bouncing off the damp walls. A party was happening a few turns away, but all we had for company was vermin. Although rats were probably better than those who Bryce had invited to his private party.

Suddenly, Zander stopped in his tracks, blocking me from going any further. "I want you to promise me something before we go in."

"We don't have time for this," I huffed, trying to shove past him. For all we knew, the others already had their eyes on Hiram and were waiting for us to make the final move.

Zander didn't let me pass. He seized my shoulders to stop me.

"Promise me that you won't do anything stupid," he said. "I meant what I said, Candy. I will not lose you too."

"I can't make that promise," I said, meeting his gaze. An intense look passed between us. His gray eyes explored mine almost pleadingly, but I couldn't give him what he wanted. "But I promise I'll try."

"That's all I can ask," he said, breaking our stare and taking my hand.

The ceiling of the tunnel widened as we neared the music. Needles and used condoms appeared on our path like a trail of breadcrumbs leading into depravity.

The Sevens had arrived.

———

For an exclusive party, I expected the guestlist to be small. I was wrong. The crowd crammed into the Maven was as large as the infamous full moon party. After his fall from grace, Bryce hadn't lost all of his supporters.

Zander was right in choosing for us to enter in a less conventional way. Coming down the staircase declared your arrival if anyone was looking in that direction, but we blended straight into the party. Zander's hand gripped mine as we headed to the dance floor.

Every motion was a snapshot under the strobe lights. The smell of liquor, cheap perfume, sweat, and next-day sex hung in the air. Around us, men slipped fifty-dollar bills into unlucky women's bras and fell away from the dance floor into the tunnels we'd left behind. Those who weren't trying to get laid had come down with a hay fever attack from the amount of coke they were snorting. We shoved past a group of men snorting a thick line of white powder from a girl's beach-ball-like breasts and shook our heads to decline two bags of pills being passed around like candies.

It's easy to see how the Maven developed its reputation. It remains the ultimate place to let loose your darkest, innermost desires. The Maven symbolizes freedom, but an untamed wilderness simmers underneath the surface. Fucking and drugs were only the tips of the iceberg.

At this point in the night, the party had been going on for hours. The good-time vibe would soon slip into something more sinister. Serious conversations about deals and business will have passed. Everyone was warming up for the main event. They were sharpening their knives, and they'd be coming for blood. If I had my way, we'd be the first to spill it.

"We need to get to a vantage point," I said.

Any kind of elevation would help. Crowds of sticky-skinned people packed together made it hard to see anything other than the circle of faces directly next to you. Without a better view, we were walking targets. Hiram could be anywhere, and he'd have eyes in every corner. Whispers would soon make their way to him about uninvited guests if they hadn't already.

"Fucking move," I hissed, winding a guy three times my size with my knee to get by.

Another slimeball leered and reached to grab my ass, but a furious glare from Zander was enough to send him scurrying back into the safety of the crowd. The Briarly name meant something, or maybe it was a perk of being the host's son. As we emerged from the dance floor pit, Bryce Briarly hovered like a prowling dog monitoring the perimeter.

"Look who it is." Bryce came over to greet us. His mouth twisted into a snarl. "You seem to have a habit of showing up to my parties uninvited, son."

"This isn't a social call," Zander spat.

"I assume you were responsible for our security breach?" Bryce said, referencing the guard bleeding out upstairs.

I looked straight past him to see West and Mieko loitering by the bar. She caught my eye and shook her head, a quick movement only I detected. Damn it. They hadn't seen Hiram either. The big man's eyes darted around the room, and his fists clenched by his sides. He was losing patience.

Mieko's hand tightened around her purse as she registered who we were talking to. Her eyes locked on Bryce's back. We may not have found Hiram, but we had another mission to complete.

"Candy," Bryce acknowledged me. "I didn't realize you'd be bringing company. Have you come to give me a gift?"

I ignored him as my stare scanned the space. A mirror propped up behind the bar reflected a familiar face in the crowd.

"We need to go." I grabbed Zander's arm and turned around. "Now."

"What did my father mean—"

Explanations could wait. I was in hunter mode. I'd caught a whiff of my prey, and everything else had fallen into insignificance. All of my focus was on a man on the opposite side of the dance pit.

"Him." I pointed at the man who hadn't moved from his position. "He's with Hiram."

I'd recognize his pock-marked face anywhere. He was one of Hiram's sadistic security guards. The misogynistic rat-faced bastard would soon regret leering at me in a wedding dress. If he was around, Hiram wouldn't be far.

Zander's shoulders tensed. He saw him before I did. The devil came into view, flanked by three of his most devout followers through the throng of bodies. He'd have more guards, but taking out those three would be a good start. We weren't the only ones staring, though. Hiram's eyes seared into mine. He raised his hand, and a sick smile spread over his twisted face. He was expecting me. We were so fucking close that I could almost smell his blood.

I dropped Zander's arm and started charging forward. As I ran, a surge of people rushed towards us. There were too many of them. They forced us further from our destination. Zander wouldn't let that stop us. He started throwing punches and flooring anyone in our way, but it was an impossible task. For everyone we took down, the tsunami of people kept coming. Why had this suddenly become the perfect spot for a fucking mosh pit?

The hairs on my arms stood on end as a guttural roar ripped through the air.

West.

My hypnotic focus lapsed, making me spin around. West towered above the crowd because of his height. A storm brewed around him. He was right in the center of a brawl. Fury blurred his features as he pummeled into everyone in touching distance like a human bulldozer. They kept coming at him, descending like a pack of rabid wolves.

"Mieko!" I turned to Zander in panic. "What about Mieko?"

A few moments ago, she'd been next to him. I craned my neck to see, but it was no use. Meiko was short, and everyone was so densely packed in that I couldn't see through the gaps in between elbows and throwing punches. Had she slipped away before the fight began?

"We need to keep going," Zander insisted, pulling me after him. "This is our chance. This is the plan."

We couldn't move. Everyone was out for blood. Fights were breaking out all over, and people kept shoving in our direction with no sign of stopping. At least fifty people stood between us and the spot where Hiram was. We'd lost sight of him in all of the commotion. Had he already made his escape?

The shouts of the crowds grew deafening. I swerved to avoid getting a fist in my face and kneed the offender in the balls, causing him to double over. Out of the corner of my eye, I saw a flash of a blade in the hands of a junkie who was blindly slashing at anyone in sight. West could hold his own in any fight, but a group of high and violent thugs was unpredictable.

We had a choice to make.

"Zander," I yelled in his ear. "We need to go back!"

I lost my reasoning ability with the Blackbird, but it gave me renewed clarity. I wanted Hiram dead, but if I had to choose between killing him now and keeping West alive, I'd pick West every fucking time. I couldn't stand by and watch him have his kidneys carved out.

"But—"

"We can't lose anyone else," I interrupted.

For all we knew, Hiram may already be on his way out of town. In which case, pounding our way through flesh would be useless. We had to focus on what we could control: getting everyone out alive.

Zander delivered a jaw-shattering blow to a stranger on his left to take out his frustration. A gold tooth flew out of the victim's mouth, which someone else snatched up, and the two of them wrestled for it.

Zander knew I was right. This wasn't how any of us wanted the night to unfold but we made an agreement that we needed to honor.

We were all going in and all coming out together.

A man dropped to the floor in front of us, and Rocky appeared behind him.

"Figured you might need a little help," Rocky said, wiping his brow.

"Where's Vixen?" Zander asked.

"I got her out," Rocky said. Vixen was a badass, but she wasn't skilled in combat. "Where's Hiram?"

"We don't know," I said. "But we need to get the fuck outta here before West gets himself killed."

West may have surrendered to the monster, but his muscles were no match for guns. Things were getting ugly fast and a pile of bodies was racking up at his feet. We already had enough enemies to deal with. We didn't need him accidentally killing someone else who'd bring more trouble to our door.

The four of us charged through the crowds. Anyone who didn't move out of our way was lucky to get away with split lips and broken wrists.

"West," I shouted above the noise as he slammed two scrawny guys' heads together and pocketed the knife that they turned on him. His head jerked upward at hearing my call.

Before we could get to him, Zander and Rocky brutally took down three men surrounding West. Seconds later, they lay unconscious on the floor. As soon as the others saw reinforcements had arrived, they started running, breaking their attack on West. One smartass ran straight into the wall and broke his fucking nose.

West threw the guy he was fighting to the floor like a toy, kicking him in the ribs to finish him off. He picked his way over the bodies to join us.

"Where's Mieko?" I asked.

"She's already gone," West panted. "She slipped away before the fight started. The fuckers came from nowhere."

I breathed a sigh of relief. Mieko was a survivor. She'd be back at the limo, curled up in Vixen's arms, worrying about the state we'd be in when we returned.

"What about Hiram?" Rocky asked.

"He got away." I said, grinding my back teeth together. "This time."

"Fuck," Rocky exploded.

"We need to go," I said, then looked to Zander to back me up. He nodded. "Now."

If Hiram was here, we would never find him now. We had to regroup. He'd gotten away this time, but we'd never let that happen again.

———

The chilly night air stung my cheeks, taking the edge off the dizziness in my head as we stumbled from the shipping container where the others had entered. Being surrounded by violence went to my head faster than any alcohol could.

"Are you hurt?" I turned to West, looking him up and down to assess the damage. It was hard to tell when he looked like he'd stepped straight out of a slasher movie. When you fight on adrenaline, you rarely realize you're hurt until it's too late.

"Don't worry." He grinned smugly, wearing his blood-soaked shirt like a badge of honor. "None of it's mine."

The three of us were lucky to only have split knuckles, a few scrapes, and bruises. We didn't have Hiram's head on a pole, but we'd walked through the fires of hell and left the shipping yard before the action spilled above ground. I wouldn't let my guard down until we were racing down the highway back to the neon lights of Lapland.

Our limo was already waiting at the gates. As we ducked under the barbed wire, the limo door flew open and Vixen burst out. At first, I thought she was glad to see us, but, as we got closer, it was clear she was frantic.

"Where's Mieko?" she screeched. "Where the fuck is she?"

A sickening dread stalked my stomach.

"You mean she's not back here with you?" Rocky asked.

Bile rose in my throat, but I didn't allow myself to react. I couldn't.

"You!" Vixen turned on West, baring her teeth like a Rottweiler. "You were supposed to be protecting her! Where is she?"

"She was right by me the whole time until a guy threw a punch. I told her to run because hell broke loose," West explained. "They were coming at me from all angles. She needed to get out, but she was nowhere near the fight. I thought she left…"

"We need to go back," Vixen screamed. "She's still inside. We need to find her!"

Rocky caught her by the waist, holding her back as she kicked out.

"You're not going back in there," Zander said, blocking her path. "It's not safe."

"I'm not leaving without her!" Vixen thrashed around in Rocky's arms. "We can't!"

"Let's all calm down—"

"Get the fuck off me, Red," she blasted, silencing his attempts at being a mediator. "Or I swear to God I'll fucking shoot you!"

She grappled around in her jacket with fumbling fingers, looking for her weapon. Rocky was already two steps ahead. He grabbed the gun and threw it for Zander to pick up. His experience as a pickpocket during his teenage years came in handy after all.

"When's the last time you saw her, West?" Vixen demanded. Her anger dissolved into a blind panic as her breathing grew short and erratic. "What about the rest of you? Where the fuck is she?"

I cast my mind back. I last saw Mieko at the bar with West right before the fight broke out. If West had told her to go, there was only one reason she wouldn't have left straight away.

Bryce.

"We were at the bar, things were getting heavy, and I told her to leave," West said. His eyes shone as he tried to remember what happened. The hot anger that had taken over his body to get him through the fight was replaced with anguish. "There was a clear path to the stairs. She had time to get away."

"We got out the moment the fight broke loose," Rocky said. His voice shook. "We didn't see her anywhere, man."

"Why didn't she leave when I told her to?" West mumbled, scrubbing his face with his hands. "We all know she has that weird thing with blood."

Vixen narrowed her eyes and snarled, "Not everyone enjoys showering in it like you."

Before she castrated West, I had to step in and say what I knew. Mieko wanted to give Bryce the contract. That had to be the reason she didn't leave when West told her to. The thought of doing something for Vixen would be the only thing that would have made her stay in a place where she was unprotected and vulnerable.

"I think I know why she didn't leave right away."

Everyone turned to stare at me.

"What?" Vixen jolted like I'd slapped her. "You better start talking, Candy. We're not talking about anyone here. She is my fucking fiancée. The girl I love!"

This isn't how I wanted this secret to come out, but I couldn't avoid it —
not now that Mieko was missing, and it felt like leeches were sucking my
emotions dry from the inside. Bryce wouldn't have stuck around during a
fight, either. He was too frail. Could they have left together?

"She went to speak to Bryce," I said.

"Bryce?" Vixen's eyebrows drew together. "Why the fuck would she
speak to *him*?"

Zander's stare burned into me. Vixen wasn't the only one looking like
they wanted to pin me to the side of the limo and rip my fingernails off.

"She was delivering a signed copy of a contract. His will."

"*His will*?" Zander spat.

"But I wouldn't sign it," Vixen stammered, shaking her head. "I told him
that at the restaurant."

"Actually…" I took a deep breath, readying for the fallout. "You did sign
it, but you didn't know it."

"What have you done, Candy?" Zander murmured.

The bitter fury in his eyes didn't make me feel bad, but the flash of disappointment at how I'd kept this from him made me want to curl into a ball. I
thought I made the right decision, but all I could think about now was how
stupid I'd been to enlist Mieko's help. If anything happened to her, I'd never
forgive myself.

My cell started vibrating like crazy in my pocket, sparing me from the
interrogation for the time being.

I looked at the screen. "It's Mieko."

"Answer it," Vixen screeched. "Put it on speaker!"

Hearing from her wouldn't prevent me from having to explain the deal I
made with Bryce, but all that mattered was her safety. As soon as I heard her
voice, I could deal with the rest later.

"Mieko?" I said into the phone. "Where are you?"

A cold laugh echoed down the line, freezing my blood solid. All the color
drained from Rocky's face as quickly as West's flushed red in anger. Vixen's
shaking hand rose to cover her mouth as she let out a whimper, which
sounded even more terrifying coming from the woman who never liked to
show weakness.

"Hello, Kitty," Hiram purred down the line. "You'd better listen closely if
you ever want to see your pretty little friend again. I took a shine to her last
time we met, remember?"

"Put Mieko on the phone." The words felt like sandpaper in my dry
mouth. "I want to hear from her myself."

Hiram tutted. "Where are your manners, Kitty?"

"Put her on, Hiram," I said, then took a deep breath. "I need to know
she's still alive."

Vixen's knees buckled. Rocky's hands were all that kept her standing.

"She is," Hiram replied, then paused. "For now."

"Prove it," I spat.

"Candy?" Mieko's voice croaked. "Tell Vixen I—"

"That's enough," Hiram hissed, taking back control. "Are you satisfied now?"

The sound of a scuffle in the background rooted me to the spot. I knew what kind of torture Hiram inflicted on his prisoners. Mieko was innocent. The only thing she was guilty of was trying to get answers for the woman she loved. Whatever happened to her would be my fault.

"Where are you?" I asked, trying to keep my voice steady despite my shaking hands. "What do you want?"

"You've been avoiding me for so long, Kitten," Hiram drawled. "Why is it you only speak to me when you want something? I thought we'd made amends after your wedding day. How do you think it made me feel when you disappeared?"

"I don't want to play your games, Hiram," I said. "Tell me what you want me to do."

"I believe you've taken something that belongs to me," Hiram said. "And I want it back."

Zander snatched the phone from me. "Name your fucking price."

"Zander Briarly, we meet again." Hiram's playful attitude changed instantly and his voice turned glacial. "I cannot be bought."

"Then what do you want?" Zander snarled. "I've helped you before. I can help you again."

"Taking my Kitten away again was never part of the plan," Hiram hissed. "I do not trust Briarly's."

I wrestled the phone from Zander before he crushed it in his fist and blew our chances at helping Mieko.

"Why don't we do a trade?" I suggested.

I had an idea, but it was fucking crazy…

"I will be sad to let her go." Hiram sighed dramatically. "I'm already starting to get attached. Do you think I want you back after everything you've done to me, Kitty?"

"I wasn't talking about me." The only thing left to do was play his bluff. "The Blackbird for Mieko. It's a fair trade. What would happen to your business operations if he died?"

The guys gawked at me like I'd lost my mind. Maybe I had, but it's the only ammunition we had.

"Isn't this nice, Kitten?" Hiram said. He hadn't hung up, so I'd piqued his interest. That was good. "We're negotiating like the old times. You've always known how to drive a hard bargain."

Vixen's eyes widened hopefully as I asked, "Do we have a deal, then?"

Hiram paused. "I don't know if I'm ready to give up one of my new toys so fast..."

"You sick bastard," Vixen's screams echoed around the clearing. "I'll fucking—"

Rocky put his hand over her mouth to silence her as tears ran down her cheeks. The more value Hiram thought Mieko had, the harder he would make it.

"I need time to consider your proposal, Kitten." Hiram chuckled. "Let me sleep on it."

"Don't think about it for too long," I threatened. "You know how impatient I can be. And don't fucking hurt her, or I will return the Blackbird lobotomized. He won't be any good to you then."

"I'll speak to you in the morning, Kitten," Hiram said. "Sleep well."

The line went dead.

There would be no sweet dreams tonight, only nightmares.

Hiram had Mieko…

"What was that?" Zander snarled. "You shouldn't have made the deal."

"Why?" Vixen rubbed her red eyes. "Red told me the Blackbird is locked in the bunker with Giles. We'll swap them back."

"That's not entirely accurate…" Rocky squirmed. "I didn't have time to fill you in on the whole story."

No fucking shit. He missed the most important part — you know, the part about him not being *alive* anymore. Vixen didn't pay Rocky any attention, though.

"Maybe the Blackbird could help us?" Vixen muttered. "He must know where Hiram is holding her, right? What's the point in having the bastard in our pockets if he can't feed us information when we need it?"

Not only was I responsible for Mieko being snatched from under our fucking noses, but I'd killed the only person who would have been able to help us. My earlier victory left a sour taste in my mouth.

"There's a small problem with that," I said, strapping on my big girl panties and preparing for the worst. Whatever Vixen threw at me couldn't be worse than what I'd put myself through. "The Blackbird is dead."

If there was a gold medal for monumental fuck-ups, I'd be standing on the podium getting showered in shit.

"What?" Vixen stammered. "How? When?"

"I killed him tonight."

I liked to believe every mistake could be a learning experience, but this was not one of them. I'd fucked up. Badly. Watching Vixen's face fall and her mascara drip down her face crushed my heart. I was the worst fucking person in the world. A true monster.

Vixen's eyes bulged in horror. "You killed the only bargaining chip we have."

"It was a…mistake," I murmured. I caught Zander's eye and hung my head. "I see that now."

Any other explanation would seem petty. Zander was right. I'd been reckless, and karma had come to whip my fucking ass. I thought I'd been doing a bad thing for the right reasons, but there was nothing good about me. No matter how hard I tried to do better, I still screwed everything up. I'd spent so long trying to convince myself there was some good in me somewhere. Convincing myself that I *deserved* to be free. Did I really belong with Hiram? Was becoming a monster and staying with him my true destiny?

"A mistake?" Vixen laughed hollowly. "How many more mistakes are you going to make, Candy? You've nearly destroyed us all, and if Mieko dies, then her blood is on your fucking hands."

She was right. Everyone and everything I touched turned to fucking ash. All the people I got close to died eventually: Crystal, Q… The Sevens would be next. I was a human version of a fly zapper, and it'd be their twitching bodies lying on the ground when the end came.

"Why make a deal with him?" Vixen asked as Rocky pulled her trembling body close. "We have nothing."

"Hiram won't kill her," I said, hoping to sound more confident than I felt. "Not when Mieko is still useful to him. He wants to get to me and, as long as he thinks the Blackbird is alive, he won't harm her."

"You're right." Zander nodded slowly in understanding. "Making that deal is the only assurance we have that he'll keep her alive."

Death wasn't the only thing we had to fear. There were fates far worse and, with most of Hiram's prisoners, being put out of your misery seemed like a five-star holiday in the Bahamas compared to the alternative. I squeezed my nails into my palm until I drew blood, trying to push away the flashbacks. Images that haunted my nightmares. We had to bring Mieko back before irreversible damage was done.

"The fight breaking out at the Maven was no accident," West said. "He knew we were there. He wanted to keep us distracted."

How hadn't I seen it? Hiram was the master of smoke and mirrors. A fight breaking out right where we were standing was too convenient to happen out of chance. When we were looking one way, Hiram moved in the other direction. He couldn't have known Mieko was going to be at the Maven tonight, but he saw her and seized the opportunity when it presented itself.

"It doesn't matter how he did it," I snapped, putting an end to the speculation. All that mattered was how we hadn't protected her when we should have. "The only thing that does is that he believes the Blackbird is still alive, and we have to keep it that way. We'll come up with a plan."

If he suspected the Blackbird was dead, Mieko would already be heading across the border with his human trafficking connections if he spared her life.

"What will he do to her when he finds out?" Vixen's bottom lip trembled, making her suddenly seem fragile. "If anything happens to her, I don't know what I'll..."

"Nothing will happen to her," Rocky reassured in soothing tones. "We'll make sure of that."

"How can you say that?" Vixen shook him off. "Look what happened to Candy. She was stuck with him for years, and you couldn't get her back."

Rocky's face fell. He opened his mouth to answer but no words came out. He couldn't argue with her on that.

"Red's not alone this time." West stepped up. "Mieko has all of us."

"What good were you in the Maven?" She snorted. "We paired her with you because you were supposed to protect her. He kidnapped her on your fucking watch."

"West made the right call by telling her to run," Zander said sharply. "There was no other way. Mieko knew what she was getting herself into when she stepped into the Maven tonight. We can't turn on each other now."

"Of course you'd say that," Vixen mocked. "I bet you're glad it's *my* girl he took this time and not yours."

Whenever Vixen got angry, her words were like poisonous bullets. Her syllables penetrated the skin multiple times, causing three times the damage that any wound would do. Her words didn't cut deep because of what she was saying. They cut deep because they were all true.

"This is my fault," I said. West tried to help her, but I'd sent her straight into danger. "I asked her to help get your signature for Bryce's will. If you want to blame anyone, blame me."

"I do," Vixen snarled. "And if anything happens to her, then I'm holding you responsible. Until then, you'd better bring her fucking back to me."

"I will," I promised, hoping she could tell from my face how sincere I was. "If it's the last thing I do."

"What do we do now?" Vixen threw her hands in the air in despair. "Sit and wait?"

"He'll be in touch again," West said. "He wants to keep us waiting."

"But we can't just do nothing." Vixen whirled around and shoved him, then started pounding her small fists into his chest. He let her, taking every punch and not flinching. "We have to do something. Mieko is with him!"

"The Blackbird may be dead," Zander said. "But there is someone who could help."

Rocky raised his eyebrows. "Do you think he's sobered up enough?"

"No!" Vixen's mouth fell open, dropping her fists like a deflated balloon. "Do you really expect *him* to help us? He burned down our fucking house."

"You didn't see him tonight, Vix," Rocky said. "He wanted to help."

"Or was he setting us up, like he has so many times before?" she seethed. "We wouldn't have set foot in that fucking cave if it wasn't for him."

That may be true, but it was my actions that caused Hiram to do what he did. I *left* him. I *betrayed* him. If Mieko never helped the Sevens get me back, Hiram would never have taken her. She was an amazing friend and was suffering because of me. If I hadn't made a deal with Bryce or agreed to work with the Sevens, they'd all be safe. This was all on me.

"We'll get the truth out of him," Zander said. "He's the only lead we have."

West cracked his knuckles. "A chat with the Blackbird will have shown him how serious we can be."

"Cooperation is not optional." Zander's mouth pressed into a thin, menacing line, and opened the door of the limo. "Let's go and speak to my cousin."

———

No one spoke on the ride back to Lapland. Vixen shot me menacing glares from her seat, but I couldn't look at her. She was furious, but it masked something else. Fear. Next to her, Rocky tried to talk about our next steps, but Zander shut him down. Our driver didn't hear our conversation outside, but we couldn't trust anyone else with the information. West buried his head in his hands, and Zander drummed his fingers on his knee like he was playing out different scenarios in his mind. We all came to the Maven together, but we were leaving one person behind. How had it all gone so wrong?

Returning to the empty club felt surreal. Zander led the way to the bunker underneath the club. As we walked, he lowered his voice so only I could hear.

"Why did you make a deal with my father?" he asked.

I didn't answer. "The only thing that matters is finding Mieko."

What was the point in telling him what deal I struck with Bryce and why? Finding out where Bryce buried her mom's body wouldn't numb Vixen's pain if Hiram posted Mieko's body parts in the mail.

After going down the hidden staircase, we arrived at the bunker. Zander punched the code into the keypad, and the steel door swung open to reveal Giles. He sat sniveling in the corner with his back pressed against the wall. It looked like he was trying to melt inside the brick. Opposite him, plastic sheeting wrapped around the Blackbird's corpse. The sides of the plastic had fallen away, revealing his ghostly face and dead eyes.

Giles's eyes widened at seeing us standing in the doorway, but he didn't move. West went to the small kitchen area and started to fill an ice bucket with water. He'd spilled enough blood, so he had a different interrogation technique in mind.

"Hello, cousin," Zander greeted him. "It's time we talk."

"But I told you all I knew!" Giles's tone was already pleading, and he started to rock back and forth. "Did you find him? Was he there?"

"Oh, he was there alright," Vixen spat. "And he took my girl. Did you have anything to do with that?"

"N-n-no!" Giles trembled, shaking his head wildly. "All I know is that he was going to the party. That's it."

"So, all of this is just a coincidence?" Vixen snarled. "Do you expect us to believe you didn't know your darling Uncle was signing away your inheritance? Sending us to the Maven where Hiram would be waiting seems like it'd be good revenge."

"What do you mean?" Giles's whisper made him sound like a small child. "Signing it away? There's nothing left to sign..."

"Do you think Bryce trusted you with everything?" Vixen mocked. "Uncle Bryce has been keeping secrets from you. All of his money is now going to me, and I'm going to enjoy spending every fucking dime."

"Tell us what you know about Hiram," Zander said, sending Vixen a glare to stand down. "You've been working for him lately. Is there somewhere he stays nearby?"

"I-I-I don't know anything," Giles stammered. "I swear—"

"West." Zander motioned for him to come forward. "Do the honors."

West grabbed Giles by the scruff of his neck and plunged his head into the ice bucket. Giles thrashed around, but West held him there. Seconds later, West yanked him out. Giles gasped for air, spitting water from his mouth.

"All you need to do is tell us the truth," Zander said. He took a seat on the reclining sofa opposite Giles like he was watching a sports game. "Tell us what you know, and this stops."

"You know everything," Giles wailed.

Zander flicked his wrist, and West plunged him into the water again. When Giles came up for air, he was heaving like a dying fish. Waterboarding was one way to sober someone up.

"I swear I don't know. He used to call me and tell me what to do. He didn't tell me anything. I don't know," Giles begged, putting his hands together in a prayer position. "Please!"

Zander gestured again, and West rammed his head back into the bucket.

"We're giving you a chance here," West growled as he pulled him up above the surface. "Other people wouldn't be so kind."

"I want Hiram gone as much as you do," Giles stuttered through chattering teeth as soon as he caught his breath. "I came here tonight because I wanted to help."

"You've done nothing to help us before," Vixen sneered, kneeling to get on his level. "Why start now?"

"If you're going to kill me," Giles said, "then get it over with already."

"I think he's telling the truth, boss," Rocky said begrudgingly, flopping down next to Zander on the sofa with a sense of defeat.

I nodded in agreement. Giles was a spineless coward. He'd have already squealed if he knew something. If this wasn't the same man whose stupidity caused the pregnant love of his life to be burned alive, I might just feel sorry for him.

"When did you last hear from Hiram directly?" I asked. If I could get a sense of his usual movements, maybe I could try to think about where he'd go? I didn't think it was likely he'd take Mieko back to Blackthorne Towers. That was too far away.

"He called me to ask if..." Giles's face crumpled, "Briarly Manor was gone."

"You've heard nothing since then?" I pressed.

Giles shook his head and started to sob uncontrollably.

Zander rose from the sofa. "That's all for tonight," he said, signaling for the rest of us to leave.

"What about me?" Giles blubbered. He shakily pointed at the Blackbird's corpse. If he'd ever had a proper conversation with the Blackbird when he was alive, he'd realize that sharing a room with him dead was better. "Don't leave me with him."

"You're not going anywhere," Zander snarled. "You could still be helpful."

Giles didn't argue. The old him would have tried to fight back, but he had no ounce of spirit left. Until we had Mieko back, we needed to keep him under our watch. He knew too much.

As soon as we were back in the penthouse, Vixen paced back and forth. "What now?" she demanded. "If we can't get to them before morning, what can we do?"

"We'll come up with something," I said.

"I'm going to call all the hotels and hospitals in town. I'll call everyone I know," Vixen muttered. "Someone might have seen them."

"Do you want us to help?" Rocky offered.

It was a pointless activity. Hiram was too clever and well-resourced, but she wanted to do something, and I couldn't blame her for that.

"The only thing all of you can do is stay the fuck out of my way," Vixen said. "All of you. You've already done enough."

Her reaction was justified, but it still stung as she slammed the door behind her and locked herself in her room. If the situation was reversed, I'd already have done a lot worse.

"Hey, C." Rocky put his arm around my shoulders. "It's okay. We'll get her back."

"You don't have to keep saying that," I snapped, stepping out of his reach. "Vixen's not around anymore. We all know what Hiram's capable of. Even if we get her back, and that's a huge fucking *if*, we both know it's what will have happened to her while she's with him that's the problem."

Rocky always tried to look on the positive side, but optimism only led to disappointment. The rising sun made the white kitchen glow, but Hiram wouldn't be in touch until later. He was nocturnal and lived for the night. He'd keep us dangling on a thread for news.

"You've come back from worse than this, C," Rocky said.

I walked over to the sofa and collapsed down.

"I don't know how long I can keep doing this," I admitted, my voice cracking. There's only so long someone can run from their past. How much fighting can you do before you lose all hope? "Wherever I go, he'll follow."

I should accept it. I'd been swimming against the tide for so long, I hadn't realized I was still miles away from shore, and water was filling my lungs. There was no escaping Hiram. Hell, I'd tried. But how many more people had to get hurt? How many more people would I let die because of me?

"I won't let him hurt you," Rocky said. He sat down and wrapped his arms around me. I didn't have the energy to resist. "You'll have to shoot me again."

"Don't you see?" I murmured. "All of this destruction is because of me. People are dead. Hiram has Mieko, and all of this is my fault. All because I dared to defy him."

"This isn't your fault," West said, sitting on my other side. "This is on Hiram. That bastard is the only one to blame."

"What about killing the Blackbird, huh?" I asked. I looked into West's eyes to see guilt reflected, matching my own. "Vix was right. I killed the only fucking chance we had of getting Mieko back."

"You didn't know what he was going to do, C," Rocky insisted, stroking my shoulder.

"I should have been smarter," I said. "Hiram has been right about me all along. I'm fucking broken, and nothing will fix it. Everything I touch falls apart."

"That's him talking," Rocky said. "You were a kid when he took you. That sick fuck brainwashed you. You didn't ask for this life. This isn't what you wanted."

"That doesn't matter," I snapped. Didn't he know wanting something wasn't enough in our world? "I'll do anything if it means getting her back. I'll do whatever it takes. I'll go back to Blackthorne Towers and live in his fucking dungeon if I have to."

Zander had been standing at the window, looking out on the street below, but spun around with ferocity at my words.

"And mean everything we've fought for has been for nothing?" Zander snarled. "Cupid died because he wanted to keep you safe. Do you want his death to be in vain? For things to go back to how they were before?"

"I can't lose anyone else," I confessed, unable to stop tears from falling. "I don't think I'd come back from it. It'll destroy me."

"That's why you don't belong with him," Zander said. He ducked down in front of me, putting his hands on my knees and staring into my face, leaving me with nowhere to hide. "That's why you are one of us. You put those you care about before yourself. Hiram would never understand that."

"You're the strongest woman I know," West said, wiping my tears away with his thumb. "You can't let him win. That's not who you are."

"He's already won, West." I sniffed. "He always does."

"Not this time," West growled. "You have us by your side."

"But we can't do this without you," Rocky said. "We need you. You know Hiram better than anyone."

"That's why I know we can't beat him," I muttered. My heart sank. "No one can. He will never let me go."

A black cloud descended over my thoughts, taking me back to my first months in Blackthorne Towers. Instead of being whisked away by a handsome prince, the devil kidnapped me. He forced me to obey. I could still feel the chains around my ankles that had been a regular feature in my life during that time. The cuffs may be gone, but Hiram still held my brain in a chokehold. A prison I couldn't escape from.

"If you give up now," Zander said, "we may as well order Mieko's tombstone and be done with it. That is, if we find the pieces of her to bury and put her back together like a jigsaw."

It wouldn't be the first time Hiram thought a treasure hunt of limbs was a good idea.

"Are you serious, Zander?" Rocky looked at him in disgust. "Our girl's hurting here and you're saying shit like that? Just look at her. She's fucking shaking."

"It's the truth, and Candy knows it," Zander said, squeezing my knees, then spoke to me directly, "The pain you're feeling is nothing compared to how you'll feel if we don't act now."

His words jolted me back to the present.

I blinked my tears away and took a deep breath. "Zander's right."

We were on a ticking clock. The only thing I'd regret more than Hiram taking her would be not trying to get her back.

Zander grinned smugly. "I always am."

He pulled me out of the pit with a few words. I may have questioned myself, but Zander didn't. He held me to account and saw me for the person I wanted to be — not a victim, but a motherfucking survivor.

I scowled at him. "Now is not the time to be an arrogant ass."

Zander's smile widened. He knew he had me. He reminded me of what really mattered. Mieko. The Sevens. They were my anchor in an endless sea with no horizon in sight.

"And she's back," Zander declared. "We need you to stay with us, little one. Can you do that?"

I nodded. "Mieko needs me."

"What are we going to do to bring Mieko home?" Zander asked. "What is Hiram's next move?"

I put myself in Hiram's shoes. I'd been around him during hostage situations in the past. What would he be thinking?

"We wait," I said without hesitation and against all of my other instincts. "He'll be in contact soon."

"How do you know?" Rocky asked.

"This isn't my first front-row seat at a Hiram circus," I said, then jumped up as another idea came to me. "In the meantime, I'm going to need all the make-up you can find and Blackbird's body moved to the freezer."

West's mouth fell open. "*Make-up?*"

"I think the Blackbird could do with a makeover." I rolled my eyes sarcastically, then turned serious. "Come on, West. Hiram will want to see proof of life."

"It may not be perfect," Zander said. "But it should buy us enough time..."

We sprung into action. Rocky set to work clearing the large chest freezer in the club's kitchen while West lugged the Blackbird's dead weight upstairs.

"Here's your delivery," West said, shoving the corpse into the open freezer.

My nose wrinkled at the smell. The bunker was damp, but not cold enough to stop decomposition from setting in.

Rocky grimaced, looking down at the Blackbird's face. "You've got a lot of work to do."

I'm no make-up artist, but Crystal taught me a thing or two. Returning the color to his face should help. I forced the Blackbird's eyes shut. Having to do this would be bad enough without his stare judging my choice of palette. The guys gathered around to watch as I lined up the products I found in the dressing room.

"You should try to rest," I told them. This was no makeover show. "You'll need your energy."

"I'm not leaving you," West insisted fiercely. "None of us are."

"You need to take time to recharge," I said. West had spent the entire night letting loose like a rampant bull. As much as he looked like a super-hero, he was still human. "Hiram will not be there alone, and we need to be at the top of our game. Despite what he said, he won't call until later in the day. He works at night."

"We'll take shifts," Zander said. "I'll take the first one."

Rocky scowled, but I could tell from his heavy eyes that he was exhausted.

"We'll wake you if we hear anything," I promised, sensing his hesitation.

The big man pouted but didn't argue. The two of them respected Zander and his orders enough to follow what he said.

When the others left, Zander sat silently and watched as I checked foundation shades against the Blackbird's skin to select a good match. I settled for a beige that took out the bluish hue. I used a beauty blender to pat the foundation into the Blackbird's sunken features. It felt like applying paint to sandpaper, but it was oddly therapeutic. It reminded me of when Crystal and I used to do each other's make-up. She was a professional, but she let me practice looks on her sometimes. I'd always found it easier to apply on other people.

"You can sleep too, you know," I said to Zander as I added pink blush to give the Blackbird a lively glow. Nothing seemed to be working. Let's face it, the ugly fucker would never have made it as a supermodel. "I don't need a babysitter, and I'm pretty sure you don't want a contouring lesson."

"Are you going to tell me now why you made a deal with my father?"

He wouldn't let it drop.

"I promise I'll tell you when this is all over," I said. "All you need to know is I did it for a good reason, and so did Mieko. Can you trust me?"

"I trust you with my life," Zander said. "But I don't trust my father."

"Zander—"

He held up his hand to silence me. "But for you, I'll do anything. As long as you try not to do anything else stupid without telling me first."

Tonight showed me what it meant to be part of a team and the importance of working together. Since I'd known the Sevens, I'd constantly defied Zander at every turn. Sometimes it was because I felt I knew better, other times it was because I didn't want to give anyone control again. Hiram showed me how orders can be used for pain and punishment, but it was different with Zander.

After seeing how he punished himself and the effects of not working together, I finally saw the truth. Zander didn't give orders and commands because he liked it. He did it because he thought of everyone. He wanted to keep us all safe.

"I'll try," I said. "I promise."

"I don't want to change you, Candy," he said, running a finger down my cheek. "But I want you to trust me. I want to do this together."

I screwed up my nose at the Blackbird's face.

"Do you think this will work?" I asked.

Zander peered at my handiwork.

"We'll make it work," he said. "There's no other way."

Twenty-Four

A text notification made me jump. Why did those fuckers let me sleep? Someone had moved me upstairs to the comfortable sofas and laid a blanket over me. Rocky, the most likely offender, snored quietly in ignorance at my feet.

"Why did you let me sleep?" I roared, throwing a cushion at Rocky's face and snatching up my phone. It was noon. Exhaustion must have taken over after the grand makeover was complete.

"You needed to rest too," Zander said from behind me. He was already wide awake and alert. West wasn't around, so I assumed he was resting or downstairs. Zander nodded at the cell. "Who is it?"

Every muscle in my body ached, but fierce resolve sharpened my senses. We may have only had a few hours of rest, but your body conserved energy in ways you didn't realize were possible during times of crisis.

I unlocked the screen and saw a message from an unknown number.

"It's from a burner," I said. Nausea stirred in my stomach as the circle icon indicated something was loading. "It's a photo."

Hiram would have destroyed Mieko's cell after they made the last call. He wouldn't want to risk us tracking him.

Zander peered over my shoulder. "Well?"

"It's still loading," I hissed back.

A download speed this slow should be made illegal. What was the point of modern technology if you couldn't open a picture at the speed of light?

We waited. I didn't take a breath until the pixels unfurled to reveal a horror scene. In the image, Mieko sat on a damp concrete floor with her legs curled underneath her to keep warm. Her wrists and ankles were bound with rope. A gag was tightly wrapped around her mouth, making her cheeks bulge. A newspaper was propped up by her feet with today's date. Evidence of her being alive... for now, anyway. Hiram's caption under the photo was an invitation: *'Your turn'*.

"Zoom in," Zander urged.

Apart from the rope burn on her wrists, a few grazes to her knees, and dark bags under her eyes, she had no other visible wounds. But a camera lens couldn't catch everything. While I scanned for injuries, Rocky's attention lingered on something else.

"It's the local paper," Rocky said. "We need to check that it's not a fake."

"They could still be close by," I murmured.

As I zoned in on Mieko's eyes, I sensed her terror through the screen. Mental wounds ran deeper than physical ones. I recognized her look of fear because it's all I used to see whenever I looked at myself in the mirror. The look of a person who isn't sure whether they would live or die.

"I need you to concentrate," Zander said. His arm on my shoulder made me blink hard, stopping me from spiraling into my memories. "What would Hiram have taught you to do if this was a job?"

I steadied my breathing, summoning the Kitten to the forefront. She is who I needed to be today. The beautiful woman in the picture was my best friend and someone I adored, but I couldn't allow my emotions to cloud my judgment. Zander approached business with ruthless precision, and I had to do the same.

Think like Hiram, Kitty.

This is the only lead we'd had since she was taken. A clue to her whereabouts could be sitting in front of us. We needed to find it. I inspected every inch of the background: a gray tiled floor and walls, no clock, no sign of light... they could be in a fucking spaceship.

"It's definitely not Blackthorne Towers," I confirmed. I knew every godforsaken inch of that hell hole, but knowing where it wasn't wouldn't help us. My hopes sank like a brick in quicksand. Recognizing *something* would be better than nothing.

"In that case, if the paper is genuine, that puts them still in the area," Zander said, echoing my suspicions. "We need to mobilize."

Zander radioed down to West over a walkie-talkie to request he join us. The poor guy was currently having the pleasure of babysitting the Blackbird. He was the worst kind of stiffy to wake up to in the morning.

"We need to show Vixen," I said.

"Do you really think she's up to seeing this?" Rocky asked, running an aggravated hand through his hair. Unlike Zander, Rocky didn't hide his emotions well. Chewing his lip until it was red raw showed his worry.

"She's been through hell and back. I don't want this to tip her over the edge…"

"See what?" Vixen emerged in the doorway. Considering she'd been avoiding everyone, she knew how to pull a Bloody Mary at the perfect time. "What is it?"

"Hiram sent a photo," I replied.

Hiding it from her wouldn't help.

"Show me," she demanded.

Her eyes were bloodshot and her cheeks pink and blotchy, as if she'd rubbed off the top layers of skin. She clenched her teeth to fight tears as she looked at the photo, but didn't let them fall. She didn't have any left to spill.

West entered wearing last night's clothes to see Vixen clutching onto the cell tightly as if it were Mieko's hand. "He's been in touch?"

I nodded.

"Does anyone recognize it?" West asked, looking over Vixen's shoulder. "The place?"

"If we did, we wouldn't be sitting here," I snapped.

"Fuck," West cursed, whirling around and punching a hole in the wall. "What do we do?"

Vixen ran a finger over Mieko's face on the screen. Her voice broke as she said, "She looks so scared."

I rose from the sofa and took her trembling frame into my arms before I changed my mind. Vixen's world hung in the balance, but I wanted her to know we were going to do everything we could. I expected her to shove me away, or slap me, or break my arm... but she didn't. Her arms closed around me.

"I'm so sorry, Vix," I murmured, stroking her back and holding her tight.

She sniffed and squeezed hard. "I know."

"I promise I'll make it right," I whispered. "I'll make this right or die trying. We'll bring her back."

A few seconds later, she pulled away and nodded sharply. The others hadn't heard my words, but she had. Her nod told me all I needed to know: she believed me. I wouldn't let her or Mieko down. Not again.

Vixen wiped her eyes, refusing to submit to her emotions. "What do we do next?"

"Red, go and find a paper," Zander ordered. "When it checks out, we will do what Hiram says."

Rocky nodded, already sprinting out the door.

I grimaced. "It's time for a photo shoot."

"I'll help," Vixen said. Her artistic flair made her the best person to take the shot. "Tell me what you need."

The Blackbird spent his life trying to blend into the shadows. In death, he'd be immortalized under our flashlight.

"We need to hurry," I said. The more irritated Hiram got, the worse it'd be for Mieko. "Hiram isn't known for his fucking patience. Let's stage a shoot."

———

"He was a pain in the ass alive, but he's even worse dead," West complained.

He stopped to wipe his brow after having to heave the body from the freezer and lie it on the kitchen floor. The nondescript background could be anywhere. Unfortunately for West, trying to pose a corpse that had already gone into rigor mortis used more energy than a triathlon. We were lucky his body hadn't frozen to the inside of the freezer already, but West still had to break a few bones to get him in position.

"Here's the paper," Rocky said, returning at the perfect time. After comparing the headlines, it confirmed our earlier suspicions. "It's a match."

Vixen dabbed extra concealer under the Blackbird's eyes as West almost snapped his fingers off trying to close them around the inky pages. Vixen would have to pick her angle well to make it look convincing, but there are only so many ways to polish a turd.

"Ready?" I asked Vixen.

She took the picture and held it out for us to inspect. "What do you think?"

"What about his eyes?" Rocky frowned. "No one's gonna buy that."

"Do we have any colored contacts?" I asked. The dancers made use of them for special performances. "That might liven them up a little."

Vixen scoffed. "I'll Photoshop the fuck out of them in perfect time, and Hiram won't even know."

"Who knew that class in juvie would come in handy?" Rocky said.

We all glared at him.

"How long do you need?" Zander asked her.

"I can work fast," she said. "I'll send it in five."

"Send the photo to me before you go," Zander ordered.

She frowned in confusion. "Why?"

"While we wait," Zander said, "there's still one person we have to show the photo to..."

Vixen did as he asked then took the phone and vanished upstairs. A lot was riding on the picture. Hiram had to believe the Blackbird was alive to organize an exchange.

———

"Gross." My nose wrinkled at the smell of the underground bunker, and I avoided looking in the direction of the ice bucket where I suspected the odor was coming from. Giles's shit, and the permeating smell of death, would reek the place out for months with its lack of airflow.

Rocky held his stomach like he was going to vomit.

West grinned and clapped Rocky on the back. "You need a stronger stomach."

"I can't help it," Rocky gasped between breaths, managing to get control of himself again. "It smells like someone died in here."

West snickered. Well, it wasn't far from the truth. Next time the Sevens built underground, Zander needed to factor an underground prison into his floor plan instead of a man cave.

"Good morning, Giles," Zander said.

Giles hadn't moved from the spot where we'd left him. He flinched at the sight of West. If I wasn't intent on bringing Mieko home, I'd have made a smart quip about how far the lofty had fallen. As much as I loved it when bad guys got their retributions, there was something pathetic about the creature he'd become.

"Did you find her?" Giles croaked through chapped lips. "Vixen's girlfriend?"

"Not yet," I replied. "We need you to look at something."

Giles's gaze shot fearfully over to West. After his interrogation last night, it'd take a while for Giles not to be jumpy around him again. Fear would work to our advantage. He had to be honest.

"We won't hurt you if you do what we ask," I said, "right, West?"

"If you insist," West grumbled.

"We need you to tell us if you recognize this place," Zander said, passing Giles the cell to show him the photograph of Mieko. He was the only one who dared get close enough to the whiff zone without a hazmat suit.

"Well?" Zander pressed. "Do you know where this is or not?"

"They could be anywhere," Giles stammered. "It's dark."

"No fucking shit," West hissed, clicking his knuckles. "This is a waste of time."

"Look again," I said.

Giles squinted at the image, and his eyes widened slightly. I'd learned to read micro-expressions, a skill honed through many hours playing poker. Something changed in Giles's face. He knew something... or thought he did.

"What is it?" I asked. "What do you see?"

"N-n-nothing," Giles stuttered too quickly.

"This isn't a time to fuck around with us, Giles," I snarled, baring my teeth. "We're not afraid to do whatever it takes to get answers. Maybe West can convince you to talk?"

West stepped forward menacingly, casting Giles in his giant shadow.

"No," Giles wailed, holding up his hands to surrender. "Okay, I'll tell you. But I can't be sure."

"You want to make Hiram pay, don't you?" I kneeled to look him in the eye and closed off my nostrils. "Think about what he did to Penelope."

"Of course I do," Giles said, shaking and pulling his knees up to his chest. "It's his fault they're both dead."

"You need to listen to every word I say very carefully," I said, talking slowly. "This is the best chance you'll ever get to bring Hiram down. The man took away your family, the woman you loved, he *tricked* you all along. You can help us make this right. Do you understand?"

He nodded, wiping his dripping nose with the back of his dirty sleeve.

"I'm going to ask you nicely one more time," I said softly. "Tell us what you think you know."

"It's too dark for me to be certain," Giles said. "There is a place out of town. I went there once with Bryce before the wedding day. He thought it'd be somewhere we could base a new operation when we started working with Hiram. He said it'd make a good production factory. It used to be a school or country club, something like that..."

"Do you know where it is?" Zander asked.

"I-I-I-I-I think so."

Zander held out his cell. He already had a GPS loaded. "Put it in."

Giles squinted, moving around the map with shaking fingers.

"I can't be sure," he said, zooming in. There was nothing labeled on the map. It was a wooded area off the highway, but the map guessed it was an hour away. "It's around here somewhere."

"This is your lucky day, Giles," I said, snatching the phone from him and standing up to get away from the smell. "If you're right about this, we may not have to kill you."

"Is that lucky?" he replied, slumping back and sinking into a pit of despair.

Most people would pity someone in this state, but we had to remember this was Giles Briarly. The man who had shot an ex-cop, albeit a crooked one, in front of us as a Christmas gift. He was no fucking angel.

Zander looked at Giles with cold indifference. "Don't burn the place down when we're gone."

As soon as we left the bunker, Zander started barking orders.

"We need to move now," he instructed. We couldn't sit around twiddling our thumbs. If Giles was correct, we had an advantage. "West, you know what to do."

West nodded. "I'll get the car."

With him behind the wheel, we could slash the estimated arrival time in half.

Vixen waited for us in the club and jumped up. She saw the purposefulness in our faces and movements, jumping to conclusions as West exited hastily. "Giles knows where she is?"

"He's not sure," I said carefully, not wanting to get her hopes up, "but it's a lead."

"I don't give a fuck what you say, Zander," Vixen said. "I'm not sitting this out. If there's a chance Mieko is with him, I'm coming with you."

Rocky opened his mouth to argue.

"Don't you fucking dare say some bullshit about protecting me," Vixen snapped, turning on him. She jabbed her finger into his chest to emphasize each word. "Or the only person who's gonna need protection is you. If it was Candy in danger, would you be happy to sit on the sidelines?"

"We don't have time to argue," Zander said. "Outside. Now."

Vixen grinned in victory, already racing out of the door with Rocky in tow. He rubbed the sore spot on his chest and grumbled, "You know that's going to bruise, right?"

As I followed, Zander grabbed my hand to pull me back.

"Before we leave," he said, "there's one more thing I have to give you."

He pulled a knife out of his suit jacket and held it out for me. I knew its slim profile instantly. The ruby adorned beauty that the Sevens had once gifted me. My secret weapon.

"You kept it." I breathed, turning it over in my hands. It felt comfortable in my grasp, and I traced my finger over the new 'Seven' engraving down its hilt. "Why give it to me now?"

The corners of his mouth twitched. "I've been saving it for a special occasion."

"Thank you," I said, looking up at him, misty-eyed. "It's perfect."

"Where are you?" Vixen's shouts from outside broke our moment. "We've got to get on the fucking road."

We nodded, hurrying out.

As soon as we slipped into the Jeep, the tires screeched as West pulled away at high speed. For all we knew, this could be the last time we ever saw Lapland.

Rocky spotted the knife in my hand and raised an eyebrow. "Who knew you could be so romantic, Zander?"

Zander didn't find it amusing. "You're lucky I just handed the blade over."

―――――

"We're getting close," West said, looking at the area where we were heading. There was only one possible turn we could make if the building was anywhere close to where Giles pointed out. "It should be around the next left."

The car took a sharp swerve, making all of us slam into the side like falling dominoes. West had been driving like we were in *Grand Theft Auto.*

"Do you think they'll still be around here?" Rocky asked, voicing what we were all thinking.

"If Hiram wanted to leave town, he'd have done it already," I replied confidently. "He'll be enjoying making us squirm. If he didn't believe the picture we sent, we'd already know about it."

"What if Giles was wrong, and this isn't the right place?" Rocky asked.

"Then we wait until Hiram gives us an address," I said. This wasn't our only opportunity, but it was the one that gave us the best odds. "But I'd rather sneak up on his ass than show up invited without the Blackbird, wouldn't you?"

Vixen hadn't said a word for the entire journey. She played with her engagement ring, twirling it around again and again. Seeing her reaction to Mieko's kidnapping only proved how true their love was. She would do anything for Mieko. They deserved their happily ever after, and I'd do whatever it took to give them it. I had watched Q change into a different person when Crystal died. I refused to let history repeat itself. It couldn't.

"We'll get her back, Vixen," I said. "We'll bring her home."

"And we'll bring that fucker to justice," West's voice came out in a low and deep rumble, fueled by bloodlust. "Once and for all."

The car continued down a badly laid road that looked like it led to nowhere. The surrounding forest grew thicker. Could Giles have been wrong? I was about to speak up when a building appeared on the horizon.

"It looks like we have company," Zander said drily, noticing five black unmarked vehicles parked ahead. Armed guards patrolled the perimeter. "This is the right place."

West's grip tightened on the wheel. "It's a good thing that this truck's bulletproof."

My cell vibrated in my pocket and a text flashed on the screen: *'See you soon.'*

I swore under my breath. "He knows we're here."

"Should we hang back?" West asked.

"No," Vixen and I roared simultaneously.

"I'm not waiting any longer," Vixen continued. "If she's in there, we need to find her."

Think like Hiram, Kitty.

"If they were going to shoot, they'd have already opened fire," I said. "That means Hiram's ready. He wants to talk."

"Whatever happens in there, we need to remember who we are," Zander said. "We are the Sevens. We go in together and out together, understood?"

"The Sevens forever," West said.

Rocky wove his fingers through mine. "Are you ready, C?"

I nodded, holding my head high. "I'm done running."

I'd been a lone wolf for so long, but I'd found my pack now. I wasn't only fighting to be free from my past, but for *our* future. A future with the Sevens. A future I realized I wanted to live for so badly that I was willing to die for it. We all were.

The main building of the old country club was crumbling apart. Half of the roof was gone, and the window frames were empty or boarded with wooden planks. Plants crawled up the walls as nature tried to take it back. The vast gardens in front of the entrance would have been impressive once, but they now resembled an overgrown jungle.

To the right of the house, guards patrolled a separate sizable outbuilding. It was in better structural condition than the main house and made up of two parts: a long thin rectangular block, that may have been a pool house, with an adjoining section. Tin sheeting had replaced the windows, meaning we couldn't get a look inside, but the heightened security signaled we were in the right location.

Our Jeep came to a halt and dust consumed the wheels in a cloud. Before we unclipped our seat belts, three guards ran over. The bastards pointed their gun barrels at our windows. I recognized their rat-like faces from my time in Blackthorne Towers. They needed a lesson on how to greet guests.

"What a charming welcoming committee, huh?" West muttered sarcastically.

I lowered the window. If they were going to shoot, the fuckers would have already tried taking out the tires. They also knew that Hiram wouldn't be happy if anyone else hurt me. That was a job for him alone.

I summoned the Kitten. My voice oozed with the entitlement of a spoilt rich brat. "Hiram is expecting me."

"He said there would be two of you," one goon said, casting a shifty glare at the other figures in the car.

"Don't pretend you don't know who I am," I warned. I flashed him my famous smile and watched him flinch at the sight of my sharp canines. "The Kitten can go wherever the fuck she likes, with whoever she wants. They are with me and, if you don't lower your weapons, it won't just be your jobs you'll lose."

They dubiously lowered their weapons. My name still meant something. They knew they were disposable. If they did something Hiram disapproved of, they'd be dead before my body was cold.

"You know it's super hot when you talk like that, right?" Rocky murmured.

"Put your tongue back in your head, Red," Vixen snapped. "This isn't foreplay!"

I kept my face impassive. I couldn't show emotion. Hiram would pounce and exploit it. I recalled a lesson he taught me.

"Let no one see what you're thinking," he'd said before he sent me on a job to extract sensitive information from a target. *"Better still, feel nothing at all. If you feel nothing, you have nothing to hide and nothing to lose."*

I nodded at the Sevens. "Let's move."

As we got out of the car, the guys formed a human shield around me and Vixen. Hiram's guards crowded around, frogmarching us to the outbuilding, hovering their fingers on triggers.

"I have orders to only let the Kitten inside," the guard standing at the entrance said.

"They all come with me," I said, planting my hands on my hips in a zero shit taking stance, "or I don't come in at all."

The guard floundered, clearly wrestling with what to do next. "Kitten, I..." He looked around at the other goons, who were also at a loss.

"You know what, this is getting old," I hissed, pushing my way past Zander to face the guard myself. I leaned close and grabbed his tiny testicles with my fist. He yelped as I squeezed hard. "You've heard the stories. Why don't you show me some respect, huh? I won't ask again. Move."

As I dropped my hold, he keeled over, clutching himself, and fell to the floor in a panting heap. We'd take each one of them out like bowling pins if we had to.

"Next time, I won't be so polite," I warned, stepping over him and opening the door for the others to pass through.

Despite the sun shining, the air in the building was heavy. It smelled damp, and the moisture made me want to clear my throat. Thin shreds of light shone through the cracks in the sheeting — enough to illuminate our path but not enough to see into the shadows at the other end of the narrow room.

"Careful!" West grabbed Vixen's arm before she stumbled over a cracked floor tile. The same tiles from the photograph.

Plastic covering concealed a large pool in the center of the room, leaving thin walkways on either side. A door at the opposite end led out of the pool house to the second half of the building.

"Mieko?" Vixen called out. "Mieko?"

Her unnerving echo bounced back to us.

"Welcome," Hiram's voice answered from the darkness. He stepped out of the door opposite us with his arms outstretched. "I don't remember sending you all an invitation."

"We saved you the trouble," I replied. My hands curled into fists at the smug grin he wore like a uniform. If I were closer, I'd tear it clean off his face and wear it as a fucking mask. "Why wait when we knew where to find you?"

"You never fail to impress me, Kitten."

"Where's Mieko?" Vixen spat. "I want to see her."

"It's impolite to make demands when you're an uninvited guest," Hiram replied coolly. "You need to learn how to fall into line."

"Easy," Rocky warned Vixen under his breath. "C knows what she's doing."

"It's a shame we couldn't see you last night," I said in a sing-song voice. "If I didn't know any better, I would have thought you were avoiding me."

Conversations with Hiram were a delicate dance. They were like a fancy dinner service. You had to move through the small talk to get to the main course.

"Did you enjoy the performance?" Hiram asked, then looked at West. "I gave one of your sidekicks a starring role. It's a shame you left so soon."

West drew himself up to full height. His muscles were bulging through his shirt, ready to tear Hiram's head off.

"We didn't feel in a party mood," I replied.

Hiram shrugged. "Pity."

"We're here to collect, Hiram." I started walking toward him. Zander stayed by my side. "Where is Mieko?"

"I've been keeping my new friend safe," Hiram purred. "Some of my guards have taken a shine to her. I can see you've shown up empty-handed, Kitten. How disappointing."

His words ignited a wild reaction in Vixen. "Let us see her," she screeched hysterically.

Hiram tutted and wagged a finger at her like he was scolding a naughty child. "If you can't stay quiet," Hiram said, "then I'll have to make you."

At his word, a group of his men stepped out of the shadows behind him and started closing in. They filed down each side of the pool, leaving us with no escape route. Hell fucking no were they getting within an inch of Vixen.

"You've already spent long enough keeping women quiet," I snarled. "Don't you think?"

"We'll see about that," Hiram said, then to his men, "leave the Kitten, but take out the spares."

Fury took over me. Hiram's goons stood no fucking chance.

The Seven men sprung into action as Hiram's guys charged, taking one each. West grabbed one by the throat and threw him against the wall with a crash like a rag doll. Zander held another in a headlock, breaking his neck in a slick maneuver without breaking a sweat. Rocky danced and dodged around his opponent, sticking out his foot to trip him up. When he was done, Rocky pinned him down and smashed his skull against the tiles. His blood flowed through the dirty grouting, turning it into a sea of red.

It was over in seconds.

"Is that all you got?" West spat on the floor.

I stepped over the growing puddle of blood spilling from the mangled head explosion. Hiram's slow, sarcastic clapping filled the space.

"Impressive." Hiram smiled, making the hairs on the back of my neck stand on end. "For small-town amateurs."

"We're no fucking amateurs," West growled.

Hiram ignored him, looking through West like he was an annoying insect. He continued to talk to me, "Tell me, did you make the Blackbird suffer? Torturing traitors used to be one of your specialties, Kitty."

My heart hammering in my chest sent blood racing to my head. I could hear it pounding through my ears like a drum.

He knew.

"We did you a favor," I replied casually. "The Blackbird was a traitor."

"And you think I didn't know?" Hiram shook his head. "You have gotten sloppy without my guidance, Kitty. Can you imagine my surprise when I retraced his steps to find a clean-up operation in place? Although, I admit I did particularly enjoy your photograph charade. I will have to frame it."

"You bastard," Rocky hissed through gritted teeth.

"I'd be careful if I were you," Hiram threatened, looking him up and down as his mouth curled into a devious snarl. "You're running out of lives, boy. When I kill you, you won't come back from the dead again."

I shot Rocky a glare. He needed to leave me to handle Hiram. I knew him best.

"We're here to make a deal," I said, starting the bargaining process. "What do you want for Mieko?"

"Don't insult my generosity, Kitten," Hiram sneered. "I've humored your rebellious phase while you've run around with a silly gang, but enough is enough. You were made for more than this. These men can't even cover up a simple murder and, now, you dare to show up empty-handed. This is not how I taught you to behave."

"I don't follow your orders anymore," I reminded him. "You released me, or have you forgotten?"

"Both of us know that contract was another one of our games." Hiram's easygoing expression turned into spine-chilling malice. I'd seen that face many times before in his workshop, right before he put a victim out of their misery. "Have you ever felt truly free, Kitten? You can't lie to me. I think you've always known you'd return to me. That's not an accident. It's because you know it's where you *belong*."

"Candy belongs with us," Zander said venomously. "She is a Seven."

"We'll see about that," Hiram clicked his fingers. "I have a surprise for you, Briarly."

At Hiram's signal, two of his deadbeat followers pulled back the pool cover. As it fell away, a bloated body floated to the surface face down. The filthy water made it hard to make out any distinguishing features. Vixen's bloodcurdling scream rattled through my core. She raced to the pool edge, grabbing the body and pulling it towards her.

Please no!

"Let this be a lesson to you all," Hiram purred victoriously. "This is what happens when people break a deal with me, Briarly."

Vixen gasped, dropping the ankle of the body and shuffling backward. She stood shivering and said, "It's Bryce."

Bryce may as well be a piece of trash floating on the water for all Zander cared. He didn't flinch, barely glancing at his father's corpse. Hiram's lip curled as he studied Zander's reaction. This is not what he'd been hoping for. The twisted fucker will have been holding out for fireworks, but Zander hadn't lit a match.

"You've made your point," Zander said with indifference. "What do you want for Mieko? Name your price."

"Like father like son," Hiram replied, searching for a weakness in Zander's cool exterior to exploit. "Only a Briarly tries to put a price on everything."

Darkness stirred behind Zander's eyes. "I'm nothing like my father."

"You're right," Hiram said with a chilling smile that looked like he was readying to attack, like a lion about to tear his prey apart. "You are far worse. Your father lied to me about his offshore accounts, but you? You broke the last deal we made and stole my *property*."

"I'm not an object you can trade," I stepped in, shaking with fury. "I'm with the Sevens because I *want* to be."

Hiram's eyes narrowed. "You don't know what you want."

"I *know* I'd rather die than come back with you."

He pretended not to hear me and shook his head. "I remember when you used to be so loyal. That gang has corrupted you. They have made you lose sight of what is important, but our bond cannot be broken."

"You've already lost her, Hiram," Zander said with a smirk. "She's one of us now."

"I will give you one final chance, Briarly," Hiram said, holding up a single finger. "I will overlook your indiscretion to make a final deal."

Zander didn't break eye contact with Hiram, asserting his dominance. Showing him how he had no fear. "You have nothing I want."

"You're wrong." Hiram pulled an envelope out of his suit pocket. "I can give you something you've been searching for. I have the answers you always wanted. This envelope contains the truth about your mother. I can tell you what your father did. I can tell you where she is buried."

"You're lying," Zander hissed, but a vein pulsed aggressively in his neck. Hiram had got under his skin like a toxic poison. He'd found Zander's vulnerability.

"Oh, Kitty. Didn't you tell him about the deal you struck with Briarly Senior?" Hiram was enjoying this. He relished having the upper hand. "Your little friend was reluctant to tell me at first, but I made her talk."

"You didn't kill Bryce because of offshore accounts," I muttered, putting the pieces together. "You killed him so you're the only one who knows Bryce's secret."

Hiram knew money wouldn't motivate Zander, but the truth about his mom? Well, that was something with immeasurable value. Hiram smirked and pulled a lighter out of his other pocket.

"Details, details!" Hiram flicked on the flames and held the envelope above it, waving it back and forth. A single jump of the flame would keep the truth buried forever. "Are you going to lose your only chance to bury your beloved mother for a girl who keeps secrets from you?"

"Is he telling the truth, Candy?" Zander asked, his voice a low rumble.

I met his searching gaze and hoped he could read what I was thinking.

"Yes," I whispered.

Zander turned back to Hiram. "What's the deal?"

"I knew you'd come around," Hiram said, tucking the envelope safely away. "Give me the Kitten forever, and you can walk away with Mieko and the answers you have been searching for."

"How do I know Mieko is still alive?" Zander asked.

"We need proof," Vixen demanded.

Hiram pressed a button on his watch, which doubled as a radio. "Bring her out."

Moments later, two beefy men dragged out a small figure by the shoulders. Her clothes were filthy, and crudely cut ropes trailed behind her ankles like undone shoelaces. They dropped her at Hiram's feet. Mieko looked around wildly. The gag over her mouth stopped her from speaking, and her hands were still bound like in the photograph. As soon as she saw us, her eyes widened like saucers and filled with tears.

She was alive. There was still hope.

"Mieko!" Vixen started to run, but West caught her. She wrestled to get out of his grip, but he held onto her thrashing body like a boa clasping its next meal. "Let me go!"

"We don't need him taking two prisoners," West murmured.

Hiram grabbed Mieko's chin and jerked it roughly to face him, then dropped her again.

"Don't fucking touch her," Vixen screamed.

"You have your proof, Briarly," Hiram said, gesturing at Mieko. "Do we have a deal?"

"Take the deal, Zander," I said. I locked eyes with my terrified friend caught in Hiram's clutches. "It's the only way."

"Listen to her, Briarly," Hiram encouraged. "She knows the power I have."

Mieko's eyebrows shot up. Despite being bound, she shook her head. Hiram caught sight of her out of the corner of his eye. He scowled and delivered a sharp blow across her cheek, sending Mieko crashing to the floor with a muffled yelp.

"No," Vixen yelled. Tears of desperation ran down her cheeks. "Don't hurt her!"

"Untie her," Zander ordered.

"As you wish," Hiram said, nudging his head for his goons to do the deed. They yanked the gag from Mieko's mouth and cut through the rope. Her skin was so pale from the blood loss she probably couldn't feel her fingers. "What's your decision, Briarly? This is my final offer."

An eerie silence stretched ahead until Zander spoke.

"I will never make a deal with you, Hiram," Zander said. "Candy is ours. I'm not leaving here without her, dead or alive. My decision is final."

"You were right." Hiram sighed in disappointment and pulled out the envelope again. He lit its edges. The paper curled and contorted; the smoke carried away Bryce's secrets. "You are nothing like your father. He wasn't so stupid."

An inferno burned behind Hiram's eyes as they met mine.

"Remember this moment, Kitten," Hiram snarled. "I'm going to kill the Sevens one by one while you watch and then bring you home, anyway. All their deaths will be for nothing."

"No," I screamed as Hiram's men flooded into the room from every door.

"Take them prisoner, but don't kill them," Hiram instructed. "I want to do that myself."

He turned and retreated into the back room. The battlefield lay ahead. We had no choice. We had to fight for our lives.

―――――

Hiram's men were divided into two groups. Unlike earlier, they were not holding back. We didn't have long to act. We stood at the edge of the pool and had to pick a direction.

"West, Red, and Vix, go left. Get Mieko and leave," Zander ordered. "Candy and I will go right. We'll get Hiram."

"But—" Rocky looked at me for approval, not wanting to leave my side.

"Do it for me," I said, hoping he could see the pleading in my eyes. "Protect Vixen and Mieko, okay?"

Rocky nodded firmly. His playful side had vanished. He'd spent years in Redlake being forced to fight in an underground ring. He knew how to survive. He'd made mistakes in the past and wouldn't let them happen again. "No one will touch them," he promised.

"See you on the other side, Pinkie," West said with a monstrous grin that would make most men shit themselves as he rubbed his hands together. He'd kept his beast caged for years, and it was finally getting its moment to shine. It lived for blood and violence. His monster wouldn't let me down.

He, Rocky, and Vixen backed away from us.

"You should have taken the deal, Zander," I murmured as we readied ourselves for the imminent attack. The men were only a few feet away now. It was too late to go back, but I had to say it. "All of this could have been over, and you could have found out what happened."

"The decision was easy, little one," Zander replied. I turned to look at him, and he was smiling. A real, sparkling smile that wouldn't look out of place on the cover of a magazine. Was he fucking insane? "There is no Sevens without you. I'll die fighting for you if I have to. We all will because we love you."

I was lost for words, torn between wanting to say it back because it might be my last chance, but afraid I'd never be able to tell Rocky or West how I felt. I could disembowel someone without blinking, but love? That was fucked up shit I didn't know how to handle, and it terrified me.

Zander raised an eyebrow, reading my thoughts. "How does love scare you more than the group of men trying to kill us?"

The first swinging punch saved me from having to answer. Zander had my back. He already had the offender by the throat, crushing his windpipe.

"No one touches our Seven girl," Zander growled, throwing the unconscious man into the pool to drown. He looked at me. "Ready?"

I pulled out my engraved knife. "More than."

The seams of my shirt tore as a sweaty arm tried to grab me. I spun and sunk my blade into his forearm to force him to loosen his grip. As my opponent wavered, I delivered a sharp blow between the legs with my knee. He doubled over in agony and fell to the floor. I loomed over him and delivered a fatal blow through his eye, killing him instantly.

At my side, three guys surrounded Zander. I launched onto one of their backs like a wildcat, stabbing at his temples like it was a game of blood spraying whack-a-mole, while Zander finished the other two. My hair would need a deep condition if we got out of this.

"Good job," Zander complimented as we raced forward.

"Thanks." I grinned, wiping the blood from my brow. "You're not so bad yourself."

I hadn't fully seen Zander in action before, but damn. He could predict our enemies' next move and stay a step ahead like everyone was moving to a tune only he could hear. The Kitten took over as we picked off the security fleet person at a time. With seven bodies behind us, we'd cleared half the room already.

"Behind you," Zander called over in warning.

I pivoted as a sneaky fucker lunged and hoisted me over his shoulder. Hadn't anyone taught him not to touch without consent? I tore straight through his ear with my teeth. The metallic taste of his blood filled my mouth. *Gross.* I spat the rubbery flesh to the ground. As well as a deep condition, I'd need to get some fucking shots too.

The man howled in pain and dropped me. He looked around frantically for his ear. Was he delusional enough to think he'd get to a hospital in time? As he dove forward to grab it, I stamped it flat and kicked him in the face to knock out his teeth for good measure.

"Let go of me," Vixen's yelling made me spin around.

Everything seemed to play in slow motion. I watched West dive to protect her from the guys who pinned her against the wall. He fought them both single-handedly. His giant hands wrenched them by their hair and slammed their skulls together so hard they knocked themselves out. Their unconscious bodies fell onto West, making him dodge and slip on a puddle of blood. He didn't act quickly enough. West lost his balance and staggered, then fell over the edge and into the murky pool water with a huge splash.

A few moments passed… nothing.

Air bubbles floated to the surface where he'd disappeared. Fuck. My throat closed as I remembered our time on the yacht.

"I can't swim," West admitted. *"Never could. If you want to throw me off, there's nothing I could do."*

"West," I screamed out his name in desperation.

He was sinking like a fucking brick, and there was nothing I could do. How long could someone survive without air? Zander tried to battle his way to the edge, but he was too busy sparring with three guys. Another gang of goons with leering faces headed towards me, blocking my entry to the water. On the other side of the pool, Vixen and Rocky were surrounded. All the while, West was still underwater... drowning.

Out of nowhere, a tiny figure sprinted to the poolside and executed a perfect dive that would be worthy of an Olympic champion. *Mieko.* She vanished under the filthy surface. Seconds later, she reappeared with West. His lips were blue, and he was gasping for air, but he was alive.

Hiram's men waited for them to emerge. They dragged them both from the water and yanked their hands behind their back into a tie. They took special care to fasten West. In his condition, he couldn't fight back even if he wanted to.

"There's too many of them," Zander panted. "We can't hold them off any longer."

He was right.

What had we done?

CHAPTER

Twenty-Six

"You don't need to be so fucking rough," I snarled at the creepy slimeball who shoved me through the door to the adjoining room where Hiram waited. Inside, the other Sevens were all being held at gunpoint by Hiram's men.

"Did you really think you could beat me, Kitten?" Hiram taunted. He nodded at the guard to drop me. I fell to my knees and forced myself to look at him. It hurt to move, but the pain had become my armor long ago. It reminded me I was still alive and of what I'd overcome. "Do you really want to choose *them* over me?"

"Don't hurt them." My voice cracked. "Please."

Hiram circled the room and stopped at each of the Sevens. First, there was Zander, who wrestled against his captor. As he resisted, Hiram's goon cracked him over the head with the butt of his gun. Blood trickled down his face, covering his Seven tattoo. Anyone else would collapse from the pain, but Zander's eyes stayed open. He refused to lose consciousness.

"Don't you remember how you meant so little to him?" Hiram mocked. "He handed you over to me. He never cared about you. He only wanted money and a name, just like his father."

Next, he moved onto West. The big man's clothes were soaked through, and his gigantic frame shivered like a tree caught in a hurricane. I'd never seen him so fragile, but I couldn't allow myself to show weakness. I had to be strong.

"Don't you remember how quickly he moved on?" Hiram continued. "He doesn't want a woman like you. What happened to the woman at the funeral? The pretty one with all the money. That's the kind of girl he wants to be with."

West's eyes met my gaze, and he opened his mouth to speak, but one of the two men holding him punched him in the ribs. He dissolved into a coughing fit, spraying water everywhere.

"He's lying, C," Rocky cried out. "Don't listen to him."

"And *you*?" Hiram whirled around and pointed at Rocky. "Are you forgetting how you abandoned her? She trusted you, and you lured her out that night. You let me take her."

Rocky held his head high. "But I won't let you take her again."

Hiram nodded, and his man punched him straight in the face. Rocky's nose exploded into a bloody mess, but he only laughed.

"I will kill you first," Hiram snarled. "I should have killed you years ago."

Hiram motioned again, and his men continued to beat Rocky until he could barely open his eyes. They took pleasure in it. Rocky had learned to take a beating, but even he couldn't last this long.

"And these two..." Hiram continued around the room, stopping at Mieko and Vixen. He surveyed Vixen with disgust. "I will have no use for her, but the other one..." He stroked Mieko's collarbone, making her shudder. "I know people who would be very keen to meet her."

"Stop," I screamed, putting an end to his theatrics. "Leave them! It's me you want!"

Hiram paused and turned to face me.

"Why defend them, Kitten?" he snarled. "Did I teach you nothing?"

"You know nothing about love," I said, rising to my feet. "Someone like you will never understand what it's like to put another person before yourself."

He struck me hard across the face, making my head snap around. His handprint would bruise.

"*This*?" Hiram gestured at all the people I loved. "This is not love. This is a weakness. Everything I did was to make you stronger."

"You turned me into a monster," I spat, averting my eyes to lock into his face.

The face of the devil who'd plagued my life.

He'd taken away my childhood.

He'd robbed me of happiness.

He'd molded me into his image, but I never asked for it.

Hiram slapped me again. The force of his blow sent me tumbling back to my knees.

"You blame me for who you've become, but all I did was make you see who you really are." Hiram yanked my hair and forced me to look into his black eyes. All I saw was darkness. He wasn't even fucking human. "All I had to do was give you the chance to shine."

"I didn't ask for it."

"But you embraced it," Hiram said softly. "I taught you everything you needed to know. I gave you everything you could have ever wanted. Is this really how you want to repay me for everything I've sacrificed for you?"

"But I never chose this life!" I refused to break down. I would die fighting. "I never wanted it!"

"Don't you see this was never a matter of choice?" Hiram said. He stroked my cheek gently. His touch made my skin burn. "This path was your destiny."

"This wasn't destiny." I pushed his hand away and staggered to my feet. "I had a normal life until you came along and destroyed everything."

"Do you think growing up in Evergreen was normal?" Hiram snarled. "You never belonged there, and you know it. You found your home in Blackthorne Towers. Do you think you would have been happy settling down with a silly boy who brought you CDs? You deserved more than that."

I looked at Rocky and he shook his head. I'd never shared that with anyone before. My mouth went dry. "How do you know about that?"

"Because I was watching," Hiram replied. "Do you think I would have gone through all of this trouble for any girl? The only reason you were in Evergreen was because *I* allowed you to be there."

"I don't understand," I stammered.

Suddenly, I felt dizzy and struggled to stay standing. My vision spun. Everything else fell away, making it feel like we were the only two people in the world.

"Let me show you," Hiram snarled. His hand closed around my throat, and he forced my head to the side to reveal the scar behind my neck. "This? This means nothing!"

Hiram slid a knife out of his sleeve and sliced my cheek. I barely registered the stinging scratch, but the liquid warmed my skin. Zander struggled against his captors, but there was no way he could escape as a goon shoved a gun underneath his collar.

"This?" Hiram held out the blade for everyone to see, allowing my blood to drip onto the floor. The droplets made a tapping noise as they bounced off the stone. "This means everything."

Vomit rose in my throat, stinging the back of my nose.

"Haven't you ever wondered why I haven't killed you like the rest of them?" Hiram asked. It's a question I used to ask myself. If anyone else acted in the way I had, Hiram would have killed them years ago. "It's your blood."

"My blood?"

"*Our* blood," Hiram corrected. "We share it. You were born to be my successor."

"What?" I couldn't find the right words. "I-I-I don't understand."

I knew nothing about my birth family. No one had ever given me information. The staff at Evergreen told me all they knew. I got dumped as a baby at the group home. No documents. Nothing.

"Let me tell you a story..." Hiram looked like he was performing onstage. "One day, I discovered my pregnant sister wanted to turn me over to the police. She didn't like what I was doing. Someone had put silly ideas in her head, and she wanted to put me away. Me! Her own brother! Her brother who'd done nothing but protect her!" I'd never seen Hiram like this before. He was out of control, his emotions turning manic. "Naturally, she had to pay for her betrayal. I killed her, of course. When I pulled you from her belly, I didn't expect you to survive, but you did."

This couldn't be happening...

It couldn't!

"That's when I knew you were the one who had to come next!" Hiram let go of my throat, and I put my hands up to my neck, gasping for air. "Do you see now? This is what you were made for."

"You were the one who dropped me at Evergreen..."

"Who else?" Hiram cackled. "I've been watching you, Kitten. All this time. I waited until the right moment to bring you back."

"It wasn't Rocky's fault," I mumbled to myself, thinking about how many years I'd spent hating him for believing he handed me over. I thought Rocky robbed me of a future, but I was wrong. I'd been dreaming of a future Hiram would never have let me have, regardless of who was in my life. "You'd have taken me anyway..."

"But turning you against him was so much more fun," Hiram said gleefully. "Wasn't it?"

"You wanted me to hate him..." I understood now. He wanted me to be like him. Bitter, twisted, betrayed. "You knew it would break me."

"You bastard," Rocky yelled, kicking out. With a flick of Hiram's wrist, he was gargling on his blood again.

"It showed me what I knew all along," Hiram said with a triumphant flourish. "That you are just like me."

I shook my head. "No... it can't be..."

"My blood flows through your veins," Hiram said. "My blood! We are family. *Real* family. Isn't that what you always wanted? A real family?"

My chest heaved as I struggled to breathe. It is what I always wanted. Something I'd been looking for my whole life.

"You have that with me, Kitten," Hiram said. He put his hands on my shoulders. "I will never let you down. It doesn't matter how far you run, you can't escape who you really are. I'll always be there to bring you home."

"Why didn't you tell me before now?" I asked. "You had years to tell me the truth."

There had been countless opportunities for him to share it, but there had been even more chances for him to kill me… and he hadn't.

"I needed to be sure you were ready," Hiram replied. "Being my successor comes with responsibility. You've shown me tonight that you're ready. You have led these men and women. You've convinced them that they're ready to die for you."

"Don't listen to him," West growled. "He's insane."

I'd been trying to avoid looking into Hiram's eyes, but I couldn't help it. I stared into the soulless abyss. The more I looked, the more similarities I saw. How hadn't I noticed it before?

"You can see now, can't you?" Hiram asked, seeing a flicker of acknowledgment across my features. "You see that we are the same."

"There's more to family than blood," Zander spoke up. "He's manipulating you."

"Just like you're trying to do?" I turned away from Hiram and addressed Zander. "It's easy for you to say that when you've always known your family. I never had that."

"They do not have your best interests at heart as I do," Hiram said. His fingers closed possessively around my shoulder to pull me back to him. "How many times will you allow them to let you down? They have served their purpose, but you've outgrown them. It's time for you to leave them behind, to let me guide you. I can give you everything. I would never betray you, you know that."

"We would never—" West began, but he was kicked in the stomach and winded instantly.

"Look at all of their faces," Hiram said, spinning around. "Each one of them would betray you in a heartbeat. How can you trust them? They've hurt you before, they'll do it again. A future with them will only end in heartbreak. Why put yourself through that? I'll only have to be there to pick up the pieces again. We are the same, you and me. We have each other. Together, we are a family. An unstoppable one."

Tears filled my eyes as the painful memories rushed back. The rejections. The betrayals. Was Hiram right? Was a future with the Sevens setting me up for misery? How could I ever be happy with them knowing who I really was? The blood running through my veins was tainted by a monster I hated, but who I was destined to become.

"You're right," I murmured.

There were cries of objections from the Sevens, but I didn't hear them. I was only listening to one person.

"I'm the only real family you will ever have," Hiram purred. "The only person who has never given up on you. Are you ready to come home for good?"

I held my head high. I'd made my decision.

"I'm ready."

"Tell them," Hiram ordered. "Tell them all."

I looked at the people who had taught me the most important lessons.

"I'm choosing to leave," I declared without wavering. "I'm choosing to go home with the only family I have."

Mieko whimpered, allowing tears to fall silently down her cheeks. Vixen shook her head, looking at Mieko but unable to reach out and console her. West and Rocky were too busy struggling and being beaten for me to see their faces, but Zander stood frozen. His shoulders slumped as if his entire universe collapsed, and all the fight left his body.

Hiram clapped and stretched his arms open for me to walk into.

I did.

"You've made the right choice," Hiram said, closing me into his embrace.

"Yes," I agreed, pulling my knife from my pocket and plunging it into his back. "I have."

His arms still held me tightly as I twisted the blade into him. I stabbed again. Again and again. I stabbed until I lost count. His gooey blood oozed between my shaking fingers until I stepped out of his grasp and let him fall. Hiram groaned, collapsing to the ground. The damage had been done. It'd be a matter of minutes before he bled out.

"You are not my family," I snarled, looking down at the man who tried to destroy and ruin every happiness I had. I wanted him to see me for who I was. The woman who took him down. His own flesh and blood. "The Sevens are my real family. Blood changes nothing, and I will fight every day of my life to be nothing like you."

"Oh, Kitten, don't you see?" Hiram smiled. A sight that would be burned into my memory forever. "You already are."

His eyelids fluttered closed as the knife slipped from my hold. I kneeled and held my fingers to his neck. His pulse slowly faded away until, finally, it stopped.

"He's dead," I whispered.

I stood up like a phoenix rising from the ashes.

"You heard Hiram," I addressed his men. "I am his successor."

They all looked around blankly at each other, unsure of what to do next. Their boss was dead. Who did the mindless morons answer to now?

"Drop your weapons and leave," I ordered, "before I kill you myself."

They had no choice. They dropped their holds on the Sevens and retreated. Their hurried footsteps faded into the distance, leaving me alone with the Sevens.

I collapsed by Hiram's side and stared at the dead smile on his face. My body trembled as I let uncontrollable tears fall. This isn't how I imagined it would feel. Killing Hiram had been my end goal. I expected to feel victorious, not like *this*.

I'd killed my only family, and worse still? Hiram was right. I was no better than him. He may be dead, but that didn't mean I'd ever be free. My blood was a curse, and whether he was alive or dead, I'd never be able to get away from him, just like he wanted.

Even in death, Hiram won. He always did.

"Y ou're the most beautiful woman I've ever seen." Rocky wrapped his arms around my waist as I flicked through my new wardrobe of Vixen-approved outfits. "Are you sure I can't tempt you back to bed?"

"Not unless you want Vix to rip your balls off for being late."

He huffed. "After she and Mieko kept us up all night, she should understand we need sleep."

There's nothing like almost dying to kickstart your libido into overdrive.

"It won't be long until they move into their own place," I reminded him. "The wedding is only a month away, remember?"

After everything that happened, they decided to move up the date. That, and Vixen had secured Ash and the Basilisks to play on their big day. Marrying Mieko was already going to be the best day of her life, and seeing her favorite band play would make it even more special.

"How could I forget?" Rocky groaned. "Did I tell you she asked me to pick up flowers today? What do I know about flowers?"

The light relief of choosing cakes and table toppers provided a slice of normalcy amongst the chaos our lives had become.

I smirked. "You're the one of us who is green-fingered."

"Weed is different," he objected. "There's a science to that."

"I'm meeting with Zander's accountant," I said, finally settling on an outfit to wear. You couldn't go wrong with a black dress. "Wanna trade?"

"Why doesn't anyone ever tell you that being an adult sucks?" Rocky collapsed onto my unmade bed with a groan, forgetting even simple movements still hurt. "Do you remember when things used to be simple?"

"You mean, when the only thing we had to worry about was someone stealing my stereo, or where our next sugar hit was coming from?" I laughed, but it sounded hollow to my ears. "It's been a long time since our lives were that simple."

Rocky grabbed me by my wrist and pulled me down on the bed next to him. I didn't resist. If I had the choice, I'd stay in bed all day and try to forget about everything else.

"I don't care that our lives aren't simple." Rocky propped himself up on an elbow and traced a finger down my stomach. "I always knew I wanted to spend my life with you."

I rolled my eyes. "You can be really fucking cheesy sometimes."

"Hey!" He tickled under my ribs, making me squeal and my bruises ache. All of us were still recovering from broken bones and injuries. "Not every guy is an asshole."

"You could have fooled me..."

"Correction," he said, kissing my neck, "not every guy is an asshole *all* the time."

Pounding on the door interrupted us, making Rocky swear under his breath.

"You've got five minutes to get your ass out of bed, Red," Vixen yelled. "We've got shopping to do."

Rocky tucked a stray strand of hair behind my ear. "Are you sure you'll be okay while I'm gone?"

"Go!" I shoved him. "I'm perfectly capable of getting dressed without supervision."

"I know..." His hand slipped further underneath my nightshirt. "But it's so much fun to help."

I slapped his hand away. "Go!"

"Fine," he relented. "But don't let Zander bore you to death today."

"I'll try."

As Rocky left, Zander stood in the doorway. How long had he been listening? He stepped inside my room and clicked the door closed. Behind my smile, he had the unnerving gift of staring straight into my soul.

"You don't have to go," he said, "if you're not ready."

"Not you too..." I shook my head. "I've already had Rocky nagging. I don't need another fucking babysitter. The only thing I need to worry about is staying awake."

"I didn't mean the appointment today," he replied quickly. "I was talking about tomorrow."

My shoulders tensed. "I already told you, I'm not missing it."

"You don't have to pretend everything is okay." Zander tilted his head and studied me closely, but I avoided his probing gray eyes. "You may fool everyone else, but you can't fool me. I know there's more going on inside your head."

"You don't have to be a fucking shrink to know that burying one of my friends tomorrow is not going to be the best day of my life," I snapped. My automatic defense mechanism to turn into a total bitch never failed when I didn't want to talk.

"It's about more than the funeral, and you know it," Zander said. "Your nightmares have been getting worse. West said you woke up screaming last night."

"Are you all comparing notes about how fucked up I am now?"

It was bad enough having one boyfriend checking in on me, but having three? They missed nothing between them.

Zander pursed his lips. "We're worried about you."

"What did you expect? Things to go straight back to normal?" I demanded. There wasn't a magic potion to drink to make everything okay. "Whoever said that the truth will set you free was talking bullshit."

I headed to my dressing table to start on my make-up, hoping it would hide what was going on underneath. Unlucky for me, lipstick couldn't fake a smile.

"Hiram was poisonous," Zander said softly. "He wanted to get inside your head. Don't let him."

I tried to thread an earring through my piercing. The damn thing wasn't going through. I gave up and launched the pearl across the room in frustration.

Zander was right by my side and wrapped his arms around my shoulders. I didn't pull away. "It'll be okay, little one."

"How am I meant to look at myself in the mirror knowing what I do now?" I whispered, keeping my gaze fixed on my lap. "Knowing that I'm part of him?"

"The same way I've learned to."

"How do you do it?"

"I remind myself that real family is who we choose, not what we are born into," he replied. "Someone once said blood changes nothing."

I pouted, cursing myself. "I can be a real smartass sometimes."

"That's why we love you." Zander grinned. "But you need to give yourself time to heal."

"How much time?"

A part of me was terrified it would never happen. Some things were too hard to come back from

"As long as it takes," he replied firmly. "And we are going to be there to help you every step of the way. We're not going anywhere."

My lips curved upward but it made my jaw ache.

"I need to get ready." I sighed, batting him away and trying to keep my focus on what needed to be done. "Or we'll be late for the meeting."

He nodded, looking like he wanted to say more but didn't.

"I'll wait for you outside."

———

"How did the meeting with the accountant go yesterday?" Mieko asked. I could tell she didn't care about the answer but wanted to keep my mind busy. It didn't work as all I could do was shrug in reply.

"I'll be right back," Vixen promised as I slipped into the first pew in the church. "There's something I need to do."

She raced off to finalize last-minute song choices. I couldn't decide whether her throwing herself into arrangements was her way of getting through the day or because of her control-freak nature.

"Cupid would be proud of you," Mieko said, sliding in next to me. She rested her head on my shoulder. "He'd be proud of everything you've done."

"I don't know about that," I replied. "If he knew the truth, I don't know if he'd have helped me at all. He wanted to take Hiram and his empire down, not help me take it over."

"You're nothing like Hiram," Mieko insisted. "You know that, don't you?"

I sighed. My bruises may have healed enough to hide under a thick layer of concealer, but other wounds were still raw. Mieko's question is one I keep asking myself. One I still didn't, and may never, know the answer to.

"He was still my uncle."

"You did what was right." Mieko squeezed my arm in reassurance. "Just like your mom did."

I cracked a small smile. Zander had hired private investigators to find out more about who my parents were, but I'm not sure whether I'll ever be ready to hear about what they uncover. The last few weeks showed me that family is *who* you choose, and sometimes you're better off not knowing...

Behind us, Giles took a seat. His suit wasn't ironed, but he didn't smell, which was an improvement from the last time we saw him. The haunted look in his eyes told me he still had a long way to go to healing. Hiram was dead, but his destruction was clear everywhere I looked.

I turned around to greet him.

"Thanks for coming," I mumbled, "and for signing the papers."

Giles nodded soberly in response. After his intelligence led to finding Hiram, we extended a peace offering and completed our 'divorce'. Our marriage may have been a sham, but Hiram made sure everything was done properly.

Vixen sat on Mieko's other side and took her hand, being careful not to rub against Mieko's fresh Seven tattoo on the inside of her wrist.

"We're ready to start now," Vixen said.

I took a deep breath as the music started playing. The bittersweet cry of the violin was almost too perfect. West, Zander, and Rocky carried Q's coffin down the aisle on their shoulders. Mieko dabbed her eyes with a tissue. I stared forward, trying my best not to think about how the only part of Q's body we could bury was his head.

My heart pounded against my skin. Hiram may be gone, but a part of him would always be with me, and I fucking hated it. I wanted to claw him out and flush my bloodstream.

"Are you okay?" Rocky took my hand as he and the guys slipped into the row alongside us.

My DNA had been programmed from childhood to survive. In school, it meant keeping my head down. In Blackthorne Towers, it involved killing on demand. After that, I did whatever I could to avoid going back there, and now? The one thing I had left to battle lived inside me.

"No," I whispered back, squeezing his fingers. Q once told me nothing worth fighting for is ever easy, and he was right. "But I will be."

The service was beautiful, but I struggled to concentrate on the speeches and poems people read out. All I wanted was to be back in Lapland with the Sevens, free of the melodramatic sobs from strippers in the back row who barely knew him. Last week, I overheard a group of dancers bragging about how they planned to use the funeral to find rich guys. We needed to rehire.

When it was over, we stood at the exit and shook hands with everyone as they left.

Zander nodded across the graveyard to a lone figure standing by a tombstone. "Who is he?"

I grimaced as the man started to approach. "That's Juliano Romano."

"Giovanni Romano's son?" Zander's eyes narrowed, and his hands went straight to rest on his gun. I'd already filled the Sevens in on how Juliano ordered a hit against his father. A hit that I'd carried out on Hiram's behalf. "What is he doing here?"

"Let me speak to him first," I said, putting my hand on Zander's wrist. Being trigger-happy at a funeral is the last thing we all needed. "I'll find out what he wants."

"You're not speaking to him alone," Rocky growled.

"Are you ever going to let me do anything without a fucking escort?"

"Nope." Rocky grinned. "You better get used to it because the Sevens are forever. You had your chance to back out and didn't take it, remember?"

West's hands curled into fists as Juliano got closer. I didn't blame him. One look at Juliano's smug, shit-eating grin would turn a nun to violence. There's a reason he cornered us here.

"Kitten," Juliano greeted me with an air kiss on both cheeks, making my guys tense. "Why do we only meet at weddings and funerals?"

"I go by Candy now," I replied coldly.

"I'm sorry for the loss of your friend," Juliano said without an ounce of real sympathy. "And Hiram, of course."

I glared at him, making it clear he wasn't welcome. "I can't pretend to be sad about the latter."

Juliano smiled, misinterpreting my remark. "We do what we have to do to get what we want, right?"

Out of respect for Q, I didn't smash his teeth out on the spot.

Zander stepped in, sensing my anger rise. "Why don't you tell us why you're here?"

"I've come to make you an offer," Juliano said. His eyes glittered with excitement. "I hear you have taken over Hiram's business."

"It's not for sale," West's deep voice rumbled. "It's under new management."

Juliano isn't the first asshole to make us an offer. After he died, we discovered Hiram got his final wish. I'd become his successor and inherited everything. The Sevens were suddenly one of the richest and most powerful gangs in the country. Vultures were already circling.

"You haven't even heard me out," Juliano replied smoothly, like a car salesman who wasn't used to being turned down. "I can assure you it's generous—"

"We don't give a fuck about the money," I interrupted, trying to keep my voice low and avoid making a scene. "We're not selling."

"But the Blackbird was very interested..."

Of course, it made sense Juliano Romano was the ambiguous other party interested in screwing Hiram over and taking everything for himself. He'd already taken over his father's business — why not acquire another and merge the two biggest crime organizations?

"Well, I'm not the Blackbird. Where is he now anyway?" I snarled. "Things didn't seem to work out well for him."

The news of his disappearance traveled fast, but what happened to him would stay a mystery as far as the world was concerned. Although, peppering a few hints about our involvement wouldn't hurt. The unknown is what people feared the most.

"Take my number," Juliano insisted, pushing his business card into my hands. "In case you want to reconsider."

I tore his card into tiny pieces and let them fall like snow. Selling would be too easy. Hiram may have thought becoming his successor was my destiny, but the only person in control of my destiny was me. I didn't want to follow in his footsteps. The Sevens may have started with a strip club, growing operation, and casino, but we had big plans and an even bigger pile of cash.

"We've made our position clear," Rocky said. "It's time for you to leave."

Unless he wanted to meet the same fate as his father…

"It was a pleasure to see you again, *Candy*," Juliano said. His lip curled menacingly, "And meet the Sevens."

"Shame we can't say the same," I rebutted.

Juliano's mask slipped as his features contorted in fury. A rejection wouldn't be something a man like him would forget. Juliano regained his control, inclined his head, and made a hasty exit.

Good fucking riddance.

West raised an eyebrow at his retreating figure. "Do you make enemies wherever you go?"

"What do you mean?" I feigned surprise. "I thought I was being charming."

West snorted. "Yeah, and we're three Prince Charmings."

"Speak for yourself." Rocky made a wobbly bow and reached out to kiss my hand. "I'm at your service, Princess."

"I'm no fucking princess."

Those whiney bitches waited around for a guy on a horse to come and save them, but me? I could break my ass out on my own.

"You're right," Zander said. "You're not a princess. You're our fucking Queen."

"And we love you," Rocky said.

I looked at the three men who changed my life. My first love, who once broke my heart but would do anything to protect it. My Hulk, who saw the darkest depths of my soul and only held me closer because of it. My equal, who understood my pain and risked everything to make our future possible. A future I couldn't imagine without them by my side.

I took a deep breath and said the words I'd been afraid to voice until now, "I love you too. All of you."

A wide grin spread over West's face as he took my arm and led me to his newest Porsche. "Your carriage awaits, my love."

Life was no fairytale, and we were heading back to a strip club instead of a palace, but none of that mattered. Q once told me to snatch happiness whenever I saw it. We may not be perfect. Hell, we were far from it. The Sevens were dysfunctional, but they were *my* dysfunctional monsters.

I smiled. "Let's go home."

The four of us had walked through the darkness together and, somewhere along the way, our broken fucked up souls made a beautiful whole. Hiram's blood may flow through my veins, but it was the Sevens who kept my heart beating.

Ever Girl
BONUS CONTENT
This short novella is set before the Lapland Underground series.

CHAPTER

One

HIRAM

S illy child.

Look up, I willed.

She didn't.

All she cared about was the goofy youth who stole candy and CDs. I thought this place would mold her into the person she needed to become. She couldn't have an easy life. That was imperative. Things would be easier if she learned life wasn't fair from a young age. It'd help with the transition later…

It wouldn't be long until she was ready.

I watched from afar as she kept her head down and didn't let her eyes stray from the ground when she walked. That could be due to the clumsiness she possessed or her apparent desire to disappear. On a subconscious level, perhaps she knew I was watching.

That something big was coming.

She was made for better things.

This town would soon be a distant place in her memories, and the person she was now? She wouldn't recognize herself. That's how I planned it and how it should be.

I can't afford a weak link. My successor has to be strong, and she will be. The strange, quiet girl who doesn't meet a stranger's eyes could be made into my image.

My sister was strong-willed too. My concerns that her child would be the same were unfounded from my observations. I could make this girl obey. I may have to break her into pieces and shatter her soul, but it would be necessary to build and make her strong again.

The curtains were closed, but light still illuminated the window through the thin fabric. Other teenagers snuck out to attend high school parties, but she didn't. The only time she ever dared to leave at night was when the boy encouraged her.

The boy may pose a problem.

Young hearts were dangerous but easily broken.

I didn't like what I saw in his eyes, or how he tried to coax her out of her comfort zone. No, I didn't like that at all.

I hoped to wait until she was sixteen, but my plans may have to be brought forward. A pot-smoking child who listened to rap music would not derail what I'd been waiting years for.

The girl had been kept alive all this time for one purpose.

I would not let my years of waiting be in vain.

No, that wouldn't do.

I would have security tail the boy. They could figure out his movements and routine. Killing him would be too simple. Anyone could see she cared for him. I needed her compliant, not drowning in a pit of pathetic sorrow. She was a fragile soul who enjoyed reading books and listening to old songs. Killing him would break her too soon. I needed to find another way. A better way of getting the boy out of the picture.

Arrangements would have to be made.

The moment was approaching.

My niece was coming home.

CHAPTER
Two

ONE YEAR EARLIER...

ROCKY

I smelled my breath behind my hand and popped the second stick of gum into my mouth. Extra minty fresh.

I'd watched what happened in the cafeteria earlier. Candy's face turned the color of a tomato after tripping over her laces in front of the cool kids' table. It wasn't her fall that made her blush but what the others said about how she should be used to being on her knees. It was complete bullshit, but a standard quip aimed at an Evergreen kid.

Candy looked cute when she blushed, not that I'd tell her that. She'd only think I was messing with her. It's a miracle she still talked to me considering I was on the football team, which she dubbed the 'asshole squad.' I mean, she was right. They *were* assholes, but it was hard to be an Evergreen kid at Rayland High, and being on the team had its perks. Plus, the team always wanted to buy weed from me, which meant I could start saving cash to get out of this dump.

I knocked on her bedroom door. "C?"

There was a shuffling on the other side as she undid three locks keeping it prized shut.

She looked me up and down. Her eyes narrowed suspiciously. "What do you want?"

"Charming!" I said, pushing past without an invitation.

"I didn't ask you in," she said in a quiet but defiant tone.

"I've got something for you."

"You don't need to bring me stuff because you feel sorry for me, you know." Her cheeks pinked again. "I know you saw what happened earlier."

I shrugged like it was nothing. "Who cares what they think?"

"Easy for you to say," she said. "You're one of them, and they like you!"

"They'd like you too if you spoke to them."

"Why would I? We all know what they think of us." Candy rolled her eyes. "What's the point of pretending?"

Candy sat in the back of the class and never raised her hand but always got straight A's. She took note of everything that went on around her and rarely spoke to other kids, preferring to get lost in her textbooks and homework.

"Don't you want to have friends?" I asked.

Her head jerked sharply, turning to face me. Shit. I screwed up. Why couldn't I keep my stupid ass mouth shut? I basically told her she had no friends.

"Look, I'm sorry," I said. "That came out wrong."

"So you didn't intend to sound like a total jerk?"

She sure could make you sit up and listen for someone who didn't talk most of the time. Other girls didn't see beyond my football jersey when they spoke to me. I was the guy on the team they wanted to screw to make their boyfriend jealous, the bad boy from the wrong side of the tracks. That, or I was the perfect person to use to annoy their parents. Dating a guy from Evergreen would make their lawyer daddies lose sleep.

Candy wasn't like the others. When she spoke to me, she really listened. She told me when I was wrong and saw past all the social hierarchy bullshit.

"I did, but I didn't mean to…" My voice trailed off. Stop talking, Rocky. You're digging yourself a hole, man! "I…"

She raised her eyebrows, making me clamp my lips shut.

"What did you bring me?" she asked, changing the subject and returning to sit down on her bed. Her skirt rode up a few inches to show off her thighs, and I cleared my throat with a cough.

"I found this in the lost and found," I said, rummaging around in my backpack and retrieving an item.

It was a lie. I'd spent most of last weekend looking around thrift stores to find the perfect gift for her. I don't know what it was about her, but part of me wanted to look after her. Maybe there was a selfish reason too. Candy didn't smile often, but when she did, her whole face lit up, and I wanted to be the one to make her smile.

"No way!" she gasped, racing across the room and taking the CD from my hands. "Why would someone leave this behind?"

I didn't have the heart to tell her she was probably the only person still listening to CDs. Everyone else had moved onto iPods.

"Some people are crazy, huh?" I said, hoping my agreement would help get me back in her good favor. "Do you like it?"

"I love it!"

She hugged me, and I felt a stirring in my pants.

Shit.

I pushed her off quickly, and her face fell.

"Sorry," she said, stepping away as a furious blush crept over her cheeks.

"I gotta go," I mumbled.

She wouldn't be embarrassed if she didn't like me, right? The thought she might see me as more than an older brother figure made me excited, but I might have fucked it all up by shoving her.

I'd have to make it up to her… if she ever let me in her room again.

For once, I was glad that Evergreen only had ice-cold showers.

———

CANDY

Why won't the ground swallow me up and suck me inside?

I bet that'll be the last time I see Rocky after basically molesting him! Why had I hugged him? He looked at me like I had a contagious disease! What was I thinking?

I collapsed on my bed and shoved my headphones in, but even Nirvana couldn't drown out my thoughts.

Hugging him wasn't even the worst part. How stupid was I to have called *him* a friend? Rocky Marshall was on the football team. He wouldn't want to be friends with someone like me. We talked sometimes, and he gave me things, but that's because he felt sorry for me. I was a quiet freak with *no friends*. He said it himself.

Rocky was like a king around here. Everyone liked him — even the popular kids thought he was funny, which he was, but not how they thought. He put on a macho facade, but there was more to him than being your typical arrogant jock. He knew how to have a real conversation. We talked about books, films… music.

I bet he never told any of his cool friends about what we discussed. They wouldn't know about the Walkman he bought me or how we once ate enough chocolate to stay awake all night. I'd bet my whole CD collection he hadn't told anyone we even spoke. It'd be too damaging for his reputation to be caught with a social outcast.

Sometimes I could go through full days without speaking to anyone. Most of the time, I didn't mind and would rather be left alone. Other days, I got so mad my head wanted to implode. Last week in math class, I snapped a pencil in two because I got so angry. No one noticed. They never looked at me for long enough. Evergreen kids were treated like shit on Jimmy Choos, but Rocky never treated me like that. Until tonight when he freaked out and slammed my door in my face.

I took my headphones out and stared at the ceiling, letting my eyes follow the cracks like a maze. It was nighttime, but the light from the street and car tail lights illuminated my bedroom wall. The curtains in Evergreen were so cheap they were transparent. I couldn't decide whether that was due to funding cuts or because they preferred us to be in a state of perpetual readiness for what might happen next.

Beyond the walls, normal people carried on with their lives. I wondered what my life would be like when I was free from my cage. I didn't know what the future would bring, but I knew I wanted to get out of Evergreen as soon as possible.

CHAPTER

Three

ROCKY

Did it make me a stalker to wait for her outside the girls' locker room? Fuck, I hoped not.

A stream of girls rushed past me, a few of them giggling and whispering behind their hands. It's not every day I loitered around, and it had piqued their interest. Then, I saw her. As usual, Candy trailed behind the rest of the group. Her hair was tied in a ponytail, but rogue blonde strands slipped away. As usual, her headphones shut out the rest of the world.

"Candy!" I called as she turned to walk in the opposite direction. "Wait!"

She didn't hear me, or she pretended not to.

She kept her head down, concentrating on each step.

I caught up to her and grabbed her arm. "Hey!"

She jumped, almost tripping over her own feet.

Way to go, Rocky. Scaring her shitless will not make you seem like any less of an asshole. Candy paled as my eyes met hers, then she turned her back on me and kept walking.

Ouch.

She *definitely* thought I was a crazy stalker now too.

"Hey, come back." I followed her, falling into step by her side. "Let's walk together."

We were both heading the same way. That wouldn't be too weird, right?

She pulled out one of her headphones at the same time as the douchiest guys on the team wolf-whistled. I'd slam his ass into the ground at our next practice.

"What do you want, Rocky?" she asked. "Are you putting on a show for your friends?"

"What?" I frowned, then realized what she meant. "No! I thought we could hang out. If you're not busy."

She eyed me warily with her sweet baby blues. Distrust lurked behind them, and I didn't blame her. Evergreen kids knew better than to trust other people.

She arched one eyebrow. "You mean busy with all my zero friends?"

I liked how she was never afraid to say exactly what was on her mind.

"You're pissed at me," I said, stating the obvious. "Look, I was a jerk last night. I shouldn't have said what I did. I'm sure you have friends."

"I don't," she replied bluntly as her hands tightened their grip on her rucksack. "Not anymore."

"What about me?" I kept pushing. "We're friends, right?"

"You don't have to keep feeling sorry for me, Rocky!" she said. "I don't need your pity. Why don't you go back to all your jock friends and joke about this whole thing? You don't want to be seen mixing with another Evergreen kid. They don't see you like the rest of us."

"They can think what they want," I said. "I speak to you because I want to."

"You couldn't stand to be in the same room as me yesterday."

"I already said I'm sorry. Why don't you let me make it up to you?" I suggested. "We could go somewhere on our way home. There's somewhere I'd like you to see."

I thought she'd say no from the way she bit her lip. I noticed she did that when she was annoyed, confused, or saw something she didn't like.

"Okay," she said eventually. "Where?"

I grinned, thinking I'd misheard. "Wait, really?"

"You asked me, didn't you?" she snapped. "Or have you changed your mind already?"

———

CANDY

I spotted him lurking outside the gym. The girls had been talking about him when they were changing, trying to decide which one of them he was going to ask out and who would say yes if he did. I tried not to think about it.

I kept walking when he called my name and hoped he'd leave me alone. I spent my days trying to blend into the background. He may be comfortable under the spotlight, but I could already feel the judgmental glares of rich girls who were calling me a whore under their breath.

It was nothing new. Evergreen guys were criminals, and girls were whores. That's how it was unless you were a unicorn like Rocky Marshall, who managed to bridge the gap between both worlds.

Rocky didn't let up, though. He followed me until I couldn't avoid him any longer. I kept waiting to be the butt of a joke and for his interest in me to be a prank. He didn't avoid me at school, but he never went out of his way to talk to me either. That could be because I spent most of my lunch in the library or sat in the corner of the yard, listening to music, counting the minutes until the final bell.

He said he wanted to make it up to me and show me somewhere. The words came out of my mouth before I could stop them, and the shock on his face made me think I said something wrong. Maybe he was only trying to be nice by inviting me and hadn't meant it.

"Are you sure you wanna come?" he asked. "I don't want to force you."

Yep, I was right. He hadn't expected me to say yes, and now he couldn't believe it.

"If you've changed your mind, that's cool," I said, realizing whoever said 'that's cool' sounded lame. "I have homework to do anyway."

"No!" he said quickly. "I mean, no… I haven't changed my mind!"

"Where do you want to go?"

"You'll see."

The sun hit his face at the perfect angle and lit up his big smile. I could see why a lot of girls had a crush on him. He may not be as tall as some of the other guys on the team, but there was *something* nice about how he was so comfortable in his skin.

Stop! I shouldn't even think about him like that. It's not like he'd ever see me that way. He was a senior! Juniors didn't even *look* at freshmen unless they had huge breasts or a reputation for putting out. He felt sorry for the loner freak kid he bought CDs for.

A guy like Rocky would never be interested in a long-term resident at Evergreen. He may live there too, but it hadn't always been that way for him. While I yo-yo'ed out of the system since I was a baby, Rocky had only been there the last two years. I never asked him about it, but I knew the rumors.

People said things started going wrong for him after his mom died from an overdose. His dad was an alcoholic until he hit the harder stuff. I'd never pressed Rocky for information, but I remember when he first arrived at Evergreen. He was beaten so badly that he could hardly walk.

———

ROCKY

I still can't believe she agreed to hang out. I must have looked like a dumb-ass. I could barely get my words out with her around. Usually, I knew exactly what to say. Around her, I suddenly lost my ability to string a sentence together.

"We're nearly there," I said, pointing in the distance.

Candy still looked unsure. Her big eyes darted around, and she clutched her rucksack tighter like she feared someone would snatch it.

She squinted to get a better closer. "What is that place?"

"That," I said proudly, "is the best-kept secret in town."

The abandoned warehouse was one of my favorite places. After my mom died, I spent a lot of time roaming the streets. It was better to wait until my dad passed out than risk returning and getting a beating. The building must have been a factory at some point, but the workers moved out long ago. All you had to do was sneak under the fence to explore.

I led her to a part of the fence where the wire was loose and flapped to the side like a small door. I held it open for her to duck under and squeeze through.

She gasped as her hair got caught on a loose wire. "Ouch!"

"Hey!" I ducked down to help. "Stay still." She froze as I carefully unraveled it and declared, "There! All done."

She didn't thank me. Once on the other side, she stormed ahead without looking back.

"Is this place even safe?" Candy asked as soon I caught up to her. Her mouth pressed into a cautious line as she surveyed the three-story building.

"No less safe than the meals we eat in Evergreen," I said. It's a miracle none of us got food poisoning more often, but we all filled up at the school canteen or lived off snacks we shook from vending machines.

"It looks like somewhere you'd take someone to kill them," she said.

My mouth fell open in shock as explosive giggles burst out of her mouth at my astonished expression. When she laughed, her eyes sparkled like they had a life of their own. She had no idea how beautiful she was. Then, her laughter stopped just as fast. She slapped her hand over her mouth like she made a huge mistake.

Someone had to teach her that having fun wasn't a crime.

"Don't worry," I said. "I'm not gonna kill you. Do you trust me?"

"I don't trust anyone."

I grinned. "That's something we'll work on."

I led the way into the building while she followed cautiously behind. She's the first person I'd shown this place to. It was where I liked to come to get my head straight, and I didn't want it to be turned into a regular rave spot. No one else needed to know.

I headed to a boarded window, swung the wood to the side, and shimmied inside. Candy swatted away my hand as I offered to help her as she squeezed through and landed unsteadily on her feet.

She exhaled slowly. "Woah!"

The place was huge on the inside, big enough to fit an Olympic-sized swimming pool.

"Pretty sweet, huh?" I said. "You've not even seen the best part yet. Come on!"

A steel staircase stood in the middle of the empty warehouse. The sound of the metal on my sneakers echoed eerily around the space as I started to climb.

Candy remained at the bottom, peering up at me. "Are you sure this isn't going to fall?"

"Come on." I held out my hand again. "You can trust me."

She looked hesitant, regarding my palm suspiciously like she was afraid I'd pull away at a moment's notice, but she took it anyway. I focused on my footing, but it was hard to think of anything other than her soft hands and how they were small against mine.

Did this mean she trusted me?

As soon as we reached the door at the top of the staircase, Candy let go. The warmth between us dissipated instantly.

"Where does this lead?" she asked.

"Close your eyes," I said.

She crossed her arms over her chest, almost pouting. "That's what someone would say if they *were* going to kill me."

"Are you always so obsessed with the idea someone is trying to kill you?"

"Only when someone takes me out to an old warehouse in the middle of nowhere," she said. "But fine!"

Candy squeezed her eyes shut.

———

CANDY

"Open them!"

A breeze hit my face as I stepped onto the warehouse's roof.

"Wow." I exhaled slowly. From up here, you got a view of the whole town. The faint outline of our school was on the horizon, and I could trace our route to Evergreen. I strolled to the edge to get a better look. "You can see everything from up here!"

"Hey!" Rocky grabbed my arm as I neared the edge. "Careful!"

If I could deal with being a target dodgeball, I could handle being up high.

I scoffed. "I'm not scared of heights."

Our world sprawled in front of us. It was all I'd ever known. It seemed so small, making my problems melt away.

I didn't notice Rocky grabbing a pair of chairs and dragging them across the roof until the horrible noise made me cringe. The metal chair legs were rusted, but they looked comfortable to sit on.

"You can sit down," he said. "If you want. You don't have to."

I couldn't figure him out. It was difficult to tell whether he wanted me around or not.

"Sure, " I said, gingerly taking a seat.

He pulled a weed baggie out of his jacket pocket.

I'd never smoked before, but I knew he did. I saw him out of my bedroom window at night. His room was on the first floor, and he scaled down the building to sneak out after curfew. I heard he started dealing recently too. It explained why he'd wait across the street for his jock friends to cruise by in their fancy-ass cars before disappearing.

Rolling a joint looked complicated. His green plastic grinder squeaked as he ground a bud, releasing a sickly sweet aroma into the air. He lined the paper with tobacco and sprinkled a generous dusting of green on top.

"Do you smoke?" he asked.

I shook my head.

"That's cool," he said.

"What's it like?"

"Tobacco tastes like shit," he said. "But it's cheaper than weed. It chills me out."

"I didn't think football players were allowed to smoke," I said, then instantly regretted it.

Could I be any more uncool?

Rocky didn't seem annoyed, though. Instead, he lit up and inhaled deeply.

"It's not weed my coach should be worried about," Rocky said. "Half the guys are coke-heads, and most of them do steroids. A bit of green never hurt anyone."

The smoke billowed around our heads.

I watched him with curiosity before mustering up the courage to ask, "Can I try it?"

ROCKY

Taking a toke instantly relaxed me.

Hopefully, this is what I needed to stop acting like a jackass. I know she'd been joking about how I'd lured her there to kill her, but shit! I didn't want her to think I was a creepy serial killer. It didn't help that I couldn't stop fidgeting since she let go of my hand, either.

"Can I try it?"

"Sure," I said. "But you don't have to."

She was usually a girl who stuck to the rules. I didn't want her to feel pressured.

"I know," Candy said. "But I want to."

I held out the joint. She took it and rested it awkwardly between her fingers.

"You'll probably cough the first time," I said. "Everyone does."

She nodded thoughtfully like she was listening to a teacher. My grades were not the best, but I was top of the stoner class.

"You want to put it between your lips and inhale," I instructed. "It might burn a little, but try to breathe in and hold it before you breathe out again."

Candy placed the joint between her lips and breathed in as the orange embers blazed. Her chest tightened as she let the smoke fill her lungs, then started spluttering a few seconds later.

"Not bad." I grinned, then added, "For your first time."

Her cheeks reddened as she passed it back.

A few minutes later, she asked to try it again. This time, she hardly coughed. Not bad at all.

"It's bitter," she commented, sniffing her nails and wrinkling her cute nose. "It makes my nails smell funny."

"That's the tobacco," I said, starting to roll another.

I'd been planning on selling this bag, but I'd pick up again later. It was worth losing some cash if it meant getting to spend time with her.

We continued to pass the joint back and forth. After smoking the second one, she said, "My head feels kinda funny."

"That's because you're high…"

"I guess I am!" She laughed, then arched her eyebrow. I couldn't tell whether she was teasing or not. "Is that why you asked me here?"

"I wanted to apologize for acting like a jerk in your room last night," I said. "I thought you'd like this place, and I like hanging out with you. We can talk about real sh-t."

———

CANDY

"What about your jock friends?" I mocked sarcastically. "I'm sure you can talk to them."

My body felt like it was swaying, but I wasn't going anywhere. My limbs were suspended in the air. Maybe Rocky was right. I was high! I'd never done anything illegal before. The cops always looked for an excuse to arrest Evergreen kids, but it felt like another world up here. The law couldn't touch us.

"I can't talk to them like I can talk to you," Rocky said. "You're different."

"You mean I'm a freak?"

"No!" For the first time, his casual, easy-going attitude vanished. "Don't say that!"

"You can quit pretending," I said. "You were right when you said I had no friends. I'm not stupid. I know what the others say about me."

He scowled. "Don't listen to those assholes."

"Why have you always been so nice to me?" I asked. "No one else is, and you don't have to be."

When he first arrived at Evergreen, I tried to ignore him like I did the others, but he never gave up trying. He always spoke when he saw me in the corridors, and that gradually progressed to us talking more.

"I know I don't have to, C," he said. "But I want to. We're... friends. Aren't we?"

"Do friends avoid each other in school?" I asked. "Or sneak into their rooms at night because they don't want other people to see them talking? Or take them to a warehouse where no one else knows that they're hanging out?"

"When you say it like that..." Rocky ran his hand through his hair and sighed. "I really am an asshole."

"It's okay." I shrugged. "I get it. I'd be embarrassed to be seen with me too."

"That's what you think?"

———

ROCKY

She seriously thought I was embarrassed to be seen with her when it was the opposite. I was cautious because I didn't want her to freeze me out. It'd taken months for her to sit and have a conversation with me. If I came on too strong, I'd scare her away.

"It's okay, Rocky," she said. "I don't mind."

"You've got it all wrong," I insisted. "I don't give a shit who sees us together. At school, I hang out with the guys because that's how it is when you're on the team. When I'm not with them, I'm selling."

Candy doesn't look at me, staring into the distance.

I gulped and mustered all my courage. It was now or never.

"I like you, C."

She waved her hand dismissively. "You don't have to keep trying to make me feel better."

"But I mean it," I said. "You're not like other girls in this town, and that's why I like you."

"Really?" she whispered, turning to face me.

I dared to look at her lips and imagined how it'd feel to kiss her, but I couldn't. Not yet.

"Trust me," I said, reaching out to take her hand to make my point clear. "I *like* you, okay?"

She looked down in surprise. "Oh…"

You stupid fucker, look what you've done! You've scared her, and now, she won't let you near her again.

"Sorry." I began to lift my hand away. "I shouldn't have—"

But Candy held on tight and slipped her fingers through mine.

"Thanks for the CD," she murmured, squeezing my hand.

CHAPTER
Four

HIRAM

The time was getting closer.

I'd been waiting since I pulled her, the screaming baby, from my traitorous sister's body. Killing her for what she did was never going to be enough. The ultimate revenge would be continuing my legacy with her blood. The girl would take her rightful place at my side, as it was destined to be.

"A girl?" The Blackbird shook his head. "You can't be serious, Hiram. What can a child do that the rest of us can't? You have all of our resources at your disposal."

The Blackbird had been one of my most loyal servants for years, but I was not blind to his shortcomings. Trusting him with a secret like this was a risk. One I was not prepared to take. Great leaders fall when a vulnerability is exposed. Revealing that this orphan was my heir could be seen as a weakness, and I'm not a man who had weaknesses.

"Do you doubt me, Blackbird?"

On my workshop bench, the writhing flesh of my victim lay in front of me. I'd already cut out his tongue, but the noise of him choking on his blood was distracting.

"No, Hiram!" the Blackbird said, casting a nervous look at my victim and reminding himself of what can happen when my orders are disobeyed. "Never! All I want to do is understand. I'm sure you have a good reason."

"I'm tired of using local whores as honey traps," I said. The ruse for taking the girl had been years in the making, and my logic was flawless. I'd meticulously planned every detail. "We need to train a girl to do more than spread her legs. Think of what an asset she could be and how much easier it would be to access men in high places."

The Blackbird scratched his chin, deep in thought. He knew I was right. I always was.

"I can assist you with selecting the child," he said. "I'm sure many of our allies would be willing to offer their daughters."

"No need," I said dismissively. "I will select the candidate myself."

The traitor struggled to free himself as his wrists rattled in their chains. I took the scalpel to his eyelids and sliced them off in response.

"How will you choose the girl?"

The Blackbird's interrogation was growing tiresome. Torturing at my leisure was how I liked to unwind after a long day, but his insolent questioning was testing my patience. He'd never dare to defy me, but I made a mental note to keep a closer eye on him. I'd given him too much power fast, and it went to his head. He would see the girl as a competition.

"That is none of your concern," I said, putting down the scalpel and hovering my hand above the rest of the tools, deciding what to use next. "But I assure you that I will pick the right one."

My trusty jigsaw never let me down. I took the serrated edge to his neck and started sawing. His convulsing stopped as his skin turned to ribbons. The blade ground against the bone, forcing the Blackbird to look away. This is what separated him from men like me. An act like this was something only people of absolute power could do. Killing was reserved for the most superior of our species, and enjoying it? That was an act of God.

"Of course, you will," he agreed hastily as the color drained from his face. "I never doubted you."

The Blackbird was spineless. He had a nose for sourcing intelligence, but his weak stomach let him down.

"But I will require your assistance with one thing," I said. "Contact Jacobson. When I find the girl, I need someone experienced to help *induct* her."

Raphael Jacobson was the best handler I knew. He made his trafficked whores compliant and took great pleasure in his job.

I wanted my niece to be my protege, but she would never learn if life was made easy for her. If she was going to follow in my footsteps, she had to walk through the fire and rise from the flames even stronger. Only the strongest survived and taking her to hell was the only way she would ever be able to fulfill her destiny... if it didn't break her first.

CHAPTER
Five

ROCKY

"You're late," Coach's voice boomed as I arrived at the locker room. "Again."

"Sorry, Coach!" I panted.

I had to do a last-minute drop and raced to get here on time.

"You owe me fifty push-ups," he said. The coach was a hard man, but he was fair. I appreciated him giving me a shot. Other teachers didn't give me a chance as soon as they knew my background. "You need to get your head in the game."

I saluted. "Yes, Coach!"

Brad slapped me on the back as I entered. "Ready for the game on Friday?"

Brad was the captain of our team, as well as a first-class douchebag. His parents had connections to the major league and paid for him to get the best training. Despite that, he wasn't a great player — not that anyone would tell him. Money could buy everything, even a captainship. It was no coincidence he secured the position after his father's generous donation to build a new school library.

"You bet," I said, peeling off my shirt and starting to change. "Those Wolves are going down."

"Damn straight!" Brad said, leaning against my locker. "Are you coming to the party after the game? It's at my place. My folks are out of town. You can hook us up, can't you?"

I nodded and lowered my voice, "Just text me what you need."

"Sweet," he said, clapping my shoulder. "It's going to be a hell of a party!"

They always were. Post-game parties were guaranteed to be full-on carnage. A rich kid's parents would inevitably be away on a business trip or vacation, and half the school would descend on a fucking mansion. Crazy shit happened every time. Trashing a house wasn't a big deal when their allowances were big enough to cover a professional cleaning crew to fix the mess before their parents returned.

"I'm gonna bring a friend if that's cool?"

"The hot blonde chick I've seen you talking to?" A sly grin spread over Brad's face that I wanted to wipe off. "The one with the porn star name?"

"Her name is Candy," I replied through gritted teeth.

"Does she fuck like a porn star too?" Brad asked. "She's a sweet piece of ass."

It took all of my self-control not to sucker punch the fucker. I hated the fact he noticed her and knew who she was.

"I've never screwed an Ever before, but I've heard they're down for anything. You'd know all about that, though," Brad continued. "Sure, you can bring your friend along to the party. Who knows, maybe it'll be the night I pop my Ever cherry?"

"Candy is with me."

"Come on, dude! We all know those girls like to share!" He winked. "But, since you're hooking me up, I'll keep my hands to myself."

He'd better. I stalked out of the locker room before I gave him permanent brain damage.

"Come on, man!" he called after me. "I was only messing! You know I'd never touch an Ever!"

Those rich bastards thought they ruled the world. I could see why Candy hated them, and I hated that I had to play along with their bullshit because I needed their cash to keep me going. If I was going to save enough money for college, I needed to rinse their wallets.

"Where do you think you're going?" Coach yelled. "Get back here! We're about to start."

I didn't look back.

CANDY

"Did practice get canceled?" I asked, looking up from my chemistry textbook. My next assignment wasn't due for a few weeks, but I wanted to get ahead. "You're back early."

"Yeah, something like that," Rocky muttered darkly.

He threw himself down on my bed and knocked all my highlighters out of disarray. When he wasn't at practice or delivering, we hung out together most days. Sometimes we studied, or rather, I tried to, and he distracted me. On other days we'd go to the warehouse. Those were my favorite days when it was the two of us up on the roof; it made everything else fade away.

"Is everything okay?"

Usually, he'd be quick to crack a joke or make fun of me for taking schoolwork seriously, but he seemed distracted.

"Are you coming to the game this weekend?" he asked.

Sports and huge crowds weren't my thing. Well, being around other people, in general, wasn't really my *thing*, but I had been considering hanging around under the bleachers to catch a glimpse of Rocky on the field. He'd been training hard, and this was the season's final game. I'd heard college scouts would attend, which, even someone with little sporting knowledge like me knew, was a big deal.

"I might," I said. "I haven't decided yet."

Plus, Rocky hadn't asked me.

"There's a party after the game," he said. "I thought you might want to come. You know, with me."

Going to the game was one thing but rubbing shoulders with the popular kids when they were wasted was another. Then again, I'd never been to a proper party, and they intrigued me. I heard whispers about them in the halls and wondered what I was missing out on.

"I don't know," I replied. "I've not been invited."

"I'm inviting you," he said. "Brad says it's cool if I bring a friend."

My heart sank at his words. *A friend.* That's all I was to him.

Sure, we hung out a lot. He held my hand and told me he liked me when we were high, but nothing else had happened between us. There was a moment last week when I thought he was going to kiss me. My pulse raced so fast I wanted to throw up, but then he picked up my headphones and started listening to music. I must have misread the signals.

"I'll think about it."

"It'll be more fun if you come," he said. "We can stay together and laugh at the stupid shit everyone does. Plus, we can have a look around Brad's house. I've heard they have a mini golf course in the basement!"

Yep, that's exactly what *friends* did.

The problem was, I'd started to like Rocky more than that. I wanted him to be more than just my friend…

"I said that I'll think about it, okay?" I turned back to my notes, gripping my pen tightly. "I need to finish my homework."

"Okay," he said. "Well, I'll catch you later then."

I needed to accept it. I was an Ever girl Rocky hung out with, but I wasn't the type of girl he wanted to kiss.

CHAPTER

Six

ROCKY

Coach tutted. "I should bench you for missing the last practice, Marshall."

Bench me? This was my final game of the season. The only one that mattered. Scouts would be watching in the stands, and, even more importantly, so would Candy. I don't know what spurred her last-minute change of heart, but it's the extra motivation I needed.

"Come on, Coach!" I pleaded. "I need this!"

He knew it too.

Other kids had fallback options, but not me. This was my best shot. Getting a scholarship would be my ticket out of town and could be the difference between ending up in jail or making something of my life.

"Final chance," Coach warned. He had a softer side under his tough exterior. "Don't make me regret this."

"You won't," I promised.

He nodded. "Suit up."

The locker room smelled of cologne and sweat, but electricity hung in the air. It was always the same before a big game. We were playing against the Wolves, our biggest rivals. Everyone on the field would be thirsty for blood and ready to tear each other apart to reach the top.

None of the guys knew how to survive better than I did, though. Adrenaline powered through my veins. I was going to bring the trophy home if it was the last thing I ever did.

The cheerleaders finished their regular pre-game performance and started to file out, which meant we were up. This was my moment. We stepped out into the bright lights, and I cast a glance into the stands. I scoured the sea of people, but I couldn't see her anywhere. Maybe she changed her mind about coming after all.

"This is the game we're going to bring it home," Brad said as we gathered into a huddle. "Are you ready to be winners?"

"Go Bears!" the team echoed.

I pulled down my helmet and got into position.

This was a game I needed to win. I'd channel all of my disappointment into it. No one would get in my fucking way, and I'd take out anyone who tried.

I threw all other thoughts away and put my sole focus on the game. Minutes passed by in a blur. Every calculated move counted, then I caught the ball in the perfect position. Suddenly, the crowd was up on their feet. They erupted into wild cheers and applause, but none of that mattered. There was only one person's applause I cared about.

I ran, swerving to avoid the other players. I kept going and didn't stop until I threw the ball down on the touchline. My teammates surrounded me with deafening yells of celebration. As much as I hated them, being part of a team was really something. For this game at least, we were all playing on the same side.

We were going to fucking win.

———

CANDY

I re-read the article for the tenth time since I dug it out of a trashcan yesterday. The magazine pages were filled with advice on all the usual bullshit: how to get a guy to notice you, what were the hottest heels for making your ass look good, and what was this month's best sex position. For the record, it was something called 'the downstroke,' which looked like a gymnastic pose. I was a virgin but, judging by the drawing, it didn't look comfortable for anyone.

I studied the beauty pages the most. I never wore make-up usually. I spent most of the day hunched over a desk, so what would be the point? Today was different, though. I was going to the game *and* a party. I wanted to look different. Nicer. Not because I cared about what the other kids thought, but because I had a point to prove to Rocky.

I wanted to show him I wasn't a kid. All the other girls in my class wore make-up and, maybe, if I looked more like them, he'd see me differently.

I never liked having to steal, but I didn't have any money, and this was an emergency. Walking from Evergreen to the local mall took over an hour. Strolling around the glossy counters made me feel like an alien. Did you know that it cost more than ten dollars to buy mascara? That's enough to buy food for a few days!

I wasn't stupid, though — that's where people often went wrong. I didn't target high-end products. Instead, I focused on cheap sample pots that were already running low. It was gross using eyeshadows other people had stuck their fingers into, but they'd only be thrown out soon. Stealing was a last resort.

When I got home, I hadn't considered that I had no idea how to apply the damn stuff. My first attempt looked like a toddler attacked my face with crayons. It didn't scream sophistication, which was the effect I was aiming for.

Rocky's game would be starting in an hour.

I threw the magazine across the room in frustration. There was no way I'd be able to master the cat-eye look without resembling a panda. I'd have to go rogue. I smudged a shimmery eyeshadow on, rubbed a hint of blush on my cheeks, wriggled a few layers of mascara on my lashes, and went for a pretty pink lip. It was subtle, but I liked it.

Usually, I wore my hair in its natural 'just rolled out of bed' state, but a girl on the floor below let me borrow her hair straightener in exchange for the mascara. It left a residual burning smell behind, but my frizz was gone, and it looked better.

All I had to do next was figure out what to wear.

I rummaged through my drawer and took out a black vest. I bought it in a yard sale a few months before but had never worn it because I worried the neckline showed too much skin.

Screw it.

I put it on, thinking it'd be nothing compared to what the cheerleaders would be wearing. I didn't have big boobs, but they looked okay in this. It showed I had a figure beneath my clothes. On a normal day, I'd throw on jeans, but it was a special occasion, so I took scissors to my oldest pair which already had holes in the knees to make shorts.

I inspected my reflection in the mirror.

It would have to do.

As soon as I arrived at school, I started to think dressing up was a mistake. I suddenly felt self-conscious around all these people. I wasn't wearing anything particularly shocking or revealing, but eyes raked over me as I walked through the stands to find a seat in the back.

"Is she new?" someone whispered as I passed.

I'd been invisible for so long that I'd forgotten what it was like to be seen.

Despite my natural instincts telling me to run, I kept going and sat down. This was Rocky's big day, and I promised I'd be there for him.

I was a few minutes late, but it was easy to spot him as the team got into position. A lot was riding on his performance.

The whistle blew, and they were off.

I wasn't sure what the rules of the game were, but I flinched as the players barreled toward each other. *Doesn't it hurt?* I winced and covered my mouth as Rocky charged at one of the Wolves. They were wearing protective clothing, but did they have to be quite so violent?

Rocky may be one of the shorter guys on the team, but what he lacked in height he made up for in speed and power. He ran like an animal released from a cage. On the field, he was nothing like the kind and gentle guy I'd gotten to know over the last few months.

The stands clapped as Rocky sprinted across the field.

Everyone rose to their feet. I could understand why people like watching football. Being there in person was different from watching it on TV. There was an energy in the air, and I jumped up. All of my inhibitions vanished as I cheered Rocky on, and he scored his second touchdown.

They'd done it!

They'd won!

ROCKY

"You killed it, man!"

"Thanks," I replied.

We had won the game, but my mood was flat.

"Shit." Brad nudged me in the ribs. "Isn't that your girl over there? Damn, that Ever is *hot*."

I followed his gaze to see the girl waiting at the edge of the field. Her arms were crossed across her chest like she was trying to protect herself from the world, but it was unmistakably her. No wonder I hadn't recognized her in the stands. As soon as I looked in her direction, she awkwardly smiled and waved, making my heart skip a beat.

I abandoned the guys and headed straight to her.

"You came," I said.

Well done, way to sound like a fucking idiot.

"I told you I would," she said.

"You look…" I swallow hard. "Different."

I'd never seen her look like… this… before. I mean, she looked good. She always did. I'd always known how beautiful she was. Only now, everyone else was paying attention to her, and it made me protective. I wouldn't let her out of my sight at the party.

She looked up at me through long eyelashes. "Is that a good kind of different?"

Damn, she had a way of staring straight into my soul. Was she flirting with me? My mouth went dry, and I suddenly felt more nervous than I had before going out on the field.

Coach's booming voice interrupted our moment, "Marshall, get over here!"

"I'll see you soon," I promised. "Wait out front for me?"

"Sure," Candy replied with a shy smile.

I joined my coach, who was deep in conversation with two men holding clipboards.

"These are the scouts I was telling you about," Coach said.

"We're pleased to meet you," one said, offering his hand for me to shake.

Men in suits holding out their hands usually wanted me to put a bag of drugs into it.

"You played a good game out there," the other complimented.

"Thank you, sir," I said.

"Rocky's our best player this season," Coach said. "One of the fastest I've seen in my career."

Holy fucking shit. Was this really happening?

"We'd like you to consider our program," one said. "We need players like you on our team."

All I could do was grin and take his business card. This is a moment I never thought would come. Just like that, a future away from crime and this town felt almost within reach.

———

CANDY

I sat on the parking lot wall waiting for Rocky as other packed cars sped away to the party. With the Bears winning, there was a lot of celebrating to go around. Even the townsfolk who came along to watch were pumped up.

I spotted Rocky. His wet, freshly-showered hair stuck to his face, but it'd soon dry in the sun. It took him nearly ten minutes to make his way over to me because everyone stopped to congratulate him on his performance.

"So, what did you think of your first game?" Rocky asked as he joined me. "Better than you thought?"

"It was great," I said, opting not to mention how terrified I'd been of him getting hurt. "You were really good."

"Good?" He put a hand to his heart. "Is that the best you got for the star player of the season?"

I rolled my eyes. "I don't want you turning into one of those arrogant football players."

"Too late!" he said. His eyes glittered with excitement. "Still up for the party?"

I nodded.

"Well, your carriage awaits!" he said, leading me over to his bicycle.

The thing was old, but it got him where he needed to be, and it wouldn't be the first time I rode on the back.

"Hey, Rocky! Want a ride?" Brad pulled up in his Porsche in front of us. "There's space for you and your chick in the back. It'll save you riding that shit heap."

His calling me Rocky's 'chick' made me want to tell him I had a name, but also… it felt kinda nice to be called Rocky's chick.

Before answering, Rocky looked at me expectantly, trying to read my expression. He didn't want to push me into anything, but I already decided I wanted to show him another side of me tonight. I wasn't going to be the scared, quiet girl who was too afraid to speak to people.

"Sure," I said to Brad. "That'd be great."

Rocky held the door open, and I slid into the back. It was the first time I'd been in a car like this. If I had to go anywhere, I either took the bus or walked. I found myself sandwiched between Rocky and the cheerleader Brad was hooking up with this week.

"I like your hair," she said. "Are you new here? I don't think I've seen you before."

Even bitchy cheerleaders were not immune to being nice after the team won a game. Why did everyone think I was new? Surely, makeup and a new outfit didn't completely alter my appearance?

"She's a freshman," Rocky said.

"Have you ever thought about cheerleading?" she asked.

Rocky snorted. Why was that so funny? It was okay for him to be in with the cool crew, but he thought it was ridiculous I'd even be considered.

"You know, I've been thinking about trying out," I lied, making Rocky choke.

There is no way in hell I'd ever be confident enough, but it served Rocky right for being an asshole.

"Let's party!" Brad yelled, cranking the stereo up and speeding away.

CHAPTER
Seven

ROCKY

Candy's eyes almost popped out of their sockets as we headed up the winding driveway to the million-dollar mansion at the end of it.

"This is insane," she whispered in my ear. "I can't believe people live like this."

It looked like the home of a movie star. From my previous visits, I knew it had a pool, cinema room, BBQ pit, DJ booth, and a jacuzzi.

"Did you get everything?" Brad turned around to face me as soon as he parked.

"It's all here," I said.

I passed him a bag of weed and pills. In exchange, he thrust a roll of cash into my palm. He paid me more than the drugs were worth. That's why I needed to keep him sweet. No business in town would employ an Evergreen kid, and there's no other way I could make a cool five hundred bucks in a night.

Brad fist-bumped me. "You're the man!"

The drugs wouldn't come out until sunset.

We followed Brad and his newest girlfriend up the steps to the entrance of the mansion.

"Everyone's staring at us," Candy said.

"I'm the best football player in the school," I joked. "What do you expect?"

In reality, I knew they were staring at the cute girl on my arm who they were noticing for the first time. Candy laughed nervously. All of this was out of her comfort zone, and even though she was putting on a damn good act, I knew her better than that.

"D'you want a drink?" I asked, hoping to help put her at ease.

She nodded fiercely.

———

CANDY

Lukewarm punch was only drinkable in sips. I had no idea what kind of drinks they'd mixed, but you'd be insane to chug it like the guys to my right, who were in the midst of a drinking challenge. Some of the senior girls cheered them on, making me question whether it was something that should impress me instead of grossing me out.

"Why don't we go hang by the pool?" Rocky suggested.

Sitting outside by the water sounded good. We'd only been at the party a few hours, but people's words were slurring, and someone passed out in a puddle of vomit. The music was super loud, the type that was nothing but a grinding bass.

"I still can't believe this is actually someone's house," I said.

I'd walked around the neighborhood a few times, but I never thought I'd get to see how the other half lived behind the gates and how quick they were to try to throw it all away. They didn't realize how lucky they were.

"Are you having fun?" Rocky asked as we sat to the side of the pool on chairs, outside of the splash zone from guys jumping in fully clothed.

"Yes," I lied.

I'd rather be sitting on the warehouse roof. I preferred it quiet and only the two of us.

"I've never seen you wear anything like this before," Rocky said.

"I've never had the occasion to dress up," I replied, flicking my hair over my shoulder. "It's not like I get invited to parties often."

"You don't have to change how you look to impress them."

"I don't want to impress *them*," I said. "There's nothing wrong with change, is there? I can look good for myself."

Alcohol loosened my tongue, and I downed the rest of my red cup to avoid saying more.

A guy on Rocky's team approached us, but I couldn't remember his name.

"Hey, babe," he said. I looked around and realized he was talking to me. "Want to dance?"

"We're talking," Rocky snarled.

"Actually," I said, "I feel like dancing."

The guy grinned, and Rocky sat up straighter. Rocky should have asked me to dance first. Besides, the magazine said a surefire way to make someone jealous was flirting with someone else.

I wanted to put that theory to the test.

———

ROCKY

What the hell was she doing?

I hated seeing her with him. Asking her to dance was an excuse to put his hands on her hips, making me more furious. Everyone knew he was a player and had a reputation for screwing around. He treated girls like dolls he collected.

What was she laughing at? He wasn't funny! He would be using a lame line he used on everyone.

There's no way I was sticking around to watch. We were supposed to be celebrating my win together. I wanted to spend the night with C, not have a front-row seat to her getting hot and heavy with an asshole who wouldn't remember her name in the morning.

I marched up to them.

"I'm leaving," I said, turning my back and storming away before she had time to answer.

I didn't even recognize her. What happened to the girl I hung out with who didn't give a shit about fitting in and liked trash-talking the rich kids? She'd been replaced by a weird cheerleader wannabe clone, and the worst part of all? I'm not sure what annoyed me more: the fact another dude was flirting with her, or how I wished it was me she chose to dance with.

———

CANDY

Rocky shouldered his way through the crowds.

"I'm gonna head off too," I said quickly.

"But we're just getting to know each other, babe!" the jock whined.

I'd had enough of his sweaty hands pawing me too.

"Sorry," I replied, wriggling out of his grasp.

He cursed under his breath, "Fucking cocktease."

"You know what," I snapped, "fuck you."

His mouth fell open in disbelief. I'd never said anything like that before, especially to a senior, but I couldn't dwell on it. I continued in the direction Rocky headed. How had he gotten down the driveway so fast? I had to run to keep up with him.

"Rocky!" I called after his pacing figure. "Wait up!"

He didn't stop or look back.

"Hey!" I yelled. He must have heard me. "Rocky!"

He didn't slow his pace.

"Didn't you hear me?" I panted, falling into line next to him.

"What do you want, C?" he sneered. "Where's your new boyfriend? You looked like you were getting pretty cozy."

I'd never seen him so angry. His eyes burned with fury, and he looked like he wanted to tear my head off.

"Is that why you're mad?" I frowned. "Because I danced with someone else?"

"He was all over you!"

"Why do you care?" My irritation rose. "It's none of your business what I do!"

"I don't want you making a fool of yourself!"

"It's called having fun, Rocky!" I couldn't win with him. "You're the one who told me I should try it."

"If you want to stay at the party, don't let me stop you!" he retaliated. "We all know what everyone will be saying about Ever girls in the morning."

―――――

ROCKY

Candy's face fell.

I may as well have slapped her.

Fuck. That was a low blow. I never should have gone there and regretted it the moment the words left my mouth.

"Is that really what you think?" she mumbled. "That I'm an 'Ever girl'?"

Her bottom lip started to tremble, making my anger melt away instantly. Seeing her upset made my chest hurt like someone had tackled me to the ground. It was my fault for being jealous.

"I shouldn't have said that," I said. "I-I-I was mad."

She turned away to sniff and wipe her eyes, refusing to cry.

"You're right," she said, holding her head high. "You shouldn't have said that."

"I'm sorry," I said. "I really am. You know I don't think that, C."

"I didn't think you thought like them," she said. "I thought you were different."

"I am!" I insisted, trying to reason with her. "I didn't mean to say that, and I'm a grade-A fucking jerk who ruined your night. I can take you back to the party if you want?"

"I don't want to go back!" Her outburst made me jump. "I wasn't having fun!"

I frowned. "But you were laughing—"

"I was trying to get you to notice me, okay?" she said. "And it worked, but not how I wanted to."

"Wait, what?" I stammered. "You wanted me to notice you?"

How couldn't she see I didn't *just* notice her? She was all I could *see*. She was the only one I noticed when we were in a room. My eyes were drawn to her like a fucking magnet, and I couldn't get her out of my head no matter how hard I tried.

———

CANDY

Don't cry, I willed myself.

"I thought if I dressed like this and danced with another guy, you'd see me," I said. The alcohol had loosened me up, letting words spew out of me. "But you've made it quite clear tonight what you think of me, and I preferred it when I didn't know."

"You've got it wrong," Rocky said.

I walked faster to try to get away from him, but it was no use when he could match my speed. Suddenly, he grabbed my arm and forced me to face him.

"You don't need to change who you are for me," he said. "I like who *you* are. I like the girl I hang out with at the warehouse."

"That's the problem!" I said. "You like me, but all you see me as is an Ever girl."

What had I expected? I'd grown up to expect disappointment.

———

ROCKY

"You're wrong."

She was wrong. So fucking wrong.

I trailed behind her as we paced the empty streets.

"Spare me your pity," she scoffed. "Everyone knows what they say about girls from Evergreen, remember? You're always telling me I should give the other kids at school a chance. When I try, you're not happy. I can't win!"

"You don't need to change who you are to do that," I said. "If they don't like who you are, they're not worth it."

"That's the thing, Rocky!" she said, stopping in her tracks. "If I was myself, no one would like me."

"I would."

She snorted. "Yeah, you sure act like it…"

Even though her eyes were filled with tears, she didn't let them fall. She was strong and unlike anyone I'd ever meet., which is why I was drawn to her. If I had any chance to make it right, I would have to be honest.

"Do you really want to know why I acted like a jerk tonight?" I asked, stepping closer to her. "Because I was jealous. I asked you to the party to hang out with me, and I didn't like seeing you with someone else. You're better than all of those assholes at the party and deserve better."

"You like me?"

I smiled and said, "You're supposed to be the smart one, C."

———

CANDY

My heart hammered so hard I thought my rib cage would shatter. The evening hadn't turned out how I hoped, but Rocky was telling me he liked me… for real, this time. I was too scared of screwing anything up by saying it back.

"You didn't ask me to dance," I muttered,

He laughed, then offered me his hand. "How about now?"

We were halfway down a random suburban street. The streetlights gave the road a warm orange glow, and everyone in the surrounding houses was fast asleep.

"Quit messing around," I said, batting him away.

"I'm not. Scouts honor!" He held up his hand. "Come on, C. I'm asking you now. Dance with me… please?"

I looked down at his hand.

"But we don't have any music," I said. "And I don't know how to dance!"

"It's okay." Rocky laced his fingers through mine. "I'll teach you."

We swayed on the spot to music only we could hear.

He raised his arm and twirled me around, before pulling me closer and placing his other hand around my waist.

ROCKY

She was so damn beautiful.

Her hands fit perfectly in mine and feeling her body against mine sent an electric bolt down to my pants. Thankfully it was dark. The last thing I wanted to do was scare her away. She had a tough exterior and put guards up to protect herself, but despite her strength and resilience, there was a gentle side to her.

My gaze rested on her lips and wondered what it would be like to kiss her as we continued to dance on the sidewalk. This was better than any party.

"Since when do you dance?" she asked.

"I have many hidden talents."

A blush spread over her cheeks as the warm breeze blew a stray strand of hair into her face. I reached out to sweep it away, making her inhale sharply at my touch. Whenever we got this close in the past, I'd made my excuses and made a hasty getaway but not tonight. Instead, I leaned in until our lips were almost touching.

After this, there would be no going back.

CANDY

His lips brushed against mine so softly that I questioned whether it happened. The lingering tingle left behind was the only trace of it.

"You have no idea how long I've wanted to kiss you," he murmured.

"Then, kiss me," I demanded.

I'd read about first kisses and the horror of guys who favored the washing machine technique, but kissing Rocky was nothing like that.

He kissed me again, with more pressing force, and there was no question that this was happening. He tasted like peppermint; his hands crept up my back and the warmth of his skin made me feel safe. All my worries over what would happen should a guy want to kiss me vanished, and my body knew exactly what to do.

The real question was, how were we ever going to stop?

CHAPTER
Eight

SIX MONTHS AFTER CANDY AND ROCKY'S FIRST
KISS...

HIRAM

"What's in it for me?" he sneered.

The acne-riddled man in front of me showed no respect for authority. If he was of no use to me, I would have no qualms about snapping his neck and leaving him to die. No one would miss him. Most of society would think I did them a favor, but I wasn't most of society.

Worthless human beings made my success possible. I learned early on that desperation didn't breed loyalty for a long time, but it would make people do anything for you in the short term. Those people were my foot soldiers. They could do my bidding and were easy to dispose of when my need for them was over. I could give them whatever they needed: cash, drugs, or whores, but no favor ever came for free.

I took out my wallet to ensure he got a good view of the cash. His greedy eyes lit up. Now he was paying attention. I hooked him in.

"Are you listening now, Mike?" I asked.

He didn't look away from my wallet but nodded like a drooling dog. His small brain was already pondering how he would spend his cash. He was hypnotized by what was in front of him.

"I need you to do a favor for me," I said.

I fanned three fifties in front of him. That was the invitation. You needed to show them you were serious and meant business.

"I'll do it," he said with zero hesitation. "Just tell me what you need me to do, man."

I cleared my throat and said, "I want you to get a new runner."

Behind me, five of my men stepped out of the shadows and surrounded us. The young man, no more than a boy really, shrunk backward, losing some of his confidence. This was another essential step in any negotiation. There was nothing like instilling fear to guarantee compliance. I wanted to give him a hint of what could happen if he dared step out of line.

"W-w-who?" Mike stammered.

It was disappointing to see him lose his nerve. It was something I often saw in small-town gangs. They got too comfortable and thought they were big fish until they met a shark. They had no real power, and when faced with men like me, they were the ones who followed orders.

I held up a photograph of Rocky Marshall on my phone.

I suspected the boy would pose problems. My niece took a shine to the street rat, but I had to play smart. If Blackthorne Towers was going to be her new home, she couldn't have anything in her past left to hold onto. I had to blow her happiness to smithereens.

"I can do that," my sniveling new partner agreed. "I'll recruit him."

"Good," I said, passing him the fifties. "Treat him like the rest and tell no one."

He shoved the cash into his pants and nodded.

"There's plenty more where that came from," I promised with a grin, making him flinch. "Don't even think of fucking me over because I will find out."

The final part of striking a deal was crucial. Pairing an incentive with a threat produced the effect I wanted.

He paled. "I w-w-wont."

I nodded, content in knowing Mike would do my bidding. "I'll be in touch with further instructions."

With a few carefully orchestrated moves, I planted the dynamite underneath Candy Green's life. She would be oblivious to what was to come until her old life crumbled around her. After that, all I had to do was help to pick up the pieces and give her a new purpose.

This wasn't my original plan, but it was better.

CHAPTER
Nine

CANDY

"You're lying to me," I said. "I can tell. You have that look on your face."

"What look?"

"*That* look!" I pointed at his guilty expression. "You told me it was just weed they wanted you to do, but I heard a girl in my Spanish class say that you're dealing meth. That destroys lives!"

His jaw clenched. "And you think I don't know that?"

Of course he did. I knew how his mom's death affected him, but that only made this worse! He knew the effects it could have. Why would he want to be part of it?

"Why do it then?" I pressed. "And why didn't you tell me?

Rocky had always been the go-to guy for supplying the rich kids. Weed, a few party drugs here and there...but no hard drugs. That was his rule. I didn't like it, but I understood it was what most Evergreen kids had to do to get by.

A few months back, a local gang reached out and recruited him as a runner. A guy who recently left Evergreen joined and gave Rocky a way in. Rocky told me he'd still be selling the same stuff, but getting paid better. Something about it didn't sit right with me, though. I watched most Evergreen guys swap these walls for jail cells because they got mixed up in the wrong shady deal. But his lying bothered me more than the dealing.

"It was just one time, okay?" Rocky sighed. "I did it as a favor, and they gave me three times as much."

"Didn't you think about what would have happened if you got caught, Rocky?" I said. "You've got a scholarship lined up! Why would you risk screwing it up?"

He put blood, sweat, and tears into securing a place at the college of his dreams. It was so close he could almost taste it.

"The scholarship won't cover everything, C," he said. "I'll still need cash for other things, and if I do a few big drops like this, it'll add up fast. I won't have to work four jobs in my first year to feed myself."

"But do you really have to do it this way?" I said. "There must be something else!"

Even as I said it, I knew there were no other options that would pay as well.

"I know you don't like it," he said. "But this won't change anything, and hey! Maybe I could get you an iPod instead of that old thing?"

"I'm happy with what I have!" I hugged my beloved Walkman close to my chest. "It's not about the money. Everyone in town knows the Jesters are bad news."

"So are the guys on the football team," he joked. "I'm used to hanging out with jerks."

"The Jesters are a gang, not trust fund brats. They're criminals!"

Money didn't matter. We both went through life having none of it. What I really cared about was making sure he didn't get himself killed or end up in prison. I didn't want him to become another Evergreen statistic. Usually, when people left at eighteen, we would put a bet on how long it'd take for them to end up in jail. We never had to wait long.

"It's only a few deals a day. We'll be able to hang out more too," he said. "Trust me, you don't need to worry about me, C."

But I did. How could I not? He was the only person in this world I truly cared about.

Rocky pulled me closer and wrapped his arms around me. I loved nestling into his neck and inhaling his scent. He knew that too and was using my kryptonite against me.

"Promise me that you'll be careful," I murmured. "You can't get caught. You need to get out of here."

"We have our plan, remember?" he said, stroking my hair. "I'll make sure we both get out of this dump for good, you hear me?"

The thought filled my chest with a warm and fuzzy feeling. One of our favorite subjects to talk about was how different life would be for us in the future. We planned it all. Rocky would go to college, become a football star, and visit me on the weekends. Until I graduated, we'd make it work long-distance while I studied and then move in together.

I often visualized how our lives could turn out. I never wanted to look back when I left this town. But, for now, sitting on the warehouse rooftop and watching the sunset on the horizon like a burst egg yolk was the closest to freedom we could get.

———

ROCKY

My stomach twisted at having to lie to Candy, but knowing the truth would make her more stressed, and I wanted to protect her. The first deal I did for the Jesters was supposed to be a one-time thing, but when you've done it once, they expect you to do it again. And again.

I've had to do three drops a day for a week. Heroin. Meth. Coke. I tried not to think about what I carried in my backpack as I moved around town. It's not kids from school I'm hooking up anymore. It's businessmen, brothel owners, and shady motherfuckers who sell porn on the internet.

But I had to focus on the positives. The money is great. It's an easy job, and I made more than I could by doing anything else. If things continued, I hoped to get my license and buy a car, which would make it easier to visit Candy after I left for college.

That's what kept me going. We needed cash for me to keep my promise to her. I wanted us to leave this place together and never come back. I had to make something of myself, and if that meant doing three drops of fuck knows what a day, I'd do it. I'd do anything to make sure I'm able to look after her. It's what she deserved and what I would make sure she'd get.

"We should be heading back soon," she murmured.

"You sure about that?" I asked, tipping her chin upward to kiss her.

We hadn't taken our relationship any further than a make-out session, and I'd wait as long as it took for her to be ready. That didn't mean self-control was easy. Hormones were no fucking joke, and cold showers were becoming a regular part of my routine. I don't think she knew how much I was into her.

She laughed, kissing me back, then caught my lip between her teeth.

Damn. She drove me wild. She groaned and pulled away.

"Come on," she said, standing up. "We'll miss curfew!"

"You're the only person in Evergreen who sticks to the rules on a Friday night, you know."

Her laughter carried through the air as my phone buzzed.

It was my burner. The Jesters gave me a new one every few weeks. They said it was safer that way. The message read *'Clubhouse. Ten minutes.'*

Candy frowned, noticing my straighter posture. "What is it?"

"It's nothing," I said, stashing my cell away.

It vibrated again, and the words '*URGENT pick-up*' flashed over my screen.

"Doesn't sound like nothing," she said.

Lying to her again would make her more annoyed than telling her the truth.

"It's the Jesters," I said. "They need me."

Candy didn't say anything. She didn't have to. I knew what was going through her mind, and I was thinking the same myself. What the fuck had I gotten myself into?

"So, you're ditching me?"

When the Jesters asked you to do something, you didn't question it unless you wanted a broken leg, which would ruin my football career forever. This wasn't a choice, but it didn't mean I had to hang around.

"The clubhouse is on the way home," I suggested. "We can detour?"

She can wait at the end of the street, and I'll grab the drugs. It won't ruin our evening.

What could go wrong, right?

———

CANDY

"Stay here," Rocky ordered. "Don't come any closer, okay?"

I didn't need to ask which house was the infamous Jesters' base of operations. The booming bass blasting through open windows, beer cans strewn over the sidewalk, and shady fuckers partying in the yard gave it away. This neighborhood wasn't a place anyone would choose to visit after dark unless you were armed with pepper spray, a rape whistle, and a bulletproof vest.

"Can't I come with you?" I asked, reluctant to stay alone.

I didn't want to go into the clubhouse either, but standing on the street corner seemed less appealing.

"I won't be long," Rocky promised. "I'll be in and out, I swear. I'll grab the package, then we can go. I'll be five minutes."

———

ROCKY

I fucking hated having to leave her outside, but I didn't want the Jesters to know about her. I wasn't stupid. I knew what they did to people who got on their wrong side, and Candy was stuck in this town for another year. I wanted to keep her off their radar.

The music made the walls vibrate, and the clubhouse was more crowded than usual. There were ten motorbikes parked outside with plates I didn't recognize. Even during the day, you never knew who you'd meet in the clubhouse. The gang leader, Mike, liked hosting all-nighters

Five minutes. That's all I needed to get the shit and get the hell outta there.

Adam fist-bumped me. "Good to see you, man."

Adam was who got me into the Jesters. He left Evergreen six months before, and his room used to be opposite mine. He helped me start dealing green when I was thirteen but convinced me now was the time to step up my game if I wanted to make serious cash.

"Where's Mike?" I asked.

He nudged his head. "In the back."

I shouldered past the drunken crowd to get to Mike's usual hangout spot in the kitchen.

"You came," Mike greeted me. "Why don't you stay for a drink now you're here?"

"I've got places to be," I said, putting my hands in my pockets.

"You don't want to insult me, do you?" he taunted, holding up a bag of coke with a street value of a thousand dollars. That would make me a sweet profit. "One drink, and then you make a special delivery."

It wasn't an invitation. It was a request.

———

CANDY

Where the hell was Rocky? So much for being five minutes!

Fifteen minutes passed, and I stood behind a tree that blocked my view of the clubhouse. Seeing the place up close made me hate it and how Rocky was involved in this world. The sooner he went to college, the better. I'd miss him like hell, but staying in this town was no good for him. He needed to get out before he got in too deep.

"Who're you hiding from, sugar?" A drunken man leered and wolf-whistled. My breathing hitched up a notch as the man approached. He didn't look like one of the Jesters. Half of his teeth were missing, his belly bulged over his pants, and he smelled like a sewer. "How much d'you want for a blow job?"

A car braked aggressively on the other side of the road, and a man got out.

"Hey!" the mysterious man called to the leering perv. "Leave her alone. She's just a kid!"

The man muttered something under his breath and staggered away into the night, already forgetting about me.

My rescuer didn't return to his car but walked over.

"You shouldn't be hanging around in a neighborhood like this," he said. "It's dangerous around here."

He was too well dressed to live in these parts. He wore a slick well-fitted black suit. If I had to guess how old he was, I'd put him in his late thirties, but he had an ageless face which made it hard to pinpoint.

"I'm waiting for a friend," I replied.

"I'll wait with you," he said. "Until they show up."

"I'll be fine. I can look after myself," I insisted. By looking after myself, I meant that I could run surprisingly fast. "Thanks for your help, but you don't have to stick around."

"I think I'll still stand and enjoy the fresh air until your friend joins us," he said. "We don't have to talk."

"If you stick around too long, someone will steal your car," I pointed out.

The guy laughed. His face was friendly and approachable. He looked like someone who would hold the door open for you in a shop. He didn't belong on this street. You could tell from his perfectly groomed stubble that he took care of his appearance.

I looked at the clubhouse, hoping Rocky would return at any minute.

"What's your name?" the stranger asked.

"I'm not telling you anything," I said. "You're a stranger."

"My name's Hiram," he said, seemingly unbothered by my rude remark. "See? I'm not a stranger now."

I smiled. I couldn't help liking him. Adults usually looked right through me. They didn't think Evergreen kids were worth talking to, but this man seemed kind. He treated me like an actual human.

"I'm Candy," I said.

"Is that a nickname?"

———

ROCKY

I drained the cup in one swallow and wiped my mouth with the back of my hand. Mike was telling me a dumb story and wouldn't shut the hell up. It's almost like the fucker could sense I wanted to go and was keeping me for fun. All I could think about was how Candy was waiting in a street grown men didn't want to come down at night.

If I'd known this would be different from my usual in-and-out pick-up, I'd never have taken her with me. It was my fault for not wanting to cut our night short and prove to her that working for the Jesters wouldn't change anything or affect our time together.

"I gotta head off," I said, grabbing the drugs. "If I wanna get there in time."

This had been the longest fifteen minutes of my life.

Mike didn't object this time. "I'll see you around."

As soon as I left, I broke into a run as my eyes scanned the street. Random people were milling around, but there was no sign of Candy. Hopefully, she stayed where I asked her to.

I sprinted as soon as I saw her and shouted, "Hey!"

She wasn't alone.

A car had pulled up alongside her. I didn't know a lot about cars, but those wheels cost serious money. Whoever owned a ride like that and drove it in a place like *this* spelled trouble. A man was talking to Candy, and I saw red as she laughed at his remark.

"You better get the fuck away from her real fast," I snarled.

"It's okay, Rocky," Candy said, taking my hand. "He was only keeping me company."

I knew Candy was tough. The girl grew up in Evergreen and yo-yo'ed out of different foster care homes as a kid, but she'd gone through life keeping her head down and trying not to get noticed, which made her vulnerable. Other people could take advantage of her naivety.

The man reminded me of a shady as fuck Wall Street banker. I didn't trust him. There was something about him that made my skin crawl. A feeling I couldn't put my finger on. I'd grown up with an alcoholic and a drug addict. At that time, my home had been like a revolving door for many people. It made me develop an intuition for sensing when something was off about people. I could spot it a mile away, and something about this man made me want to drag Candy by the arm and run in the other direction.

"I'm here now," I said. I may be younger than him, but I'd guarantee I was faster and stronger. "You can leave now."

"Sorry about him," Candy said, smiling apologetically. "He's... protective."

She was on his side? That made me hate the smarmy bastard more. I'd throw him to the ground if we were on the football field.

"He's right to be protective," the man said. "It's good to have someone looking out for you."

"Damn right it is," I said, biting my tongue to stop myself from adding that she needs someone looking out for her when creeps like you are roaming the streets.

"Thanks again," Candy said to the man.

"My pleasure," he said, heading to his shiny car. "Enjoy your evening, Candy."

Something about his tone made the hairs on my arms stand on end. I was glad to see him going back to whichever rich kingdom he came from.

"You didn't have to be so rude," she said as he sped off. "If you hadn't taken so long, he wouldn't have needed to save me from a perv."

"Shit, C!" My anger dissipated. All thoughts of the rich stranger vanished and were replaced by guilt for dragging her over here. I'd put her in danger, and there was no way I'd make that mistake again. "Are you okay?"

"I'm fine," she said, waving her hand dismissively. Even if she wasn't, she wouldn't admit it. "Can we go now?"

I nodded. All I had to do was drop off the coke then I'd be able to return to my and Candy's world. The only place where I was truly happy.

CHAPTER
Ten

CANDY

Rocky rolled on top of me as we kissed. I wrapped one of my legs around him to draw him closer. He hardened against me, warming between my legs. I liked knowing I'd done that to him and he wanted me.

"C," he murmured, pausing reluctantly. "We're supposed to be doing homework…"

I pulled him back. "Who cares about homework?"

I was wearing a short skirt, and his hand slid up my thigh. I wanted to feel his touch. I craved it. I wanted *more*. We fooled around before, but he hadn't touched me…down there… yet. I pushed my hips upward, which he seemed to like, judging by his groan. He's all I wanted.

"I think I'm ready," I whispered.

Sex was a strange new world I only read about in books or saw hinted at in movies. I knew everyone else in Evergreen screwed around all the time. That's part of the reason why we had a curfew. After a string of unplanned pregnancies, a rule was put in place to ban us from being in each other's rooms. That didn't mean there weren't ways around it if you were smart enough not to get caught.

Rocky froze. "Are you sure?"

He knew what I was talking about. We discussed it a few times before. Rocky had hooked up with girls in the past, but he never tried to pressure me and told me he was happy to wait until I was ready.

I nodded as my heart raced. "Yes."

I slid my hand further down to meet his zipper.

He grabbed my wrist to stop me. "Not now."

"But—"

Had I completely misread his signals? I'd read somewhere that guys liked it when girls took charge.

"It's not that I don't want to," he said quickly. "But I don't want your first time to be like this. I want it to be special."

"I don't need a five-star hotel or rose petals," I said. Although, it would be nice to lose my virginity without having to worry about the Evergreen fire drill going off for the third time in as many hours. "I want you."

"And you'll have me," Rocky promised. "Tomorrow night."

———

ROCKY

It took every ounce of my self-control to stop her from touching me, but I didn't want her first time to be a quick fuck. I wanted to make it special for her. You couldn't get your virginity back, and I wanted to make sure my girl's first time would be the best.

I also wanted to be able to tell her something else.

Something I'd never told anyone before.

If Candy wanted to open her body to me, I was ready to open my heart to her. I was in love with her. I had been for a long time, long before she ever took an interest in me, but I hadn't told her yet.

Tomorrow night, I'd prove it to her.

———

CANDY

After my conversation with Rocky, I tossed and turned all night. Butterflies fluttered in my stomach from a mixture of nerves and excitement. All day in school I'd been thinking about what would happen...

What did you wear to lose your virginity?

Would he expect me to have fancy underwear?

Would I disappoint him?

I tied my hair up, then tore the band out, and let my hair fall around my face. I screwed my nose up in the mirror at my reflection. Whatever style I tried didn't look right.

Would sex hurt?

Would I like it? Would *he* like it?

Would I be...bad?

Amongst my nervous anticipation, there was something else too. A warm glow. Rocky wasn't treating me like a casual fling. He wanted to make it *special*.

My turbulent childhood taught me that the only person you can rely on is yourself, but Rocky changed that. He was the first person I'd been able to fully put my trust into.

———

ROCKY

She waited for me outside Evergreen as we agreed. My eyes lit up as soon as I saw her.

"I've planned something special," I said, taking her hand. "We're going to the warehouse."

Candy raised an eyebrow in bemusement. "The warehouse?"

"You'll see," I said.

It would be a step up from our habit of smoking joints and eating snacks. When we arrived, I made her pause at the entrance.

"I know it's no hotel, but close your eyes."

She put her hands on her hips, standing her ground. "Do I have to?"

"Yes," I insisted. "Close them."

Candy sighed and did as I asked. Her stubbornness and underlying fiery spirit only made her more attractive. I led her through the warehouse and upstairs to our usual hang-out spot.

"Okay, now open them!"

I removed my hands. She gasped and a giggle burst from her mouth at the sight in front of us.

"A tent?"

It's not every day you see a yellow tent pitched on the roof of an abandoned building.

"Not just any tent," I said, ducking to unzip the door.

Inside, I filled it with blankets and set up a makeshift picnic with some of her favorite food. It may not be a fine-dining restaurant, but she wasn't the kind of girl who would be impressed by their hard-to-pronounce dishes.

"So?" I cast a nervous glance at her unreadable expression. "What do you think?"

Had I screwed this up?

"It's perfect," she whispered.

———

CANDY

We climbed inside the tent, and Rocky opened a can of lukewarm soda for each of us. The bright glow of the tent made everything appear glowing and magical. The warehouse was our special place, but this made it feel cut off from the rest of the world like our own private island.

"I'm glad you like it," Rocky said. "Not bad for my first date, huh?"

"Your first date?" I frowned, reclining on the pillows. "But you've dated lots of girls."

He laughed. "You listen to the rumors too much. I've been dragged along with some of the guys, but I've never asked another girl out before."

My insides felt warm and fuzzy as the bubbles went to my head. "Really?"

"You're the only girl I've ever wanted to take out on a date," he said, staring into my eyes. "I thought you'd have already realized that by now."

I smiled, put the soda down, and shuffled over to him.

______

ROCKY

Candy slipped onto my lap, wrapping her legs around my middle. In the small space, I was consumed by the smell of her sweet peachy shampoo and a hint of vanilla perfume I knew she saved for special occasions.

"Hey," I said, pausing before she could kiss me. "Are you sure about this?"

"Yes." Her voice came out a little breathless as she unbuttoned her shirt. "I don't want to wait anymore."

Her fingers reached the final button, and the glimpse of her skin made my cock strain against my pants. She had no idea how fucking beautiful she was. Candy took a deep breath, letting her shirt drop from her shoulders to the blankets. Her white bra hugged her breasts, and my eyes widened as she unhooked it and let it fall too.

Holy fucking shit.

"You're perfect," I admired, putting my hands around her and pulling her close.

She kissed me hungrily. Her soft hands slid under my T-shirt and caressed my back, yanking the hem to push it upward. I took it off, and she let out a small gasp as I gently laid her back into the pile of cushions. Her blonde hair fanned out around her face making her resemble an angel.

______

CANDY

Rocky started to kiss my neck and slowly move downwards. His kisses left a tingling trail down my collarbone as his hands cupped my breast. He continued, leaving kisses as he went until he reached my nipple and began to play with it gently. He took it into his mouth and sucked gently, then squeezed it between his thumb and forefinger, coaxing a moan from my lips.

His eyes darted to mine to check I was okay, and I smiled to reassure him. This is what I wanted.

His hair tickled my skin as he slid down my body, kissing along my hip bone as his hand glided up my thigh. I willed him to go higher, but he stopped at the edge of my skirt.

"Can I take it off?" he asked.

"Yes," I breathed, helping him tug my skirt down and leaving me in my panties.

———

ROCKY

I paused to take in all of her beauty. This is what I dreamed about every time I saw her in a short skirt.

"Are you sure you want to do this?" I asked as my fingers caressed her inner thigh.

"Yes," she replied with zero hesitation.

I slid two fingers down the front of her panties. I was already rock hard, but feeling the damp fabric and outline of her pussy lips sent an electric shock down to my core.

Candy gasped as my fingers found her clit and slowly circled it. "Oh!"

"Is this okay?" I asked, stopping what I was doing.

"Yes," she breathed, rolling her hips against my hand. "I want…more."

"More?" I grinned. "I can do that."

I pulled her panties down, and Candy's body tensed for a second before letting her legs fall apart. She had nothing to feel self-conscious about. She was fucking perfect.

"I'll be gentle, okay?" I said as I positioned my face between my legs.

I could spend hours exploring her body. I wanted to learn what she liked, how she liked to be touched, and how I could make her moan my name.

———

CANDY

Rocky touching me through my panties was one thing, but new worries were starting to emerge.

Does it smell weird? Does he think it looks strange? Does he…

"Fuck!" I cried involuntarily as his tongue licked along my slit, making my toes curl from a dizzying pleasure I'd never experienced before.

Rocky paused to ask, "Is that okay?"

I blushed, embarrassed at my loud outburst. "Yeah, it's…good."

Really fucking good.

He grinned as his tongue explored me again. Why didn't anyone talk about how *good* this felt? Why had I waited so long? Rocky's fingers circled my entrance and slowly entered me as he continued to play with his tongue.

I moaned and writhed, unable to control myself as my desire was building. He slid a second finger inside me. I inhaled sharply at the sudden feeling of fullness and being stretched, but he didn't rush.

———

ROCKY

Her moans drove me crazy as her tight pussy hugged my fingers. I didn't think there would be enough room for two, but she opened up, and her wetness coated my fingers.

Her thigh muscles twitched around my head as her hands stroked the back of my head.

"Rocky!"

Fuck. I loved hearing her say my name and the taste of her on my tongue.

Her self-consciousness disappeared, and she parted her legs wider to open herself. Her breathing grew short and rapid. This moment was all about her. I wanted to make her feel the best she'd ever felt.

———

CANDY

It's a good thing we weren't in Evergreen because the experience took me by surprise. I'd made myself orgasm before, but nothing like this. My whole body seemed to fold in on itself as Rocky's tongue tipped me over the edge in a climax which made me clench on his fingers so tightly that I didn't know whether he'd be able to get them out again.

When I'd finished, Rocky sat up with a smug smirk on his face. "You liked that, huh?"

"It was okay," I said with a cheeky grin. "I guess…"

He raised one eyebrow. "Just okay?"

"Don't worry," I said. "We're not done yet."

He bent down to kiss me, laying on top of me and taking the weight of his body with his elbows. It was weird to taste myself, but I also liked it. It was a reminder of what we'd done together.

His erection pressed into me through his jeans, and I reached down to unbutton them. Brushing against the warm bulge in his pants made me nervous again. It felt…big.

"Take these off," I demanded, hoping to sound more confident than I felt. I didn't know much about being dominating, but I also knew I didn't want to chafe against denim.

Watching him shrug off his jeans inside the small tent made me giggle. He couldn't stand straight, and there was only enough room for us to lie down without touching the sides. My laughter soon stopped when I saw the size of the tent he was pitching in his boxers. Fitting two fingers inside me was just about possible, but something like that was more of a weapon.

"It's okay," he said, sensing my nervousness. "We'll go real slow."

My eyes almost popped out of my head as he pulled his shorts down to reveal his cock.

Holy shit.

Where was that going to go?

―――――

ROCKY

We didn't need to rush.

I wanted her to feel comfortable.

Candy's eyes scanned my body. I'd always been confident in how I looked but knowing she was looking at me made me nervous. I knew other girls thought I was attractive, but Candy wasn't like any other girl I'd met.

What happened if she didn't like what she saw?

"You're…" she says, blushing, "…big."

Well, that's not what I was expecting.

I laid next to her, and she turned over, so we were on our sides facing each other. The warmth of her naked body radiated toward me. Her hand reached down to stroke the head of my cock.

"What do I do with it?" she blurted out.

I smiled. "Don't worry, I'll show you."

———

CANDY

I wrapped my hand around Rocky's cock. He placed his hand over my own and moved to show me how he liked it. It was softer than I expected, like smooth velvet. Rocky's hand let go of mine, and he moaned as I continued to work his shaft.

"Stop," he groaned.

"Have I done something wrong?" I said, dropping his dick like it was on fire.

"Hell no," he growled. "You'll make me cum if you keep doing that, and I want to make love to you."

"Make love?"

Rocky was the kind of guy who called sex 'fucking' or 'screwing'. Making love was a whole other language.

He cleared his throat. It was the first time I'd seen him look nervous since I met him.

"Yes," he said, rolling on top of me. "I love you, C."

I wanted to play it cool, but I couldn't stop the giant smile from spreading over my face and making my cheeks hurt.

"I love you too," I replied.

He was the only person I wanted to be with. The only person I ever trusted and could rely on. I was ready to give myself to him completely.

"Are you sure this is what you want?" he said, reaching to grab a condom packet.

I nodded eagerly, watching as he expertly rolled it down himself in seconds. "I want you, Rocky."

I wasn't sure what to expect as I parted my legs for him. I heard losing your virginity was like being torn in two, but Rocky was gentle. There was an initial sting as he pushed inside, making my body go rigid.

"Do you want me to stop?"

"No," I insisted, wrapping my arms around him so he couldn't go anywhere. "I want this."

He started to thrust slowly. It was a strange feeling, but kinda nice too. It made me complete in a way I didn't think was possible and more whole than I ever had been before. Now, we'd shared every part of ourselves with each other, and there was no going back.

CHAPTER
Eleven

HIRAM

The time had come.

She was sixteen and an adult in my eyes. I would not let the boy corrupt her any longer. My blood would not slip through my fingers because of an arrogant football player with nothing to offer.

Candy was born for a bigger purpose than being the token girlfriend on the arm of someone inferior. When I finished with her, she would be feared by everyone. I would ensure she was strong enough to carry the legacy she was destined for.

I was reminded of my sister when I watched her. Helena had been so wrapped up in her first love, she'd been willing to give her only brother over to the cops for him. A mistake that cost both of them their lives. I would make sure their daughter never did the same.

I tasked Q, the technical genius who worked for me, to research the boy and inform me if he received a scholarship. For a boy in his position, that was the same as holding a winning lottery ticket. That gave me leverage. He may care for Candy, but a boy of his age would put his life over hers. He'd only ever get one chance at a better life, but girls? He could take his pick.

Her feelings for him could easily be erased. It was time for me to meet Mike, the Jesters' leader, again. It paid to have him in my pocket. He lulled Rocky Marshall into a false sense of security and found a way to make him a runner upon my request. Now, I would reap the rewards of my investment.

Candy may think the boy cared for her, but I would show her how wrong she was.

Whatever she felt for him would be torn into pieces. His betrayal would fuel her. From her ashes, a phoenix would rise and be reborn. But, first, Mike would bring the boy to me. It was time I met the boy my niece had grown so fond of.

CHAPTER
Twelve

ROCKY

She *loved* me too.

Even though we left the warehouse hours ago, I replayed the moment repeatedly in my head. I couldn't believe how lucky I was. How often in life does your dream girl, who you've been crushing on for years, tell you she feels the same?

Taking our relationship to the next level only proved what I'd known all along. No one else would ever compare to her. She would be the only girl for me.

Leaving her at Evergreen to go to the clubhouse for my regular nightly pick-up didn't fill me with as much dread as usual. Nothing could happen today to ruin my good mood, even dealing with Mike.

The clubhouse was surprisingly quiet. Usually, it was a non-stop party, and music could be heard from the end of the block, but only a few passed-out revelers lay in the yard. Maybe the Jesters needed a day to chill.

"Hello?" I pushed open the clubhouse door. "Anyone there?"

"Through here," Mike called. "In the kitchen."

I made my way through the house to find Mike wasn't alone or surrounded by his usual heavies. Instead, a man in a suit stood by his side.

"What is he doing here?" I demanded.

I never forgot a face. It was a handy skill to have in my line of work, and I knew who to avoid. This man was someone I'd almost forgotten about, but seeing him for the second time reinforced my initial opinion that I never wanted to see him again.

"Nice to see you again, Rocky," the strange man said. "I've been waiting for you."

A few months ago, he spoke to Candy while she waited outside the clubhouse for me. Something about him didn't feel right then, and it sure as hell didn't feel right now. The fact he knew my name only pissed me off more. I don't know what game he was playing, but he wanted to rattle me.

"Who are you?" I spat, already on the defense. You didn't fuck around or show weakness at the first battle. "What do you want?"

"I want something you have."

"I have nothing a man like you can't buy."

"But you haven't even asked me what it is yet," the man sneered.

I didn't need to. I could sense he was trouble and, whatever he wanted, I wasn't interested.

"I want to make a deal with you," he said. "I think you'll be interested in my proposition. I want you to bring Candy to me."

I'd been right about him. He was one of those fucking creeps who traded young girls like Pokemon cards.

"No fucking way," I snarled.

"I think you may change your mind when you learn who I am," he said, extending his hand. "I'm Hiram."

"So?" I crossed my arms over my chest. "Is that supposed to mean something?"

Hiram shot me a twisted smile.

"C'mon, Rocky," Mike said, speaking for the first time since my arrival. He normally acted like the big man, but even he was cowering in Hiram's presence. "You've heard about Blackthorne Towers, haven't you?"

Of course I had. I may live in Evergreen, but I hadn't grown up under a fucking rock.

Realization dawned on me. Shit. Holy mother fucking shit. It couldn't be...this was *the* Hiram?

Hiram was the biggest kingpin in the state. I heard whispers about him in shady circles. He was the guy who wasn't afraid to rip your eyeballs out of your head and put them in a cocktail for you to drink afterward.

"Now that I have your attention," Hiram drawled. "I'm sure you know I'm not a man who likes to be kept waiting."

My palms broke out in a cold sweat. "What do you want with her? Why her?"

"That is none of your business," Hiram snapped. "The only thing you need to know is that you are the one who will deliver her to me. After that, you are going to pretend she never existed."

"It's not happening," I said. "No fucking way."

This was *Candy* we were talking about, not a fucking bag of coke or speed! I loved her more than anything and anyone. I wasn't handing her over to a monster. Over my dead body.

"You have two choices," Hiram said, holding up two fingers to count them out. "You either bring her to me, and she lives, or I have to find her myself, and she dies."

But what if he couldn't find her? We could go on the run. I saved enough cash from dealing that we could leave town and hop on the next train or bus.

Hiram laughed again, chilling my blood ice cold.

"You can't run from me," Hiram said, reading my mind. "No one can. You want her to live, don't you?"

What kind of stupid question was that?

"Yes," I spat through gritted teeth.

"Then you *will* do what I say," Hiram said. "If you bring her to me, no one has to get hurt. If I have to hunt you down, I won't be so kind. I'll kill every person in Evergreen, including Candy, and get you thrown in jail for murder. What would happen to your football career then?"

A man like Hiram had more power and influence than a high schooler could imagine. He could do whatever he wanted, and no one would question it. He'd have contacts in the legal system and within law enforcement. I had no doubt he could pin a murder on me, and no one would even question it.

"How do you know I play football?"

I don't know why I asked when I already knew the answer. He watched me. Watched us. How long had he planned to take her? Had he decided to take her after the conversation he had with Candy the night I made the mistake of bringing her to the clubhouse?

"I know everything about you, Rocky," Hiram said. "I know you care about her. I know you don't want to waste away in jail knowing she's dead, and you're responsible."

"Why go through all of this trouble to get her if you'd kill her in a heartbeat?" I demanded. "You're bluffing. You don't want her dead."

"Try me," Hiram snarled. "The only way Candy's heart keeps beating is if she stays with me. I will make sure no harm comes to her. You have my word on that. If she isn't with me, I have no use for her. She's better off dead."

"Maybe she would be better off dead than going with you," I replied viciously.

Hiram grabbed me by the throat. I resisted, but his grip was stronger than a mechanical arm. There was no way I could pry his gloved fingers off.

"I would *never* hurt her," Hiram said, releasing his hold. "Candy will be safe if you follow my orders. I could even pay your school fees to show you my appreciation."

"I don't want your fucking money," I gasped, massaging my neck.

"But you want Candy to have a better life, don't you?" Hiram said. The bastard was manipulative, trying to get into my head and twist my thoughts. "I can give her that."

"I've heard about Blackthorne Towers," I said. "It's not a fucking summer camp."

"What you think is irrelevant." Hiram tutted. "You're not going to stand in my way. If you want both of you to be alive by the end of the week, you'll bring her to me tomorrow night."

Hiram may be presenting this as a choice, but what options did I have? Someone like me stood no chance against him. If he wanted Candy, he was going to get her regardless. Trying to defend her and run would only put her at risk of greater harm.

I wanted to sink to my knees, but I stood straighter.

"I'll see you later," Hiram said, clapping me on the back like we were old friends. "Remember, I'll be watching. One wrong move and my men will slit that pretty throat of hers."

If I didn't bring Candy to him, he'd kill whoever stood in his way.

What the fuck was I going to do?

CHAPTER
Thirteen

CANDY

"You're quiet today," I said, lacing my hands through Rocky's.

Since last night's drop, he'd been more reserved than usual. I knew him well enough to know something was on his mind.

"Sorry, C," he murmured. "Just tired."

When he did his deliveries, I watched from the window to make sure he got home safely. I stayed up until four a.m. before falling asleep, so he must have gotten back even later.

I didn't want to pry. We had an unspoken rule about his dealings with the Jesters. He didn't mention it, and I didn't bring it up. Lecturing him about the dangers wouldn't change his mind about working with them. He'd only have to do it for a few more months and promised to be careful. I trusted him to do what was right.

"The sky looks beautiful tonight, doesn't it?" I said.

It was a mix of brilliant pinks and oranges. We'd have a perfect view of the sunset from the warehouse roof.

Rocky didn't look up. "Yeah, it is…"

"Okay, now I know something's up." I stopped walking. "Are you going to tell me what's wrong, or will I have to force it out of you?"

Our route to the warehouse wove through a disused field which was more of a desert as the grass had turned a patchy yellow. An old dust road cut through it, and a large black car was heading down the path toward us.

"I'm sorry, C," he murmured. "I'm so fucking sorry."

"Sorry, for what?"

The car stopped in front of us, and a figure stepped out.

―――――

ROCKY

"Remember me, Candy?"

Candy's brow furrowed in thought, then she smiled brightly as she remembered him. She had no idea who we were standing with. She was an innocent deer coming face to face with a bloodthirsty lion and expecting them to be friends. The most infamous criminal in the state didn't deserve her smile. That fucker didn't deserve to breathe the same air as her.

"Sure," Candy replied. "You're my knight in shining armor, right?"

Hiram laughed. She had no idea that he couldn't be any further from a knight in shining armor if he tried. He was a sadistic bastard who wanted to take her away from everything she knew and the life she wanted to have.

"Rocky?" Candy looked down at our linked hands. I held hers so tightly that my knuckles turned white, hoping that if I clutched onto her hard enough, I'd never have to let her go. "Are you okay?"

I was caught in a catch-22. If I brought her to Hiram, she'd live. If I didn't, he'd hunt her down, and she'd die. I don't know which fate would be kinder, but I couldn't continue to live in a world where she didn't exist.

Three other cars hurtled down the road after Hiram from all directions, blocking off any escape route. Hiram wouldn't leave anything to chance. Even though I knew she wouldn't get away and her fate had already been decided, I couldn't stand by in our final moments and do nothing.

"We made a deal, Rocky." Hiram stepped forward. "I am here to collect."

"What is he talking about?" Candy asked, turning to me. I was the only person she trusted to give her answers. "I don't understand. What's going on?"

"This town is no longer your home, Candy." Hiram put a firm hand on her shoulder. "You are going to get into the car with me."

"No," she stammered, shaking him off. "I live here. I'm not going anywhere! You must think I'm someone else. Rocky? Tell them. There must be some kind of mistake!"

Five armed men jumped out of the cars surrounding us, pointing guns in our direction.

"There is no mistake," Hiram said. "Rocky is the one who brought you to me."

"Rocky?" Candy's beautiful eyes widened in horror. She may not understand what I did yet, but she'd soon learn how I betrayed her. It'd shatter any feelings she ever had for me.

"Candy—"

Before I could say more, two men lunged forward and grabbed Candy's arms. She struggled and screamed. Those gorillas were being too rough with her. I dove forward, trying to pull them off her but another smashed my jaw and sent me flying.

"Rocky!" Candy's eyes were wild. "Rocky! Make them stop!"

She thrashed in their arms, trying to kick them away, but they were too strong. Her heels left a trail as they dug into the dirt as they dragged her into the back of a van and slammed the door. Her screams begging me to do something rattled around my ears.

Uncontrollable tears rolled down my cheeks, and I fell to my knees. It was the first time I cried in years.

"What now?" I screamed at Hiram. "Are you going to kill me? Fucking do it!"

I wanted him to. It's what I deserved for being part of this. I betrayed her trust that had taken years to build. I helped to crush any hopes she had for a future.

"Killing you wouldn't be worth my time." Hiram regarded me with disgust and stepped past me. "It was a pleasure doing business with you."

Dust stung my eyes as the convoy of cars rolled away, leaving me alone in the dirt. All I could do was watch as they disappeared into the distance, taking the only girl I'd ever love with them.

Without her, all I had left was a beautiful sunset haunted by her desperate cries for help.

———

About the Author

Holly Bloom has a degree in English Literature, but don't let that fool you... she would pick a steamy romance over a Shakespeare play any day!

Holly writes contemporary romance - the dark, gritty and twisty kind. She loves creating badass babe characters, who aren't afraid to speak their minds, and writing about the men who can handle them - often, there is more than one! Why choose, right?

When she isn't working on her next project, Holly spends an unhealthy amount of time watching true crime and roaming around the woods near her home in the UK.

As well as gooey chocolate brownies, Holly's favourite thing in the world is hearing from her readers - her characters may bite, but she doesn't! Promise!

Find out more about Holly Bloom's books at:
www.hollybloomauthor.com

instagram.com/hollybloomauthor
facebook.com/hollybloomauthor
tiktok.com/@hollybloomauthor

9 781916 588097